FAVOURITE CAT STORIES

FAVOURITE CAT STORIES

Foreword by Nerys Hughes

COMPILED BY

LESLEY O'MARA

ILLUSTRATED BY

WILLIAM GELDART

MICHAEL O'MARA BOOKS LIMITED

This extended edition published in 1995 by
Michael O'Mara Books Limited, 9 Lion Yard,
Tremadoc Road, London SW4 7NQ

First published in Great Britain in 1992

A CIP catalogue record for this book is
available from the British Library

ISBN 1–85479–778–6

Endpapers: William Geldart

Typeset by Florencetype Ltd, Stoodleigh, Devon

Printed in England by Clays Ltd, St Ives plc

Contents

FOREWORD 7
Nerys Hughes

THE CAT THAT COULD FLY 9
Stella Whitelaw

CATS OF MY CHILDHOOD 22
May Eustace

A VET'S LIFE 32
John Bower

GERSHWIN 40
Judy Gardiner

THE CHERRY TREE 55
Derek Tangye

CAT'S CRUISE 66
Mazo de la Roche

AMOURS 79
Colette

THE CHESHIRE CAT 83
Lewis Carroll

THE YELLOW TERROR 91
W. L. Alden

C STANDS FOR CUISINE 101
Beverley Nichols

THE COAT 106
Mary Williams

THE ACHIEVEMENT OF THE CAT 128
Saki

INCIDENT ON EAST NINTH 130
Jill Drower

YE MARVELOUS LEGEND OF
TOM CONNOR'S CAT 138
Samuel Lover

RUFUS THE SURVIVOR 147
Doris Lessing

THE HOME LIFE OF A HOLY CAT 164
Arthur Wiegall

SOLOMON AND SHEBA 172
Doreen Tovey

PANGUR BAN 187
Irish Monk

CALVIN, THE CAT 188
Charles Dudley Warner

PUSS IN BOOTS 198
Charles Perrault

THE TOTEM OF AMARILLO 203
Emma-Lindsay Squier

MY BOSS THE CAT 218
Paul Gallico

LA MENAGERIE INTIME 223
Théophile Gautier

MINNA MINNA MOWBRAY 224
Michael Joseph

THE SLUM CAT 240
Ernest Thompson Seton

COME, LOVELY CAT 255
Charles Baudelaire

CHILDHOOD OF MISS CHURT 256
F. R. Buckley

THE CAT THAT WALKED BY HIMSELF 269
Rudyard Kipling

HOW A CAT PLAYED ROBINSON CRUSOE 279
Charles G. D. Roberts

ACKNOWLEDGMENTS 288

Foreword

NERYS HUGHES

There were two small orange kittens in the RSPCA Cattery eight Christmases ago. We chose the shivering tiniest one, and his brother stared at us in a lonely bewildered way as we left. On Boxing Day we went back and got him. My daughter Mari-Claire, who was four at the time, called the little one Cuddles – a name which did inhibit me a bit when I was desperately calling his name up and down our street when we lost him once. Fearless and loyal, more like a dog than a cat, he follows Mari-Claire everywhere through thick and thin and even through snow. My son Ben called the other kitten Twm-Twm (Welsh for Tom Tom) after a much-loved long-ago cat my Auntie Gwen befriended in Wales.

Having muttered and grumbled about cats' hairs in favourite chairs, settee backs used as scratching posts, and tortured mice by the kitchen door, I was taken aback by the total desolation I felt when Cuddles got run over, and we thought we were going to lose him. His sense of adventure and curiosity had taken him along the road to play dodgems with the traffic, and he got knocked down by a motorbike, breaking some bones and shattering his pelvis. We were all sobbing as we left the emergency vet's that night, having been told to leave him overnight so that the vet could test if his bladder had been pierced, if so he wouldn't survive. The next morning we were stricken to be told that he hadn't passed water, so the vet feared the worst. As we were going out of the door, gazing at him with love and despair, he smiled at us, gave a little bark, and relieved himself hugely and copiously all over his cage. We whooped and cheered and took him home. Patrick, my husband, made a little hospital cage out of an old cot and some wire netting so we could restrict his movements for a few weeks. He made a complete recovery, growing muscle tissue instead of bone over his pelvis, as cats do, and is now as daring and as lively as ever. Cuddles the Survivor. Perhaps that is why I identified so strongly with Doris Lessing in her beautifully written story about Rufus, her orange cat. The subtle but determined inroads that cats make into our hearts and homes! The doors that have to be left just ajar, creating thin draughts, the chairs that are forfeited, the meals on wheels and company that has to be organized when we go away, and the cross orange backs that are turned on me when we get back.

Certainly Doreen and Charles Tovey adjusted their friendships and lifestyle to accommodate two very naughty cats, I'm not sure I would have the patience to live with the beautiful and wicked Siamese Solomon and Sheba! Charles Dudley Warner celebrates the life of a mysterious and exceptional cat called Calvin. 'Incident on East Ninth' is a clever thriller – but then all the stories are evocative and readable.

If you don't like cats you'll enjoy reading this book. If you like cats you'll love it.

The Cat That Could Fly

STELLA WHITELAW

IT BEGAN on a curiously still morning when not a leaf stirred and even the butterflies seemed to hover over the flowers without moving. The dead elm stretched its ashen branches skywards waiting for the chop that was a long time in coming. A mile up a chartered Tri-Star ferried yawning early starters to a package holiday in Majorca, its gentle hum followed by vapour trails in the sky.

Leopold trod the dew-hung clover with delicate paws. He was a big ginger and white cat with a wide, surprised face and fluffed cheeks. His eyes were very green and brilliant which added to his startled look. He lived an uncomplicated life: he ate and slept; he caught the occasional bird or shrew just to keep his hand in.

The family that he lived with were what Leopold called sleek. They had everything – two cars, two colour television sets, a video recorder, wall to wall stereos, a deep freeze that could take a whale, every domestic appliance on the market, and yet they were as mean as a cross-eyed snake. They bought him unbranded cat food, a mish-mash of wet cereal and unmentionable animal parts; he never got a taste of fresh liver or fish. They drank the cheapest coffee, bought broken biscuits, and cut all the 10p-off coupons out of the paper. They were sleek all right.

They were sleek on affection too. If Leopold jumped on to a vacant lap, he was hastily brushed off.

'Gerroff my suit! I don't want your hairs all over me. Shoo. Shoo,' said the sleek man impatiently.

The sleek woman was as bad. Her clothes were also uncatable. The one person who liked Leopold was the daughter, Dana, but she was preoccupied with O levels and boy friends, and the only time Leopold saw her was when she came in late from a disco and they shared the cosy quietness of a 2 am kitchen.

As Leopold took his early morning stroll down the garden, he heard a faint chirp, chirp. The sound made his stomach contract. He was hungry. Last night's supper was best forgotten, and they would not give him a breakfast until he had been outside for at least an hour. Leopold did not understand these rules. It was another of their odd ways. He noticed that they ate broken biscuits whenever they felt like it.

Leopold crept up on the sound. It was a baby thrush, softly speckled brown and white, a big fluffy, helpless creature, looking straight at Leopold with bright, trusting eyes. It staggered a few inches and fell forward on to its plump breast. Leopold's surprised expression sharpened with delight. This was obviously some sort of game. He patted the soft feathers with a tentative paw. The bird chirped encouragingly and hopped another few inches. A few trees away, the mother bird heard her baby's call but was not alarmed. It had to learn to fly by itself.

Suddenly Leopold pounced. The baby's neck hung limp between his jaws. Leopold growled, a low rumbling jungle sound echoing back from his wild ancestors. He paraded his victim, the feathers stuck out round his mouth like an Air Force moustache. He crunched the tiny body thoughtfully, blood on the short white fur under his nose.

The mother bird went crazy. She flew from branch to branch in distress. She swooped over the ginger cat and what was left of her baby, her cries loud and distraught. But it was too late. There was nothing she could do. She took one last look at the big cat and flew blindly into the empty air.

There was a great oak which Leopold liked to climb. He never went very far because he knew his limits. But today the baby bird lay heavily in his stomach, and Leopold climbed higher, hoping to leave the uncomfortable feeling behind. The thick tangled branches gave no hint of how high he was climbing. He went on, up and up, leaping from one claw-hold to the next. Because there was no wind, the branches barely moved, again giving Leopold an unfounded sense of security. When a broken branch revealed a glimpse of the land below, Leopold was quite amazed. He could see the tops of other trees, padded with green-like cushions beneath him. The garden of his house was a smudge of blurred colours. In the distance was the church spire, almost eye level. A helicopter whirled into sight, coming straight towards the oak, its rotor blades clattering discordantly.

Leopold leaped back. He forgot he was on a branch, up a tree. He took off backwards, falling head between heels, somersaulting through a cascade of leaves and broken twigs, the wind rushing through his whiskers, flashes of sky and earth alternately in vision as he hurtled towards the ground.

He spread his paws helplessly in a gesture of supplication to the great cat god in the sky. He closed his eyes tightly. He did not want to see what was coming to him.

Leopold first became aware of a change when the swift rushing wind in his ears slowed to the merest whisper. He was still falling, but no longer that shattering, pummelling plunge earthwards. He seemed to be drifting. Perhaps he had died.

He opened one eye the merest slit. He saw the Japanese maple, a beech hedge and below him a bed of button dahlias, prim and tight-headed. He landed right in the middle of the flowers and shook himself.

'Gerroff my dahlias!' the sleek woman yelled from a bedroom window.

Leopold extracted himself from the damaged flowers with dignity and walked away, a curled yellow petal behind one ear like a Hawaiian hula dancer. He had too much to think about to be worried by appearances.

After breakfast he sat looking at the oak tree. It did look very high. What had happened to him? How could he have fallen all that way and survived? He knew that cats could fall from the roof of a house and land unhurt on four paws, but that tree was at least three houses high, or so it seemed to Leopold. Eventually Leopold wandered into the wood to the far end where it was secluded and the blackened stump of a tree struck by lightning stood lonely and unloved.

He climbed the black stump, sniffing the lingering smell of sulphur. He sat in the fork and looked down on the carpet of pine needles below. It was about eight feet high. He could either scramble down the charred bark, or he could jump.

He jumped. He expected to land on the bed of needles in about one and a half seconds flat. But strangely he seemed to float. It took four seconds to land. It was puzzling.

He thought about it for a time, then decided to climb the stump again. He jumped off from the fork. This time it took six seconds and he landed some yards away on dry bracken.

Leopold was beginning to enjoy himself. After all, what harm was there if he wanted to spend the afternoon jumping off an old tree? What the hell! He climbed again, rapidly, like a Red Arrow. He jumped again, quite merrily, paws spread, wondering where he would land.

Suddenly he saw a clump of nettles right below him. Despite his thick fur, he knew all about nettles. His pink nose was particularly vulnerable. He stretched wide his paws in horror and sailed over the top of the clump. Without thinking, he lifted both his right legs and wheeled away in a shallow curve towards an open patch of ground.

When he returned that evening, the family scolded him and said he was too late for supper. They sat round the television, dunking broken biscuits into watery coffee. Leopold licked at the dried bits still stuck on his breakfast saucer. His drinking bowl had not been changed and the water was practically growing algae. He jumped on the draining board and stretched his neck towards a dripping tap.

'Gerroff the draining board, you wicked cat,' the woman shouted. Leopold obligingly removed himself. For a split second, as he jumped, he almost spread his paws but an inner caution stiffened this action and he landed awkwardly, unbalanced.

'Now don't do that again! I won't allow it.'

He sat on the front steps in the dark until Dana came home from her date. She was sniffing into a twisted scrap of handkerchief and her mascara had run into panda smudges. She made herself a mug of milky cocoa and poured a large saucerful for

Leopold. She knew where her father kept a hidden packet of chocolate biscuits and she helped herself, spreading out the remainder so that he would not notice the difference.

'Of course, I can never tell them about Roger,' she said to the cat, stroking his ears. 'They wouldn't understand about him not having any money, or a job. They'd never understand.'

Leopold daintily mopped up the fallen crumbs. No, they would never understand. The next morning, he was at the door, waiting to be let out, and streaked through the moment there was a crack. He spent all day practising, graduating from tree to taller tree. It was exhilarating. By mid-afternoon, he acknowledged what he had been wondering about ever since his miraculous escape from the big oak.

It was not simply this new skill which filled him with joy and excitement, but the fact that it held the key to something far more important – escape. He walked back to the house quite jauntily, not caring that his supper would not make up for missing breakfast.

'Caught yourself a little mouse for breakfast, did you?' asked the sleek woman, scraping the last globule of mush from the tin. 'There's a good pussy.'

Good pussy swallowed the revolting food. It was important now to keep up his strength. When he saw the family go out for the evening, he climbed on to the roof of the house, skirting the television aerial and leaping up on to the flat top of the chimney. He sat there for a long time, his tail neatly curled over his feet. It was not that he lacked courage; it was just that this was the first time he had contemplated jumping from anything other than a tree. And it might be that trees were a vital ingredient . . . however, he would never find out just by sitting.

He stepped off into space, automatically widening his paws, claws outstretched, tail stiffened, lifting his head. These movements slowed his free fall, then he leaned carefully into a wide arc, his brilliant eyes almost crossed with concentration. He glided across their garden, passed the dahlias, rising over the hedge, then soaring up as he came face to face with an overgrown rhododendron bush. The evening air was cool and peaceful as he locked into a pure, straight, calculated climb, his whiskers twitching as the wind resistance began to increase. He winked as he passed two alarmed starlings flying home to roost. As he topped the climb, he closed his paws, tucked his head down and streamlined his descent on to the flat roof of a neighbour's garage. Shaking with relief, he sat down and began to lick back his ruffled fur. He had done it. He did not need a tree.

After that, there was no stopping Leopold. He jumped off anything and everything. His greatest day was when he managed to climb into the church belfry and then up the narrow ladder that was steel-pinned to the side of the spire. There was precious little room at the top for him and the weathervane. The dim metal cock spun round, creaking, obviously out of control, almost knocking Leopold off his perch. Leopold took off in a perfect swallow, levelling out at about 100 feet without any effort. The thermals of air took him up higher and he gloried in the feeling of space and freedom. Below the neat rows of houses and gardens stretched for miles. Dark green patches of woodland were all that were left of the great forests which had once covered the hills. He flew over the top of the ugly grey gasometer, tracking for fun the snake-like train that swayed along the line. People were so small, wobbling along on matchstick legs, heads down, wrapped up in their worries and dreams. No one noticed a large ginger-and-white cat flying casually overhead.

He began to get more adventurous, exploring the countryside and neighbouring towns. He followed the river Thames to London, but did not stay long among the high-rise flats and skyscraper office blocks. The air traffic bothered him and the pigeons were rude.

'I've just seen a cat fly by,' said a stunned window cleaner in a cradle at the 21st floor of some offices.

'Fell out a winder,' said his pal morosely, wiping a dark mirrored pane of glass. 'Probably pushed.'

'It was flying. It was a ginger cat.'

'We gotta little tabby. Company for the missus.'

The window cleaner screwed up his eyes against the sun. Whatever it was was almost out of sight, skimming over the top of St Paul's dome, the cross sparkling in the bright rays.

Perhaps it was a ginger bird. He clamped his mouth shut and turned back to his work. He did not want to get his cards.

Of course, Leopold could not keep his secret forever. He began to get careless. The family gave a party with watered gin and cut-price whisky to celebrate the sleek man's latest promotion. As they cleared up, Leopold slid among the chairs looking for morsels of cocktail snacks. If they were anything like the general standard of catering in the house, most of the guests would have dropped them. He found a pathetic shrimp on a soggy toast finger stuffed behind a pot plant. It wasn't bad. The cheese they had used had been so stale and crumbly, it had parted company from the cubes of pineapple and there were lots of bits on the floor.

The sleek woman had also lashed out on a dip made from dried chicken soup and tinned cream. Not many people had dipped so there was a lot left. As she was scraping it all together and wondering if she could turn it back into soup, a big dollop slopped off her finger and fell on to the carpet. Leopold raced to the rescue.

'Gerrout the way! You damned cat! Look what you've made me do,' she stormed. She swiped at him with her morocco-bound visitors' book. (Someone had signed: 'Unbelievable party, darling.')

The book caught Leopold on the side of his head. Swift as a flash he spread his paws and leaped to the safety of the pelmet. The woman was furious and did not notice anything unusual about the ascent. She lashed out at him again and he took off, flying right across the room to a shelf on the other side.

'You wicked thing,' she shrieked, wondering if she had watered the gin enough.

'Mummy,' said Dana, opening the french doors to let out the smoke-laden air. 'I think Leopold can fly.'

Leopold soared out into the night air. He shared a gnarled oak with an old owl and contemplated the future. They knew now. Perhaps it would not matter. After all, what could it possibly mean to them? Habit was hard to break and, at breakfast time, Leopold nodded to the sleepy owl and took off for home. He flew down into the garden and sauntered up to the back door, casually twitching his tail.

'Darling,' cooed the woman, scooping him into her arms.

'Darling Leopold, you've come back to mummikins! Nice pussy, come and have some lovely milk.'

Leopold was thoroughly alarmed, squashed against her second-best jumper with the sequin buttons. She smelled of musk and face cream. He struggled but she was holding him very tightly. He heard the back door shut and it was the thud of doom.

They sold him to a circus. As he was being driven away in the back of the circus owner's Cortina estate, the sleek family was hugging each other with glee, waving the fat cheque and planning to buy more cars, more televisions and a holiday in the Bahamas.

Leopold quite liked the circus for about two days. They put him in a large cage that smelt of bear, and people came and looked at him, bringing delicious things like fish and chips, beefburgers and anchovy pizzas.

Then the circus owner put him on the scales and declared a diet. Leopold must not gain a single ounce. Aerodynamics he called it.

Leopold did not understand the circus. It was so bright and noisy with strange animals growling in the night. They did feed him better food than he was used to, though he suspected it was left over from the lion's share.

The trouble started when Miss Dora, the trapeze artist, refused to carry Leopold up the ladder to her platform high in the roof of the big tent. She absolutely refused even to touch him.

'I shall come out in a rash all over,' she said, every rhinestone on her brief costume quivering with indignation.

The circus hands rigged up a basket affair in which to hoist Leopold up to the platform. Leopold hated it. He felt sick as it swayed and jerked higher and higher up into the dim black regions of the roof. He stepped out on to the narrow platform and looked round politely. It was very high up indeed. Miss Dora stood as far away from him as possible.

'Shoo, shoo,' she said, her feathered headdress nodding with each word. 'Go away.'

Someone switched on a spotlight, blinding Leopold. He stepped sideways to avoid the brilliant white light and, disorientated, he fell off the platform. He fell, paralysed with fear, like a stone, and landed with a bounce in the safety net, all four paws and his head stuck through the mesh; it was very undignified.

'Now, Leopold,' said the circus owner, speaking slowly and deliberately. 'When you get up there on the platform I want you to fly across to the other platform.' Leopold looked back at him with puzzled green eyes. 'Fly across, like Miss Dora. Only you're a clever pussy and you don't need a trapeze bar.'

Miss Dora scowled. 'I don't like sharing my act with a cat. It's ignominious.'

Again Leopold was put into the elevator and swung up to the platform. Again he fell into the net. The sweat began to come out on the owner's brow. He had gambled a fortune.

This time Leopold rolled over and got into such a mess in the netting they had to cut it to get him out. He tried not to look smug as he returned to his cage.

'Please, pussy,' said the circus owner the next day, wringing his hands. 'Fly for me. I gotta lotta money tied up in you. You wouldn't want to see old Joss go bankrupt, would you?'

Miss Dora had covered her body thickly with an antibite ointment in order to protect herself from Leopold's deadly rash. The smell was awful. He couldn't stand it for two seconds. He launched himself off the platform at speed, did two fast circuits of the arena then, spotting the exit sign, made a beeline for the opening. He dipped stylishly over the big top before heading off towards the far country. He felt the faintest twinges in his paws as he climbed higher in the sky. He had never reached this altitude before. His tail streamed out behind him, his fur filled with air and the loose flaps of skin under his armpits belled out like a parachute.

Leopold was looking for the sea. He had had in mind for some time to learn to fly properly. He was a bit afraid of going to the mountains to find an eagle or a condor. They were so big and unpredictable. But seagulls, now they were a different kettle of fish. And there was no doubt about it, they could fly. Leopold's capacity would be one of an ardent observer.

He was quite surprised when he eventually found the sea. It was not at all as he had expected, just miles and miles of heaving wet blue waste. But the seagulls were there in their thousands, screeching and diving and squabbling among themselves. Leopold particularly admired their precision take-offs and landings on water.

He went down to the pebble beach to practise a few low-level take-offs, but each time he nose-dived straight into the sea. It was horrid, and he soon discovered that he could not fly very well if his fur was wet.

'Scram, scram,' shrieked the seagulls as Leopold went headlong into the waves yet again. He gathered his dignity round him like a wet bathrobe and climbed into the heather to dry off.

When he found the cliffs, he knew he had the answer. Their sheer height was impressive; the grandeur of the craggy rock face filled Leopold with quivering pride. This was going to be his home. He was going to be a cliff cat; he saw himself leaping about the rock face as sure-footed as Tarzan, catching his food among the gorse on the headland, sleeping in a small cave. He could watch the seagulls all day and learn their secrets. He would practise diligently from his cliff-top take-off, experimenting, and adapting their flight to his. It was going to be wonderful.

The seagulls were a bit alarmed by this peculiar, flying ginger thing. They knew cats ate birds but what sort of cat was this? They resorted to a Mafia-style protection racket, dropping Leopold the odd, freshly caught mackerel in return for paws-off. This suited Leopold admirably. He did not fancy a mouthful of wet feathers.

Leopold ate well. Fresh fish, rabbits and mice; the dew to drink from fragrant morning puddles shot with silvery sunshine. He was very happy.

His flying improved. He could stay in the air for much longer and with a lot less effort. He could glide in for touch-down with fanatical precision. He experimented with stalling in the air, letting himself fall, heart in mouth, then pulling himself out of it moments before hitting the waves. He skimmed along the surface of the sea with carefree abandon. He learned to loop the loop, to power dive like a blazing meteor; he perfected a victory roll, coming out of it to soar up into the blue sky until everything was so translucently blue that he could no longer tell which was sea and which were the heavens.

He was sailing along on one such routine flight, his thoughts to himself, when he discovered he could no longer see land. He circled around, his green eyes searching the horizon. He could see nothing solid or familiar. He flew slowly, wondering in which direction to make tracks. He had no idea how far this sea stuff went.

He began to get tired, flying in ever wider circles. Then he realized that the sun had gone and it was getting darker. He was not alarmed by this as he could see very well in the dark. But this was not the night. It was another kind of foreboding, grey gloom; the gathering of thunder clouds laden with rain.

Leopold looked up as he heard far-off rumbling. There was going to be one heck of a storm, and he was going to be caught in it. He knew what would happen when his fur got wet. He knew what would happen if he had to land on water. Zwat. Caput. End of Leopold.

He flew on bravely, his body aching. The first big drop of rain hit him squarely between his eyes. He blinked and adjusted his speed. He had to keep his head or this thing would beat him.

He tried to climb higher to get above the storm but it was too late. The thunder clouds were dark and menacing; flashes of lightning lit up the rolling masses of horror. He began to wish he had stayed with the circus, or perhaps even the sleek family.

The storm gathered into a seething black mass overhead; the rain began hitting him like sledgehammers. In minutes he was soaked, his fluffy fur plastered to his skin. He lifted his head, trying to maintain height. Fiercely Leopold fought to hold his own, relying on the months of practice to come to his aid now. But he was losing speed and losing height. The dark water below was surging in great white frothed waves, deep gullies sucking and swallowing each other. One bedraggled ginger-and-white cat would soon disappear beneath that hungry sea.

Leopold could hardly see now. His lids were glued by the onslaught of rain. He began to fall. As he fell, he mewed piteously . . .

'Jumping Jehova, if it isn't raining cats and dogs! There, my fine fellow, don't struggle. Mike Kelly's got you safe enough.'

Leopold found himself caught by strong arms that took the impact of his fall. It was a miracle. He must have fallen straight into the arms of a saint.

The saint was wearing glistening yellow oilskins and a brimmed sou'wester off which the rain was dripping. His lined and crinkled brown face had a pair of the bluest eyes Leopold had ever seen.

'And where did you come from? I suppose you done drop out of one of them aeroplanes? My word, we'd better take you down below and dry you off before you catch your death.'

Mike Kelly carried Leopold down into the tiny cabin and began to rub his coat with a rough towel. It was the smallest room Leopold had ever seen, cat-sized in fact. He looked around with interest. The room pitched and rolled in the strangest way, but it did not seem to disturb the man so it must be all right.

'Well, you're stuck here now,' Mike Kelly went on. 'Whether you like it or not. I'm sailing round the world and I shan't make landfall for weeks. You can get off then if you want to, or you can come back to Ireland with me. Please yourself. I'm easy. What do you think?'

Leopold had already made up his mind. No one had ever consulted him before, or treated him as an equal.

'I'm needing a ship's cat and a bit of company,' said Mike, opening a tin of evaporated milk. 'So you dropped in just right. You'll earn your keep and I reckon we'll get on . . .'

It was the beginning of a lifetime of devotion and mutual companionship. Leopold sailed all over the world with Mike, following him round strange foreign places and wintering sometimes in Southern Ireland in Mike's cottage while his catamaran was docked for repairs or maintenance, and the next voyage was planned.

The circus owner sued the sleek family for misrepresentation and the wrangling went on in court for years. Eventually the judge dismissed the case, saying it was useless to go on when neither party could produce the evidence, ie, the cat in question. The costs were enormous and the sleek family, who had spent the cheque, were rather silent as they made an appointment to see their bank manager. Dana did not go. Instead she ran off with Roger and went to live with him in a caravan.

Leopold did not entirely give up flying, though it took him some time to get his nerve back after that terrible storm. He made sure he did not fly too high, or too far away, realising that navigation was his weak point. He even perfected a new technique of a low level approach for a deck landing.

If Mike ever noticed his cat flying round the masthead, he was too tactful to mention it. Occasionally he was heard to mutter unsaintly comments about the Blarney Stone, or wonder if it was the Irish whiskey.

One day he vowed he'd write a book about Leopold, but then, who would believe him?

Cats of My Childhood

MAY EUSTACE

THE NOSTALGIC longing for childhood days superimposes itself on everything I write.

> Why do I write,
> What sin to me unknown,
> Dipt me in ink,
> My parents' or my own?
>
> *Alexander Pope*

Looking back on my yesterdays is to me an exercise in solace and inspiration. No other human experience fills me with such delight. When I reminisce I forget all the cares of the world. I forget that I am getting old. I forget that I am now nearly altogether alone. I forget that I have tax forms to fill in and pension books to sign. I forget all the irritations of the present and enjoy again the old familiar haunts, with the old folks and the animals who first taught me how to live.

> I remember, I remember,
> The house where I was born,
> The little windows where the
> sun,
> Came peeping in at dawn.

Yes, those were the days. Clearly, as through a looking-glass, I see the old home, the gardens, the paddocks and rivulets. And I see the pathway, too, which leads to the river and the woods carpeted with bluebells, primroses and cowslips. And then – as if I ever could forget – I see my mother and father again. Mother's long black skirt is trailing in the dust and my father's moustache seems longer and bushier than before. They are speaking in whispers, as if they still have some unfinished business in hand. It was the business of love and sex. Our family was not yet complete.

And, fortunately for us children, our parents were so taken up with each other that they left us very much to our own devices. Within reason we could do what we liked. The same good fortune followed the cats. They were everywhere, males and females together, just living their own lives in their own sweet ways. I know that mother never had a kitten destroyed and there were many of them coming and going in all directions. If I had today's official standards of points I am sure I would have found, amongst them, Rexes and Havanas, Silver Tabbies and British Blues and Bi-coloureds galore.

I was only a small child when the seeds of cat enchantment were sown within me. Not in a namby-pamby way but in a studious and interested fashion, more becoming to an older child. And I repeat again that cats were everywhere. On a sunny day they came out in number, each selecting its very own sheltered and sunny spot. Ostensibly, none of these outdoor cats could claim from us a roof for their heads. We had our own recognized cat dynasty, which included the cat belonging to Rosey, our old housekeeper, and one or two others who scrounged their own kind of living. But we had plenty of surplus rations which we handed out freely to the strays.

But how many of these multi-coloured or self-coloured cats were really strays? There was one little tabby who always had her afternoon nap on my window sill. She basked in the sunshine like an oriental goddess. She felt and smelled good. Her ears stood up sharply and she had wisdom written all over her little striped face. She had a cute black nose which seemed to direct her always to the sun. I would not say that she was an over-friendly cat. she did not permit too many familiarities—one or two little rubs, a tickle under her chin, a gentle touch to her little thick tail. No more. She let me know she did not like my overtures and stood up and went away. I thought that an apt name for her would be Winny Silly.

Our next sunbather was the doorstep cat. He was pure black

and every inch a male. I was sure of this because I often heard Rosey using bad language towards him; nevertheless, he sat it out though his noxious presence angered the humans. He was quite an agreeable old fellow and permitted me to rub him down and tickle his chin. We called him Steptoe, not after the TV character we know today, but because of his location preference and also after our uncle. He was a very rich farmer and came to Kilkenny once a year. He did not trust anyone to do his buying and selling and when he came down the road on a fair day he had the biggest herd of cattle of all the farmers. He specialized in the Herefordshires and congratulated himself on being a quality breeder. He had only one weakness: he always celebrated a good sale with a good drink. He liked his whiskey neat and always ordered it in doubles. Mother did not seem to mind for she said it was his own money he spent and he could do what he liked with it – his pockets always bulged with £5 and £10 notes. When my father helped him into his cart he just dropped down in the straw like an asphyxiated pig and the pony went along home without any direction, keeping to his own side of the road and negotiating his entrance to the drive carefully.

But Steptoe held onto the step no matter who was coming and going, so long as it was sunny and warm. You were at liberty to step over him but not to displace him.

The barn cat was a black and white one and the most determined sunbather of the lot. He was not so distinguished-looking as Steptoe. His coat was rather coarse, there were odd smudges of white on his tummy and the tip of his tail was white for a good half-inch. He was domesticated, too, and never objected to having his whiskers pulled. Like the others, whose names were associated with their own selected habitat, we found that Barny was a heaven-ordained name for him. He always hung round the barn and it would appear that he had a special friendship for the little black Kerry cow who was house-bound until her calf was born. She was known to wander and had her calves in the most unlikely places. Once she actually gave birth while standing in a stream. Only by the merest fluke was she found in time. In the meantime, if the sun shone, Barny came out to enjoy it and, if the weather was bad, he went into the straw with the cow. Sometimes we did not see him around for a couple of weeks. He did not smell so much of cat as of cow dung.

With regard to smells and scents country folk are more discriminating than those born in towns. The scents of lilacs and roses could never obliterate the smells associated with animals. But Rosey had a town nose, really, and particularly disliked tom cat odour. If she got the slightest whiff she was away for the dog or for her switch.

Then there was the most beautiful of all the cats – the white Persian. I say 'beautiful', but I ought to have said 'could have been beautiful', for her coat was always very dirty. Her lovely fan-like tail was trailed in the dirt too. I am absolutely certain that she had blue eyes which she used to advantage – if ever a cat winked an acknowledgment it was Persi. Her favourite haunt was the stable where we kept the big brown stallion. He was an enormous fellow and generated a special kind of heat which appealed to cats. Persi did not have to cuddle up to him; you could always see the perspiration coming from his body. Though he was a noble beast, full of puissance and fertility, the occasion for him to prove himself never arose.

Besides those named there were also more cats hiding in the hay lofts and it only needed the sun to bring them out. It was interesting to see how the various cats reacted to weather changes. I do not know what Kilkenny weather is like now but I remember that, half a century ago, it was always raining. My mother pointed out that the ever-green grass and the lush vegetation everywhere was the result of the pleasant moist climate. She loved the rain. Once she went on a holiday to her brother in Wembley and she said the weather was too clammy and dry; she longed for the drip, drip, drip, that seemed to be going on forever round our old home. I can remember standing so often in the porch waiting for the sun to shine and my pal and I chanted the popular dirge, 'Rain, rain, go to Spain, and never come back again'. During these wet periods the cats disappeared altogether. All, of course, except our own cats who had managed to sequester themselves in some quiet corners. But no stray cats were allowed the comfort of Rosey's kitchen. She did not keep her hearth so beautifully polished and the surrounding brasses so exquisitely radiant and shining to dazzle the eyes of the strays. This inviting spot was hers and for her little cat alone. Even the house dogs on the payroll were not encouraged to loiter in the comforting glow from the turf fire and the logs.

It was really Nan that set our project in action. Nan was one of the songsters who was with me singing in the rain. She was also one of my best school friends and had a big heart for all cats.

'Where is Winny Silly today?' she asked, seeing the vacant corner.

'Funny you should ask as I was just wondering the same myself. Every time it rains she goes away. Suppose we try to find out where her second home is?' I replied.

'Yes,' said Nan, 'we will run after her next time she comes and decides to leave.'

'And there are others, too, who sit around in the sun for days at a time and as soon as the weather breaks – away they go. It would be fun to find out where they all live.' And there and then we embarked on a project which would establish for all time the true homes of all our visiting felines.

It was quite a few days before we could get our plan started. The weather had been most inviting and we saw all the cats in their sunbathing haunts. I told Nan that mother had prophesied that the low clouds now in the sky meant that rain was on the way. And she was right. Nan had barely arrived when the first drops fell. The first to really get the message was Winny Silly. She was away in a flash with the two of us after her. She jumped over the garden gate like a born athlete, wound her way along the hedge, through the woodside, in and out amongst the trees. We were both out of breath trying to keep up with her. To make matters worse Nan fell down a marshy slope and commenced to cry, 'I think I will go home. We'll never catch her, and I am so tired.'

But I dismissed her complaints and she soon stopped them and came running on with the same zest as she had at the start. We had Winny in sight when she took a sharp turn into the lane leading to the priest's house. We watched her let herself in through the window with such aplomb that we knew she was home. We waited round for a bit and she did not come out. So that was that. Our first query was solved: Winny Silly was the

priest's cat. Sunbathing on my windowsill meant nothing to her. She was there because she liked the shelter it afforded her. She had no love for stray humans. When life suddenly became hard, and the cruel winds of winter buffeted her about, she knew where she could find comfort – on the welcoming knees of the priest's housekeeper. Here food was plentiful and warmth abundant.

Finding Steptoe's domicile took a more exhaustive search. In the first place a few drops of rain were not enough to displace him. We watched him while he crouched miserably against the wall, while the rain lashed all about him.

'Come on Nan,' I whispered, 'I think he has had enough.' Yes. That was so. He was moving. First, he looked appealingly into Rosey's kitchen. The fire was sending out rays of warmth and light which made Steptoe's skin tickle in anticipation. But before he had as much as put a foot forward Rosey was after him like a ton of bricks.

'No stray cats here, please!' said Rosey in a language that Steptoe understood. He walked sulkily away. We wore heavy rain wear and Wellington boots and continued in Steptoe's wake. Once again he took the same route as Winny, but this time he passed the priest's house and went in the direction of the river. It was like a funeral march for, rain or no rain, Steptoe was in no hurry. He stopped several times for a smell of this and that. Then, quite unexpectedly, he stood in front of his own halldoor but this time it was not the usual kind of door – it was a door that one had to jump over and this abode was a houseboat of sorts. There didn't seem to be any welcoming hands coming out to fondle him; nevertheless, he climbed into the cabin, displaying a proprietorial air, and sat himself down. It was evident that this was his real home. No matter how desolate and dreary everything looked in the rain, we were satisfied that this was where Steptoe lived. Later, mother told us that an old fellow known as Joxer had laid claim to the boat after the death of the real owner. He was known to be respectable and did odd jobs for the farmers. He did quite a good bit of fishing, too, and if anyone wanted a nice fresh trout Joxer was their man.

We were very pleased to have found Steptoe's home. Now we had traced back two of our sunbathers. After that I often purloined some of Rosey's cat food for poor Steptoe because I felt he had a lean time on the boat. Miss Winny Silly needed no extra rations for she lived the life of a lady when she was not on our windowsill. She was well fed and well nourished from the generous table of the fat parish priest.

Now for Barny. His conduct was not always predictable. Sometimes for days he disappeared and then we saw him surreptitiously climb through the window of the cow shed. It was certain there was some sort of affinity between the little Kerry cow and him. When we did approach him he was always amiable and we were sure that he was not an abandoned stray. He was never ravenously hungry like Steptoe, so Nan and I agreed that he came from a good home. Yet we had not a single clue. Finding his home would be a hit-or-miss matter. Unlike Winny and Steptoe he was not driven away by the rain. When his sunbathing was disturbed he just went inside and played the waiting game with the little cow. He lay comfortably in the straw as if time did not matter. Nan and I decided that all we could do was wait. Surely this was wise, for by waiting we found out all we wanted to know about Barny. We were coming home from school one day when a little fellow called Tommy Docherty asked us if we would play a game of marbles with him. As we had never before been asked favours from boys, we agreed to do this.

'Hold on a minute,' said Tommy, 'I see Jimmy, our cat, coming home for his dinner.' And at that very moment we looked into the eyes of Cowshed Barny. So that was that, Barny – alias Jimmy – had a good home.

As we walked back Nan and I congratulated ourselves on establishing the real identity of Cat Number Three – Barny of the old barn – a cat who had fallen in love with our little cow.

The fourth cat, the dirty white Persian, was the most difficult of all to trace, for she never left the stable. When she was not sunbathing on the roof she was inside with the big horse. She really was a homeless stray as she never left our yard and she was the one cat that was never missing. She was always hungry and ate ravenously in a manner more becoming to a waif and stray than to her Persian forebears. I could never catch her. Nan and I saw her several times a day and we decided that, if we could catch her and clean her up, she would gain entry in to any society – and most certainly into Rosey's kitchen. The word 'Persian' was magic.

We told mother of the lovely white cat we saw in the stable and we were sure she was a Persian.

'Persian, indeed,' said mother, 'and how could a Persian cat be turned into a waif or stray?'

So 'Persian, indeed' was our most difficult quarry. To trace her was not going to be easy.

About this time Nan and I started our education proper at the convent school. No more frolics with Tommy Docherty and his kind. Every morning we walked nearly two miles, along footpaths, leafy lanes, through the woods and fields, passing the old church and graveyard, and up the hill to the convent. A little later mother got us our own pony and trap and we took him to school every day. It was very difficult getting permission to tie him up at the back gate and there was one thing we had to promise and that was that we must clean up every evening. The little nun who was in charge of the roses welcomed the good manure we placed so liberally on her rose trees. Driving backwards and forwards to school, with a car full of scholars, was amongst the proudest and happiest experiences of my early school life.

And soon, very soon indeed, there occurred the last and final key to our cat project. Reverend Mother's first address to the assembly included a request pupils to keep an eye out for her own very special white Persian cat, which had been missing for about a month.

'Did you hear that, Nan?' I whispered, 'could it possibly be Persi?'

Trembling all over I put my hand up to speak. 'Please, Mother, I think I know where there is a white Persian.'

'Speak up, child,' was her reply but I was not able to speak any louder and I was summoned to the table.

Then everything changed. Suddenly her voice sounded more kindly and the next thing I knew was that I was being sent home with big Alice, the convent cook. Yes, she immediately identified Fluffie, the convent cat. While the chase was on she told mother that she was a very special cat, having been imported (or rather smuggled in) from the home of a viscount in Le Mans – a special gift to Reverend Mother for services rendered to his daughter while boarding in the convent. Then Alice took mother aside and said that, being a female, she was becoming a real annoyance, especially when the male cat population of the town serenaded her all night. It took quite a little while to catch Fluffie as her month's freedom and life as a waif and stray had whetted her appetite for adventure. With the whole of our working staff guarding every exit from the stable, Alice dived headlong under the horse's belly and emerged with a much-bedraggled Fluffie.

Instead of settling down to be the angelic, white-robed creature she used to be, her stay in the outside world had unsettled her. She was no longer content to listen quietly to the angelus bells and the clanking of the rosary beads as the nuns came and went from their devotions. Celibate and happy though her owners might be, Fluffie was now rebellious. The quiet of the convent was shaken. After a serious conference in the community it was decided that Fluffie would have to move on – not as a horse's mate in a dull and depressing stable but as a companion for someone of importance in the town.

When Reverend Mother's wishes were made public the convent bell rang loud and often as hopeful hearts sought ownership of the most important cat in town. From several applicants Fluffie was presented to the mayor, for who better than the first citizen to win such a prize?

But now the real fun started. On the night of arrival Fluffie escaped up the chimney and it looked as if she would be impossible to catch, so the First Lady sent out a series of SOS. The mayor himself was quickly on the scene and, when he looked up the chimney, he was soon blinded by soot that had been displaced by the cat. More and more SOS to civic dignitaries and others. The district nurse outran the doctor and arrived in time to shout: 'Oh, your Lordship! Your poor, dear Lordship! Water, soap, castor oil and brandy! Quick!'

It did not take Ellen, the district nurse, many minutes to get things under control. She cleaned up the mayor, cheered up the mayoress, nipped the wee brandy and went after the cat. By this time Fluffie was in a more agreeable mood and was not so difficult to catch.

'You may take her if you want,' stammered the mayor, 'she is too much for me with my civic duties.'

And so Fluffie became the nurse's cat.

It is so many years ago that I cannot remember all the details but I know that, after her weekly bath, her coat was as white as snow. She was as sweet as she was handsome – and nurse watched carefully over her morals. The occasional tom who picked up her trail ran for his life if ever he saw nurse appear, so there were never any little Fluffies to carry on the name.

And that was how it was in my youth. Cats and everything to do with them were so much fun.

A Vet's Life

JOHN BOWER

'Mrs Jones is on the telephone. Apparently her cat has just jumped off the sofa and its tail has dropped off!' My very able nurse had never delivered a more unusual or macabre message than that. At this stage I decided to speak to Mrs Jones myself as obviously there was some mistake – such a thing could not happen. It had! Mrs Jones's description of the furry object, about nine inches long, which was no longer part of Blackie the cat, left me in no doubt at all. I suggested she should bring both parts of Blackie in to my surgery where I hoped I could resolve the problem.

Blackie had indeed jumped off the sofa and lost his tail. About three weeks earlier, Blackie had been involved in a road accident from which he appeared to recover fairly rapidly. He had not regained the use of his tail, however, due to a 'stretch fracture' at the base of the tail. This type of fracture is caused by a car tyre trapping the tail while a cat is still crossing the road at speed. This had, in this case, led to the death of the tail but not of Blackie. A minor cosmetic operation was needed to tidy up what was left of Blackie's tail and Blackie was as good as new – certainly a few inches better off than a Manx cat.

Cats do have problems with their tails. They seem to pay dearly for the extra bit of balance that the tail may give them. I always think of tail injuries as happening to cats that nearly got away with it. The tail, as I mentioned, is a fairly common site for a road accident injury. It is also often involved in injuries sustained in fights with other cats – presumably, either in cowardly cats which were running away at the time (too slowly), or possibly in cases in which the aggressor unfairly pounced from behind.

In the surgery, cats can be more difficult to handle and restrain than dogs. If a dog is a little fractious it is possible to muzzle it to prevent a bite and, of course, its claws are relatively harmless. A cat, however, can only be muzzled with extreme difficulty and usually distress is caused. The result is less co-operation than if it were not muzzled, and its claws can inflict most unpleasant wounds to the veterinary surgeon, the nurse or the owner. To reprimand a dog when necessary can help; in the case of cats it only makes the situation worse. Patience is the only real answer apart from a sedative when really necessary. Luckily for the profession, the attitude of the owner of an unco-operative cat is usually sympathetic to the veterinary surgeon. This varies from the mild, 'Do be careful, he may bite and scratch you', to the blunt, 'Don't trust him—he's a tiger.' This latter type of cat is usually brought in to the surgery trussed up in a small bag with perhaps his head protruding. One client of mine brings his cross-Siamese (very cross Siamese!) into the surgery from the waiting room by holding onto the scruff of the neck only. In this way the cat is brought in with all four legs and eighteen claws rigidly extended, teeth bared and a continuous, meaningful, warning growl coming from its mouth. I was horrified the first time this happened and tried to explain to the client that there were better ways of carrying his cat. However, a short abortive attempt to demonstrate other ways with his cat convinced me otherwise! I now see this cat only at his home, where he is considerably better behaved.

Some cats are great believers in the saying that attack is the best method of defence. The minute they are placed on the consulting table they make a determined attempt to climb up the person examining them. This is a highly effective method of avoiding an examination. Equally effective is the raised attacking forepaw when a hand comes anywhere near them. But once the cat is restrained by the scruff of the neck gently on the table, then it is usually possible to carry out a thorough examination.

A separate waiting room for cats away from their canine cousins is a sound idea in a veterinary practice, although this is not always possible owing to shortage of space. Certainly cats are more relaxed in such surroundings than sandwiched between a great dane and a wolfhound. It is always much safer to bring a cat to a surgery in a cat basket or zipper bag than just to carry it or wrap it in a towel. This minimizes any risk of escape which we all know can and does happen, and also ensures that the cat does not obtain such a close view of his neighbours in the waiting room.

I recall one escape with amusement now but great concern at the time that it happened. The surgery had finished and I was just contemplating a quiet evening when the door bell rang. At the time I lived above the surgery so there was no escape during off-duty hours. I answered the door and found a client holding her cat closely to her without even so much as a towel wrapped round it. The owner had misread the surgery hours and was presenting the cat for a routine check on a fractured leg which I had encased in a plaster cast the previous week. The poor cat took one look at me, realized immediately who I was and took off. The owner struggled to hold it but to no avail and within three seconds the cat had disappeared down the path, limping at lightning pace. I say limping because a quick look at the owner revealed that she was still holding the plaster cast! This was the one part of the cat that she had grasped when he struggled, to try to prevent him from escaping, but the Houdini had pulled his leg out of it and bolted! The story has a happy ending which is why I can now look back on it with amusement. Houdini limped straight home and was promptly returned to the surgery in a zipper bag. I applied a further plaster cast and within four weeks his leg was as good as new.

The most astonishing escapologist I ever handled was a ginger tom called Sandy. Sandy lived in a small coastal fishing village and, true to form on a Saturday evening, ate a piece of mackerel which unfortunately still contained the hook. This inevitably caught in Sandy's throat and my services were needed. This was no simple matter; the hook was anchored firmly in the throat and Sandy was in no way appreciative of my efforts to remove it. There was no alternative but to take him back to the surgery for a general anaesthetic in order to remove the hook. Sandy was popped into a strong wicker basket and placed in the back of my estate car. The sliding windows of the estate were closed. After a few miles I decided to telephone the surgery to make sure there were no further urgent calls on the way back. Luckily there were not. On my arrival at the surgery, I lifted the basket out of the car and noticed that it was surprisingly light. Sandy had gone! The car, of course – he must be in the car! But I could feel myself beginning to panic. Mislaying a patient is not a common occurrence and I was hoping that this was a false alarm. It was not – Sandy was not in the car either. One sliding back window was now open. While I had stopped to make the telephone call, Sandy had escaped from an escape-proof basket (I have since decided that no wicker baskets are escape-proof!), opened one of the sliding windows and absconded. All of this at least ten miles from his home, on the wrong side of a very wide estuary, and with a fish hook in his mouth. I think it was at this stage that I nearly joined the Ministry – and not the Ministry of Agriculture at that!

How was I to explain this to his devoted owners? I decided that there was no substitute for the truth, which I proceeded to tell them over the telephone. The news was received with unbelievable calm and equanimity, and apologies for not telling me that Sandy would open sliding doors, cupboards and windows. I assured them that I would alert all the other veterinary practices, RSPCA and police. This I proceeded to do but, of course, none of them at this stage could help.

Three weeks later the RSPCA inspector arrived out of the blue with Sandy (dear, lovable Sandy) whom he had just picked up on the other side of the estuary from that on which he had been lost. I cannot explain to this day whether Sandy is a strong swimmer or had, in fact, jumped out of the moving car nearer to my surgery than I originally thought. Anyway, Sandy was back and looking fat and healthy at that, but with the fish hook still firmly embedded in the back of his mouth. He had obviously managed to eat well despite the presence of the hook. I rapidly administered a general anaesthetic and removed the hook. Sandy was then returned to his surprisingly

grateful owners and I exchanged all my wicker cat baskets for fibreglass ones.

I suppose this escapology is one aspect of intelligence in cats. It varies from cat to cat and my own three Siamese demonstrate quite clearly how the application of intelligence can vary. Guilia and Sadie are mother and daughter, and make up a very efficient door-opening team. They cannot open a door with a round knob but are experts at door handles. Sadie, being younger and fitter, jumps up at the handle and pulls it down with both forepaws as she falls to the ground, while Guilia, with precision timing, scrapes at the base of the door when the handle is depressed and opens it. They are so good at this that I have had to reverse the door handles of rooms which are forbidden to cats. The lounge falls into this category as the cats regard the lounge suite as their scratching posts. Rudyk, our third Siamese, has found an answer to this door provided we are in the lounge. He has noticed that, when the front door bell rings, we open the lounge door to go to answer it, which is when he nips in. He has also noticed that, in the bedroom upstairs, is an old-fashioned tassel pull to a bell which used to summon the maid in some past era, and that both bells sound alike. Amazingly, he has put two and two together and, when he wishes to come into the lounge, he runs upstairs, pulls the tassel, waits until one of us opens the lounge door to answer the front door and into the lounge he goes. We had not the heart to disconnect this bell.

Some of the more amusing incidents in the course of a working day are concerned with the sex of the cat and the problems arising if the owner is wrong about it. I see male cats called Sue and females called Jason but, luckily, a substantial proportion of Fluffys and Blackies, names which could apply to either sex. Owners can become quite indignant if told that the cat is not the sex that they thought it was. I recall a huge, obviously masculine, tabby with the typical male development of the cheeks and wide head, being presented at the surgery for the spay operation. I pointed out tactfully that spaying was the term applied to the female operation but that the male operation was called castration. To this the owner pointedly replied that she was aware of this and her cat was, of course, female. I rapidly checked that my original impression of the masculinity of the cat was biologically correct (which it was) and, feeling quite relieved, reassured the owner that the cat was indeed male. 'But it can't be,' replied the owner, 'it's called Tinkerbelle.'

The terms used for these routine operations are also great fun when modified by clients. Female cats are brought in to be splayed or sprayed; males to be incarcerated or castigated, while either sex can be brought in to the surgery to be neutralized or nurtured. One proud owner presented a superb little kitten and exclaimed, 'I want to know whether it is a boy or a girl and if it is a girl I want it incarcerated.' She was obviously terribly confused!

These operations are perfectly routine and side-effects are virtually nonexistent. In the case of dogs, bitches occasionally put on weight when spayed but only if fed too much of the wrong food. Cats, however, seem to regulate their body weight by correct feeding and exercise. Very few cats become highly overweight. An exception is a neuter male I am at present treating for a bladder complaint. He weighs 36 lbs. When one considers that 10lbs is a fairly healthy weight for a normal male, this one is obviously grossly overweight. He somewhat resembles a miniature seal and is so wide that, when he sits lengthways along a wall, one front leg hangs down on each side of the wall. How he manages to climb the wall I have no idea! Apart from his present problem, which is not associated with his obesity, he remains active and healthy and loving with his owners. He does, however, resent my presence and interference for some reason and tries to make life difficult. Because of the amount of fat under his skin, he has no scruff, as this is obliterated by the fat. The scruff of the neck in cats was designed purely and simply for veterinary surgeons to hold onto while examining the cat and, when it is nonexistent, restraint of the cat becomes a major problem.

Some cats, however, appear to like and respect us. A colleague tells me of a blue-point Siamese cat called Buttons, brought to his surgery by his owners who live only a few doors away. Buttons had an injury to one ear, causing a large blood blister which had to be drained under an anaesthetic and then sutured to prevent its filling up again. The sutures are passed through the ear flap and knotted through a button to prevent the nylon suture pulling through the skin. Thereafter, Buttons used to arrive on his own at the surgery about every third day to have his buttons checked and finally removed. The only time his owners came with him was the first time.

The life we lead is sometimes exhausting but invariably rewarding. It is very satisfying to see patients recovering: to see Ginger running and climbing again after having sustained a broken leg in a road accident; to see Suki and kittens thriving after a Caesarean operation; to see Sandy recover from the slug-bait poisoning or even feline influenza. We do get attached to our patients but, as cats do not live to our life span, we necessarily see most of our patients pass on eventually over the years. It is very sad to see an old patient pass away when one can remember delivering him or her what seems like only yesterday. It is an interesting life, however, and the many bright moments brought about by such incidents as I have mentioned, either by the apparent wit of the cat or often the wit of the owner, send one home chuckling at the end of a hard day.

Gershwin

JUDY GARDINER

LADDY SILVER sat looking out of the window and thinking that next year he would be seventy. The idea struck him as preposterous. He didn't look old, neither did he feel it except for a tendency towards heartburn when he stooped. Then it occurred to him that it wasn't people who changed so much as the things they did. Once he had been a dance-band leader, Laddy Silver and his Syncopated Rhythm, playing at the Savoy, the Dorchester, the Trocadero and once at Buckingham Palace at a private supper party. And he was still capable of running a band if anyone wanted him to. He was a good tenor sax player, musical arranger and businessman, but nobody wanted dance bands any more because nobody wanted to dance. At least, not properly.

So Laddy lived a life of enforced retirement in a block of flats in North Finchley with his wife Dolly. And Dolly hadn't changed either, except to become a little fatter and a little more disparaging. They had met when she auditioned as a girl vocalist, and they still had the record she made of *Two Dreams Met* in a very young voice with a throb in it. But he hadn't let her sing any more after they were married because it would have been bad for her status as Mrs Laddy Silver.

He looked across at her now, on this long sunny afternoon filled with nothing but thoughts and the prospect of a cup of tea and a slice of chocolate torte at four o'clock. She was lying back in her chair with her shoes off and her mouth slightly open, and one hand was curved protectively round Gershwin, their cat.

'Gershhh . . .' whispered Laddy, forming his lips into a funnel. The cat opened lazy eyes and regarded him speculatively for a moment before going back to sleep.

'Who's Daddy's lovely boy then, eh? Daddy's lovely big boy, are we? . . .' His whispering seemed to float on the air and he watched it tickle at Gershwin's ears with a beady satisfaction. 'Coming for a little walkies, Gersh?'

'Why don't you shut up?' mumbled Dolly without opening her eyes. The hand that was round Gershwin moved upwards and began to rub the area around his neck with a drowsy expertise.

'He oughtn't to sleep so much,' Laddy complained. 'He's a fine strong cat and he ought to get about more.'

He turned his attention to the window, craning down to see into the garden. 'Here comes little Miss Whatsit. She's got a string bag full of shopping – looks like mainly vegetables.'

'Go and put the kettle on.'

'Which could be why she's so thin. Vegetables don't give you an ounce of fat, they just pass straight through.'

He went out to the kitchen, which was as warm and torpid as the lounge. A lone fly buzzed on the window. He made the tea, then stacked the tray with cups and saucers, milk and sugar and two plates each containing a hefty slice of chocolate torte.

Dolly was awake now and pushing her flimsy, silver-pink curls back into position. She gave Laddy a calm, distant look.

'Got his as well?'

Without replying Laddy placed the saucer of milk on the carpet between them, then bent down and stirred half a teaspoonful of sugar into it. Dolly poured the tea, and they drank it in silence while Gershwin strolled over to his saucer and inspected its contents with care.

'There's been a train disaster in Canada,' Dolly said through a mouthful of torte. 'But I don't think it's anywhere near Joe.'

'Canada's a big place,' Laddy said.

'Joe's thirty-five.'

'Thirty-six on the 5th of September.'

'I know when my own son's birthday is.'

'He's my son too.'

'We must remember to send him a card this year . . .'

Gershwin finished his milk and wiped round the saucer with his tongue. He washed his hands and face then went over to Laddy and jumped on his lap.

'Where's Daddy's lovely boy, eh? Go little walkies, shall we?'

'I wonder if Joe's got a girl,' Dolly said. Then added sharply: 'Don't hold him upside down when he's full of milk.'

'He's not upside down. He's just lying on his back in my arms.'

'For an animal to lie on its back *is* being upside down to *it*,' Dolly said, and although Laddy continued to rub Gershwin under the chin for a few moments longer, he restored him to an upright position.

'More tea?'

'No thanks.'

Conversation died.

Between the block of flats and its driveway there was a wide strip of garden which had been planted with grass, roses, and some silver birches. Considering that the North Circular was only round the corner, the sound of traffic was minimal.

Having walked as far as the garages at the back of the flats, Laddy turned and began to pace back again, pausing every now and then for Gershwin to stare at whatever caught his attention.

'It must take a lot of patience to train a cat to a collar and lead,' said a voice, and Laddy recognized little Miss Whatsit who lived somewhere on the fourth floor. Seen close to, she had a fresh-skinned face with a bright, rather artless expression, and her age was probably no more than twenty. He noticed that she had changed her dress for a pair of jeans and that she was carrying a magazine. They had never spoken before, only smiled.

'It depends on the cat,' Laddy said. 'This one's very intelligent.'

She bent down and held out her fingers to Gershwin who sniffed them courteously before turning away.

'If animals can't adapt to an urban society they're doomed.'

'You could say the same for humans,' Laddy said. 'If you

brought Queen Victoria back she'd choke to death on diesel fumes within a couple of hours.'

'Not if she was at Balmoral,' the girl said. Then added: 'What's your cat's name?'

'Gershwin. After my favourite composer.'

'I like Tchaikovsky,' she said, 'but you couldn't call a cat that, could you?'

'Don't see why not,' Laddy replied, and wished she would go away. To discourage her he sat down on one of the garden seats and stared hard at a bed of roses, but she sat down beside him, riffling the pages of her magazine.

'I work at the Maudsley Hospital,' she said, 'and I finish at three every afternoon this week.'

'That's nice,' he murmured, and couldn't be bothered to ask what sort of work she did. Or even to ask what her name was. It struck him that he had grown to prefer Gershwin's company to that of almost everyone else.

'I'm a physiotherapist,' she said.

'Uh-huh . . .'

Having examined the four legs of the seat with scrupulous care, Gershwin sprang lightly on to Laddy's lap and began butting his head gently against his hand. Late sunlight smiled in his eyes.

The girl opened her magazine and began to study a knitting pattern, then her attention wandered and she sat watching Laddy's hand caressing Gershwin's ears with an easy rhythm.

'Have you got any children, Mr, er—?'

'A son called Joe who lives in Canada. And the name's Laddy Silver.'

He didn't expect it to mean anything to her, not at her age. With every year that passed, fewer and fewer people betrayed any sign of recognition when his name was mentioned. Nevertheless, something made him add: 'At one time I had a dance band.'

She closed her magazine and sat looking at him with unashamed curiosity.

'How interesting. My grandad once had a letter from Roy Fox.'

'Did he,' said Laddy on a falling note. Not wishing to hear any more he uncoiled Gershwin's lead, set him on his feet and led him back home. Going up in the lift to the first floor he wondered whether the girl knew that Roy Fox had been dead for quite a while.

'Nice to talk to, is she?' asked Dolly, who was in the kitchen mashing Gershwin's boiled fish with a fork.

'Who?'

'Little Miss Whatsit.'

Several answers came to mind. *About on a level with you,* was one of them, but it seemed that she didn't expect him to reply because she began calling Gershwin to come for his supper.

And that was it: Gershwin never needed calling for supper, especially when the scent of boiled fish tinted the atmosphere. He was always present and correct, weaving a vigilant arabesque in and out of her feet and exhorting her to hurry in his high eunuch miaow.

But not this evening. Without speaking they hurried through the flat – the lounge, the bedroom and the bathroom, but there was no sign of him. Only the ping-pong ball by the coffee table and a round flattened patch on Laddy's bathrobe, where he sometimes liked to sleep for a change.

'Gershwin! . . . Gershie, *Gershie!*—'

Simultaneously they arrived at the open front door, open no more than a couple of inches. They glared at one another with hate.

'You didn't close it when you brought him back—'

'Look—' Laddy said, darting back to the lounge to seize the freshly folded evening paper. 'You opened the door to the newsboy while I was in the john—'

'I didn't – that was last night—'

Frantically they tried to disentangle one uneventful evening from another. Sometimes one of them opened the door to the newsboy and other times he shoved the paper through the letterbox.

'Never mind – it doesn't *matter!*'

Without waiting for the lift Laddy sped downstairs with Dolly scuttling rapidly behind him. They flung themselves through the big swing doors that gave on to the drive, and there was a moment of summer evening sweetness with even a blackbird singing before the squeal of tyres and the slam of a car door. And the silence that followed was total. Even the blackbird stopped in mid-phrase.

The car was a blue Renault and the man had come to a party in flat 63. He got up from his knees in front of the car holding Gershwin in his hands like a little fur rug.

'I didn't stand a chance . . .' Although he was a large man he sounded like a shocked child. 'I'd slowed right down but he ran straight under the front wheels . . .'

Ashen-faced, Laddy took Gershwin on his outstretched arms and stumbled away, conscious that Dolly was gasping and trying to touch the motionless body.

Without saying anything to the man, or to one another, they took him back to the flat and laid him tenderly on the kitchen table. There was no movement, no sound. He looked as if he were asleep except that his eyes – their habitual vivid green—were still half-open.

'Gershie . . . Oh, little Gershie . . .'

'Get the vet – ring the vet—'

'What've they done to you, little baby?'

No movement, no sound. A soft, still-warm body encased in sleek fur. Helplessly, Laddy groped between the front paws for the heart but couldn't find it.

'The kiss of life!—' Dolly tried to insert a trembling, red-nailed finger between the jaws, then bent her head and blew explosively into the neat little pink nostrils. Dazed as he was, it struck Laddy as a ludicrous thing to do.

'Don't,' he rasped. 'Can't you see he's already gone?'

She gave a deep choking sob and they stood shoulder to shoulder, watching the light fade from the green silver of Gershwin's eyes. It was like watching night fall.

'He's really died,' Dolly said in a disbelieving croak and, although the tears were running down their cheeks, it was a terrible effort to move, or even to think.

'Come on,' Laddy managed to say finally, and blunderingly dried Dolly's face with the tea towel that hung on the airer. It was the first physical contact between them since Christmas, when he had kissed her on the ear and given her a bottle of bath oil. Passively she allowed him to lead her back into the lounge, and even attempted to swallow a little brandy when he pressed the glass to her lips.

'He's dead. One minute he was alive and now he's dead,' she intoned like a woman in a trance.

'I can't take it in,' Laddy said brokenly. 'It'll be years before I can really take it in . . .'

They had two brandies each before they were able to go back to the kitchen, steeling themselves to face the horror of Gershwin lying dead on the table. But there he was, and the coldness of death was already overtaking the warm supple beauty around which had been built two private, middle-aged worlds.

Dolly wanted to have him buried under one of the silver birches down in the garden and became furiously indignant when permission was witheld on the pretext that, if everyone in the flats wanted a pet interred in the garden, it would cause a health hazard. Then they learned that, in Golders Green, there was an animal cemetery where Gershwin could be laid to rest in a plot reserved especially for cats, with dogs buried at a discreet distance away and the more non-conformist creatures such as guinea pigs and parrots planted in a corner by the entrance gate.

The foam-quilted box cost them £15 and the little headstone with his name engraved on it another £25 (cheques made payable to Elysian Fields Ltd), but at least it was somewhere peaceful and beautiful, and the thought of it brought them comfort.

Returning home from the funeral they found themselves confronted by Gershwin's basket, his collar and lead and his plate and saucer. The basket they hid away, but the empty space it left was so poignant that they brought it out again, even though they avoided looking at it.

'It's all so empty without him.'

'You've still got me,' Laddy said, attempting a joke. They sat looking at one another dubiously.

At tea-time Laddy went out to the kitchen and prepared the tray, wincing when his hand automatically reached for Gershwin's saucer. He cut two large slices of apple cake.

'They said we can go back there any time we like,' Dolly said. She was sitting in her chair with her shoes kicked off. 'They said they like to feel that people go back there any time they want to be with their – their little . . .' Her eyes filled.

'We'll visit him once a week,' Laddy said. 'Twice, if you like.'

Sniffing, she poured the tea, and they both sat staring at the floor between them where Gershwin's saucer was normally placed. They wondered what they were going to do with the rest of their lives.

'A lot of people from the flats have stopped me and said how sorry they were to hear about him. They all said how much they'll miss seeing him go for his little walk in the garden with me.'

'I used to take him sometimes,' Dolly said. 'I used to love taking him for a little walk whenever you'd let me.'

'I never stopped you. You always said you couldn't walk because of your feet.'

'I've got very high insteps.'

'Drink your tea,' he said. 'And eat your cake.'

She tried to, then pushed them aside. 'I can't. I feel I'd choke.'

During the silence that ensued Laddy turned and looked out of the window. The silver birches were swaying in a soft breeze.

'We've got to pull ourselves together,' he said finally. 'The show's still got to go on.'

'Sounds like the old days,' Dolly said tonelessly. 'Broken-hearted clowns, and all that.'

'Which reminds me of a slow foxtrot,' Laddy said, and began to hum in a quavering, experimental way.

'Eat your cake and drink your tea.'

'I can't,' he said. 'I can't, any more than you can.'

'Well, stop making that stupid noise.'

The next silence lasted for five minutes and was only broken by the creak of Laddy's kneecap as he got up from his chair. He went over to the cocktail cabinet and returned with the bottle of brandy and two glasses.

'What's that for?'

'Us. If we can't face tea, we'd better find a substitute.'

Dolly looked doubtful. 'That's what we had on the day – on the day—'

'He died. Yes, I know.' Laddy poured two tots and passed

one across to her. 'Drink up. It's just to help us over the worst.'

They sat listening to the distant murmur of the North Circular.

'I had a rabbit when I was a little girl,' Dolly said in a calmer voice. 'But the dog next door got it.'

'That was awful,' Laddy studied her with sudden attention. 'Didn't your Dad complain?'

'He couldn't. He was away.'

'He was away a lot, wasn't he?'

That's how it is with commercial travellers.'

'Ah, yes,' said Laddy. 'Mine was a gents' outfitter and he had his busy times, too. Just before Ascot he never slept at all.'

'You're talking as if I never met him. I met him at our wedding and when Joe was christened, only I don't think he liked me.'

'He liked you very much.'

'I sometimes get the feeling that nobody likes me very much.'

'I like you,' Laddy said. Then he gave a heavy sigh when he remembered that this was the time of day when he always took Gershwin for a walk.

As there was no point in going on his own he poured another brandy for them both. The summer light faded and lonely shadows gathered in the corners of the room.

'I wish you'd let me go on singing,' Dolly said. 'I'd only just got started when I had to stop.'

'You got married.'

'I could still have gone on singing.'

'Then you had Joe. What about him?'

'Girls manage careers these days as well as husbands and children, so why couldn't they then?'

'Because everything was different. Men liked looking after their wives in those days.'

'You married beneath you,' Dolly said. 'That's why you kept me in the background.'

'Baloney,' said Laddy. 'There's no social difference between a commercial traveller and a gents' outfitter, is there?'

'No, but you were Laddy Silver, weren't you?'

'Laddy Silver.' Raising his hands he stroked with sudden

bitterness at the little wisps of hair still struggling to maintain a foothold on his cranium. 'Who the hell was Laddy Silver?'

Without replying Dolly got up from her chair and went through to the bedroom. He heard the squeak of the cupboard doors, then she returned with a heavy leather suitcase thickly covered with travel labels. She put it on the floor between them and, puffing slightly, sat down beside it. The locks clicked open and she began to rummage beneath the open lid.

'Don't,' Laddy said.

'That was Laddy Silver,' she said, and laid a photograph on his lap. The man in it had thick black hair that gleamed like a wet roof, a white bow tie poised on an immaculate dress-shirt and a cigarette holder held between delicately manicured fingers.

'When I told my mother we were getting married, she said, what's the catch? What's he marrying you for when he could have a debutante? I said I didn't know, and she said, well, watch your step. A man in his position wouldn't marry a girl like you if he hadn't got some ulterior motive.'

'You were little and thin, with big eyes and a way of putting over a lyric that no other girl ever had except Ella,' Laddy said. Leaning forward he drew out a handful of publicity stills, of old dinner-dance programmes and a photograph of the band waving from the deck of the *Queen Mary*.

'It hurts,' he said, looking through them. 'No use pretending it doesn't.'

'We haven't been through them for years,' Dolly said. 'Not since Joe was in a skiffle group.'

'Little boy Joe,' Laddy said. 'Remember how I used to play him a lullaby?'

'I remember. He was the only person I wasn't jealous of.'

'There was never any need to be jealous. I only ever loved you, and I dressed you in mink to prove it, didn't I? All mink you were, from head to toe.'

'But all those women who wouldn't leave you alone. Society women giving you gold cigarette cases, waiting outside the hotel suite and freezing me with hate when I came out instead of you . . .'

She sat by the suitcase absently rubbing the cramp in her bulbous calves, unaware that he had left the room until the first notes of music crept through the open door. He was hunched on the side of the bed with the tenor sax catching the last gleam of light. He hadn't played for years, and the first experimental scale sounded husky and hesitant, then like the moon sliding from behind a bank of cloud the notes sang clear and silver sweet.

Speechlessly she staggered to her feet and stood leaning against the bedroom doorway with her face tilted blindly towards the sound. He played the lullaby for little Joe, breathing the sounds like a sigh before wandering on through the tunes that still carried the elegant dinner-jacket charm of the Savoy, the Dorchester and the old Trocadero.

She sang with him, but only in her mind, and when the final tune was no more than a bitter-sweet echo in the room she opened her eyes like someone awakening from a long sleep.

'That was Gershwin.'

'I know,' he said, laying the sax carefully back in its velvet-lined case. 'I meant it as a kind of tribute.'

She went over to him and he opened his arms. Sitting on the bed he only came up to her chest, and she found herself kissing with sudden passion the bony cranium with its poor little wisps of hair.

They fell backwards, sideways, crying because of Gershwin and laughing because it was all so crazy and because they weren't sure whether they still could any more.

'Listen, sweetie,' Laddy said next day. 'I've got news.'

'Uh-huh?'

They were having breakfast in their bathrobes, a thing they hadn't done for years. The voice of the blackbird came in through the open window.

'We're going to Canada to see Joe. We'll phone him tonight. We could fix a cheap flight, and now that we're – we've no commitments—'

'Now that Gershwin's dead,' she said, dry-eyed.

'Now that we're free, what's to stop us? After all, Joe's our baby. Our real baby—'

'Suppose he doesn't want us? Maybe he's tied up with some woman—'

'Aahh—' Busily he buttered his toast. 'You women are always on about other women. So maybe Joe's got a woman—after all, he's thirty-five and human – but what's that got to do with his poor old Momma and Poppa going to pay him a visit, huh?'

The years had fallen away; Joe was in the forefront of their thoughts in the same way that Laddy had unwittingly slipped back into the transatlantic slang of the dance-band days. He looked across at Dolly in her white towelling bathrobe and silver-pink curls and called her a cutie.

They discussed the idea of going to Canada with steadily increasing enthusiasm, and after more coffee and toast worked out that it would be silly not to ring Joe with the good news straight away. So they rang him, oblivious of the fact that for him it was three o'clock in the morning.

'Joe – hey, Joey – this is Daddy! This is your old Poppa—'

'Christ, England,' said a blurred voice. 'What's wrong?'

'Nothing's wrong,' roared Laddy, 'except that the old gal and I are coming out to see you! We can come any time, so just give the word . . .'

They talked for fifteen minutes, during which time Joe woke up and said he'd be glad to see them only they mustn't expect things to be the same as they were when he went away. He was a grown man now, and things changed, didn't they?

'Of course they do—' cried Dolly, leaning over Laddy's shoulder and blasting his eardrum. 'Things have changed for us, too, and we'd so love to see you, Joe baby—'

When the line clicked they stood looking at one another with happy tears in their eyes, then Laddy shaved and dressed and set off for the travel agent while Dolly washed the breakfast things and dusted around.

'But I still think it's a risk,' she said, when he returned with a collection of coloured brochures. 'We haven't seen Joe since he was twenty-two—'

'And we're going to be there for his birthday on the 5th of September,' Laddy said.

They sat down and began to plan the details.

'We'll be there to see the Indian summer and you'll have to set to and make him a birthday cake. I bet he's never had a bit of decent cake since he left home.'

'What'll I wear? He'll think I'm so old . . .'

'He'll love you,' Laddy said, very seriously. 'Just as much as I do.'

If only he'll love me like he did when he was little, she thought. She could see him so clearly, even without closing her eyes.

They booked the flight, checked the state of their bank account and laughed incredulously at their old passport photographs. Then Laddy sat down to write a long letter to Joe, telling him, among many, many other things, when to expect them.

The doorbell rang when Dolly was in the bedroom trying on an old evening dress. Through layers of flame-coloured chiffon she heard Laddy answer it, and then the muffled sound of voices. One belonged to a woman, and Dolly's head burst through the gathered neckline in time to hear it say: 'It just seems like fate, somehow.'

Silent in stockinged feet she went through to the lounge, then halted abruptly. Little Miss Whatsit in jeans and T-shirt was standing close to Laddy and gently brushing his cheek with something held in her cupped hands.

'She says someone found it outside the Maudsley Hospital,' he said helplessly, 'and she wants to give it to us.'

Without speaking, Dolly stood watching while the girl placed the kitten on Laddy's shoulder. She watched the way it stood up, arching its tiny back and mewing shrilly.

'But we can't—' she heard Laddy say.

'Oh, Mr Silver, you *must*! The only way to get over losing a pet is to have another one in its memory—' Her bright, silly face beamed at him persuasively. 'And if you don't have him, he'll have to be destroyed.'

'Yes, but—'

'I know you're going to love him just like the way you loved the other one,' she said, then with a brief little wave in Dolly's direction, added: 'Don't worry, I'll see myself out.'

The kitten teetered on Laddy's shoulder, continuing to mew. Carefully he detached its claws from his shirt and stood looking at the way it tried to nestle in the hollow of his hands.

'It wouldn't make any difference,' he said at length. 'We'd still go.'

'Of course it makes a difference,' Dolly said. 'You heard her say it'll be destroyed if we don't keep it.'

'We could put it in a boarding place.'

'No, we couldn't. It'd get fleas and things.'

'But what about Joe?'

'We won't be going,' she said.

He looked up from the kitten and met the accusation in her eyes. The old, old accusation that went back to the days of society women giving him gold cigarette cases and waiting outside the hotel suite.

'Look, it's only a little helpless kitten,' he said. 'And she meant it for both of us.'

'Put it in Gershwin's basket while I warm some milk for it.'

But the kitten had gone trustfully to sleep in his hands, so he sat quietly on the arm of the chair until she returned, looking sleazy and dishevelled in the old evening dress that was far too tight and all the wrong colour.

'Don't hold him like that, he can't breathe.'

'But we don't want another cat!' he cried, suddenly desperate. 'Honest to Christ, we don't want another one!'

She put the milk down on the floor, then removed the kitten from his hands in a brusque, proprietorial fashion.

'That's what we said about Gershwin,' she said. 'Remember?'

The Cherry Tree

DEREK TANGYE

THE FOG came down again as we were having lunch, and, by the time we had finished, was clinging around the porch where we were sitting. I mentioned a photograph album at this point which contained photographs of my brother's previous visit; and Jeannie said she knew where it was, that it was in her studio, and it would not take a minute for her to fetch it.

She was away several minutes.

'What have you been doing?' asked my brother on her return. 'Feeding the birds?'

'Always doing that!'

I sensed, however, that she was in a state of excitement; and I could not understand why. Whatever the cause she was not going to disclose it in front of my brother.

I had to wait until we were alone.

'When I left you both,' she then told me, 'I went down the path feeling sad that the fog was thick again. Then I saw something which I could not believe was real.'

'What was it?'

'I saw a little black cat looking like the double of Lama and Oliver . . . curled up on the grass at the foot of the cherry tree.'

I reacted in the way that might be expected of me.

'I hope you chased it away,' I said.

'It ran away on its own.'

'Good.'

I sensed, however, that there could be trouble between Jeannie and me. There were danger signs. The following morning, for instance, the morning when my brother Colin was to leave for his Guildford home on the Cornish Riviera from Penzance station, there was the first danger sign. She did not wait for me to make her a cup of tea, but she was out of bed and dressed within five minutes. Then, through the bedroom window, I saw her disappear up the lane with a saucer in her hand.

'She's being unfaithful,' I murmured to Ambrose who was curled on the bed beside me.

I could, of course, understand her interest in the cat. If, when living some distance away from any habitation, one has already had two black cats coming uninvited to the door, it is natural to be intrigued by the appearance of yet a third. It was also specially intriguing that the arrivals were always black. When I was a fervent anti-cat person I always acted in friendly fashion towards a black cat, almost as if I was in awe of a black cat. I had this superstitious corner in my nature. The act of a black cat crossing my path gave me encouragement. Any other coloured cat, in those fervent anti-cat days, seemed to me to be vermin.

There had been, besides Lama and Oliver, two other black cats who had sought a home at Minack, but their efforts had failed because their timing was wrong.

The first of these cats was called Felix. He had been abandoned when the farm where he lived was sold, and the farmhouse was left empty. True, a neighbour had agreed to look after him, but the arrangements as far as Felix was concerned were unsatisfactory. Hence he began looking around for another home, and chose Minack as the most suitable.

His method of approach was persistent, aggressive and, for that matter, heart-rending. We first saw his face eagerly looking through the sitting-room window, and when I opened the door he dashed past me indoors, and came face to face with Lama. He would have pounced on Lama in the manner of a heavyweight boxer on a flyweight if I had not instinctively picked him up and thrown him out.

Since we knew where he came from and the circumstances in which he was being cared for, we decided to return him by driving him there in the car. Ten minutes away by road, five minutes across the fields, we deposited him there at midday. At one o'clock he was back on the window sill, his eager face pressed against the glass.

This situation was repeated several times until we decided we had to act drastically. We discovered the address of the new owner of the farm, contacted him and explained that he had bought a black cat as well as the farm. 'Bring him along to me,' said the man immediately – and that was the last we saw of Felix.

The second black cat began roaming around Minack soon after Oliver had died, and when Ambrose was acclimatizing himself to being on his own. He was a small, compact cat and, in contrast to Felix, timid. For no special reason Jeannie called him Fergus.

I became attached to the sight of him coming prancing up the lane, or passing along the stable meadow, or finding him stalking a mouse in the wood. But he was not domineering like Felix. Fergus seemed content just to stay in the neighbourhood without thrusting his personality upon us. Or perhaps he was

watching us, waiting to see whether a home with us, and Ambrose, was possible.

Then came the day I found him curled up in a corner of the Orlyt greenhouse in front of the cottage; and I was so excited that I behaved very clumsily. I shut the greenhouse door and rushed to tell Jeannie. When we returned Fergus was in such terror that he was trying to throw himself through the glass. After that incident he never appeared at Minack again.

There was, however, a happy ending. Margaret and George, the potters who live at the end of the lane, had just lost their old cat. Her basket was still in place in their kitchen when one morning, a few days after the Orlyt greenhouse incident, Fergus walked in through their front door and straight away settled himself in the basket. A wise cat.

We said goodbye to my brother at Penzance station, then drove back home, and when we reached the turn by the gate which leads to Oliver land, Jeannie asked me to stop.

'The saucer, I suppose,' I said grumpily.

'Yes,' she said, getting out of the car, and fetching the saucer.

It hadn't been touched.

'There,' I said, 'you were wasting your time.'

Stray cats the world over are courted, and so I could not blame Jeannie for doing so. There are thousands of stray cats at this very moment who are wandering in the neighbourhood of potential homes, watching the occupants, studying their habits, making up their minds whether such occupants would cater for their requirements to their satisfaction. Cats appear to be loners and many a time you will hear someone, as I used to do, complain that, unlike a dog, a cat is incapable of love; and that it is a selfish, demanding animal which only a fool would pander to.

There is a certain truth in this viewpoint, but I think it is unfair to compare a cat to a dog. I have been a dog person from a child, always will be, but there are circumstances which can make a cat a more suitable companion.

In my case the circumstances concern the change in my attitude towards wildlife since we first came to Minack. In the first years I behaved as I had always been ready to do since, as a teenager, my father gave me my first gun. In those youthful days nothing gave me more pleasure than early morning wanderings, a dog, an old English Sheepdog, in fact, beside me while I kept my gun at the ready to shoot any game bird or rabbit on sight. Rough shooting, as it is called, had almost a poetic quality in its pleasure for me. I was a hunter. Killing provided no sense of guilt.

Then slowly, like an ivy creeping up a building, I began at Minack to become aware of the wonder of life in the countryside, and of its struggle to survive; and when, one hard winter, I heard on the other side of the valley the frenetic gunshots of men shooting, the barks of dogs being urged on to retrieve the ducks, the plovers, the snipe which had been killed or half-killed, I knew I no longer subscribed to the attitude of my youth.

As often happens when there is such a change in the attitude of a person's beliefs, there is always a chance he might go to the other extreme. I have not done that. I could never condone, for instance, a politically motivated animal rights group; or accept that fox hunting is worse than gin trapping. I just do not intend to kill. Nor do I wish to disturb wildlife in its natural habitation. I want pheasants to roam around our land without fear, and birds to nest without disturbance, and badgers to be free of Ministry of Agriculture persecution. It means, too, that a dog is out of place at Minack. I would never be able to give it the free run, the free chase, the free barking, that I would have done if I had been at Minack in my youth.

A cat, I find therefore, is an easier companion than a dog. A cat's sense of independence also enables oneself to be independent. A cat can amuse itself on its own and, if it feels like a walk, off it will go. A dog, of course, will demonstrate its love to someone much more obviously than a cat, but then a dog will wag its tail at anyone who pays it attention. A cat will not do that. A cat, on most occasions, will remain aloof; and this aloofness, curiously, often maddens those very people who profess to adore cats. Such people, with their baby-language noises as they try to coax a cat to take notice of them, are infuriated with the cat which ignores them.

We have been fortunate in that we have never had a cat which caught birds as a pastime; and yet, if I wish to be fair, I do not condemn cats for being bird catchers. I look upon their cats as another example of nature's way of maintaining the balance of nature. There is, after all, continuous warfare in the world of nature, and cats catching birds is part of it.

Nonetheless, I am thankful that our cats have never shown signs of wishing to catch birds; and this thankfulness has always made me hesitate to welcome any new cat arrival at Minack. I would not be able to tolerate such a cat after the peaceful times of Monty, Lama, Oliver and Ambrose.

There was no sign of the cherry tree cat that day, and no sign of it the following day.

'It's returned to wherever it came from,' I said to Jeannie, 'and a good thing too.'

I had no wish for Ambrose's life to be disturbed.

On the Wednesday, however, I went into the hut where once we used to force, by paraffin heat, daffodil buds into full bloom, and I made a disturbing discovery. The hut, among other uses, had become a cat's kitchen. It was here that Jeannie would painstakingly, on a discarded calor-gas stove, boil the coley for Ambrose. The coley came in 10 lb frozen slabs, and Jeannie, the night before, would lay the slab out to de-freeze.

On the Tuesday evening she had laid out such a slab – but when, on the Wednesday, I had gone into the hut I found a part of the still frozen slab gnawed away. The hut door was shut, but there was a small gap between door and floor level. Something had got through it. What?

I said to Jeannie that it must have been a rat, but we never had previous evidence of a rat. The very mention of such a possibility provoked Jeannie into making an extravagant outburst on behalf of the cherry tree cat.

'It was a starving cat that did that,' she said, with all the conviction of a besotted cat lover. 'Only a starving cat would have clawed at frozen fish!'

'How could it have got there? The door was shut.'

'But there was the gap at the bottom, you silly. The cat is a small one, almost a kitten perhaps, and it could easily have got through such a gap.'

I have never tried to pursue my own point of view when Jeannie is in a cat mood. Wise for me to keep silent.

Thursday was a beautiful sunny day, and we got up leisurely, and I said to Jeannie that we should not waste such a lovely day on work, and that we should relax. It is this pure joy of being free to choose the pattern of a day that makes one a millionaire in real terms. No question of what deal to do next, no question of how to spend money to boost one's ego, just the question of whether to take the donkeys first for a walk, or to take Ambrose.

Then, when such pleasurable duties have been decided upon, then completed, there is the question, keeping a sense of guilt always out of sight, as to what to have for lunch – and where.

On this Thursday, Jeannie, because it was like a summer day in October, decided to have our lunch, consisting of Brie from Paxton and Whitfield, on the bridge. We were sitting there, enjoying ourselves, gossiping, making remarks that strangers to us would not understand, when suddenly I saw the cherry tree cat for the first time.

Surrounding Jeannie's studio, which was several yards below where we were sitting, is a high stone wall, high enough to hide the studio from sight. It was on the top of this high wall that I first saw a little black head, then a thin little black body.

'The cat's back!' I called out loudly, loud enough to scare it and make it disappear.

There had been such excitement in the tone of my voice that Jeannie jumped to the conclusion I was pleased to have seen it.

'A little black cat at Minack again! You are pleased, aren't you?'

'No,' I replied, recovering my composure, 'it's going to be a nuisance hovering around, and anyhow where has it come from? It must have come from somewhere.'

My irritation, I have to admit, was superficial only. I was intrigued. I was not, however, going to give Jeannie any encouragement.

'I wonder where it has been since I saw it on Sunday.'

'It is possible,' I said, 'that it is one of Walter's or it belongs to Tregurnow, and it's just a wandering cat.'

Walter Grose, a Pied Piper of cats, had a collection of them at the farm at the top of the lane. Tregurnow was further away, and also had a number of cats.

'Walter,' said Jeannie, 'has never had a black cat.'

'Anyhow,' I said, and felt relieved as I spoke, 'it shows no sign of wishing to be friendly. It is only a shadow at the moment, and long may it remain so.'

Jeannie was silent. Then she said: 'I have a hunch that Cherry is not always going to be a shadow.'

'So you've christened it already.'

'Cherry is the right name for her, finding her under the cherry tree.'

'So it is a her?'

'I'm sure. Small cats are usually female.'

There was no sign of the cat during the rest of the day, no sign of it the following morning, and Jeannie kept wondering where it could have been hiding. In the afternoon, however, she had a pleasant surprise. She had decided to take to Ambrose a saucer of milk in which she had mixed a raw egg, a favourite concoction of his; and as during the day, when he was not hunting, he was usually curled up in the hay which we kept for the donkeys in the Orlyt, she carried it down to him there. Instead of being curled in the hay, however, he was at the far bottom end of the Orlyt staring intently at something. She walked along to him and found, to her astonishment, the cherry tree cat curled up in a round ball, sound asleep, and only a few feet from him.

'Ambrose was absolutely calm,' she told me later, 'but when she woke up and saw me, she bolted. Ambrose didn't chase her. That's a good sign, isn't it?'

Jeannie knew very well that my main objection to any cat infiltration was the question of Ambrose's reaction to it. My own form of loyalty.

'And where did she go?'

'No idea. Completely disappeared.'

'I refuse to believe that Ambrose would ever enjoy the company of another cat.'

'But he didn't chase her, I tell you.'

I guessed that Jeannie had now decided to carry out a secret wooing campaign; saucers containing an assortment of delicacies would be placed at strategic points around Minack. The game would amuse her. She had done it before. I remember when Oliver was hovering in the neighbourhood she left a saucer containing sliced roast chicken halfway up the lane. I happened to look down that way a little later and saw a fox at the saucer, an astonished fox.

I spent the Saturday morning of that week fiddling with my brush cutter. The brush cutter is like an outdoor vacuum cleaner, just as important, even more so because, although you can manually dust and clean a house, it is quite impossible to keep cliff meadows manually in trim. The brush cutter is an instrument you sling over your shoulders, has a six-foot-long frame with a circular blade at the end of it. At this time of year, early autumn, it is my special companion. I use it to cut away the undergrowth of our numerous small meadows in readiness for the February daffodil season. Unfortunately my brush cutter would not operate properly. I had bought an early model and it was now tired. I would have to get a new one, I realized.

After lunch, when Jeannie told me she was going for a walk with Fred and Merlin on Oliver land, I said I would have a Churchill. This meant a rest. Churchill was always in favour of a rest after lunch.

I lay down on our bed, and ruminated. Such a rumination can cover a multitude of subjects in quick succession. A long-ago memory can merge into a present-day conflict I might be having with someone who had part control of my future. A flash, no logical reason for it, recalls a time when I stayed for a month in 956 Sacramento Street, San Francisco, then suddenly comes the recall of the occasion when, preparing the ground for early potatoes, the rotovator upset and one of the spikes pierced my foot. I was lying on the same bed as on that first night we stayed at Minack, rain dripping through the roof and Monty, companion on the journey in the Land Rover from Mortlake, beside us. Suddenly I was aware of a whisper noise on the carpet beside me. I looked down and there was the cherry tree cat.

The sight of her had an effect on me. It suggested that she was more than just a cat wandering around in the hope of food, and that she was indeed a cat who was looking for a home. Hence, when next I saw Jeannie, my attitude was a different one. I said to her we had a moral duty to perform. Somebody, I said, must have lost the little cat and would be searching for her at this very moment. Instead of amusing ourselves by thinking she might be another Minack cat, we had to take steps to see if we could find out who might have lost her.

After her inspection of the bedroom she kept out of sight for a couple of days, and we thought she had possibly left the neighbourhood. Perhaps she had just been making use of us, a pause in a journey. But the following Monday Jeannie, still leaving saucers around, suddenly saw her at a saucer opposite the water butt at the corner of the cottage. Jeannie had placed the saucer of temptation in the miniature bed of a rockery; and there, to Jeannie's delight around eight in the morning, she saw the cherry tree cat gulping its contents.

Jeannie left her at the saucer, and came back to tell me what she had seen. Then we both went out to have a look.

There was no cat; and there appeared to be no saucer.

'Look,' said Jeannie, who had bent down, 'she's covered it up! She's covered it up with old grass, like a wild animal hiding its prey.'

'Perhaps that's the explanation,' I said. 'Perhaps she is a wild cat, just as Lama was wild when she first appeared.'

We did not see her again that day until evening time when Jeannie caught sight of her on the path, and promptly filled another saucer; she placed it in the same place as the morning saucer. The incident was repeated. The cat soon came to consume its contents, left a little, and covered it up again with old grass. She was very nervous and, when she caught sight of us, she immediately ran away. A pity, because we were harmless. It was Ambrose she had to be scared of.

The first public confrontation with Ambrose came two mornings later. There may have been a previous confrontation, perhaps a meeting during the night, but this we did not know. The public confrontation, however, was horrific.

Ambrose came serenely out of the porch after a breakfast of coley, strolled confidently past the water butt at the corner of the cottage . . . and saw her. He arched his back, growled, spat, then, when the lady saw him and fled, he raced after her. She fled up the path to the clothes line – the clothes line with the most beautiful view in the country, looking across Mount's Bay and with sea breezes drying the clothes – she fled towards it, and seconds later there were such screams that I thought Ambrose was killing her. I followed the two of them and found the lady high up on a privet bush, looking down upon a furious Ambrose.

The incident made me determined to get rid of her.

'Impossible for her to stay around here another day,' I said firmly to Jeannie. 'I just won't tolerate Ambrose being upset.'

'I don't want him upset either.'

'All right then, we are both agreed . . . But don't feed that cat again.'

'I will,' replied Jeannie defiantly.

'Absurd, quarrelling over an unknown cat.'

Our collision of views did not last long. We compromised. The cherry tree cat would continue to be fed.

The search for her origin would immediately begin.

Cat's Cruise

MAZO DE LA ROCHE

CAT was as black as a crow. This very blackness made her presence desired by sailors who were sure it brought them good luck. She was not pretty but she had charm which she had spent her life in exercising to get what she wanted. She was eight years old and she had woven into that eight years more travel and more adventure than most humans achieve in eighty. She had also brought forty-five kittens into the world.

She had been born on board a coaling-vessel, the *Sultara*, in the midst of a terrible storm when the crew thought that every moment would be their last. Her mother was ginger-coloured; and she had, while the vessel floundered in distress, produced three ginger-coloured kittens besides this last one, black as the coal which formed the cargo. The stoker, looking gloomily at their squirming bodies, had growled:

'There'll be no need for us to drown *them*. The bloomin' sea'll do it!'

He picked up the black midget and held it in his hand. He felt an instant's compassion for it. It had come out of darkness and was so soon to return; yet there it lay, curved in his palm, bullet-headed, its intricate mechanism of tiny organs and delicate bones padded with good flesh, the flesh covered by thick silky fur, the whole animated by a spirit so vigorous that already ten little claws made themselves felt on his palm.

'If I could find a bottle the right size,' he said, 'I'd put you into it and chuck you into the sea. I'll bet you'd get to land!'

But there was no need to try the experiment. Miraculously, it seemed, the storm began to abate. The waves subsided; the vessel was got under control. One and all declared that they had been saved by the timely birth of the black kitten. It became the mascot, the idol of the ship.

They could not agree on a name for it. Some wanted a simple one, easy to say and descriptive of its colour, such as Smut, Darkie, Jet or Nigger. Others insisted on some name which would suggest the rescue of their lives by the kitten's timely birth. One offered Nick-o'-Time, with Nick for short. But they could not agree. Then someone called her simply 'Cat', and the others, in spite of themselves, acquiesced, as is often the case with names. From then on she was proudly, affectionately, known as 'Cat' wherever she went.

She had a very round head, with small ears and narrow, clear green eyes. She had exceptionally long, glossy whiskers above a large mouth that displayed needle-sharp teeth in a three-cornered smile or a ferocious grin when her emotions were stirred. Her tail was sleek and sinuous and almost never still. Happy was the sailor round whose neck she wound it. Her attentions were known to bring good luck.

As she grew up she reigned supreme on the vessel. Nothing was too good for her. If what she wanted was not given her at once, she climbed on to the neck of the man who withheld it and put both arms (you could not call them forelegs, because she used them exactly like arms) round his neck and peered into his eyes out of the narrow green slits of her own. If he did not at once surrender, she pressed her stubby nose on first one side of his face then on the other, while with her claws she massaged the weather-beaten back of his neck. If he were still obdurate, or perhaps mischievous enough still to deny her, she reversed her position and put her claws into his thigh. Gladly he gave her then whatever she desired.

She had a loud vibrant purr and when she moved gracefully along whatever deck she was favouring with her presence, purring and swaying her long tail, a feeling of reassurance and tranquillity came to all on board . . . It was a bitter thing to the crew of the coaling-vessel on which she had been born when, at the time of her first litter, she deserted them for a Norwegian schooner. The captain could scarcely persuade the crew to sail. The docks at Liverpool were combed for her without success. The voyage was one of rough weather and general dissatisfaction.

At that time the Norwegians had not heard of her. They had their own cat and did not want another. But she soon won them over and they had the most successful voyage they had ever known. When they next called at Liverpool the mate boasted of Cat in the hearing of one of the crew of the *Sultara*. He boasted of her intelligence, of her blackness, of the luck she brought.

On board the *Sultara* there was joy when they learned that she was safe, rage when they heard that she was living with the Norwegians. They visited the foreigners and saw for themselves that the cat was Cat. They found that she had a litter of ginger-coloured kittens. But the Norwegians would not give her up. They would give up one or all of her ginger-coloured litter but they would not give up 'Katts'.

The crew of the *Sultara* hung about the docks with scraps of kipper in their pockets, because Cat had a weakness for kippers; but the Norwegians guarded Katt with terrible efficiency. When, however, she chose to go ashore, nothing could stop her. A morsel of kipper was proffered her at the right moment. She mounted the shoulder of the giver and was borne in triumph to her birthplace. She gave evidence of the greatest pleasure in her reunion with the crew who were ready to weep with joy at recovering her.

Cat remained with them for two voyages. Then again she disappeared, this time in favour of an oil-tanker bound for the East . . . And so it went on, this life of change and adventure. She chose her ships. She remained on them till her love of variety prompted her to seek another lodging. But wherever she sailed she brought good luck and, at regular intervals, she returned to the *Sultara*. On all the Seven Seas she produced litters of ginger or grey kittens but never one of her own glittering black. She held herself unique. She was Cat.

Now, on a morning in late February, she glided down the gangway of the *Greyhound* which had just limped into port after an Antarctic relief expedition. The voyage had lasted for six months, and had been one of the mistakes of Cat's life, so far as her own pleasure was concerned.

The captain and crew of the *Greyhound* had been delighted when she sauntered aboard. The seal of success, they felt, had been set on the expedition. And they were right. The lost explorers had been discovered, living, though in desperate plight. Cat's reputation was still more enhanced.

But she herself was disgruntled through and through. She had never in all her years of travel experienced such a voyage. She felt disillusioned; she felt ill. She felt like scratching the first hand that was stretched out to pat her.

'Hullo, Cat!' exclaimed a burly dock-hand. 'So you're back from the Pole? And what captain are you going to sign up with next?' He bent to scratch her neck but she eluded him and glided off with waving tail.

'Cat don't look very bright,' observed another dock-hand.

'She's fed up, I expect, with the length of the last voyage,' said the first speaker, staring after her. 'She don't generally go for such long ones. *And* the weather! *And* the grub! She could have done much better for herself and she knows it.'

He turned to one of a crew which was about to sail for Norway.

'Hi, Bob! Here's Cat! Just back from the South Pole. P'raps you can make up to her.'

Bob approached, grinning. He planted himself in Cat's way and held two thick tarry hands down to her.

'Puss, puss!' he wheedled. 'Coom along wi' us. Tha can have whativer tha wants. Tha knows me, Cat.'

She knew Bob well and liked him. She suffered herself to be laid across his breast and she gave him a long look out of her narrow green eyes. He felt her ribs with his blunt fingers.

'She's naught but fur and bone,' he declared.

'Her's been frettin' fer home,' said the first.

'The sea is her home,' said Bob. 'But she's a dainty feeder. S'll I carry thee off, Cat?'

She began softly to purr. She relaxed in every fibre. The tip of her tongue showed between her lips. She closed her eyes.

'She'll go with you,' said the dock-hand and Bob began to pick his way among crates and bales, carrying Cat hopefully in his arms.

She heard the varied sounds of the docks, the shouts, the hoarse whistles of ships, the rattle of chains, smelled the familiar smells. It was music and sweetness to her after her long absence. She surrendered herself to the rhythmic movement of Bob's big chest.

In triumph he deposited her on his own deck. The rest of the crew stopped in their work for a moment to welcome her. The cook brought her a brace of sardines.

For politeness' sake she ate one but left the other on the deck. She arched herself against the legs of the first mate and gave her three-cornered smile. A ray of feeble sunlight struggled through the wintry fog and fell across her. She began to think she might sail with his crew.

'Keep an eye on her,' said the mate to a cabin-boy. 'Don't let her out of your sight till we're away.'

All about was hurry and noise. Cat sat on the deck washing the oil of the sardine from her whiskers. The pale sunshine surrounded her but deep within her there was dissatisfaction growing. This was not what she wanted and soon it would be too late to return to the docks. She would be in for another long, cold voyage.

Her little round black head looked very innocent. Her eyes were tight shut. Methodically she moved her curved paw over her face.

Someone called the boy and, forgetting the earlier order, he ran off. Cat was galvanized into life and movement. She flew along the deck. In another instant she would be on the docks.

But Bob saw her and caught her in his huge hands. She liked him; still she did not weaken. She thrust her claws into his hands and, with a yell of triumph and every hair erect, escaped.

It was some time before she regained her calm. She slunk among legs, among trucks, through scattered straw and trampled mud. The fog thickened again, settling clammily on her fur. It was bitterly cold. What she wanted was solitude. She was sick of the sight and sound of men and their doings.

She entered a warehouse and passed between tiers of wooden boxes and bales, stopping to sniff now and again when some smell attracted her. The cold in this building was very penetrating. Was she never to know warmth again?

In a dim shed she found stalls, all empty except one in which a prize ram was awaiting shipment to America where he was to be used for breeding. She clambered up the partition of the stall and perched there, gazing down at him. She did not remember having seen anything like him before. His yellow gaze was as inscrutable as hers.

With paws tucked under her breast she sat, enjoying the sight of him. She stared at his massive woolly shoulders, his curly horns, his restless pawing hoofs. He lowered his head and butted the manger in front of him with his hard skull. Cat felt that she could watch him for ever.

The gruff whistles of the ships shook the hoary air. The faint sunlight coming in at the cobwebbed window was shut off by a curtain of grey dusk. Cat and the ram were wrapped about by a strange intimacy. The chill increased. The docks became almost silent. The ram gave a bereft *baa* and sank to his knees.

Now he was only a pale mound in the dusk but Cat still stared at him. He was conscious of her too and, like some earth-bound spirit, he raised his yellow gaze to the glimmering stars of her eyes.

Towards midnight the cold became unbearable to her. On the Antarctic expedition she had slept in a bunk with a well-fleshed sailor. Now a thin rime was stiffening every hair of her coat. She rose stiffly and stretched. Her tail hung powerless. Some message, some understanding passed between her and the ram.

She leaped from the partition and landed between his shoulders. She sank into the deep oily warmth of his wool. He remained motionless, silent as the hill where he had pastured.

She stretched herself out on him with a purr of delight. She sought to feel his flesh with the fine points of her claws through the depth of his wool. A smell new to her rose from his body and the beginning of a *baa* stirred in his throat. Their two bodies united in the quiet breathing of sleep. Her sleep was light, of a pale luminous quality, always just on the edge of waking; but his was dark and heavy, as though he were surrounded by shaggy furze and thick heather.

A dense fog rose from the sea at dawn and pressed thickly into the stall. With it crept a long grey cat with a white blaze on his face and his ears torn by fighting. He scrambled up the partition of the stall and peered down at the two below. He dropped to the manger and from there to the straw. He touched Cat tentatively.

She had been conscious of his approach. It had brought into her dreams a vague vision of a tawny striped cat she had met in Rio de Janeiro, where the relief ship had called. But the touch of the paw galvanized her. She gave a shriek and, driving her hind claws into the ram's back, she reared herself and struck at the intruder's face as though she would put her mark on it for ever.

But he was not easily frightened off. He sprang to the ram's back also and through the fog Cat saw his white face grinning at her. He set his teeth in the back of her neck. They both shrieked.

The ram's deep, dark, warm slumber was shattered into fright. He bounded up with a clatter of hoofs, overthrowing the cats. His white eyelashes flickered. He glared in primeval rage and lowered his head to charge.

The cats scrambled agilely over the partition and dropped to the stone floor outside, their tails enormous. They sped in opposite directions into dim corners of the shed. The battering of the ram's head against the door of the stall echoed through the fog.

As Cat reached her corner a mouse flickered out of the gloom, squeaking in an agony of fear, and shot past her. With a graceful flourish of her limber body she turned completely round and captured the mouse with one effective movement. She picked it up delicately in her teeth and crouched in the corner.

After a time the door opened and two men came in. They turned on a light and the interior of the shed was revealed in foggy pallor. The men entered the stall where the ram was. There came strange bumping sounds. The men cursed. Then they appeared leading the ram, roped by the horns. He was led out helpless, his little hoofs pattering on the stone floor. He uttered a plaintive, lamb-like *baa*. The men left the door open behind them.

Cat discovered the body of the mouse. It now meant nothing to her. She glided out on to the docks, wondering what ship she would sail in. She passed among them as they were dimly revealed, cargoes being loaded or unloaded, men working like ants. She felt a dim wonder at their activity, a faint disdain for their heaving bodies.

Towards noon, when a shabby blurred disc showed where the sun was, she came upon a passenger ship just departing on a West India cruise. She had never sailed on a passenger ship. They were an untrustworthy and strange world and she hated the sight of women.

As she stood pessimistically surveying it a kitchen worker tossed a slice of chicken-breast through a porthole to her. She crouched on the pier devouring it while shivers of delight made her separate hairs quiver. She had not known that such food existed. After it was gone she sat beaming towards the porthole but nothing more was thrown out.

Luggage was being loaded on to the ship and a throng of people, of a sort she had never before seen, hastened up the gangway. One of them, a man, bent and gently massaged the muscles in the back of her neck, before he passed on. She beamed after him. She had not known such hands existed, so smooth, so tender. They were like the breast of chicken she had just devoured.

She rose, chilled by the clammy cold, and glided up the gangway on to the ship.

She knew that she was a stranger here and some instinct told her that quite possibly she might not be welcome. She slunk along the innumerable white passages, making herself as nearly invisible as possible. She glanced in at the doors of staterooms as she passed. Generally there were women inside and sometimes the rather disgusting smell of flowers was on the air.

Cat heard the thunder of the whistle. She felt a quiver go through the ship. She had a mind to get off it while there was yet time but she felt powerless to turn herself away from the delicious warmth that was radiated from every corner of the liner. It made her feel yielding, soft. She wanted something cosy to lie down on.

She paused at the door of a cabin that was empty except for the promise of a man's coat and hat thrown on the berth. She went in and walked round it, purring. She held her tail stiffly erect, all but the tip which moved constantly as though it were, in some subtle way, gauging the spiritual atmosphere of the cabin.

Gregg, the swimming-instructor, found her there curled up on his coat. They had left the docks so she could not be put ashore. He recognized her as the cat he had caressed and supposed that she belonged on the liner. He tucked her under his arm and carried her to the kitchen quarters. The boy who had thrown her the morsel of chicken recognized her. He had once been galley-boy on an oil-tanker she had favoured with her presence.

'It's Cat,' he explained. ' 'Aven't yer never 'eard tell of Cat?

W'y, we're in luck, mister! And yer ought to be proud to share your berth wiv 'er!'

But Gregg did not want to share his berth with Cat, even after he had heard her history and virtues. He dumped her down and rather glumly retraced his steps. He felt a shrinking from the long cruise that stretched ahead of him. To be sociable was a part of his job and he hated the thought of sociability.

He had, in fact, seen too much of people. He had had more experience of society than was good for him. He was not yet thirty but he had lost a fair-sized fortune, the woman he loved and, worst of all, his hope and fortitude. He had been at his wits' end to find a job when a friend had got him this post as swimming-instructor. He was in a state bordering on despair but, here he was, bound to seem cheerful and gay, to take a passionate interest in the flounderings of fat passengers in the pool.

No one on board was so out of sympathy with the cruise as was he. Indeed, everyone on board was in sympathy with the cruise but Gregg and Cat, who did not at all understand cruising for pleasure.

She was there in his berth waiting for him when he returned to his cabin that night, having found her way through all the intricacy of glittering passages. He was a little drunk, for he was very attractive and people insisted on treating him. The sight of Cat lying there on his bed angered him. He was about to put her out roughly when she rolled over on her back, turned up her black velvet belly and round little face with the glittering eyes narrowed and the three-cornered smile showing her pink tongue. He bent over her, pleased in spite of himself.

'You're a rogue,' he said. 'But you can't get around me like that.'

For answer she clasped her forepaws round his neck and with her hind paws clawed gently on his shirt front. She pressed her face to his and purred loudly in his ear.

'Cheek to cheek, eh?' said Gregg, and gave himself up to her hypnotic overtures.

Morning found them snuggled close together. He sent the steward for a dish of milk for her. He appeared at the swimming-pool with her on his shoulder. She basked in the heavenly warmth of the place.

From that time she spent her days by the pool. Tolerantly, almost benignly, she watched the skill or awkwardness of the swimmers. When the pool was deserted she crouched by its brink gazing at her reflection, dreaming of lovely fish that might have graced it. At night she slept with Gregg. She thrived immensely.

When they were in sparkling southern waters, Cat disappeared early one evening. She met Gregg at the door of his cabin with a tremulously excited air. She advanced towards him, purring, then turned her back and flaunted her sinuous black tail. She looked back at him over her shoulder. Her head and tail met. She caught the tip of it in her mouth and lay down on her back, rolling coyly from side to side. She looked strangely slender.

'So you've been and gone and done it,' said Gregg. 'Not on the bed, I hope!'

No, not on the bed. In the wardrobe, where Gregg's soft dressing-gown had somehow fallen from its peg. There were three of them, all plump, all tawny like the gentleman in Rio de Janeiro.

Next day Gregg got a nice box with a cushion and put the kittens in it. He carried them to the balmy warmth of the air that surrounded the swimming-pool, and all the bathers gathered to admire and stroke them. They were the pets of the ship. But Cat cared only for Gregg. She fussed over him far more than she did over her kittens. She refused to stay with them by the pool at night, so the box had to be carried to his cabin. There she would sit waiting for him, her glowing eyes fixed on the door, every nerve tuned for his coming.

But on one night he did not come. She waited and waited but he did not come. At last she sprang up from suckling her kittens, and they fell back like three tawny balls. The door was fixed ajar. She glided through the opening and began her search for him.

The smoke-room was closed; the lounge was empty, the decks deserted except for a pacing figure in uniform. At last Cat saw Gregg standing, still as a statue, in a secluded corner where a lifeboat hung. Silent as the shadows cast by moonlight, she drew near to him. But she did not rub herself against his leg as usual. She climbed into the lifeboat and over its edge peered down into his face.

That night Gregg felt alone – lost. In spite of the moonlight, the myriad glittering waves, the world was black to him. The life on this luxurious liner, among these spoiled shallow people, was suffocating him; he could not breathe. He looked back on his own life as a waste, on his future with despair. He had made up his mind to end it all.

Cat watched him intently as he leaned against the rail. If he had been her prey she could not have observed him with more meticulous concentration as he mounted it. Just before he would have leaped over the side she sprang on to his shoulders with a shriek that curdled the blood of those whose staterooms gave on to that deck. She not only shrieked but she drove every claw into Gregg. She turned herself into a black fury whose every hair stood on end, whose eyes glared with hate and fear at that gulf below . . .

'I don't know what the devil is the matter with her,' Gregg said to the officer who hastened up. 'She's as temperamental as a prima donna.' His hand shook as he stroked her.

But she had saved him from his black mood, saved him from his despairing self. When he was undressed, he looked in wonder at the little bloody spots on his shoulders . . . Cat slept on his chest.

He made up his mind that he would never part with her. He owed her a debt which could only be repaid by the certainty of affection and gentle living for the rest of her days. He would find lodgings where she would be welcome.

But Gregg reckoned without Cat. By the time they reached port she was sick to death of the luxury liner. There was not a smell on board that pleased her. She liked Gregg but she could do without him. She liked her three plump kittens, but the quality of real mother love did not exist in her. She loved the sea and the men who spent their days in strenuous work on the sea. She disliked women and scent and all daintiness. She was Cat; she could not change herself.

In the confusion of landing no one saw her slip ashore. She vanished like a puff of black smoke. It was as lovely a morning as any they had seen on the cruise. The air was balmy, the sky above the dock blue as a periwinkle. When Cat reached the places she was accustomed to she purred loudly and rubbed herself against tarry trouser-legs, arched her neck to horny hands. But she was coy. She would not commit herself. For a fortnight she lived on the dock, absorbing the satisfying smells of fresh timber, straw, tar, salt fish, hemp, beer, oil and sweat. She even renewed acquaintance, this time more amiably though with loud screams, with the grey-furred gentleman who had called on her in the ram's stall.

At last she sailed on a cattle ship, and all her past was as nothing to her!

Amours

COLETTE

THE ROBIN had won. Now he celebrated his victory in little dry chirps, safe in the depths of a chestnut tree. He was proud that he had not fled from the cat. He had hovered above her buzzing like an angry bee. His taunts, to anyone who understood his chirping, were fiercesome.

'I, Robin red-breast, will peck out your eyes if you take one more step towards the nest which holds my precious eggs.'

I was watching, ready to intervene, but the cat understands that the robin is not to be touched. She understands so many things. Still, she thinks that in allowing the bird to insult her with impunity, she risks being made to look a fool. So, she thrashes her tail like a lion and arches her back. In the end she leaves the frantic bird and we continue on our walk through the dusk.

It is a slow, pleasurable amble in which we both make discoveries. Well, she is making discoveries to be honest. She stops and stares fixedly at something in the distance which I cannot see. She crouches and leaps at a noise I do not hear. I have to guess what she is finding so fascinating.

Being with a cat is always stimulating but did I set out fifty years ago to seek the company of cats? It never seemed that I had to look for them. They were always there at my feet. They came in so many guises: lost and starving, hunting and being hunted, the library cat embalmed in ink, dairy cats and butcher's cats well-fed but with paws cold from the tiled floor. There are flabby bourgeois cats, self-satisfied cats and despot cats who tyrannize over Paul Morand, Claude Farrere and me. They all come to me with pleasure but without surprise.

One day I noticed a poor thin cat being pushed to and fro by the crowd which pours each evening out of the Autreuil metro. In fact it was she who recognized me. 'There you are at last,' she said. 'You are very late. Where is your home? Do not worry, I will follow you.'

When we got home my house seemed to frighten her, perhaps because I lived there with someone else. She soon settled in, however. She lived with me for four years before dying in an accident.

But I must not forget my dogs, just as loving, just as vulnerable. How could I live without you? I am indispensable to you. You make me realise how truly valuable I am to you. Is there anyone else of whom I can say the same? You comfort me with your devotion though maybe you are almost too loving, your eyes too beseeching. I do not know much about a dog's sex life because, out of my favourite ten breeds, I prefer those unable to breed. For instance, sometimes the bitch of the Brabant terrier, the French type of bulldog – pug-nosed with a huge head – instinctively refuses to mate. It knows that giving birth is dangerous because of its size and shape.

Two bitches I had, used to bite dogs who tried to mate outside 'safe periods'. One poodle was happy to feed a rubber puppy instead of the real thing. Though I have owned many dogs, cats have always been more important to me. From them I have learnt to be reserved, self-disciplined and intolerant of noise.

The cat which has meant most to me and was different from all others was the one I mentioned at the beginning. And yet, because she was so special I cannot say too much about her. Only when she was sexually active did she cease to be mine and rejoined the cat world. I can only guess what she saw in the tomcat who raped and abused her. Sex not love brought forth her terrible wails and birdlike cries, insulting and threatening her mate.

In the country she is flirtatious and promiscuous, delighting in her freedom to be truly catlike and not the human's 'best

friend'. To me she is warm, faithful and sensitive – the opposite of all she is to her cat lovers.

In town, in the narrow walled garden of my Paris house, she played happily, sometimes full of energy, sometimes content to dream. She restrained her natural instincts haughtily rejecting would-be mates. There is the old striped conqueror, thin as a rake, bald in places but highly experienced. He is decisive, respected by his rivals, confident of success.

Then there is a young cat, stupid and self-satisfied, enjoying his own beauty – the beauty of the tiger. Finally, there is the farm cat who appears on the top of the wall as though awakened from a dream by an urgent mating call.

She gives all three a hard time using her paws without mercy to slap their faces when they push too hard. Then she rolls around in front of them but follows that exhibition with freezing contempt. She climbs onto a crumbling pillar from which she can pour scorn on her assailants. When she decides to rejoin her three slaves she does so with hauteur. She allows one of her admirers to kiss her nose but when this goes on too long she puts a stop to it with an imperious cry impossible to describe.

The three tomcats jump back in surprise. My cat, seeming to forget her lovers, goes back to grooming herself. Depressed by their long courtship, the male cats begin to fight amongst themselves to pass the time. My cat leaves them to it, renouncing her flirtatious games, pleased to rejoin the humans.

While I work, my cat lies beside me under the warmth of the reading lamp, silent, watchful, content – my she-cat, my friend.

The Cheshire Cat

LEWIS CARROLL

THE ONLY things in the kitchen that did not sneeze were the cook, and a large cat which was sitting on the hearth and grinning from ear to ear.

'Please, would you tell me,' said Alice a little timidly, for she was not quite sure whether it was good manners for her to speak first, 'why your cat grins like that?'

'It's a Cheshire cat,' said the Duchess, 'and that's why. Pig!'

She said the last word with such sudden violence that Alice quite jumped; but she saw in another moment that it was addressed to the baby, and not to her, so she took courage and went on again:

'I didn't know that Cheshire cats always grinned; in fact, I didn't know that cats *could* grin.'

'They all can,' said the Duchess, 'and most of 'em do.'

'I don't know of any that do,' Alice said very politely, feeling quite pleased to have got into a conversation.

'You don't know much,' said the Duchess, 'and that's a fact.'

Alice did not at all like the tone of this remark, and thought it would be as well to introduce some other subject of conversation. While she was trying to fix on one, the cook took the cauldron of soup off the fire, and at once set to work throwing everything within her reach at the Duchess and the baby – the fire-irons came first; then followed a shower of saucepans, plates and dishes. The Duchess took no notice of them even when they hit her; and the baby was howling so much already that it was quite impossible to say whether the blows hurt it or not.

'Oh, *please* mind what you're doing!' cried Alice, jumping up and down in an agony of terror. 'Oh, there goes his *precious* nose,' as an unusually large saucepan flew close by it, and very nearly carried it off.

'If everybody minded their own business,' the Duchess said in a hoarse growl, 'the world would go round a deal faster than it does.'

'Which would *not* be an advantage,' said Alice, who felt very glad to get an opportunity of showing off a little of her knowledge. 'Just think what work it would make with the day and night! You see the earth takes twenty-four hours to turn round on its axis —'

'Talking of axes,' said the Duchess, 'chop off her head!'

Alice glanced rather anxiously at the cook, to see if she meant to take the hint; but the cook was busily engaged in stirring the soup, and did not seem to be listening, so she ventured to go on again: 'Twenty-four hours, I *think*; or is it twelve? I —'

'Oh, don't bother *me*,' said the Duchess. 'I never could abide figures!' And with that she began nursing her child again, singing a sort of lullaby to it as she did so, and giving it a violent shake at the end of every line:

Speak roughly to your little boy,
And beat him when he sneezes:
He only does it to annoy,
  Because he knows it teases.

Chorus (which the cook and the baby joined):

Wow! wow! wow!

While the Duchess sang the second verse of the song, she kept tossing the baby violently up and down, and the poor little thing howled so, that Alice could hardly hear the words:

I speak severely to my boy,
I beat him when he sneezes;
For he can thoroughly enjoy
The pepper when he pleases!

Chorus:

Wow! wow! wow!

'Here! You may nurse it a bit, if you like!' the Duchess said to Alice, flinging the baby at her as she spoke. 'I must go and get ready to play croquet with the Queen,' and she hurried out of the room. The cook threw a frying-pan after her as she went out, but it just missed her.

Alice caught the baby with some difficulty, as it was a queer-shaped little creature and held out its arms and legs in all directions, 'just like a star-fish', thought Alice. The poor little thing was snorting like a steam-engine when she caught it, and kept doubling itself up and straightening itself out again, so that altogether, for the first minute or two, it was as much as she could do to hold it.

As soon as she made out the proper way of nursing it (which was to twist it up into a sort of knot, and then keep tight hold of its right ear and left foot, so as to prevent its undoing itself), she carried it out into the open air. 'If I don't take this child away with me,' thought Alice, 'they're sure to kill it in a day or two; wouldn't it be murder to leave it behind?' She said the last words out loud, and the little thing grunted in reply (it had left off sneezing by this time). 'Don't grunt,' said Alice, 'that's not at all a proper way of expressing yourself.'

The baby grunted again, and Alice looked very anxiously into its face to see what was the matter with it. There could be no doubt that it had a *very* turn-up nose, much more like a snout than a real nose; also its eyes were getting extremely small for a baby. Altogether, Alice did not like the look of the thing at all. 'But perhaps it was only sobbing,' she thought, and looked into its eyes again to see if there were any tears.

No, there were no tears. 'If you're going to turn into a pig, my dear,' said Alice, seriously, 'I'll have nothing more to do with you. Mind now!' The poor little thing sobbed again (or grunted, it was impossible to say which), and they went on for some while in silence.

Alice was just beginning to think to herself, 'Now, what am I to do with this creature when I get it home?' when it grunted again, so violently, that she looked down into its face in some alarm. This time there could be *no* mistake about it: it was neither more nor less than a pig, and she felt that it would be quite absurd for her to carry it any further.

So she set the little creature down, and felt quite relieved to see it trot away quietly into the wood. 'If it had grown up,' she said to herself, 'it would have made a dreadfully ugly child; but it makes rather a handsome pig, I think.' And she began thinking over other children she knew, who might do very well as pigs, and was just saying to herself, 'If one only knew the right way to change them –' when she was a little startled by seeing the Cheshire Cat sitting on a bough of a tree a few yards off.

The Cat only grinned when it saw Alice. It looked good-natured, she thought; still, it had *very* long claws and a great many teeth, so she felt that it ought to be treated with respect.

'Cheshire Puss,' she began, rather timidly, as she did not at all know whether it would like the name; however, it only grinned a little wider. 'Come, it's pleased so far,' thought Alice, and she went on: 'Would you tell me, please, which way I ought to go from here?'

'That depends a good deal on where you want to get to,' said the Cat.

'I don't much care where –' said Alice.

'Then it doesn't matter which way you go,' said the Cat.

'– so long as I get *somewhere*,' Alice added as an explanation.

'Oh, you're sure to do that,' said the Cat, 'if you only walk long enough.'

Alice felt that this could not be denied so, she tried another question: 'What sort of people live about here?'

'In *that* direction,' the Cat said, waving its right paw round, 'lives a Hatter; and in *that* direction,' waving the other paw, 'lives a March Hare. Visit either you like; they're both mad.'

'But I don't want to go among mad people,' Alice remarked.

'Oh, but you can't help that,' said the Cat: 'We're all mad here. I'm mad. You're mad.'

'How do you know I'm mad?' said Alice.

'You must be,' said the Cat, 'or you wouldn't have come here.'

Alice didn't think that proved it at all; however, she went on. 'And how do you know that you're mad?'

'To begin with,' said the Cat, 'a dog's not mad. You grant that?'

'I suppose so,' said Alice.

'Well, then,' the Cat went on, 'you see a dog growls when it's angry, and wags its tail when it's pleased. Now *I* growl when I'm pleased, and wag my tail when I'm angry. Therefore, I'm mad.'

'I call it purring. not growling,' said Alice.

'Call it what you like,' said the Cat. 'Do you play croquet with the Queen today?'

'I should like it very much,' said Alice, 'but I haven't been invited yet.'

'You'll see me there,' said the Cat, and vanished.

Alice was not much surprised at this, she was getting so used to queer things happening. While she was looking at the place where it had been, it suddenly appeared again.

'By the by, what became of the baby?' said the Cat. 'I'd nearly forgotten to ask.'

'It turned into a pig,' Alice quietly said, just as if it had come back in a natural way.

'I thought it would,' said the Cat, and vanished again.

Alice waited a little, half expecting to see it again, but it did not appear, and after a minute or two she walked on in the direction in which the March Hare was said to live. 'I've seen hatters before,' she said to herself; 'the March Hare will be much the most interesting, and perhaps, as this is May, it won't be raving mad – at least not so mad as it was in March.' As she said this, she looked up, and there was the Cat again, sitting on a branch of a tree.

'Did you say pig, or fig?' said the Cat.

'I said pig,' replied Alice, 'and I wish you wouldn't keep appearing and vanishing so suddenly. You make one quite giddy.'

'All right,' said the Cat; and this time it vanished quite slowly, beginning with the end of the tail and ending with the grin, which remained some time after the rest of it had gone.

'Well! I've often seen a cat without a grin,' thought Alice, 'but a grin without a cat! It's the most curious thing I ever saw in all my life!'

Alice began to feel very uneasy; to be sure she had not, as yet, had any dispute with the Queen, but she knew that it might happen any minute, 'and then,' thought she, 'what would become of me? They're dreadfully fond of beheading people here; the great wonder is that there's anyone left alive!'

She was looking about for some way of escape, and wondering whether she could get away without being seen, when she noticed a curious appearance in the air. It puzzled her very much at first, but, after watching it a minute or two, she made it out to be a grin, and she said to herself, 'It's the Cheshire Cat; now I shall have somebody to talk to.'

'How are you getting on?' said the Cat, as soon as there was mouth enough for it to speak with.

Alice waited till the eyes appeared, and then nodded, 'It's no use speaking to it,' she thought, 'till its ears have come, or at least one of them.' In another minute the whole head appeared, and then Alice put down her flamingo and began an account of the game, feeling very glad she had someone to listen to her. The Cat seemed to think that there was enough of it now in sight, and no more of it appeared.

'I don't think they play at all fairly.' Alice began, in rather a complaining tone, 'and they all quarrel so dreadfully one can't hear oneself speak – and they don't seem to have any rules in particular; at least, if there are, nobody attends to them – and you've no idea how confusing it is all the things being alive; for instance, there's the arch I've got to go through next walking about at the other end of the ground – and I should have croqueted the Queen's hedgehog just now, only it ran away when it saw mine coming!'

'How do you like the Queen?' said the Cat in a low voice.

'Not at all,' said Alice; 'she's so extremely —' Just then she noticed that the Queen was close behind her listening, so she went on, ' – likely to win, that it's hardly worth while finishing the game.'

The Queen smiled and passed on.

'Who *are* you talking to?' said the King, coming up to Alice, and looking at the Cat's head with great curiosity.

'It's a friend of mine – a Cheshire Cat,' said Alice, 'allow me to introduce it.'

'I don't like the look of it at all,' said the King; 'however, it may kiss my hand if it likes.'

'I'd rather not,' the Cat remarked.

'Don't be impertinent,' said the King, 'and don't look at me like that!' He got behind Alice as he spoke.

'A cat may look at a king,' said Alice. 'I've read that in some book, but I don't remember where.'

'Well, it must be removed,' said the King very decidedly, and he called to the Queen who was passing at the moment. 'My dear! I wish you would have this cat removed!'

The Queen had only one way of settling all difficulties, great or small. 'Off with his head!' she said, without even looking around.

'I'll fetch the executioner myself,' said the King eagerly, and he hurried off.

Alice thought she might as well go back and see how the game was going on as she heard the Queen's voice in the distance, screaming with passion. She had already heard her sentence three of the players to be executed for having missed their turns, and she did not like the look of things at all, as the game was in such confusion that she never knew whether it was her turn or not. So she went in search of her hedgehog.

The hedgehog was engaged in a fight with another hedgehog, which seemed to Alice an excellent opportunity for croqueting one of them with the other; the only difficulty was that her flamingo was gone across to the other side of the garden where Alice could see it trying in a helpless sort of way to fly up into one of the trees.

By the time she had caught the flamingo and brought it back, the fight was over and both the hedgehogs were out of sight. 'But it doesn't matter much,' thought Alice, 'as all the arches are gone from this side of the ground.' So she tucked it under her arm, that it might not escape again, and went back for a little more conversation with her friend.

When she got back to the Cheshire Cat she was surprised to find quite a large crowd collected around it; there was a dispute going on between the executioner, the King, and the Queen, who were all talking at once, while all the rest were quite silent and looked very uncomfortable.

The moment Alice appeared, she was appealed to by all

three to settle the question, and they repeated their arguments to her, though as they all spoke at once, she found it very hard to make out exactly what they said.

The executioner's argument was, that you couldn't cut off a head unless there was a body to cut it off from; that he had never had to do such a thing before, and he wasn't going to begin at *his* time of life.

The King's argument was, that anything that had a head could be beheaded, and that you weren't to talk nonsense.

The Queen's argument was, that if something wasn't done about it in less than no time, she'd have everybody executed, all round. (It was this last remark that had made the whole party look so grave and anxious.)

Alice could think of nothing else to say but, 'It belongs to the Duchess; you'd better ask *her* about it.'

'She's in prison,' the Queen said to the executioner, 'fetch her here.' And the executioner went off like an arrow.

The Cat's head began fading away the moment he was gone and, by the time he had come back with the Duchess, it had entirely disappeared.

The Yellow Terror

W. L. ALDEN

'SPEAKING OF CATS,' said Captain Foster, 'I'm free to say that I don't like 'em. I don't care to be looked down on by any person, whether he be man or cat. I know I ain't the President of the United States, nor yet a millionaire, nor yet the Boss of New York, but all the same I calculate that I'm a man, and entitled to be treated as such. Now, I never knew a cat yet that didn't look down on me, same as cats do on everybody. A cat considers that men are just dirt under his or her paws, as the case may be. I can't see what it is that makes a cat believe that he is so everlastingly superior to all the men that have ever lived, but there's no denying the fact that such is his belief, and he acts accordingly. There was a Professor here one day, lecturing on all sorts of animals, and I asked him if he could explain this aggravating conduct of cats. He said that it was because cats used to be gods, thousands of years ago in the land of Egypt; but I didn't believe him. Egypt is a Scripture country, and consequently we ought not to believe anything about it that we don't read in the Bible. Show me anywhere in the Bible that Egyptian cats are mentioned as having practised as gods, and I'll believe it. Till you show it to me, I'll take the liberty of disbelieving any worldly statements that Professors or anybody else may make about Egypt.

'The most notorious cat I ever met was old Captain Smedley's Yellow Terror. His real legal name was just plain Tom: but being yellow, and being a holy terror in many respects, it got to be the fashion among his acquaintances to call him "The Yellow Terror". He was a tremendous big cat, and he had been with Captain Smedley for five years before I saw him.

'Smedley was one of the best men I ever knew. I'll admit that he was a middling hard man on his sailors, so that his ship got the reputation of being a slaughter-house, which it didn't really deserve. And there is no denying that he was a very religious man, which was another thing which made him unpopular with the men. I'm a religious man myself, even when I'm at sea, but I never held with serving out religion to a crew, and making them swallow it with belaying pins. That's what old Smedley used to do. He was in command of the barque *Medford*, out of Boston, when I knew him. I mean the city of Boston in Massachusetts, and not the little town that folks over in England call Boston: and I must say that I can't see why they should copy the names of our cities, no matter how celebrated they may be. Well! The *Medford* used to sail from Boston to London with grain, where she discharged her cargo and loaded again for China. On the outward passage we used to stop at Madeira, and the Cape, and generally Bangkok, and so on to Canton, where we filled up with tea, and then sailed for home direct.

'Now thishyer Yellow Terror had been on the ship's books for upwards of five years when I first met him. Smedley had him regularly shipped, and signed his name to the ship articles, and held a pen in his paw while he made a cross, same as if he had been a Dago. You see, in those days the underwriters wouldn't let a ship go to sea without a cat, so as to keep the rats from getting at the cargo. I don't know what a land cat may do, but there ain't a seafaring cat that would look at a rat. What with the steward, and the cook and the men forrard, being always ready to give the ship's cat a bite, the cat is generally full from kelson to deck, and wouldn't take the trouble to speak to a rat, unless one was to bite her tail. But, then, underwriters never know anything about what goes on at sea, and it's a shame that a sailorman should be compelled to give in to their ideas. The Yellow Terror had the general idea that the *Medford* was his private yacht, and that all hands were there to wait on him. And Smedley sort of confirmed him in that idea, by treating him with more respect than he treated his owners, when he was ashore. I don't blame the cat, and after I got to know what sort of a person the cat really was, I can't say as I blamed Smedley to any great extent.

'Tom, which I think I told you was the cat's real name, was far and away the best fighter of all cats in Europe, Asia, Africa, and America. Whenever we sighted land he would get himself up in his best fur, spending hours brushing and polishing it, and biting his claws so as to make sure that they were as sharp as they could be made. As soon as the ship was made fast to the quay, or anchored in the harbour, the Yellow Terror went ashore to look for trouble. He always got it too, though he had such a reputation as a fighter, that whenever he showed himself, every cat that recognised him broke for cover. Why, the gatekeeper at the London Docks – I mean the one at the Shadwell entrance – told me that he always knew when the *Medford* was warping into dock, by the stream of cats that went out of the gate, as if a pack of hounds were after them. You see that as soon as the *Medford* was reported, and word passed among the cats belonging to the ships in dock that the Yellow Terror had arrived, they judged that it was time for them to go ashore, and stop till the *Medford* should sail. Whitechapel used to be regularly overflowed with cats, and the newspapers used to have letters from scientific chaps trying to account for what they called the wave of cats that had spread over East London.

'I remember that once we laid alongside of a Russian brig, down in the basin by Old Gravel Lane. There was a tremendous big black cat sitting on the poop, and as soon as he caught sight of our Tom, he sung out to him, remarking that he was able and ready to wipe the deck up with him at any time. We all understood that the Russian was a new arrival who hadn't ever heard of the Yellow Terror, and we knew that he was, as the good book says, rushing on his fate. Tom was sitting on the rail near the mizzen rigging when the Russian made his remarks, and he didn't seem to hear them. But presently we saw him going slowly aloft till he reached our crossjack yard. He laid out on the yard arm till he was near enough to jump on to the mainyard of the Russian, and the first thing that the Russian cat knew Tom landed square on his back. The fight didn't last more than one round, and at the end of that, the remains of the Russian cat sneaked behind a water cask, and the Yellow

Terror came back by the way of the crossjack yard and went on fur brushing, as if nothing had happened.

'When Tom went ashore in a foreign port he generally stopped ashore till we sailed. A few hours before we cast off hawsers, Tom would come aboard. He always knew when we were going to sail, and he never once got left. I remember one time when we were just getting up anchor in Cape Town harbour, and we all reckoned that this time we should have to sail without Tom, he having evidently stopped ashore just a little too long. But presently alongside comes a boat, with Tom lying back at full length in the sternsheets, for all the world like a drunken sailor who has been delaying the ship, and is proud of it. The boatman said that Tom had come down to the pier and jumped into his boat, knowing that the man would row him off to the ship, and calculating that Smedley would be glad to pay the damage. It's my belief that if Tom hadn't found a boatman, he would have chartered the government launch. He had the cheek to do that or anything else.

'Fighting was really Tom's only vice; and it could hardly be called a vice, seeing as he always licked the other cat, and hardly ever came out of a fight with a torn ear or a black eye. Smedley always said that Tom was religious. I used to think that was rubbish; but after I had been with Tom for a couple of voyages I began to believe what Smedley said about him. Every Sunday when the weather permitted, Smedley used to hold service on the quarter-deck. He was a Methodist, and when it came to ladling out Scripture, or singing a hymn, he could give odds to almost any preacher. All hands, except the man at the wheel, and the lookout, were required to attend service on Sunday morning, which naturally caused considerable grumbling, as the watch below considered they had a right to sleep in peace, instead of being dragged aft for service. But they had to knock under, and what they considered even worse, they had to sing, for the old man kept a bright lookout while the singing was going on, and if he caught any man malingering and not doing his full part of the singing he would have a few words to say to that man with a belaying pin, or a rope's end, after the service was over.

'Now Tom never failed to attend service, and to do his level best to help. He would sit somewhere near the old man and pay attention to what was going on better than I've seen some folks do in first-class churches ashore. When the men sang, Tom would start in and let out a yell here and there, which showed that he meant well even if he had never been to a singing-school, and didn't exactly understand singing according to Gunter. First along, I thought that it was all an accident that the cat came to service, and I calculated that his yelling during the singing meant that he didn't like it. But after a while I had to admit that Tom enjoyed the Sunday service as much as the Captain himself, and I agreed with Smedley that the cat was a thoroughgoing Methodist.

'Now after I'd been with Smedley for about six years, he got married all of a sudden. I didn't blame him, for in the first place it wasn't any of my business; and, in the next place, I hold that a ship's captain ought to have a wife, and the underwriters would be a sight wiser if they insisted that all captains should be married, instead of insisting that all ships should carry cats. You see that if a ship's captain has a wife, he is naturally anxious to get back to her, and have his best clothes mended, and his food cooked to suit him. Consequently he wants to make good passages and he don't want to run the risk of drowning himself, or of getting into trouble with his owners, and losing his berth. You'll find, if you look into it, that married captains live longer, and get on better than unmarried men, as it stands to reason that they ought to do.

'But it happened that the woman Smedley married was an Agonyostic, which is a sort of person that doesn't believe in anything, except the multiplication table, and such-like human vanities. She didn't lose any time in getting Smedley round to her way of thinking, and instead of being the religious man he used to be, he chucked the whole thing, and used to argue with me by the hour at a time, to prove that religion was a waste of time, and that he hadn't any soul, and had never been created, but had just descended from a family of seafaring monkeys. It made me sick to hear a respectable sailorman talking such rubbish, but of course, seeing as he was my commanding officer, I had to be careful about contradicting him. I wouldn't ever yield an inch to his arguments, and I told him as respectfully as I could, that he was making the biggest mistake of his life. "Why, look at the cat," I used to say, "he's got sense enough to be religious, and if you was to tell him that he was descended from a monkey, he'd consider himself insulted." But it wasn't any use. Smedley was full of his new agonyostical theories, and the more I disagreed with him, the more set he was in his way.

'Of course he knocked off holding Sunday morning services; and the men ought to have been delighted, considering how they used to grumble at having to come aft and sing hymns, when they wanted to be below. But there is no accounting for sailors. They were actually disappointed when Sunday came and there wasn't any service. They said that we should have an unlucky voyage, and that the old man, now that he had got a rich wife, didn't consider sailors good enough to come aft on the quarter-deck, and take a hand in singing. Smedley didn't care for their opinion, but he was some considerable worried about the Yellow Terror. Tom missed the Sunday morning service, and he said so as plain as he could. Every Sunday, for three or four weeks, he came on deck, and took his usual seat near the captain, and waited for the service to begin. When he found out that there was no use in waiting for it, he showed that he disapproved of Smedley's conduct in the strongest way. He gave up being intimate with the old man, and once when Smedley tried to pat him, and be friendly, he swore at him, and bit him on the leg – not in an angry way, you understand, but just to show his disapproval of Smedley's irreligious conduct.

'When we got to London, Tom never once went ashore, and he hadn't a single fight. He seemed to have lost all interest in worldly things. He'd sit on the poop in a melancholy sort of way, never minding how his fur looked, and never so much as answering if a strange cat sang out to him. After we left London he kept below most of the time, and finally, about the time that we were crossing the line, he took to his bed, as you might say, and got to be as thin and weak as if he had been living in the forecastle of a lime-juicer. And he was that melancholy that you couldn't get him to take an interest in anything. Smedley got to be so anxious about him that he read up in his medical book to try and find out what was the matter with him; and finally made up his mind that the cat had a first-class disease with a big name something like spinal menagerie. That was some little satisfaction to Smedley, but it didn't benefit the cat any; for nothing that Smedley could do would induce Tom to take medicine. He wouldn't so much as sniff at salts, and when Smedley tried to poultice his neck, he considered himself insulted, and roused up enough to take a piece out of the old man's ear.

'About that time we touched at Funchal, and Smedley sent ashore to lay in another tom-cat, thinking that perhaps a fight would brace Tom up a little. But when the new cat was put down alongside of Tom, and swore at him in the most impudent sort of way, Tom just turned over on his other side, and pretended to go asleep. After that we all felt that the Yellow Terror was done for. Smedley sent the new cat ashore again, and told me that Tom was booked for the other world, and that there wouldn't be any more luck for us on that voyage.

'I went down to see the cat, and though he was thin and weak, I couldn't see any signs of serious disease about him. So I says to Smedley that I didn't believe the cat was sick at all.

' "Then what's the matter with him?" says the old man. "You saw yourself that he wouldn't fight, and when he's got to that point I consider that he is about done with this world and its joys and sorrows."

' "His nose is all right," said I. "When I felt it just now it was as cool as a teetotaller's."

' "That does look as if he hadn't any fever to speak of," says Smedley, "and the book says that if you've got spinal menagerie you're bound to have a fever."

' "The trouble with Tom," says I, "is mental: that's what it is. He's got something on his mind that is wearing him out."

' "What can he have on his mind?" says the captain. "He's got everything to suit him aboard this ship. If he was a millionaire he couldn't be better fixed. He won all his fights while we were in Boston, and hasn't had a fight since, which shows that he can't be low-spirited on account of a licking. No, sir! You'll find that Tom's mind is all right."

' "Then what gives him such a mournful look out of his eyes?" says I. "When you spoke to him this morning he looked at you as if he was on the point of crying over your misfortunes – that is to say, if you've got any. Come to think of it, Tom begun to go into thishyer decline just after you were married. Perhaps that's what's the matter with him."

'But there was no convincing Smedley that Tom's trouble was mental, and he was so sure that the cat was going to die, that he got to be about as low-spirited as Tom himself. "I begin to wish," says Smedley to me one morning, "that I was a Methodist again, and believed in a hereafter. It does seem kind of hard that a first-class cat-fighter like Tom shouldn't have a chance when he dies. He was a good religious cat if ever there was one, and I'd like to think that he was going to a better world."

'Just then an idea struck me. "Captain Smedley," says I, "you remember how Tom enjoyed the meetings that we used to have aboard here on Sunday mornings!"

' "He did so," said Smedley. "I never saw a person who took more pleasure in his Sunday privileges than Tom did."

' "Captain Smedley," says I, putting my hand on the old man's sleeve. "All that's the matter with Tom is seeing you deserting the religion that you was brought up in, and turning agonyostical, or whatever you call it. I call it turning plain infidel. Tom's mourning about your soul, and he's miserable because you don't have any more Sunday morning meetings. I told you the trouble was mental, and now you know it is."

' "Mebbe you're right," says Smedley, taking what I'd said in a peaceable way, instead of flying into a rage, as I expected he would. "To tell you the truth, I ain't so well satisfied in my own mind as I used to be, and I was thinking last night, when I started in to say 'Now I lay me' – just from habit you know—that if I'd stuck to the Methodist persuasion I should be a blamed sight happier than I am now."

' "To-morrow's Sunday," says I, "and if I was you, Captain, I should have the bell rung for service, same as you used to do, and bring Tom up on deck, and let him have the comfort of hearing the rippingest hymns you can lay your hand to. It can't hurt you, and it may do him a heap of good. Anyway, it's worth trying, if you really want the Yellow Terror to get well."

' "I don't mind saying," says Smedley, "that I'd do almost anything to save his life. He's been with me now going on for seven years, and we've never had a hard word. If a Sunday morning meeting will be any comfort to him, he shall have it. Mebbe if it doesn't cure him, it may sort of smooth his hatchway to the tomb."

' "Now the very next day was Sunday, and at six the Captain had the bell rung for service, and the men were told to lay aft. The bell hadn't fairly stopped ringing, when Tom comes up the companion way, one step at a time, looking as if he was on his way to his own funeral. He came up to his usual place alongside of the capstan, and lay down on his side at the old man's feet, and sort of looked up at him with what anybody would have said was a grateful look. I could see that Smedley was feeling pretty serious. He understood what the cat wanted to say, and when he started in to give out a hymn, his voice sort of choked. It was a ripping good hymn, with a regular hurricane chorus, and the men sung it for all they were worth, hoping that it would meet Tom's views. He was too weak to join in with any of his old-time yells, but he sort of flopped the deck with his tail, and you could see he was enjoying it down to the ground.

'Well, the service went on just as it used to do in old times, and Smedley sort of warmed up as it went along, and by and by he'd got the regular old Methodist glow on his face. When it was all through, and the men had gone forrard again, Smedley stooped down, and picked up Tom, and kissed him, and the cat nestled up in the old man's neck and licked his chin. Smedley carried Tom down into the saloon, and sung out to the steward to bring some fresh meat. The cat turned to and ate as good a dinner as he'd ever eaten in his best days, and after he was through, he went into Smedley's own cabin, and curled up in the old man's bunk, and went to sleep purring fit to take the deck off. From that day Tom improved steadily, and by the time we got to Cape Town he was well enough to go ashore, though he was still considerable weak. I went ashore at the same time, and kept an eye on Tom, to see what he would do. I saw him pick out a small measly-looking cat, that couldn't have stood up to a full-grown mouse, and lick him in less than a minute. Then I knew that Tom was all right again, and I admired his judgment in picking out a small cat that was suited to his weak condition. By the time that we got to Canton, Tom was as well in body and mind as he had ever been; and when we sailed, he came aboard with two inches of his tail missing, and his starboard ear carried away, but he had the air of having licked all creation, which I don't doubt he had done, that is to say, so far as all creation could be found in Canton.

'I never heard any more of Smedley's agonyostical nonsense. He went back to the Methodists again, and he always said that Tom had been the blessed means of showing him the error of his ways. I heard that when he got back to Boston, he gave Mrs Smedley notice that he expected her to go to the Methodist meeting with him every Sunday, and that if she didn't, he should consider that it was a breach of wedding articles, and equivalent to mutiny. I don't know how she took it, or what the consequences were, for I left the *Medford* just then, and took command of a barque that traded between Boston and the West Indies. And I never heard of the Yellow Terror after that voyage, though I often thought of him, and always held that for a cat he was the ablest cat, afloat or ashore, that any man ever met.'

C Stands for Cuisine

BEVERLEY NICHOLS

EVERY PUSSY, if given a chance, is an epicure. The pussy who has been brought up with love and understanding never gobbles her food, and though on rising from the table she may not send her compliments to the chef in so many words, she makes it very clear if she has been pleased or not. Even non-Fs will agree that this demeanour is in striking contrast to the behaviour of dogs who gulp their meals in a grossly animal manner, and very seldom complain even if they are offered the sort of fare which used to be provided on British Railways. In which their conduct strikingly resembles that of their masters.

My own cats have always been fortunate in the fact that they have been served by a first-class chef in the form of Gaskin. He takes as much trouble with their meals as with mine, and would be as distressed if their whiting were not *à point* as if my soufflé had failed to rise. I need hardly say that, in the course of twenty-five years, neither of these disasters has yet occurred.

Moreover, Gaskin takes almost as much trouble with what might be called the general arrangements of the table as with the actual preparation of the dishes. Thus, he regards placing as of vital importance. Many of us have probably attended dinner parties in Paris where there have been frightful *froideurs* about procedure, when some obscure but legitimate count has threatened to leave the room because he has been placed in an inferior position to an equally obscure, but bastard, marquis.

Throughout history, members of the French aristocracy have always been so busy fussing about where they sit at table that they usually have failed to notice that the entire country is sinking rapidly into the abyss. Gaskin's seating arrangements for the pussies arise from no such foolish snobbishness; he has merely learned, from long experience, that there are certain places where they like to dine and certain places where they do not, and that is that. Why they have chosen these places, nobody knows, and, as far as I am aware, nobody has ever been so vulgar as to ask them.

Thus, 'Four' insists on breakfasting under the kitchen sink, 'Five' on the kitchen table, and Oscar in a corner by the side of the dresser. Were the plates to be placed in any other position, they would be ignored. There would be pained expressions, lashings of the tail, shruggings of the shoulders and exits into the garden, and no food would be partaken until Gaskin had come to his senses.

This fastidiousness has its drawbacks. There have been a few unhappy occasions when I have been abroad, and when Gaskin has gone away for the night. Needless to say, before doing so, he has engaged a reliable woman as a 'temporary' to attend to the cats' menus. He has inquired into her antecedents, vetted her character and thoroughly coached her in the technique. The fish must be cooked just so long, and no more. The milk must be warmed. There must be a large bowl of fresh water. The times for breakfast and dinner must be strictly observed: 7.45 for breakfast, 4.15 for dinner. Above all, the position of the plates must never vary . . . 'Four' under the sink, 'Five' on the kitchen table, and Oscar by the dresser. 'You understand?' says Gaskin. Yes, says the temporary, she understands. Whereupon Gaskin, with a last beetling glance, hands her the latchkeys keys and departs, not without forebodings.

Alas, the forebodings have sometimes been justified. Even reliable women, with clean aprons and rosy faces, may have a sinister streak of non-Fness in their characters. Such a one was Mrs . . . never mind, we will call her Mrs X. How was Gaskin to know that Mrs X, who had impeccable references, with duchesses raving about her soufflés across pages of coroneted writing paper, could possibly be so wickedly incompetent about feeding the cats? No – it was not incompetence, it was

done with deliberation. For Mrs X, arriving on the following morning in the empty house – admittedly on time – suddenly decided that the cats were 'pampered'. (In subsequent cross-examination she actually *confessed* to this.) And so, having cooked the fish, she set it all on a large plate in the centre of the floor and left the cats to it, under the astonishing impression that they would eat it. She had some odd, barbaric notion that she was 'teaching them a lesson'. I am not suggesting that she was actually a sadist, and I believe that she was quite a good mother to her own three very plain and sniffly children who would probably have eaten with the greatest relish off a communal plate in the middle of the floor. All the same, I really do think it a great pity that there should be such women in the world.

Cats, of course, have exquisite table manners, though their etiquette differs somewhat from the more restricted human variety. I wonder if any of the following customs are shared by the pets of other Fs?

1. *Dabbing*. This is permissible in the best circles. My own principal dabber is 'Five'. He usually decides to dab when offered a small piece of the dish one is eating oneself. He enters the dining-room, sits by one's chair, and subjects one to a steady stare. Needless to say, he would never do anything so impolite as to mew, or to reach up to the table. The stare is duly rewarded by a small portion of chicken or steak or whatever one may be eating. This is cut up, as a *bonne bouche*, and placed before him. Whereupon 'Five' lowers his head and contemplates the *bonne bouche*. This contemplation may last for several minutes. 'Really, "Five", you are a spoilt cat,' one says. 'That is a beautiful piece of chicken. There are many cats, sleeping on the Embankment, who would be most grateful for . . .' But one does not finish the sentence, for if one begins to think of cats sleeping on the Embankment one will have a wretched night and get no sleep oneself. However, the reproof seems to have registered, for 'Five' suddenly emerges from contemplation and gives the piece of chicken a sharp dab with his right paw. It slides to the edge of the plate; then it is dabbed back again with the left paw. For all I know, this may be 'Five's' retort to one's remark about the Embankment; it may be his way of saying that such painful subjects should not be mentioned at meal

times. Whatever the reason, he eventually eats the piece of chicken. Having done so, he sits down and makes his toilet. He never asks for more.

2. *Growling*. This habit may seem to non-Fs to conflict with the claim for 'exquisite table manners'. I do not think so, for two reasons. Firstly, because there is only one dish – at least as far as my own cats are concerned – which gives rise to growling . . . rabbit. Why this should be, I do not pretend to understand. I can only register the fact that, when rabbit is on the menu, growls are in the air. They are very fierce growls, accompanied by dramatic movements of the head over the shoulder, as though seeking some imaginary enemy.

The other reason why I am, as it were, pro-growling, is because I think it would greatly enliven human dinner parties if it were generally adopted. I would not growl over most of the dishes one is offered in British households, but I would certainly growl over caviare. If one is the least important guest, as one usually is, and if one is sitting in Starvation Corner, and if one sees great dollops of this ambrosia being ladled out to fat rich ladies who could well afford to buy it by the bucket, and if one is eventually given a tiny reluctant scraping from the bottom of the jar . . . surely one *should* growl? One should not only growl, but scratch and pounce and hiss. One dies, in spirit, but not in fact, and repression, as we all know, ties the psyche up in knots.

3. *Leaving a small piece uneaten*. All delicately nurtured felines do this. It is the ultimate proof of good breeding. Even if one adopts the scruffiest alley cat, as soon as he has been plumped out and given the blessed assurance that his days of scrummaging in dustbins are over, he will leave a little bit of dinner uneaten. I have never known any exceptions to this rule. It is absolutely *de rigueur* and it suggests that somewhere, in the Feline Archives, there must be some venerated volume of Etiquette for Cats, thumbed by countless paws and sniffed over by hosts of little noses, whose lessons are passed down from generation to generation.

The Coat

MARY WILLIAMS

AT FIRST, I didn't mind. The cat had been Fay's mascot during her theatrical career, and I realized there was a strong bond between them. So when we got married, and Fay Lester 'gave up her career' . . . her own words . . . to live with me in the wilds of Cornwall, where I was mining engineer to a flourishing tin company, it seemed quite natural for her to bring her pet along.

She was ten years my senior, although she didn't look it . . . being a natural blonde: slight, fair, with large hazel eyes glittering gold one moment and green the next between thick dark lashes that owed nothing to artifice.

I *should* have realized, but didn't, that, despite her appearance, her grip on audiences was beginning to wane, owing perhaps to a slightly over-emotional old-fashioned style of acting, and possibly a subtle deterioration of physical vitality that left occasional gaps in communication. But I never thought of it, being far too infatuated to delve into abstruse whys and wherefores. It was sufficient that she cared enough to jump into matrimony so promptly, and with such apparent zest.

I'm not denying that, at thirty-two, women hadn't liked me before . . . they had, in the way the frail type often go for strong men six-footers of the rugged kind. But until Fay came along I'd managed to avoid any long-term commitment.

Anyway, after the wedding which had all the glamorous, corny trappings of a famous stage beauty stepping off into the romantic unknown with, to quote . . . 'the *one* man this time . . . the love of her life' . . . we went straight back, at her wish, to Port Erith, and our new home which stood on a hill overlooking the sea, two miles from the little town and four from St Tude's where I had my job.

The house, originally a large cottage which had been converted recently to modern standards and added on to considerably, cost me a packet, but I didn't mind.

'But darling, it's *heavenly,*' Fay had exclaimed the first time I'd taken her round. 'How did you *know* so *exactly* what I'd like? And the garden! Quite, gorgeous. Sheba will love it. Everything she needs . . . trees, little secret hidey-holes, and that darling little copse at the end . . .'

Her voice had trailed off dreamily into a 'little girl' vision of her own which amused me in a mild way . . . *then.*

Sheba, of course, was the cat; a spayed Persian queen . . . pure white with glinting green eyes, staring enigmatically with a kind of remote contempt from an abundance of thick fur. No one could have denied she was quite a beauty, and for the first few weeks at Moongate – Fay's name for our house – the sight of her padding proudly around, fine tail erect, added a certain air of feline luxury to the new premises, although Fay eventually was always her target . . . the object of her passion and desire.

It didn't worry me in the least, during those early days, to go off each day leaving the curled-up white form on Fay's lap in a lounge chair, or wandering by her side in the garden when I returned. Sheba, after all, was just a pet, and Fay was a very feminine type of woman; the kind that needed something to cuddle, in solitary moments. Maybe, I thought . . . just *maybe* perhaps, there could be a child if we didn't leave it too late. Women around forty had been known to have children without much trouble.

I was kidding myself, though. Fay didn't want any. And as the weeks passed it was all too obvious, though she did her best not to show it.

I didn't blame her really. It would have been wrong, I suppose. But there were other ways of getting over that hurdle than the one she chose . . . a certain withdrawal of passion, too subtle at first to be conclusive . . . just . . . 'Oh darling. I've had a hard day . . . Mrs Thomas was late, and I had to get down to the chores myself . . .' Mrs Thomas was our 'daily' who came three hours each morning to tackle the domestic work. Or, on other occasions . . . 'I'm tired. Really exhausted, Rod. Guess it's all the excitement . . .' and she'd looked at me with the frail imploring gaze that I just couldn't argue with. So I'd accepted it at first. I had to. But eventually, after a month or two, it was just too much.

It happened to be a Saturday and, as it was fine, with the pungent, heady magic of early autumn in the air, I suggested a picnic out, on the moors somewhere.

'What about it?' I asked Fay, early. 'Let's take off like a couple of kids and eat sandwiches in the bracken.' Although of course there was more to it in my mind than that.

I thought for a moment her eyes were wary; they had a kind of sideways glance . . . a bit critical, as though she doubted my masculine motive. Then she said, gaily . . . too gaily, I suppose, though I'd shrugged off the thought at the time, 'All right darling. Just as you say. It'll be fun for Sheba too. She's not had a real sniff of the moors yet.'

'*Sheba*?' I echoed sharply, 'surely, for once, that cat of yours can make shift for herself in the house. She has a box, all our silk cushions, a bed, eiderdown and armchairs to choose from; and a choice of chicken and rabbit to guzzle at. For God's sake darling, let's be *free* for once.'

'*Free*? From Sheba? Don't be *mean*, Rod.' Her voice was suddenly cold. 'The house is still strange to her. And if there was a storm or anything . . . she'd be *terrified* alone. No. If we can't have Sheba, I shan't go either.'

And so, of course, Sheba went along with us. Possibly if I'd been cleverer and more cooperative, the outing might have worked. But from the time we found a suitable place sheltered from the breeze by rocks, and clumps of bushes, making it a kind of bower, Sheba took charge, claiming the first taste of our sandwiches . . . chicken, and, as usual, crouching close to Fay with her green eyes glinting adoringly from her furry face. Once, as I watched the two of them in feline communication, I said irritably to the creature, 'Go on . . . shoo! *Shoo*! . . .' waving a paper napkin at its nose. 'Take a walk, can't you?'

The cat merely blinked, while Fay said defensively, 'How *can* you! Don't be so cruel, Rod. I thought you *liked* animals.'

'I do in their place,' I said shortly.

'Then why . . .?' Her voice trailed off. She shrugged before adding, 'Sheba's place is *here*; with me. It always has been. So please, darling, don't interfere.'

'Interfere?' I thought, savagely, grabbing a sandwich. Fay was my wife, wasn't she? And I bloody well hadn't gone with her on an outing like a couple of scouts with a mascot, to make a friendly threesome.

There was the scent of heather, fallen blackberries, and brine in the air. The bracken beneath us was a bed for lovers. I desired her urgently, with a sudden thrusting need. Always before, I'd managed to be gentle; now restraint was gone and I was suddenly on top of her, my hands about her breasts, locating through the thin blouse she wore. She struggled, screamed . . . at least, I thought it was a scream, or it could have been a cat's cry.

The next moment a smothering ball of soft fur had landed on my head, and streaks of pain were seering my cheek. One fist shot out, as I managed to free myself and jump up. Blood splashed my shirt, trickling down my jaw from jagged, clawed scars.

I didn't speak, just mopped my face, while Fay sat up, arranged her clothes again, and said with a mixture of triumph and contrition, in smug, well-bred tones, 'I'm sorry you're hurt, Rod. Sheba didn't *mean* that . . . did you, my sweet . . .?' Her voice, like her eyes, were liquid with love for the wild brute.

'No?' I said harshly.

'Of course not. She's protective that's all. You shouldn't have . . . have . . . tried to . . . to . . .'

'Seduce my wife?' I finished for her. 'No, I shouldn't. Not in the presence of that damned animal. Well . . . I'm telling you Fay, it'll have to *go*.'

'Sheba will never go, unless I go with her,' Fay said coldly. 'Obviously you resent her. You haven't the first inkling of how to treat animals, and they always *know*. If you were more tolerant . . .'

'Tolerant?' I snapped, 'What, for God's sake, have I been for weeks now? When was it we last made love? Tell me that.

You've been a pretty tired woman where I've been concerned lately, and that's a fact. But Sheba! . . . Oh *no*. Sheba comes first, doesn't she? Love me, love my cat. That's about the size of it. But get this into your head, darling, and I mean it . . . no more of it. In future, when I want you, you'll grin and bear it, whether you like it or not. And no *cat* around. Understand?'

She didn't reply. But I knew I'd made my point.

And that night, following the travesty of the picnic, I proved it.

Fay was lying between the pink sheets, with a book, when I went upstairs and, as usual, Sheba huddled close to her. She glanced at me as I undressed, and maybe there was a hint of fear in her eyes as I went to the bed. But I didn't say anything; just lifted the cat up . . . I'd taken the precaution of wearing gloves . . . and threw her, hissing, out of the room on to the landing.

Then I went to Fay, very deliberately pulled back the sheets, and took the lacy thing from her body, revealing the almost childlike breasts and slender thighs pressed together protectingly.

'Don't,' she whispered. 'Don't you *dare* . . . Rod . . .'

But I did dare. I took her as ruthlessly as I'd have taken a petulant mistress, forgetting temporarily that this was the delicately cherished glamorous woman I'd adored and felt so privileged to marry.

Afterwards, of course, I was ashamed . . . not for showing her once and for all how things were going to be when I felt that way . . . but of my manner of showing it. I tried to apologize but she lay simply staring at the ceiling, moaning a little, though tearlessly. It was as though I didn't exist for her any more, and that one act . . . induced by my resentment of the cat, had alienated and divided us completely.

She was withdrawn and silent the next morning, refusing breakfast which I took up to her on a tray.

'Fay . . .' I said, trying to ignore the malicious gleam of Sheba's eyes . . . the sickening sight of white fur curled against my wife's shoulders . . . 'be sensible, *please*. We've got to adjust a bit . . . both of us. In marriage these things do happen sometimes. It can't always be one or the other. It's *both* of us.

Our life together.' She didn't answer. 'So please do eat something. You'll feel better then.'

'I'll eat when I feel like it,' she answered, coldly remote. 'Mrs Thomas will be here presently. If I want anything, she'll get it.'

Smothering a hot retort, I kissed her forehead lightly and left for St Tude's. When I returned that evening she was nowhere in the house; everywhere seemed strangely quiet and still. The days were closing in now and, though fine, the autumn sky was already yellowing to grey behind the copse bordering the garden. As I stared across the lawn a leaf dropped soundlessly from a nearby chestnut, leaving the networked branches dark and exposed, except for the last remaining foliage grouped in hanging fingered shapes . . . the shapes of dead hands . . . which would soon be gone.

I felt uneasy. Chilled by foreboding. And then I saw them . . . two white shapes, Fay and Sheba, strolling slowly, almost glidingly, from the trees, along the path bordering the lawn. The cat was in her arms when they reached the house.

'Oh hullo, Rod,' she said absently. 'You're early, aren't you?'

'No,' I answered abruptly. 'Late if anything, and hungry.'

'I'll get you something.' Her voice was quiet; very cold and composed. I'd have preferred her to be edgy or sharp.

'Don't let it worry you,' I told her. 'I can fend for myself if necessary. I expect you're tired after your ramble.' My heavy sarcasm seemed to escape her. 'Oh no,' she said, sweetly reasonable. 'Sheba and I have just been gorgeously aimless and at peace . . . haven't we, my pet?'

Churning inwardly with mounting rage and resentment, I managed to say briefly, 'What is it then . . . the meal?'

'Oh . . .' she paused, wiping a strand of pale hair vaguely from her forehead. 'There's cold pie in the fridge . . . or eggs . . . we've had ours. But . . .' Her voice trailed off.

I turned on my heel savagely and went to the kitchen. 'We'! It was then I knew I was going to kill Sheba. And as the days went by my resolve intensified. Possibly if Fay had shown the slightest warmth to me . . . even once let me touch her without wincing, I might have weakened. But she didn't. She remained outwardly poised, cool and remote . . . though what went on in her mind I never knew . . . could only guess at the emotional yearnings over that damned cat.

It was unnatural. I knew I had to end it.

And so one evening when Fay was having her bath and Sheba, as usual, waiting for her in the bedroom, I took a syringe . . . and with all the skill I'd learned in an early brief training as a vet . . . very deliberately put her painlessly to sleep. She was an oldish cat. It didn't take long . . . no more than a minute. And, when it was over, I went downstairs, leaving her there, curled up on the pink eiderdown, waiting for Fay.

Even now, so long afterwards, I consider I was quite justified, arguing that, with Sheba gone, Fay and I would have the chance of a new beginning and a normal life ahead.

But it didn't work out that way.

She didn't fight me. Oh no; it would have been better if she had. She just accepted my explanation that cats did die like that sometimes . . . just curled up and went to sleep . . . 'or maybe she could have picked up something that disagreed with her', I concluded. It made no difference at all. Fay was beyond theorizing or argument. She just fretted and went about in a bemused way, as though nothing mattered any more. I buried Sheba at the bottom of the garden on the edge of the copse, because there had to be a stone, suitably inscribed, according to my wife . . . although I thought it pretty mawkish and morbid. Still, if that was what she wanted, I made no objection, and was thankful when the whole thing was over.

At least I *thought* it was over.

As it happened, it was only the beginning.

With the approach of winter, I made tentative overtures to Fay and, once or twice, made love to her, if you could call it lovemaking. She didn't resist but lay there cold, rigid and unresponsive, while I tried desperately to rouse some emotion . . . even anger, rather than such dead negation of body and spirit.

One evening, when we lay afterwards side by side without warmth or words between us, she turned her head suddenly, gave me a long searching look, and then said, 'Did *you* kill Sheba?'

Though taken aback, I managed to answer calmly enough, 'Don't be silly. If I'd wanted to get rid of her I'd have put her in a sack and chucked her over the cliffs into the sea . . . or at least drowned and buried her. You'd never have known then, would you? You'd have thought she'd just wandered off like cats do and got lost . . . or injured.'

'Not Sheba,' she said firmly.

'Fay! For heaven's sake,' I prevaricated . . . 'do I look like a murderer?' She stared at me reflectively before answering in a queer, contemptuous sort of way, 'Yes, I think you do.'

'Then get your thoughts straight,' I said abruptly, 'and don't mention that bloody animal to me again.'

Nothing more was said that night. But all the next day I couldn't get the incident out of my mind. Work was impossible; I just mooched about, smoked, and toyed unsuccessfully with books of figures that didn't make sense at all. I felt so browned off, in fact, that I gave Fay a ring telling her not to keep a meal for me, I'd be dining out – business appointment.

There was no business, of course. I just went to a place I knew on the harbour where they had slap-up meals to candlelight, with all the expensive trappings that attracted the select few who could afford to pay for it. There weren't many in . . . just half a dozen or so, including a girl I used to know, Cora Ellis. She was an artist and, at one time, I'd toyed with the idea of taking the plunge with her . . . not necessarily marriage, but at least some sort of steady relationship that would have satisfied our wandering libidos. Cora was dark, picturesque, and quite luscious in her own particular way. Clever too. She had a mind of her own that saw things clearly, which probably accounted for her considerable success as an abstract painter.

That night she was wearing an orange cape over some dark green maxi thing . . . kaftans they call them, don't they? . . . Immense silver ear-rings swung below her black hair. Yes, her hair was truly black. Maybe she had gipsy blood in her; she liked to think so, but had told me once, 'It's all an act, darling. Good publicity.'

She was very honest with her friends. This was one of the things I liked about her, and several times I'd thought lately what a fool I'd been not to marry her instead of Fay. But then our chemistries, I suppose, hadn't clicked. There'd been no mystery . . . no subtle conquest of the unknown. Whereas with Fay . . . *Fay*! I pulled myself together, and went to Cora's table.

'Mind if I join you?' I asked.

'Darling Rod, of course not. Thrilled.' She indicated a chair. I took it and glanced at the menu, a fantastic crimson affair embossed with gold. 'What's up?' Cora said after a brief pause. 'You look a bit . . .'

'Browned off,' I finished for her. 'That's putting it mildly.'

'No. I wasn't going to say that,' she remarked. 'Belligerent, I think . . . like someone wanting a fight, who can't find anyone to fight with.'

I couldn't help smiling. She had so completely hit the nail on the head. Well, naturally, after I'd ordered a meal that would have burned a hole in anyone's pocket, I gave her the rough outline of my married history.

'Hm.' Cora commented when the story was finished . . . and I admit it must have sounded a pretty adolescent situation, the way I told it. 'You have got yourself into a state. I wouldn't have believed it, honest I wouldn't . . . a down-to-earth hefty male like you shattered by a cat . . .'

'The cat's dead,' I interrupted.

'It makes no difference. You've got it on your mind still . . . a kind of guilt complex, I suppose. And there's no need. You had to do something; well, you did it. But that's not your problem, is it, Rod?'

'What do you mean?'

'The real trouble's Fay.'

'I don't need telling that.'

'Yes you do, darling, so you can see straight.' She shrugged. 'Or maybe you'd rather go round in circles. But that's not like you.'

'Go on.'

'She's a whole ten years older than you. I know what you're going to say . . . she doesn't look it, she's beautiful, and famous and very, very feminine. True enough. But forty plus doesn't always go for passion. Some women are frigid then. I do know, my father's a doctor. Remember? In any case, I shouldn't have to tell you this.' She stubbed a cigarette on the tray and lit another, stared at me thoughtfully for a moment or two, then concluded, 'You've either got to play things gently, *her* way, or not at all. That is, unless you want a divorce . . .'

'I don't,' I replied.

A wry smile touched her lips. 'I thought not. Some women don't know their luck . . .'

'Cora. I . . .' for a moment I wondered; just played again with the idea of what it would be like to go to bed with her, have something for once that was mutual and unrestricted by fears and frustration! She had a beautiful body, and despite her diamond-bright mind, those limpid eyes of hers, full, perfectly modelled lips indicated an inner sensuality that could be exciting. And yet . . . my thoughts wavered off doubtfully, which she must have sensed, because she remarked apropos of nothing I'd spoken aloud . . . 'Don't, Rod.' Her hand touched mine lightly. 'I know you like me. So let's leave it that way. There could be more if you were that kind. But you're not, Fay's still the only one, I can see that . . .'

'Yes,' I admitted. 'I love her.'

'Then why not go home and tell her so . . . say it the way you've just said it to me, and try your damnedest, darling, to believe things will adjust in time. Maybe they will; I hope so, because I know that's what you want.'

I doubted that her advice would work; still, I decided to give it a try, and half an hour later was on my way back to Moongate.

As I walked up the path to the front door I thought Fay's name for the house had been an apt choice. The moon, indeed, was bright that night, spilling a luminous pattern of light and shade across the landscape, in which the cottage crouched, looking curiously alone and bereft.

At moments, the windows that side were lit to momentary pale clarity . . . then just as quickly became bleak and dark as though an immense hand had washed all vestige of life away.

I went in. Fay was nowhere about; I was puzzled, briefly, and a little frightened, until I went to the lounge windows, opened the curtains, and saw a white shape at the end of the garden, standing perfectly motionless by Sheba's grave. The sight of her back, so grief-stricken somehow, filled me with remorse; yet behind the sympathy jealousy still lingered, because of her concentration . . . her overwhelming passionate devotion to the creature that had for so long shared her life. Can desire, if strong enough, resurrect the dead? Since then I have never really been able to make up my mind. But, at one point, I could have sworn a ghostly feline shape emerged round the stone, tail waving in the sudden unclouded light, as it moved and curled round Fay's still form. Her head was slightly bent, her hands, I imagined, clasped in an attitude of prayer. The sight was unnerving; my whole body felt cold suddenly, as though death itself had touched me.

Then the moon slipped behind a veil of cloud, and I jerked myself to reality. It was a cold night. Fay was not robust. She could catch pneumonia out there in only her night things and flimsy wrap. As I went to bring her in I blamed myself for not getting a specialist to see her earlier; obviously she was ill . . . physically and mentally depleted through her unwholesome love and grief for Sheba.

When I reached the copse where the headstone stood like some pagan memorial to an ancient god, Fay turned and looked at me.

I was shocked by her expression . . . the dead, transfixed stare of her eyes, which in the moonlight glinted pure green, with no flicker of movement . . . no recognition, or even surprise. She could have been in a trance. Catalepsy or something, and I thought how apt was the word.

I took her hand. It was ice-cold. 'Fay,' I said, 'come along . . . come back darling. You'll catch your death. You shouldn't . . . you really shouldn't do this sort of thing . . .'

I don't know whether she heard me or understood. She made no response, but allowed herself to be led compliantly back to the house. I guided her upstairs to bed, then got a hot drink for her which she took without demur.

She went to sleep quite soon, and lay there breathing deeply and evenly like a child, apparently at peace. I wondered, then, how I could ever have desired her so remorselessly and with such savage physical urgency. There was nothing of her at that moment I wanted, or could imagine I would want again. Before I switched off the light I noticed the tiny lines networking the corner of her closed eyes . . . the faintly sunken upper lip, and too thin neck already faintly creased. Cora's words echoed through my mind . . . 'She's a whole ten years older than you . . .' and for the first time I recognized their truth.

I was swamped by pity that held no passion or need, except the need in myself to expiate what I'd done. I would get her another pet, I thought, as I lay wakeful and ill at ease . . . a kitten, or puppy perhaps . . . something she could lavish her affection on, leaving me free of the burden of guilt and loving.

Or . . . had I ever really loved her?

A man does not like to doubt himself or his motives. But that night I faced a whole lot of them; and, when at last I went to sleep, it was not of Fay I dreamed but of a vibrant, clear-eyed young woman of warmth and generosity. Cora . . . who wanted me, and had sent me back to my own sterile illusion, and . . . though she did not know it . . . to so much else that was unspeakable and degrading.

By a strange quirk of fate, Fay's mood was subtly different the next morning. Although still quiet and remote, her eyes held awareness, as though for the first time since our early married days she was seeing me as a person . . . or even as a man. There was something discomforting about it. I usually took up her breakfast first, and had mine on my own, but that day she came down herself, made tea and toast, sat opposite me at the breakfast table, pouring from the pot, with all the grace displayed so effectively in the past on the stage. She was, I remembered, looking more than usually glamourous . . . and I was quite aware that she knew it and had laid it on for my benefit. It was all rather creepy; I couldn't help wondering if I'd talked in my sleep, or if, with some sixth sense, she guessed about Cora. The guilt complex flooded back in me. I could feel her watching me all the time even when my eyes were turned away.

'Oh damn!' I thought. 'Why *now*? Why for God's sake has she to soften at this point and make me feel a real heel . . .?'

I couldn't fathom it; couldn't make out myself either . . . why, when such a short time ago one warm glance from her could have made me cock-a-hoop . . . all it gave me now was a smothering sense of irritation and longing to be out of the house.

I did my best to appear appreciative, of course, an attempt which encouraged her even to go to the door when I left, with her face tilted slightly upwards, obviously expecting me to kiss her . . . a habit which for weeks she'd discouraged.

I did so very briefly and lightly on the cheek. She smiled, and said, 'Bye darling. Try not to be late tonight.'

As I walked down the lane to the shed where I kept the car I tried to puzzle things out; tried to fathom the reason for my sudden change of heart from Fay to Cora. In the restaurant the previous evening, Cora had registered primarily as a good friend, an attractive confidante of my woes who hadn't counted in any way as a rival to my wife. Now, suddenly, everything was different and, as I traced events retrospectively, I knew the crucial moment had been when Fay and I had stood in the moonlight, face to face by Sheba's grave.

For those few momentous seconds, an empty shell had confronted me. Then, afterwards . . . I recollected the tired, aged look of her in sleep . . . followed, only an hour ago, by an inexplicable decision to make breakfast . . . the look of almost coy supplication when she stood at the door, waiting. I didn't like it. And, at the same time, I didn't know why. After all, it could be she was making an effort at last; had decided to end the 'war' between us, and really try.

But it wasn't that. And deep down I knew it. Fay was not Fay any more. She'd gone, replaced by . . . what? I pulled myself together with an effort. The idea was monstrous, absurd. But at the back of my mind the fantastic idea still niggled and tormented me. And when I returned in the evening she was waiting for me; luxuriously dressed in one of those cream and satiny looking affairs bought at an expensive store for dining and wining in secret . . . a kind of dual-purpose outfit that could be respectably worn in company, or seductively displayed on private occasions. Ours, of course, was intended to be *very* private that evening and, as she bent over the table putting the plate before me, the dress, gown, or whatever they called it, slipped provocatively below the curved breasts, revealing one pink nipple . . . as pink and probing as a . . . a loving cat's tongue.

I pretended not to notice. But I was revolted. Unduly so. And when she didn't zip up properly, I said sharply, 'Fay, your dress is undone.'

She gave a little moue of surprise, arched her eyebrows and replied in a soft, silky voice, 'Darling . . . I'm so *sorry*. But you don't mind, do you? Not as it's just us?'

She returned to a place right behind my chair, and twined

her arms round my neck. I could feel her soft hair brush my face by the ear, and I lifted one hand irritably.

'For heaven's sake, Fay. Let me eat. I'm hungry.'

She moved away, and took her place at the table, facing me.

'So am I,' she said, with a meaningful, repelling glance. 'Terribly, *terribly* hungry, darling.'

And that night her hunger consumed me. Not in the normal way of a woman in love with a man, but with sickening possessive lust that made me loathe her soft white limbs, the pressure of her body against mine . . . close, so close, I nearly suffocated.

It was not until early morning that I had any sleep at all and, when I got up, I found Fay was already downstairs with an excellent breakfast prepared and, as before, looking quite glamorous in a nauseating way.

After that things intensified. When I was at home she could not leave me alone, but was forever fawning and purring over me, pressing her lips against my face, and her thighs against mine. As the days passed though, those thighs weren't so slender any more. She was putting on weight, and gradually becoming more luscious and overbearing.

One evening I met Cora by chance as I was about to get into the car. In contrast to Fay she now looked almost coltish in her youthful safari trouser-suit showing blue beneath her green anorak.

'Hullo,' she said, half timidly. 'How are things, Rod?'

I paused before replying . . . 'They're . . . different.'

'Oh.' I thought she looked briefly disappointed, then she said, quite gaily, though the gaiety was probably forced. 'I'm glad.'

'You needn't be,' I retorted curtly.

'How come?'

Looking her straight in the eyes, I answered:

'Because I made one hell of a mistake, Cora.'

'You mean . . . she doesn't want you? But you've just said . . .'

'Oh she *wants* me,' I retorted bitterly. 'She wants me too much. The trouble is, I don't want *her* any more. I . . . loathe her, Cora . . .'

She stared at me blankly, uncomprehendingly for a moment, then she said, 'What do you propose to do about it?'

'Nothing. Not for the moment,' I told her. 'Except just get into this car, drive straight back so I'm there in time for our tasty little meal together.'

'Rod . . . you're not well,' she protested. 'What is it? Do explain . . . just a little. I've no right to ask, I know; but . . .'

'You have, Cora. You've every right. The snag is, it's too late now. I'm hooked. For good. By a *cat*. A feline sickening cat of a woman who won't let me alone . . . even at work, she's *there*, in my mind. And I don't know how long I can stand it.'

As I drove away I glanced back once and saw Cora standing motionless watching me, most probably thinking I'd gone quite off my chump. Recalling a little of our conversation I thought so myself.

Shortly before Christmas when I returned in the evening I saw a furry pale shape poking about a holly bush in the garden. My heart lurched, and almost stopped for a moment, then bounded on again as the form straightened and came towards me. The half light was already quickly fading into darkness, but when she straightened, lifting her head, I saw it was Fay, wearing a coat I'd not seen before . . . a long-haired, very thick and soft affair, with a hood in purest white.

'How do you like it?' she cooed under the light when we went in, turning this way and that . . . prancing and preening herself like any prize feline animal on show. From the hood her hazel eyes had a green covetous look, and it seemed to me for a sickening second that the fur on her head was slightly pointed above each ear, reminding me of the one thing I wanted to forget. 'I bought it for a song . . .' she went on, 'honestly. Don't you think it's the most gorgeous creation on earth?'

'Take it off,' I shouted, unable to control myself. 'Take it off, do you hear? And never let me see you wearing it again.'

She looked temporarily stupefied but, after a brief pause, did what I said, muttering almost under her breath, 'I don't understand you, darling. I believe you're jealous.' She sidled up to me, touching my arm fawningly. '*Is* that it, Rod? Are you really jealous of a coat?'

I did then what I'd not done before, pushed her quite roughly away, so that she fell against a chair. She straightened herself, one hand to her side, while I found grace enough to say, 'I'm sorry, I didn't mean to do that.'

She came towards me stealthily, and very maliciously, her eyes narrowed and fiery-cold . . . 'Then don't ever do it again, darling,' she said through her teeth, with a hissing sound. 'I have very sharp claws, you know.'

Yes, I knew. I think I'd known it for quite a time.

The question was . . . how to clip them.

At Christmas, mercifully, I went down with a touch of flu which meant that Fay's amours, to a certain extent, were curtailed, though at nights I was aware of her sexual and emotional yearnings as she lay beside me, plump and white limbed, with her hair occasionally tickling my face. I had a slight temperature which probably accounted for the illusion that she was growing down round her mouth and contours of her chin. Even her arms sometimes seemed to have the sheen of silky hair on them, and occasionally, when she went out at night, 'for a little wander', in her own words, because she couldn't sleep, I would watch her from the window cross the lawn to the copse where she would stand briefly by Sheba's grave, looking for all the world like a great cat herself, in her white coat, before passing on down a path through the trees which led eventually to a picturesque but dangerous place . . . an abandoned quarry of precipitious depth where sheep in the past had fallen and died.

It was thinking of the quarry that gave me the idea, although I would not at first acknowledge it, even to myself. However, when I came round to facing things squarely, the idea seemed reasonable and a very practical solution to a situation that had become intolerable.

If I could have tackled Fay honestly, and said frankly, 'Look Fay . . . our marriage isn't a success. We're not suited to each other . . . I don't love you as I thought I did; will you, for both our sakes, consider a divorce? I'll be generous . . . fit in with any arrangements you want, financially speaking, and we could remain good friends . . .'

But I couldn't. Several times I tried, with the words on the tip of my tongue. Then my courage faltered. She was so intimidating, facing me in the way she'd had lately, of devouring me with her eyes, hands half extended towards me, palms upwards, with fingers slightly curved, pearly pointed nails held inwards . . . though graspingly, waiting for what she could have of me. Yes, it was *me* she wanted . . . and only me. Money, security . . . friendship . . . these had no meaning for Fay any more. I was her 'thing' . . . her possession, or, as some would say, her 'familiar'.

And so I coldly and calculatingly formulated my plan.

As time passed Fay's nightly jaunts through the copse became more frequent . . . a procedure which did not escape the vigilant eyes of the scattered local population. I was well aware that she was becoming known as an eccentric who, whatever the weather, went about always smothered in white fur, poor thing, and mostly at night when ordinary folk were asleep in bed. This opinion suited me perfectly, and when a farmer's wife suggested to me one day that, although it wasn't her business and she didn't like interfering, it had occurred to her that my wife perhaps ought to see a doctor, I agreed, with a show of worried concern.

'I wouldn't have said a *word*,' the woman emphasized, 'except that my husband saw her wandering about by that quarry place the other night . . . quite clear it was, moonlight . . . anyway, he thought it a bit dangerous. So he went up to her and she was acting kind of strange . . . making funny little sort of mewing noises, and didn't seem to recognize him. So I thought . . .' her voice wavered off uncertainly.

'Thank you for telling me, Mrs Carver,' I answered. 'I'm most grateful, and I'm afraid you're right. My wife isn't at all well.'

'I expect it's only temporary,' she said encouragingly. 'Sometimes at her age . . . forgive me . . . she *is* older than you, isn't she, sir? . . . Well, women have funny ideas, if you know what I mean. Just a phase. We all go through it one way or another.'

But not in Fay's way, I thought, with savage irony, when the woman had gone. And there was nothing temporary about it. That's why it had to be ended, once and for all . . . the whole morbid uncanny business of Fay and Sheba.

I chose a night that was not too clear or dark . . . just a film of cloud passing intermittently over a ringed moon.

Fay had been amorous in bed, entwining me by her white, now fleshy thighs, pushing her face suffocatingly against my own, so the down on it, almost whiskers now, tickled and half stifled me. I had tried once to push her off, but she was on top of me, and around me, luscious, soft, and demanding, and there was nothing I could do but let her have her way. When it was over, she stretched, sighed, and presently, thinking I was asleep, got up, went to the wardrobe for her furry white coat, put it on, slunk downstairs, and let herself out.

I was only a minute behind, having put my dark coat ready with a pair of rubber-soled black shoes that should make no sound above the moaning of the rising wind. Her hooded white shape was quite visible crossing the lawn; but I kept to the side path, well in the shadow of the bushes, and waited as she paused by Sheba's grave. Then, after a moment, she went on and I followed.

Really, what happened after that was incredibly simple.

It was so easy to keep track of her figure ahead, padding almost slidingly along the winding thread of path which led eventually to a sudden clearing of trees, and the precipitous edge of the quarry.

I waited in the darkness of undergrowth and tangled branches until I was certain of her direction . . . of whether or not she intended to prowl around a bit before returning or if, with luck, she would make straight for the quarry which seemed to hold for her such fascination.

My luck was in and I grabbed it. She must have heard me before she fell; I had a glimpse of a pale, cat-like face turned quickly, with baleful terrified eyes staring accusingly from its furry hood. Then my arm shot out, and she was gone, screaming, into the darkness of the pit.

Her body was found in the morning by the farmer owning the adjoining land.

Naturally, Fay's death caused a stir in the district; there was gossip which, despite sympathetic concern for the 'poor husband', held a hint of relish in it. After all, the poor thing had been crazy, hadn't she? Always wandering off like that. It was obvious . . . folk had said for some time . . . that she'd end up, sooner or later, by taking a header over the cliff.

And so it was.

The verdict at the inquest a week later was recorded as 'Death by misadventure' and sympathy accorded, as was customary, to the bereaved husband, myself.

Everything was properly rounded off, I thought, as I walked up the path of Moongate that cold February evening following the inquiry. I was alone now. Free for the first time since my marriage, which, on looking back, seemed an eternity. Now all that remained for me to do was, first, to get rid of every trace of Fay's clothes and possessions, and have that odious stone removed from Sheba's grave, so that no reminder of either lingered. Later, probably, I would sell the cottage too. But that would be when I'd had a holiday to restore health and equilibrium.

It was a cold night; the house felt chill and damp when I went in. Wan light streaked through the windows where the curtains were still open, revealing a landscape bereft of life or colour . . . just dull, quickly fading grey, merging into the yellowing darkness of enveloping twilight. I felt the heaters in hall and lounge. They were full on, but no warmth seemed to penetrate the atmosphere. So I pulled the curtains close, switched on three bars of the electric fire, got a stiff whisky, and settled down to enjoy it as warmth spread through my body again, making me feel once more a human being.

Then I turned on the television.

Everything was silent at first. I waited one minute, two. No picture, no sound; nothing. Then rather faintly, as though from a great distance, the announcer's voice started its ritual of evening news. The screen flickered, shot with dancing lines which suggested there was a technical fault somewhere, then, gradually, the distortion resolved into the dim outlines of the newsreader's face. But the screen was misty and, as the voice droned on, my muscles and senses stiffened with horror, because clouding the male features were those of another, so that the impression given was of a badly taken photograph with one film overlaying a first. I rubbed my eyes with a shaking hand, trying to get the thing . . . whatever it was, either erased completely or properly into focus so that I knew what I was dealing with.

When I looked again though, there was no difference, except that the slant, amber-green eyes staring from the woolly white hood were slightly more defined. *Fay*! . . . or Sheba . . . it didn't matter any more. The features were there, overlapping those of the broadcaster . . . mouth malicious and mocking, moving silently, to the ordinary accompaniment of the programme.

I sat rooted to the chair for a minute, then I struggled to my feet, and smashed my fist against the screen. 'Go away. Damn you,' I shouted, with my heart thumping unevenly against my ribs, and in my ears. 'Leave me alone . . . can't you?' I was breathing heavily, and staggered back to the chair with sweat trickling from my face down the collar of my shirt.

There was a soft kind of feline chuckle; followed by a cessation of all sound. When the giddiness had passed and I could see properly again, everything was perfectly normal. The announcer's face was in proper perspective, as I knew it, and relief flooded me. An hallucination, I told myself, when I'd steadied my nerves with a second whisky; and it was a wonder I'd not shattered the screen with the lunge I'd delivered.

All the same, I switched off presently, taking no chance of a repetition.

I slept badly that night. Once or twice I woke, with the nightmare sensation of Fay's body pressing against mine . . . of her silky hair tickling my face, creeping everywhere, up my nostrils . . . my ears . . . in my throat even, choking me. But when I switched on the light there was nothing. Only the sound of the clock ticking and my own heart pumping. Tomorrow, I decided, I would move into the spare room, or sleep on the divan downstairs. It was obvious that the sooner I got away on a holiday jaunt the better.

I saw Cora in the morning and, although I didn't say anything about the morbid incident, which, in the light of day I convinced myself had been imagination . . . I told her I was taking off that evening for a brief break in the south of France and, if she'd care to come along too, it would do a whole lot for me.

'Dear Rod,' she said regretfully, 'I'd love to. But I'm on an important commission, and I just can't get away at the moment. It isn't only the money, don't think that. But I've *pro-*

mised to deliver the designs by Tuesday, and it means working half the nights anyway. So you see . . .'

'It's OK,' I said, taking her hand and giving it a little squeeze. 'I understand.'

'Anyway,' she went on consolingly, 'maybe you should be on your own for a bit. Just to get things into perspective again. I'm sure I'm right.'

But she wasn't.

No one could have been more chillingly wrong.

I travelled from one place to another . . . from pension to pension, Brittany first, then further south in France where I thought, at last, I'd found a haven free from Fay's haunting presence. It was a small picturesque place on the outskirts of a village in the Bordeaux district, with lush slopes and vineyards behind, and a café place in front, overlooking the river, frequented every evening by holiday-makers and colourful inhabitants who did their best to entertain tourists with wine and song.

I slept well the first night.

But on the second I was restless, and when I got up to look out of the window she was there, a perfectly static shape, standing in the moonlight, all furry-white but with satiny soft limbs desirous, I knew, beneath the obscene thick coat.

I pulled the curtains to, shuddering went back to bed and lay with hands clenched, body rigid and sweating with fear. I dozed a little at last but, when I woke, suddenly alert, I could feel a soft arm stir round my stomach. I sat up, tore myself free wildly, and jumped out of bed, rushing to the window, which I opened wide, for air.

When I looked back there was no one there. Nothing but my own clothes flung over the back of a chair, an indentation in the sheets, where a body, or *two*, had been lying, and the eiderdown, pink silk, rumpled on the floor.

This was too much for me.

I packed up and left the same day, catching the first possible plane flight for home.

The next day I was back at Moongate, and I know now that I shall never leave.

I am, in fact, beginning to adjust to my new way of life. Fay, at least, never troubles me in the daytime now; and although some nights we are together, at others she prefers to wander aimlessly over the moors and through the copse, pausing for a motionless interlude by Sheba's grave for comfort and sustenance. It is, you see, her home. And while I am there, too, she is a comparatively peaceful ghost.

Cora, of course, can't understand why I never go away . . . why our friendship has never matured into the deeper relationship that once, at the time of Fay's death, seemed inevitable. People consider it unnatural living as I do, a confirmed widower. But then they have no linking of the truth . . . that when I lie in my bed I have frequent company . . . the pressure of soft white limbs entwining mine, and the tickle of fine hair against my cheek.

The Achievement of the Cat

SAKI

(Hector Hugo Munro)

THE ANIMAL which the Egyptians worshipped as divine, which the Romans venerated as a symbol of liberty, which Europeans in the ignorant Middle Ages anathematized as an agent of demonology, has displayed to all ages two closely blended characteristics – courage and self-respect. No matter how unfavourable the circumstances, both qualities are always to the fore.

Confront a child, a puppy, and a kitten with a sudden danger; the child will turn instinctively for assistance, the puppy will grovel in abject submission to the impending visitation, the kitten will brace its tiny body for a frantic resistance. And disassociate the luxury-loving cat from the atmosphere of social comfort in which it usually contrives to move, and observe it critically under the adverse conditions of civilization – that civilization which can impel a man to the degradation of clothing himself in tawdry ribald garments and capering mountebank dances in the streets for the earning of the few coins that keep him on the respectable, or non-criminal, side of society. The cat of the slums and alleys, starved, outcast, harried, still keeps amid the prowlings of its adversity the bold, free, panther-tread with which it paced of yore the temple courts of Thebes, still displays the self-reliant watchfulness which man has never taught it to lay aside.

And when its shifts and clever managings have not sufficed to stave off inexorable fate, when its enemies have proved too strong or too many for its defensive powers, it dies fighting to the last, quivering with the choking rage of mastered resistance, and voicing in its death-yell that agony of bitter remonstrance which human animals, too, have flung at the powers that may be; the last protest against a destiny that might have made them happy – and has not.

Incident on East Ninth

JILL DROWER

I LEANED my head against the cool metal of the reinforced door. Something was digging into my temple – the spy-hole. I pictured Arnold peeping through from the other side, squinting at me with a cold, cold eye, resentful, gloating, wishing me dead. He loathed me. I realized it the first moment we were introduced. Arnold got me into this. It was all his fault.

It was hot – somewhere in the eighties. This was a smart apartment block in the East Village, but the corridor still looked like it belonged to cell block B at a state pen. It was stifling but I was shaking more than a leaf on a Dutch elm. Was it embarrassment or shock? Every few minutes the elevator would chime and ping out another group of homecomers. They would glance over in my direction and then look away indifferently. What was the matter? Didn't I look weird enough for them? Dishevelled, furtive, I pressed up close to the apartment door in a feeble attempt to conceal myself behind the architrave.

The T-shirt I was wearing was a little tatty, but it was as bright-white as new. It came down just below my navel and it had giant sans serif letters across the chest which spelt out the word 'RELAX'. This was my first night in New York and I was locked out of my friend's apartment. I was telling myself to calm down. Difficult. Apart from the T-shirt, all I was wearing was a pair of gold-hoop earrings.

Arnold's relationship with Laura was entirely platonic. Having shared the apartment for some years they were now as close as brother and sister. Laura was relieved to find a flatmate who accepted her as she was, someone who didn't squabble about petty things like who did the washing-up. Besides, living in New York was a lonely business and Arnold was entertaining company. The problem was, he was jealous of her friends. Maybe he thought that, if she found someone and fell in love, she might want to get married and 'the other man' would boot him out. Whatever it was, Arnold made it his business to frighten away any friends whom she invited in. She had taken to visiting singles bars, and this brought a fairly high number of invitations from her to 'come back to my place for coffee'. Arnold developed what he called his 'spooking-out technique' which, after a couple of evenings, he had down to a fine art. Laura, unsuspecting, would disappear into the kitchen to fix the percolator. Arnold, very friendly, would join the visitor on the sofa and, at a given moment, he would put on this stare and become strangely menacing. When Laura returned with the tray, he was back to being the nice guy and would make a big ceremony of leaving the room tactfully to let them sit alone together on the sofa. After one visit, these poor hopefuls never returned.

I was in New York principally to meet a number of old friends who were now living there but, as this was my first visit to the city, I wanted to see as much of Manhattan as possible in the ten days I had.

'You're welcome to stay at my place, if you like, so long as you don't mind sleeping on the sofa.' I took Laura up on her offer. She lived on East Ninth, somewhere near the bottom of Fifth Avenue and near enough to Washington Square Park for us to go jogging there every morning.

The journey from La Guardia to Laura's apartment had me in a trance. It was all exactly like those cop shows and Scorcese films I'd seen, only much more so. It was all so different from the ribbons of mock Tudor en route from Heathrow or Gatwick. I took it all in: the weatherboard houses, the freeways, the automobiles, the 'last exit to . . .' signs and the bluntness of the yellow cab driver who took me from the bus terminal to Laura's place. Like the uninitiated in any major city,

I saw the place as a series of clichés. All that was missing was the steam coming out of subway gratings, but I suppose I had the wrong time of year for that. This was summer in the city and fire-hydrant-unlocking time. Firecrackers snapped all around, a constant reminder that July the 4th was only a day away.

Laura was a model host. She took me for brunch and a short walk through the Village. Being an architect, she was able to talk interestingly about the brownstone buildings around. She did warn me briefly about Arnold, saying he was a bit fractious, but no more was said about him that afternoon. Anyway, I reckoned I could manage to soften him up easily enough and that, in no time, we'd be getting along fine.

That first evening a whole group of us ate out in Little Italy to celebrate the reunion of an old gang of friends. I had Conchiglie alla Siciliana which seemed to me the most wonderful dish I had ever tried. We toasted the chef and then drank to absent friends. The man who served us was attentive and gave me a special smile which made him look like a member of the Corleone family. 'I haven't said goodbye to the waiter,' I exclaimed as we were leaving the building. 'He'll live,' said the manageress in the kind of Brooklyn accent I'd kill for if I were an actress. We all laughed and linked arms walking briskly back past the down and outs on the Bowery.

'Do come with us,' said Emil. 'You're only here for a few days.' He wanted me to join them for a late-night showing of *Kiss Me Kate* in 3D. 'No, I'm really too tired, I haven't slept for nineteen hours,' I made my excuses, trying to draw some sympathy. 'I'll see you all tomorrow when the jet lag's worn off.' They accompanied me as far as the junction of Astor Place and Broadway. Laura explained once more how the spare key worked. 'If you get stuck, ask the super.' I looked blank. 'The janitor,' she translated. 'What's a janitor?' I joked in my most pompous English accent.

I let myself in without difficulty and walked over to the window. It was wide open. Just level with the bottom of the frame was a large expanse of flat roofing. At the far end was the ironwork of a fire escape. 'Fire escapes,' I thought. 'Now I *know* I'm in New York. Cookie, elevator, faucet, super, janitor, I wonder if they have their own word for fire escape too.'

On the sofa was a neat pile of sheets. I managed to assemble it all into some sort of order and struggle into my T-shirt ready for bed. As I lay there half-asleep, I wondered mildly why Laura was so lax about security, but I was too sleepy to get up and close the window. I sank under the cover and within a few seconds I had drifted into sleep.

I woke with a start and lay there for several minutes listening to the whoop-whoop-whoop of police patrol cars and watching the thin curtains billow in the grimy night air.

At some point, I realized I was not alone. The intruder was there somewhere in the room. I stumbled through the darkness towards the door, upsetting a table as I went. I felt something sharp slash my flesh as I groped madly around the wall for a light switch and found it. Then we were looking straight at each other in the lighted room. My attacker, with his vicious penetrating eyes, was standing a few feet away, holding my gaze with his, pinning me to the spot with nothing more than his burning, piercing, hating eyes.

I knew that, if I moved, my assailant would try another slash. We stayed frozen like that for a few moments – musical statues without the music – blood dripping down from the deep gashes in my legs. I had to protect my body from the next attack. Beside me on the floor was a pile of old copies of *Rolling Stone* magazine. Moving quickly, I tried to whip the newsprint in front of me as a shield, but he was far quicker on the draw and cut through the backs of my hands in a trice. He was now taking systematic swipes at any exposed part of me that he could reach. I was no match.

I grappled with the front-door latch and shot through to the hallway. This time Arnold was not quite quick enough. I pulled the door until I heard a gentle click as the latch locked home.

I don't know how long I stood there in that Greenwich Village hallway, half-naked, in a state of trembling indecision.

At last, I crept down to the basement by the back stairs and followed the sound of an early hours news channel reporting preparations for the Independence Day celebration fireworks on the West Side. The janitor looked me slowly up and down, but more down than up.

'Do you happen to have a first-aid box?' I asked meekly. 'And something for me to wear?' He shuffled about and produced a large paint-spattered sheet which I wrapped around me like a toga. After further searching he came up with an old rag, stiff with dried metal polish. After dabbing at the gashes with it for a few moments, I managed to work out that it had once been some kind of undergarment.

'I've been attacked by a cat,' I explained. 'Lady,' he replied, 'you got problems.' He wasn't planning to solve them for me, just commenting. He went back to listening to the broadcast. 'I've also been locked out of apartment number 208. I don't suppose you've got a spare key, have you?'

He dug a credit card out of his wallet and I followed him back up to the flat. He started to work away with the plastic. He seemed amazingly skilled at breaking in and I began to wonder what he did for a living before he was a janitor. Still, this was not the moment to doubt the man whose help I badly needed. My assistant was the silent type, so I did all the talking. 'As soon as the door opens, I'll throw this in.' I waved the polishing-rag undies. 'Don't leave until I've got past him into the bedroom.' I rolled them up tight into a ball and got ready to throw.

The door swung wide open. Arnold was across the other side, eyeing me, quivering in readiness. Ignoring the janitor, he waited for me to make my move. I bowled the brasso ball, medium speed, with a bit of spin. While he was savaging it, I slipped past into Laura's bedroom and shut the door, calling out my thanks to the indifferent janitor. Wasting no time, I took a ladderback chair and tucked it smartly under the door handle.

I switched on the TV. It was tuned to a Spanish language programme. 'Adónde vas? A que no te atreves a besarme?' I flicked the button to the next channel number. Behind me the bedroom-door handle was rattling and jerking. I checked the chair back was still tightly wedged in position, and then settled down to the programme. It was a threesome gameshow. The secretary was called Barbara. She knew far more about husband Bob than wife Connie did. Still, Connie was being very sporting about it; even when it emerged that it was Barbara, not Bob, who had chosen her tenth anniversary present, she

laughed ecstatically and applauded her humiliation along with the studio audience.

All this time, Arnold was still pounding on the handle, trying to hurry up the metal fatigue. I turned the volume up to maximum and set my face to the screen. Then suddenly, nothing. Silence outside.

I heard the front latch turn and heard Laura's voice. 'Hi, Arnold, how yer been?' She walked in to greet me wearing cardboard glasses, one red side, one green. She stopped in her tracks. 'Looks like you've been having some 3D effects in here.' She looked round at all the furniture in disarray.

Over the next few days Laura did what she could to try to make Arnold see me in a more positive light. These efforts included getting me to give him a bowl of Nine Lives Formula, a plan which went disastrously wrong. Simple tasks like walking to the bathroom or making a cup of coffee were now a nerve-wracking ordeal. 'Try and relax,' Laura would encourage me as I started my journey across the room. 'Are you sure this is a good idea? Couldn't we lock Arnold away just till I go out?' I pleaded. Then I'd hear him scurrying along after me and feel his claws as they found their way through the denim to my tender flesh.

Laura eventually brought in a cat psychiatrist because she was seriously worried about his worsening behaviour. A neighbour had already threatened litigation after Arnold took a swipe one afternoon. 'I'd better do something or, sooner or later, someone is going to take me to court. Suing someone you know is our most popular national pastime. People take classes in it at night school.'

A series of appointments were set up with a very nice Argentinian therapist called Graciela. 'She says I am Arnold's emotional blanket,' Laura confided after one of these consultations. 'And she thinks he's suffering from an abandonment complex.' I felt this was all a very pricey way to find out the obvious, but I kept these thoughts to myself.

The therapist explained what single-cat syndrome was, and suggested that Laura buy Arnold his own little kitten to play with. He was also put on a course of Valium. With half a tablet he was still attacking me. On one whole pill he couldn't quite coordinate enough, so he would just stare at me. In fact, Arnold did a lot of staring over the next few days. At primary school, I can remember a huge portrait of the Queen which hung in the dining-room. I noticed that it didn't matter which table I sat at, her eyes would always be looking directly at me. Having Arnold around was a bit like that, only it wasn't a case of wherever I looked from but whenever I looked. From time to time, it might be two minutes or twenty, I would glance up from my guide book or Manhattan street plan, and there he'd be, eyeballing me. I never saw him blink.

Laura followed all the advice she was given except the bit about buying Arnold his own little kitten. Somehow, she never got around to visiting that pet store on Hudson Street. It would, on reflection, have been a bad idea. Picture Arnold patting and putting the fluffy little thing around the room like an outsize mouse.

This story does have a happy ending (for Arnold at any rate) because, after a few days, I gave up and moved to a hotel. He celebrated his victory by becoming docile and lovable once more. He continued to preside over Laura's spinsterhood, but now with increased confidence.

As for Laura, she carried on her social life outside the flat and rarely invited people back. The offers of a bed to visiting tourist friends ceased after my trip which, for someone living in such a sought-after spot on the globe, must have come as something of a relief. It certainly gave her more time to concentrate on her work and later that year she was promoted, so I suppose there was a happy ending for her too.

'I've landed this incredible job,' she phoned me about a year later. 'It's a complete renovation of an art gallery in SoHo.'

'How's Arnold these days?' I asked.

'Oh, he couldn't be better. He's right by my side, can't you hear him purring?'

Ye Marvelous Legend of Tom Connor's Cat

SAMUEL LOVER

THERE WAS a man in these parts, sir, you must know, called Tom Connor, and he had a cat that was equal to any dozen of rat traps, and he was proud of the baste, and with rayson; for she was worth her weight in goold to him in saving his sacks of meal from the thievery of the rats and mice; for Tom was an extensive dealer in corn, and influenced the rise and fall of that article in the market, to the extent of a full dozen of sacks at a time, which he either kept or sold, as the spirit of free trade or monopoly came over him. Indeed, at one time, Tom had serious thoughts of applying to the government for a military force to protect his granary when there was a threatened famine in the country.

'Pooh, pooh, sir!' said the matter-of-fact little man. 'As if a dozen sacks could be of the smallest consequence in a whole country – pooh, pooh!'

'Well, sir,' said Murtough, 'I can't help you if you don't believe; but it's truth what I'm telling you, and pray don't interrupt me, though you may not believe; by the time the story's done you'll have heard more wonderful things than *that* – and besides, remember you're a stranger in these parts, and have no notion of the extraordinary things, physical, metaphysical and magical, which constitute the idiosyncrasy of rural destiny.'

The little man did not know the meaning of Murtough's last

sentence – nor Murtough either; but, having stopped the little man's throat with big words, he proceeded:

'This cat, sir, you must know, was a great pet, and was so up to everything, that Tom swore she was a'most like a Christian, only she couldn't speak, and had so sensible a look in her eyes, that he was sartin sure the cat knew every word that was said to her. Well, she used to set by him at breakfast every morning, and the eloquent cock of her tail, as she used to rub against his leg, said. "Give me some milk, Tom Connor," as plain as print, and the plentitude of her purr afterwards spoke a gratitude beyond language. Well, one morning, Tom was going to the neighbouring town to market, and he had promised the wife to bring home shoes to the childre' out o' the price of the corn; and sure enough before he sat down to breakfast, there was Tom taking the measure of the children's feet, by cutting notches on a bit of stick; and the wife gave him so many cautions about getting a "nate fit" for "Billy's purty feet," that Tom, in his anxiety to nick the closest possible measure, cut off the child's toe. This disturbed the harmony of the party and Tom was obliged to breakfast alone, while the mother was endeavouring to cure Billy; in short, trying to make a *heal* of his *toe*. Well, sir, all the time Tom was taking measure for the shoes, the cat was observing him with that luminous peculiarity of eye for which her tribe is remarkable; and when Tom sat down to breakfast the cat rubbed up against him more vigorously than usual; but Tom being bewildered, between his expected gain in corn and the positive loss of his child's toe, kept never minding her, until the cat, with a sort of caterwauling growl, gave Tom a dab of her claws, that went clean through his leathers, and a little further. 'Wow!' says Tom, with a jump, clapping his hand on the part, and rubbing it. 'By this and that, you drew the blood out o' me,' says Tom. 'You wicked divil – tish! – go along!' says he, making a kick at her. With that the cat gave a reproachful look at him, and her eyes glared just like a pair of mail-coach lamps in a fog. With that, sir, the cat, with a mysterious "meow", fixed a most penetrating glance on Tom and distinctly uttered his name.

'Tom felt every hair on his head as stiff as a pump handle; and scarcely crediting his ears, he returned a searching look at the cat, who very quietly proceeded in a sort of nasal twang:

' "Tom Connor," says she.

' "The Lord be good to me!" says Tom. "If it isn't spakin' she is!"

' "Tom Connor," says she again.

' "Yes, ma'am," says Tom.

' "Come here," says she. "Whisper – I want to talk to you, Tom," says she, "the laste taste in private," says she – rising on her hams and beckoning him with her paw out o' the door, with a wink and a toss o' the head aiqual to a milliner.

'Well, as you may suppose, Tom didn't know whether he was on his head or his heels, but he followed the cat, and off she went and squatted herself under the hedge of a little paddock at the back of Tom's house; and as he came round the corner, she held up her paw again, and laid it on her mouth, as much as to say "Be cautious, Tom." Well, divil a word Tom could say at all, with the fright, so up he goes to the cat, and says she:

' "Tom," says she, "I have a great respect for you, and there's something I must tell you, because you're losing character with your neighbours," says she, "by your goin's on," says she, "and it's out o' the respect that I have for you, that I must tell you," says she.

' "Thank you, ma'am," says Tom.

' "You're going off to the town," says she, "to buy shoes for the childre'," says she, "and never thought o' getting me a pair."

' "You!" says Tom.

' "Yis, me, Tom Connor," says she, "and the neighbours wondhers that a respectable man like you allows your cat to go about the counthry barefutted," says she.

' "Is it a cat to ware shoes?" says Tom.

' "Why not?" says she. "Doesn't horses ware shoes? And I have a prettier foot than a horse, I hope," says she with a toss of her head.

' "Faix, she spakes like a woman; so proud of her feet," says Tom to himself, astonished, as you may suppose, but pretending never to think it remarkable all the time; and so he went on discoursin'; and says he: "It's thrue for you, ma'am," says he, "that horses ware shoes – but that stands to rayson, ma'am, you see – seeing the hardship their feet has to go through on the hard roads."

' "And how do you know what hardship my feet has to go through?" says the cat, mighty sharp.

' "But, ma'am," says Tom, "I don't well see how you could fasten a shoe on you," says he.

' "Lave that to me," says the cat.

' "Did anyone ever stick walnut shells on you, pussy?" says Tom, with a grin.

' "Don't be disrespectful, Tom Connor," says the cat, with a frown.

' "I ax your pard'n, ma'am," says he, ". . . as for the horses you wor spakin' about warin' shoes, you know their shoes is fastened on with nails, and how would your shoes be fastened on?"

' "Ah, you stupid thief!" says she, "haven't I illigant nails o' my own?" and with that she gave him a dab of her claw, that made him roar.

' "Ow! murdher!" says he.

' "Now no more of your palaver, Misther Connor," says the cat. "Just be off and get me the shoes."

' "Tare and ouns!" says Tom. "What'll become o' me if I'm to get shoes for my cats?" says he. "For you increase your family four times a year, and you have six or seven every time," says he; "and then you must all have two pair apiece – wirra! wirra! – I'll be ruined in shoeleather," says Tom.

' "No more o' your stuff," says the cat, "don't be standin' here undher the hedge talkin' or we'll lose our characters – for I've remarked your wife is jealous, Tom."

' "'Pon my sowl, that's thrue," says Tom, with a smirk.

' "More fool she," says the cat, "for 'pon my conscience, Tom, you're as ugly as if you wor bespoke."

'Off ran the cat with these words, leaving Tom in amazement. He said nothing to the family, for fear of fright'ning them, and off he went to the town, as he pretended – for he saw the cat watching him through a hole in the hedge; but when he came to a turn at the end of the road, the dickings a mind he minded the market, good or bad, but went off to Squire Botherum's, the magisthrit, to swear examinations agen the cat.'

'Pooh, pooh – nonsense!' broke in the little man, who had listened thus far to Murtough with an expression of mingled wonder and contempt, while the rest of the party willingly gave up the reins to nonsense, and enjoyed Murtough's legend and their companion's more absurd common-sense.

'Don't interrupt him, Coggins,' said Mr Wiggins.

'How can you listen to such nonsense!' returned Coggins. 'Swear examinations against a cat, indeed! Pooh pooh!'

'My dear sir,' said Murtough, 'remember this is a fairy story, and that the country all round here is full of enchantment. As I was telling you, Tom went off to swear examinations.'

'Ay, ay!' shouted all but Coggins. 'Go on with the story.'

'And when Tom was asked to relate the events of the morning, which brought him before Squire Botherum, his brain was so bewildered between his corn, and his cat, his child's toe, that he made a very confused account of it.

' "Begin your story from the beginning," said the magistrate to Tom.

' "Well, your honour," says Tom, "I was goin' to market this mornin', to sell the child's corn – I beg your pard'n – my own toes, I mane, sir.'

' "Sell your toes!" said the Squire.

' "No, sir, takin' the cat to market, I mane —"

' "Take a cat to market!" said the Squire. "You're drunk, man."

' "No, your honour, only confused a little; for when the toes began to spake to me – the cat, I mane – I was bothered clane —"

' "The cat speak to you!" said the Squire. "Phew! Worse than before. You're drunk, Tom."

' "No, your honour; it's on the strength of the cat I come to spake to you —"

' "I think it's on the strength of a pint of whiskey, Tom."

' "By the vartue o' my oath, your honour, it's nothin' but the cat." And so Tom then told him all about the affair, and the Squire was regularly astonished. Just then the bishop of the diocese and the priest of the parish happened to call in, and heard the story; and the bishop and the priest had a tough argument for two hours on the subject: the former swearing she must be a witch; but the priest denying *that*, and maintaining she was *only* enchanted, and that part of the argument was afterwards referred to the primate, and subsequently to the conclave at Rome; but the Pope declined interfering about cats, saying he had quite enough to do minding his own bulls.

' "In the meantime, what are we to do with the cat?" says Botherum.

' "Burn her," says the bishop. "She's a witch."

' "*Only* enchanted," says the priest, "and the ecclesiastical court maintains that —"

' "Bother the ecclesiastical court!" says the magistrate; "I can only proceed on the statutes;" and with that he pulls down all the law books in his library and hunts the laws from Queen Elizabeth down, and he finds that they made laws against everything in Ireland, *except a cat*. The divil a thing escaped them but a cat, which did *not* come within the meaning of any Act of Parliament – *the cats only had escaped*.

' "There's the alien act, to be sure," says the magistrate, "and she was missin', I remember, all last Spy Wednesday."

' "That's suspicious," says the Squire, "but conviction might be difficult; and I have a fresh idea," says Botherum.

' "Faith, it won't keep fresh long, this hot weather," says Tom, "so your honour had betther make use of it at wanst."

' "Right," says Botherum. "We'll make her a subject to the game laws; we'll hunt her," says he.

' "Ow! Elegant!" says Tom; "we'll have a brave run out of her."

' "Meet me at the crossroads," says the Squire, "in the morning, and I'll have the hounds ready."

'Well, off Tom went home; and he was racking his brain what excuse he could make to the cat for not bringing the shoes; and at last he hit one off, just as he saw her cantering up to him, half a mile before he got home.

' "Where's the shoes, Tom?" says she.

' "I have not got them today, ma'am," says he.

' "Is that the way you keep your promise, Tom?" says she. "I'll tell you what it is, Tom – I'll tare the eyes out o' the childre' if you don't get me those shoes."

' "Whist, whist!" says Tom, frightened out his life for his children's eyes. "Don't be in a passion, pussy. The shoemaker said he had not a shoe in his shop, nor a last that would make one to fit you; and he says I must bring you into the town for him to take your measure."

' "And when am I to go?" says the cat, looking savage.

' "Tomorrow," says Tom.

' "It's well you said that, Tom," says the car, "or the divil an eye I'd leave in your family this night," and off she hopped.

'Tom thrimbled at the wicked look she gave.

' "Remember!" says she, over the hedge, with a bitter caterwaul.

' "Never fear," says Tom.

'Well, sure enough, the next mornin' there was the cat at cockcrow, licking herself as nate as a new pin, to go into the town, and out came Tom with a bag undher his arm and the cat after him.

' "Now git into this, and I'll carry you into the town," says Tom, opening the bag.

' "Sure, I can walk with you," says the cat.

' "Oh, that wouldn't do," says Tom. "The people in the town is curious and slandherous people, and sure it would rise ugly remarks if I was seen with a cat afther me – a dog is a man's companion by nature, but cats does not stand to rayson."

'Well, the cat, seeing there was no use in argument, got into the bag, and off Tom set to the crossroads with the bag over his shoulder, and he came up, quite innocent-like, to the corner, where the Squire, and his huntsman, and the hounds, and a pack of people were waitin'. Out came the Squire on a sudden, just as if it was all by accident.

' "God save you, Tom," says he.

' "God save you kindly, sir," says Tom.

' "What's that bag you have at your back?" says the Squire.

' "Oh, nothin' at all, sir," says Tom, makin' a face all the time, as much as to say, I have her safe.

' "Oh, there's something in that bag, I think," says the Squire. "You must let me see it."

' "If you bethray me, Tom Connor," says the cat, in a low voice, "by this and that I'll never spake to you again!"

' "Pon my honour, sir," says Tom, with a wink and a twitch of his thumb towards the bag, "I haven't anything in it."

' "I have been missing my praties of late," says the Squire, "and I'd just like to examine that bag," says he.

' "Is it doubting my character you'd be, sir?" says Tom, pretending to be in a passion.

' "Tom, your sowl!" says the voice in the sack. "If you let the cat out of the bag, I'll murther you."

' "An honest man would make no objection to be sarched," said the Squire, "and I insist on it," says he, laying hold o' the bag, and Tom purtending to fight all the time; but, my jewel! Before two minutes, they shook the cat out o' the bag, sure enough, and off she went with her tail as big as a sweeping brush, and the Squire, with a thundering view halloo after her, clapped the dogs at her heels, and away they went for the bare life. Never was there seen such running as that day – the cat made for a shaking bog, the loneliest place in the whole country, and there the riders were all thrown out, barrin' the huntsman who had a web-footed horse on purpose for soft places, and the priest whose horse could go anywhere by reason of the priest's blessing; and, sure enough, the huntsman and his riverence stuck to the hunt like wax; and just as the cat got on the border of the bog, they saw her give a twist as the foremost dog closed with her, for he gave her a nip in the flank. Still she went on, however, and headed them well, towards an old mud cabin in the middle of the bog, and there they saw her jump in at the window, and up came the dogs the next minit, and gathered round the house with the most horrid howling ever was heard. The huntsman alighted and went into the house to turn the cat out again, when what should he see but an old hag lying in bed in the corner!

' "Did you see a cat come in here?" says he.

' "Oh, no-o-o-o!" squeals the old hag in a trembling voice. "There's no cat here," says she.

' "Yelp, yelp, yelp!" went the dogs outside.

' "Oh, keep the dogs out of this," says the old hag – "Oh-o-o-o!" and the huntsman saw her eyes glare under the blanket, just like a cat's.

' "Hillo!" says the huntsman, pulling down the blanket – and what should he see but the old hag's flank all in a gore of blood.

' "Ow, ow! you old divil – is it you? You old cat!" says he, opening the door.

'In rushed the dogs. Up jumped the old hag and, changing into a cat before their eyes, out she darted through the window again, and made another run for it; but she couldn't escape, and the dogs gobbled her while you could say "Jack Robinson." But the most remarkable part of this extraordinary story, gentlemen, is that the pack was ruined from that day out; for after having eaten the enchanted cat, *the divil a thing they would ever hunt afterwards but mice.*'

Rufus the Survivor

DORIS LESSING

EVENTS DID cast their shadow, months before. All that spring and summer, as I went past on the pavement, a shabby orange-coloured cat would emerge from under a car or from a front garden, and he stood looking intently up at me, not to be ignored. He wanted something, but what? Cats on pavements, cats on garden walls, or coming towards you from doorways, stretch and wave their tails, they greet you, walk a few steps with you. They want companionship or, if they are shut out by heartless owners, as they often are all day or all night, they appeal for help with the loud insistent demanding miaow that means they are hungry or thirsty or cold. A cat winding around your legs at a street corner might be wondering if he can exchange a poor home for a better one. But this cat did not miaow, he only looked, a thoughtful, hard stare from yellow-grey eyes. Then he began following me along the pavement in a tentative way, looking up at me. He presented himself to me when I came in and when I went out, and he was on my conscience. Was he hungry? I took some food out to him and put it under a car, and he ate a little, but left the rest. Yet he was necessitous, desperate, I knew that. Did he have a home in our street, and was it a bad one? He seemed most often to be near a house some doors down from ours and, once, when an old woman went in, he went in too. So he was not homeless. Yet he took to following me to our gate and once, when the pavement filled with a surge of shouting schoolchildren, he scrambled into our little front garden, terrified, and watched me at the door.

He was thirsty, not hungry. Or so thirsty, hunger was the lesser demand. That was the summer of 1984, with long stretches of warm weather. Cats locked out of their homes all day without water suffered. I put down a basin of water on my front porch one night and in the morning it was empty. Then, as the hot weather went on, I put another basin on my back balcony, reached by way of a lilac tree and a big jump up from a small roof. And this basin, too, was empty every morning. One hot dusty day there was the orange cat on the back balcony crouched over the water basin, drinking, drinking . . . He finished all the water and wanted more. I refilled the basin and again he crouched down and emptied that. This meant there must be something wrong with his kidneys. Now I could take my time looking at him. A scruffy cat, his dirty fur rough over knobbly bones. But he was a wonderful colour, fire colour, like a fox. He was, as they put it, a whole cat, he had his two neat furry balls under his tail. His ears were torn, scarred with fighting. Now, when I came in and out of the house, he was no longer there in the street, he had moved from the fronts of the houses and the precarious life there with the speeding cars and the shouting, running children, to the back scene of long untidy gardens and shrubs and trees, and many birds and cats. He was on our little balcony where there are plants in pots, bounded by a low wall. Over this the lilac tree holds out its boughs, always full of birds. He lay in the strip of shade under the wall, and the water bowl was always empty, and when he saw me he stood up and waited beside it for more.

By now the people in the house had understood we must make a decision. Did we want another cat? We already had two beautiful, large, lazy, neutered toms, who had always had it so good they believed that food, comfort, warmth, safety were what life owed them, for they never had had to fight for anything. No, we did not want another cat, and certainly not a sick one. But now we took out food as well as water to this old derelict, putting it on the balcony so he would know this was a favour and not a right, and that he did not belong to us, and could not come into the house. We joked that he was our outdoor cat.

The hot weather went on.

He ought to be taken to the vet. But that would mean he was our cat, we would have three cats, and our own were being huffy and wary and offended because of this newcomer who seemed to have rights over us, even if limited ones. Besides, what about the old woman whom he did sometimes visit? We watched him go stiffly along a path, turn right to crawl under a fence, cross a garden and then another, his orangeness brilliant against the dulling grass of late summer, and then he vanished and was presumably at the back door of a house where he was welcome.

The hot weather ended and it began to rain. The orange cat stood out in the rain on the balcony, his fur streaked dark with running water, and looked at me. I opened the kitchen door and he came in. I said to him, he could use this chair, but only this chair; this was his chair, and he must not ask for more. He climbed on to the chair and lay down and looked steadily at me. He had the air of one who knows he must make the most of what Fate offers before it is withdrawn.

When it was not raining the door was still open on to the balcony, the trees, the garden. We hate shutting it all out with glass and curtains. And he could still use the lilac tree to get down into the garden for his toilet. He lay all that day on the chair in the kitchen, sometimes getting clumsily off it to drink yet another bowl of water. He was eating a lot now. He could not pass a food or water bowl without eating or drinking something, for he knew he could never take anything for granted.

This was a cat who had had a home, but lost it. He knew

what it was to be a house cat, a pet. He wanted to be caressed. His story was a familiar one. He had had a home, human friends who loved him, or thought they did, but it was not a good home because the people went away a lot and left him to find food and shelter for himself, or who looked after him as long as it suited them and then left the neighbourhood, abandoning him. For some time he had been fed at the old woman's place but, it seemed, not enough, or had not been given water to drink. Now he was looking better. But he was not cleaning himself. He was stiff, of course, but he had been demoralized, hopeless. Perhaps he had believed he would never have a home again? After a few days, when he knew we would not throw him out of the kitchen, he began to purr whenever we came into it. Never have I, or anyone else who visited the house, heard any cat purr as loudly as he did. He lay on the chair and his sides went up and down and his purring rumbled through the house. He wanted us to know he was grateful. It was a calculated purr.

We brushed him. We cleaned his fur for him. We gave him a name. We took him to the vet, thus acknowledging that we had a third cat. His kidneys were bad. He had an ulcer in one ear. Some of his teeth had gone. He had arthritis or rheumatism. His heart could be better. But no, he was not an old cat, probably eight or nine years old, in his prime if he had been looked after, but he had been living as he could, and perhaps for some time. Cats who have to scavenge and cadge and sleep out in bad weather in the big cities do not live long. He would soon have died if we had not rescued him. He took his antibiotics and the vitamins, and soon after his first visit to the vet began the painful process of cleaning himself. But parts of himself he was too stiff to reach, and he had to labour and struggle to be a clean and civilized cat.

All this went on in the kitchen, and mostly on the chair, which he was afraid of leaving. His place. His little place. His toehold on life. And when he went out on to the balcony he watched us all in case we shut the door on him, for he feared being locked out more than anything, and if we made movements that looked as if the door might be shutting he scrambled painfully in and on to his chair.

He liked to sit on my lap and, when this happened, he set

himself in motion, purring, and he looked up with those clever greyish-yellow eyes: Look, I am grateful, and I am telling you so.

One day, when the arbiters of his fate were in the kitchen drinking tea, he hopped off his chair and walked slowly to the door into the rest of the house. There he stopped and turned and most deliberately looked at us. He could not have asked more clearly: Can I go further into the house? Can I be a proper house cat? By now we would have been happy to invite him in, but our other two cats seemed able to tolerate him if he stayed where he was, a kitchen cat. We pointed to his chair and he climbed patiently back on to it, where he lay silent and disappointed for a while, and then set his sides heaving in a purr.

Needless to say, this made us feel terrible.

A few days later, he got carefully off his chair and went to the same door and stopped there, looking back at us for directions. This time we did not say he must come back, so he went on into the house, but not far. He found a sheltered place under a bath and that was where he stayed. The other cats went to check where he was, and enquired of us what we thought of it, but what we thought was, these two young princes could share their good fortune. Outside the house it was autumn, and then winter, and we needed to shut the kitchen door. But what about this new cat's lavatory problems? These days he waited at the kitchen door when he needed to go out, but once there he did not want to jump down on to the little roof, or climb down the lilac tree, for he was too stiff. He used the pots the plants were trying to grow in, so I put down a big box filled with peat, and he understood and used it. A nuisance, having to empty the peat box. There is a cat door right at the bottom of the house into the garden, and our two young cats had never, not once, made a mess inside the house. Come rain or snow or high winds, they go out.

And so that was the situation as winter began. In the evenings people and the two resident cats, the rightful cats, were in the sitting-room, and Rufus was under the bath. And then, one evening, Rufus appeared in the doorway of the sitting-room and it was a dramatic apparition, for here was the embodiment of the dispossessed, the insulted, the injured, making himself felt by the warm, the fed, the privileged. He glanced at the two cats who were his rivals, but kept his intelligent eyes on us. What were we going to say? We said, Very well, he could use the old leather beanbag near the radiator, the warmth would help his aching bones. We made a hollow in the beanbag and he climbed into the hollow and curled up, but carefully, and he purred. He purred, he purred, he purred so loudly and so long we had to beg him to stop, for we could not hear ourselves speak. Literally. We had to turn up the television. But he knew he was lucky and wanted us to know he understood the value of what he was getting. When I was at the top of the house, two floors up, I could hear the rhythmic rumbling that meant Rufus was awake and telling us of his gratitude. Or perhaps he was asleep and purring in his sleep, for once he had started he did not stop but lay there curled up, eyes shut, his sides pumping up and down. There was something inordinate and scandalous about Rufus's purring, because it was so calculated. And we were reminded, as we watched, and listened to this old survivor, who was only alive now because he had used his wits, of the hazards and adventures and hardships he had undergone.

But our other two cats were not pleased. One is called Charles, originally Prince Charlie, not after the present holder of that title, but after earlier romantic princes for he is a dashing and handsome tabby who knows how to present himself. About his character the less said the better – but this chronicle is not about Charles. The other cat, the older brother, with the character of one, has a full ceremonial name, bestowed when he first left kittenhood and his qualities had become evident. We called him General Pinknose the Third, paying tribute and perhaps reminding ourselves that even the best looked-after cat is going to leave you. We had seen that icecream-pink tinge, but on the tips of noses with a less noble curve, on earlier, less imposing cats. Like some people he acquires new names as time makes its revelations, and recently, because of his moral force and his ability to impose silent judgements on a scene, he became for a time a bishop and was known as Bishop Butchkin. Reserving comment, these two cats lay in their respective places, noses on their paws, and watched Rufus. Charles is always under a radiator, but Butchkin likes the top of a tall basket where he can keep an eye on things. He is a magnificent cat. Familiarity had dulled my eyes: I knew he was handsome, but I came back from a trip somewhere to be dazzled by this enormous cat boldly patterned in his shining black and immaculate white, yellow-eyed, with white whiskers, and I thought that this beauty had been bred out of common-or-garden mog-material by good feeding and care. Left unneutered, a cat who had to roam around in all weathers to compete for a mate, he would not look like this, but would be a smaller, or at least gaunt, rangy, war-bitten cat. No, I am not happy about neutering cats, far from it.

But this tale is not about El Magnifico, the name that suits him best.

When he thought we didn't know, Charles would try to get Rufus into a corner and threaten him. But Charles has never had to fight and compete, and Rufus has, all his life. Rufus was so rickety he could be knocked over by the swipe of a determined paw. But he sat back and defended himself with hard experienced stares, with his wary patience, his indomitability. There was no doubt what would happen to Charles if he got within hitting distance. As for El Magnifico, he was above competing on this level.

During all those early weeks, while he was recovering strength, Rufus never went out of the house, except to the peat box on the balcony, and there he did his business, keeping his gaze on us and even now, if it seemed the door might shut him out, he gave a little grunt of panic and then hobbled back indoors. He was so afraid, even now, he might lose this refuge gained after long homelessness, after such torments of thirst. He was afraid to put a paw outside.

The winter slowly went by. Rufus lay in his beanbag and purred every time he thought of it, and he watched us, and watched the two other cats watching him. Then he made a new move. By now we knew he never did anything without very good reason, that first he worked things out, and then acted. The black and white cat, Butchkin, is the boss cat. He was born in this house, one of six kittens. He brought up his siblings as much as his mother did; she was not a bad mother so much as an exhausted one. There was never any question about who was the boss kitten of the litter. Now Rufus decided to make a bid for the position of boss cat. Not by strength, because he did not have that, but by using his position as a sick cat, given so much attention. Every evening The General, El Magnifico Butchkin, came to lie by me on the sofa for a while, to establish his right to this position, before going to his favourite place on top of the basket. This place by me was the best place, because Butchkin thought it was. Charles, for instance, was not allowed it. But now, just as he had walked deliberately to the kitchen door and then looked back to see if we would allow him to the house itself, just as he had stood in the sitting-room door to find out if we would let him in to join the family, so now Rufus deliberately stepped down off the beanbag, came to where I sat, pulled himself up, first front legs, and then, with difficulty, his back legs and sat down beside me. He looked at Butchkin. Then at the humans. Finally, a careless look at Charles. I did not throw him off. I could not. Butchkin only looked at him and then slowly (and magnificently) yawned. I felt it was he who should make Rufus return to the beanbag. But he did nothing, only watched. Was he waiting for me to act? Rufus lay down, carefully, because of his painful joints. And purred. All people who live with animals have moments when they long to share a language. And this was one. What had happened to him, how had he learned to plan and calculate, how had he become such a thinking cat? All right, so he was born intelligent, but then so was Butchkin, and so was Charles. (And there are very stupid cats.) All right, so he was born with such and such a nature. But I have never known a cat so capable of thought, of planning his next move, as Rufus.

Lying beside me, having achieved the best place in the sitting-room after only a few weeks from being an outcast, he purred. 'Shhh Rufus, we can't hear ourselves think.' But we did not share a language, could not explain that we would not throw him out if he stopped purring, saying thank you.

When we made him swallow pills he made little grunts of protest; he probably saw this as the price he had to pay for a refuge. Sometimes, when we swabbed his ear and it hurt, he swore, but not at us; it was a generally directed curse from one who had much occasion to use curses. Then he licked our hands to show he didn't mean us, and set his purr going again. We stroked him and he gave his rusty grunt of acknowledgement.

Meanwhile, Butchkin the Magnificent watched and thought his own thoughts. His character had a lot to do with Rufus's fate. He is too proud to compete. If he is in intimate conversation with me at the top of the house, and Charles comes in, he simply jumps down off the bed or chair and goes off downstairs. He will not only not tolerate competition felt to be unworthy of him, he won't put up with thoughts not centred on him. Holding him, stroking him, I have to keep my thoughts on him. No such thing, with Butchkin, as stroking him while I read. The moment my thoughts have wandered, he knows it and jumps down and is off. But he doesn't bear grudges. When Charles behaves badly, tormenting him, he might give him a swipe, but then bestows a forgiving lick, *noblesse oblige*.

Such a character is not going to lower himself by fighting any cat for first place.

One day I was standing in the middle of the room addressing myself to Butchkin who was curled on his basket top, when Rufus got down off the sofa and came to stand just in front of my legs, looking at Butchkin as if to say, She prefers me. This was done slowly and deliberately, he was not being emotional or rash or impulsive, all qualities that Charles had too much of. He had planned it, was calm and thoughtful. He had decided to make a final bid to be top cat, my favourite, with Butchkin in second place. But I wasn't going to have this. I pointed at the sofa and he looked up at me in a way which, had he been human, would have said, well, it was worth having a go. And he went back to the sofa.

Butchkin had noted my decisiveness in his favour and did not remark on it more than by getting down off his place, coming to wind himself around my legs, and then going back again.

Rufus had made his bid to be first cat, and failed.

He had not put a paw downstairs for months, but now I saw him trying a clumsy jump on to the roof, and there he looked back, still afraid I might not let him back in, then he eyed the lilac tree, working out how to get down it. Spring had come. The tree was freshly green and the flowers, still in bud, hung in whitish-green fronds. He decided against the tree and jumped painfully back up to the balcony. I picked him up, carried him downstairs, showed him the cat door. He was terrified, thinking it was a trap. I gently pushed him through while he swore and struggled. I went out after him, picked him up, and pushed him back. At once he scrambled up the stairs, thinking I wanted to throw him out altogether. This performance was repeated on successive days and Rufus hated it. In between I petted and praised him so he would know I was not trying to get rid of him.

He thought it over. I saw him get up from his place on the sofa and slowly go down the stairs. He went to the cat door. There he stood, his tail twitching in indecision, examining it. He was afraid; fear drove him back. He made himself stop, return . . . several times he did this, then reached the flap itself, and tried to force himself to jump through it, but his instincts rose up in him and forced him away. Again and again this was repeated. And then he made himself do it. Like a person jumping into the deep end, he pushed his head through, then his body, and was in the garden that was full of the scents and sounds of spring, birds jubilating because they had made it through another winter, children reclaiming their playgrounds. The old vagabond stood there, snuffing the air which seemed to fill him with new life, one paw raised, turning his head to catch the smell-messages (what someone in the house calls smellograms) that brought him reminders of former friends, both feline and human, brought him memories. Easy then to see him as a young cat, handsome and full of vigour. Off he went in his deliberate way, limping a little, to the end of the garden. Under the old fruit trees he looked to the right and he looked to the left. Memories tugged him both ways. He went under the fence to the right, in the direction of the old woman's house – or so we supposed. There he stayed for an hour or so, and then I watched him squeezing his way back under the fences into our garden, and he came back down the path and stood at the back door by the cat flap and looked up at me: Please open it, I've had enough for one day. I gave in and opened the door. But next day he made himself go out through the flap, and he came back through the flap, and after that there was no need for a cat box, not even when it rained or snowed or the garden was full of wind and noise. Not, that is, unless he was ill and too weak.

Most often he went visiting to the right, but sometimes off to the left, a longer journey, and I watched him through binoculars, till I lost him in the shrubs. When he returned from either trip he always came at once to be petted, and he set his purring machinery in motion . . . it was then we realized his purring was no longer the very loud, insistent, prolonged noise it had been when he first came. Now he purred adequately, with moderation, as befitted a cat who wanted us to be sure he valued us and his place with us, even though he was not top cat and we would not give him first place. For a long time he had been afraid we would prove capricious and throw him out, or lock him out, but now he felt more secure. But at that stage he never went visiting without coming at once to one of us, and purring, and sitting by our legs, or pushing his forehead against us, which meant he would like his ears rubbed, particularly the sore one which would not heal.

That spring and summer were good for Rufus. He was well, as far as he could be. He was sure of us, even though once I incautiously picked up an old broom handle, which lay on the back porch, and I saw him jump down on to the roof, falling over, and he scrambled down the tree and was at the end of the garden in one wild panicky rush. Someone in the past had thrown sticks at him, had beaten him. I ran down into the garden and found him terrified, hiding in a bush. I picked him up, brought him back, showed him the harmless broom handle, apologized, petted him. He understood it was a mistake.

Rufus made me think about the different kinds of cat intelligence. Before that I had recognized that cats had different temperaments. His is the intelligence of the survivor. Charles has the scientific intelligence, curious about everything, human affairs, the people who come to the house, and, in particular, our gadgets. Tape recorders, a turning gramophone table, the television, a radio, fascinate him. You can see him wondering why a disembodied human voice emerges from a box. When he was a kitten, before he gave up, he used to stop a turning record with a paw . . . release it . . . stop it again . . . look at us, miaow an enquiry. He would walk to the back of the radio set to find out if he could see what he heard, go behind the television set, turn over a tape recorder with his paw, sniff at it, miaow, *What* is this? He is the talkative cat. He talks you down the stairs and out of the house, talks you in again and up the stairs, he comments on everything that happens. When he comes in from the garden you can hear him from the top of the house. 'Here I am at last,' he cries, 'Charles the adorable, and how you must have missed me! Just imagine what has happened to me, you'll never believe it . . .' Into the room you are sitting in he comes, and stands in the doorway, his head slightly on one side, and waits for you to admire him. 'Am I not the prettiest cat in this house?' he demands, vibrating all over. Winsome, that's the word for Charles.

The General has his intuitive intelligence, knowing what you are thinking and what you are going to do next. He is not interested in science, how things work; he does not bother to impress you with his looks. He talks when he has something to say and only when he is alone with you 'Ah,' he says, finding that the other cats are elsewhere, 'so we are alone at last.' And he permits a duet of mutual admiration. When I come back from somewhere he rushes from the end of the garden, crying out, 'There you are, I've missed you! How could you go away and leave me for so long?' He leaps into my arms, licks my face and, unable to contain his joy, rushes all over the house like a kitten. Then he returns to being his grave and dignified self.

By the time autumn began Rufus had been behaving like a strong, well cat for some months, visiting friends, sometimes staying away for a day or two. But then he did not go out, he was a sick cat and lay in a warm place, a sad cat with sores on his paws, shaking his head because of the ulcer in his ear, drinking, drinking . . . Back to the vet. Verdict: not good, very bad, in fact, sores like these a bad sign. More antibiotics, more vitamins, and Rufus should not go out in the cold and wet. For months Rufus made no attempt to go out. He lay near the radiator, and his hair came out in great thick rusty wads. Wherever he lay, even for a few minutes, was a nest of orange hair, and you could see his skin through the thin fur. Slowly, he got better.

By ill luck it happened that another cat, not ours, needed medicating at the same time. It got itself run over, had a serious operation and convalesced in our house being fussed over and our own two cats did not like it, and took themselves off into the garden away from the upsetting sight. And then Butchkin too seemed ill. When I went into the garden or the sitting-room he was stretching out his neck and coughing in a delicate but gloomy way, suffering nobly borne. I took him to the vet, but there was nothing wrong. A mystery. He went on coughing. In the garden I could not pick up a trowel or pull out a weed without hearing hoarse and hollow coughing. Very odd indeed. One day, when I had petted poor Butchkin and enquired after his health, and given up, and come indoors, I was struck by unpleasant suspicion. I went to the top of the house and watched him through the binoculars. Not a sign of coughing, he was stretched out enjoying the early spring sunlight. Down I went into the garden and, when he saw me, he got into a crouching position, his throat extended, coughing and suffering. I returned to the balcony with the spy glass, and there he lay, his beautiful black and white coat a-dazzle in the sun, yawning. Luckily, the second sick cat recovered and went off to his new home and we were again a three-cat family. Butchkin's cough mysteriously disappeared, and he acquired another name: for a time he was known as Sir Laurence Olivier Butchkin.

Now all three cats enjoyed the garden in their various ways, but pursued in it three parallel existences; if their paths crossed they politely ignored each other.

One sunny morning I saw two orange cats on the fresh grass of the next-door lawn. One was Rufus. His fur had grown back, but thinner than before. He sat firmly upright, confronting a very young male cat who was challenging him. This cat was bright orange, like an apricot in sunlight, a plumy, feathery cat who made delicate jabs, first with one paw and then the other, not actually touching Rufus but, or so it looked, aiming at an imaginary or invisible cat just in front to Rufus. This lovely young cat seemed to be dancing as it sat, it wavered and sidled and patted and prodded the air, and the foxfire shine of its fur made Rufus look dingy. They were alike; this was Rufus's son, I was sure, and in him I was seeing the poor old ragbag Rufus as he had been before the unkindness of humans had done him in. The scene went on for minutes, half an hour. As male cats often do, they seemed to be staging a joust or duel as a matter of form, with no intention of actually hurting each other. The young cat did let out a yowl or two, but Rufus remained silent, sitting solidly on his bottom. The young cat went on feinting with his fringed red paws, then stopped and hastily licked his side as if losing interest in the business, but then, reminded by Rufus's stolid presence that he had an obligation to fight Rufus, he sat up again, all style and pose, like an heraldic cat, a feline on a coat of arms, and resumed his feinting dance. Rufus continued to sit, neither fighting nor refusing to fight. The young cat got bored and wandered off down the garden, prancing at shadows, rolling over and lolling on the grass, chasing insects. Rufus waited until he had gone, and then set off in his quiet way in the direction he was going, this spring, not to the right, to the old lady, but to the left where he might stay hours or even overnight. For he was well again and it was spring, mating time. When he came home he was hungry and thirsty, and that meant he was not making human friends. But then, as spring went on, he stayed longer, perhaps two days, three. He had, I was pretty sure, a cat friend.

Tetchy and petulant Grey Cat had been unfriendly with other cats. Before she was spayed she was unloving with her mates and hostile even to cats living a long time in the same house. She did not have cat friends, only human friends. When she became friendly with a cat for the first time she was old, about thirteen. I was living then in a small flat at the top of a house that had no cat doors, only a staircase to the front door. From there she made her way to the garden at the back of the house. She could push the door open to come in, but had to be let out. She began admitting an old grey cat who would ascend the stairs just behind her, then wait at the door to our flat for her to say he could come up further, and waited at the top to be invited into my room: waited for her invitations, not mine. She liked him. For the first time she was liking a cat who had not begun as her kitten. He would advance quietly into my room – her room, as he saw it – and then went towards her. At first she sat facing him with her back to a big old chair for protection; she wasn't going to trust anyone, not she! He stopped a short way from her and softly miaowed. When she gave a hasty, reluctant mew in reply – for she had become like an old woman who is querulous and bad tempered, but does not know it – he crouched down a foot or so away from her, and looked steadily at her. She too crouched down. They might stay like that for an hour, two hours.

Later she became more relaxed about it all, and they sat crouched side by side, close but not touching. They did not converse, except for soft little sounds of greeting. They liked each other, wanted to sit together. Who was he? Where did he live? I never found out. He was old, a cat who had not had an easy life, for he came up in your hands like a shadow, and his fur was lustreless. But he was a whole cat, a gentlemanly old cat, grey with white whiskers, polite, courtly, not expecting special treatment or, indeed anything much from life. He would eat a little of her food, drink some milk if offered some, but did not seem hungry. Often when I came back from somewhere he was waiting at the outside door and he miaowed a little, very softly, looking up at me, then came in after me, followed me up the stairs to the door of our flat, miaowed again, and came up the final stairs to the top where he went straight to Grey Cat who let out her cross little miaow when she saw him, but then permitted him a trill of welcome. He spent long evenings with her. She was a changed cat, less prickly and ready to take offence. I used to watch the two of them sitting together like two old people who don't need to talk. Never in my life have I so badly wanted to share a language with an animal. 'Why this cat?' I wanted to ask her. 'Why this cat and no other cat? What is it in this old polite cat that makes you fond of him? For I suppose you will admit you are? All these fine cats in the house, all your life, and you've never liked one of them, but now . . .'

One evening, he did not come. Not the next. Grey Cat waited for him. She sat watching the door all evening. Then she waited downstairs at the door into the house. She searched the garden. But he did not come, not ever again. And she was never again friends with a cat. Another cat, a male cat who visited the cat downstairs, took refuge with us when he became ill, a few weeks before he died, and lived out the end of his life in my room – her room; but she never acknowledged his existence. She behaved as if only I and she were there.

I believed that Rufus had such a friend, and that was where he was going off to visit.

One evening in late summer he stayed on the sofa by me, and he was there next morning in exactly the same position. When at last he got down, he walked holding up a limp and dangling back leg. The vet said he had been run over: one could tell by his claws, for cats instinctively extend their claws to grip when the wheel drags at them. His claws were broken and split. He had a bad fracture of a back leg.

The cast went on from his ankle to the top of his thigh, and he was put into a quiet room with food and water and a dirt box. There he was happy to stay overnight, but then wanted to come out. We opened the door and watched him clumsily descend the stairs, flight after flight, to the bottom of the house where he swore and cursed as he manoeuvred that sticking-out leg through the cat door, then hopped and hobbled up the path, and swore a lot more as he edged himself and the leg under a fence. Off to the left, to his friend. He was away for about half an hour; he had been to report to someone, feline or human, about his mishap. When he came back, he was pleased to be put back into his refuge. He was shaken, shocked, and his eyes showed he was in pain. His fur, made healthy by summer and good feeding, looked harsh, and he was again a poor old cat who could not easily clean himself. Poor old ragbag! Poor Calamity Cat! He accumulated names as Butchkin does, but they were sad ones. But he was indomitable. He set himself to the task of removing his cast, succeeded, and was returned to the vet to have another put on, which he could not take off. But he tried. And, everyday he made his trip down the stairs, to the cat door, where he hesitated, his leg stuck out behind him, then went through it cursing, because he always knocked his leg on it, and we watched him hobble up the garden through the puddles and leaves of the autumn. He had to lie almost flat to get under the fence. Every day he went to report, and came back exhausted and went to sleep. When awake, he laboured at the task of getting his cast off. Where he sat was white with bits of cast.

In a month it came off, the leg was stiff but usable, and Rufus became himself, a gallant adventuring cat who used us as a base, but then got ill again. For a couple of years this cycle went on. He got well, and was off, got ill and came home. But his illnesses were getting worse. His ear ulcer would not heal. He would return from somewhere to ask for help. He would put his paw delicately to his suppurating ear, retch delicately at the smell on his paw, and look helplessly at his nurses. He gave little grunts of protest as we washed it out, but he wanted us to, and he took his medicaments, and he lay around and allowed himself to get well. Under our hands his was a tough, muscled body and he was a strong old cat, in spite of his ailments. It was only at the end of his life, his much too short life, when he was ill and could hardly walk, that he stayed home and did not attempt to go out at all. He lay on the sofa and seemed to think, or dream, when he was not asleep. Once, when he was asleep, I stroked him awake to take his medicine, and he came up out of sleep with the confiding, loving trill greeting cats use for the people they love, the cats they love. But when he saw it was me he became his normal polite and grateful self, and I realized that this was the only time I had heard him make this special sound – in a house where it was heard all day. This is how mother cats greet their kittens, kittens greet their mothers. Had he been dreaming of when he was a kitten? Or perhaps even of the human who had owned him as a kitten, or a young cat, but then had gone off and abandoned him? I shocked, and hurt, this ultimate sound, for he had not made it even when he was purring like a machine to show gratitude. During all the time he had known us, nearly four years, several times nursed back to health, or near-health, he had never really believed he could not lose this home and have to fend for himself, become a cat maddened by thirst and aching with cold. His confidence in someone, his love, had once been so badly betrayed that he could not allow himself ever to love again.

Knowing cats, a lifetime of cats, what is left is a sediment of sorrow quite different from that due to humans: compounded of pain for their helplessness, of guilt on behalf of us all.

The Home Life of a Holy Cat

ARTHUR WIEGALL

ONE SUMMER during a heat wave, when the temperature in the shade of my veranda in Luxor was 125° Fahrenheit, I went down to cooler Lower Egypt to pay a visit to an English friend of mine stationed at Zagazig, the native city which stands beside the ruins of ancient Bubastis.

He was about to leave Egypt and asked me whether I would like to have his cat, a dignified, mystical-minded, long-legged, small-headed, green-eyed female, whose orange-yellow hair, marked with greyish-black stripes in tabby pattern, was so short that she gave the impression of being naked – an impression, however, which did not in any way detract from her air of virginal chastity.

Her name was Basta, and though her more recent ancestors had lived wild amongst the ruins, she was so obviously a descendant of the holy cats of ancient times, who were incarnations, of the goddess Basta, that I thought it only right to accept the offer and take her up to Luxor to live with me. To be the expert in charge of Egyptian antiquities and not have an ancient Egyptian cat to give an air of mystery to my headquarters had, indeed, always seemed to me to be somewhat wanting in showmanship on my part.

Thus it came about that, on my departure, I drove off to the railroad station with the usually dignified Basta bumping around and uttering unearthly howls inside a cardboard hat box, in the side of which I had cut a small round hole for ventilation. The people in the streets and on the station platform seemed to be under the impression that the noises were digestive and that I was in dire need of a doctor; and it was a great relief to my embarrassment when the hot and panting train steamed into Zagazig.

Fortunately, I found myself alone in the compartment, and the hatbox at my side had begun to cause me less anxiety, when suddenly Basta was seized with a sort of religious frenzy. The box rocked about, and presently out through the airhole came a long, snake-like paw which waved weirdly to and fro in space for a moment and then was withdrawn, its place being taken by a pink nose which pushed itself outward with such frantic force that the sides of the hole gave way, and out burst the entire sandy, sacred head.

She then began to choke, for the cardboard was pressing tightly around her neck; and to save her from strangulation I was obliged to tear the aperture open, whereupon she wriggled out, leaped in divine frenzy up the side of the carriage and prostrated herself on the network of the baggage-rack, where her hysteria caused her to lose all control of her internal arrangements if and I say modestly that she was overcome with nausea, I shall be telling but a part of the dreadful tale.

The rest of the journey was like a bad dream; but at the Cairo terminus, where I had to change into the night express for Luxor, I got the help of a native policeman who secured a large laundry basket from the sleeping-car department, and after a prolonged struggle, during which the train was shunted into a distant siding, we imprisoned the struggling Basta again.

The perspiring policeman and I then carried the basket at a run along the tracks back to the station in the sweltering heat of the late afternoon, and I just managed to catch my train; but during this second part of my journey Basta travelled in the baggage-van whence, in the hot and silent night, whenever we were at a standstill, her appalling incantations came drifting to my ears.

I opened the basket in an unfurnished spare room in my house, and like a flash Basta was up the bare wall and on to the curtain pole above the window. There she remained all day, in a sort of hypnotic trance; but at sunset the saucer of milk and plate of fish which I had provided for her at last enticed her down, and in the end she reconciled herself to her new surroundings and indicated by her behaviour that she was willing to accept my house as her earthly temple.

With Pedro, my pariah dog, there was not the slightest trouble; he had no strong feelings about cats, and she on her part graciously deigned to acknowledge his status – as, I believe, is generally the case in native households. She sometimes condescended to visit my horse and donkey in their stalls; and for Laura, my camel, she quickly developed a real regard, often sleeping for hours in her stable.

I was not worried as to how she would treat the chickens and pigeons, because her former owner at Zagazig had insisted upon her respecting his hen coop and pigeon cote; but I was a little anxious about the ducks, for she had not previously known any, and in ancient times her ancestors used to be trained to hunt wild geese and ducks and were fed with *pâté de foie gras*, or whatever it was called then, on holy days and anniversaries.

In a corner of the garden I had made a miniature duck pond which was sunk rather deeply in the ground and down to which I had cut a narrow, steeply sloping passage, or gangway. During the day, after the ducks had been up and down this slope several times, the surface used to become wet and slippery, and the ducks, having waddled down the first few inches, were forced to toboggan down the rest of it on their tails, with their two feet sticking out in front of them and their heads well up.

Basta was always fascinated by this slide and by the splash at the bottom, and used to sit and watch it all for hours, which made me think at first that she would one day spring at one of them; but she never did. Field mice, and water rats down by the Nile, were her only prey; and in connection with the former I may mention a curious occurrence.

One hot night I was sitting smoking my pipe on the veranda when my attention was attracted by two mice which had crept into the patch of brilliant moonlight before my feet and were boldly nibbling some crumbs left over from a cracker thrown to Pedro earlier in the evening. I watched them silently for a while and did not notice that Basta had seen them and was preparing to spring, nor did I observe a large white owl sitting aloft amongst the overhanging roses and also preparing to pounce.

Suddenly, and precisely at the same moment, the owl shot down on the mice from above and Basta leaped at them from beside me. There was a collision and a wild scuffle; fur and feathers flew; I fell out of my chair; and then the owl made off screeching in one direction and the cat dashed away in the other; while the mice, practically clinging to each other, remained for a moment or so too terrified to move.

During the early days of her residence in Luxor, Basta often used to go down to the edge of the Nile to fish with her paw; but she never caught anything, and in the end she got a fright and gave it up. I was sitting by the river watching her trying to catch one of a little shoal of small fish which were sunning themselves in the shallow water when there came swimming into view a twelve or fourteen-inch fish which I recognized (by its whiskers and the absence of a dorsal fin) as the electric cat fish, pretty common in the Nile – a strange creature able to give you an electric shock like hitting your funny bone.

These fish obtain their food in a curious way: they hang round any shoal of small fry engaged in feeding, and then glide quietly into their midst and throw out this electric shock, whereupon the little fellows are all sick to the stomach, and the big fellow gets their disgorged dinners.

I was just waiting to see this happen with my own eyes – for it had always seemed a bit far-fetched – when Basta made a dart at the intruder with her paw and got a shock. She uttered a yowl as though somebody had trodden on her and leaped high in the air; and never again did she put her foot near the water. She was content after that with our daily offering of a fish brought from the market and fried for her like a burnt sacrifice.

Basta had a most unearthly voice, and when she was feeling emotional would let out a wail which at first was like the crying of a phantom baby and then became the tuneless song of a lunatic, and finally developed into the blood-curdling howl of a soul in torment. And when she spat, the percussion was like that of a spring-gun.

There were some wild cats or, rather, domestic cats who, like Basta's own forebears, had taken to a wild life, living in a grove of trees beside the river just beyond my garden wall; and it was generally the proximity of one of these which started her off;

but sometimes the outburst was caused by her own unfathomable thoughts as she went her mysterious ways in the darkness of the night.

I think she must have been clairvoyant, for she often seemed to be seeing things not visible to me. Sometimes, perhaps when she was cleaning fish or mouse from her face, she would pause with one foot off the ground and stare in front of her, and then back away with bristling hair or go forward with friendly little mewing noises; and sometimes she would leap off a chair or sofa, her tail lashing and her green eyes dilated. But it may have been worms.

Once I saw her standing absolutely rigid and tense on the lawn, staring at the rising moon; and then all of a sudden she did a sort of dance such as cats sometimes do when they are playing with other cats. But there was no other cat and, any way, Basta never played; she never forgot that she was a holy cat.

Her chaste hauteur was so great that she would not move out of the way when people were walking about, and many a time her demoniacal shriek and perhaps a crash of breaking glass informed the household that somebody had tripped over her. It was astonishing, however, how quickly she recovered her dignity and how well she maintained the pretence that whatever happened to her was at her own celestial wish and was not our doing.

If I called her she would pretend not to hear, but would come a few moments later when it could appear that she had thought of doing so first; and if I lifted her off a chair she would jump back on to it and then descend with dignity as though of her own free will. But in this, of course, she was more like a woman than like a divinity.

The Egyptian cat is a domesticated species of the African wild-cat, and no doubt its strange behaviour and its weird voice were the cause of it being regarded as sacred in ancient times; but, although the old gods and their worship have been forgotten these many centuries, the traditional sanctity of the race has survived.

Modern Egyptians think it unlucky to hurt a cat and, in the native quarters of Cairo and other cities, hundreds of cats are daily fed at the expense of benevolent citizens. They say that they do this because cats are so useful to mankind in killing off mice and other pests; but actually it is an unrecognized survival of the old beliefs.

In the days of the Pharaohs, when a cat died the men of the household shaved off their eyebrows and sat around wailing and rocking themselves to and fro in simulated anguish. The body was embalmed and buried with solemn rites in the local cats' cemetery, or was sent down to Bubastis to rest in the shadow of the temple of their patron goddess. I myself have dug up hundreds of mummified cats; and once, when I had a couple of dozen of the best specimens standing on my veranda waiting to be dispatched to the Cairo Museum, Basta was most excited about it, and walked around sniffing at them all day. They certainly smelled awful.

On my lawn there was a square slab of stone which had once been the top of an altar dedicated to the sun god, but was now used as a sort of low garden table; and sometimes when she had caught a mouse she used to deposit the chewed corpse upon this slab – nobody could think why, unless, as I always told people, she was really making an offering to the sun. It was most mysterious of her; but it led once to a very unfortunate episode.

A famous French antiquarian, who was paying a polite call, was sitting with me beside this sacred stone, drinking afternoon tea and eating fresh dates, when Basta appeared on the scene with a small dead mouse in her mouth, which in her usual way she deposited upon the slab – only on this occasion she laid it on my guest's plate, which was standing on the slab.

We were talking at the moment and did not see her do this and, anyhow, the Frenchman was as blind as a bat; and, of course, as luck would have it, he immediately picked up the wet, mole-coloured mouse instead of a ripe brown date, and the thing had almost gone into his mouth before he saw what it was and, with a yell, flung it into the air.

It fell into his upturned sun helmet which was lying on the grass beside him; but he did not see where it had gone and, jumping angrily to his feet in the momentary belief that I had played a schoolboy joke on him, he snatched up his helmet and was in the act of putting it on his head when the mouse tumbled out on to the front of his shirt and slipped down inside his buttoned jacket.

At this he went more or less mad, danced about, shook himself, and finally trod on Basta, who completed his frenzy by uttering a fiendish howl and digging her claws into his leg. The dead mouse, I am glad to say, fell on to the grass during the dance without passing through his roomy trousers, as I had feared it might; and Basta, recovering her dignity, picked it up and walked off with it.

It is a remarkable fact that, during the five or six years she spent with me, she showed no desire to be anything but a spinster all her life, and when I arranged a marriage for her she displayed such dignified but violent antipathy towards the bridegroom that the match was a failure. In the end, however, she fell in love with one of the wild cats who lived among the trees beyond my wall, and nothing could prevent her going off to visit him from time to time, generally at dead of night.

He did not care a hoot about her sanctity, and she was feminine enough to enjoy the novelty of being roughly treated. I never actually saw him, for he did not venture into the garden, but I used to hear him knocking her about outside my gates; and when she came home, scratched and bitten and muttering something about holy cats, it was plain that she was desperately happy. She licked her wounds, indeed, with deep and voluptuous satisfaction.

A dreadful change came over her. She lost her precious dignity and was restless and inclined to be savage; her digestion played embarrassing tricks on her; and once she mortally offended Laura by clawing her nose. There was a new glint in her green eyes as she watched the ducks sliding into the pond; the pigeons interested her for the first time; and for the first time, too, she *ate* the mice she had caught.

Then she began to disappear for a whole day or night at a time, and once when I went in search of her amongst the trees outside and found her sharpening her claws on a branch above my head, she put her ears back and hissed at me until I could see every one of her teeth and halfway down her pink throat. I tried by every method to keep her at home when she came back, but it was all in vain, and at last she left me forever.

Weeks afterwards I caught sight of her once again amongst

the trees, and it was evident that she was soon to become a mother. She gave me a friendly little mew this time, but she would not let me touch her; and presently she slipped away into the undergrowth. I never knew what became of her.

Solomon and Sheba

DOREEN TOVEY

THE DAY Sheba chased a gnat behind the picture over the bureau and left a row of black footprints up the wall Charles said it wasn't fair to blame the cats for everything. It wasn't her fault, he said, that when it flew past she happened to be looking up the chimney and had her paws covered in soot. I must remember that Siamese were not as other cats, and make allowance for their verve and curiosity.

He didn't say that when we put down the new stair-carpet and Solomon, busily showing Sheba how Strong he was, ripped the daylights out of the bottom-tread while we were still hammering down the top. He said Solomon was a damblasted little pest and if he wasn't careful he'd end up in the Cats' Home. Neither did it improve matters when I, to protect the rest of the carpet until Solomon got tired of sharpening his claws on it, made a set of stair-pads out of folded copies of *The Times*. The idea was to put a pad on each stair whenever we were going out. It worked for a few days – then one morning Charles, dashing up at the last moment to fetch his wallet, slipped on the top copy and slid from top to bottom on his neck. Both Solomon and I were in the dog-house then, and although it didn't worry me unduly – Charles, who is six feet tall, falls down the cottage stairs, which are steep and narrow, quite regularly, and I would get the blame even if I were on the top of Everest at the time – Solomon was quite put out about it.

While Sheba comforted Charles in the hall, walking up and

down on his stomach and asking anxiously if he were Dead, Solomon sat at the top of the stairs delivering a long Siamese monologue about the injustice of it all. Sheba Clawed Things, he said, and Nobody Complained About Her. She did too. The underside of the spare room arm chair sagged like a jelly bag where Sheba, when she first woke up in the morning, dragged herself round and round on her back by way of exercise – and all Charles said about that was that we had to make allowance for her high spirits.

She Knocked Things Down and Hit People Too, wailed Solomon. You could tell when he got to that bit by the pitch of his voice. Always powerful, it rose to an ear-shattering roar when he was in the right and knew it. Solomon didn't knock things down and hit people. He couldn't climb high enough to start with. But Sheba, shinning like a mountain goat up the bookshelves either side of the fireplace, was always bombarding unwary visitors with dislodged encyclopaedias or law books. Lately I had begun to wonder whether that, too, was quite the accident she claimed it to be. It had certainly been no accident the night I was just in time to stop her crowning Solomon with a Benares brass pitcher. When I caught her she was standing on the arm of a chair trying as hard as she could to hook it off the mantelpiece with her paw while he, stretched out full length to warm his stomach, lay innocently asleep on the rug below.

Now, craning his neck over the landing to make sure everybody heard him, Solomon continued his tale of woe. Charles was Clumsy, he wailed, staring reproachfully down at the spot where Sheba, relieved to find that Charles was good for a few more years yet, was making the most of the occasion by treading vigorously on his waistcoat and assuring him that *she* was a good girl. Charles would have Fallen Down the Stairs even without the newspapers, yelled Solomon. Charles Fell Over Everything. Charles Fell Off the Ladder only last Saturday. Nobody, said Solomon, with the mournful wail-cum-sniffle which meant that at that moment he was feeling particularly hard done by, could blame him for that. Charles had done it All By Himself.

Charles had indeed. He had been painting the eaves of the cottage, perched on the sloping hall roof, on a ladder that had a cracked leg and was – despite Father Adams's warning that he knew several blokes who had killed themselves like that—suspended by faith and a piece of ancient rope from the chimney-stack. Charles's own version of what happened was that he was just reaching up to put on the last brushful of paint, thinking to himself (he was given to making up tense little dramas to amuse himself while he worked), 'And at that moment, just as he reached out for the final handhold, there was a sharp crack of breaking rope and he fell like a stone into the abyss below' – when the rope did break. Not with a sharp crack. It unravelled slowly and sadistically before his very eyes as he stood helplessly on the top rung. He didn't fall into any abyss either. He landed on the hall roof with a thump that shook the cottage to its poor old foundations. When I rushed out, convinced that I was a widow at last, he was sitting despondently on the roof in a pool of pale-blue paint while, standing side by side on top of the coal-house, craning their necks like a couple of spectators at a Lord Mayor's Show, Solomon and Sheba anxiously inquired what he wanted to do that for.

Charles said I might not believe it, but as he slid down the roof after the crash he had seen – actually *seen* – that pair gallop down the path and scramble up on to the coal-house as if it were a grandstand. I believed it all right. So often in trouble themselves, there was nothing they liked better than sitting smugly by, tails wrapped primly round their front paws and expressions of pained incredulity on their faces, when somebody else was in the soup. I remember once when a dog chased a neighbour's kitten up the electricity post outside our garden wall. Solomon was hardly in a position to talk, after the incident of the fire brigade, while Sheba had lately developed her mother's habit of demanding to be rescued by Charles from every tree she came across. It made no difference. While Charles and I tried to solve the problem of getting a ladder safely balanced against the rounded post they sat side by side at the foot, their necks stuck out like giraffes to emphasize What A Long Way Up She Was, their eyes round as bottle stops, yelling encouragingly up at her that she was Very Silly To Do A Thing Like That and They Didn't Suppose We'd Ever Get Her Down Again. The fact that no sooner had Charles rescued the kitten than he had to go up again to fetch Solomon, who had meanwhile climbed the ladder himself by way of an experiment and was now stuck half way up bellowing his own head off, was quite incidental. It still left Sheba at the bottom nattering away happily about what a long way up *he* was and she didn't suppose we'd ever get *him* down either.

It was inevitable, of course, that their rubber-necking would one day lead them into trouble. It happened at a time when we had new neighbours in the next cottage and Sol and Sheba, consumed with their usual curiosity, were going up every day to see how they were getting on. We warned the people not to encourage them. Disaster, we said, would unfailingly follow. Solomon would wreck their stair-carpet or raid their pantry and Sheba would either go up their chimney or fall down their lavatory. They wouldn't listen. They hadn't met any Siamese before and they were fascinated, they said, by the way our two marched one behind the other down the garden path, greeted them with an airy bellow and proceeded to inspect the place as if they owned it. Which, so far as we could see, made it entirely the Westons' own fault when they tried to fill their water-butt during a drought by means of a hosepipe sneaking illicitly through the delphiniums and lupins to the kitchen tap and Solomon and Sheba promptly gave them away to the entire village by sitting on the outhouse roof, gazing wide-eyed down at the bubbles, and loudly inviting passers by to come and see what they'd found. Father Adams, who was one of the people who did – years ago his grandfather had lived in the Westons' cottage and that, according to country politics, really gave him more right to walk up the front path than the Westons themselves, who were newcomers from town – said old man Weston turned all the colours of a shammylon when he saw he'd been found out. He hadn't been there long enough to know that practically everybody else – certainly Father Adams – filled their water-butts in exactly the same way, and for days he went round hardly daring to look anybody in the face. Which, as Aunt Ethel said the day Solomon ate her guinea pot of beauty cream, just showed the folly of having anything to do with Siamese at all.

We never managed to get the better of them ourselves. Every time we thought we had them weighed off, up they came with something new. Mouse-catching, for instance. No sooner had we got used to the routine of Sheba catching them and Solomon slinging them round our heads for hours than Sheba, feeling that Solomon was getting too much limelight, decided that she'd better tell us when she caught a mouse in future, so there would be no mistaking it was hers. The first time Solomon heard her coming under the new system, moaning like a travelling air-raid siren, he said it was ghosts and hid under the bath and we had an awful job to coax him out; but it wasn't long before he, in turn, thought up an even better gimmick. He ate the mouse. Not quietly, in a corner, but noisily on the hearth-rug, leaving us the head and tail as souvenirs. The next thing was that Sheba ate a mouse too, but her stomach wasn't as strong as Solomon's and she went straight out and sicked it up on the stairs. And so, as Charles said, life went on.

There was a period, just after Sugieh died and the kittens were beginning to feel their feet as individuals, when if we had visitors we just couldn't move for them, sitting solidly in people's laps, licking their iced cakes when they weren't looking, investigating their handbags and chatting to them under the bathroom door. They liked people so much that when we shut them in the hall one night because one of Charles's friends had a dark suit on and wasn't very fond of cats anyway they climbed the curtains, got out through a transom window which we didn't know was open, and appeared suddenly with their small smudgy faces pressed to the window of the sitting-room, gazing wistfully in like orphans of the storm.

A great success that was. Everybody cooed over them and gave them ice-cream and Charles's friend went home with a suit that looked as if it were made of angora. The next time they were shut out on account of visitors Solomon, remembering the ice-cream, promptly jumped out of a window again. This time, however, as all the hall windows were shut, old Bat Brains went upstairs and jumped out of the bedroom window. One visitor fainted on the spot when she saw him coming down, but he landed in a hydrangea and was quite unharmed. The only thing was that now Solomon had discovered that he could open windows by putting his fat little bullet-head under the catches and pushing them up, in addition to spreading twelve copies of *The Times* on the stairs any time we shut them out, we now had to tie up all the window-catches with string as well.

Though the cats drove visitors nearly mad with their attention when they first arrived, however, if anybody stayed after eleven o'clock things were very different. Then, retiring to the most comfortable armchair (if anybody was sitting in it they just squeezed down behind him and kept turning round and round till he got out; it never failed), they curled up and ostentatiously tried to go to sleep. Tried was the operative word. Any time anybody looked across at the chair there would be at least one Siamese regarding them with half-raised head, one eye open and a pained expression that clearly indicated it was time they went home, Some People were tired. If this had no effect, in due course Solomon would sit up, yawn noisily and subside again with a loud sigh on top of Sheba. Few visitors missed that hint. Solomon yawned like fat men belch—long, loudly and with gusto. What was most embarrassing, though, was the way – after lying for hours as if they'd been working all day in a chain gang – they suddenly perked up the moment people did start to go. It wouldn't have been so bad if they'd just politely seen them off at the door, the way Sugieh used to do. These two sat in the hall and bawled to people to hurry up – and as we shepherded people to the front gate they could be seen quite plainly through the window, hilariously chasing one another over the chairs by way of celebration.

To be quite honest, by that time the visitors usually weren't looking with such a kindly eye on the cats either. There was the friend, for instance, who brought an old pair of stockings for playing with the cats and left her best ones in our bedroom for safety. She expected the old ones to be ruined, and she was right. Solomon gave her a friendly nip in the ankle while we were having tea and bang they went. Unfortunately the bedroom door wasn't properly shut and while Sheba was, of her own accord, bringing the new ones down for the lady they went bang too, hitched up in a snag on the stairs.

There was the friend who unthinkingly left her car keys on the hall table. An innocent enough gesture – except that that was the time when Solomon was being an Alsatian dog and carrying things round in his mouth and it took us two hours to find where he had put them. Down the clock-golf hole on the lawn.

There was the cactus which disappeared mysteriously from its pot while its owner, who had just been given it by another friend, was calling on us for a cup of tea. Charles said if that didn't prove Solomon wasn't right in the head nothing did—but as a matter of fact it wasn't Solomon. It was Sheba, as we discovered later when we started raising cactus ourselves and had to lock them in the bathroom every night for safety while she howled under the door for just a little one to play marbles with.

It was Solomon, though, alone and unaided, who killed the fur coat. We laughed at the look of awe on his face the first time he saw it, and the way he immediately put up his back and offered to fight. We didn't give it a thought as the owner, patting him on the head and saying it was only a coat little man, tossed it nonchalantly on to the hall chair. But Solomon did. As soon as he'd had his share of the crab sandwiches he went out and killed it so dead I shudder even now to think how much it cost us to have it repaired.

We kept a strong guard on fur coats after that. Whenever one arrived Charles held Solomon in the kitchen while I personally locked it in the wardrobe and then locked the bedroom door. Even so I had qualms the night someone arrived wearing a particularly fine leopard coat and Solomon, as soon as supper was over, disappeared quietly into the hall. As soon as I could I slipped out too, to check. Everything seemed all right. The bedroom door was still firmly locked and when I spoke to him Solomon, sitting innocently on the hall table and gazing out into the night, said he was only looking for foxes.

It wasn't until the visitor, getting ready to go, started looking round the hall saying it was funny but she could have *sworn* she left it on the chest that I realized I hadn't taken her hat up to the bedroom as well – and by that time it was too late. It had – or rather it had had – a smart black cocksfeather cockade on one side. When we picked it up, from under the same chair that had once concealed Aunt Ethel's famous telegram, all the feathers fell off.

By the time Solomon was six months old he had, despite his unpromising beginnings, grown into one of the most handsome Siamese we had ever seen. True he still had spotted whiskers and big feet and walked like Charlie Chaplin. But he had lost his puppy fat and was as lithe and sleek as a panther. His black, triangular mask – except for one solitary white hair right in the middle which he said he'd got through worrying over Sheba – shone like polished ebony. His eyes, set slantwise above high, Oriental cheekbones, were a brilliant sapphire and remarkable even for a Siamese. When he lay on the garden wall with his long black legs drooping elegantly over the edge he looked, according to Father Adams, exactly like a sheik in one of them Eastern palaces.

Father Adams, who was a great fan of Ethel M. Dell's, would have liked Solomon to be a sheik in the real romantic sense of the word. At that time he was still dreaming of making a fortune from cat-breeding and Solomon was so magnificent that there was nothing he would have liked more than to see him drag Mimi off into the hills by the scruff of her sleek cream neck and there found a race of Siamese that would, as he was always telling us, fetch ten quid apiece as easy as pie.

He was so disgusted when we had Solomon neutered that he wouldn't speak to us for a week – which was all very well; we didn't want to spoil Solomon's life either, but we had to share it with him and even our best friends wouldn't have lasted long in a house with an un-neutered Siamese. The only way we could have kept him – unless we let him wander, in which case a Siamese tom usually develops into a terrible fighter and rarely comes home at all – would have been outside in a stud-house.

When we asked Solomon about it he said he'd rather have beetles than girls. And cream cakes, he added, casting a speculative eye at the tea-trolley. And sleeping in our bed, he said that night, burrowing determinedly under the blankets to find my head.

That settled it. We could as soon imagine Solomon a stud-tom as pretending to be a lion at the zoo. The following week-end he was neutered, and Sheba along with him, and not a scrap of trouble did we have with either of them except in the matter of Sheba's stitches. Two she had, and the vet who did the operation – a town one this time; not for one moment did we attach any blame to the vet who did Sugieh's operation, but it seemed fairer all round to have Sheba done by someone else – said we could easily take them out ourselves on the tenth day. Just snip here and there, he said, pull smartly – and the job was done.

It might have been with normal cats, but not with Sheba. She wasn't going to have any ham-fisted amateurs handling her, she said. Every time we approached her with the scissors she fled to the top shelf of the bookcase and barricaded herself in. Even Charles couldn't get her to come down. She liked him very much, she assured him from behind the Britannicas – but not her stitches, if he didn't mind. He could practise on Solomon, Mimi or even me. She wanted a real doctor. After the night when the stitches began to itch and she lay on our bed first trying to get them out herself and then letting Solomon have a go until the perpetual snick-snicking nearly drove us mad she got one, too. We could hardly ask the local vet to do the job, as he hadn't done the operation, so the next morning we rang Doctor Tucker, who came over and obliged at once. Sheba didn't run away from him. She told him at great length what we'd tried to do to her and did he think he ought to report it to the Medical Association. Then, while he snipped and pulled with the self-same scissors we had tried to use, she stood quietly on the table, her eyes happily crossed, and purred.

That, we thought, was the end of our troubles. The cats were growing up now. They had their little idiosyncrasies of course. Like Sheba's habit of turning out the vegetable rack every night, followed by complaints from our new help that it wasn't her job in other houses to fish sprouts and squashed tomatoes from under the cooker every morning. Not that it mattered much because she gave us notice quite soon anyway on account of Solomon's habit of walking over floors as soon as she'd scrubbed them.

Sheba was jolly pleased when she went. Now, she said – and how right she was – she'd be able to file sprouts under the stove until they smelled real high before anybody moved them. Solomon was pleased. She kept throwing the floor-cloth at him, he said, and if he hadn't been a gentleman – in the *highest* sense of the word, he said, ignoring Sheba's aside to Charles that he Wasn't Any More Was He, Not Since His Operation?—he'd have bitten her. Charles was pleased. If she hadn't gone, her said, judging by the looks she gave him when he asked her to empty the ashtrays, she'd have been throwing the floor-cloth at him next. The only one who wasn't pleased was me – and I was too busy doing the housework to complain.

There was Solomon's keen interest in things mechanical which led him to follow the vacuum-cleaner like a bloodhound, with his nose glued firmly to the carpet, watching the bits disappear inside. Come to think of it, it was a good thing the help wasn't around the day he decided to experiment with that and, while I was moving a chair, poked his ball of silver paper curiously into the works. I turned round just in time to see a long black paw disappearing under the front and to hurl myself at the switch like a bomb.

Mrs Terry wouldn't have done that. She'd have screamed, thrown her apron over her head and fainted, the way she did when she removed the guard from the electric fire in the sitting-room for cleaning and Solomon, with happy memories of Mum, promptly walked over and stuck his rear against it. The only result of that incident had been that, for a while, Solomon's tail, indented in two places by the electric bars, had looked more like that of a poodle than a Siamese and Sheba had made him cross by pretending to be frightened every time she saw it. What might have happened with the vacuum I hardly dared to think.

These though, as I have said, were idiosyncrasies such as all Siamese owners experience. So long as we got up at five in the morning to let them out – otherwise Sheba knocked the lamp off the dressing-table and Solomon bit us; so long as we only ate chocolates wrapped in silver paper and let Solomon have every single piece – he sulked like mad when somebody gave us a 4lb box for Christmas without an inch of silver paper among them: Done It On Purpose he said they had, watching disconsolately every time the box was opened, and couldn't we eat them faster than that; so long as we kept a box of All Bran permanently on the kitchen floor to fill the corners when he felt peckish – if we didn't he was liable to get in the cupboard and look for it himself with disastrous results; so long as we remembered little things like that we had no trouble at all. Real little home birds they were. Always running in to see that we hadn't gone for a walk without them – or even more important, that we weren't eating something behind their backs.

Which made it all the more worrying the morning I called the cats and instead of the usual mad stampede to see what was for breakfast only Sheba appeared, looking very small and forlorn and nattering anxiously that Solomon had vanished; she'd looked all over the place for him and she didn't know where he could be.

We didn't know it then but Solomon, tired of the chains of civilization, had gone to be an explorer – and, as explorers sometimes do, he had met with a hazard. When I found him an hour later, after scouring the countryside till I was practically on my knees, he was in a field more than a mile away with a pair of large and angry geese. When I panted up he was crouching in a corner bawling his head off about what he'd do if they came any nearer, but he didn't fool them – or me. He was scared stiff. His ears stuck up like a pair of horrified exclamation marks. His eyes were nearly popping out of his head. When I called him he gave a long, despairing wail which clearly signified that if I didn't hurry up the cannibals would get him, and he wasn't half in a fix.

I got him out of that by wading knee-deep in a bed of stinging-nettles, leaning over a barbed-wire fence and hauling him out by the scruff of his neck. From the look on the faces of those geese it was obvious there wasn't time to go round by the gate. He never learned, of course. No sooner was he safely on my shoulder and the geese out of earshot than the old bounce was back. All the way home I had a monologue right in my ear about what they said to him and what he said back—punctuated halfway by a decision, which I nipped in the bud by grabbing his tail and hanging on to it firmly, to go right back and tell them some more.

By the time we got home Solomon, in his own mind at least, was a budding Marco Polo. And from then on we had hardly a moment's peace. Summoned by a wail that turned my blood cold when I heard it, I rescued him from one emergency after another. Once, under the impression that she was running away from *him*, he chased a cow that was being tormented by flies. That was fine fun while it lasted, tearing across the field with the wind in his tail and his long black legs going like a racehorse – until the cow turned round, saw Buffalo Bill capering cockily at her heels, and chased him instead.

I rescued him that time from a handy wall, doing a fine imitation of the Stag at Bay with the cow's horns about an inch from his trembling black nose. The time he frightened a little lamb, though, he wasn't so lucky. His nearest point of escape then was through a hedge which topped a steep bank above the woods, and by the time he made it the lamb's mother was so close behind he couldn't stop to look for a proper way through. As I toiled wearily up through the woods in answer to his yell for help he appeared dramatically on the skyline, leapt into space, and landed ignominiously in a pool of mud.

That taught him nothing either. The very next day I saw him – in his own inimitable way, which meant laboriously hiding behind every blade of grass he came across and crawling across the open bits on his stomach – tracking a small kitten into the self-same woods. I let him go that time. His dusky face was alight with eagerness, there was such an Excelsior light in his eyes – and he couldn't, I thought, get into trouble with a little kitten like that.

That was where I was wrong. A few minutes later there was a volcanic explosion, a mad crashing of branches, silence – and then, once more, the familiar sound of Solomon yelling for help. Creeping stealthily through the woods he had, it seemed, come across his enemy from the farmyard, doing a bit of mousing. Judging by the way the tom went streaking up the road as I dashed into the woods he was just as alarmed as Solomon by the encounter – and indeed it wasn't that that Columbus was belly-aching about. It was that, just as he had taken refuge up a tree, so had the kitten. Up the same tree, Solomon had made it first and was clinging for dear life six feet up while the kitten, unable to pass him, was directly under his tail. Solomon, in all his glory, a magnificent, intimidating specimen of a male Siamese, was howling because a tiny kitten no bigger than a flea wouldn't let him get down.

After that Solomon kept away from the woods for a while. He took to sitting on the garden wall instead, pretending, when we asked him why he hadn't gone exploring, that he was Waiting for a Friend. That, unfortunately, was how he came to get interested in horses. Unfortunately – because when Solomon got interested in anything he invariably wanted a closer look. Unfortunately – because it wasn't long before the owner of the local riding-school was ringing us up to ask whether we would mind keeping him in while her pupils went by. He was frightening the horses, she said. Little Patricia had already fallen into our stinging-nettles twice, and her mother didn't like it.

When we said, somewhat indignantly, that cats didn't frighten horses, she said ours did. She said he lurked in the grass until the first one had gone by, then dashed out into the road and pranced along behind him. It looked, she said, almost as if he was imitating the horse – though that of course was ridiculous. The first horse was all right because he couldn't see the cat; the ones behind, she said – and we could quite see her point – nearly had hysterics.

We saw to it that, after that, Solomon did his imitations from the hall window when the riding-school went by. Unfortunately, while it was easy enough to tell when they were coming – what with the trampling of hoofs and instructions to people to watch their knees or keep their eyes on their elbows they made, according to Father Adams, more noise than the ruddy Campbells – solitary riders were different. Sometimes we were in time to stop Trigger the Second following his latest idol down the lane. More often the first we knew that a horse had passed that way was when once again Solomon was missing.

It was very worrying. Sometimes it would be a couple of hours or more before he came plodding back on his long thin legs, looking rather sheepish and trying to slip through the gate so that he could pretend he'd been there all the time. We tried everything we could think of, short of a cage, to curb this latest craze. We even bought some goldfish, seeing it was things that moved he liked, and set up a special tank for him in the sitting-room.

Sheba and Charles thought they were wonderful. They sat in front of the tank for ages goggling like a couple of tennis fans as the fish flipped and glided lazily through the water. Solomon, however, when he found there was no way in at the top or sides and that they didn't run away when he looked at them, lost interest and slipped silently out. Charles was too intent on the fish to see him go, or to notice the lone, red-coated rider clopping up the lane; and I was in the kitchen. The first I knew of his latest escapade was when the phone rang and a farmer from the other end of the valley said he didn't know whether I knew it but that black-faced cat of ours had just gone by following one of the huntsmen. He was going it well, he said, stepping it out like a proper little Arab. But the horse was a kicker with a red ribbon on its tail and he didn't . . .

I didn't wait to hear any more. I dropped the phone and ran. When I caught up with them Solomon was still, unknown to the rider, following doggedly along behind that pair of wicked-looking hoofs. The huntsman stared in admiration as I picked him up. Plucky little devil, he said, to have followed all that way. Ought to have been a horse himself.

He didn't know me, of course, or Solomon, from Adam. He looked a little alarmed when, holding old Bat Ears firmly by the scruff of his neck, I said it was a remark like that which started all this horse business in the first place.

Pangur Bán

IRISH MONK

8th century

I and Pangur Bán, my cat,
'Tis a like task we are at;
Hunting mice is his delight,
Hunting words I sit all night.

Better far than praise of men
'Tis to sit with book and pen;
Pangur bears me no ill-will,
He too plies his simple skill.

'Tis a merry thing to see
At our tasks how glad are we,
When at home we sit and find
Entertainment to our mind.

Oftentimes a mouse will stray
In the hero Pangur's way;
Oftentimes my keen thought set
Takes a meaning in its net.

'Gainst the wall he sets his eye
Full and fierce and sharp and sly;
'Gainst the wall of knowledge I
All my little wisdom try.

When a mouse darts from its den,
Oh, how glad is Pangur then!
Oh, what gladness do I prove
When I solve the doubts I love!

So in peace our task we ply,
Pangur Bán – my cat – and I;
In our arts we find our bliss,
I have mine and he has his.

Practice every day has made
Pangur perfect in his trade;
I get wisdom day and night
Turning darkness into light.

Calvin, the Cat

CHARLES DUDLEY WARNER

CALVIN is dead. His life, long to him, but short for the rest of us, was not marked by startling adventures, but his character was so uncommon and his qualities were so worthy of imitation that I have been asked by those who personally knew him to set down my recollections of his career.

His origin and ancestry were shrouded in mystery; even his age was a matter of pure conjecture. Although he was of the Maltese race, I have reason to suppose that he was American by birth as he certainly was in sympathy. Calvin was given to me eight years ago by Mrs Stowe, but she knew nothing of his age or origin. He walked into her house one day out of the great unknown and became at once at home, as if he had been always a friend of the family. He appeared to have artistic and literary tastes, and it was as if he had enquired at the door if that was the residence of the author of *Uncle Tom's Cabin* and, upon being assured that it was, had decided to dwell there. This is, of course, fanciful, for his antecedents were wholly unknown, but in his time he could hardly have been in any household where he would not have heard *Uncle Tom's Cabin* talked about.

When he came to Mrs Stowe, he was as large as he ever was, and apparently as old as he ever became. Yet there was in him no appearance of age; he was in the happy maturity of all his powers and you would rather have said, in that maturity, he had found the secret of perpetual youth. And it was as difficult to believe that he would ever be aged as it was to imagine that he had ever been in immature youth. There was in him a mysterious perpetuity.

After some years, when Mrs Stowe made her winter home in Florida, Calvin came to live with us. From the first moment, he fell into the ways of the house and assumed a recognized position in the family – I say recognized, because after he became known he was always enquired for by visitors, and in the letters from other members of the family he always received a message. Although the least obtrusive of beings, his individuality always made itself felt.

His personal appearance had much to do with this, for he was of royal mould and had an air of high breeding. He was large, but he had nothing of the fat grossness of the celebrated Angora family; though powerful, he was exquisitely proportioned and as graceful in every movement as a young leopard. When he stood up to open a door – he opened all the doors with old-fashioned latches – he was portentously tall, and when he stretched on the rug before the fire he seemed too long for this world – as indeed he was. His coat was the finest and softest I have ever seen, a shade of quiet Maltese; and from his throat downwards, underneath, to the white tips of his feet, he wore the whitest and most delicate ermine; and no person was ever more fastidiously neat. In his finely formed head you saw something of his aristocratic character; the ears were small and cleanly cut, there was a tinge of pink in the nostrils, his face was handsome and the expression of his countenance exceedingly intelligent – I should call it even a sweet expression if the term were not inconsistent with his look of alertness and sagacity.

It is difficult to convey a just idea of his gaiety in connection with his dignity and gravity, which his name expressed. As we know nothing of his family, of course it will be understood that Calvin was his Christian name. He had times of relaxation into utter playfulness, delighting in a ball of yarn, catching sportively at stray ribbons when his mistress was at her toilet, and pursuing his own tail, with hilarity, for lack of anything better. He could amuse himself by the hour, and he did not care for children; perhaps something in his past was present to his memory. He had absolutely no bad habits, and his disposition was perfect I never saw him exactly angry, though I have seen his tail grow to an enormous size when a strange cat appeared upon his lawn. He disliked cats, evidently regarding them as feline and treacherous, and he had no association with them. Occasionally there would be heard a night concert in the shrubbery. Calvin would ask to have the door opened, and then you would hear a rush and a 'pestzt', and the concert would explode, and Calvin would quietly come in and resume his seat on the hearth. There was no trace of anger in his manner, but he wouldn't have any of that about the house.

He had the rare virtue of magnanimity. Although he had fixed notions about his own rights, and extraordinary persistency in getting them, he never showed temper at a repulse; he simply and firmly persisted till he had what he wanted. His diet was one point; his idea was that of the scholars about dictionaries – to 'get the best'. He knew as well as anyone what was in the house, and would refuse beef if turkey was to be had; and if there were oysters, he would wait over the turkey to see if the oysters would not be forthcoming. And yet he was not a gross gourmand; he would eat bread if he saw me eating it, and thought he was not being imposed on. His habits of feeding, also, were refined; he never used a knife, and he would put up his hand and draw the fork down to his mouth as gracefully as a grown person. Unless necessity compelled, he would not eat in the kitchen, but insisted upon his meals in the dining-room, and would wait patiently, unless a stranger were present; and then he was sure to importune the visitor, hoping that the latter was ignorant of the rule of the house, and would give him something. They used to say that he preferred as his tablecloth on the floor a certain well-known Church journal; but this was said by an Episcopalian.

So far as I know, he had no religious prejudices, except that he did not like the association with Romanists. He tolerated the servants, because they belonged to the house, and would sometimes linger by the kitchen stove; but the moment visitors came in he arose, opened the door and marched into the drawing-room. Yet he enjoyed the company of his equals, and never withdrew, no matter how many callers – whom he recognized as of his society – might come into the drawing-room. Calvin was fond of company, but he wanted to choose it;

and I have no doubt that his was an aristocratic fastidiousness rather than one of faith. It is so with most people.

The intelligence of Calvin was something phenomenal, in his rank of life. He established a method of communicating his wants, and even some of his sentiments; and he could help himself in many things. There was a furnace register in a retired room, where he used to go when he wished to be alone, that he always opened when he desired more heat; but never shut it, any more than he shut the door after himself. He could do almost everything but speak; and you would declare sometimes that you could see a pathetic longing to do that in his intelligent face. I have no desire to overdraw his qualities but, if there was one thing in him more noticeable than another, it was his fondness for nature. He could content himself for hours at a low window, looking into the ravine and at the great trees, noting the smallest stir there; he delighted, above all things, to accompany me walking about the garden, hearing the birds, getting the smell of the fresh earth, and rejoicing in the sunshine. He followed me and gambolled like a dog, rolling over on the turf and exhibiting his delight in a hundred ways. If I worked, he sat and watched me, or looked off over the bank and kept his ear open to the twitter in the cherry trees. When it stormed, he was sure to sit at the windows, keenly watching the rain or the snow, glancing up and down at its falling; and a winter tempest always delighted him.

I think he was genuinely fond of birds but, so far as I know, he usually confined himself to one a day; he never killed, as some sportsmen do, for the sake of killing, but only as civilized people do – from necessity. He was intimate with the flying-squirrels who dwelt in the chestnut tree – too intimate, for almost every day in the summer he would bring in one, until he nearly discouraged them. He was, indeed, a superb hunter, and would have been a devastating one if his bump of destructiveness had not been offset by a bump of moderation. There was very little of the brutality of the lower animals about him; I don't think he enjoyed rats for themselves, but he knew his business and, for the first few months of his residence with us, waged an awful campaign against the horde and, after that, his simple presence was sufficient to deter them from coming on the premises. Mice amused him, but he usually considered them too small game to be taken seriously; I have seen him play for an hour with a mouse and then let him go with a royal condescension. In this whole matter of 'getting a living', Calvin was a great contrast to the rapacity of the age in which he lived.

I hesitate to speak of his capacity for friendship and the affectionateness of his nature, for I know from his own reserve that he would not care to have it much talked about. We understood each other perfectly, but we never made any fuss about it; when I spoke his name and snapped my fingers, he came to me; when I returned home at night, he was pretty sure to be waiting for me near the gate, and would rise and saunter along the walk, as if his being there were purely accidental – so shy was he commonly of showing feeling; and when I opened the door he never rushed in, like a cat, but loitered and lounged, as if he had had no intention of going in, but would condescend to. And yet, the fact was, he knew dinner was ready, and he was bound to be there. He kept the run of dinner-time. It happened sometimes, during our absence in the summer, that dinner would be early, and Calvin, walking about the grounds, missed it and came in late. But he never made a mistake the second day. There was one thing he never did – he never rushed through an open doorway. He never forgot his dignity. If he had asked to have the door opened, and was eager to go out, he always went deliberately; I can see him now, standing on the sill, looking about at the sky as if he was thinking whether it were worth while to take an umbrella, until he was near having his tail shut in.

His friendship was rather constant than demonstrative. When we returned from an absence of nearly two years Calvin welcomed us with evident pleasure, but showed his satisfaction rather by tranquil happiness than by fuming about. He had the faculty of making us glad to get home. It was his constancy that was so attractive. He liked companionship, but he wouldn't be petted, or fussed over, or sit in anyone's lap a moment; he always extricated himself from such familiarity with dignity and with no show of temper. If there was any petting to be done, however, he chose to do it. Often he would sit looking at me and then, moved by a delicate affection, come and pull at my coat and sleeve until he could touch my face with his nose, and then go away contented. He had a habit of coming to my study in the morning sitting quietly by my side or on the table for hours, watching the pen run over the paper, occasionally swinging his tail round for a blotter and then going to sleep among the papers by the inkstand. Or, more rarely, he would watch the writing from a perch on my shoulder. Writing always interested him and, until he understood it, he wanted to hold the pen.

He always held himself in a kind of reserve with his friend, as if he had said, 'Let us respect our personality and not make a "mess" of friendship.' He saw, with Emerson, the risk of degrading it to trivial conveniency. 'Why insist on rash personal relations with your friends. Leave this touching and clawing.' Yet I would not give an unfair notion of his aloofness, his fine sense of the sacredness of the me and the not-me. And, at the risk of not being believed, I will relate an incident which was often repeated. Calvin had the practice of passing a portion of the night in the contemplation of its beauties and would come into our chamber over the roof of the conservatory through the open window, summer and winter, and go to sleep at the foot of my bed. He would do this always exactly in this way; he never was content to stay in the chamber if we compelled him to go upstairs and through the door. He had the obstinacy of General Grant. But this is by the way. In the morning, he performed his toilet and went down to breakfast with the rest of the family. Now, when the mistress was absent from home, and at no other time, Calvin would come in the morning, when the bell rang, to the head of the bed, put up his feet and look into my face, follow me about when I rose, 'assist' at the dressing, and in many purring ways show his fondness, as if he had plainly said, 'I know that she has gone away, but I am here.' Such was Calvin in rare moments.

He had his limitations. Whatever passion he had for nature, he had no conception of art. There was sent to him once a fine and very expressive cat's head in bronze, by Frémiet. I placed it on the floor. He regarded it intently, approached it cautiously and crouchingly, touched it with his nose, perceived the fraud, turned away abruptly and never would notice it afterwards.

On the whole, his life was not only a successful one, but a

happy one. He never had but one fear, so far as I know; he had a mortal and a reasonable terror of plumbers. He would never stay in the house when they were here. No coaxing could quiet him. Of course, he didn't share our fear about their charges, but he must have had some dreadful experience with them in that portion of his life which is unknown to us. A plumber was to him the devil, and I have no doubt that, in his scheme, plumbers were foreordained to do him mischief.

In speaking of his worth, it has never occurred to me to estimate Calvin by the worldly standard. I know that it is customary now, when anyone dies, to ask how much he was worth, and that no obituary in the newspapers is considered complete without such an estimate. The plumbers in our house were one day overheard to say that, 'They say that *she* says that *he* says that he wouldn't take $100 for him.' It is unnecessary to say that I never made such a remark, and that, so far as Calvin was concerned, there was no purchase in money.

As I look back upon it, Calvin's life seems to me a fortunate one, for it was natural and unforced. He ate when he was hungry, slept when he was sleepy, and enjoyed existence to the very tips of his toes and the end of his expressive and slow-moving tail. He delighted to roam about the garden, and stroll among the trees, and to lie on the green grass and luxuriate in all the sweet influences of summer. You could never accuse him of idleness, and yet he knew the secret of repose. The poet who wrote so prettily of him that his little life was rounded with a sleep, understated his felicity; it was rounded with a good many. His conscience never seemed to interfere with his slumbers. In fact, he had good habits and a contented mind. I can see him now walk in at the study door, sit down by my chair, bring his tail artistically about his feet, and look up at me with unspeakable happiness in his handsome face.

I often thought that he felt the dumb limitation which denied him the power of language. But since he was denied speech, he scorned the inarticulate mouthings of the lower animals. The vulgar mewing and yowling of the cat species was beneath him; he sometimes uttered a sort of articulate and well-bred ejaculation, when he wished to call attention to something that he considered remarkable, or to some want of his, but he never went whining about. He would sit for hours at a closed window, when he desired to enter, without a murmur, and when it was opened he never admitted that he had been impatient by 'bolting' in. Though speech he had not, and the unpleasant kind of utterance given to his race he would not use, he had a mighty power of purr to express his measureless content with congenial society. There was in him a musical organ with stops of varied power and expression, upon which I have no doubt he could have performed Scarlatti's celebrated cat's fugue.

Whether Calvin died of old age, or was carried off by one of the diseases incident to youth, it is impossible to say; for his departure was as quiet as his advent was mysterious. I only know that he appeared to us in the world in his perfect stature and beauty, and that after a time, like Lohengrin, he withdrew. In his illness there was nothing more to be regretted than in all his blameless life. I suppose there never was an illness that had more dignity and sweetness and resignation in it. It came on gradually, in a kind of listlessness and want of appetite. An alarming symptom was his preference for the warmth of a furnace register to the lively sparkle of the open wood fire. Whatever pain he suffered, he bore it in silence, and seemed only anxious not to obtrude his malady. We tempted him with the delicacies of the season, but it soon became impossible for him to eat, and for two weeks he ate or drank scarcely anything. Sometimes he made an effort to take something, but it was evident that he made the effort to please us. The neighbours – and I am convinced that the advice of neighbours is never good for anything – suggested catnip. He wouldn't even smell it. We had the attendance of an amateur practitioner of medicine, whose real office was the cure of souls, but nothing touched his case. He took what was offered, but it was with the air of one to whom the time for pellets was passed. He sat or lay day after day almost motionless, never once making a display of those vulgar convulsions or contortions of pain which are so disagreeable to society. His favourite place was on the brightest spot of a Smyrna rug by the conservatory, where the sunlight fell and he could hear the fountain play. If we went to him and exhibited our interest in his condition, he always purred in recognition of our sympathy. And when

I spoke his name, he looked up with an expression that said, 'I understand it, old fellow, but it's no use.' He was to all who came to visit him a model of calmness and patience in affliction.

I was absent from home at the last, but heard by daily postal card of his failing condition; and never again saw him alive. One sunny morning he rose from his rug, went into the conservatory (he was very thin then), walked around it deliberately, looking at all the plants he knew, and then went to the bay-window in the dining-room and stood a long time looking out upon the little field, now brown and sere, and towards the garden where perhaps the happiest hours of his life had been spent. It was a last look. He turned and walked away, laid himself down upon the bright spot in the rug, and quietly died.

It is not too much to say that a little shock went through the neighbourhood when it was known that Calvin was dead, so marked was his individuality; and his friends, one after another, came in to see him. There was no sentimental nonsense about his obsequies; it was felt that any parade would have been distasteful to him. John, who acted as undertaker, prepared a candle-box for him, and I believe assumed a professional decorum; but there may have been the usual levity underneath, for I heard that he remarked in the kitchen that it was the 'driest wake he ever attended'. Everybody, however, felt a fondness for Calvin and regarded him with a certain respect. Between him and Bertha there existed a great friendship, and she apprehended his nature; she used to say that sometimes she was afraid of him, he looked at her so intelligently; she was never certain that he was what he appeared to be.

When I returned, they had laid Calvin on a table in an upper chamber by an open window. It was February. He reposed in a candle-box, lined about the edge with evergreen, and at his head stood a little wine glass with flowers. He lay with his head tucked down in his arms – a favourite position of his before the fire – as if asleep in the comfort of his soft and exquisite fur. It was the involuntary exclamation of those who saw him, 'How natural he looks!' As for myself, I said nothing. John buried him under the twin hawthorn trees – one white and the other pink – in a spot where Calvin was fond of lying and listening to the hum of summer insects and the twitter of birds.

Perhaps I have failed to make appear the individuality of character that was so evident to those who knew him. At any rate, I have set down nothing concerning him but the literal truth. He was always a mystery. I did not know whence he came; I do not know whither he has gone. I would not weave one spray of falsehood in the wreath I lay upon his grave.

Puss in Boots

CHARLES PERRAULT

THERE WAS a miller, who had left no more estate to the three sons he had, than his mill, his ass and his cat. The partition was soon made. Neither the scrivener nor attorney were sent for. They would soon have eaten up all the patrimony. The eldest had the mill, the second the ass, and the youngest nothing but the cat.

The poor young fellow was quite comfortless at having so poor a lot. 'My brothers (said he) may get their living handsomely enough, by joining their stocks together; but for my part, when I have eaten up my cat, and made me a muff of his skin, I must die with hunger.' The cat, who heard all this, but made as if he did not, said to him with a grave and serious air, 'Do not thus afflict yourself, my good master; you have nothing else to do but to give me a bag, and get a pair of boots made for me, that I may scamper through the dirt and brambles, and you shall see that you have not so bad a portion of me as you imagine.'

Though the cat's master did not build very much upon what he said, he had, however, often seen him play a great many cunning tricks to catch rats and mice; as when he used to hang by the heels, or hide himself in the meal, and make as if he were dead; so that he did not altogether despair of his affording him some help in his miserable condition. When the cat had what he asked for, he booted himself very gallantly; and, putting his bag about his neck, he held the strings of it in his forepaws, and went into a warren where was great abundance of rabbits. He put bran and sow thistle into his bag and, stretching himself out at length, as if he had been dead, he waited for some young rabbits, not yet acquainted with the deceits of the world, to come and rummage his bag for what he had put into it.

Scarce was he laid down, but he had what he wanted; a rash and foolish young rabbit jumped into his bag and Monsieur Puss, immediately drawing close the strings, took and killed him without pity. Proud of his prey, he went with it to the palace, and asked to speak with his Majesty. He was shown upstairs into the King's apartments and, making a low reverence, said to him, 'I have brought you, Sir, a rabbit of the warren, which my noble Lord, the Marquis of Carabas (for that was the title which Puss was pleased to give his master) has commanded me to present to your Majesty from him.'

'Tell thy master (said the King) that I thank him, and that he does me a great deal of pleasure.'

Another time he went and hid himself among some standing corn, holding still his bag open; and when a brace of partridges ran into it, he drew the strings, and so caught them both. He went and made a present of them to the King, as he had done before of the rabbits which he took in the warren. The King, in like manner, received the partridges with great pleasure, and ordered him some money to drink.

The cat continued for two or three months thus to carry his Majesty, from time to time, game of his master's taking. One day in particular, when he knew for certain that he was to take the air, along the riverside, with his daughter, the most beautiful princess in the world, he said to his master, 'If you will follow my advice, your fortune is made; you have nothing else to do, but go and wash yourself in the river, in that part I shall show you, and leave the rest to me.' The Marquis of Carabas did what the cat advised him to, without knowing why or wherefore.

While he was washing, the King passed by, and the cat began to cry out as loud as he could, 'Help, help, my Lord Marquis of Carabas is going to be drowned.' At this noise the King put his head out of the coach window and, finding it was the cat who had often brought him such good game, he commanded his guards to run immediately to the assistance of his Lordship the Marquis of Carabas.

While they were drawing the poor Marquis out of the river, the cat came up to the coach, and told the King that, 'While his master was washing there came by some rogues who went off with his clothes, though he had cried out, "Thieves! Thieves!" several times, as loud as he could.' This cunning cat had hidden them under a great stone. The King immediately commanded the officers of his wardrobe to run and fetch one of his best suits for the Lord Marquis of Carabas.

The King caressed him after a very extraordinary manner; and, as the fine clothes he had given him extremely set off his good mien (for he was well made and very handsome in his person), the King's daughter took a secret inclination to him, and the Marquis of Carabas had no sooner cast two or three respectful and somewhat tender glances, but she fell in love with him to distraction. The King would needs have him come into the coach, and partake of the airing. The cat, quite overjoyed to see his project begin to succeed, marched on before and, meeting some countrymen who were mowing a meadow, he said to them, 'Good people, you who are mowing, if you do not tell the King that the meadow you mow belongs to my Lord Marquis of Carabas, you shall be chopped as small as herbs for the pot.'

The King did not fail of asking of the mowers, to whom the meadow they were mowing belonged. 'To my Lord Marquis of Carabas,' answered they all together; for the cat's threats had made them terribly afraid. 'You see, Sir (said the Marquis), this is a meadow which never fails to yield a plentiful harvest every year.' The master cat, who went still on before, met some reapers, and said to them, 'Good people, you who are reaping, if you do not tell the King that all this corn belongs to the Marquis of Carabas, you shall be chopped as small as herbs for the pot.'

The King, who passed by a moment after, would needs know to whom all that corn, which he then saw, did belong. 'To my Lord Marquis of Carabas,' replied the reapers; and the King was very well pleased with it, as well as the Marquis, whom he congratulated thereupon. The master cat, who went always before, said the same words to all he met; and the King was astonished at the vast estates of my Lord Marquis of Carabas.

Monsieur Puss came at last to a stately castle, the master of which was an ogre, the richest that had ever been known; for all the lands which the King had then gone over belonged, with this castle, to him. The cat, who had taken care to inform himself who this ogre was, and what he could do, asked to speak to him, saying, 'he could not pass so near the castle without having the honour of paying his respects to him.'

The ogre received him as civilly as an ogre could do, and made him sit down. 'I have been assured (said the cat) that you have the gift of being able to change yourself into all sorts of creatures you have a mind to; you can, for example, transform yourself into a lion, or elephant, and the like.' 'This is true (answered the ogre very briskly), and to convince you, you shall see me now become a lion.' Puss was so sadly terrified at the sight of a lion so near him, that he immediately got into the gutter, not without abundance of trouble and danger because of his boots, which were of no use at all to him in walking upon the tiles. A little while after, when Puss saw that the ogre had resumed his natural form, he came down and owned he had been very much frightened.

'I have been moreover informed (said the cat), but I know not how to believe it, that you have also the power to take upon you the shape of the smallest animals; for example, to change yourself into a rat or a mouse; but I must own to you, I take this to be impossible.'

'Impossible! (cried the Ogre). You shall see that presently,' and at the same time changed himself into a mouse and began to run about the floor. Puss no sooner perceived this, but he fell upon him and ate him up.

Meanwhile the King who saw, as he passed, this fine castle of the ogre, had a mind to go into it. Puss, who heard the noise of his Majesty's coach running over the drawbridge, ran out and said to the King, 'Your Majesty is welcome to the castle of my Lord Marquis of Carabas.'

'What! My Lord Marquis (cried the King), and does this castle also belong to you? There can be nothing finer than this court, and all the stately buildings which surround it; let us go into it, if you please.' The Marquis gave his hand to the

Princess, and followed the King, who went up first. They passed into a spacious hall where they found a magnificent collation, which the ogre had prepared for his friends, who were that very day to visit him, but dared not enter, knowing the King was there.

His Majesty was perfectly charmed with the good qualities of my Lord Marquis of Carabas, as was his daughter who was fallen violently in love with him; and, seeing the vast estate he possessed, said to him, after having drunk five or six glasses, 'It will be owing to yourself only, my Lord Marquis, if you are not my son-in-law.' The Marquis, making several low bows, accepted the honour which his Majesty conferred upon him, and forthwith, that very same day, married the Princess.

Puss became a great lord and never ran after mice any more, only for his diversion.

The Totem of Amarillo

EMMA-LINDSAY SQUIER

PERHAPS you have heard me speak of Amarillo before. He was a yellow cat who came to us from out of the woods when Brother and I still lived in the little log cabin on the shores of Puget Sound. And he was, in those days, our very special friend. His coming to our home was most spectacular, and his departure was equally dramatic. As for the grand finale of his story, as I learned it from those who cared for him in his last years, it is so curious and hints so much of melodrama that I am afraid that some will doubt it. I offer in explanation of my belief that it is true, only the fact that Amarillo was always a most unusual cat. And the proof of it is that he is perpetuated for ever in the village of Old Man House in a totem pole, carved and painted. Only the truly great are thus honoured by the tribe of Skokomish.

Amarillo, the yellow one, was born, I think, in the woods. And I further believe that complete savagery was only a short generation behind him. For his ears were tufted as are the ears of a bobcat, and his eyes were slanted and amber so that, in moments of complete repose, he resembled a Chinese mandarin pleasantly absorbed in thought.

He had grown up in a region where the law was that only the strongest survived. He had fought many battles and won them, and so had grown to a size unbelievable in an ordinary cat, another fact which hinted strongly at a parentage having nothing to do with domesticity and quiet firesides.

Still, he had within him the instinct of association with man. For when he first came to us, his lovely fur all draggled and covered with blood, he was sorely hurt and dragged a torn and wounded leg. He mewed pitifully and crawled to us, yet was afraid to let us touch him, and sprang back spitting venomously. But the instinct that had brought him down from the woods to the little cabin, where he knew he would find succour for his hurt, finally made him accept us. He let us examine the wounded leg, suffered us to bathe it and anoint it with salve. Then, being completely unable to hunt or care for himself, he allowed us to extend to him the hospitality of our home. He came to love us, and adopted us, and when he was well he stayed with us and became our friend.

Now Brother and I were so fond of Amarillo, the yellow cat, that we saw none of his faults; and when they were called to our attention by the grown-ups, we made excuses for them and pretended that they did not matter. For he was our constant companion during the day and, when I slept out of doors on the camp bed, I would, sometimes during the night, hear his soft 'Prr-t,' which signified that he was about to jump up beside me, and then feel the thud of his soft, heavy body, as he leaped. But the grown-ups did not share our unqualified approval of Amarillo and his ways. For he, never having had any knowledge of civilization, did not know, and could not be taught, that chickens were to be respected, and not stalked and devoured whenever he happened to be hungry. Neither was it permissible that he should molest the pigeons, climb up to the nests and kill their young. So, after all persuasion had failed and many attempts at discipline, it was decreed that Amarillo must go. And Brother and I were very sad because of it.

It was not hard to find a new home for him. He was admired by all who saw him and many places were open to our choosing. But it was deemed best that he be given into the kindly care of a fisherman friend of ours. A huge, dark man with kindly smiling eyes, a man whose descent was traced from Indian and Spanish blood, and whose wife and kinsfolk were of the tribe of Skokomish. They lived in the far-off village of Old Man House, called by the Indians, Suquamish.

They would, we knew, be kind to Amarillo. They had no chickens or pigeons for him to kill unlawfully, and there were rats and much small game in the woods to satisfy his hunting instincts.

So, on the day set for his departure, we took our friend, the Yellow One, down to the fishing launch which anchored at our float, and it was with heavy hearts that we set a dish of milk for him upon the deck. We hoped that eating would occupy his attention and that he would not realize until too late that he was going away from us. The Indian fisherman shoved off very gently from the wharf and did not start the engine until the launch had drifted for a hundred feet or more. But when the whirring of the fly wheel startled Amarillo, and the churning of the propeller whirled the water into eddies of white and green – then he knew that he was being taken away without his will or knowledge.

He sprang to the gunwale and stood, for an instant, gazing out at us, his slanted, amber eyes wide with alarm. The Indian fisherman spoke to him soothingly and moved towards him with friendly hand outstretched. But it was too late. For Amarillo, without an instant's hesitation, had leaped. We saw the flash of his yellow body as he sprang and the splash as he sank from sight. We cried out, because we thought he would drown. But he had no idea of coming to such an inglorious end. For the next instant he was swimming towards us, easily, powerfully, his tufted ears flattened back on his head, his body a lithe, yellow streak in the blueness of the water. When he reached the float, he climbed upon it, sat down with perfect composure, and commenced to wash himself with great earnestness and poise. He appeared to think nothing whatsoever of the swim he had taken. And that day, because of our entreaties, he was allowed to remain with us.

But it was, we knew, only a stay of sentence. On the next day we bade our friend goodbye once more. This time the Yellow One was fastened in a sack and, when the launch started its chugging way out into the blueness of the bay, we saw the frenzied contortions of the burlap bag and dimly heard protesting yowls above the throbbing of the engine. We watched sadly from the float until the fishing launch was but a speck of black athwart the jutting greenery of the Point. Then it was lost to sight and we knew that Amarillo had gone from us for ever.

In the years that followed, we heard of our yellow friend

from time to time. Once the Indian fisherman chugged around the Point and into our tiny cove specially to give us news of him. And once the old fisherman, who made his home with us, put into the village of Suquamish to learn at first hand of Amarillo's welfare. We were assured, each time, that the Yellow One was well and happy, and that he had established a kingship among the lesser cats of the village so that there was none to dispute his authority. But the details of his tempestuous life I did not fully learn until, grown out of childhood and many years away from the country of grey waters and singing pine trees, I came back to the woods and waters of Puget Sound; found at Suquamish our beloved old fisherman, with no trace of time upon the pinkness of his cheeks or within the clear twinkling of his eyes; found, too, the Indian fisherman and his wife who had given Amarillo shelter; and learned from him, and from the blind boy who was their son, the story of the Yellow One's tragic, triumphant career.

Now, the blind boy was a carver of totems. And in the great darkness, where there was no light, he found solace in bringing to remembrance the strange, almost forgotten tales of the Indians of the Sound. He made them live again, cunningly carved into symbols upon pine poles, and he painted them carefully, under the watchful eye of those who could see. There is today, in the open square of the village, a totem pole that the blind boy made. Upon it is depicted the story of how Teet' Motl, with his sweetheart, Hoo Han Hoo, rode upon a dolphin's back towards a far country where the Great Spirit promised them rest and prosperity. Their progress was barred by a school of blackfish, those tigers of the water called by the Indians 'killers'. But the brave dolphin, with a word of encouragement to those upon his back, dived into the depths of the sea, scraping up pebbles in his mouth. Then there came a great storm, and Teet' Motl and Hoo Han Hoo crept into the dolphin's mouth for safety. Inside they found the shining pebbles scraped up by the giant fish. And when at last the storm abated, the dolphin had indeed brought them safely to a pleasant country, green with trees and fruitful with berries. The Indians who inhabited the country used for currency shining pebbles. And Teet' Motl and Hoo Han Hoo, having many of them, were rich and for ever prosperous. Even to this day, said the blind boy, when the killers come from the south, then a storm will rise. So he portrayed upon the totem Teet' Motl and his sweetheart safe in the belly of the dolphin.

It was while the blind boy still carved the story upon the totem pole that Amarillo was brought into the household. And curiously enough, it was to the child who lived in darkness that the Yellow One gave his love and never-ending loyalty. He liked very well indeed the Indian fisherman and his wife, who was of the tribe of Skokomish. He obligingly caught the rats that had formerly made merry under the cabin, and once in the dead of night he gave alarm of fire that had started from a chance spark, by mewing and rubbing his cold nose against the Indian fisherman's face. He repaid the hospitality they offered him with a friendship that was staunch and true. But it was only the blind boy that he loved – and I believe, and would have you believe, that it was because he knew of the darkness in which the blind boy lived, and because he knew that in some ways his friend was helpless.

But because he loved the little blind boy so well, Amarillo was jealous of everything to which he gave his attention. During the long evenings, when the blind boy carved the totem pole, the Yellow One would sit on the table beside him, watching with slanted amber eyes, while the childish, sensitive fingers crept over the long pine pole, feeling out with a sharp knife the contours of the dolphin, the killer blackfish, and the rude figures of Teet' Motl and his sweetheart. When Amarillo thought his friend given too much attention to the work of carving, he would reach out a padded, yellow paw and pat the blind boy's hand. If there was no response, he would yawn prodigiously, get up and stretch, and rub his broad back against the blind boy's face, deliberately walking on the pole, so that he could not carve. Then, if his friend persisted in his work, Amarillo would mew sharply, a little angry sound that ended in a snarl. He would switch his tail violently, jump down from the table with a loud thump, and sulk under the stove, refusing to come out for commands or cajoling words.

Now, Amarillo was not the only four-footed guest in the household of the Indian fisherman and his wife. The hospitality of their little cabin was offered freely to any living thing that needed shelter or aid, and there was rarely a time when they were not caring for some boarder from the wood who had come to grief. Once they found a pheasant's nest with the mother's dead body beside it, bullet-riddled, and the tiny, brown chicks scarcely out of their shells. They took the tiny things to their cabin and fed them so carefully that all of them lived, and would have grown eventually to adult pheasant-hood – had it not been for Amarillo.

At first, it was not difficult to keep the wee brown pheasant chicks secluded. They learned very soon to run briskly to the door of their wire coop when they heard a footstep approaching, and they were as friendly as if their parents had never lived in the wilds. Amarillo watched them with sullen, amber eyes, his tail twitching ever so little, his shoulder muscles moving slightly whenever he saw the baby pheasants running about in the safety of the wire enclosure. But he never attempted to molest them. And even when they grew so large that the coop was deemed too small to hold them comfortably, and so were permitted to roam at liberty, he did not try to pounce upon them – having perhaps in mind the punishment meted out to him at our cabin the day when he tried to kill the chickens.

But upon the day when the little blind boy made his way out to the wire enclosure and called to the pheasants, who came running to peck at the crumbs he held in his hand – upon that day did Amarillo declare war upon the brown invaders. Never did the Indian fisherman or his wife actually catch him doing violence to the pheasant boarders, but one by one they disappeared with only a bunch of feathers left to tell of their passing. And once the Yellow One came into the cabin with one tiny feather still hanging from his whiskers – he had forgotten to remove the evidence. It was the last feather of the last pheasant. So they spanked him soundly, and he snarled and spat, and ran away into the woods, and did not come back for two days, during which time the blind boy missed him sorely. When he returned, it was with sullen, padding steps, and his amber eyes were rather furtive as if he doubted whether he would be welcomed. But the family forgave him the pheasants, and made much of him, and the blind boy cried, holding the yellow cat close against his cheek. So Amarillo purred deeply, like an organ, and dug his toes comfortably into his friend's shoulders, and that night slept upon the blind boy's bed, unrebuked. For a week he would not let the child go out of his sight, but followed him like a dog, and every evening sat near him when he carved upon the totem pole.

It was soon after the incident of the pheasants that another woods friend was brought into the kindly care of the Indian fisherman and his wife. One day the Indian fisherman saw in the woods, near the village of Suquamish, a little lady racoon who had been caught in a trap such as they set for racoons in the Puget Sound country. A hole had been bored in a small log, and honeycomb had been put deep inside it. Then nails had been set in such a way that a racoon hand, reaching inside for the honeycomb, could not pull itself out without tearing the skin completely away. So the Indian fisherman found the racoon lady with one arm inside the hole, her bright eyes blinking worriedly through the black marking that ran completely across her face like a highwayman's mask. She was really very foolish to have kept her clutch on the honeycomb, for by releasing it and squeezing her little black hand together, she could have brought it through the nail barricade without mishap. But she wanted the honeycomb and so she kept her hold of it, thus keeping herself prisoner – as, indeed, those who set the trap knew she would do.

But the Indian fisherman could not bear to see the little lady racoon thus a captive. For she was soon to have babies. He drew out the nails, very carefully, while she stood rigidly alert to all he was doing, but stubbornly refusing to let go her hold on the sweetness that was in the hole. He slipped his hat over her; then, in her sudden alarm, she withdrew her hand, all sticky with honeycomb, and the Indian fisherman brought her to the cabin, wriggling and squeaking in protest.

He saw to it that she had a comfortable pen to live in, and all the family made much of her. By the time her tiny children were born, she was quite at home in her new environment, and accepted philosophically all the kindly attentions bestowed upon her.

They named her Betty, and her children were born in a box behind the kitchen stove. Soon afterwards she was put into a comfortable cage in the woodshed. But one day she escaped from the pen and came into the house, with her three babies following her in single file, their tails curled up high over their backs as if they had been taught just the correct way of holding them thus, and on every tiny face was a black mask through which bright eyes blinked in friendly curiosity at the new world in which they found themselves.

Now, Amarillo saw this strange procession with astonishment not unmixed with alarm. He had been away hunting in the woods when Betty was brought to the cabin and the Indian fisherman had taken care that he had had no access to her cage or to her box behind the kitchen stove. Certainly he had never seen a racoon baby, with a black mask on its face and its tail curling up neatly over its head. He leaped upon a chair and spat vigorously as the little procession trundled across the kitchen floor to a saucer of milk behind the stove. Betty took no notice of him and pursued her even course, her three babies following in a line, one directly behind the other.

Amarillo leaned over the edge of the chair and growled terrifically. Betty looked up at him from behind her highwayman's mask, and her eyes glittered at him. She showed a line of white, menacing teeth. The Yellow One continued to snarl deep in his throat, but made no move, except to settle down on his haunches and watch and speculate. If Betty and her babies had been out in the open, he would have set upon them without delay. But their presence in the kitchen disturbed him, made him vaguely uncertain as to their standing. For he had been punished many times for interfering with domestic friends. He licked his chops and continued to growl.

Then, suddenly, his temper getting the better of him – he sprang. The Indian Fisherman moved to protect the racoon lady, whose life he thought in peril. But Betty was quite capable of defending herself and her family. Although she had apparently given no heed to the yellow cat, yet she was ready for his pounce. She gave a shrill squeal and darted to one side so quickly that even Amarillo's swiftness was not equalled by it. Before the yellow cat could realize what had happened, she was upon him, her black little hands clutching at his neck, her sharp teeth digging through his thick fur and into the flesh beneath. Amarillo snarled and yowled with pain. He rolled over and over, seeking vainly to fasten his claws on the alert, darting body of the lady racoon. The racoon babies scuttled under the stove where they sat and peeped with bright, inquisitive eyes at the rolling, scrambling whirlwind of fur—yellow fur and brown. It was Amarillo who finally cried 'enough' in the unequal battle. His authority had been undisputed for such a long time that it made his surrender the more complete. He bolted for the open door, yowling in wholehearted terror, with Betty astride him like a jockey, her hands deep in his fur, her eyes viciously sardonic through the black highwayman's mask.

Amarillo finally rid himself of his unwelcome rider by rolling with despairing energy. Having freed himself, he climbed a tree, spitting at every step, and found shelter on a limb, very high above the ground, where he snarled and spat, and licked his wounds, and had many harsh and bitter thoughts towards racoons and the world in general.

Betty, on the other hand, took her victory with modest simplicity. She curled her tail high over her head and marched sedately back to the kitchen and her babies. And after taking a refreshing drink of milk from the saucer, she proceeded to give her children their lunch, while she tidied her disordered coat, pulling from it the bits of twigs and tufts of yellow fur that had clung to it in the battle.

Amarillo went away into the woods, as was his custom when insulted, and he stayed so long that the family feared that his nose had been put permanently out of joint. But he came back at last, very sulky and bad-tempered until he found that he was really welcomed, especially by the blind boy who had missed him greatly. So he purred and rolled on the floor like a kitten, and slept at night on the little boy's bed. The racoon family—who now lived under the house – he did not molest. Betty and her children came at will into the kitchen and the room adjoining, they even received food from the hand of the blind boy—and Amarillo did not seek to prevent them. Sometimes he would growl and spit softly, but when Betty glanced at him sharply from behind her menacing mask, he would blink and look away, and pretend that he had not said a word.

The racoons were very cleanly folk. There was a big pan of water for them always upon the black porch, and into it they would dip every morsel of food before they ate it. They would bathe regularly, too, sitting up around the pan like little, furry toys, dipping their black hands in the water and washing their faces and necks very daintily and properly. They knew where the Indian fisherman beached the flat-bottomed boat in which he carried fish to sell. It was his custom to leave a few small fish in it after the day's work, just for the pleasure of seeing Betty lead her children down through the woods to the gravelled shore, the four of them in single file with their tails curled over their heads, and all of them humming a curious little monotone of a song, such as racoons sing when they are journeying and are contented with life.

When the fall came the racoon babies, quite well grown by that time, went away, into the woods, and later Betty, too, slipped away, to be gone for the whole winter. They expected that she would return in the spring. But she did not, and they never knew what became of the intrepid little lady.

Her absence, as you can readily imagine, was no grief at all to Amarillo. His kingship was once more undisputed, and he was happy in the friendship of the Indian fisherman and his wife, and in the affection that the blind boy gave him. The two were more inseparable than ever. It was rarely now that the Yellow One went away to hunt in the woods. He preferred, instead, to remain with the little boy he loved, to follow when the child walked about in the yard with the halting, uncertain steps of those who cannot see, and to sleep on his bed at night.

In due course of time he found a lady cat to his liking, and he brought her to live at the cabin of the Indian fisherman. Only one kitten did the lady cat give birth to, a kitten who was almost as golden in colour as Amarillo himself. And Amarillo as a father, I am glad to say, emulated his savage ancestors rather than his immediate domestic forebears. He cared for the kitten much more tenderly than the mother cat did, for she proved after all to be a careless jade, totally unworthy of Amarillo's affections. Soon after her daughter was weaned she went away into the woods and the kitten, to whom the Indian fisherman gave the outrageous name of 'Whiskey Susan', grew up entirely under her father's supervision.

Whiskey Susan was the only one beside himself whom Amarillo would suffer the family to pet. He was not jealous of the affection they gave her, and even the blind boy could hold the snuggling, yellow kitten in his lap while he carved upon the totem pole, and Amarillo would sit on the table beside him, purring deep in his throat, his eyes closed to mere slits of contentment.

But one day, many months later, there came another, and this time a final, disturbing factor in the life of the Yellow One. The Indian fisherman had found a small mallard duck caught in the meshes of his nets, and one leg had been broken so that he floundered there, helpless, beating the water with his wings. The Indian fisherman released him gently and brought him to the cabin where his wife took kindly charge of the invalid, set the hurt leg in splints, and tended to his wants. It was upon the first evening of his stay that Amarillo, coming in from out-of-doors, spied the newcomer. The blind boy, who could not see the Yellow One's approach, was bending over the wounded duck, stroking him gently. And at the sight Amarillo hissed sharply – and sprang. His leap did no more than knock the astonished duck over on the floor, but the Fisherman's wife was impatient that her invalid should be so treated. She cuffed Amarillo sharply and he stared at her with furious, amber eyes, then laid his ears back on his head and trotted out of the house, his fur in thick, outraged ruffles, and headed straight for the woods.

He did not come back for one week, nor for the two weeks. And the blind boy grew daily more worried and more lonely. He took to wandering about the yard, calling for Amarillo, and when his mother was busy, so that he could not prevent him, he would feel his way through the gate and set off up the trail that led into the deep woods, walking very slowly with his hands outstretched before him, calling Amarillo's name, hoping that the yellow cat would hear and come to him.

Now, it was not safe to go alone or unarmed into the thickness of those forests, for many dangers lurked in the shadowed depths of them and many were the tales told of bold attacks made by cougars and bobcats driven down from the high mountains by hunger or forest fires. Yet always the blind boy came back safely, for he ventured only a little way and returned before his absence could be noticed.

But one day he slipped away, having acquired some confidence in his knowledge of the trail. He went farther and farther, calling to Amarillo with louder tones as he felt himself out of hearing distance from the cabin. The trail became rougher and was unfamiliar to his feet. But still he went on and, at last, he realized that there was a chill in the air that spoke of coming night. The woods were very still, with only the light dropping of pine needles to dot the silence, or the distant call of a heron flying to a tall pine-tree nest. A little frightened, the blind boy turned towards home. But his feet had lost their confidence. He turned into a ragged, wandering trail that led away from the true path. And as the night grew colder, and his feet stumbled over sprawling roots, and low-hanging branches struck his face, he knew that he was lost, lost and helpless.

Then he ceased to call for Amarillo, but sent up his voice in a thin, wavering cry such as the Indians use. It is a sound which carries clearly across great spaces, and the Indians know it for a signal of distress.

Down in the cabin it was nearly sunset before the absence ofthe blind boy had been discovered, for both the Indian fisherman and his wife were at work mending nets upon the beach. When evening came, and they returned home, they looked at each other with startled eyes, and a great fear was in their hearts. For they knew the menace of the dark woods behind them.

The Indian fisherman called the others of the tribe of Skokomish and, with that cunning that Indians possess, they found the child's light, halting footprints in the softness of the earth, and followed them into the forest, until it was too dark for them to see further.

They listened, and presently, from far away, a thin, wavering cry came to their ears. They responded mightily and plunged along the trail, the glimmering of their lanterns throwing dark, grotesque shadows on the path before them.

But suddenly they heard another cry, and they stood breathless for a moment, tingling cold with horror. For it was the savage, hunting cry of the bobcat – the cry he gives as he springs upon his prey.

Firing their guns and shouting fiercely, they set off at a run towards the direction from which the two cries – the call for help and the call of death – had come. It was easy to guide themselves so, for the woods were alive with the savage sounds of fighting – eerie screams that set the birds to twittering nervously and made the men grit their teeth with fear at what they should find.

When they turned down the ragged, wandering trail, they heard above the snarls and shrieks a child's voice sobbing in fear. And the gleam of the lanterns caught a wild tangle of blazing eyes, white, snapping teeth, and rolling, twisting, furry bodies upon the ground. The blind boy crouched in the ferns at the side of the trail and crawled towards them, his arms lifted to his unseen rescuers. His father caught him up with a fierce sobbing of breath. And there came a fusillade of shots barking viciously into the whirl of writhing bodies. There was a sharp, sudden silence. The bodies dropped down loosely, twitched for a moment, then lay still.

Then the child screamed sharply. 'Don't shoot,' he cried, 'don't shoot – you'll hurt Amarillo!'

The men stared. And for once the Indian fisherman was glad that his child could not see. For there before them, in the trail, lay the tawny, dead body of a bobcat its cruel claws clenched about the yellow body of a cat – the gallant body of Amarillo. The body of the Yellow One was torn almost to shreds, and he lay in a pool of blood. But the wildcat had suffered too, for Amarillo's teeth were buried in his throat and even death had not sufficed to loosen the hold.

They carried the poor, torn body very tenderly back to the cabin, and the blind boy sobbed on his father's shoulder. He told them later how, in that cold darkness, he had heard a light swishing of leaves, and then a well-known 'Prr-t,' which told him that Amarillo had heard him at last and was coming to him. But even as he had knelt, his arms outstretched to welcome the Yellow One to his heart, there had come a stirring in the branches over his head – and the wild, savage shriek of a bobcat. Then had come the leap that had knocked him upon his face. But before the bloodthirsty creature could spring again, Amarillo was upon him, fighting savagely, and the bobcat, surprised at the sudden attack, had fought back, for the moment forgetting the human prey whom he had stalked.

So it was that many years later, when I came to the village of Old Man House, known by the Indians as Suquamish, I found the old fisherman, and the Indian fisherman, and his wife who was of the tribe of Skokomish. I met the blind boy, grown now almost to manhood, and I saw in the open square of the village the totem telling the story of how Teet' Motl and Hoo Han Hoo found the promised land.

There, in the cabin yard, is a little grave. It bears no headstone, such as a white man would erect to a well-remembered friend. It has a nobler, more fitting monument of gratitude and love – a carved and painted totem pole. At the bottom of the totem is the fierce, snarling face of a wildcat with white, cruel fangs displayed. Over the snarling face sits the stolid figure of a mallard duck, with one leg stiffly wrapped in splints. Above this are two closed eyes – eyes that cannot see the light. And at the very top, in the place of honour, is the carved portrait of Amarillo himself – his yellow face benign and almost smiling – his tufted ears erect and alert . . .

If he could know this, I am sure he would be proud. For only the truly great are thus honoured by the tribe of Skokomish.

My Boss the Cat

PAUL GALLICO

IF YOU are thinking of acquiring a cat at your house and would care for a quick sketch of what your life will be like under *Felis domesticus*, you have come to the right party. I have figured out that, to date, I have worked for – and I mean *worked* for – thirty-nine of these four-legged characters, including one memorable period when I was doing the bidding of some twenty-three assorted resident felines all at the same time.

Cats are, of course, no good. They're chisellers and panhandlers, sharpers and shameless flatterers. They're as full of schemes and plans, plots and counterplots, wiles and guiles as any confidence man. They can read your character better than a $50-an-hour psychiatrist. They know to a milligram how much of the old oil to pour on to break you down. They are definitely smarter than I am, which is one reason why I love 'em.

Cat-haters will try to floor you with the old argument, 'If cats are so smart, why can't they do tricks, the way dogs do?' It isn't that cats can't do tricks; it's that they *won't*. They're far too hep to stand up and beg for food when they know in advance you'll give it to them anyway. And as for rolling over, or playing dead, or 'speaking', what's in it for pussy that isn't already hers?

Cats, incidentally, are a great warm-up for a successful marriage – they teach you your place in the household. The first thing Kitty does is to organize your home on a comfortable

basis – *her* basis. She'll eat when she wants to; she'll go out at her pleasure. She'll come in when she gets good and ready, if at all.

She wants attention when she wants it and darned well means to be let alone when she has other things on her mind. She is jealous; she won't have you showering attentions or caresses on any other minxes, whether two or four-footed.

She gets upset when you come home late and when you go away on a business trip. But when *she* decides to stay out a couple of nights, it is none of your darned business where she's been or what she's been up to. Either you trust her or you don't.

She hates dirt, bad smells, poor food, loud noises and people you bring home unexpectedly to dinner.

Kitty also has her share of small-child obstinacy. She enjoys seeing you flustered, fussed, red in the face and losing your temper. Sometimes, as she hangs about watching, you get the feeling that it is all she can do to keep from busting out laughing. And she's got the darndest knack for putting the entire responsibility for everything on *you*.

For instance, Kitty pretends that she can neither talk nor understand you, and that she is therefore nothing but a poor helpless dumb animal. What a laugh! Any self-respecting racket-working cat can make you understand at all times exactly what she wants. She has one voice for 'Let's eat,' another for wanting out, still a third for 'You don't happen to have seen my toy mouse around here, the one with the tail chewed off?' and a host of other easily identifiable speeches. She can also understand you perfectly, if she thinks there's profit in it.

I once had a cat I suspected of being able to read. This was a gent named Morris, a big tabby with topaz eyes who lived with me when I was batching it in a New York apartment. One day I had just finished writing to a lady who at that time was the object of my devotion. Naturally I brought considerable of the writer's art into telling her this. I was called to the telephone for a few minutes. When I returned, Morris was sitting on my desk reading the letter. At least, he was staring down at it, looking a little ill. He gave me that long, baffled look of which cats are capable, and immediately meowed to be let out. He didn't come back for three days. Thereafter I kept my private correspondence locked up.

The incident reminds me of another highly discriminating cat I had down on the farm by the name of Tante Hedwig. One Sunday a guest asked me whether I could make a cocktail called a Mexican. I said I thought I could, and proceeded to blend a horror of gin, pineapple juice, vermouth, bitters, and other ill-assorted ingredients. Pouring out a trial glass, I spilled it on the grass. Tante Hedwig came over, sniffed and, with a look of shameful embarrassment, solicitously covered it over. Everybody agreed later that she had something there.

Let me warn you not to put too much stock in the theory that animals do not think and that they act only by instinct. Did you ever try to keep a cat out that wanted to come in, or vice versa? I once locked a cat in the cellar. *He* climbed a straight, smooth cement wall, hung on with his paws (I saw the claw marks to prove it); unfastened the window-hook with his nose and climbed out.

Cats have fabulous memories, I maintain, and also the ability to measure and evaluate what they remember. Take, for instance, our two Ukrainian greys, Chin and Chilla. My wife brought them up on a medicine dropper. We gave them love and care and a good home on a farm in New Jersey.

Eventually we had to travel abroad, so Chin and Chilla went to live with friends in Glenview, Ill., a pretty snazzy place. Back in the United States, we went out to spend Thanksgiving in Glenview. We looked forward, among other things, to seeing our two cats. When we arrived at the house, Chin and Chilla were squatting at the top of a broad flight of stairs. As we called up a tender greeting to them, we saw an expression of horror come over their faces. 'Great heavens! It's those *paupers*! Run!' With that, they vanished and could not be found for five hours. They were frightened to death we had come to take them back to the squalor of a country estate in New Jersey, and deprive them of a room of their own in Illinois, with glassed-in sun porch, screens for their toilets and similar super-luxuries.

After a time they made a grudging appearance and consented to play the old games and talk over old times, guardedly. But when the hour arrived for our departure, they vanished once more. Our hostess wrote us that apparently they got hold of a timetable somewhere and waited until our train was past Elkhart before coming out.

It was this same Chilla who, one day on the farm after our big ginger cat, Wuzzy, had been missing for forty-eight hours, led us to where he was, a half mile away, out of sight and out of hearing, caught in a trap. Every so often Chilla would look back to see if we were coming. Old Wuz was half-dead when we got there, but when he saw Chilla he started to purr.

Two-Timing, or Leading the Double Life, is something you may be called upon to face with your cat. It means simply that Kitty manages to divide her time between two homes sufficiently far apart that each home-owner thinks she is his.

I discovered this when trying to check up on the unaccountable absences of Lulu II, a seal-point Siamese. I finally located her at the other end of the bay, mooching on an amiable spinster. When I said, 'Oh, I hope that my Lulu hasn't been imposing on you,' she replied indignantly, *'Your* Lulu! You mean *our* dear little Pitipoo! We've been wondering where she went when she disappeared occasionally. We do hope she hasn't been annoying *you*.'

The shocking part of this story, of course, is that, for the sake of a hand-out, Lulu, with a pedigree as long as your arm, was willing to submit to being called Pitipoo.

Of all things a smart cat does to whip you into line, the gift of the captured mouse is the cleverest and most touching. There was Limpy, the wild barn cat down on the farm who lived off what she caught in the fields. We were already supporting four cats, but in the winter, when we went to town, we brought her along.

We had not been inside the apartment ten minutes before Limpy caught a mouse, or probably *the* mouse, and at once brought it over and laid it at our feet. Now, as indicated before, Limpy had hunted to survive. To Limpy a dead mouse was Big and Little Casino, a touch-down home run and Grand Slam. Yet this one she gave to us.

How can you mark it up except as rent, or thanks, or 'Here, looka; this is the most important thing I do. You take it because I like you'? You can teach a dog to retrieve and bring you game, but only a cat will voluntarily hand over its kill to you as an unsolicited gift.

How come Kitty acts not like the beast of prey she is but like a better-class human being? I don't know the answer. The point is, she does it – and makes you her slave ever after. Once you have been presented with a mouse by your cat, you will never be the same again. She can use you for a door-mat. And she will, too.

La Ménagerie Intime

THÉOPHILE GAUTIER

IT IS no easy task to win the friendship of a cat. He is a philosopher, sedate, tranquil, a creature of habit, a lover of decency and order. He does not bestow his regard lightly, and, though he may consent to be your companion, he will never be your slave. Even in his most affectionate moods he preserves his freedom, and refuses a servile obedience. But once gain his confidence, and he is a friend for life. He shares your hours of work, of solitude, of melancholy. He spends whole evenings on your knee, purring and dozing, content with your silence, and spurning for your sake the society of his kind.

Minna Minna Mowbray

MICHAEL JOSEPH

AMONG ALL my cats, past and present, Minna Minna Mowbray was an outstanding personality. Except to a connoisseur of cats Minna was not physically impressive. She was a short-haired tortoiseshell tabby, with tiny white paws to match her piquant white face. Her head was small but beautifully shaped. The rather large ears were grey, and streaks of orange fur ran down between her amber eyes and on either side to the under part of her delicate jaw, forming a regularly designed tortoiseshell frame for her white face. A flash of coral pink was visible when she opened her dainty mouth. Her teeth were white and strong. The under part of her body was pure white and even in the soot and grime of London this was nearly always spotlessly clean. At kitten time it was dazzlingly white. This part of her was domestically known as her 'ermine'. When she was feeling particularly sociable, certain favoured members of the household were permitted, sometimes even encouraged, to massage it gently.

Minna was small, as cats go, but exquisitely proportioned. All her movements were graceful. She would sit upright, with her tiny forepaws close together, her long, rather full tail coiled round. Her favourite position for sleep was a crouch, the hind legs drawn up close and head resting on the outstretched forepaws which she converted into cushions by turning them inwards. Sometimes she preferred to lie on her side, legs outstretched luxuriously at queer angles. Various attitudes I learned to recognize as meditative (often assumed, this one), ecstatic, proud (both these when kittens were on view), majestically indignant (accompanied by business with tail), enquiring (as when she wanted to know what I was eating – this was primarily curiosity, for as often as not she rejected after close scrutiny the morsel I offered her) and leave-me-alone-please. This last was indicated by a haughty turning aside of her head; if this failed she would calmly turn her back and if *that* gesture had no effect she would walk off with the air of an offended dowager.

Like her mother, Lady Dudley, she had no voice, her vocal chord being partially paralysed. Oddly enough – for such a physical defect is presumably not hereditary – her kittens seldom cried, except when they were very young. Minna opened her mouth when, for instance, she wanted a door open, but no sound emerged. When she was greatly agitated about something a faint squeak was audible if you listened carefully. She could purr loudly enough but did not purr often. She could also swear, in delicate but determined fashion, but this again was reserved for special occasions.

Minna Minna Mowbray was a gentle cat. She never attempted to scratch a human. Babies and small boys could do what they liked with her. Like all self-respecting cats she disliked rough handling but she never attempted retaliation. If her tail were pulled or her long, sensitive whiskers touched she showed displeasure by asking silently to be allowed to go.

Contrary to expert advice, Minna wore a collar – an elegant green collar with an identity disc and two brass bells. A collar, I have heard, is undesirable because it may catch in the spikes of railings or the branches of a tree, but in my experience this risk is negligible if a cat is trained to a collar when very young. It is possible that a grown cat may so resent the introduction of a collar that he will try to drag it off and thereby injure himself, but I have never heard of an instance.

Minna was proud of her collar and plainly enjoyed wearing it. She put the bells to practical use, whenever she wanted to be admitted to a room, by shaking her head outside the closed door. She never worried if she were late for breakfast, knowing that the tinkle of her bell would cause the door to be opened. Sometimes when she rang outside the door I delayed, for the satisfaction of hearing her tinkle imperiously repeated. And with what an air of affronted majesty she stalked into the room if she had been thus kept waiting! Custom brought her to the dining-room at breakfast time, not hunger, for as often as not she turned up her aristocratic nose at the fish or milk offered her.

Minna also learned to summon her kittens by sounding her bells. When the babies got to the exploring stage and escaped from the maternal eye in house or garden Minna recalled them by an agitated peal. They usually answered the summons promptly but Minna would continue to ring until they did.

Minna could silence her bell as effectively as she could ring it. Not a sound was to be heard when she stalked a bird. What a waste of time it is to 'bell the cat' with the intention of suppressing natural instincts!

The real owner of my house in those days was Minna. She walked about with the manner of a landed proprietor surveying his domain; on the whole proud, but reserving the right to be critical. The day nursery and the kitchen were her favourite rooms. The dining-room and what my family insisted on calling 'the study' were frequently patronized. Her appearances in the other rooms were rare, with the exception of my bedroom in the winter when warm milk was usually to be coaxed from me last thing at night.

When she was younger the bathroom enchanted her. She soon discovered it to be a magic, fascinating and deliciously dangerous place with a queer contraption which was often filled with water. As a kitten, Minna used to insist on stalking round the edge of the bath when there was water in it, balancing precariously at the rounded corners. Running water fascinated her and she would play with a dripping tap for hours. Her mother, and some of Minna's own kittens, shared this fondness for running water; and so did my favourite Siamese, Charles. Micky Jos, one of Minna's most spirited kittens, had a passion for water and thoroughly enjoyed being soaked to the skin. But when she was grown up, with matronly responsibilities, Minna seldom played with water. It was beneath her dignity.

Another forsaken attraction in her middle age was the piano. As a kitten she took a great interest in it. As soon as it was opened she would jump on the keyboard. A series of spirited discords marked her progress from bass to treble and back again. She much preferred the bass, possibly because the deeper volume of sound or the stronger vibration took her fancy. But, as she grew up, Minna tired of the piano and took no notice of it.

Minna had a curious aversion to whistling. If I tried to whistle (it is not one of my accomplishments) Minna was at once agitated and tried to stop it by putting her paw on my lips. So long as I continued she behaved as one would expect an operatic tenor to behave within hearing of a mouth organ. It was not often that I outraged Minna's artistic susceptibilities but, when I did, her agitation was intense.

Flowers had a curious attraction for Minna. She could never resist nibbling at them. Spring flowers particularly; if not prevented she would drag daffodils and tulips to the ground for the aesthetic satisfaction of sampling their flavour at her leisure. It was not that she required vegetable diet for grass, which cats eat regularly when they can get it, was easily accessible. Minna's taste for flowers was not utilitarian.

If there was one thing Minna disliked more than any other it was preparation for a journey. As soon as suitcases were produced she made a prompt and plaintive appearance on the scene. Her agitation always increased when packing began. She would sit mournfully looking on while cupboards and drawers shed their contents, every now and then making a timid and reproachful attempt to interfere with our progress. Even the perfunctory packing of a suitcase for a weekend disturbed her. As for the wholesale removal of the family during the summer, that was a terrible ordeal. On one occasion, when boxes and cases were being brushed as a preliminary to their annual excursion, Minna, shaking her bell in protest, disappeared downstairs, to reappear a few minutes later with Peter, our wire-haired terrier. And then the pair of them sat gazing lugubriously at the signs of departure.

Minna, like most cats, disliked travelling. She had a very commodious basket (I was always annoyed by people who called it a dog basket) and entered it with a poor grace. Poor dear, she knew what was coming. However comfortably the basket was lined, the taxi jolted her up and down and the noise of passing traffic frightened her. The ignominy of being deposited on the platform of a railway station was bad enough, but worse was to follow. The train was the climax of her ordeal.

It was only when Minna was with me in a railway carriage that the sensation of being cooped up in a swiftly moving box oppressed me. To the more sensitive creature, who was my cat, the jolting, swaying movement of the small compartment which carried us so swiftly and mysteriously to an unknown destination must have been a paralysing torture. It was only then that I realized how uncomfortable even the most modern railway carriage is. Poor Minna! She would emerge timidly from her basket, grateful for release, but terrified of the unknown. Even in her fear curiosity compelled her to climb for a view of the rushing landscape. A glimpse was enough, and down on to the floor she would spring, crouching and panting, her little tongue hanging from her mouth like a signal of distress.

Only once do I remember Minna facing a railway journey with equanimity – and that, I am sure, was more apparent than real. On that occasion Minna was the proud mother of five kittens, who had also to be transported. The booking-office clerk stared when I told him I had six cats with me. When I added that they were infants in arms and enquired if there were any reduction on account of either age or quantity, or both, he grinned comprehendingly. I was mad, of course. He gave me one ticket and took my half-crown with cheerful tolerance. I betook myself and my cat basket off hastily before he could change his mind.

Minna, evidently determined to conquer her fears for the sake of her kittens, was remarkably self-possessed. She submitted without anxiety to imprisonment in the basket and made no fuss when it was lifted into the taxi and dumped on the floor. Not until the train was speeding southwards and she was allowed the freedom of the carriage did she betray her usual agitation. And then, I observed, only when she was well clear of the basket and its tiny occupants. On the seat beside me, snatching a furtive look out of the window from time to time, Minna went through the familiar performance of crying silently, appealing to me with a troubled paw to bring the dreadful and mysterious train to a standstill. But she had one eye all the time on the basket below and, at the first whimpering sound, she was back again, comforting her babies with soft maternal purring.

Minna was always an exemplary mother. But cats vary considerably in this respect. I have already mentioned Meestah, an earlier kitten of Lady Dudley's and therefore a half-sister to Minna. Meestah was worse than neglectful. Her nomenclature, by the way, was based on an Arab word meaning 'to hide', for she had a strange habit of hiding away in odd corners.

It was so long before Meestah became a mother that we began to think she would escape the destiny of female cats, but one day the family arrived – two beautiful kittens. Meestah was most resentful. She would have nothing to do with them. All our coaxing was of no avail. Fortunately, this was when I had fourteen cats. About nine of them were females and the kittens problem was rapidly becoming serious. But, luckily for Meestah's kittens, another of my large cat family accommodatingly had kittens just then and, as the litter was small, we were able to add Meestah's offspring to the new nursery. This was met with the complete approval of both mothers. Meestah was enormously relieved. That was her sole venture into motherhood. How Minna must have disapproved of her!

Minna adored having kittens. Indeed, a cynical friend once remarked that it was her life's work. Her kittens were invariably beautiful and never commonplace. Tortoiseshell tabby, orange, and prettily marked black and white were the usual arrivals, and there were often black flecked with bronze, and kittens mottled distinctively which I am at a loss to describe. Sometimes they were long-haired but usually they inherited the smooth, short-haired coat of their mother. Lest it be thought that I was prejudiced in their favour I must add that Minna's kittens excited admiration even in people usually indifferent to cats.

The fame of my Minna's kittens spread far and wide. Her offspring grew into handsome cats in households all over the country. As my work brought me into touch with a large number of authors, several of her kittens were transferred to literary ownership. Other kittens went to more modest family circles. Our milkman was a regular customer. He had been rather unlucky with his kittens and we cheerfully replaced them. The fishmonger begged for one which captivated him; and the little orange tabby which went to the greengrocer's wife was the recipient of so much affection that I am sure he did not begrudge the others the natural advantages of their respective establishments.

Several times we resolved to keep for ourselves a particularly charming kitten. There was Dinah, a fluffy, sentimental and very attractive young lady whom we brought from the country when we went to live in Regent's Park. I was especially fond of Dinah; whenever Minna held herself aloof – and that was often – Dinah could be depended on to stay purring blissfully on my knee. Dinah was as affectionate as she was decorative.

Not long after our arrival in London Dinah was reported missing. The usual frantic search followed, with no result. Dinah's virtues were magnified with the passing days and, when at last I had to admit there was no longer any hope of finding her, my loss seemed irreparable. I can write of my lost Dinah in this lighthearted way on account of what followed.

One Sunday morning, some weeks later, someone looking out of a window said, 'Isn't that Dinah?' I must explain that the back of our house faced the backs of a crescent of other houses, with small gardens abutting on each other. In these gardens were trees and on a low-lying bough there was a cat. It certainly did look like Dinah.

I ran down to the garden and, climbing on to the wall, made my way along until I was close enough to identify the cat. It *was* Dinah. She watched me coming and when I called her name looked down at me with mild interest. I noticed, with relief, that she had evidently been well fed and cared for. If she recognized me she did not show it. Balancing precariously, I tried to coax her down. Dinah took no notice. So, feeling rather foolish, I retired, in the vain hope that she would follow.

Then I had an inspiration. Dinah might have transferred her affections to another human being, but what about her mother? I dashed into the house, picked up Minna and returned to the garden wall. To reach the tree I had to pass along the tops of several garden walls, on some of which my neighbours had erected trelliswork, wire and such-like impediments. With Minna doing her best to escape it was no easy matter to negotiate these obstacles but, apart from blacking my hands and face and tearing my trousers on a nail, I completed the journey safely. I was confident that Dinah would eagerly come down as soon as she saw Minna; and that Minna would be overjoyed to find her lost baby.

I held Minna up in my arms, balancing on tiptoe, so that the two cats could see each other face to face. Dinah looked down on us with surprise, as if to remark what a strange world this was, with human beings performing antics with other cats on the tops of walls. Her innocent eyes looked at Minna with an expression which clearly said, 'I don't know you, madam, and I don't want to know you.' Minna, on the other hand, recognized her offspring at once. Was she overjoyed? Did she utter the crooning call, half purr, half squeak, with which she had always summoned her kittens? Not she. She spat viciously and began to swear under her breath, in a suppressed note of unmistakable feline hate. She kept it up in a steady crescendo until I lowered her on to the wall and let her go; and then she sprang to the ground, lashing her tail with fury.

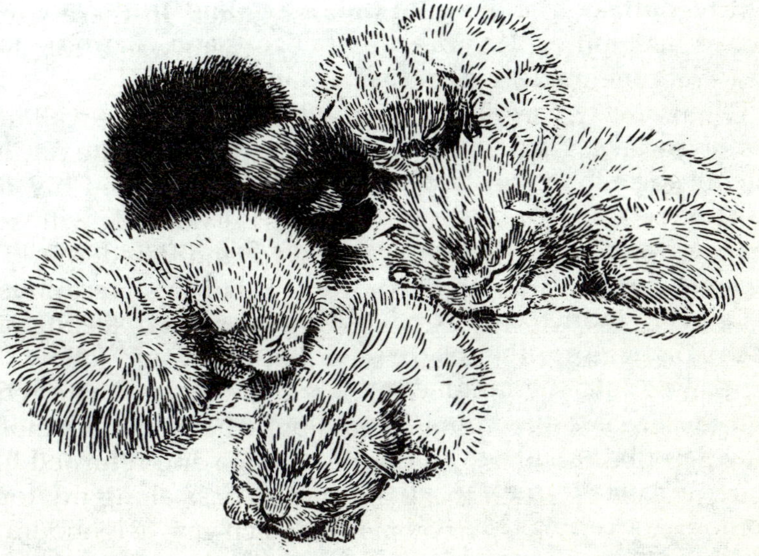

At the time I was amazed at this unmotherly behaviour. Dinah was still a kitten and only a few weeks before had been the apple of her mother's eye. It was inconceivable that she could have become a stranger in so short a time. I knew that grown cats fail to recognize their parents, and vice versa, but there was Minna behaving in a way most unnatural and offensive.

Later, I became suspicious. It dawned on me that there was something odd about these disappearances of favourite kittens. Whenever we tried to keep one of a litter, it invariably left us before it was many months old. Everyone who has had anything to do with cats knows how distressed the mother cat is when a kitten is lost or taken away, especially if it is the sole survivor of a litter. Now, it struck me as curious that Minna showed no anxiety when these mysterious departures occurred. We all searched high and low, but Minna was quite unconcerned.

It was when Fowey vanished that my suspicions were confirmed. Fowey (named after the Cornish seaport) was a mischievous orange rascal with china-blue eyes, the throatiest purr I have ever heard, an insatiable appetite and absurd fluffy paws which contrasted oddly with the dainty and aristocratic white feet of his mother. He was an intelligent and charming kitten and everyone made a great fuss of him.

When Fowey was about three months old, Minna took him for long walks. On one occasion I discovered them in a field by the railway a long way from the house. No doubt these expeditions were a source of delight to little Fowey, who wanted to see the world, but there seemed to me to be something sinister about them.

One day mother and son left the house together, Fowey as usual prancing with delight at the prospect of yet another expedition into the fascinating unknown. I watched them go, and there was a queer look in Minna's eye, a look which I can only describe as sinister. Maybe it was only my fancy but it was enough to make me ask at once for Fowey when I returned home that evening. My fears were realized; Minna was there, smirking triumphantly, I fancied, but Fowey was missing.

The days went by and Fowey did not return. We searched in vain. When I asked Minna she looked up at me with an expression so blandly innocent that I am sure she understood perfectly well what I was talking about. Now there is no doubt whatever in my mind that what happened was this. Minna took Fowey to some unfamiliar, deserted spot and there turned round and attacked her unsuspecting offspring. Most probably she said something like this to him:

'Look here, young Fowey (*bang*) you understand this (*scratch*). I'm the only cat wanted in Their house (*biff*) and I'm not (*scratch*) going to have you on the premises. (*Bite, scratch, bang*.) You go and find a home of your own. (*Spit*.) You're not wanted, d'you hear me? (*Bang, spit, bite, scratch, and general fireworks*.)'

No wonder poor Fowey beat a retreat like all the others! He reappeared a few weeks later in one of the gardens at the back and I discovered that he was lording it over one of the houses in the neighbouring crescent. He had grown into a magnificent cat with a long coat (carefully brushed, I was glad to note) and a huge plume of a tail which I could see daily fluttering in the trees when I was shaving in my bathroom. He was, to judge by appearances, a happy cat and played joyously in the gardens most of the day. But he never came into ours.

Minna was an expert in the art of getting her own way. I can recall only two occasions when she was defeated and then I think she allowed herself to be. The first occasion was the little matter of Peter's basket.

Peter belonged to my wife before I knew her and, incidentally, there were times when that dog made me feel as a second husband must feel when his wife describes the virtues of his predecessor. Who is this interloper? Peter seemed to say. Well, when Peter became part of the new *ménage* the basket came along too, but in the excitement of meeting Minna Minna Mowbray and the consequent revolution in his habits and ideas of home life, Peter apparently forgot about the basket.

My wife was upset. She said that Peter was so intelligent he wouldn't go to sleep anywhere but in his basket. (That was before she knew the change Minna could produce.) So it came about that Peter slept – I suspect uneasily – on the mat outside her bedroom door. Then one day my wife said, '*Poor* Peter! No wonder he looks unhappy. He hasn't got his basket.' So the basket was dug out of the pile of miscellaneous kit which was awaiting disposal in the new house, and was ceremoniously put outside the door for Peter's accommodation. I rather liked the look of it and reflected aloud, to my wife's indignation, that Minna Minna Mowbray could just do with a basket like that.

Peter wagged his stump, looked intelligent and barked. That night he occupied the basket according to plan. We knew something was wrong (from Peter's point of view) when he scratched at the door the next morning about an hour before his usual time. He came in with the air of an ill-used dog, his stump registering dejection.

We had not long to wait for the explanation. Shortly after tea Minna Minna Mowbray stalked upstairs and leisurely installed herself in the basket. By the time we turned off the radio and went upstairs to bed she was coiled up fast asleep (or ostensibly so) while Peter, squatting on the landing, regarded her balefully from a discreet distance.

That was the beginning of the basket war. The old Trojan War, the Hundred Years War, and the Great War faded into insignificance. Our household was promptly divided into two factions – the pro-Peterites, led by my wife, and the pro-Minnaites, which was me. The cook thought it was too bad, the parlourmaid echoed, 'Poor Peter.' It is true the postman grinned unsympathetically when he heard about it, but he and Peter are traditional enemies so that he was more anti-Peter than pro-Minna.

The fact that numbers were against her did not daunt my Minna. Her tiny stature was deceptive. In action she could give points to any Amazon. So that Peter's fugitive attempts to regain possession of his sleeping quarters are scarcely worth recording. Except perhaps the day when, bloated with tea and Dutch courage, he made a spirited attempt to get in while Minna dozed peacefully on the cushion. The battle was swiftly over; Peter emerged from the regions of the coal cellar only after an interval of two days and much coaxing.

Then other and more important domestic affairs took precedence over the Minna-Peter feud. While the rest of the household talked of other things it rumbled on in a state of trench warfare, with Minna securely dug in and Peter making occasional raids across no-man's-landing. Indeed, we all regarded the basket war as a permanent feature of our domestic life.

Actually it lasted for just over two years. Armistice was declared only when our baby daughter Shirley crawled out of the bedroom door, seized Minna by the scruff of her furry neck, neatly ejected her and solemnly climbed into the basket.

Peter was present at the ceremony and (presumably) gave a loud doggy guffaw. Minna withdrew with dignity. She then turned the day nursery into her sleeping quarters and Peter retired to the kitchen. The basket was 'reconstructed' after the war and for a long time was occupied by a teddy bear, a musical duck and a woolly rabbit. There was peace in our time.

The other occasion when Minna graciously surrendered was the advent of Charles O'Malley, my Siamese cat. I have written another book about Charles and I shall not say much about him here; although readers of that book may understand my feeling that this is Hamlet without the Prince of Denmark.

Charles O'Malley was the first Siamese I had had. Minna Minna Mowbray was furious when I brought him home and always looked upon him as an intruder. It was quite clear that she would never forgive me for adopting another cat. As for Charles himself, Minna at first swore and spat vigorously at his approach. But she soon decided to tolerate him and after a fortnight or so the two cats were drinking peaceably from the same saucer. Charles, as a ten-week-old kitten, was enormously impressed by Minna Minna Mowbray. No amount of bad language or threats deterred him from the pursuit of her tail but it was several weeks before Minna permitted him to play with her.

Charles O'Malley was aristocratically bred, and looked it. With his sapphire-blue eyes, delicate cream coat, chocolate-pointed ears, feet, tail and 'mask', he was a truly handsome creature.

There are differences between Siamese and other cats, apart from their shape and colouring. The Siamese voice is quite distinctive. When Minna first heard Charles's raucous squeak she visibly shuddered. Siamese cats have the reputation of being ferocious fighters; they are certainly stronger than ordinary cats. I do not think they are so graceful when walking or jumping. Indeed, Charles would land on his feet with a thud which was positively canine. Siamese are exquisite animals, however; sensitive, intelligent and responsive. Charles O'Malley (whom I confess I adopted partly to annoy Minna, who had been treating me very cavalierly at the time) was indeed a most lovable and charming cat and, as readers of his story* will know, he was destined to become my best loved cat.

However, no despot ever ruled his kingdom with more certainty of getting his own way than Minna Minna Mowbray did the house which we then lived in. It was a benevolent tyranny, this rule of Minna's; often amusing, never malicious, always sure and precise. She was clearly a believer in the divine right of cats, exercising her power with due regard to the niceties and obligations of her position.

To the uninitiated it may appear that I was merely foolish about my cat. However, I was not Minna's only subject. She bossed everyone in the house with the exception of my little daughter, Shirley, who occasionally did a bit of bossing herself. But Minna was quite happy about that. Shirley was privileged to stroke her fur the wrong way, to play with her tail and to carry her round the nursery suspended at all sorts of queer angles. I fancy that Minna rather enjoyed it all. Shirley was very fond of her and if Minna was accidentally hurt when they were playing together – this rarely happened, for Shirley knew she must be careful – the ensuing ceremony of contrite apology on the part of one and gracious forgiveness of the other was delightful to watch.

When Minna had kittens Shirley was a privileged visitor from the time of their birth. Minna allowed her to stroke them, knowing that Shirley would only touch them with gentleness. As soon as the babies reached the romping age Shirley was in her element. The nursery was transformed into an arena, in which young tigers leaped and raced swiftly in all directions, with Shirley's attempts at pursuit interrupted by her gurgles of excited laughter. Minna used to look on quite happily at these performances.

Like all cats who are happily accommodated in a human household Minna was a docile creature. But she insisted on having her own way. She would observe, with well-bred interest, my wife's painstaking preparations to provide her with a comfortable and secluded bed for her kittens. A large cardboard box, of the kind she loved, carefully lined with successive layers of newspaper, tissue paper and soft linen, and placed in one of her favourite cupboards, which was conveniently warm, well ventilated and discreetly dark – this was dutifully prepared at certain times by one of us. Whoever prepared her bed, however comfortably made and conveniently placed it might be, we could be sure of one thing – Minna would not use it.

Minna deceived several generations of interested cooks and house-parlourmaids by her tactics on these occasions. It was her custom to inspect at intervals the box or basket which had been so thoughtfully made ready for her, even to occupy it for forty winks every now and again as if to advertise her satisfaction. Many a beaming domestic servant announced the good news that 'Minnie is very pleased with her new box.' But these premature expectations were invariably disappointed. Minna knew what she was about. The attention of our expectant domestic staff being thus publicly drawn to a particular spot, Minna had her kittens elsewhere.

In this respect most cats, I believe, behave in the same independent way. Is it yet another survival of jungle instinct, this hiding away from prying eyes at important times? Or merely a gesture of independence, a rejection of our human proprietorship, a challenge to man and his stupid ways? Minna, although intensely secretive about her plans, made no further attempt at concealment when her kittens were born. She was then embarrassingly anxious that they should be seen and admired. In this I think she may have differed from other cats who, reasonably enough, do not like to be disturbed for some days. Minna, however, scorned further camouflage. She unmistakably invited us to pay our respects to the new arrivals. Nor did she object to their being touched. Our praise was clearly to her liking; she would purr loudly if we admired the little, squealing, almost invisible babies.

Naturally enough she would resent it if we overstayed our welcome, or if any stranger intruded on her privacy. And what a calamity if there should be any attempt to move her family! In that event, as soon as the coast was clear, Minna would remove them methodically, one by one, to what she obviously trusted would be a place less liable to disturbance. She was quite capable of registering a protest if disturbed by strangers; this usually took the form of depositing her kittens under the cover of my bed. There were times when I arrived home to find the house in a state of agitation because Minna and her kittens had disappeared. Nearly always they were to be found huddled together at the end of my bed comfortably asleep under the warm and sheltering darkness of the eiderdown.

Minna brooked no interference in her private affairs. At an early age she began to take an active interest in the opposite sex and all our well-meant efforts to influence her in the direction of a more lady-like modesty were frustrated. If the doors were shut she climbed out of a window. Nor were our attempts to find her a worthy husband any more successful. Whether the so-called attraction of opposites is responsible or not, it is a lamentable fact that Minna invariably chose the most disreputable gentleman friends. Any ugly, one-eyed, torn-eared tom-cat seemed to have an irresistible attraction for our Minna Minna Mowbray.

The uglier they were, the more eligible they appeared to be. She had, I remember, a disgraceful passion for an old roué with a lacerated tail, fractional ears, a permanently closed left eye and a pronounced limp. At his approach Minna behaved in a shameless and otherwise indescribable fashion. On such occasions I used to pretend she was not my cat.

When we were living in Surrey we did our best to reform her. It was not successful. Within a few days of our arrival the news had spread in some mysterious fashion that a new and comely lady cat had taken up her residence and that she had a decided preference for experienced lovers. Somehow Minna had made it known to the cats of all Surrey (and part of Sussex, too, I fancy) that she liked to choose her followers from the ranks of the veterans and middle-aged. She had no use for boy friends, it appeared.

We discovered this, and were considerably humiliated thereby, when we introduced her to a young orange cat from a neighbouring house. As soon as we set eyes on this cat, we decided that here was an ideal husband for Minna. He was a strikingly handsome cat, young and, so far as we could see, perfectly eligible. Minna, however, thought not. She promptly spat at him in a most unladylike way. Our candidate let us down badly. He fled for his life. After that we left Minna to her own devices – and to the reprobate toms of the neighbourhood.

To look at Minna Minna Mowbray as she sat demurely on the arm of my chair, her little white paws set neatly together in a modest pose, you would never imagine that she favoured the toughs and tramps of the tom cat world. In every other respect she was fastidious to the point of absurdity. She would refuse to drink from a saucer that was not spotlessly clean; would spend hours industriously making her toilet, until every hair was in its proper place; insisted on her milk being at exactly the right temperature; and objected to being touched, making a pretence of exquisite discomfort if I happened to stroke her when she didn't feel like it or to lay hands, however gently, on any part of her sensitive anatomy. Yet, ten minutes later, she could be observed (if you cared to gaze on the unedifying spectacle) in the garden below, being rolled playfully about in the mud by a caveman lover from the slums of Camden Town.

The Slum Cat

ERNEST THOMPSON SETON

LIFE I

THE LITTLE slum kitten was not six weeks old yet, but she was alone in the old junk-yard. Her mother had gone to seek food among the garbage-boxes the night before, and had never returned, so when the second evening came she was very hungry. A deep-laid instinct drove her forth from the old cracker-box to seek something to eat. Feeling her way silently among the rubbish she smelt everything that seemed eatable, but without finding food. At length she reached the wooden steps leading down into Jap Malee's bird store underground at the far end of the yard. The door was open a little, and she walked in. A Negro sitting idly on a box in a corner watched her curiously. She wandered past some rabbits; they paid no heed. She came to a wide-barred cage in which was a fox. He crouched low; his eyes glowed. The kitten wandered, sniffing, up to the bars, put her head in, sniffed again, then made straight toward the feed-pan, to be seized in a flash by the crouching fox. She gave a frightened 'mew', and the Negro also sprang forward, spitting with such copious vigour in the Fox's face that he dropped the kitten and returned to the corner, there to sit blinking his eyes in sullen fear.

The Negro pulled the kitten out. She tottered in a circle a few times, then revived, and a few minutes later, when Jap Malee came back, she was purring in the Negro's lap, apparently none the worse.

Jap was not an Oriental; he was a full-blooded Cockney; but his eyes were such little accidental slits aslant in his round, flat face that his first name was forgotten in the highly descriptive title of 'Jap'. He was not especially unkind to the birds and beasts which furnished his living, but he did not want the slum kitten.

The Negro gave her all the food she could eat and then carried her to a distant block and dropped her in an iron-yard. Here she lived and somehow found food enough to grow till, weeks later, an extended exploration brought her back to her old quarters in the junk-yard and, glad to be at home, she at once settled down.

Kitty was now fully grown. She was a striking-looking cat of the tiger type. Her marks were black on a pale grey, and the four beauty spots of white, on nose, ears and tail-tip, lent a certain distinction. She was expert now at getting a living, yet she had some days of starvation and had so far failed in her ambition to catch a sparrow. She was quite alone, but a new force was coming into her life.

She was lying in the sun one September day when a large black cat came walking along the top of a wall in her direction. By his torn ear she recognized him at once as an old enemy. She slunk into her box and hid. He picked his way gingerly, bounded lightly to a shed that was at the end of the yard, and was crossing the roof when a yellow cat rose up. The black tom glared and growled; so did the yellow tom. Their tails lashed from side to side. Strong throats growled and yowled. They approached with ears laid back, with muscles a-tense.

'Yow – yow – ow,' said the black one.

'Wow – w – w —' was the slightly deeper answer.

'Ya – wow – wow – wow —' said the black one, edging up an inch nearer.

'Yow – w – w —' was the yellow answer, as the blond cat rose to full height and stepped with vast dignity a whole inch forward. 'Yow – w,' and he went another inch, while his tail went swish, thump, from one side to the other.

'Ya – wow – yow – w,' screamed the black in a rising tone,

and he backed the eighth of an inch as he marked the broad, unshrinking beast before him.

Windows opened all around, human voices were heard, but the cat scene went on.

'Yow – yow – ow,' rumbled the yellow peril, his voice deepening as the other's rose. 'Yow,' and he advanced another step.

Now their noses were but three inches apart; they stood sidewise, both ready to clinch, but each waiting for the other. They glared at each other for three minutes in silence, and like statues, except that each tail-tip was twisting.

The yellow began again. 'Yow – ow – ow,' in deep tone.

'Ya-a-a-a,' screamed the black with intent to strike terror by his yell, but he retreated one-sixteenth of an inch. The yellow walked up a whole long inch; their whiskers were mixing now; another advance, and their noses almost touched.

'Yo – w – w,' said yellow like a deep moan.

'Ya-a-a-a-a,' screamed black, but he retreated a thirty-second of an inch, and the yellow warrior closed and clinched like a demon.

Oh, how they rolled and bit and tore – especially the yellow one!

How they pitched and gripped and hugged – but especially the yellow one!

Over and over, sometimes one on top, sometimes the other, but usually the yellow one, and over they rolled till off the roof, amid cheers from all the windows. They lost not a second in that fall into the junk-yard; they tore and clawed all the way down, but especially the yellow one; and when they struck the ground, still fighting, the one on top was chiefly the yellow one; and before they separated both had had as much as they wanted, especially the black one! He scaled the wall and, bleeding and growling, disappeared, while the news was passed from window to window that Cayley's 'Nig' had been licked by 'Orange Billy'.

Either the yellow cat was a very clever seeker, or else slum Kitty did not hide very hard, for he discovered her among the boxes and she made no attempt to get away, probably because she had witnessed the fight. There is nothing like success in warfare to win the female heart, and thereafter the yellow tom and Kitty became very good friends, not sharing each other's lives or food – cats do not do that much – but recognizing each other as entitled to special friendly privileges.

When October's shortening days were on an event took place in the old cracker-box. If 'Orange Billy' had come he would have seen five little kittens curled up in the embrace of their mother, the little slum Kitty. It was a wonderful thing for her. She felt all the elation an animal mother can feel – all the delight – as she tenderly loved them and licked them.

She had added a joy to her joyless life, but she had also added a heavy burden. All her strength was taken now to find food. And one day, led by a tempting smell, she wandered into the bird cellar and into an open cage. Everything was still, there was meat ahead, and she reached forward to seize it; the cage door fell with a snap and she was a prisoner. That night the Negro put an end to the kittens and was about to do the same with the mother when her unusual markings attracted the attention of the bird man, who decided to keep her.

LIFE II

Jap Malee was as disreputable a little Cockney bantam as ever sold cheap canary birds in a cellar. He was extremely poor, and the Negro lived with him because the 'Henglishman' was willing to share bed and board. Jap was perfectly honest, according to his lights, but he had no lights and there is little doubt that his chief revenue was derived from storing and restoring stolen dogs and cats. The fox and the half a dozen canaries were mere blinds. The 'Lost and Found' columns of the papers were the only ones of interest to Jap, but he noticed and saved a clipping about breeding for fur. This was stuck on the wall of his den and, under its influence, he set about making an experiment with the slum cat. First he soaked her dirty fur with stuff to kill the two or three kinds of creepers she wore and, when it had done its work, he washed her thoroughly. Kitty was savagely indignant, but a warm and happy glow spread over her as she dried off in a cage near the stove, and her fur began to fluff out with wonderful softness and whiteness. Jap and his assistant were much pleased. But this was preparatory. 'Nothing is so good for growing fur as plenty of oily food and continued exposure to cold weather,' said the clipping. Winter was at hand, and Jap Malee put Kitty's cage out in the yard, protected only from the rain and the direct wind, and fed her with all the oil cake and fish heads she could eat. In a week the change began to show. She was rapidly getting fat. She had nothing to do but get fat and dress her fur. Her cage was kept clean, and Nature responded to the chill weather and oily food by making Kitty's coat thicker and glossier every day so that, by Christmas, she was an unusually beautiful cat in the fullest and finest of fur with markings that were at least a rarity.

Why not send the slum cat to the show now coming on?

"T'won't do, ye kneow, Sammy, to henter 'er as a Tramp Cat, ye kneow,' Jap observed to his help; 'but it kin be arranged to suit the Knickerbockers. Nothink like a good noime, ye kneow. Ye see now, it had orter be "Royal" somethink or other – nothink goes with the Knickerbockers like "Royal" anythink. Now, "Royal Dick" or "Royal Sam": 'ow's that? But 'owld on: them's tom names. Oi say, Sammy, wot's the noime of that island where you were born?'

'Analostan Island, sah, was my native vicinity, sah.'

'Oi say, now, that's good, ye kneow. "Royal Analostan," by Jove! The onliest pedigreed Royal Analostan in the howle sheow, ye kneow. Ain't that capital?' and they mingled their cackles.

'But we'll 'ave to 'ave a pedigree, ye kneow;' so a very long fake pedigree on the recognized lines was prepared.

One afternoon Sam, in a borrowed silk hat, delivered the cat and the pedigree at the show door. He had been a barber, and he could put on more pomp in five minutes than Jap Malee could have displayed in a lifetime, and this, doubtless, was one reason for the respectful reception awarded the Royal Analostan at the cat show.

Jap had all the Cockney's reverence for the upper class. He was proud to be an exhibitor but when, on the opening day, he went to the door he was overpowered to see the array of carriages and silk hats. The gateman looked at him sharply but passed him on his ticket, doubtless taking him for a stable boy to some exhibitor. The hall had velvet carpets before the long rows of cages. Jap was sneaking down the side row, glancing at the cats of all kinds, noting the blue ribbons and the reds, glancing about but not daring to ask for his own exhibit, inwardly trembling to think what the gorgeous gathering of fashion would say if they discovered the trick he was playing on them. But he saw no sign of slum Kitty.

In the middle of the centre aisle were the high-class cats. A great throng was there. The passage was roped and two policemen were there to keep the crowd moving. Jap wriggled in among them; he was too short to see over, but he gathered from the remarks that the gem of the show was there.

'Oh, isn't she a beauty!' said one tall woman.

'Ah! what distinction!' was the reply.

'One cannot mistake the air that comes only from ages of the most refined surroundings.'

'How I should like to own that superb creature!'

Jap pushed near enough to get a glimpse of the cage and read a placard which announced that 'The Blue Ribbon and Gold Medal of the Knickerbocker High Society Cat and Pet Show had been awarded to the thoroughbred pedigreed Royal Analostan, imported and exhibited by J. Malee, Esquire, the well-known fancier. Not for sale.' Jap caught his breath; he stared – yes, surely, there, high in a gilded cage on velvet cushions, with two policemen for guards, her fur bright black and pale grey, her bluish eyes slightly closed, was his slum Kitty, looking the picture of a cat that was bored to death.

Jap Malee lingered around that cage for hours, drinking a draught of glory such as he had never before known. But he saw that it would be wise for him to remain unknown; his 'butler' must do all the business.

It was slum Kitty who made that show a success. Each day her value went up in the owner's eye. He did not know what prices had been given for cats and thought that he was touching a record pitch when his 'butler' gave the director authority to sell the cat for $100.

This is how it came about that the slum cat found herself transferred to a Fifth Avenue mansion. She showed a most unaccountable wildness, as well as other peculiarities. Her retreat from the lap dog to the centre of the dinner-table was understood to express a deep-rooted, though mistaken, idea of avoiding a defiling touch. The patrician way in which she would get the cover off a milk-can was especially applauded, while her frequent wallowings in the garbage-pail were understood to be the manifestation of a little pardonable high-born eccentricity. She was fed and pampered, shown and praised, but she was not happy. She clawed at that blue ribbon around her neck till she got it off; she jumped against the plate glass because that seemed the road to outside; and she would sit and gaze out on the roofs and back yards at the other side of the window and wish she could be among them for a change.

She was strictly watched – was never allowed outside – so that all the happy garbage-pail moments occurred while these receptacles of joy were indoors. But one night in March, as they were being set out a-row for the early scavenger, the Royal Analostan saw her chance, slipped out of the door, and was lost to view.

Of course there was a grand stir, but pussy neither knew nor cared anything about that. Her one thought was to go home. A raw east wind had been rising and now it came to her with a particularly friendly message. Man would have called it an unpleasant smell of the docks, but to pussy it was a welcome message from her own country. She trotted on down the long street due east, threading the rails of front gardens, stopping like a statue for an instant, or crossing the street in search of the darkest side. She came at length to the docks and to the water, but the place was strange. She could go north or south; something turned her southward and, dodging among docks and dogs, carts and cats, crooked arms of the bay and straight board fences, she got in an hour or two into familiar scenes and smells and, before the sun came up, she crawled back, weary and footsore, through the same old hole in the same old fence, and over a wall into her junk-yard back of the bird cellar, yes, back into the very cracker-box where she was born.

After a long rest she came quietly down from the cracker-box towards the steps leading to the cellar, and engaged in her old-time pursuit of seeking for eatables. The door opened and there stood the Negro. He shouted to the bird-man inside:

'Say, Boss, come hyar! Ef dere ain't dat dar Royal Ankalostan comed back!'

Jap came in time to see the Cat jumping the wall. The Royal Analostan had been a windfall for him; had been the means of adding many comforts to the cellar and several prisoners to the cages. It was now of the utmost importance to recapture Her Majesty. Stale fish heads and other infallible lures were put out till pussy was induced to chew at a large fish head in a box trap. The Negro, in watching, pulled the string that dropped the lid, and a minute later the Analostan was again in a cage in the cellar. Meanwhile, Jap had been watching the 'Lost and Found' column. There it was: 'Twenty-five dollars reward,' etc. That night Mr Malee's 'butler' called at the Fifth Avenue mansion with the missing cat. 'Mr Malee's compliments, sah.' Of course, Mr Malee would not be rewarded, but the 'butler' was evidently open to any offer.

Kitty was guarded carefully after that but, so far from being disgusted with the old life of starving and glad of her care, she became wilder and more dissatisfied.

The spring was on in full power now and the Fifth Avenue family were thinking of their country residence. They packed up, closed house and moved off to the summer home some fifty miles away, and Pussy, in a basket, went with them.

The basket was put on the back seat of a carriage. New sounds and passing smells were entered and left. Then a roaring of many feet, more swinging of the basket, then some clicks, some bangs, a long, shrill whistle, and door-bells of a very big front door, a rumbling, a whizzling, an unpleasant smell; then there was a succession of jolts, roars, jars, stops, clicks, clacks, smells, jumps, shakes, more smells, more shakes, big shakes, little shakes, gases, smoke, screeches, door-bells, tremblings; roars, thunders, and some new smells, raps, taps, heavings, rumbling and more smells. When at last it all stopped the sun came twinkling through the basket lid. The Royal Cat was lifted into another carriage and they turned aside from their past course. Very soon the carriage swerved, the noises of its wheels were grittings and rattlings, a new and horrible sound was added – the barking of dogs, big and little, and dreadfully close. The basket was lifted, and slum Kitty had reached her country home.

Everyone was officiously kind. All wanted to please the Royal Cat, but, somehow, none of them did, except possibly the big, fat cook that Kitty discovered on wandering into the kitchen. That greasy woman smelt more like a slum than anything she had met for months and the Royal Analostan was proportionately attracted. The cook, when she learned that fears were entertained about the cat's staying, said: 'Shure, she'd 'tind to thot; wanst a cat licks her futs shure she's at home.' So she deftly caught the unapproachable Royalty in her apron and committed the horrible sacrilege of greasing the soles of her feet with pot grease. Of course, Kitty resented it; she resented everything in the place; but, on being set down, she began to dress her paws and found evident satisfaction in that grease. She licked all four feet for an hour, and the cook triumphantly announced that now 'shure she's be apt to sthay'; and stay she did, but she showed a most surprising and disgusting preference for the kitchen and the cook and the garbage-pail.

The family, though distressed by these high-born eccentricities, were glad to see the Royal Analostan more contented and approachable. They guarded her from every menace. The dogs were taught to respect her; no man or boy about the place would have dreamed of throwing a stone at the famous pedigreed cat, and she had all the food she wanted, but still she was not happy. She was hankering for many things, she scarcely knew what. She had everything – yes, but she wanted something else. Plenty to eat and drink – yes, but milk does not taste the same when you can go and drink all you want from a saucer; it has to be stolen out of a tin pail when one is pinched with hunger, or it does not have the tang – it is not milk.

How pussy did hate it all! True, there was one sweet smelling shrub in the whole horrible place – one that she did enjoy nipping and rubbing against it; it was the only bright spot in her country life.

One day, after a summer of discontent, a succession of things happened that stirred anew the slum instincts of the Royal prisoner. A great bundle of stuff from the docks had reached the country mansion. What it contained was of little moment, but it was rich with the most piquant of slum smells. The chords of memory surely dwell in the nose, and pussy's past was conjured up with dangerous force. Next day the cook left through some trouble. That evening the youngest boy of the house, a horrid little American with no proper appreciation of Royalty, was tying a tin to the blue-blooded one's tail, doubtless in furtherance of some altruistic project, when pussy resented it with a paw that wore five big fish-hooks for the occasion. The howl of down-trodden America roused America's mother; the deft and womanly blow she aimed with her book was miraculously avoided and pussy took flight, upstairs, of course. A hunted rat runs downstairs, a hunted dog goes on the level, a hunted cat runs up. She hid in the garret and waited till night came. Then, gliding downstairs, she tried the screen doors, found one unlatched and escaped into black August night. Pitch black to man's eyes, it was simply grey to her, and she glided through the disgusting shrubbery and flower-beds, had a final nip at that one little bush that had been an attractive spot in the garden, and boldly took her back track of the spring.

How could she take a back track that she never saw? There is in all animals some sense of direction. It is low in man and high in horses, but cats have a large gift, and this mysterious guide took her westward, not clearly and definitely, but with a general impulse that was made definite because the easiest travel was on the road. In an hour she had reached the Hudson River. Her nose had told her many times that the course was true. Smell after smell came back.

At the river was the railroad. She could not go on the water; she must go north or south. This was a case where her sense of direction was clear: it said 'go south'; and Kitty trotted down the footpath between the iron rails and the fence.

LIFE III

Cats can go very fast up a tree or over a wall, but when it comes to the long, steady trot that reels off mile after mile, hour after hour, it is not the cat-hop but the dog-trot that counts. She became tired and a little footsore. She was thinking of a rest when a dog came running to the fence near by and broke out into such a horrible barking close to her ear that pussy leaped in terror. She ran as hard as she could down the path. The barking seemed to grow into a low rumble – a louder rumble and roaring – a terrifying thunder. A light shone; Kitty glanced back to see, not the dog, but a huge black thing with a blazing eye, coming on yowling and spitting like a yard full of tom cats. She put forth all her power to run, made such time as she never had made before, but dared not leap the fence. She was running like a dog – was flying, but all in vain: the monstrous pursuer overtook her, but missed her in the darkness, and hurried past to be lost in the night, while Kitty sat gasping for breath.

This was only the first encounter with the strange monsters – strange to her eyes – her nose seemed to know them, and told her that this was another landmark on the home trail. But pussy learned that they were very stupid and could not find her at all if she hid by slipping quietly under a fence and lying still. Before morning she had encountered many of them, but escaped unharmed from all.

About sunrise she reached a nice little slum on her home trail and was lucky enough to find several unsterilized eatables in an ash-heap. She spent the day around a stable. It was very like home, but she had no idea of staying there. She was driven by an inner craving that was neither hunger nor fear, and next evening set out as before. She had seen the 'One-eyed Thunder-rollers' all day going by, and was getting used to them. That night passed much like the first one. The days went by in skulking in barns, hiding from dogs and small boys, and the nights in limping along the track, for she was getting footsore; but on she went, mile after mile, southward, ever southward – dogs, boys, roarers, hunger – dogs, boys, roarers, hunger – but day after day with increasing weariness on she went, and her nose from time to time cheered her by confidently reporting, 'This surely is a smell we passed last spring.'

So week after week went by, and pussy, dirty, ribbonless, footsore and weary, arrived at the Harlem Bridge. Though it was enveloped in delicious smells she did not like the look of that bridge. For half the night she wandered up and down the shore without discovering any other means of going south excepting some other bridges. Somehow she had to come back to it; not only its smells were familiar, but from time to time when a 'One-eye' ran over it there was the peculiar rumbling roar that was a sensation in the springtime trip. She leaped to the timber stringer and glided out over the water. She had got less than a third of the way over when a 'Thundering One-eye' came roaring at her from the opposite end. She was much frightened but, knowing their blindness, she dropped to a low side beam and there crouched in hiding. Of course, the stupid monster missed her and passed on, and all would have been well but it turned back, or another just like it, and came suddenly roaring behind her. Pussy leaped to the long track and made for the home shore. She might have got there, but a third of the red-eye terrors came roaring down at her from that side. She was running her hardest, but was caught between two foes. There was nothing for it but a desperate leap from the timbers into – she did not know what. Down – down – down – plop! splash! plunge – into the deep water, not cold, for it was August, but oh! so horrible. She spluttered and coughed and struck out for the shore. She had never learned to swim, and yet she swam, for the simple reason that a cat's position and attitude in swimming are the same as her position and attitude in walking. She had fallen into a place she did not like; naturally she tried to walk out, and the result was that she swam ashore. Which shore? It never fails – the south – the shore nearest home. She scrambled out all dripping wet, up the muddy bank and through coal-piles and dust-heaps, looking as black, dirty and unroyal as it was possible for a cat to look.

Once the shock was over the Royal pedigreed slummer began to feel better for the plunge. A genial glow without from the bath, a genial sense of triumph within, for had she not outwitted three of the big terrors?

Her nose, her memory and her instinct of direction inclined her to get on the track again, but the place was infested with the big thunder-rollers, and prudence led her to turn aside and follow the river bank with its musky home reminders.

She was more than two days learning the infinite dangers and complexities of the East River docks, and at length, on the third night, she reached familiar ground, the place she had passed the night of her first escape. From that her course was sure and rapid. She knew just where she was going and how to get there. She knew even the most prominent features in the dogscape now. She went faster, felt happier. In a little while she would be curled up in the old junk-yard. Another turn and the block was in sight –

But – what – it was gone. Kitty could not believe her eyes. There, where had stood, or leaned, or slouched, or straggled – the houses of the block – was a great broken wilderness of stone, lumber and holes in the ground.

Kitty walked all around it. She knew by the bearings and by the local colour of the pavement that she was in her home; that there had lived the bird-man, and there was the old junk-yard; but all were gone, completely gone, taking the familiar odours with them; and pussy turned sick at heart in the utter hopelessness of the case. Her home love was her master mood. She had given up all to come to a home that no longer existed, and for once her brave little spirit was cast down. She wandered over the silent heaps of rubbish and found neither consolation nor eatables. The ruin had covered several of the blocks and reached back from the water. It was not a fire. Kitty had seen one of these things once. Pussy knew nothing of the great bridge that was to rise from this very spot.

When the sun came up Kitty sought for cover. An adjoining block still stood with little change, and the Royal Analostan retired to that. She knew some of its trails, but once there was unpleasantly surprised to find the place swarming with cats that, like herself, were driven from their old grounds, and when the garbage-cans came out there were several cats to each. It meant a famine in the land and pussy, after standing it a few days, set out to find her other home in Fifth Avenue. She got there to find it shut up and deserted, and the next night she returned to the crowded slum.

September and October wore away. Many of the cats died of starvation or were too weak to escape their natural enemies. But Kitty, young and strong, still lived.

Great changes had come over the ruined blocks. Though silent the night she saw them, they were crowded with noisy workmen all day. A tall building was completed by the end of October, and slum Kitty, driven by hunger, went sneaking up to a pail that a Negro had set outside. The pail, unfortunately, was not garbage, but a new thing in that region, a scrubbing-pail – a sad disappointment, but it had a sense of comfort: there was a trace of a familiar touch on the handle. While she was studying it the Negro elevator boy came out again. In spite of his blue clothes his odorous person confirmed the good impression of the handle. Kitty had retreated across the street. He gazed at her.

'Sho ef dat don't look like de Royal Ankalostan – Hya, pussy – pussy – pussy – pus-s-s-y, co-o-ome – pus-s-s-y, hya! I specs she's sho hungry.'

Hungry! She had not had a real meal for a month. The Negro went into the hall and reappeared with a portion of his own lunch.

'Hya, pussy, puss – puss – puss.' At length he laid the meat on the pavement and went back to the door. Slum Kitty came, found it savoury; sniffed at the meat, seized it, and fled like a little tigress to eat her prize in peace.

LIFE IV

This was the beginning of a new era. Pussy came to the door of the building now when pinched by hunger, and the good feeling for the Negro grew. She had never understood that man before. Now he was her friend, the only one she had.

One week pussy caught a rat. She was crossing the street in front of the new building when her friend opened the door for a well-dressed man to come out.

'Hell, look at that for a cat,' said the man.

'Yes, sah,' answered the Negro; 'dat's ma cat, sah; she's a terror on rats, sah. Hez 'em 'bout cleaned up, sah; dat's why she so thin.'

'Well, don't let her starve,' said the man, with the air of a landlord. 'Can't you feed her?'

'De liver-meat man comes reg'lar, sah, quatah dollar a week, sah,' said the Negro, realizing that he was entitled to the extra fifteen cents for 'the idea'.

'That's all right; I'll stand it.'

Since then the Negro has sold her a number of times with a perfectly clear conscience, because he knows quite well that it is only a question of a few days before the Royal Analostan comes back again. She has learned to tolerate the elevator and even to ride up and down on it. The Negro stoutly maintains that once she heard the meat man while she was on the top floor and managed to press the button that called the elevator to take her down.

She is sleek and beautiful again. She is not only one of 400 that form the inner circle about the liverman's barrow, but she is recognized as the star pensioner as well.

But in spite of her prosperity, her social position, her Royal name and fake pedigree, the greatest pleasure of her life is to slip out and go a-slumming in the gloaming, for now, as in her previous lives, she is at heart, and likely to be, nothing but a dirty little slum cat.

Come, Lovely Cat

CHARLES BAUDELAIRE

Come, lovely cat, and rest upon my heart,
  And let my gaze dive in the cold
Live pools of thine enchanted eyes that dart
  Metallic rays of green and gold.

My fascinated hands caress at leisure
  Thy head and supple back, and when
Thy soft electric body fills with pleasure
  My thrilled and drunken fingers, then

Thou changest to my woman; for her glance,
  Like thine, most lovable of creatures,
Is icy, deep, and cleaving as a lance.

  And round her hair and sphinx-like features
And round her dusky form float, vaguely blent,
  A subtle air and dangerous scent.

Childhood of Miss Churt

F. R. BUCKLEY

MISS CHURT – British, like everyone else aboard the *Malvern* – sat on the storm sill of the galley and with glazed eyes surveyed the North Atlantic.

Miss Churt was meditating sombrely on the rump steak the cook had given her. 'Eat it up, Kitty; good!' the cook had said, and Miss Churt had followed the suggestion.

Now – although the steak had been delicious – Miss Churt was experiencing certain qualms; a sensation, as of cannon balls in the midriff, had assailed her. . . .

Miss Churt decided that she would get a little fresh air and drop in on her friend Mr Wharton.

She dropped from her perch and, with tail at its meridian height, walked unsteadily toward the cuddy stairway.

The *Malvern* was moving unsteadily also, and likewise because of a heavy feeling in the midriff; caused not by cannon balls but by much more modern munitions of war. Never on very cordial terms with her rudder, she had now been be-shelled and be-packing-cased and be-airplane-parted until she would just as soon go anywhere as anywhere else, and was constantly trying to do so.

In a room on the boat deck, the first officer and the chief engineer were discussing this phenomenon and others related to the comfort and well-being of the ship's company. Mr McIvor, who was naturally the engineer, had joined in New York and was absorbing pessimism from Mr Wharton.

'He's a kind of mixed product of the flu and the board room,' said the first mate, alluding to his captain. 'He's – well, you saw him.'

'I saw *something*,' said Mr McIvor, cautiously.

'That'd be him. Chairman's nephew; on the beach for years; war come along – old Stokes gets flu – hand o' Providence – an' here I am sayin' "Aye, aye, sir!" to *that*. If he'd got eyelashes I wouldn't mind it so much, but – '

Mr McIvor nodded, and his unclean pipe said, 'Cluck, cluck.'

'Have any trouble comin' over?'

'Subs, you mean? Naw. Hello, sweetheart! Hello! Come to see Poppa?'

Mr McIvor, thunderstruck, made an instinctive motion to smooth his hair, but it was only Miss Churt. Mr Wharton went over, picked her up out of the aperture of the hooked door and before sitting down again on his berth spread a month-old newspaper carefully on the carpet. The page uppermost bore a picture of Lady Somebody's wedding to Captain Gossakes-Whosis of the guards; Mr Wharton, bending with Miss Churt sprawled over his palm, surveyed orange blossoms, smiles, teeth, tonsils and the arch of swords with a nitric eye.

'There, sweetheart,' he said, putting Miss Churt down on them.

'You a morried mon?' asked Mr McIvor.

'Nah. But I *will* be. That's her.'

The engineer rolled an eye at the picture on the bureau.

'Nice gurrul.'

'You said it. Canon Hobson an' all. Speakin' of cannon, have you seen our 4.7 on the poop deck?'

'To my grief. But what's this', said Mr McIvor, whose intake of personal news was disproportionate to his output, 'aboot a canon? The young leddy's no got a smash on um?'

'On old Hobson? Not *that* kind,' said Mr Wharton; and his look made Mr McIvor wonder whether he should have asked. 'Fact is – that's a good little sweetheart! Come to Poppa! 'At's a girlie!'

'Ye seem fond o' yon kitten.'

'I'm mad about her. And she's just wild about Harry, aren't you, pet?'

Miss Churt licked a gnarled and knotted hand. It tasted

something like the rump steak, flavoured with tar, salt, tobacco and Mallinson's Wonder Ointment for superficial cuts and bruises. . . .

'Then whaur *does* this canon come in?'

'All the girls round our way in Liverpool are mad about him. See – he had us all in Sunday school; children's choral guild, he called it; us boys got away after we'd been confirmed, of course, but you can believe it or not, I've never been the swearer I ought to have.'

'I noticed that when we was warpin' into the stream,' said Mr McIvor. 'I thocht maybe ye was a nance.'

A sudden squeezing of Miss Churt's ribs evoked a mew.

'Did I hurt ums bellah?' asked Mr Wharton. 'Dere Snuzzle down, a good girlie; such a full ickle tummy . . . Ho, you did, hah?'

'Until we met,' said Mr McIvor in haste. 'But – he canna be a young mon, this parson?'

'Canon,' said Mr Wharton. 'Naw, an' he's no beauty neither. But he's the bee's knees so far's Annie's concerned, an' she's goin' to be married by him or nobody, so so far it's been nobody – an' now they go an' put this pink-whiskered nincompoop in over my head – '

'What's it matter who morries ye? It takes no longer than havin' a tooth out.'

'Ho, doesn't it? That's where *you* drop your tow. Old Hobson's strong for the ritual and all that; and that means veils an' orange flowers for Annie an' a top hat an' tails for me.'

'But not in wartime!'

'How do *you* know?'

'I'd go,' said Mr McIvor after reflection, 'an' see the old mon an' say "Fush!" to um.'

'You would *not*,' said Mr Wharton darkly, 'not if you saw him. He's only five foot six, but I've seen him sober, an' askin' for coffee. He's got one o' those kissers you carve out o' granite with a road drill. Looks something like you.'

The chief engineer considered this judicially, and put his glass down.

'Awheel,' he said, rising. 'It's the wull o' Allah, I suppawse, that some of us should be morried an' hae bairns, while ithers lovish their possions on tobby cots. Guid nicht, Mr Wharton.'

In the doorway he turned to see the burst of this Glaswegian bomb. Miss Churt, who had been awakened by something that felt like an earth tremor, blinked at him and went to sleep again.

'We've naval ratings aboard to work yon gun?' McIvor asked, to cover his more morbid curiosity.

'We have,' said Mr Wharton, 'an' if anybody asks you who's in command o' that gun crew, it's me. Naval reserve.'

'You bein' in turn commanded by Captain Timbs. Weel – guid nicht.'

'You heard about that timber ship gettin' torpedoed?' Wharton asked.

'No. What was that?'

'Oh, just that they thought she mightn't have sunk properly, an' be derelict hereabouts. Timbs has been radioin' everybody bar Churchill an' President Roosevelt, but nobody's seen her. Dark night, too. Well – pleasant dreams.'

A certain pensiveness marked Mr McIvor's departure but the first mate seemed to feel better.

He extracted Miss Churt gently from the land of nod, held her up with forelegs dangling, treated her to a gigantic smile and kissed her unhygienically on the nose.

'Azza booful girlie!' said Mr Wharton. 'You like Poppa go home to his other girl an' get married, please, an' zen you have lovely house an' garden to scratch in?'

Miss Churt was exceedingly drowsy; moreover that rump steak seemed still to be clogging her articulation. She opened her pink mouth, but no sound issued.

'I'll bet you,' said Mr Wharton. 'And that reminds me – '

He had just risen to pick up the newspaper with the wedding on it when from for'ard, out in the starry dark, there came a thunderous crash.

The *Malvern* stopped in her tracks like a dowager smitten in the breadbasket.

Simultaneously, the lights went out.

It was, of course, that derelict, floating bottom up at what the French so prettily call the flower of the water, or, in Anglo-Saxon sea talk, awash.

Having accomplished the destiny given her by those heavenly lights overhead – Neptune afflicted by Mars, perhaps; who knows? – and buckled the *Malvern*'s blunt bows backward like the bellows of a concertina, the timber ship rolled, spewed a few hundred thousand board feet from a new gash and sank; while down behind the forepeak of the *Malvern*, Mr Wharton and a number of nearly naked shipmates strove to save their tub from doing likewise.

It was a question of strengthening a bulkhead, and strengthening bulkheads is uneasy work in the pitch dark.

It was an hour before Mr McIvor and his horde got the uprooted dynamo going again; and then what was revealed by hand lights led into the hold was the reverse of encouraging.

Not only was the bulkhead spouting water through the holes of deracinated rivets; it was bulging bodily and visibly inward, so that it was obvious that no time remained for carpenter work and fancy shoring.

Mr Wharton's eyes, under a mop of embattled hair, shuttled desperately about the hold. The port and starboard sides were solid-packed with minor munitions, forming admirable buttresses for the wings of the forward wall. But in the midst stood two cases that had taxed the stevedores; they were large and heavy enough to have contained whippet tanks, and the *Malvern*'s notorious instability had caused them to be stowed well aft of the bulkhead.

The space between was filled with this and that, in packets weighing mere hundreds of pounds.

'Get that junk out o' the way!' roared Mr Wharton. 'C'mon, boys!'

He himself was about to seize a crate when the third mate grabbed his shoulder.

'I say – Wharton – '

'The hell you do. Muck in an' shift something. I'm going' to shove these locomotives up, or whatever they are'.

'Listen! The Old Man's in a sweat of funk – sendin' out SOS till the ether's got clots in it – '

'To hell with him!'

'An' now he's getting ready to abandon ship.'

Mr Wharton disposed of his current crate and dashed forward to cut the key case out of a jam. Somehow or other his shirt had disintegrated, and his trousers consisted of but a breechclout and one leg, but still he was not swearing.

Canon Hobson, at that moment asleep in far-off Liverpool, his craglike nose in a soft pillow made for him by a parishioner, would have been gratified could he have known.

'What are you going' to do?' demanded the third officer. 'He's got all the ship's papers ready, an' he says his duty's to his men, an' unless we get help by dawn he's gonna take to the boats.'

'If you don't get outa my dog-rammed way we won't be afloat till dawn,' said Mr Wharton. 'Hey – '

'But you got to stop him!'

'An' risk my ticket – mutiny? No, sir; I obey – get that stuff movin,' you bunch o' lobsters! Come along aft here, you knobeyed slackers – want me to shove this myself? You Fawdry – you Wilson – '

A cleared space now lay between the bulkhead and the first tank, which, of course, was not really a tank, it just felt like one. Anyway, the problem was to get it up to that bulkhead – and the other one up behind it, if possible. And the bulkhead was remarking, in the language of tortured steel, that it would be damned if it was going to wait for such support much longer.

'You can't shift 'em,' said the third mate weakly, 'an' if you do, you'll shove her bow down an' we'll slide.'

'Like the *Tornado* at Coney Island,' gasped Mr Wharton, grinning.' "Down went McGinty" – ready, boys? Line up, get your shoulders against it. It's shove or grow gills! Now – one – two – '

The case didn't move.

'The Old Man says – ' gasped the third mate.

'Give us a shanty,' grunted one of the men; and Mr Wharton obliged. It might almost be said that out of the fullness of the heart the mouth spoke. It could hardly be called singing, and the verbiage was bald and incomplete; yet in topicality, direction and – yes – the passion of love denied, Mr Wharton's shanty might have claimed kinship with the romances of the troubadours.

'Ca-a-a-ptain Ti-i-i-mbs,' he emitted in a wavering roar, 'is a son of a – *heave*!'

The men had had their leave stopped in Staten Island.

'Ca-a-a-ptain Ti-i-i-mbs,' they agreed fulsomely, 'is a son of a – *heave*!'

The case budged.

'Ca-a-a-ptain Timbs – *heave*!'

It moved six inches.

' – son of a – *heave*!'

Six inches more.

Up on the bridge, the subject of the shanty was talking to three naval ratings who seemed not to like him. They were the men responsible for the 4.7 aft, and they seemed to be suffering from the spirit of Nelson, or Collingwood or somebody.

All they did about it, though, was to say they didn't think –

'You don't have to think!' said Captain Timbs.

'You're not our officer, sir,' said the senior rating.

'You're under my orders! If I say to abandon ship, we'll abandon ship!'

This made it the turn of the junior rating.

'Aye, aye, sir,' said he. 'If you say so.'

Captain Timbs swallowed a large and visible lump in the throat. 'That's the order,' he said. 'Soon's it's dawn. We're ripped wide open.'

'Roughish sea, sir,' said the senior rating impassively.

'I've got a Swedish freighter on the radio – she'll be here by then, standing by. Who the hell are you, questioning my orders?'

'Nobody, sir,' said the second rating.

'Get to hell out!'

'Aye, aye, sir,' said the third; and out they went.

What they said as they went below is nobody's business; such low speculations about the sums payable by government to bereaved ship owners; so much plain, vulgar swearing. One may, however, make extracts to the extent that the senior remarked that dawn was breaking already; the second said that the old gal felt like taking the high dive, at that; while the junior, peering aft, remarked sentimentally that anyhow she'd go down with her flag up and her gun shotted.

'Might go an' fire her off for once,' said he.

'Might go down an' give Wharton a hand,' said his senior severely; and so they did.

Some time later, Miss Churt, whose rump steak had filled slumber with dreams of gigantic rats chasing her down unending alleyways, awoke with a start and a bad taste in her mouth.

She yawned and decided that a little fresh air, again, would do her good. Jumping down from the settee, she found that the floor was not exactly where she had left it – it sloped downward now, and before she could correct her stance her for'ard legs had given way and she had rolled into a corner.

Picking herself thence, and reaching the door-sill, she rolled forth in search of company. It was light, so she gave the yawn and stretch by which cats thank God for each night spent in shelter – but something appeared to be wrong.

Where was everybody, to start with?

And why wasn't the deck vibrating as it always had, except just before and after mother left? And then the cargo winches had been working, with a roar that set one's ears back; now there was stillness – and behold! as one crossed behind the charthouse the bulwark of boats was gone and the wind smote one unimpeded.

Just some ropes trailing . . .

Miss Churt walked forward a few more paces and sat down, like the treble clef in a musical stave. Far in the misty distance she could see a ship standing still; and as for the *Malvern*'s boats, they were on the water – swimming, actually, and swimming away from her.

And in one of them, along with the three naval ratings and some other able-bodied gentlemen who disapproved of Captain Timbs and were saying so, Mr Wharton was at this identical moment remembering that he had left Miss Churt aboard.

'Noah's nails!' he ejaculated; and Canon Hobson, still sleeping, smiled in his distant dreams. 'Why – '

The oars lifted.

'Forgot something, sir?' asked the senior rating.

'Forgotten something?' said Mr Wharton. 'I've left my cat behind!'

From the bow of the boat came an imperfectly stifled chuckle.

'You laugh at me and I'll put a head on you,' said the first officer; and silence redescended on the ocean.

'Want to go back, sir?'

'I – think I will,' said Mr Wharton. 'If we're to save our dirty hides when there's no need to, I don't see why a poor dumb animal should suffer. Unless these gentlemen object? Pull stabbud, back port! Come on, you bunch of tailors!'

'Captain's boat's stopped rowin', sir,' said the bow oar.

'Ne'er mind,' said Mr Wharton, 'we can rat just as well in ten minutes' time. An' that Swede can wait. Some expensive nephew for – c'mon, put some beef into it!'

A distant hail came over the water – which, by the way, was now astonishingly calm.

'I'll just swarm up the falls an' be back in a jiffy,' said Mr Wharton – not knowing that a mile the other side of the *Malvern* the sea, hidden from him by the wallowing bulk of that ship, was just being broken by the conning tower of a submarine.

Her commander, a pleasant enough fellow named Koenig, usually resident in Munich, Glocknergasse No. 8, had heard the frantic distress signals wirelessed by Captain Timbs and had wondered if perchance they might portend something in his line of business. There was, he knew, a temporary scarcity of destroyers in this area, but the event was turning out better than his hopes. Through the periscope he had watched the crew abandoning ship, and, when the *Malvern* failed to slide precipitately out of sight, had commented soul-ticklingly to his men on the unsea-to-dare-worthiness of British sailors.

That this was no Q-ship he was well assured, both by the presence of the Swedish ship and the perilous trim of the *Malvern* herself. So it was his intent to combine business with pleasure by letting the fleeing crew watch him use their vessel for target practice. He thought he would use percussion fuse and blow the funnel out of her first.

As the submarine came awash her gun crew tumbled up, ran for'ard and proceeded to clear their gun.

And simultaneously, the longing gaze of Miss Churt was gratified by the spectacle of Mr Wharton, shaggier than ever. Miss Churt liked shagginess, it gave one more corners to nestle in.

Her master, landing on the boat deck from the falls, didn't seem as cheery as usual; something seemed to be bothering him; he didn't smile.

But Miss Churt knew how to remedy that. When anybody looked sad, she ran away, and Mr Wharton ran after her and picked her up and called her a little devil and corrected himself and said 'weevil' and kissed her on the end of the nose.

Miss Churt therefore ran away now, skidding slightly because of the slant of the deck; her ears cocked for the sound of beloved footsteps pursuing.

And here they came.

But here came something else.

Something terrible. A long, increasing noise, coming out of the middle of a distant thump, boring into her ears – so terrifying – and then – a vast flash of light, taking up the whole world and tearing it to pieces, shaking her stomach so that the steak didn't matter any more. . . .

Mr Wharton, rushing from behind the wireless house, paused a moment.

He saw a very large scorched hole in the boat deck planking, around which he had to pick his way.

While thus engaged, he saw Captain Koenig's submarine, lying perhaps three quarters of a mile off.

But what he was looking for was a small ball of soiled fur; and this he found, very limp, just for'ard of the bridge deck ladder. The curious thing is that Captain Koenig also adored cats, and had three at home in the Glocknergasse.

But that's war.

Mr Wharton took up in his very large hand what war had left of Miss Churt, and he laid the other hand over her like the lid of a little coffin and cursed Captain Koenig and his superiors and inferiors; and then he lifted both his arms and, still holding the limp form in his right hand, raised in a voice that almost carried the distance.

Indeed – in St Mary's Rectory, Canon Hobson awoke with a start; looked at his bedside clock and found it was 5.25; rolled over – but somehow was disinclined to go to sleep again.

'You bloody, sneaking *bloody* butcher!' Mr Wharton was now shouting; and there came a sudden crack in his voice. 'My little – '

A voice spoke from just behind him. It had not seemed quite proper to the naval ratings that their officer should go aboard without escort, so they had swarmed up the falls also and here they were. The voice was the voice of the senior rating, as was proper.

'How about giving 'em a packet, sir?' he inquired.

Mr Wharton had forgotten the 4.7 gun aft. Now he remembered and gave a perfect snarl of assent.

The body of Miss Churt he crammed into the side pocket of his coat; and then down the ladder he went, and after him came the ratings.

They had to descend another ladder and cross the aft welldeck and then climb the poop; and it was now that Captain Koenig saw them.

With a welter of ow sounds and a swamp of terminations in ch, he directed his men to shift target and give Wharton *et al.* a packet; so that the question resolved itself roughly into one of who should give whom a packet first.

The U-boat, being in the groove, got her shot off the earlier; but the hastily altered aim was high and the shell went to miss the Swedish ship by no more than half a mile. (Memorandum of 27 March 1940, paragraph 2.)

Meantime, the senior rating had done various manipulations of various things; and now, with a nod of the head, he expressed himself satisfied. Quite unnecessarily, he looked at Mr Wharton, opened his mouth and was just about to ask if he should open fire when the officer (not a regular navy man, of course) shoved him aside, seized the firing lever and got the shot off himself.

It was just luck, blind luck, for all concerned; but the fact remains that the unconventional, almost illegitimate, shell flew as through a tube to the barrel of the U-boat's gun, bent it, zoomed thereoff without touching Captain Koenig or his men, and smote the lip of the conning tower, where it exploded with the abandon peculiar to high explosive.

Nobody was hurt, save Seaman Albrecht Otto of Bremen (deafness and scratches) – but the conning tower was impossible to close. That meant no submersion –

And on the southern sky line there had appeared, and was approaching, a smudge of smoke, which betokened destroyers. The ratings pointed this out to one another.

Meanwhile Mr Wharton, at the other rail, was expressing his completely berserk opinion of Captain Timbs and all men who would take to boats leaving cats on perfectly sound ships full of badly needed munitions.

This expression, in addition to blistering (if the third officer may be believed) the paint on the thwarts of Lifeboat No. 1, left Mr Wharton rather exhausted. And softened in mood.

He put his hand into his pocket and pulled out the mortal envelope of Miss Churt. The bluish eyes were closed, the furry head rolled on the neck, and all her whiskers had been singed away.

'You want us to come back, sir?' came a hail from the boats.

'You can go to hell!' roared Mr Wharton; so they started toward him.

But a voice pitched to carry a quarter of a mile is tremendous at close range.

Miss Churt vibrated in every cell.

Her stomach began to trouble her again. There was a familiar smell in her nostrils, seeping past the stench of burned whiskers – tobacco, tar and Mallinson's –

She opened her eyes and said: 'Mew!'

For all it was wartime, the parish church of St Mary's was properly decorated for this wedding; though in view of the circumstances, Canon Hobson had consented to relax the clothing rules so far as the bridegroom was concerned.

Miss Woollard, however, was in the prescribed raiment even down to the seventy-ninth orange blossom; albeit inclined, apparently, to take nervous bites out of her veil. She was more nervous than brides usually are; more nervous even than seemed warranted by the fact that her bridegroom had three best men – the senior, junior and middle naval ratings, all with medals but one degree inferior to that which had been bestowed on Mr Wharton.

The cause for this uneasiness came to light when Canon Hobson, opening his prayer book, first glanced, then looked, then stared at the bridegroom's right-hand coat pocket.

It should perhaps be mentioned here that in addition to a granite face and an extraordinarily soft heart, the reverend gentleman was equipped with eyes that seemed to have been chipped out of adamant and ground to fine points.

He furled the prayer book and spoke in a low, dazed voice.

'Henry,' said he, while the congregation craned, 'that cannot be a cat you have in your coat pocket? Not a *cat*?'

This was rather an exaggeration of the status of Miss Churt, who was six weeks old that day and had just put her shell-shaven face out for a little air. But the general proposition was undeniable.

'Yes,' said Mr Wharton. 'It is.'

'He *would* bring it – he *would* – I said – ' quavered the bride; but Canon Hobson paid no attention to her, though she began to sob.

Meeting the bluish eyes of Miss Churt, however, his adamantine orbs underwent a peculiar process. First they flickered from their condemning stare; then, as it were, they liquefied, so that their penetrative qualities became nil.

He spoke:

'Am I to presume that – this – is some kind of mascot? Connected perhaps with the recent – ? What has happened to her whiskers?'

'I'll tell you about it in the vestry,' said Mr Wharton; and, meeting the canon's gaze, mourned for the misjudgments of his youth.

Canon Hobson nodded; opened the book which he had closed on a probationary thumb, and cleared his throat.

'Dearly beloved,' he proclaimed, 'we are gathered together – '

Miss Churt could not quite identify all the smells (largely lilies) or sounds (mostly Canon Hobson) that were going on.

They were interesting, and she had a vague idea that something of the same general purport might be her personal concern one day.

But not now.

Not for a long time yet.

And meantime she had had enough air.

She withdrew her head from the atmosphere of St Mary's into the warm tweediness of Mr Wharton's pocket and composed herself to sleep.

The Cat that Walked by Himself

RUDYARD KIPLING

THIS BEFELL and behappened and became and was, O, my Best Beloved, when the tame animals were wild. The Dog was wild, and the Horse was wild, and the Cow was wild, and the Sheep was wild, and the Pig was wild – as wild as could be – and they walked in the wet wild woods by their wild lones, but the wildest of all the wild animals was the Cat. He walked by himself, and all places were alike to him.

Of course the Man was wild too. He was dreadfully wild. He didn't even begin to be tame till he met the Woman and she did not like living in his wild ways. She picked out a nice dry cave, instead of a heap of wet leaves, to lie down in, and she strewed clean sand on the floor, and she lit a nice fire of wood at the back of the cave, and she hung a dried Wild Horse skin, tail down, across the opening of the cave, and she said: 'Wipe your feet when you come in, and now we'll keep house.'

That night, Best Beloved, they ate Wild Sheep roasted on the hot stones and flavoured with wild garlic and wild pepper, and Wild Duck stuffed with wild rice, and wild fenugreek and wild coriander, and marrowbones of Wild Oxen, and wild cherries and wild granadillas. Then the Man went to sleep in front of the fire ever so happy, but the Woman sat up, combing. She took the bone of the shoulder of mutton, the big flat blade bone, and she looked at the wonderful marks on it, and she threw more wood on the fire and she made a magic. She made the first Singing Magic in the world.

Out in the wet wild woods all the wild animals gathered together where they could see the light of the fire a long way off, and they wondered what it meant.

Then Wild Horse stamped with his foot and said: 'O, my friends and my enemies, why have the Man and the Woman made that great light in that great cave, and what harm will it do us?'

Wild Dog lifted up his nose and smelled the smell of the roast mutton and said: 'I will go up and see and look and stay: for I think it is good. Cat, come with me.'

'Nenni,' said the Cat. 'I am the Cat who walks by himself, and all places are alike to me. I will not come.'

'Then we will never be friends again,' said Wild Dog, and he trotted off to the cave.

But when he had gone a little way, the Cat said to himself: 'All places are alike to me. Why should I not go too and see and look and come away?' So he slipped after Wild Dog softly, very softly, and hid himself where he could hear everything.

When Wild Dog reached the mouth of the cave he lifted up the dried Horse skin with his nose a little bit and sniffed the beautiful smell of the roast mutton, and the Woman heard him and laughed and said: 'Here comes the first wild thing out of the wild woods. What do you want?'

Wild Dog said: 'O, my enemy and wife of my enemy, what is this that smells so good in the wild woods?'

Then the Woman picked up a roasted mutton bone and threw it to Wild Dog and said: 'Wild thing out of the wild woods, taste and try.' Wild Dog gnawed the bone and it was more delicious than anything he had ever tasted, and he said: 'O, my enemy and wife of my enemy, give me another.'

The Woman said: 'Wild thing out of the wild woods, help my Man to hunt through the day and guard this cave at night and I will give you as many roast bones as you need.'

'Ah!' said the Cat listening, 'this is a very wise Woman, but she is not so wise as I am.'

Wild Dog crawled into the cave and laid his head on the Woman's lap and said: 'O, my friend and wife of my friend, I will help your Man to hunt through the day, and at night I will guard your cave.'

'Ah!' said the Cat listening, 'that is a very foolish Dog.' And he went back through the wet wild woods waving his tail and walking by his wild lone. But he never told anybody.

When the Man woke up he said: 'What is Wild Dog doing here?' And the Woman said: 'His name is not Wild Dog anymore, but the First Friend because he will be our friend for always and always and always. Take him with you when you go hunting.'

Next night the Woman cut great green armfuls of fresh grass from the water meadows and dried it before the fire so that it smelled like new-mown hay, and she sat at the mouth of the cave and plaited a halter out of horsehide, and she looked at the shoulder of mutton bone – at the big broad blade bone – and she made a magic. She made the second Singing Magic in the world.

Out in the wild woods all the wild animals wondered what had happened to Wild Dog, and at last Wild Horse stamped with his foot and said: 'I will go and see why Wild Dog has not returned. Cat, come with me.'

'Nenni,' said the Cat. 'I am the Cat who walks by himself, and all places are alike to me. I will not come.' But all the same he followed Wild Horse softly, very softly, and hid himself where he could hear everything.

When the Woman heard Wild Horse tripping and stumbling on his long mane she laughed and said: 'Here comes the second wild thing out of the wild woods. What do you want?'

Wild Horse said: 'O, my enemy and wife of my enemy, where is Wild Dog?'

The Woman laughed and picked up the blade bone and looked at it and said: 'Wild thing out of the wild woods, you did not come here for Wild Dog, but for the sake of this good grass.'

And Wild Horse, tripping and stumbling on his long mane, said: 'That is true, give it to me to eat.'

The Woman said: 'Wild thing out of the wild woods, bend your wild head and wear what I give you and you shall eat the wonderful grass three times a day.'

'Ah,' said the Cat listening, 'this is a clever Woman, but she is not so clever as I am.'

Wild Horse bent his wild head and the Woman slipped the plaited hide halter over it, and Wild Horse breathed on the woman's feet and said: 'O, my mistress and wife of my master, I will be your servant for the sake of the wonderful grass.'

'Ah,' said the Cat listening, 'that is a very foolish Horse.' And he went back through the wet wild woods, waving his wild tail and walking by his wild lone.

When the Man and the Dog came back from hunting, the Man said: 'What is Wild Horse doing here?' And the Woman said: 'His name is not Wild Horse anymore, but the First Servant because he will carry us from place to place for always and always and always. Take him with you when you go hunting.'

Next day, holding her wild head high that her wild horns should not catch in the wild trees, Wild Cow came up to the cave, and the Cat followed and hid himself just the same as before; and everything happened just the same as before; and the Cat said the same things as before, and when Wild Cow had promised to give her milk to the Woman every day in exchange for the wonderful grass, the Cat went back through the wet wild woods walking by his lone just the same as before.

And when the Man and the Horse and the Dog came home from hunting and asked the same questions, same as before, the Woman said: 'Her name is not Wild Cow anymore, but the Giver of Good Things. She will give us the warm white milk for always and always and always, and I will take care of her while you three go hunting.'

Next day the Cat waited to see if any other wild thing would go up to the cave, but no one moved, so the Cat walked there by himself, and he saw the Woman milking the Cow, and he saw the light of the fire in the cave, and he smelled the smell of the warm white milk.

Cat said: 'O, my enemy and wife of my enemy, where did Wild Cow go?'

The Woman laughed and said: 'Wild thing out of the wild woods, go back to the woods again, for I have braided up my hair and I have put away the blade bone, and we have no more need of either friends or servants in our cave.'

Cat said: 'I am not a friend and I am not a servant. I am the Cat who walks by himself and I want to come into your cave.'

The Woman said: 'Then why did you not come with First Friend on the first night?'

Cat grew very angry and said: 'Has Wild Dog told tales of me?'

Then the Woman laughed and said: 'You are the Cat who walks by himself and all places are alike to you. You are neither a friend nor a servant. You have said it yourself. Go away and walk by yourself in all places alike.'

Then the Cat pretended to be sorry and said: 'Must I never come into the cave? Must I never sit by the warm fire? Must I never drink the warm white milk? You are very wise and very beautiful. You should not be cruel even to a Cat.'

Then the Woman said: 'I knew I was wise but I did not know I was beautiful. So I will make a bargain with you. If ever I say one word in your praise you may come into the cave.'

'And if you say two words in my praise?' said the Cat.

'I never shall,' said the Woman, 'but if I say two words you may sit by the fire in the cave.'

'And if you say three words?' said the Cat.

'I never shall,' said the Woman, 'but if I do you may drink the warm white milk three times a day for always and always and always.'

Then the Cat arched his back and said: 'Now let the curtain at the mouth of the cave, and the fire at the back of the cave, and the milk pots that stand beside the fire remember what my enemy and the wife of my enemy has said.' And he went away through the wet wild woods waving his wild tail and walking by his wild lone.

That night when the Man and the Horse and the Dog came home from hunting, the Woman did not tell them of the bargain she had made because she was afraid that they might not like it.

Cat went far and far away and hid himself in the wet wild woods by his wild lone for a long time till the Woman forgot all about him. Only the Bat – the little upside-down Bat – that hung inside the cave knew where Cat hid, and every evening he would fly to Cat with the news.

One evening the Bat said: 'There is a Baby in the cave. He is new and pink and fat and small, and the Woman is very fond of him.'

'Ah,' said the Cat listening, 'but what is the Baby fond of?'

'He is fond of things that are soft and tickle,' said the Bat. 'He is fond of warm things to hold in his arms when he goes to sleep. He is fond of being played with. He is fond of all those things.'

'Ah,' said the Cat, 'then my time has come.'

Next night Cat walked through the wet wild woods and hid very near the cave till morning time. The woman was very busy cooking, and the Baby cried and interrupted; so she carried him outside the cave and gave him a handful of pebbles to play with. But still the Baby cried.

Then the Cat put out his paddy-paw and patted the Baby on the cheek, and it cooed; and the Cat rubbed against its fat knees and tickled it under its fat chin with his tail. And the Baby laughed; and the Woman heard him and smiled.

Then the Bat – the little upside-down Bat – that hung in the mouth of the cave said: 'O, my hostess and wife of my host and mother of my host, a wild thing from the wild woods is most beautifully playing with your Baby.'

'A blessing on that wild thing whoever he may be,' said the Woman straightening her back, 'for I was a busy Woman this morning and he has done me a service.'

That very minute and second, Best Beloved, the dried horse-skin curtain that was stretched tail-down at the mouth of the cave fell down – *So!* – because it remembered the bargain, and when the Woman went to pick it up – lo and behold! – the Cat was sitting quite comfy inside the cave.

'O, my enemy and wife of my enemy and mother of my enemy,' said the Cat, 'it is I, for you have spoken a word in my praise, and now I can sit within the cave for always and always and always. But still I am the Cat who walks by himself and all places are alike to me.'

The Woman was very angry and shut her lips tight and took up her spinning wheel and began to spin.

But the Baby cried because the Cat had gone away, and the Woman could not hush him for he struggled and kicked and grew black in the face.

'O, my enemy and wife of my enemy and mother of my enemy,' said the Cat, 'take a strand of the thread that you are spinning and tie it to your spindle wheel and drag it on the floor and I will show you a magic that shall make your Baby laugh as loudly as he is now crying.'

'I will do so,' said the Woman, 'because I am at my wits' end, but I will not thank you for it.'

She tied the thread to the little pot spindle wheel and drew it across the floor and the Cat ran after it and patted it with his paws, and rolled head over heels, and tossed it backward over his shoulder, and chased it between his hind legs, and pretended to lose it, and pounced down upon it again till the Baby laughed as loudly as he had been crying, and scrambled after the Cat and frolicked all over the cave till he grew tired and settled down to sleep with the Cat in his arms.

'Now,' said the Cat, 'I will sing the Baby a song that shall keep him asleep for an hour.' And he began to purr loud and low, low and loud, till the Baby fell fast asleep. The Woman smiled as she looked down upon the two of them and said: 'That was wonderfully done. Surely you are very clever, O, Cat.'

That very minute and second, Best Beloved, the smoke of the

fire at the back of the cave came down in clouds from the roof because it remembered the bargain, and when it had cleared away – lo and behold! – the Cat was sitting, quite comfy, close to the fire.

'O, my enemy and wife of my enemy and mother of my enemy,' said the Cat, 'it is I, for you have spoken a second word in my praise, and now I can sit by the warm fire at the back of the cave for always and always and always. But still I am the Cat who walks by himself and all places are alike to me.'

Then the Woman was very, very angry and let down her hair and put more wood on the fire and brought out the broad blade bone of the shoulder of mutton and began to make a magic that should prevent her from saying a third word in praise of the Cat. It was not a Singing Magic, Best Beloved, it was a Still Magic; and by and by the cave grew so still that a little we-wee Mouse crept out of a corner and ran across the floor.

'O, my enemy and wife of my enemy and mother of my enemy,' said the Cat, 'is that little Mouse part of your magic?'

'No,' said the Woman, and she dropped the blade bone and jumped upon a footstool in front of the fire and braided up her hair very quick for fear that the Mouse should run up it.

'Ah,' said the Cat listening, 'then the Mouse will do me no harm if I eat it?'

'No,' said the Woman, braiding up her hair, 'eat it quick and I will always be grateful to you.'

Cat made one jump and caught the little Mouse, and the Woman said: 'A hundred thanks to you, O, Cat. Even the First Friend is not quick enough to catch little Mice as you have done. You must be very wise.'

That very moment and second, O, Best Beloved, the milk pot that stood by the fire cracked in two pieces – *So!* – because it remembered the bargain, and when the Woman jumped down from the footstool – lo and behold! – the Cat was lapping up the warm white milk that lay in one of the broken pieces.

'O, my enemy and wife of my enemy and mother of my enemy,' said the Cat, 'it is I, for you have spoken three words in my praise, and now I can drink the warm white milk three times a day for always and always and always. But still I am the Cat who walks by himself and all places are alike to me.'

Then the Woman laughed and set him a bowl of the warm

white milk and said: 'O, Cat, you are as clever as a Man, but remember that the bargain was not made with the Man or the Dog, and I do not know what they will do when they come home.'

'What is that to me?' said the Cat. 'If I have my place by the fire and my milk three times a day I do not care what the Man or the Dog can do.'

That evening when the Man and the Dog came into the cave the Woman told them all the story of the bargain, and the Man said: 'Yes, but he has not made a bargain with me or with all proper Men after me.' And he took off his two leather boots and he took up his little stone axe (that makes three) and he fetched a piece of wood and a hatchet (that is five altogether), and he set them out in a row and he said: 'Now we will make a bargain. If you do not catch Mice when you are in the cave, for always and always and always, I will throw these five things at you whenever I see you, and so shall all proper Men do after me.'

'Ah,' said the Woman listening. 'This is a very clever Cat, but he is not so clever as my Man.'

The Cat counted the five things (and they looked very knobby) and he said: 'I will catch Mice when I am in the cave for always and always and always: but still I am the Cat that walks by himself and all places are alike to me.'

'Not when I am near,' said the Man. 'If you had not said that I would have put all these things away (for always and always and always), but now I am going to throw my two boots and my little stone axe (that makes three) at you whenever I meet you, and so shall all proper Men do after me.'

Then the Dog said: 'Wait a minute. He has not made a bargain with me.' And he sat down and growled dreadfully and showed all his teeth and said: 'If you are not kind to the Baby while I am in the cave for always and always and always I will chase you till I catch you, and when I catch you I will bite you, and so shall all proper Dogs do after me.'

'Ah,' said the Woman listening. 'This is a very clever Cat, but he is not so clever as the Dog.'

Cat counted the Dog's teeth (and they looked very pointed) and he said: 'I will be kind to the Baby while I am in the cave as long as he does not pull my tail too hard for always and always and always. But still I am the Cat that walks by himself and all places are alike to me.'

'Not when I am near,' said the Dog. 'If you had not said that I would have shut my mouth for always and always and always, but now I am going to chase you up a tree whenever I meet you, and so shall all proper Dogs do after me.'

Then the Man threw his two boots and his little stone axe (that makes three) at the Cat, and the Cat ran out of the cave and the Dog chased him up a tree, and from that day to this, Best Beloved, three proper Men out of five will always throw things at a Cat whenever they meet him, and all proper Dogs will chase him up a tree. But the Cat keeps his side of the bargain too. He will kill Mice and he will be kind to Babies when he is in the house, as long as they do not pull his tail too hard. But when he has done that, and between times, he is the Cat that walks by himself and all places are alike to him, and if you look out at nights you can see him waving his wild tail and walking by his wild lone – just the same as before.

How a Cat Played Robinson Crusoe

CHARLES G. D. ROBERTS

THE ISLAND was a mere sandbank off the low, flat coast. Not a tree broke its bleak levels – not even a shrub. But the long, gritty stalks of the marsh grass clothed it everywhere above tide-mark; and a tiny rivulet of sweet water, flowing from a spring at its centre, drew a ribbon of inland herbage and tenderer green across the harsh and sombre yellow grey of the grass. Few would have chosen the island as a place to live, yet at its seaward end, where the changing tides were never still, stood a spacious, one-storied, wide-verandaed cottage, with a low shed behind it. The virtue of this lone plot of sand was coolness. When the neighbour mainland would be sweltering day and night alike under a breathless heat, out here on the island there was always a cool wind blowing. Therefore a wise city dweller had appropriated the sea waif and built his summer home thereon, where the tonic airs might bring back the rose to the pale cheeks of his children.

The family came to the island toward the end of June. In the first week of September they went away, leaving every door and window of house and shed securely shuttered, bolted or barred against the winter's storms. A roomy boat, rowed by two fishermen, carried them across the half mile of racing tides that separated them from the mainland. The elders of the household were not sorry to get back to the world of men, after two months of mere wind, and sun, and waves, and waving grass tops. But the children went with tear-stained faces. They were leaving behind them their favourite pet, the accustomed comrade of their migrations, a handsome, moon-faced cat, striped like a tiger. The animal had mysteriously disappeared two days before, vanishing from the face of the island without leaving a trace behind. The only reasonable explanation seemed to be that she had been snapped up by a passing eagle. The cat, meanwhile, was a fast prisoner at the other end of the island, hidden beneath a broken barrel and some hundredweight of drifted sand.

The old barrel, with the staves battered out of one side, had stood, half buried, on the crest of a sand ridge raised by a long prevailing wind. Under its lee the cat had found a sheltered hollow, full of sun, where she had been wont to lie curled up for hours at a time, basking and sleeping. Meanwhile the sand had been steadily piling itself higher and higher behind the unstable barrier. At last it had piled too high; and suddenly, before a stronger gust, the barrel had come toppling over beneath a mass of sand, burying the sleeping cat out of sight and light. But at the same time the sound half of the barrel had formed a safe roof to her prison, and she was neither crushed nor smothered. When the children in their anxious search all over the island chanced upon the mound of fine, white sand they gave it but one careless look. They could not hear the faint cries that came, at intervals, from the close darkness within. So they went away sorrowfully, little dreaming that their friend was imprisoned almost beneath their feet.

For three days the prisoner kept up her appeals for help. On the third day the wind changed and presently blew up a gale. In a few hours it had uncovered the barrel. At one corner a tiny spot of light appeared.

Eagerly the cat stuck her paw through the hole. When she withdrew it again the hole was much enlarged. She took the hint and fell to scratching. At first her efforts were rather aimless; but presently, whether by good luck or quick sagacity, she learned to make her scratching more effective. The opening rapidly enlarged, and at last she was able to squeeze her way out.

The wind was tearing madly across the island, filled with flying sand. The seas hurled themselves trampling up the beach, with the uproar of a bombardment. The grasses lay bowed flat in long quivering ranks. Over the turmoil the sun stared down from a deep, unclouded blue. The cat, when first she met the full force of the gale, was fairly blown off her feet. As soon as she could recover herself she crouched low and darted into the grasses for shelter. But there was little shelter there, the long stalks being held down almost level. Through their lashed lines, however, she sped straight before the gale, making for the cottage at the other end of the island, where she would find, as she fondly imagined, not only food and shelter but also loving comfort to make her forget her terrors.

Still and desolate in the bright sunshine and the tearing wind, the house frightened her. She could not understand the tight-closed shutters, the blind, unresponding doors that would no longer open to her anxious appeal. The wind swept her savagely across the naked veranda. Climbing with difficulty to the dining-room windowsill, where so often she had been let in, she clung there a few moments and yowled heartbrokenly. Then, in a sudden panic, she jumped down and ran to the shed. That, too, was closed. Never before had she seen the shed doors closed, and she could not understand it. Cautiously she crept around the foundations – but those had been built honestly: there was no such thing as getting in that way. On every side it was nothing but a blank, forbidding face that the old familiar house confronted her with.

The cat had always been so coddled and pampered by the children that she had had no need to forage for herself; but, fortunately for her, she had learned to hunt the marsh mice and grass sparrows for amusement. So now, being ravenous from her long fast under the sand, she slunk mournfully away from the deserted house and crept along under the lee of a sand ridge to a little grassy hollow which she knew. Here the gale caught only the tops of the grasses; and here, in the warmth and comparative calm, the furry little marsh folk, mice and shrews, were going about their business undisturbed.

The cat, quick and stealthy, soon caught one and eased her hunger. She caught several. And then, making her way back to the house, she spent hours in heartsick prowling around it and around, sniffing and peering, yowling piteously on the threshold and windowsill; and every now and then being blown ignominiously across the smooth, naked expanse of the veranda floor. At last, hopelessly discouraged, she curled herself up beneath the children's window and went to sleep.

In spite of her loneliness and grief the life of the island prisoner during the next two or three weeks was by no means one of hardship. Besides her abundant food of birds and mice she quickly learned to catch tiny fish in the mouth of the rivulet, where salt water and fresh water met. It was an exciting game, and she became expert at dashing the grey tom-cod and blue-and-silver sand-lance far up the slope with a sweep of her armed paw. But when the equinoctial storms roared down upon the island, with furious rain, and low, black clouds torn to shreds, then life became more difficult for her. Game all took to cover, where it was hard to find. It was difficult to get around in the drenched and lashing grass; and, moreover, she loathed wet. Most of the time she went hungry, sitting sullen and desolate under the lee of the house, glaring out defiantly at the rush and battling tumult of the waves.

The storm lasted nearly ten days before it blew itself clean out. On the eighth day the abandoned wreck of a small Nova Scotia schooner drove ashore, battered out of all likeness to a ship. But hulk as it was it had passengers of a sort. A horde of rats got through the surf and scurried into the hiding of the grass roots. They promptly made themselves at home, burrowing under the grass and beneath old, half-buried timbers, and carrying panic into the ranks of the mice and shrews.

When the storm was over the cat had a decided surprise in her first long hunting expedition. Something had rustled the grass heavily and she trailed it, expecting a particularly large, fat marsh mouse. When she pounced and alighted upon an immense old ship's rat, many-voyaged and many-battled, she got badly bitten. Such an experience had never before fallen to her lot. At first she felt so injured that she was on the point of backing out and running away. Then her latent pugnacity awoke, and the fire of far-off ancestors. She flung herself into the fight with a rage that took no accounting of the wounds she got; and the struggle was soon over. Her wounds, faithfully licked, quickly healed themselves in that clean and tonic air; and after that, having learned how to handle such big game, she no more got bitten.

During the first full moon after her abandonment – the first week in October – the island was visited by still weather with sharp night frosts. The cat discovered then that it was most exciting to hunt by night and do her sleeping in the daytime. She found that now, under the strange whiteness of the moon, all her game was astir – except the birds, which had fled to the mainland during the storm, gathering for the southward flight. The blanched grasses, she found, were now everywhere a-rustle; and everywhere dim little shapes went darting with thin squeaks across ghostly-white sands. Also she made the acquaintance of a new bird, which she regarded at first uneasily and then with vengeful wrath. This was the brown marsh owl, which came over from the mainland to do some autumn mouse hunting. There were two pairs of these big, downy-winged, round-eyed hunters, and they did not know there was a cat on the island.

The cat, spying one of them as it swooped soundlessly hither and thither over the silvered grass tops, crouched with flattened ears. With its wide spread of wing it looked bigger than herself; and the great round face, with hooked beak and wild, staring eyes, appeared extremely formidable. However, she was no coward; and presently, though not without reasonable caution, she went about her hunting. Suddenly the owl caught a partial glimpse of her in the grass – probably of her ears or head. He swooped; and at the same instant she sprang upward to meet the assault, spitting and growling harshly and striking with unsheathed claws. With a frantic flapping of his great wings the owl checked himself and drew back into the air, just escaping the clutch of those indignant claws. After that the marsh owls were careful to give her a wide berth. They realized that the black-striped animal with the quick spring and the clutching claws was not to be interfered with. They perceived that she was some relation to that ferocious prowler, the lynx.

In spite of all this hunting, however, the furry life of the marsh grass was so teeming, so inexhaustible, that the depredations of cat, rats and owls were powerless to make more than a passing impression upon it. So the hunting and the merry-making went on side by side under the indifferent moon.

As the winter deepened – with bursts of sharp cold and changing winds that forced the cat to be continually changing her refuge – she grew more and more unhappy. She felt her homelessness keenly. Nowhere on the whole island could she find a nook where she might feel secure from both wind and rain. As for the old barrel, the first cause of her misfortunes, there was no help in that. The winds had long ago turned it completely over, open to the sky, then drifted it full of sand and reburied it. And in any case the cat would have been afraid to go near it again. So it came about that she alone of all the island dwellers had no shelter to turn to when the real winter arrived, with snows that smothered the grass tops out of sight, and frosts that lined the shore with grinding ice cakes. The rats had their holes under the buried fragments of wreckage; the mice and shrews had their deep, warm tunnels; the owls had nests in hollow trees far away in the forests of the mainland. But the cat, shivering and frightened, could do nothing but crouch against the blind walls of the unrelenting house and let the snow whirl itself and pile itself about her.

And now, in her misery, she found her food cut off. The mice ran secure in their hidden runways, where the grass roots on each side of them gave them easy and abundant provender. The rats, too, were out of sight – digging burrows themselves in the soft snow in the hope of intercepting some of the tunnels of the mice, and now and then snapping up an unwary passer-by. The ice fringe, crumbling and heaving under the ruthless tide, put an end to her fishing. She would have tried to capture one of the formidable owls in her hunger, but the owls no longer came to the island. They would return, no doubt, later in the season when the snow had hardened and the mice had begun to come out and play on the surface. But for the present they were following an easier chase in the deeps of the upland forest.

When the snow stopped falling and the sun came out again there fell such keen cold as the cat had never felt before. The day, as it chanced, was Christmas; and if the cat had had any idea as to the calendar she would certainly have marked the day in her memory as it was an eventful one for her. Starving as she was she could not sleep, but kept ceaselessly on the prowl. This was fortunate, for had she gone to sleep without any more shelter than the wall of the house she would never have wakened again. In her restlessness she wandered to the farther side of the island where, in a somewhat sheltered and sunny recess of the shore facing the mainland, she found a patch of bare sand, free of ice cakes and just uncovered by the tide. Opening upon this recess were the tiny entrances to several of the mouse tunnels.

Close beside one of these holes in the snow the cat crouched, quiveringly intent. For ten minutes or more she waited, never so much as twitching a whisker. At last a mouse thrust out its little pointed head. Not daring to give it time to change its mind or take alarm, she pounced. The mouse, glimpsing the doom ere it fell, doubled back upon itself in the narrow runway. Hardly realizing what she did in her desperation the cat plunged head and shoulders into the snow, reaching blindly after the vanished prize. By great good luck she caught it.

It was her first meal in four bitter days. The children had always tried to share with her their Christmas cheer and enthusiasm, and had usually succeeded in interesting her by an agreeable lavishness in the matter of cream; but never before had she found a Christmas feast so good.

Now she had learned a lesson. Being naturally clever and her wits sharpened by her fierce necessities, she had grasped the idea that it was possible to follow her prey a little way into the snow. She had not realized that the snow was so penetrable. She had quite wiped out the door of this particular runway; so she went and crouched beside a similar one, but here she had to wait a long time before an adventurous mouse came to peer out. But this time she showed that she had grasped her lesson. It was straight at the side of the entrance that she pounced, where instinct told her that the body of the mouse would be. One outstretched paw thus cut off the quarry's retreat. Her tactics were completely successful; and as her head went plunging into the fluffy whiteness she felt the prize between her paws.

Her hunger now fairly appeased, she found herself immensely excited over this new fashion of hunting. Often before had she waited at mouse holes, but never had she found it possible to break down the walls and invade the holes themselves. It was a thrilling idea. As she crept toward another hole a mouse scurried swiftly up the sand and darted into it. The cat, too late to catch him before he disappeared, tried to follow him. Scratching clumsily but hopefully she succeeded in forcing the full length of her body into the snow. She found no sign of the fugitive, which was by this time racing in safety down some dim transverse tunnel. Her eyes, mouth, whiskers and fur full of the powdery white particles, she backed out, much disappointed. But in that moment she had realized that it was much warmer in there beneath the snow than out in the stinging air. It was a second and vitally important lesson; and though she was probably unconscious of having learned it she instinctively put the new lore into practice a little while later.

Having succeeded in catching yet another mouse for which her appetite made no immediate demand, she carried it back to the house and laid it down in tribute on the veranda steps while she meowed and stared hopefully at the desolate, snow-draped door. Getting no response she carried the mouse down with her to the hollow behind the drift which had been caused by the bulging front of the bay-window on the end of the house. Here she curled herself up forlornly, thinking to have a wink of sleep.

But the still cold was too searching. She looked at the sloping wall of snow beside her and cautiously thrust her paw into it. It was very soft and light. It seemed to offer practically no resistance. She pawed away in an awkward fashion till she had scooped out a sort of tiny cave. Gently she pushed herself into it, pressing back the snow on every side till she had room to turn around.

Then turn around she did several times, as dogs do in getting their beds arranged to their liking. In this process she not only packed down the snow beneath her, but she also rounded out for herself a snug chamber with a comparatively narrow doorway. From this snowy retreat she gazed forth with a solemn air of possession; then she went to sleep with a sense of comfort, of 'homeyness', such as she had never before felt since the disappearance of her friends.

Having thus conquered misfortune and won herself the freedom of the winter wild, her life though strenuous was no longer one of any terrible hardship. With patience at the mouse holes she could catch enough to eat; and in her snowy den she slept warm and secure. In a little while, when a crust had formed over the surface, the mice took to coming out at night and holding revels on the snow. Then the owls, too, came back; and the cat, having tried to catch one, got sharply bitten and clawed before she realized the propriety of letting it go. After this experience she decided that owls, on the whole, were meant to be let alone. But for all that she found it fine hunting, out there on the bleak, unfenced, white reaches of the snow.

Thus, mistress of the situation, she found the winter slipping by without further serious trials. Only once, toward the end of January, did Fate send her another bad quarter of an hour. On the heels of a peculiarly bitter cold snap a huge white owl from the Arctic Barrens came one night to the island. The cat, taking observations from the corner of the veranda, caught sight of him. One look was enough to assure her that this was a very different kind of visitor from the brown marsh owls. She slipped inconspicuously down into her burrow; and until the great white owl went away, some twenty-four hours later, she kept herself discreetly out of sight.

When spring came back to the island, with the nightly shrill chorus of fluting frogs in the shallow, sedgy pools and the young grass alive with nesting birds, the prisoner's life became almost luxurious in its easy abundance. But now she was once more homeless, since her snug den had vanished with the snow. This did not much matter to her, however, for the weather grew warmer and more tranquil day by day; and moreover, she herself, in being forced back upon her instincts, had learned to be as contented as a tramp. Nevertheless, with all her capacity for learning and adapting herself she had not forgotten anything. So when, one day in June, a crowded boat came over from the mainland, and children's voices, clamouring across the grass tops, broke the desolate silence of the island, the cat heard and sprang up out of her sleep on the veranda steps.

For one second she stood, listening intently. Then, almost as a dog would have done, and as few of her supercilious tribe ever condescend to do, she went racing across to the landing place – to be snatched up into the arms of four happy children at once, and to have her fine fur ruffled to a state which it would cost her an hour's assiduous toilet to put in order.

ACKNOWLEDGMENTS

All possible care has been taken to make full acknowledgment in every case where material is still in copyright. If errors have occurred, they will be corrected in subsequent editions if notification is sent to the publisher. Grateful acknowledgment is made for permission to reprint the following:

'A Vet's Life' by John M Bower BVSc MRCVS, reproduced by permission of the author.

'Amours' from *Les Vrilles de la Vigne* by Colette, reproduced by permission of John Johnson Limited, translation copyright © 1992 by Michael O'Mara Books.

'Incident on East Ninth' by Jill Dower, reproduced by permission of the author.

'My Boss the Cat' by Paul Gallico, reproduced by permission of Aitken and Stone and Harold Ober Associates Incorporated.

'Gershwin' by Judy Gardiner, reproduced by permission of Rupert Crew Limited. Copyright © 1983 by Judy Gardiner.

'Minna Minna Mowbray' by Michael Joseph, reproduced by permission of Hugh Joseph and Richard Joseph Publishers Ltd.

'Rufus the Survivor' by Doris Lessing from *Particularly Cats and More Cats*, reproduced by permission of Michael Joseph Ltd and Jonathan Clowes Ltd, on behalf of Doris Lessing. Copyright © 1989 by Doris Lessing.

'Cat's Cruise' from *The Sacred Bullock and Other Stories of Animals* by Mazo de la Roche, reproduced by permission of Pan Macmillan Ltd.

'C Stands for Cuisine' from *Cats' A-Z* by Beverley Nichols, reproduced by permission of Eric Glass Ltd.

Extract from 'The Cherry Tree' by Derek Tangye, reproduced by permission of Michael Joseph Ltd. Copyright © 1986 by Derek Tangye.

'Solomon and Sheba' from *Cats in the Belfry* by Doreen Tovey, reproduced by permission of Serafina Clarke.

'The Cat that Could Fly' by Stella Whitelaw, reproduced by permission of Rupert Crew Limited. Copyright © 1983 by Stella Whitelaw.

'The Coat' by Mary Williams, reproduced by permission of Laurence Pollinger Limited. Copyright © 1976 by Mary Williams.

Grateful thanks also go to Joan Moore of Cat World and the librarians of Northcote Road Library, Wandsworth, London for their help in finding stories.

PRESIDENT'S FOREWORD

'Revolution: Russian Art 1917–1932' explores the extraordinary diversity of art made in Russia during one of the most turbulent periods in modern history. In October 1917 Vladimir Lenin and the socialist Bolshevik party swept to power, ending centuries of autocratic rule under the Tsars. During the heady days after the Revolution, Kazimir Malevich, Vasily Kandinsky and others pursued their experiments in pure colour and form to create new art for a new world. But the euphoria was not to last. Increasingly, the Soviet state demanded art that was representational and that could be easily understood by the masses. In 1932 Joseph Stalin issued a decree that all art should express Soviet ideology.

While many exhibitions have focused on the great achievements of the Russian avant-garde, ours is the first in Britain to reassess and to engage fully with the complexity of this fascinating period. In addition to famous avant-garde artists, audiences will discover the work of such figurative artists as Kuzma Petrov-Vodkin and Alexander Deineka who, although conforming to the demand for Socialist Realist art, produced highly original works that go far beyond propaganda, and who until now have been relatively unknown in the West.

The ideal that art should not be elitist, but useful and available to all, led to an explosion of creativity in many different media. In addition to paintings, 'Revolution: Russian Art 1917–1932' includes the groundbreaking films of Dziga Vertov and Sergei Eisenstein, the architectural schemes of El Lissitzky, Tatlin's famous glider *Letatlin*, Rodchenko's daring photographs, innovative graphic design, and beautiful porcelain decorated by Malevich and his followers.

Such an ambitious exhibition relies on the inspiration and talent of many individuals. Firstly, I would like to thank the exhibition's curators, Natalia Murray, who first proposed the idea for the exhibition and has worked closely with John Milner, and Ann Dumas, the curator at the Royal Academy, in developing the concept and selecting the works of art. We are grateful to Ian Christie for advising us on the films that are shown in the exhibition and their presentation.

At the Royal Academy, Tim Marlow, Artistic Director; Andrea Tarsia, Head of Exhibitions; Flora Fricker, Exhibitions Manager; Rebecca Bray, Jasmine Fenn, Curatorial Assistants; Belén Lasheras Díaz, Exhibitions Assistant; and Giulia Ariete and Caroline Arno, Rights and Reproductions Co-ordinators, have all worked hard to turn the vision into a reality. We are grateful to RA Publications for producing this handsome catalogue, and to the authors for their excellent contributions. We thank Kathrin Jacobsen for the book's elegant design.

Mike Hawkes has created the exhibition's spectacular design that reflects the radical spirit of the times in which the art was made. We are most grateful to Henry Milner who has skilfully made the re-creations of El Lissitzky's apartment and Tatlin's glider. Tim Harvey is responsible for the imaginative graphic design of the gallery texts.

An exhibition such as this cannot be realised without the generous support of the lenders who are willing to part with great works of art from their collections, both public and private. We are greatly indebted to our Russian colleagues and would like to thank especially Vladimir Gusev, Director, and Evgenia Petrova, Deputy Director for Science, of the State Russian Museum in St Petersburg, and Zelfira Tregulova, Director of the Tretyakov Gallery in Moscow, not only for their generous loan of paintings, many of which are seen in Britain for the first time, but also for their advice and support throughout the project. We thank the State Museum and Exhibition Center, ROSIZO, who together with a number of individual museums in Russia, have facilitated the loan of a number of works. We would also like to thank Mikhail Piotrovsky, Director of the State Hermitage Museum, St Petersburg.

We are very grateful to Petr Aven, to Alex Lachmann and to Vladimir Tsarenkov for their loans. We also thank Jenny Dugan-Chapman, and Elena Sudakova, Director of the Gallery for Russian Arts and Design, for lending so generously.

Finally, we owe a great debt of gratitude to the exhibition's supporters, LetterOne, the Blavatnik Family Foundation, The Polonsky Foundation and to Petr Aven for their support.

It is our hope that this display of the brilliantly inventive art that flourished in Russia in the darkest of political times will be a revelation to our public.

Christopher Le Brun PRA
President, Royal Academy of Arts

SPONSOR'S PREFACE

LetterOne is proud to sponsor 'Revolution: Russian Art 1917–1932', a once-in-a-lifetime exhibition of a unique moment in the history of Russian art, when for fifteen years following the Revolution, artists explored the possibilities of new types of art for the new state, before Stalin began his violent suppression of the avant-garde.

During this period there was an incredible outburst of artistic creativity and optimism as well as a wish to redefine art, with an avant-garde movement existing alongside the emerging Socialist Realism. For the first time in the UK, this exhibition combines and contrasts the diverse array of art forms that flourished during this complex post-revolutionary period.

This short-lived Russian artistic renaissance had an immense impact on European and American art in the twentieth century. Many artists who lived through the revolutionary years emigrated to the West, influencing art, theatre companies, architecture, films and international exhibitions.

This art is the culmination of centuries of artistic and cultural exchange across Europe, and a wonderful illustration of the rich cultural heritage we share. We hope that visitors will enjoy the chance to experience the exhibition's rich themes, which explore the interaction between art and politics during this turbulent period of Russian history.

Mikhail Fridman
Chairman, LetterOne, International Investment Business

ПЕТЕРБУРГ
-РОСТА-
НЕСМОТРЯ НА ТРЕХЛЕТНИЯ
УСИЛИЯ ВРАГОВ ВСЕГО МИРА
РЕВОЛЮЦИЯ ИДЕТ
ГИГАНТСКИМИ ШАГАМИ!

Fig. 16
Works by members of the Society of Easel Painters (OST) in 'Fifteen Years of Artists of the Russian Soviet Republic', State Russian Museum, Leningrad, 1932. Photo Archives of the State Russian Museum, St Petersburg

Fig. 17
Installation of paintings by Alexander Deineka in 'Fifteen Years of Artists of the Russian Soviet Republic', State Russian Museum, Leningrad, 1932. Photo Archives of the State Russian Museum, St Petersburg

and to demonstrate that Soviet artists were now 'working peacefully together as a single front'. Although art historians have long viewed the April resolution as a repressive measure intended to deprive Soviet artists of their last creative freedoms under the increasingly totalitarian Stalinist regime, historical evidence shows that in fact it had a broad base of support among artists and critics. They counted on the resolution to put an end to the bitter rivalry and infighting between numerous groups that had nearly halted artistic production during the late 1920s and early 1930s. This massive survey was seen as a valuable opportunity to perform a practical assessment of their work and to find common ground. Yet in fact the competition between the artists for inclusion in the canon of the history of Soviet art was fiercer than ever. As the photorealist painter Evgeny Katsman punned, decisions were being made about 'whom to exhibit and whom to throw out' ('kogo vystavliat', a kogo vystavit').[11]

The exhibition presented a stately spectacle. Visitors ascended a grand staircase decorated with flowers and large banners emblazoned with agitational slogans (fig. 13). Red carpets were rolled out down the staircase and across all the galleries, where greenery added to the festive spirit. Paintings and sculpture shared the same spaces, while the graphic and applied arts were shown in smaller adjacent rooms. The physical layout of the exhibition space presented significant challenges, as Grabar recalled: 'It was confusing, full of dead ends and lacked through passage.'[12] Curators found an apt solution to the latter problem by creating a circular historical trajectory for the display, which established a symbolic continuity between its starting and ending points, the galleries showing Lenin's revolutionary activity and Stalin's industrialisation respectively (figs 14, 15). The second gallery was originally supposed to showcase the period of War Communism, dominated by leftist art. The Exhibition Committee decided to cut it for reasons of space and thus no longer had to include any abstract or Constructivist works, which were left in storage. Instead, Lenin's room was followed by three large galleries showcasing works by members of the Society of Easel Painters (OST) (figs 16, 17). One of these was dominated by David Shterenberg, with 50 exhibited works, while the others were given to Andrei Goncharov and Alexander Labas respectively. The evolution of each of these artists' work was intended to exemplify 'a healthy development' from an excessive preoccupation with form and colour to the soundness of Soviet subject-matter.

Following Matsa's proposal to show the history of artistic development dialectically, the formally innovative paintings by members of the Society of Easel Painters were counterbalanced by the more aesthetically conservative works by members of the former 'World of Art' group and its more contemporary equivalent, the group '4 Arts'. Next came works by members of the Leningrad groups 'Circle of Artists' and 'Machine Shop'. The largest part of the exhibition was dedicated to artists from the Association of Artists of Revolutionary Russia (AKhRR), whose works were shown in a dialectical interaction with those of members of the Society of Moscow Artists (OMKh). Punin described how these two groups affected each other: The Artists of Revolutionary Russia artists learned to lighten up their paintings by looking at the legacy of Paul Cézanne and other Western modernists in the works of the Society of Moscow Artists, while the latter were inspired by the realist tendencies of the late nineteenth-century Russian painters known as the Wanderers, and also to focus more on Soviet themes, the staple of AKhRR painting.[13] Finally, in the last gallery, a few artists were shown to support the collective push toward industrialisation under Stalin's watchful leadership.

The Exhibition Committee's decision to leave out the period of War Communism and thus to dispense with the need to show any works by avant-garde artists was a significant shift that was glossed over by being hardly discussed in public. An acknowledgement of this bias – and some resistance to it – came from the organisers at the State Russian Museum itself. Thus Punin, who undoubtedly even if cautiously advocated the inclusion of leftist art in the exhibition, acknowledged and attempted to justify its very limited representation in his catalogue essay: 'Of course the present exhibition cannot lay claim to a strict historical continuity; much of what "came and went" is not represented at all; in the same way historical proportions are not preserved. But "continuity" and "historicism" are not what's most important now; we are building a new life, a new artistic culture and therefore prefer to look ahead, rather than to pedantically count every step of our historical past.'[14] Grabar did not mention the omission in his catalogue text, but articulated his position in an unpublished review of the exhibition: 'these movements that came to us across the divide of the October Revolution directly from the shops of art dealers in Paris and Berlin, were in no way the long-sought proletarian art, as they were presented to us back then, but, quite on the contrary, they were the last style of a culture in its twilight that had come to a dead end.'[15]

Only two galleries in the retrospective were devoted to artists perceived as leftist: the Analytical painter Pavel Filonov (fig. 18) and the founder of Suprematism, Kazimir Malevich (fig. 66). Their exceptional inclusion was most likely due to their continued presence in Leningrad: both had tight-knit groups of students and Malevich had just been given a research laboratory at the State Russian Museum, in which he continued to work on his architectons.[16] It was also enabled by the direct patronage of the State Russian Museum's director Iosif Gurvich, who, in his turn, relied on the support of the Leningrad Communist

Fig. 18
Installation of works by Pavel Filonov, including *Formula of the Petrograd Proletariat* (cat. 53) and *Tractor Workshop at the Putilov Factory* (cat. 20) in 'Fifteen Years of Artists of the Russian Soviet Republic', State Russian Museum, Leningrad, 1932. Photo Archives of the State Russian Museum, St Petersburg

Party leader Sergei Kirov. Ultimately, it was only thanks to Kirov's direct intervention on the eve of the exhibition's opening that the 'extreme-left' works were allowed to remain on the walls, despite the Government Committee's last-minute request that they be removed.[17]

The inclusion of works by Filonov and Malevich did not necessarily play to their advantage, however, for their galleries were dead-end spaces located outside the main circulation of the exhibition, and their work was thus presented as a deviation from the main course of Soviet artistic development. Nevertheless, Malevich used this opportunity to create a conceptually uniform display of his pictorial language, not as an evolution but as a total system of non-objectivity, which, at this point in his thinking, went beyond the distinction between figuration and abstraction. As such, the display was consistent with Malevich's goal, since his return to painting in the late 1920s, to offer his viewers a cure from mimetic naturalism, which was increasingly dominating Soviet art.[18] Yet even though he was not giving up his struggle for what he called New Art, Malevich was painfully aware of the false recognition he was receiving. He expressed as much in a letter to his old friend and confidant the artist Ivan Klyun: 'The arts administrators' attitude towards me took a very malicious form – general recognition, honour, respect, but not a thing more; they don't let me in anywhere and don't give me anything … a blockade all around.'[19] The absence of any other avant-garde works in the exhibition was a severe blow for many artists, especially since a good number took it as the personal verdict of their colleagues rather than a generalised prohibition on the part of the administrators. Vladimir Tatlin, for instance, voiced a telling grievance at a public debate about the retrospective held at the newly formed Moscow Union of Soviet Artists: 'I attributed a great deal of importance to the "15 years" exhibition, but my work was not displayed, which was wrong, since I really should have some place in the history of art. By not exhibiting me, artists seem to have excluded me from their ranks.'[20]

The dismissal of the avant-garde legacy at the 1932 exhibition was accomplished in two steps: first by relegating it to the first few years after the Revolution in the historical account and then by its removal from public view, with only two exceptions, both of which were taken out of their historical context. By completely obliterating the legacies of Constructivism or Production Art, the exhibition restored the traditional division between artistic mediums and shifted the focus back to painting, sculpture and the graphic arts. Figuration was ubiquitous, and in the absence of any more radical works, painters from the former Society of Easel Painters, especially Alexander Labas and Alexander Tyshler, were censured for being too subjective and too absorbed in the formal aspects of painting by a group of critics who mounted an orchestrated attack against 'formalism' in the months immediately following the Leningrad exhibition.[21] Unlike earlier debates about the future of Soviet art, which had been formulated largely in theoretical terms, these essays focused on visual analysis of specific paintings – an important discursive shift that the huge retrospective made possible. Evidently, the Moscow authorities were not satisfied with the outcome of the Leningrad exhibition. The Soviet press barely mentioned it, leading even the traditionalist Grabar to speak out about its 'deliberate silencing'.[22]

The show's sequel in Moscow was meant to rectify its shortcomings. By the time a substantially modified and expanded version of the exhibition opened at the State Historical Museum on Red Square in June 1933 – comprising 3,500 works by nearly 500 artists – the Soviet art world had changed significantly: it was considerably more centralised and hierarchical, and artists' autonomy had been substantially curtailed. Critics had become the main mouthpieces both of the artists and of the mass of Soviet viewers, and their own opinions had to be much more closely tailored to the official line of those in power.

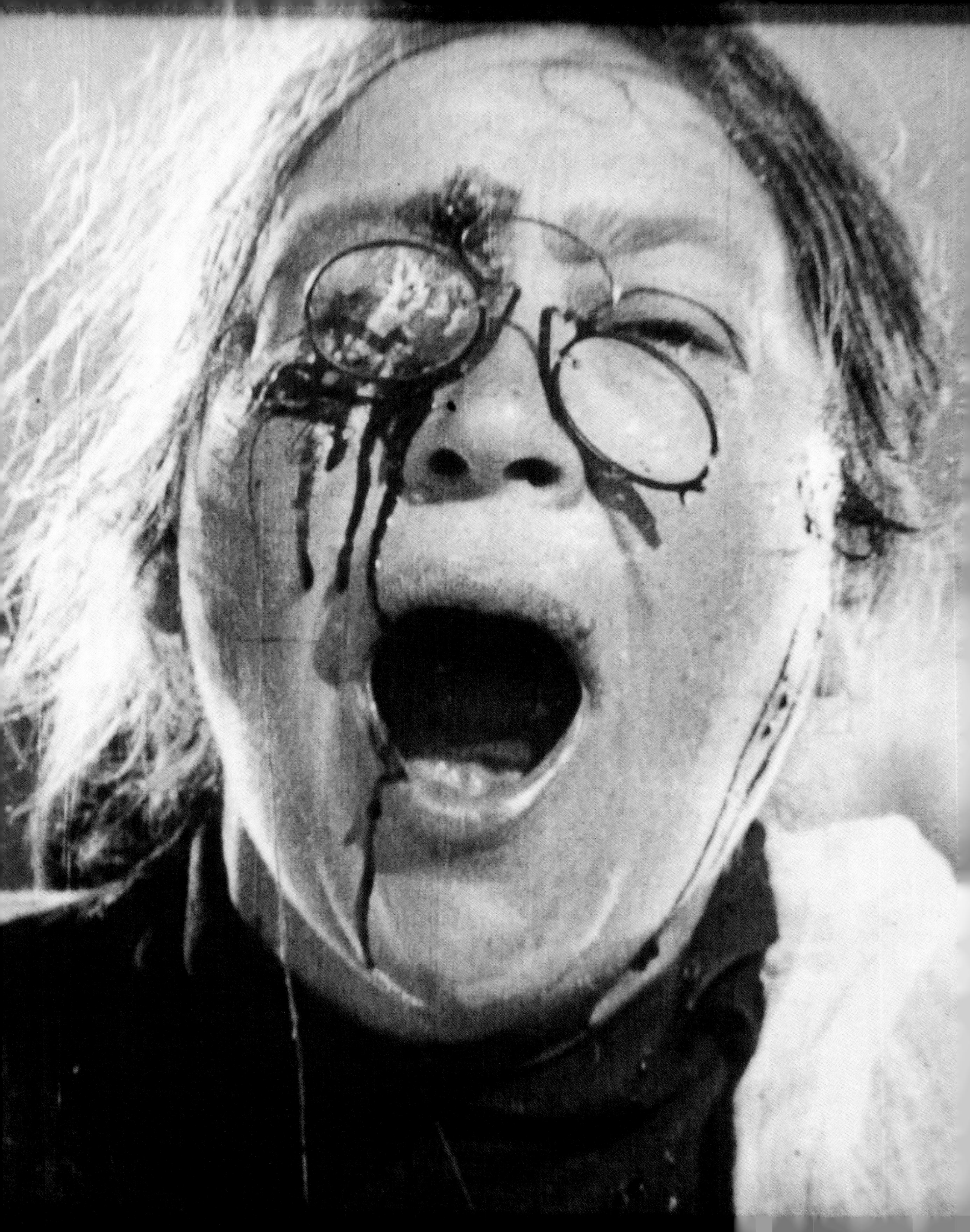

'THE MOST IMPORTANT ART'? SOVIET FILM-MAKING IN THE 1920S

Ian Christie

NOTHING BETTER ILLUSTRATES THE CRUCIAL role of film in proclaiming the success of the October Revolution than the triumphant international reception of its most famous director, Sergei Eisenstein, in 1929–30. Throughout Western Europe, and subsequently in New York, Los Angeles and Mexico City, celebrities in all branches of the arts clamoured to meet the maker of *The Battleship Potemkin* (1925, fig. 19), which had become, simultaneously, the most admired and most notorious film of the post-First World War world. Six months before Eisenstein and his co-director Grigori Alexandrov left for their tour, they were apparently summoned for an interview with Stalin, who wanted changes made in their latest film, *The General Line* (1929), but also to impress upon the pair that 'the significance of Soviet film art is very great', especially abroad, where 'they all watch Soviet films with attention and all understand them'.[1]

It would seem that Stalin must have been aware that Soviet films enjoyed high prestige in the late 1920s, at a time when very little art in other media had reached a world that was avid for contact with post-revolutionary Russia – a fascination that Lev Kuleshov had already exploited and parodied in his 1924 comedy *The Extraordinary Adventures of Mr West in the Land of the Bolsheviks* (fig. 20). But the films that won highest praise were hardly the products of any systematic Soviet policy towards the medium during the 1920s. Although Lenin long continued to be quoted claiming that 'of all the arts, for us the cinema is the most important', his nationalisation of the remains of a shattered industry in 1919 had little practical effect. Most of Russia's established film-makers initially headed south as the Soviet regime stabilised its grip on power, often sabotaging or removing their equipment before they left to resume business in Paris or Berlin. Those who stayed faced acute shortages of necessary materials amid the general privations caused by an effective Allied blockade following Russia's withdrawal from the war with Germany in late 1917, yet managed to make a number of short 'agitational' films (*agitki*), with titles such as *Hunger... Hunger... Hunger, Days of Struggle* and *Sickle and Hammer.* Some of these, with the earliest newsreels recording the Civil War, were shown on the agit-trains and river ships that carried the Bolshevik message to far-flung areas of Russia and became an integral part of Soviet cinema's romantic founding mythology.

None of this early production was seen abroad, although the Norwegian polar explorer Fridtjof Nansen made a documentary account of the 1921 Volga disaster, *The Famine in Russia*, which was widely shown and helped raise charitable funds for relief. Under Lenin's New Economic Policy (NEP), foreign films began to appear in the cinemas alongside a few pre-revolutionary Russian titles that remained in circulation. Although Lenin's own taste was as conservative in film as in literature and the visual arts, he recognised the need to encourage production of entertainment films ('for advertising and revenue, of course with no indecency or counter-revolution'), while insisting on a 'proportional' policy that would ensure that films with 'a specifically propagandist content' were also widely shown.

What actually transpired during the five years after 1924 was an unruly yet highly creative struggle between competing models for what 'Soviet cinema' should be, at a time when the new government had more important priorities. Yet understanding of this period was long dominated by the extraordinary prestige of a handful of 'revolutionary' films, led by Eisenstein's *The Battleship Potemkin* and *October* (1928, fig. 29), together with Vsevolod Pudovkin's *The Mother* (1926) and *The End of St Petersburg* (1927), and the Ukrainian Alexander Dovzhenko, with his *Zvenigora*

Fig. 19
Sergei Eisenstein, *The Battleship Potemkin* (Mosfilm, USSR), 1925. Film still. Deutsche Kinemathek, Berlin

Fig. 20
Lev Kuleshov, *The Extraordinary Adventures of Mr West in the Land of the Bolsheviks* (Goskino, USSR), 1924. Film still. The Kobal Collection, London

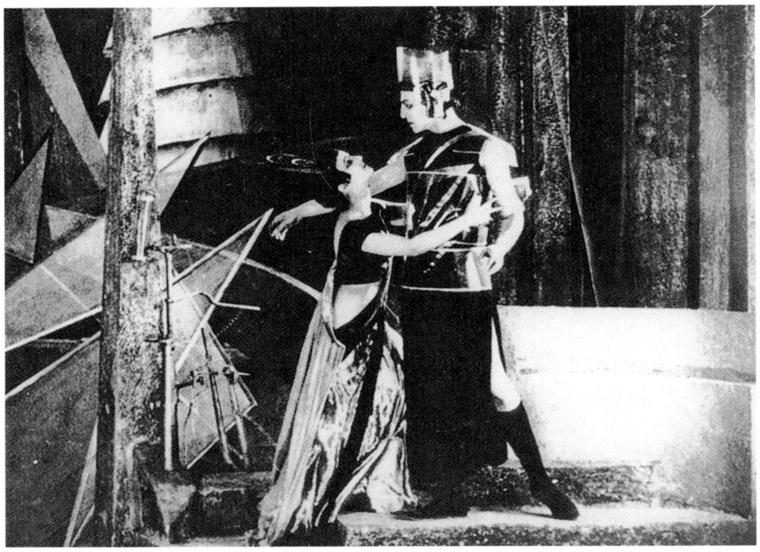

Fig. 21
Yakov Protazanov, *Aelita* (Mezrabpom-Rus, USSR), 1924. Film still. Deutsche Kinemathek, Berlin

Fig. 22
Grigory Kozintsev and Leonid Trauberg, *The Adventures of Oktyabrina* (Sevzapkino, USSR), 1924. Film still. Private collection

(1928) and *Arsenal* (1929), and his first sound film, *Ivan* (1932). These were to form the core of a pantheon of early Soviet classics shared by official Russian history and by a tradition of Western connoisseurship that had been shaped by the film-society movement, which had welcomed these directors and promoted them as among the greatest in world cinema. Authorities as diverse as Charlie Chaplin, the educator Alfred H. Barr, founder of New York's Museum of Modern Art, and the English director Thorold Dickinson, Britain's first film academic, all accepted the idea articulated by Eisenstein that his generation had arrived 'like Bedouin or gold-seekers' to create Soviet cinema from scratch.[2]

In fact, there was rather more continuity with the thriving pre-revolutionary cinema than many wanted to acknowledge. Two of its most successful directors, Vladimir Gardin and Protazanov, resumed their place at the forefront of making dramatic features that tackled new political imperatives in essentially traditional narrative forms. Protazanov had returned from a period of exile in Western Europe, and his Soviet debut *Aelita* (1924, fig. 21) offered a remarkable synthesis of themes and styles. Subverting a science-fiction novel by another repentant émigré, Alexei Tolstoy, he parodied the vogue for 'interplanetary revolution' with a story set in both the shady real world of the NEP economy and on a vividly imagined Mars, with Cubo-Futurist sets and costumes by the avant-garde artist Alexandra Exter. Protazanov went on to make some of the most admired comedies and literary adaptations of the next fifteen years, developing the actor Igor Ilyinsky as the archetypal 'little man' and giving Vsevolod Meyerhold his sole screen acting role in the Soviet era, as a Tsarist official in *The White Eagle* (1928).

Another key figure in the transition, Kuleshov, had previously been an art director for the leading pre-revolutionary director Evgeni Bauer before agreeing to run an experimental workshop in the pioneering film school set up by Gardin in 1920. In this workshop his demonstration of the power of association and contrast between successive images through 'montage' proved seminal, influencing both Pudovkin and Eisenstein, and giving Soviet cinema its claim to originality, as developed by these and other film-makers. His *Extraordinary Adventures of Mr West* gave Soviet production one of its first popular successes, featuring Pudovkin as a grotesque villain and another future director, Boris Barnet, as Mr West's faithful servant 'Cowboy Jeddy', while a stark Jack London adaptation, *By the Law* (1926), was greatly admired by modernist writers associated with the journal *Close Up*.[3]

Eisenstein's path towards cinema lay through theatre design and direction. Working with a variety of short-lived theatre groups during 1920–24, he managed to insert a slapstick short film, *Glumov's Diary* (1923), into his acrobatic production of a venerable classic play by Alexander Ostrovsky. A similar background in Futurist-inspired performance brought Grigory Kozintsev and Leonid Trauberg, founders of the Factory of the Eccentric Actor (FEKS) in Petrograd in 1921, to their first film, *The Adventures of Oktyabrina* (1924, fig. 22), a parody of the popular cliff-hanger serials of the time. Thereafter, Eisenstein, as well as Kozintsev and Trauberg, quickly seized new opportunities for full-scale film-making with *The Strike* (1925, fig. 23) and *The Devil's Wheel* (1926). Both films made exuberant use of real locations, a factory and a fairground respectively, with a battery of 'trick' devices signalling their makers' awareness of contemporary European and especially American popular cinema. Their ostentatious rejection of what they considered the decadent gloom of Tsarist cinema was indeed cultural rather than political revolution.

It was, however, challenged by the first of the Soviet-era pioneers, who had adopted the striking pseudonym of Dziga Vertov.[4] Having served his apprenticeship compiling film reportage during the Civil War, Vertov launched two major newsreel series, *Film Weekly* (*Kino-nedelia*, 1918–19) and the more famous and formally ambitious *Film Truth* (*Kino-pravda*, 1922–25, fig. 24). Deliberately named to evoke the party newspaper, *Pravda*, and using Constructivist-style intertitles designed by Alexander Rodchenko, the second series aimed to be much more than a record of contemporary events. As Vertov declared in a 1923 manifesto:

Fig. 23
Sergei Eisenstein, *The Strike* (Goskino, USSR), 1925. Film still. Deutsche Kinemathek, Berlin

Fig. 24
Dziga Vertov, *Film Truth (Kino-pravda)* (Kultkino, USSR), no. 18, March 1924. Film still. Private collection

> FROM TODAY *neither psychological*
> *nor detective dramas are needed in cinema*
> FROM TODAY *filmed theatrical productions*
> *are unnecessary*
> FROM TODAY *neither Dostoyevsky*
> *nor Nat Pinkerton will be filmed*
> *Everything will be included in the new*
> *definition of film newsreel.*[5]

Speaking in the name of the Kinoki, or 'Soviet of Three' (which comprised his wife and editor Elizabeta Svilova and his brother Mikhail), Vertov denounced all forms of fictional or dramatic cinema as illusory, even 'leprous', insisting that the 'mechanical eye' of the camera is 'more perfect than the human eye for examining the chaos of visual phenomena'. In typically utopian terms, Vertov claimed cinema would offer nothing less than a truly 'Communist deciphering' of 'the world that you do not know'. While few could accept the extremism of his call for the abolition of all that cinema had come to mean – and Eisenstein mocked Vertov's 'cine-eye' by contrasting it with his 'cine-fist' – the pluralism of the mid-1920s ensured that his manifestos were published in a range of journals, such as Vladimir Mayakovsky's LEF and the Constructivist *Kino-fot*. His first feature-length compilation, *Cine-eye* (*Kino-glaz*, 1924, fig. 25) was entered in the 1925 Paris 'Exposition Internationale des Arts Décoratifs et Industriels Modernes', along with Eisenstein's *The Strike*, and both received medals. With increasing difficulty, Vertov continued to find backing for five more non-fiction features, culminating in what was to become his best known: *The Man with a Movie Camera* (1929, fig. 32). This advertised itself in the opening titles as 'an experiment in absolute kinography [based on] its complete separation from the language of theatre and literature'.[6]

Among the early Soviet avant-gardes, Vertov can be seen as the filmic exponent of radical Productivist or Factographic tendencies within Constructivism. Less radical, yet perhaps ultimately more influential, was the work of Esfir Shub, who had been employed in the early 1920s to re-edit imported entertainment films to 'correct' or even reverse their ideologies. (Fritz Lang's crime thriller *Dr Mabuse the Gambler* [1922] became the polemical *Gilded Rot* in 1924, at the hands of Shub and her apprentice Sergei Eisenstein.) In a 'factographic' spirit, Shub went on to collect surviving pre-revolutionary footage and edit it into *The Fall of the Romanov Dynasty* (1927), which became part of Soviet cinema's contribution to celebrating the Revolution's tenth anniversary, showing the regime that had been overthrown. Shub would follow this with more compilation films, including *Leo Tolstoy and the Russia of Nicholas II* (1928), and a pioneering sound manifesto, *The Komsomol – Sponsor of Electrification* (1932), which included an opening demonstration of the technique of recording sound onto film. Other forms of what would now be called 'documentary' were also flourishing under the broad influence of Constructivism, and Viktor Turin's *Turksib* (1929, fig. 26), celebrating the completion of a rail link between Turkestan and Siberia, became a model for the nascent British documentary-film movement, strongly championed by its founding impresario John Grierson.[7]

The Soviet films that commanded most attention abroad were undoubtedly those that commemorated protests and massacres, such as Eisenstein's *The Battleship Potemkin*, Pudovkin's *The Mother* and Kozintsev's and Trauberg's memorial for the Paris Commune, *New Babylon* (1929, fig. 27). But the later 1920s saw the emergence of a trend that spoke more eloquently to domestic audiences: films that dealt with the realities and new dilemmas, especially sexual, of Soviet life. The key film-makers responsible for this trend were Fridrikh Ermler (one of the few Party members among film directors at this time), with *Katka's Reinette Apples* (1926) and *The Parisian Cobbler* (1928); Abram Room, in his *Bed and Sofa* (1927); and in a comedic vein, through no less attuned to the new customs and tensions, Boris Barnet, in *The Girl with the Hat-box* (1927) and *The House on Trubnaya Street* (1928, fig. 38). The development of this reflective genre was, however, interrupted by a combination of events that began in 1929 and diverted Soviet cinema away from one of its

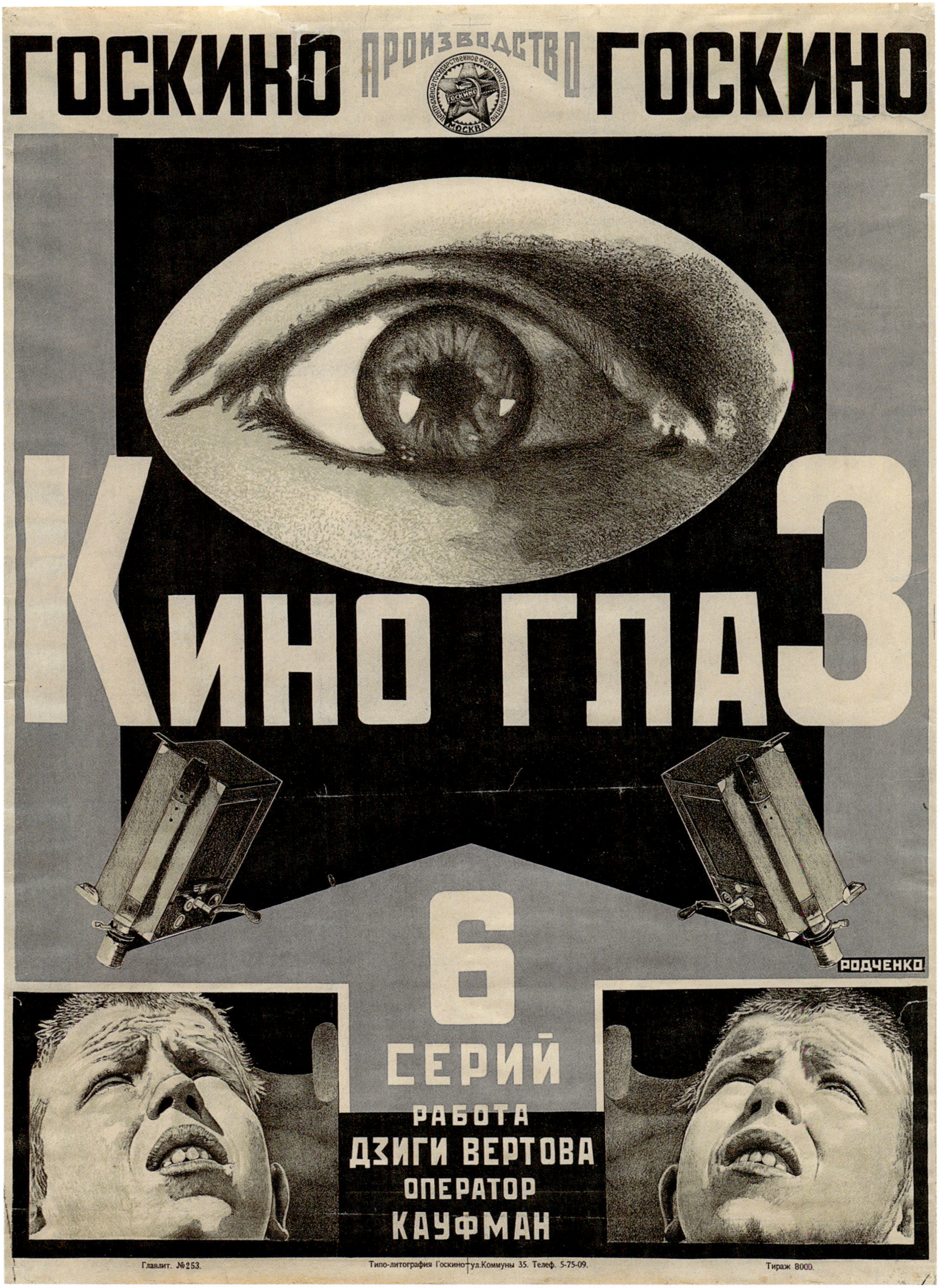
ГОСКИНО
ПРОИЗВОДСТВО
ГОСКИНО
ГОСКИНО
МОСКВА
КИНО ГЛАЗ
РОДЧЕНКО
6
СЕРИЙ
РАБОТА
ДЗИГИ ВЕРТОВА
ОПЕРАТОР
КАУФМАН
Главлит. №253.
Типо-литография Госкино ул.Коммуны 35. Телеф. 5-75-09.
Тираж 8000.

Fig. 25
Alexander Rodchenko, poster for Dziga Vertov's *Cine-eye (Kino-glaz)*, 1924. Lithograph, 92.7 × 69.9 cm. The Museum of Modern Art (MoMA), New York

Fig. 26
Viktor Turin, *Turksib* (Vostokkino, USSR), 1929. Film still. Society for the Co-operation in Russian and Soviet Studies (SCRSS), London

Fig. 27
Grigory Kozintsev and Leonid Trauberg, *New Babylon* (Sovkino, USSR), 1929. Film still. Sovkino collection

most intriguing directions: the investigation of private life within a radically restructured society. One film that continued this path into the 1930s, Room's *A Severe Young Man* (1935), addressed sexuality and the new class distinctions in Soviet society, and paid the price for its temerity by being emphatically banned.[8]

After a decade of relative neglect since Lenin's nationalisation, cinema was to occupy the focus of State attention with a week-long Party conference held in March 1928. Greater ideological direction was demanded, so that 'fiction film [would] actually become a medium of Communist enlightenment and agitation'.[9] Specifically, film-makers were now expected to play their part in 'educating and organising the masses around the basic tasks … of socialist construction', within the framework of the first Five-Year Plan. All this reflected not only Stalin's increasingly authoritarian attitude towards agriculture and industry, as well as the worldwide Communist movement, but also his personal interest in cinema.[10] In late 1927 he had apparently intervened in the editing of Eisenstein's and Alexandrov's *October* to ensure that Trotsky was eliminated from this chronicle of events leading up to the Bolshevik Revolution; and their *The General Line* bore the brunt of his changing attitude towards collectivisation, finally emerging as *The Old and the New* in late 1929, before being quietly suppressed in a purge of films considered ideologically or aesthetically dubious. This increasing degree of control also coincided with Stalin's desire to accelerate the adoption of synchronised sound in Soviet cinema, two years after *The Jazz Singer* had launched the 'talkies' throughout the non-Soviet world. One early beneficiary was Vertov, whose *Enthusiasm* (1930) celebrated the industrial fervour of the Donbas region as a showpiece of the Five-Year Plan, while also demonstrating how the natural sounds of industry could be combined with music and radio speech in a new matrix of audiovisual montage.

Others set out to follow the new line with apparent conviction, grateful for clearer guidance from the State, even if it came at a price. Among a group of films converted to sound during production, Kozintsev's and Trauberg's *Alone* (1931) showed a graduating teacher in Leningrad abruptly assigned to distant Mongolia, far from her fiancé, where she has to battle against prejudice and superstition. Some of the 'eccentric' invention of the original FEKS group returned in their next film, conceived as a 'talkie' from the outset. *The Youth of Maxim* (1935) followed a young worker's induction into the Bolshevik underground in pre-revolutionary St Petersburg, and became not only a template for the new genre of 'Socialist Realism' but an immense popular success, leading to two sequels featuring its attractive hero. It joined *Chapaev* (1934), made by two of Eisenstein's pupils, Georgi and Sergei Vasiliev, and set during the Civil War, which had become Soviet cinema's equivalent of the American West as an arena for adventure, capable of reflecting different ideological emphases. *Chapaev* is a charismatic but uneducated Red Army commander, who accepts the guidance of his political commissar, enabling him to lead his peasant force to victory.

One other film from the early sound period set an unexpected new direction in Soviet cinema: the popular musical. After Eisenstein, Alexandrov and the cameraman Eduard Tisse returned from a two-year leave in Europe and the Americas, having been forced to abandon their Mexican film *¡Que viva México!*, they parted company and Alexandrov directed *Jolly Fellows* (1934). Also known abroad as *Jazz Comedy* or *Moscow Laughs*, this surreal musical fantasy invited comparison with contemporary Hollywood films by the Marx Brothers and Busby Berkeley, and was to launch a new vein of popular music, as well as a new kind of glamorous star, Lyuba Orlova, soon to become Alexandrov's wife. For Eisenstein, as for many Western admirers of 'revolutionary' Soviet cinema, this amounted to apostasy.[11] But Joseph Stalin and Andrei Zhdanov welcomed *Jolly Fellows* as enthusiastically as *Chapaev* and *The Youth of Maxim*, even if several of its key creators would be arrested in the purges of the mid-1930s. Stalin's new-style Soviet cinema had found its models, and when Eisenstein, its most famous director, finally succeeded in returning to production after a series of rejected projects and the banning of a completed film (*Bezhin Meadow*, 1937), he was working within a fundamentally new aesthetic of 'revolutionary romanticism' for his *Alexander Nevsky* (1938) and *Ivan the Terrible* (1944/56).[12]

CHRONOLOGY

Natalia and Nicholas Murray

**Since this chronology spans both pre- and post-revolutionary years the Old Style (Julian) calendar is used for the dates before February 1918 and the New Style (Gregorian) calendar – for the subsequent dates.*

1917

EVENTS IN THE POLITICAL SPHERE

23 FEBRUARY (JULIAN CALENDAR)*
The first Revolution of 1917 starts on International Women's Day. Women factory workers in Petrograd strike for 'Bread and Peace', demanding an end to the First World War and food shortages. The government orders troops to fire on the rioters but the troops mutiny and the city falls into a state of chaos.

27 FEBRUARY
The first Revolution peaks.

2 MARCH
Tsar Nicholas II abdicates after the Cossacks and Moscow join the uprising.

7 MARCH
The new Provisional Government imprisons the Tsar and his wife Alexandra.

9 MARCH
The Tsar and his family are sent to the Alexander Palace in Tsarskoe Selo.

3 APRIL
Lenin arrives at Petrograd's Finland Station on a sealed train financed by Germany, which knew of his plan to withdraw Russia from the 'imperialist' war. In a speech to Bolshevik supporters, he condemns the Provisional Government and calls for a Europe-wide proletarian revolution. Over the next days Lenin speaks at Bolshevik meetings, shocking many supporters by ridiculing those who want

EVENTS IN THE VISUAL ARTS

4 MARCH
Commission for the Protection of Art Valuables established on Maxim Gorky's initiative. Its members, including Alexandre Benois, Fedor Chaliapin and Kuzma Petrov-Vodkin, focus on the pressing need to save palaces and works of art from the threat of war and revolution.

10 MARCH
Artists persistently vote for the separation of art from the State. Nikolai Punin, Natan Altman, Lev Bruni, Alexander Rodchenko, Vsevolod Meyerhold, Vladimir Tatlin and others establish a new union, the Freedom of Arts (Svoboda Iskusstv). Founding of the All-Arts Union (Souz Deiatelei Vsekh Iskusstv), an overarching organisation uniting the majority of Russian artists – from Realists to Futurists.

23 MARCH
The first non-religious procession is mounted in Petrograd, honouring the funerals of the 184 victims of the February Revolution. A million people (half the city's total population) march to the Field of Mars.

4 APRIL
Anatoly Lunacharsky, future Commissar of Public Enlightenment, arrives in Petrograd in a sealed train following Lenin from Switzerland.

10 APRIL
The All-Arts Union issues a petition to the Provisional Government demanding that the development of art in Russia be managed by the artists themselves.

1917

EVENTS IN THE POLITICAL SPHERE

reconciliation with the Mensheviks and reveals his April Theses, an outline of his plans for the Bolsheviks.

5 MAY
The Provisional Government under Prince Georgy Lvov is sworn in and a Constituent Assembly formed, which spans highly divergent interests, from nationalist ex-Duma members to agitators for an international socialist world. 'Dual power' (Soviets and Provisional Government attempting to work in parallel) is agreed.

1 JUNE
The First All-Russian Congress of Soviets takes place.

3–4 JULY (THE 'JULY DAYS')
Workers and soldiers demand that the Soviet takes power. Sporadic fighting follows (fig. 28).

18 JULY
Lenin flees to Finland. A warrant for his arrest is issued, naming him a German agent provocateur.

24 JULY
The second Provisional Government is sworn in under Alexander Kerensky.

AUGUST
The Bolsheviks win control over the Petrograd and Moscow Soviets. Early August: the Tsar and his family are exiled to Tobolsk in Siberia by order of the Provisional Government, which then moves into the Tsar's former private rooms.

30 AUGUST
General Kornilov's attempted putsch fails. Kerensky, who is seen as complicit, loses support and later resigns.

1 SEPTEMBER
Russia is declared a republic, with Kerensky in charge.

SEPTEMBER
Lenin returns to Russia. Peasant land-seizure continues, reaching near-insurrection in Tambov province.

EVENTS IN THE VISUAL ARTS

18 APRIL
The first legal celebration of International Workers' Solidarity Day is marked by demonstrations and street-theatre performances in Petrograd and Moscow.

26 APRIL
Decree of the Provisional Government 'On the transition of all significant portraits of Russian Tsars and their families from government institutions to the Winter Palace'.

1 JUNE
Petrograd newspapers announce that most museums have closed for the summer due to the absence of visitors.

1 JULY
The government declares the nationalisation of all imperial palaces in Petrograd and sets up an Art Historical Committee to list the treasures in the Winter Palace and other imperial property.

7 AUGUST
The first meeting of the Moscow branch of the Union of Artistic Affairs is held at the Tretyakov Gallery in Moscow. Protection of monuments becomes the highest priority.

20 AUGUST
The Petrograd press announces new designs for postage stamps by such artists as Ivan Bilibin and Sergei Chekhonin.

SEPTEMBER
Works of art from the Hermitage, Russian Museum and Imperial Academy of Arts are urgently evacuated to Moscow.

EVENTS IN THE POLITICAL SPHERE

EVENTS IN THE VISUAL ARTS

1917

5 OCTOBER
In Petrograd Lunacharsky gives the first of a series of lectures 'Proletariat and Culture'.

16–19 OCTOBER
Lunacharsky (by then President of the Culture and Education Committee of the Petrograd Party) calls the first conference of proletarian cultural-education organisations. The Petrograd Proletkult (Proletarian Culture Organisation) is formed, led by Alexander Bogdanov.

24 OCTOBER
The recently formed Bolshevik Military Revolutionary Committee seizes control of Petrograd's key transport, communication, printing and utilities hubs, and overthrows the Provisional Government on the eve of the second meeting of the All-Russia Congress of Soviets.

25 OCTOBER
The virtually bloodless storming of the Winter Palace, seat of the Provisional Government, occurs.

26–27 OCTOBER
Lenin announces the formation of a new government at the Second All-Russia Congress of Soviets. Menshevik attendees protest at the 'illegal' seizure of power and risk of Civil War.

27 OCTOBER
Soviet proclamations are made on land and peace. Ceasefire is declared, together with a law to hand over land to village communities.

30 OCTOBER
Lunacharsky proclaims the Winter Palace in Petrograd the state museum.

2 NOVEMBER
Lunacharsky issues a decree on the inspection of all the art treasures in Petrograd collections. On the same day, following reports about the destruction of palaces in Moscow, he sends a letter of resignation, which is declined by Lenin.

12 NOVEMBER
Lunacharsky makes his first declaration as Commissar of Enlightenment, proclaiming an abdication of the powers of Soviet governmental institutions into a directorate of cultural affairs named NARKOMPROS (People's Commissariat of Enlightenment).

17 NOVEMBER
Civil War, an event seen as inevitable by Lenin, breaks out.

NOVEMBER
The All-Russia Collegium of Museum Affairs and Preservation of Works of Art and Antiquity is formed within NARKOMPROS.

DECEMBER
The new government sets up the Cheka (the military and security arm of the Bolshevik Communist Party, to be led by Felix Dzerzhinsky), the Vesenkha (Central Economic Council) and Sovnarkom, the All-Bolshevik Council of the People's Commissars, the highest government authority. When the Bolsheviks came to power in October 1917, theirs was not a mass movement – the Party then contained at best 350,000 (0.25%) people in a country of 140 million.

1918

5 JANUARY
Despite recent events, the Constituent Assembly opens. The Bolsheviks poll third behind the Social Revolutionaries and Mensheviks. The Assembly rejects a Bolshevik resolution, the session is adjourned and the building locked.

6 JANUARY
The Constituent Assembly is dissolved.

EVENTS IN THE POLITICAL SPHERE

EVENTS IN THE VISUAL ARTS

1918

12 JANUARY
Declaration of the Rights of Working and Exploited People.

14 JANUARY
An attempt is made on Lenin's life; his car is shot at, supposedly by a group of former army officers.

15 JANUARY
Sovnarkom formally establishes the Workers' and Peasants' Red Army.

JANUARY
Petrograd is in dire straits: electricity is cut off, the trams stop and the sewage system fails, leading to an epidemic of stomach diseases. The State monetary system collapses and strictly rationed food coupons replace money. Political posters fill empty shop windows. To make matters worse, starving, desperate people are prevented from leaving the city. The only chance to flee is to join the Red Army.

29 JANUARY
A Department of Visual Arts (IZO) is formed within NARKOMPROS and established in the Petrograd Winter Palace. Representatives of the more radical, leftist groups gather around IZO. The artist David Shterenberg is appointed head of IZO NARKOMPROS. Between 1918 and 1920 IZO organises 28 exhibitions and acquires a total of 1,926 works by 415 artists.
The Winter Palace is re-named the Palace of Arts.
The Imperial Porcelain Factory is nationalised and re-named the State Porcelain Factory (GFZ). It produces propaganda wares, ranging from plates to figurines.

FEBRUARY
Mobilisation of the Red Army begins. The Gregorian calendar is adopted by dropping the Julian dates of 1–13 February 1918.
The new government enters formal negotiations with Germany to end Russia's participation in the First World War.

3 MARCH
After long delays and under threat, the Bolshevik leaders sign the Brest-Litovsk Treaty with Germany, ceding major areas of former Russian territory.

5 MARCH
The capital is moved to Moscow due to risk of German attack on Petrograd. the Bolshevik Party is re-named the Communist Party.

13 MARCH
Trotsky is appointed People's Commissar of Army and Navy Affairs.

MARCH
'War Communism' is announced. Industries are nationalised, a state trading monopoly created, financial transactions suspended and peasant grain and food surpluses requisitioned. War Communism causes major disillusionment, dissent and poverty, but beneficially focuses resources on the Red Army.

APRIL
The White Army, led by anti-Bolshevik former Tsarist officers, approaches Tobolsk, prompting the Bolsheviks to move the imperial family west to Ekaterinburg in the Urals.

12 APRIL
The Imperial Academy of Arts is closed down and replaced by the Petrograd State Free Artistic Workshops (PEGOSKhUM). Entrance exams are abolished to encourage students from all ranks of society to enrol.
Lenin announces the Plan for Monumental Propaganda – a strategy employing visual monumental art (revolutionary slogans and monumental sculpture) as a means of propagating revolutionary and Communist ideas. Between 1918 and 1920, 25 monuments are erected in Moscow, and 15 in Petrograd.

MAY DAY
First military parade under the Bolsheviks. Petrograd is decorated by avant-garde artists.

Page 40:
Fig. 28
Viktor Bulla, *The Shooting of Demonstrators on Nevsky Prospect, Petrograd*, 4 July 1917. Photograph. State Central Museum of Contemporary History of Russia, Moscow, 36864/29

Fig. 29
The storming of the Winter Palace as portrayed by Sergei Eisenstein in *October*, 1928. Film still. Lobster Films, Paris

1918

EVENTS IN THE POLITICAL SPHERE

10 JULY
The Fifth All-Russian Congress of Workers, Peasants and Cossack Deputies establishes the first constitution of the RSFSR (Russian Soviet Federative Socialist Republic). The new coat of arms with hammer and sickle in the centre is adopted.
17 JULY
The Tsar and his family are murdered by the Bolsheviks in Ekaterinburg. Around the same date, a Socialist Revolutionary attempt to take power fails, timed to coincide with an Allied landing in Arhkangelsk, which is postponed. An anti-Bolshevik uprising in Ekaterinburg is put down.
30 AUGUST
Second attempt on Lenin's life by the Socialist Revolutionary Fanya Kaplan.

EVENTS IN THE VISUAL ARTS

1 JUNE
NARKOMPROS announces plans for a Museum of Artistic Culture with two central branches in Moscow and Petrograd and smaller collections across Russia. Between 1918 and 1921, 36 museums and art schools are allocated or receive works, thus setting up important collections of modern Russian art that could be seen across the country.
3 JUNE
Decree of the Soviet of People's Commissars on the nationalisation of the Tretyakov Gallery in Moscow.

1918

EVENTS IN THE POLITICAL SPHERE

5 SEPTEMBER
In response to the failed assassination of Lenin and to the successful assassination of the Petrograd Cheka chief Moisei Uritsky on 17 August 1918, the Bolsheviks instruct Dzerzhinsky to commence the Red Terror, which had been announced in the 1 September 1918 issue of *Krasnaya Gazeta* (*The Red Newspaper*). Under Lenin's instructions, 'anyone who dares to spread the slightest rumour against the Soviet regime will be arrested immediately and sent to a concentration camp'. This edict technically ceases in October 1918, but actually runs until 1923. In the period 1917 to 1923 between 50,000 and 200,000 people are killed.

EVENTS IN THE VISUAL ARTS

SEPTEMBER
Kazimir Malevich drafts a list of paintings for State purchase, including the works of 40 avant-garde Russian artists, plus Pablo Picasso and André Derain. Lunacharsky broadens the list to 143 artists including representatives of the World of Art and the Wanderers movements. Orphans are housed in the grand rooms of the Palace of Art (Winter Palace), now re-named the Palace of the Poor.
5 SEPTEMBER
The Moscow SVOMAS (Free State Art Studios) are founded from an amalgamation of Moscow School of Painting, Sculpture and Architecture with Stroganov Art School.
15–20 SEPTEMBER
First All-Russian Proletkult Conference.
1 OCTOBER
PEGOSKhUM, the Petrograd State Free Artistic Workshops, re-named the Petrograd SVOMAS.
5 OCTOBER
A decree on the registration and preservation of works of art and antiquity in the possession of private citizens, societies and institutions allows Soviets to confiscate works of art from private collections.

EVENTS IN THE POLITICAL SPHERE

1918

NOVEMBER
Germany withdraws from Russian territory.

21 NOVEMBER
Sovnarkom forbids all private food trade and establishes a rationed distribution of food in accordance with people's class: workers and officials are allowed 1/2 pound of bread per day; public servants 1/4 pound; the bourgeoisie 1/8 pound; and dependants 1/16 pound.

18 DECEMBER
The city of Perm falls to the Whites. Leon Trotsky reorganises the Red Army, recruiting former imperial officers.

1919

FEBRUARY
The White Armies make a coordinated multi-front attack but are driven back by the Red Army, which captures Kiev.
Russian–Polish war breaks out.
MARCH
Eighth Party Congress. Formation of the Politburo (the executive committee of the Communist Party) and Orgburo (the Organisational Bureau of the Central Committee of the Communist Party).

28 JUNE
The Treaty of Versailles is signed, bringing the First World War to an end.
15 AUGUST
Corrective prison camps are established by Party decree.

EVENTS IN THE VISUAL ARTS

1918

NOVEMBER
The International Office of IZO is established to 'effect the unification of the progressive fighters of the new art in the name of constructing a new universal artistic culture'.
5 NOVEMBER
Lenin signs a Sovnarkom decree nationalising the Shchukin Gallery, and later also the Morosov and Ostroukhov private collections.
7 NOVEMBER
The first anniversary of the October Revolution is celebrated throughout Russia. Artists from all artistic movements contribute to the decoration of cities.
Vladimir Mayakovsky's play *Mystery Bouffe* is premiered in the Petrograd Musical Drama Theatre.
11 NOVEMBER
The People's Art School is opened in Vitebsk by Marc Chagall, then Commissar of Artistic Affairs for the Vitebsk region.
14 NOVEMBER
A new decree states that no works of art given to the Hermitage for restoration, valuation or temporary conservation can be taken out of the museum.
26 NOVEMBER
Decree on the recognition of scientific, literary, musical and artistic works as State property.
5 DECEMBER
First issue published of the Futurist newspaper *Art of the Commune* (*Iskusstvo Kommuny*).
Vasily Kandinsky (at the time a leading member of IZO in Moscow) publishes his autobiography *Steps*, declaring himself the inventor of abstract painting.

1919

FEBRUARY
At the All-Russian Museum Conference in Petrograd, a general concept for museums of contemporary art is approved.

10 APRIL
A decree of the Petrograd Soviet orders the removal of the 'left' artists of IZO NARKOMPROS from involvement in May Day street decorations.
13 APRIL
The 'First State Free Exhibition of Works of Art' opens in the former Winter Palace in Petrograd. It includes 1,826 works of art by 299 artists from the World of Art to Suprematists.
MAY
El Lissitzky accepts an invitation from Chagall and travels to Vitebsk, where he teaches at the People's Art School.
The first exhibition of the Young Artists Society (OBMOKhU), organised by students from the Free State Art Studios, opens in the former Stroganov Art School in Moscow.
25 MAY
The first parade of athletes and Universal Military Training troops is held in Moscow's Red Square.
SUMMER
The Museum of Artistic Culture opens in Moscow, directed by Kandinsky, Rodchenko and Petr Vilyams.

EVENTS IN THE POLITICAL SPHERE

1919

OCTOBER
The White Army and General Yudenich reach the suburbs of Petrograd.

1920

FEBRUARY
Polish–Soviet War over the control of an area equivalent to today's Ukraine and parts of modern-day Belarus intensifies.

9 MARCH
Party Congress held, at which the Nomenklatura process, a system for listing potential recruits for Party roles, is set in motion.
29 MARCH–5 APRIL
During the Ninth Congress of the Russian Communist Party, Trotsky openly criticises Stalin's behaviour. The new Workers' Opposition group emerges amid concern over the 'growing chasm' between workers and the Party which claims to act in their name.
7 APRIL
The Third All-Russia Congress of Trade Unions decrees that all salaries will be paid in food, cloth, shoes and soap vouchers, the amount received depending on the recipient's category.
25 APRIL
Poland invades Ukraine.

19 JULY
Second Congress of the Third International in Moscow.
AUGUST
Polish–Russian Armistice. Outbreak of peasant insurrection at Tambov.

EVENTS IN THE VISUAL ARTS

1919

AUTUMN
Propaganda posters created by artists and poets under the supervision of the Chief Committee for Political Education are displayed in the windows of the Russian Telegraph Agency (ROSTA).

1920

JANUARY
Foundation of the Decorative Institute in Petrograd with various workshops producing posters, agitprop and theatre designs. Malevich is appointed director in 1925. Employees of the institute at various times include Tatlin, Ilya Chashnik, Mikhail Matiushin and Punin.
11 JANUARY
The Museum of the October Revolution is established in the private rooms of the imperial family in the former Winter Palace.

6 FEBRUARY
First performance of the *Suprematist Ballet* with set designs by Nina Kogan.

17 MARCH
The newspaper *Izvestiia* in Vitebsk publishes the manifesto of the Affirmers of the New Art (UNOVIS), an art association set up by students and followers of Malevich at the People's Art School in Vitebsk.

MAY
The Institute of Artistic Culture (INKhUK) is established in Moscow within IZO NARKOMPROS to determine the course of artistic experiment in post-revolutionary Russia. Its first director is Kandinsky.
SVOMAS is reorganised into the Higher State Artistic and Technical Workshops (VKhUTEMAS) of the re-established Academy of Art and entrance exams are reinstated. 'Left' artists are gradually replaced by more traditional academicians.
JULY
A new 'political-educational sector' of NARKOMPROS, Glavpolitprosvet (the Main Political-Educational Committee), is formed.
AUGUST
Naum Gabo issues with his brother Antoine Pevsner a 'Realistic Manifesto' proclaiming the tenets of pure Constructivism.
SEPTEMBER
VKhUTEMAS is founded in Moscow, replacing the Free State Art Studios (SVOMAS).

EVENTS IN THE POLITICAL SPHERE

1920

NOVEMBER
White Army troops led by General Wrangel are defeated in the Crimea by the Red Army. Contemporaries describe Petrograd in 1920 as a starving, ragged city – half-empty, without electricity, cars or cabmen. Some 775 factories had been closed down due to lack of oil. Only 722,000 people remain in Petrograd, compared with the 1918 population of two million.

22–29 DECEMBER
The Eighth All-Russian Congress of Soviets adopts the plan of the State Commission for the Electrification of Russia (GOELRO), envisaged for 10 to 15 years.

1921

FEBRUARY
Foundation of Gosplan, responsible for central economic planning.

MARCH
Further cuts in the bread ration lead to worker unrest and extreme urban poverty across Russia.

EVENTS IN THE VISUAL ARTS

1920

5–12 OCTOBER
The Central Committee issues a directive to incorporate Proletkult into NARKOMPROS.

7 NOVEMBER
The mass spectacle 'The Storming of the Winter Palace' is presented on Palace Square (now Uritsky Square) in Petrograd with 6,000 performers – far more dramatically than the event it commemorates.

8 NOVEMBER
Tatlin unveils his *Model for the Monument to the Third International* (fig. 46).

1 DECEMBER
In a letter 'On the Proletkult', Lenin severely criticises the concept put forward by Proletkult ideology of creating purely 'proletarian art'.

EVENTS IN THE POLITICAL SPHERE

1921

1 MARCH
Mutiny of the 'loyal' Kronstadt Garrison, demanding free election to the Soviets.

15 MARCH
The Tenth Party Congress approves the resolution 'On Political Enlightenment and Agitational Tasks of the Party'. In addition, the New Economic Policy (NEP), 'state capitalism', is launched in an attempt to reduce peasant unrest by allowing freer trading giving peasants rights to sell surplus grain. This helps restore the shattered economy, increases productivity and organises commerce.

17 MARCH
The Kronstadt mutiny is suppressed by force. About 1,000 soldiers are killed in the revolt and between 1,200 and 2,168 people executed. Following the mutiny a more centralised authority is established, resulting in the loss of freedom of speech, even within the Party. The Workers' Opposition movement is censured.

18 MARCH
Signing of The Peace of Riga, a formal peace treaty dividing the disputed territories between Poland and Soviet Russia.

EVENTS IN THE VISUAL ARTS

1921

SPRING
The Union of Poets and Painters (Makovets) is founded in Moscow by former members of the Moscow Salon, World of Art and Jack of Diamonds groups. Its 20 members aspire to capture a new reality in a romantic manner.

Fig. 30
El Lissitzky, *Beat the Whites with the Red Wedge*, 1920. Lithograph in red and black

Fig. 31
Dmitry Moor, *Help!*, 1921. Lithograph

Fig. 32
Dziga Vertov's *The Man with a Movie Camera* (Vufku, Ukraine), 1929. Spinning spools of thread. Film still. Lobster Films, Paris

Fig. 33
Alexander Dovzhenko
Earth (Wufku, Ukraine),
1930. Excited peasants
welcoming the arrival of
their first tractor. Film still.
Lobster Films, Paris

Fig. 34
Alexander Rodchenko,
'Beer Beats Poteen!'
(Advertisement for
Mosselprom Store), 1923.
Colour lithograph

Fig. 35
Vladimir Lebedev, *The Red*
Vision of Communism is
Sweeping Over Europe,
1923. Colour lithograph

Fig. 36
Alexander Rodchenko and
Vladimir Mayakovsky,
'Workers: Expensiveness
and NEP Don't Scare Us'
(Bread Advertisement
for Mosselprom Store),
1923. Colour lithograph.
Russian State Library,
Moscow

1921

EVENTS IN THE POLITICAL SPHERE

JUNE
the ongoing peasant uprising in Tambov province is suppressed. Maxim Gorky returns to Sorrento in Italy (from 1906 to 1913 he lived on Capri), diagnosed with tuberculosis.

AUTUMN
famine strikes the Volga, leading the government to demand surrender of church valuables for famine relief.

EVENTS IN THE VISUAL ARTS

3 APRIL
The Museum of Artistic Culture in Petrograd (founded in 1920) opens to the public.
3 AUGUST
Punin and the Symbolist poet Nikolai Gumilev are arrested in distant connection with the Kronstadt mutiny. Punin is released with Lunacharsky's help but Gumilev is shot.
7 AUGUST
The death of Alexander Blok signals the end of artistic freedom.
SEPTEMBER
Two-part art exhibition '5 × 5 = 25' opens in Moscow. Alexandra Exter, Lyubov Popova, Rodchenko, Varvara Stepanova and Alexander Vesnin present highly abstracted geometric work and announce the 'end' or 'death' of art.
AUTUMN
The IZO department of NARKOMPROS is closed down.
DECEMBER
Vasily Kandinsky travels to Germany to organise a branch of the Russian Academy of Artistic Sciences (of which he was vice-president) in Berlin. He never returns to Russia. Formation of the new art groups Bytie (Being) and the New Society of Painters (NOZh) in Moscow. Bytie is established by a group of VKhUTEMAS graduates along with former members of the Jack of Diamonds group. NOZh artists, whose members include Samuil Adlivankin and Grigory Riazhsky, show a satirical bias (for example mocking 'NEP-men').

1922

EVENTS IN THE POLITICAL SPHERE

FEBRUARY
The Cheka is reorganised as the GPU, a more centralised bureau, but still under Dzerzhinsky.
MARCH
Stalin is appointed General Secretary at the Eleventh Party Congress.
APRIL
Patriarch Tikhon, Patriarch of Moscow and All Russia of the Orthodox Church, is put under house arrest.

JUNE
Trial of Metropolitan Veniamin, the most senior Petrograd bishop in the Orthodox Church, followed by his execution (and later, canonisation).

EVENTS IN THE VISUAL ARTS

MARCH
Kandinsky starts teaching at the Bauhaus in Weimar.

MAY
Opening of 'Paintings by Realist Artists to Help the Starving', the first exhibition of the newly formed Association of Artists of Revolutionary Russia (AKhRR), which brings together painters, graphic artists and sculptors and is the predecessor of the future Union of Artists of the USSR. Members include Abram Arkhipov, Isaak Brodsky, Boris Kustodiev and Konstantin Yuon.
JUNE
The 'Association of New Trends in Art' exhibition opens at the Museum of Artistic Culture in Petrograd.

1922

EVENTS IN THE POLITICAL SPHERE

SEPTEMBER
160 intellectuals are expelled to Riga on the first 'Philosophers' ship'.

OCTOBER
Civil War finally ends with the defeat of the White Army in Crimea.

DECEMBER
Formation of the Union of Soviet Socialist Republics (USSR). Lenin's relationship with Stalin deteriorates over Stalin's heavy-handed and chauvinistic handling of the merger of Soviet republics into one federal state.

29 DECEMBER
The First Congress of Soviets of the USSR adopts the Declaration of the Creation of the USSR.

EVENTS IN THE VISUAL ARTS

SEPTEMBER
Chagall applies for an exit visa for France.

15 OCTOBER
The 'First Russian Art Exhibition' opens at the Galerie Van Diemen in Berlin. More than 700 works by 167 artists are shown, including Kandinsky, Altman and El Lissitzky.

1923

12 APRIL
Party Conference held. The USSR Constitution is published.

SUMMER
The 'Scissors crisis' breaks out, comprising bitter arguments over economic investment priorities (industry versus agriculture).

13 OCTOBER
A secret decree of Sovnarkom establishes a prison on the Solovetsky Islands.

NOVEMBER
A second 'Philosophers' ship' leaves for Odessa.
About this time the cult of 'Leninism' is initiated, Lenin now being largely detached from government, too ill to read or write. Leninism is managed as a flexible concept by the Politburo and subsequently used to define 'good' and 'bad' adherence to Party policy.

APRIL
Chagall arrives in France.

MAY
The 'Exhibition of Works of Petrograd Artists of All Trends, 1918–1923' opens at the Academy of Arts in Petrograd, with 263 artists displaying 1,621 works.

19 AUGUST
The 'First All-Russian Agricultural and Handicraft Industries Exhibition' opens in Moscow on the future site of Gorky Park (founded in March 1928). Pavilions are built by such architects as Konstantin Melnikov and Fedor Shekhtel and decorated by artists including Petrov-Vodkin.

AUGUST
Malevich is appointed director of the Museum of Artistic Culture in Petrograd.
Establishment of *LEF* – the journal of the Left Front of the Arts – an association of avant-garde writers, photographers, critics, artists and designers, aiming 'to shape revolutionary art'. (It runs until 1925 as *LEF* and from 1929 as *New LEF*.)

1924

21 JANUARY
Lenin dies.

24 JANUARY
Petrograd is re-named Leningrad. Shortly afterwards, Trotsky is defeated in the Politburo by a triumvirate of Stalin, Lev Kamenev and Grigory Zinoviev.

26 JANUARY
The Second All-Union Congress of Soviets opens in commemoration of Lenin. In a speech on behalf of the Bolshevik Party, Stalin vows to fulfil Lenin's behest.

1924
The Museum of Artistic Culture in Moscow becomes a branch of the State Tretyakov Gallery.

EVENTS IN THE POLITICAL SPHERE

MAY
At the Thirteenth Party Congress Lenin's 'Letter to Congress' rejecting Stalin as his successor is read out, but dropped from the minutes and later declared a forgery by Stalin.

JUNE
A resolution of the Central Committee on 'Party Policy in the Field of Artistic Literature' is passed, determining the Party's approach towards the activities of the artistic associations of the time.

EVENTS IN THE VISUAL ARTS

1 JUNE
The last exhibition of the World of Art group of artists opens at the Municipal Museum (the former Anichkov Palace) in Leningrad.

1 OCTOBER
The Museum of Artistic Culture in Leningrad is reformed into the State Institute of Artistic Culture (GINKhUK).

OCTOBER
The Painters of Moscow group is established to make a true synthesis of content and modern form. It attracts up to 40 artists, including Igor Grabar, Alexander Drevin, Nadezhda Udaltsova, Ilya Mashkov and Kuprin.

18 OCTOBER
The 'First German Exhibition' opens at the Historical Museum in Moscow before travelling to Leningrad and Saratov.
The Society of Artists Named After Ilya Repin, founded by Repin's students, includes new members Brodsky, Grabar and Filip Maliavin.

5 DECEMBER
Seven icon painters from the village of Palekh organise an Artel of Ancient Painting, using their skill to produce decorative art with Soviet subject-matter.

1925

JANUARY
Trotsky is dismissed as War Commissar.

18 MARCH
The law of obligatory military service is accepted.

10 APRIL
The city of Tsaritsyn is re-named Stalingrad.

18–31 DECEMBER
At the Fourteenth Party Conference, 'Socialism in One Country' is proclaimed, implying 'build USSR first, the rest later'. The country is set on a course for industrialisation.

8 FEBRUARY
The seventh AKhRR exhibition, 'Revolution, Daily Life and Labour', opens in Moscow.
The 4 Arts Society is set up by Bruni, Pavel Kuznetsov, Petr Miturich, Petrov-Vodkin and others, uniting more than 70 painters, draughtsmen, sculptors and architects.

8 MARCH
The 'Woman in Art' exhibition opens at the State Tretyakov Gallery in Moscow.

APRIL
First exhibition of the 4 Arts Society at the Museum of Visual Arts in Moscow.

26 APRIL
The first exhibition of the Society of Easel Painters (OST) opens in Moscow.
The Masters of Analytical Art (MAI) group is formed in Leningrad, uniting Pavel Filonov's students. At its peak, it has 70 members.
The Society of Russian Sculptors (ORS) is established. Its members and exhibitors include Altman and Nikolai Andreev.

21 DECEMBER
Premiere of *The Battleship Potemkin*, a silent film about a mutiny, directed by Sergei Eisenstein.

EVENTS IN THE POLITICAL SPHERE

1926

24 APRIL
Germany and the Soviet Union sign a treaty pledging neutrality in the event of an attack on the other by a third party for a period of five years.

23 OCTOBER
Trotsky and another founding member of the Bolshevik Party, Lev Kamenev, are expelled from the Politburo.

3 NOVEMBER
A further founding member of the Bolshevik Party, Sergo Ordzhonikidze, is expelled from the Politburo.

1927

25 FEBRUARY
Article 58 is adopted, giving authorities a free hand to make arrests and resulting in the imprisonment and execution of many prominent people, as well as numerous ordinary innocents.

MAY
A rupture in diplomatic relations with Britain leads to growing fear of an international war.

OCTOBER
Trotsky and Zinoviev are expelled from the Central Committee. The United Opposition attempts to organise independent demonstrations commemorating The tenth anniversary of the Bolshevik seizure of power, but the demonstrators are dispersed by force.

EVENTS IN THE VISUAL ARTS

1926
The Decorative Institute in Leningrad becomes part of GINKhUK.

FEBRUARY
Malevich is dismissed as director of GINKhUK.

MARCH
Graduates of VKhUTEIN establish the Circle of Artists group in Leningrad. It attracts more than 40 members.

3 MAY
The AKhRR opens its eighth exhibition 'Life and Customs of the USSR Peoples' in the grounds of the Agricultural Exhibition in Moscow (now Gorky Park).

16 MAY
The 'Revolutionary Art of the West' exhibition opens at the former Rumiantsev Museum in Moscow. The Painters of Moscow group merges with AKhRR.

7 NOVEMBER
The first completed monument to Lenin is erected in front of the Finland station in Leningrad.

1 DECEMBER
GINKhUK is closed down.

15 DECEMBER
GINKhUK's staff, funds and property are handed over to the State Institute of the History of Art. Punin moves its collection to the recently opened Department of Newest Trends at the Russian Museum and the State Museum Fund.

1927

MARCH
Malevich travels to Warsaw for his first foreign exhibition and on to Berlin for a retrospective, finally bringing him international recognition. He leaves most of the paintings, architectural models and manuscripts in these exhibitions in Germany. Some members of Makovets form the Path of Painting Society; others join the 4 Arts Society and the Society of Moscow Artists.

APRIL
Opening of the 'Latest Trends in Art' exhibition at the State Russian Museum in Leningrad.

17 APRIL
Exhibition of MAI group held at the House of the Press in the centre of Leningrad.

8 MAY
First exhibition of the Circle of Artists group opens at the State Russian Museum in Leningrad.

AUGUST
The State Museum Fund, responsible for the purchase of contemporary art, is abolished. VKhUTEMAS is replaced with VKhUTEIN (Higher State Artistic and Technical Institute). Society of Moscow Artists (OMKh) founded in Moscow. Comprising former members of the Jack of Diamonds, Painters of Moscow, Bytie and Makovets groups, it views art as 'a tool for the active reconstruction of life'. Led by Aristarkh Lentulov OMKh's 70 members include Mashkov, Georgy Rublev and Igor Grabar.

EVENTS IN THE POLITICAL SPHERE

1927

12 NOVEMBER
Trotsky and Zinoviev are expelled from the Communist Party.

2–19 DECEMBER
Party Congress, at which the Collectivisation of Agriculture is decreed.

1928

SPRING
A grain procurement crisis occurs following a two-million-ton shortfall in grains bought by the State. Hoarding by kulaks (land-owning, wealthier peasants) is blamed.

7 APRIL
Death of Lenin's old adversary Alexander Bogdanov.

MAY
Trial in Shakhty of 'bourgeois intellectuals' accused (on flimsy evidence) of wrecking agricultural equipment: eleven death sentences are passed; five are executed.

SUMMER
Launch of the Cultural Revolution. Anti-intelligentsia, anti-bureaucrat Class War is initiated, followed by purges. The search to promote an educated proletarian-based professional class is set in motion to modernise industry. NEP ends.

OCTOBER
The first Five-Year Plan is launched (it runs to December 1932).

1929

FEBRUARY
Trotsky is deported from the Soviet Union.

APRIL
New laws on 'religious associations' are passed, forbidding the promotion of religion. The mass closure of churches begins.

SEPTEMBER
Harvest Day is re-named 'Day of Harvest and Collectivisation' to remove traditional religious connotations.

AUTUMN
Forced collectivisation of agriculture starts. Nikolai Bukharin and Alexei Rykov (President of the Soviet Union) oppose collectivisation of agriculture and advocate a return to the NEP, but the rest of the Politburo sides with Stalin.

NOVEMBER
Having initially allied himself and his 'Centre' faction with Bukharin, to defeat Trotsky and the Left, Stalin turns on his former allies.

EVENTS IN THE VISUAL ARTS

1927

1 NOVEMBER
Opening of the 'Latest Trends in Art' exhibition at the State Russian Museum in Leningrad.

7 NOVEMBER
Premiere at the Bolshoi Theatre in Moscow of *October* (fig. 29), a silent film produced by Eisenstein and Grigori Alexandrov (a celebratory dramatisation of the 1917 October Revolution commissioned for the tenth anniversary of the event).

28 NOVEMBER
500 paintings from the Hermitage are transferred to Moscow, including works by Rembrandt, Rubens, Van Dyck, Poussin and Veronese (70 more are sent later, most of which are sold to Western museums and collectors).

1928

FEBRUARY
The 'Permanent Exhibition of Avant-garde Art' opens at the State Tretyakov Gallery in Moscow.

13 APRIL
The government issues the resolution 'On setting up an agency for ideological and organisational control of development in the field of literature and art' (GLAVISKUSSTVO).

MAY
RAPP (Russian Association of Proletarian Writers) is formed, working to unmask the 'rightist danger' in the arts.

16 SEPTEMBER
An exhibition of modern French art opens at the State Museum of New Western Art, Moscow, with the participation of Russian artists living in France, including Yury Annenkov, Goncharova, Mikhail Larionov, Ivan Puni, Chagall and Exter.

1929

27 APRIL
The third exhibition of the Circle of Artists group opens at the State Russian Museum in Leningrad.

SEPTEMBER
Lunacharsky is dismissed as Commissar for Enlightenment and replaced by the Party apparatchik Andrei Bubnov.

AUTUMN
Filonov's one-man exhibition is organised at the State Russian Museum in Moscow. The paintings are hung and a catalogue prepared but the exhibition never opens to the public.

1 NOVEMBER
Malevich's last one-man exhibition opens at the State Tretyakov Gallery in Moscow.

EVENTS IN THE POLITICAL SPHERE

EVENTS IN THE VISUAL ARTS

1929

17 NOVEMBER
Bukharin is expelled from the Politburo; the 'Right Opposition' inside the Communist movement is defeated, accused of representing the influence of the peasantry and the danger of capitalist restoration.

21 NOVEMBER
The 'Law on Defectors' is accepted: from now on anyone who refuses to return to the USSR will be announced a criminal and if caught will be shot within 24 hours.

1930

30 JANUARY
Decree by the Politburo of the Central Committee of the All-Russian Communist Party 'on measures aimed at liquidating the *kulak* economies in areas of total collectivisation'. This document serves as legal grounds for mass repression of the Russian peasantry, which is fulfilled with great cruelty.

2 MARCH
Pravda publishes Stalin's article 'Dizzy with Success', praising the success of the collectivisation programme, despite the fact that grain production is still below the 1913 level.

1930
VKhUTEIN is dissolved, following political and internal pressures. The Oktiabr (October) group is formed in Moscow and Leningrad. With more than 100 members, it plays an important role in the development of posters, design and architecture. Founder members include Deineka, Eisenstein, Alexei Gan, Gustavs Klucis and Moisei Ginzburg.

EVENTS IN THE POLITICAL SPHERE

EVENTS IN THE VISUAL ARTS

1930

Lunacharsky is further removed from power and sent to represent the Soviet Union at the League of Nations. (He is later appointed to be Soviet Ambassador in Spain but dies en route in December 1933.)

25 APRIL
Foundation of the Directorate of Camps (ULAG) of the Joint State Political Directorate (OGPU).

JUNE
Work on the White Sea Canal commences, mainly using prisoners.

OCTOBER
ULAG is re-organised as the Chief Directorate of Camps (GULAG).

NOVEMBER–DECEMBER
The show trial of the 'Industrial Party' takes place. Several Soviet scientists and economists are accused and convicted of plotting a coup (with foreign help) against the government.

APRIL
The formerly Bolshevik-dedicated poet Mayakovsky commits suicide. Malevich's one-man show travels to Kiev Picture Gallery.

18 JUNE
Creation of the Federation of Groups of Soviet Artists.

AUGUST
The 'Permanent Exhibition of Avant-garde Art' is closed at the State Tretyakov Gallery in Moscow.

OCTOBER
Opening of the Mausoleum of V. I. Lenin designed by the architect Alexei Shchusev.

AUTUMN
Malevich is arrested as a German spy and held in prison for two months for 'anti-Soviet propaganda'.

Fig. 37
Dimitri Bulanov, *Advertisements in the Tram Are Read by Millions of People Every Day*, 1927. Colour lithograph. Russian State Library, Moscow

Fig. 38
Residents on the landings of their crowded tenement, from Boris Barnet's *The House on Trubnaya Street* (Mezhrabpom, USSR), 1928. Film still. Lobster Films, Paris

1930–1931

EVENTS IN THE POLITICAL SPHERE

DECEMBER (1930)
Rykov is fired and replaced by Vyacheslav Molotov on Stalin's recommendation.

MARCH (1931)
Trial of ex-Menshevik bureaucrats accused of having attempted 'criminally' to retard the country's industrial development.

JUNE
The Central Committee approves the plan to build an underground railway in Moscow.

5 DECEMBER
The Cathedral of Christ the Saviour in Moscow is dynamited and reduced to rubble.

EVENTS IN THE VISUAL ARTS

1931
The State Russian Museum's Department of Newest Trends is closed down.
MAY
The Association of the Workers of Revolutionary Posters (ORPP) is established with 153 members including Dmitry Moor, Viktor Deni and Deineka.
The State Tretyakov Gallery creates the Soviet Art group (later transformed into a department).
10 MAY
The Russian Association of Proletarian Artists (RAPKh) is established.
15 JUNE
The 'Russian Art of the Imperialist Era' exhibition, including works by avant-garde artists, opens at the State Russian Museum in Leningrad.
14 JULY
The RAPKh secretariat approves the decision to 'work on the artistic depiction of the heroes of the Five-Year Plan without delay'.
NOVEMBER
The 'Experimental Comprehensive Exhibition of the Art of the Capitalist Era' opens at the State Tretyakov Gallery in Moscow. Avant-garde works are still exhibited but now presented as capitalist or bourgeois art.

1932

EVENTS IN THE POLITICAL SPHERE

23 APRIL
The Central Committee passes the resolution 'On the Reformation of Literary-Artistic Organisations'.

15 MAY
Stalin signs a government decree for a 'Godless Five-Year Plan' with the aim that by 1 May 1937, 'the name of God should be forgotten in the territory of the country'.
Famine crisis in Ukraine and elsewhere (until 1934).

EVENTS IN THE VISUAL ARTS

1932
RAPP is closed down
The 4 Arts Society, Masters of Analytical Art Group (MAI) and Society of Moscow Artists (OMKh) are closed down.
Malevich is appointed as Head of Experimental Laboratory at the State Russian Museum in Leningrad. He starts working on the painting Socialist City, which was never finished.
The Suprematist Nikolai Suetin is appointed chief painter at the State Porcelain Factory in Leningrad.
20 MAY
The term Socialist Realism is used for the first time at a meeting of core USSR writers. It is adopted as the 'culmination of all the best literary currents of the past', effectively defining its identification with the Party.
Tatlin's one-man show opens at the State Museum of Fine Arts in Moscow. His work *Letatlin* (cat. 179) is exhibited for the first time.
25 JUNE
The Moscow Regional Union of Soviet Artists is created. Yuon, Deineka, Ryazhsky and Lentulov are among its first members.
2 AUGUST
The Leningrad Regional Union of Soviet Artists (LOSSKh) is formed. The first president is Petrov-Vodkin.
All artistic organisations are dissolved and replaced by the State-controlled Union of Soviet Artists.
NOVEMBER
The 'Art of the Great Industrial Bourgeoisie on the Eve of the Proletarian Revolution' exhibition opens at the State Tretyakov Gallery in Moscow.
13 NOVEMBER
The 'Fifteen Years of Artists of the Russian Soviet Republic' exhibition opens at the State Russian Museum in Leningrad. (On 27 June 1933, the exhibition moves to Moscow but with far fewer paintings by avant-garde artists.)

Fig. 39
Vladimir Mayakovsky, *Blacksmith*, 1921. Stencil print. Private collection

Fig. 40
2 Stenberg 2 (Vladimir and Georgi Stenberg), poster for the film *Fragment of an Empire* directed by Fridrikh Ermler (detail), 1929. Chromolithograph, 95 × 62 cm. Russian State Library, Moscow

РЕЖИССЕР
ФРИДРИХ
ЭРМЛЕР
ПРОИЗВОДСТВО
СОВКИНО

1

SALUTE THE LEADER

1
Boris Kustodiev
Demonstration on Uritsky Square on the Day of the Opening of the Second Comintern Congress in July 1920, 1921
Oil on canvas, 133 × 268 cm
State Russian Museum, St Petersburg

2
Mikhail Adamovich, Dulevo Porcelain Factory, Moscow
Plate with Depiction of the Second Interim Wooden Mausoleum of Vladimir Lenin, which Preceded the Present Granite Mausoleum, 1924
Vitrified enamel paint on porcelain, gilding, diameter 25.3 cm
The Petr Aven Collection

3
Rudolf Vilde, State Porcelain Factory, Petrograd
Plate with the Inscription 'Workers' Victory 25 Oct.' on a Red Banner, 1919
Vitrified enamel paint on porcelain, silvering, gilding, etching on gold, diameter 24 cm
The Petr Aven Collection

4
Mikhail Adamovich,
State Porcelain Factory,
Petrograd
Cup with Leon Trotsky's Portrait and a Red Star in the Background with the inscription 'Red Army Workers' Defence', 1923
Vitrified enamel paint on porcelain, height 9.4 cm
The Petr Aven Collection

5
Maria Lebedeva,
State Porcelain Factory,
Leningrad
Decorative Vase 'The Liberated People' with Vladimir Lenin's Portrait under Banners and Depictions of Scenes of Life in Different Nations, 1929. Vitrified enamel paint on porcelain, gilding, etching on gold, height 31.5 cm
The Petr Aven Collection

6
Natalia Danko, State Porcelain Factory, Petrograd
Woman Embroidering a Banner, 1919
Vitrified enamel paint on porcelain, height 15.5 cm
The Petr Aven Collection

7
Nikolai Terpsikhorov
First Motto, 1924
Oil on canvas, 88 × 103 cm
State Tretyakov Gallery, Moscow

8
Vera Mukhina
Flame of the Revolution,
1922–23
Bronze-toned cast of 1954,
90 × 43 × 50 cm
State Tretyakov Gallery,
Moscow

9
Isaak Brodsky
Vladimir Lenin and a Demonstration, 1919
Oil on canvas, 90 × 135 cm
The State Historical Museum, Moscow

10
Isaak Brodsky
Lenin in Smolny, 1930
Oil on canvas, 190 × 285 cm
State Tretyakov Gallery,
Moscow

11
Moisey Nappelbaum
Vladimir Ilyich Lenin, 1922
Gelatin silver print,
28.5 × 22.5 cm
Alex Lachmann
Collection, London

12
Arkady Shaiket
Red Square, 1926
Gelatin silver print,
21.4 × 19 cm
Alex Lachmann
Collection, London

13
Kuzma Petrov-Vodkin
Beside Lenin's Coffin, 1924
Oil on canvas, 71 × 88.5 cm
State Tretyakov Gallery, Moscow

14
Nikolai Demkov
Kerchief with Portrait of Lenin in the Centre and Trotsky's Corner Portrait Cut Out, 1924
Cotton, 70 × 79 cm
The Burilin Ivanovo Museum of Local History, Ivanovo

15
Kliment Redko
Insurrection, 1925
Oil on canvas,
170.5 × 212 cm
State Tretyakov Gallery,
Moscow

16
Unknown
Stalin as the Glorious Leader, 1928
Lacquer, tempera and gold paint on papier mâché, diameter 39 cm
The Petr Aven Collection

17
Isaak Brodsky
Portrait of Joseph Stalin,
1927
Oil on canvas, 116 × 85 cm
The Russian Academy
of Fine Arts Museum,
St Petersburg

18
Georgy Rublev
Portrait of Joseph Stalin,
c. 1930
Oil on canvas,
152 × 152 cm
State Tretyakov Gallery,
Moscow

ПРАВДА

2

MAN AND MACHINE

MECHANISATION TAKES COMMAND

John Milner

THE FALL OF THE EMPIRE AND THE ABDICATION of the Tsar in 1917 led to a cultural crisis in Russia. Under the Dictatorship of the Proletariat the workers assumed a central importance. Somehow they would have to find a visual language embedded in their own experiences and achievements. Furthermore, there would be only one patron and one client: the State and the mass of the people. This demanded a culture that was collective in its production, political in its content and public in its manifestation, a culture that attempted, at least in theory, to erase distinctions of class, race and gender, and to remove inequalities of wealth. Imperial, spiritual and commercial power were ridiculed grotesquely in posters, and portrayed as class enemies.

Vasily Kandinsky, Marc Chagall, Vladimir Tatlin, Alexander Rodchenko and Lyubov Popova all sought a role in creating this new visual culture. Painting as fine art, with its connotations of individual genius, wealth and commerce, could go to the museums. The Revolution intended the *physical* realisation of a new classless and collective society. The workers' new world was to be distinctly materialist. The spiritual soul would give way to scientific study of the brain, and icons were to be studied and no longer worshipped. Intellectual work and physical labour had to find a new understanding of this, providing the workers with a new image and new status after 1917.

As divisions between intellectual workers and physical labourers were increasingly examined and debated, so the barriers between them were scrutinised. The apportionment of food coupons, for example, was determined by the number of calories each category of work required. The painter Malevich consistently argued for more coupons, and there were even Suprematist designs for them. The art of painting could now be valued in food coupons.

In 1920 the Russian engineer Vladimir Shukhov completed the latest of his innovative structures, an immensely high radio tower made of spiralling elements of metal crossing to right and left.[1] Each section had diagonally leaning struts rising from a circular base up to the next, smaller metal ring. Shukhov's struts formed a tall openwork lattice that was both as light and as strong as he could make it. The mast rose in height as each section was raised into place with pulleys. Built without scaffolding, the structure seemed to grow of its free own will. Arkady Shaiket's photograph of the radio mast (fig. 45) shows its height and slender shape.

Shukhov may have had no cultural ideas about his tower: he simply reached the right height as economically as possible. But his engineering achievement in Moscow is contemporary with the tower devised by Tatlin for Petrograd (fig. 46), and the two make an informative comparison. Initially intended as a Monument to the Revolution, Tatlin's tower was soon re-named the *Monument to the Third International*. Tatlin constructed a large wood and metal model in studios at the former Academy of Arts beside the Neva River. The

Fig. 45
Arkady Shaiket, *Moscow Radio Mast*, 1920s. Gelatin silver print, 15 × 9.5 cm. Richard Saltoun Gallery, London. Tosca Photographic Fund, inv. 1739

Fig. 46
Vladimir Tatlin, *Model for the Monument to the Third International*, 1920. Photograph. The Museum of Modern Art (MoMA), New York

colossal scale envisaged by Tatlin for his tower would have made it the largest structure ever built. His model consisted of struts supporting two wooden spirals rising from a circular wooden base across which he attached a wide paper strip to indicate the Neva. The tower would have been big enough to straddle the width of the river, from the square beside the Hermitage to the Proletarian sector of Petrograd. By building the greatest wonder of the modern world, Tatlin – or those who commissioned him – aimed to acknowledge, preserve and dominate the city that Peter the Great had created. Although Tatlin may have envisaged its actual construction, his tower also provided a structure from which to lead the world.

Whereas Shukhov's tower was designed and built by a trained and experienced engineer, Tatlin's model was made with pieces of wood connected with cut-metal fixings. But his ambition was immense. Shukhov's tower was engineering, Tatlin's was a vision of a new world.

The reason for the gigantic scale of Tatlin's tower lay in its purpose: to house the International Government of the entire planet. Here *Workers of the World, Unite!* was to be taken literally. The two great spirals of Tatlin's tower superficially recall the interlacing spirals of Shukhov's, but Tatlin envisaged a spinal structure as well as immense rotating halls suspended within the structure to accommodate the highest committees of the International Government. These would resolve all political difficulties and broadcast their decisions to the population of the planet via the radio station at the tower's apex. Tatlin was not a trained engineer. His tower was an immensely influential idea masquerading as engineering: it excited the imagination and it lived in the mind, and remains unforgettable. It was also the first construction to incorporate Communist government bodily into its workings. Tatlin's attempt to marry politics and engineering in this way was unique and certainly utopian, a persuasive project that might one day perhaps be realised, just as a unitary government of the planet might one day perhaps be possible.

The daring ambition of the project, part machine, part building, part monument, has lingered in the mind, East and West, for a hundred years. It was a start more than a closure, a first gigantic step for communal humanity, the beginning and not the end. In this vast machine Tatlin counted mankind among its materials, debating in its halls and rising in its elevators to the double-glazed meeting rooms. Tatlin had designed a kind of giant astrolabe in which meetings were fixed by the movements of planets. In this cockpit of Planet Earth all past and future history would be recalled and all conflicts resolved. The structure has the skeleton and organs of a great striding figure, which Tatlin's friend Nikolai Punin said was *not* an idealised human figure, and *not* a typical human figure, but the embodiment of the *collective* human figure. Woman, man and machine have a special relationship in this three-dimensional wooden diagram of Communist thinking, which fired the imagination as a first step into a Soviet culture. The gigantic project was reflected in works by El Lissitzky, Naum Gabo, Gustavs Klucis, Rodchenko and others. It provided a basis for the concept of 'Engineer-constructors, the inventors of objects, the organisers of materials, [and] the workers of form'.[2]

The celebrated painter Boris Kustodiev in his canvas *The Bolshevik* (cat. 50) showed the giant figure of Revolution striding through the city, clumsier than Tatlin's giant but easier to understand. The graphic designer Vladimir Kozlinsky showed a great red figure taking gigantic strides as he scatters the little black figures of rotund bankers and capitalists at his feet (fig. 1). The graphic designer and architect Vladimir Krinsky came closest, however, to Tatlin's idea of the collective human in his graphic image of an enormous striding figure made up entirely of small, anonymous workers moving around like cogs in a machine (fig. 47).

Krinsky also made a simplified graphic diagram of Shukhov's tower soaring above and pushing aside the tiny towers of an Orthodox church, a Western church and a mosque. Shukhov's tower broadcast its materialist message to the world: *Vsem, Vsem* ('To everyone'), a call to move beyond the spiritual differences that make unity impossible. Krinsky's design effectively added a cultural significance to Shukhov's tower and in doing so brought it closer to the function of Tatlin's tower. But Shukhov thought as a structural engineer, and his design said nothing about his political beliefs. By contrast, Tatlin and Krinsky declaimed as loudly as possible their allegiance to revolutionary ideals.[3]

There were also bold egalitarian messages to spread. Factories were frequently presented as a setting for the organisation of work in which women as well as men undertook heavy labour in construction and production, in fabric mills and clothing. In the red-and-black poster designed by Nikolai Kogout in 1920–21 (fig. 48), male and female workers are given balanced roles in the factory. Against the backdrop of industrial buildings, smoke, an arching metal bridge and a crane, workers struggle in the physical tasks of production, labouring with wheels, levers and hammers. In the foreground two large-scale figures, a woman and a man, work at an anvil. She holds a red-hot piece of metal with a heavy pincer, while he swings a great hammer

Fig. 47
Vladimir Krinsky, *Collective Figure*, illustration for the magazine *Bolsheviks*, 1922. Pencil, watercolour and white body-colour on paper, 58.9 × 39.8 cm. The Schusev State Museum of Architecture, Moscow, Pla 9150/1.2

Fig. 48
Nikolai Kogout, *With the Rifle We Defeated the Enemy. With Our Labour, Comrades, We Shall Win Our Bread. Everyone to Work! Workers of the World Unite!*, 1920–21. Lithograph in red and black, 70 × 50.5 cm. Russian State Library, Moscow

to strike it. Each has a role in the manual work of the factory. But there is a second message here. Behind the man, three rifles stand ready in a tripod format, showing that these same workers were fighting in the People's Army in the Civil War. His pointed Red Army hat with its red star lies ready next to the cogwheel of industrial mechanisation. Her strong boot touches both hammer and sickle. She, it suggests, has come to industrial labour from the countryside, which is signified by the sickle of harvest work. Together, the two stand for industry and agriculture, the union of workers and peasants that was intended to own and control the means of production. The slogan reads: 'With the Rifle We Defeated the Enemy. With Our Labour, Comrades, We Shall Win Our Bread.'

The theme of women workers recurs throughout the 1920s and 1930s. In his large canvas *Textile Workers* (cat. 23), the painter Alexander Deineka was adapting his image from collage, photography and photomontage techniques to attain the clarity and immediacy of contemporary posters. His Constructivist design principles made an immediate and accessible appeal to his public. The scale, light and colour of the painting *Textile Workers* make it a distinctive and spectacular example of what painting could achieve in the era of new Soviet photography.

Photography and film together provided an unsurpassed medium for documentary observation and record. Documentary film used fragmentary factual material assembled into a filmic construction – in itself a form of production. In Dziga Vertov's film *The Man with a Movie Camera* (fig. 32), the image of the working woman is woven into a film montage of spinning bobbins of thread interlacing her actions with those of her machine. The woman's smiling face and the footage of spinning bobbins were filmed separately, then juxtaposed and assembled to suggest a synthesis of woman and machine.

Photomontage in these years, especially in the posters of Klucis, readily acknowledged the pasting together of photographic and printed graphic material. Klucis's poster *Long Live Our Happy Socialist Motherland* (1935) is constructed from fragmentary elements of factual material. Rodchenko, Varvara Stepanova, Solomon Telingater and others also used this technique, and it was evident in the subtle and brilliant montage and double exposures of Lissitzky's photomontages and photo-murals.

Conversely, there were painters devoted to revolutionary themes who transferred conventional skills to new themes as opportunities arose. Isaak Brodsky's painting of an anonymous shock-worker from Dneprostroi (cat. 19), the great Dnepr (Dneiper) River dam construction of 1932, is filled with a dark and intense drama of physical labour. The structure of the scaffolding in this construction site frames the figure's sheer strength and determination.

Fig. 49
Vladimir Tatlin standing beside his *Model for the Monument to the Third International*, 1919–20. Photograph. Punin Family Archive, St Petersburg

Fig. 50
Mikhail Kaufman, Alexander Rodchenko in his studio standing in front of his dismantled *Spatial Constructions*, 1924. Photograph. Moscow Photo Museum (House of Photography)

Shaiket's photograph *Komsomol at the Wheel* (cat. 35) predates Brodsky's painting by three years. Both show the physical strength of anonymous workers, and together they reveal what painting could learn from the new photography. The Komsomol, a young Soviet worker, is shown here at the wheel of some great industrial machine. The photograph is carefully posed and not spontaneous. Its theme is physical labour enhanced by the power of machine technology. The low viewpoint effectively raises the status of the anonymous worker, making him a heroic figure, despite the small scale of the photographic print. The message is visually clear and legible to the illiterate, even without words. In the midst of debates about non-objective art, new Soviet photographers revealed the accessibility and persuasiveness of photographs of people. Photojournalists recognised this as did former painters, who both worked with and learnt from them. In this respect, the avant-garde and photojournalists shared a common goal.

Looking up to the Komsomol is like looking at a monument. The viewer feels he or she is part of a crowd, although here the crowd is anyone who encounters the photograph. The heroic Komsomol is a politically committed figure who, like a vigorous athlete or a disciplined soldier, is part of the team fighting for the new society. Shaiket's photograph sent a visual message about the determination and physical strength of the Soviet Union by embodying them in this image of an unknown youth. He also ensured the collective reception of this message through the image's publication. It conjures up loyalty 'to the team', and so contributes to the process of making the masses self-aware. The people are both subject and spectator in a visualised political process.

Both man and machine here inhabit the same material, physical world. This photograph is independent of imperial patronage, commerce, spiritual enlightenment or even self-expression – all are effectively dismissed as mystical or introspective delusions. In this material world, man acquires the strength of a machine by designing, creating and controlling it. Together they demonstrate the strength that is Soviet power: worker + machine = labour + mechanisation. Machines of iron and steel are in physical contact with the biological mechanism of the human being: they work together. The photographer Boris Ignatovich made this specific point with clarity and simplicity in his 1930 image *Tightening the Bolt: Lever Controls for Tramways* (cat. 37).

Individual photographic prints are flimsy and fragile, but photographic negatives permit the image to be printed or projected to any size: either reduced or vastly enlarged. It can be seen as a small and precious object in an album, or shown large on a street hoarding. Visually it can address the masses, or be featured in a magazine with a wide circulation. The

Fig. 51
Semyon Fridlyand (Simon Fridland), *Construction at the Cherepovets Factory: Welding*, c. 1930. Vintage gelatin silver print. Richard Saltoun Gallery, London. Tosca Photographic Fund, inv. 1082

Fig. 52
Boris Ignatovich, *Young Worker*, 1930. Photograph. Private collection

power of the photographic image lies in its potential for multiplication, dispersal and wide intelligibility.

Individual paintings could never achieve the multiplicity of photography and film. The proletarian worker, no longer selling his labour on the open market, was now, notionally, a central element in the so-called Dictatorship of the Proletariat, a new kind of collective patron, an essential new subject, and the new collective consumer.

An understanding of the heroic narratives of elite academic history painting required a specialised and lengthy education. Addressing the masses in Revolutionary Russia was very different: a good education could be seen as elitist, and committed intellectuals had to forge solidarity with the people in order to demonstrate their allegiance. Anatoly Lunacharsky's drive for literacy was part of this process; he distributed books so that recipients would learn to read them and pass on their knowledge – and the books – to others. The young teaching the old is a recurrent theme in contemporary Soviet photography, posters and even in revolutionary ceramics.

In this period, man, woman, machine and politics were interwoven. Photographs of Tatlin (fig. 49), Lissitzky (cat. 59) and Rodchenko (fig. 50) show creative intellectuals pretending to be manual workers. Of these three, only Lissitzky was trained as an engineer, and he probably made only one building. Yet all three had a profound and dynamic cultural influence and, significantly, we know their names. In photographs, manual workers are rarely, if ever, named: they are simply part of the proletariat at work, and as anonymous as the machines in Semyon Fridlyand's *Construction at the Cherepovets Factory: Welding* (fig. 51). Ignatovich's photograph of a young man in a flat cap as he works at the machine maintains his subject's anonymity even while acknowledging the dignity of his labour (fig. 52).

There is an imbalance here that points to difference of background, aims and status between known creative photojournalists and the anonymous workers that they photographed. Ignatovich, Rodchenko and Lissitzky were all educated and experienced photographers, so Ignatovich was, like them, one of the educated types who observed and recorded the workers. This professional status raised them above the workers' industrious anonymity that they appeared so much to admire.

19
Isaak Brodsky
Shock-worker from Dneprostroi, 1932
Oil on canvas, 98 × 125 cm
The Russian Academy of Fine Arts Museum, St Petersburg

20
Pavel Filonov
Tractor Workshop at the Putilov Factory, 1931–32
Oil on canvas mounted on cardboard, 73 × 99 cm
State Russian Museum, St Petersburg

21
Vyacheslav Pakulin
Turbine Shop at the Factory 'Elektrosila', 1931–32
Oil on canvas, 118 × 91 cm
State Russian Museum, St Petersburg

22
Ekaterina Zernova
Tomato Paste Factory, 1929
Oil on canvas, 141 × 110 cm
The Astrakhan State Art Gallery

23
Alexander Deineka
Textile Workers, 1927
Oil on canvas,
161.5 × 185 cm
State Russian Museum,
St Petersburg

24
Alexander Deineka
Construction of New Workshops, 1926
Oil on canvas,
212.8 × 201.8 cm
State Tretyakov Gallery,
Moscow

25
Alexander Deineka
Let's Mechanise Donbass,
c. 1930
Gouache and collage
on paper, 117 × 83 cm
Alex Lachmann
Collection, London

26
Nikolai Denisovsky
Cast Iron Output, 1930
Oil on canvas,
124 × 99.5 cm
State Tretyakov Gallery,
Moscow

27
Natan Altman
Russia. Labour, 1921
Paper, enamel and charcoal on mahogany, 98.5 × 49 cm
State Tretyakov Gallery, Moscow

28
Mikhail Mokh, State Porcelain Factory, Leningrad
Tea Set 'Metal': Tray, Teapot, Sugar-bowl, Milk Jug, Two Cups with Saucers, 1930
Vitrified enamel paint on porcelain, gilding, etching on gold,
tray: diameter 35.7 cm; teapot: height 14 cm; sugar-bowl: height 10.2 cm; milk jug: height 13.8 cm; cups: height 5.4 cm; saucers: diameter 14.7 cm
The Petr Aven Collection

29
Liudmila Protopopova
A Cup for Serving Tea,
1931
Vitrified enamel paint on
porcelain, height 6.4 cm
The Petr Aven Collection

30
Unknown, State Porcelain
Factory, Leningrad
Dish 'Moulding Workshop',
1931
Vitrified enamel paint
on porcelain, diameter
51.7 cm
The Petr Aven Collection

31
Andrey Golubev
Red Spinner, 1930
Cotton print fabric, chintz, 17.5 × 27 cm
The Burilin Ivanovo Museum of Local History, Ivanovo

32
Daria Preobrazhenskaya
Five Years in Four, 1930
Chintz, cotton fabric, 17.5 × 27 cm
The Burilin Ivanovo Museum of Local History, Ivanovo

33
Unknown
Kerchief Commemorating the Second Congress of the Trekhgornaya Textile Workers, 1930s
Cotton fabric, 89 × 94.5 cm
JSC Trekhgornaya Manufactura, Moscow

34
Arkady Shaiket
Construction of the Moscow Telegraphic Centre, 1928
Gelatin silver print, 45.6 × 34 cm
Alex Lachmann Collection, London

35
Arkady Shaiket
Komsomol at the Wheel, 1929
Print from the 1950s, 78 × 57.5 cm
Alex Lachmann Collection, London

36
Georgi Zelma
Crane Operator, c. 1930
Gelatin silver print,
35.3 × 48.5 cm
Alex Lachmann
Collection, London

37
Boris Ignatovich
Tightening the Bolt: Lever Controls for Tramways,
1930
Gelatin silver print,
17.7 × 24.2 cm
Alex Lachmann
Collection, London

38
Boris Ignatovich
Stretching Cables, 1930
Gelatin silver print,
23.7 × 17.9 cm
Alex Lachmann
Collection, London

39
Alexander Rodchenko
Steering Wheels, 1929
Gelatin silver print,
21.7 × 29.8 cm
Alex Lachmann
Collection, London

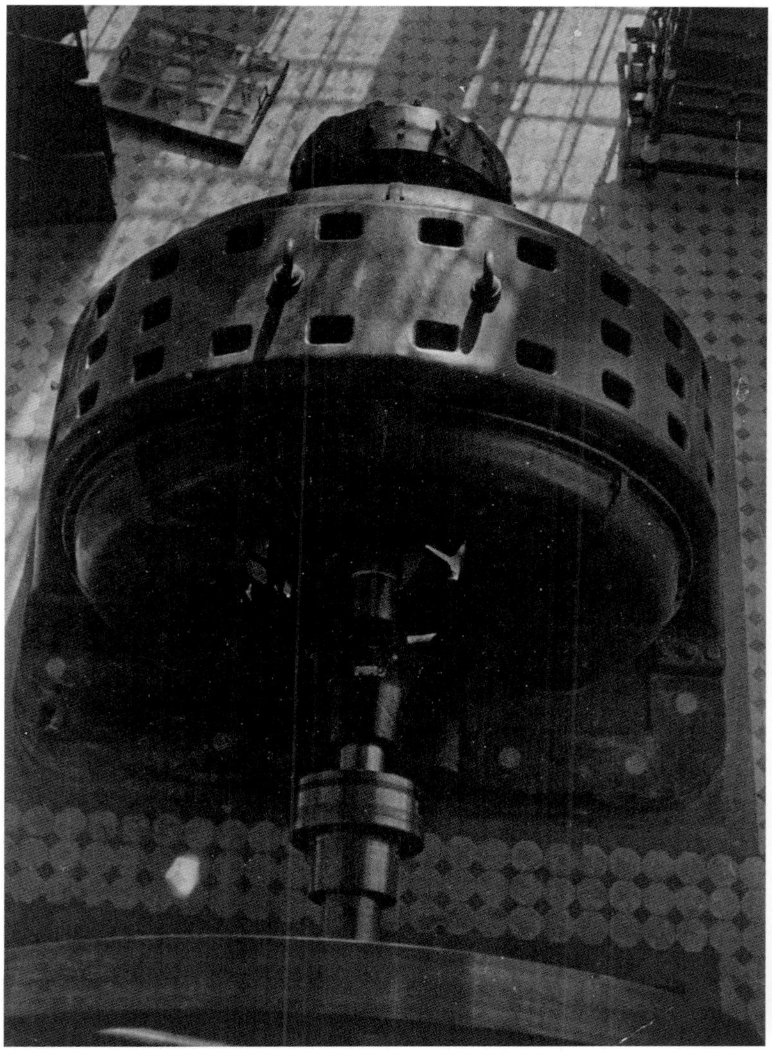

40
Boris Ignatovich
Generator, 1929
Gelatin silver print (stamped), 24 × 18 cm
Alex Lachmann Collection, London

41
Boris Ignatovich
Crankshafts, 1930
Gelatin silver print, 24.2 × 16 cm
Alex Lachmann Collection, London

Пролетарии всех стран, соединяйтесь!
Премия
за упорное
стремление

42
Arkady Shaiket
Brigade of Shock-workers, 1928
Gelatin silver print, 16.4 × 11.6 cm
Alex Lachmann Collection, London

43
Georgi Zelma
Red Army Soldiers by Power Cable, 1931
Gelatin silver print, 40.6 × 29.6 cm
Alex Lachmann Collection, London

3

BRAVE NEW WORLD

CONSTRUCTORS OF THE FUTURE IN SEARCH OF THE NEW

Zelfira Tregulova and Faina Balakhovskaya

As it was, is now, and ever shall be?
We do not want rich patrons
We do not want favourable reviews
We do not want to be privileged.
... We want equality and freedom in art.
Nadezhda Udaltsova, 'We Want', 1918[1]

Remake everything. Organise it so as to make everything new, so that our false, dirty, boring, ugly life becomes just, clean, happy and beautiful.
Alexander Blok, 'The Intelligentsia and the Revolution', 1918[2]

Detail of cat. 53B

'VICTORY ON THE ART FRONT MAY BE ONE OF THE most substantial elements of the Bolshevik victory. The Civil War will live for centuries within the frame given to it by the arts. Alexander Blok's poem "The Twelve" will always act as a preface to the history of the October Revolution,' wrote Georgy Fedotov, summing up fifteen years of Bolshevik government.[3] This achievement was largely made possible by the lack of definition and the diversity of what was demanded from creative people loyal to the new power. Despite periodic calls from the Party elite – and even from cultural figures themselves – for a Party line on literature and art, it was a long time before the Party acted on its responsibility for cultural issues. It refused to 'connect itself to any particular school in the field of literary [or artistic] form', as a resolution of the Central Committee of the Russian Communist Party (Bolsheviks) put it on 18 June 1925.[4] The People's Commissar of Enlightenment, Anatoly Lunacharsky (cat. 61), maintained in February 1928 that 'the government ... is obliged to support all forms of contemporary art until the style of the new epoch becomes clear'.[5] The vague formula of the 'new and only true method' of Socialist Realism was not announced until the First Writers' Congress in 1934. The professional unions for creative people, such as the Union of Writers or the Union of Artists, had not yet been formed, nor were their debates on formalism and naturalism to take place until 1936. In the meantime, creative people were largely free to compete for 'a monopoly on revolutionary culture', to propose new concepts of content and form reflecting the most immense political changes.[6]

Most published debate concerned an alliance with the 'innovators', masters of the avant-garde who were the real proponents of change. But the new government also tried to engage the 'old' classics, distinguished and celebrated writers and artists, a process that culminated in the return of Maxim Gorky (cat. 73), but also Ilya Repin's refusal to return.[7] 'The joy of destruction and the chance to create something from nothing, apparently given by the Revolution'[8] took hold of the leftists, but even if the right shared this joy it was mixed with fear for the end of the old world and the beginning of the new, and both groups described this change in biblical and cosmic terms. As El Lissitzky (cat. 75) put it, 'We are now experiencing an exceptional epoch when a new, real and cosmic birth in the world within ourselves enters our consciousness.'[9] As might be expected, the old guard, who were now the bearers of a useless cultural heritage, were guided by past experience and tradition, and Leon Trotsky feared their influence on the construction of the new. They presented highly ambiguous works. Konstantin Yuon's apocalyptic

Fig. 53
Konstantin Yuon, *Study for a Theatre Curtain for the State Academic Bolshoi Theatre*, 1920. Oil on canvas, 86 × 109 cm. Museum of the State Academic Bolshoi Theatre, Moscow

New Planet (cat. 52) and the superhuman size of Boris Kustodiev's *The Bolshevik* (cat. 50) could be read either as a will for change or as a fear of what was to come. In the practical language of the new world order they were either Soviet or anti-Soviet. These images of figures rising from their graves at the end of the world, and also the huge flag-bearer, are just as ambiguous as the figure of Jesus Christ in Blok's 'The Twelve' (cat. 69), 'in a white wreath of roses' leading a procession of a dozen ruffians. In depicting a cataclysm, when 'Communism appeared with the morning',[10] those dedicated to realism borrowed symbolic language and signs from many sources including the Bible and frescoes in churches. Yuon and Kustodiev referred to their works at the time of the 1905 Revolution in Russia: Yuon had made drawings for *The Creation of the World: The Realm of the Living* (1908–09; State Tretyakov Gallery, Moscow) and Kustodiev had depicted death striding through a blood-soaked Moscow in *Moscow I. Entry* (fig. 54). But Kustodiev was attempting a more realistic, almost documentary, image of the events of October 1917, which evidently had a completely different effect on him from that of the February Revolution of 1917: 'The reality was incredible. I, of course, [being bed-ridden], saw very little, only what happened in the square under my windows, but what the eyes saw the brain could not yet interpret. It was like a dream or even clearer. The ancient extravaganza [*féerie*] fell apart. What we had feared to see yesterday was no longer frightening, it simply evaporated like smoke.'[11] Kustodiev's *Bolshevik* and Yuon's *New Planet*, and other images of global catastrophe, known now mostly in poor reproductions, marked an episode in the work of artists who later returned to depictions of their favoured landscapes, to history painting and to bucolic scenes from village life. For Yuon this was also the start of a long relationship with the government, culminating in a Stalin Prize in 1943 and membership of the Communist Party in 1951.

THE ART OF THE WORD

The clearest signs of the new were words from the revolutionary repertoire in lettering, slogans and rhetoric. Despite their disconcertingly obvious applied nature, they offered direct proof that art could be useful. Political reality had encroached upon 'high art': newspaper texts in collages provided a direct means to convey useful messages transferred straight onto the canvas. In depicting letters, words, phrases and quotations from the classics, artists of the new Russia were scarcely learning from the experiments of the Cubists; they were destroying the logic and the familiar construction of the world with charades.[12]

In the post-revolutionary reality, slogans became an independent visual element, a distinctive feature of the new actuality.

The 'patch of cloth' in Blok's 'The Twelve' was damaged beyond use, its slogan incomprehensible. It was not simply a message, but a foretaste of that art of agitation and propaganda: 'They sewed crooked letters on a bright red piece of calico; they painted "Workers of the World, Unite" on fences; and they cobbled together five-pointed stars made from boards ... Their aesthetic was "the brighter the better". They wanted only for everyone to feel that the circular, sleepy Russian plain was transformed into a spinning, turning, noisy wheel of movement.'[13] The eradication of illiteracy was one of the aims of the new government, and verbal texts put them ahead of the game, explaining and agitating, taking over every possible surface, invading the theatre, and increasingly the cinema, even decorating chinaware – the last place one would expect to see a slogan, an appeal, or political propaganda. This post-revolutionary lettering was not just pictorial material; first and foremost, these

Fig. 54
Boris Kustodiev, *Moscow I. Entry*, 1905. Ink and watercolour on paper, 26 × 26 cm. State Tretyakov Gallery, Moscow. Illustration for the satirical journal *Zhupel*, no. 2, 1905, p. 4

44
Sofya Dymshits-Tolstaya
Propaganda Glass
'Workers of the World, Unite!', 1919–21
Oil on glass,
53.2 × 40 cm
State Russian Museum,
St Petersburg

45
Sofya Dymshits-Tolstaya
Propaganda Glass
'Peace to the Sheds, War on the Palaces', 1919–21
Oil on glass,
40 × 53.5 cm
State Russian Museum,
St Petersburg

46
Sofya Dymshits-Tolstaya
Propaganda Glass
'Labour is the Foundation of the RSFSR [Russian Soviet Federative Socialist Republic]', 1919–21
Oil on glass, 40 × 53 cm
State Russian Museum, St Petersburg

50
Boris Kustodiev
The Bolshevik, 1920
Oil on canvas,
101 × 140.5 cm
State Tretyakov
Gallery, Moscow

51
Ivan Puni
Spectrum: Flight of Forms, 1919
Oil on canvas, 127 × 124 cm
State Russian Museum, St Petersburg

52
Konstantin Yuon
New Planet, 1921
Tempera on cardboard, 71 × 100.8 cm
State Tretyakov Gallery, Moscow

53A
Pavel Filonov
Formula of Spring,
1927–29
Oil on canvas,
106 × 72 cm
State Russian Museum,
St Petersburg

53B
Pavel Filonov
Formula of the Petrograd Proletariat, 1920–21
Oil on canvas,
154 × 117 cm
State Russian Museum,
St Petersburg

54
Pavel Filonov
Heads (Human in the World), 1925–26
Oil on paper mounted
on canvas, 109 × 72.7 cm
State Russian Museum,
St Petersburg

55
Lyubov Popova
Space-force Construction, 1921
Oil, tessellation on plywood, 124 × 82.3 cm
State Tretyakov Gallery, Moscow

56
Lyubov Popova
Space-force Construction, 1921
Oil with metallic powder on plywood, 70.2 × 52 cm
State Tretyakov Gallery, Moscow

57
Alexander Deineka
The Defence of Petrograd,
1928
Oil on canvas,
210 × 238 cm
The Central Armed Forces
Museum of the Russian
Federation, Moscow

Дейнека 1928

58
Mikhail Matiushin
Movement in Space,
c. 1921
Oil on canvas,
124 × 168 cm
State Russian Museum,
St Petersburg

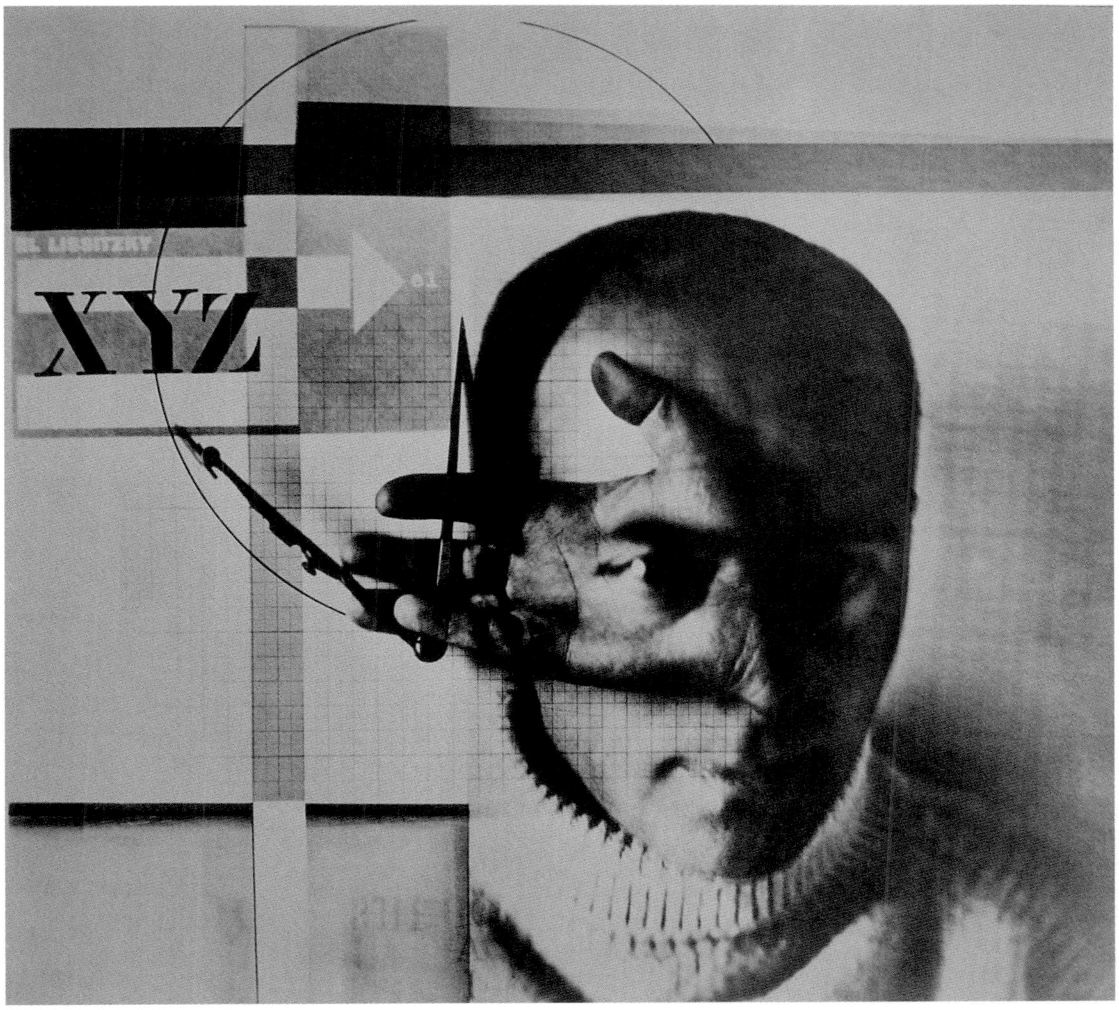

59
El Lissitzky
Constructor (Self-portrait with Dividers), 1924
Gelatin silver print,
26.3 × 29.5 cm
Alex Lachmann
Collection, London

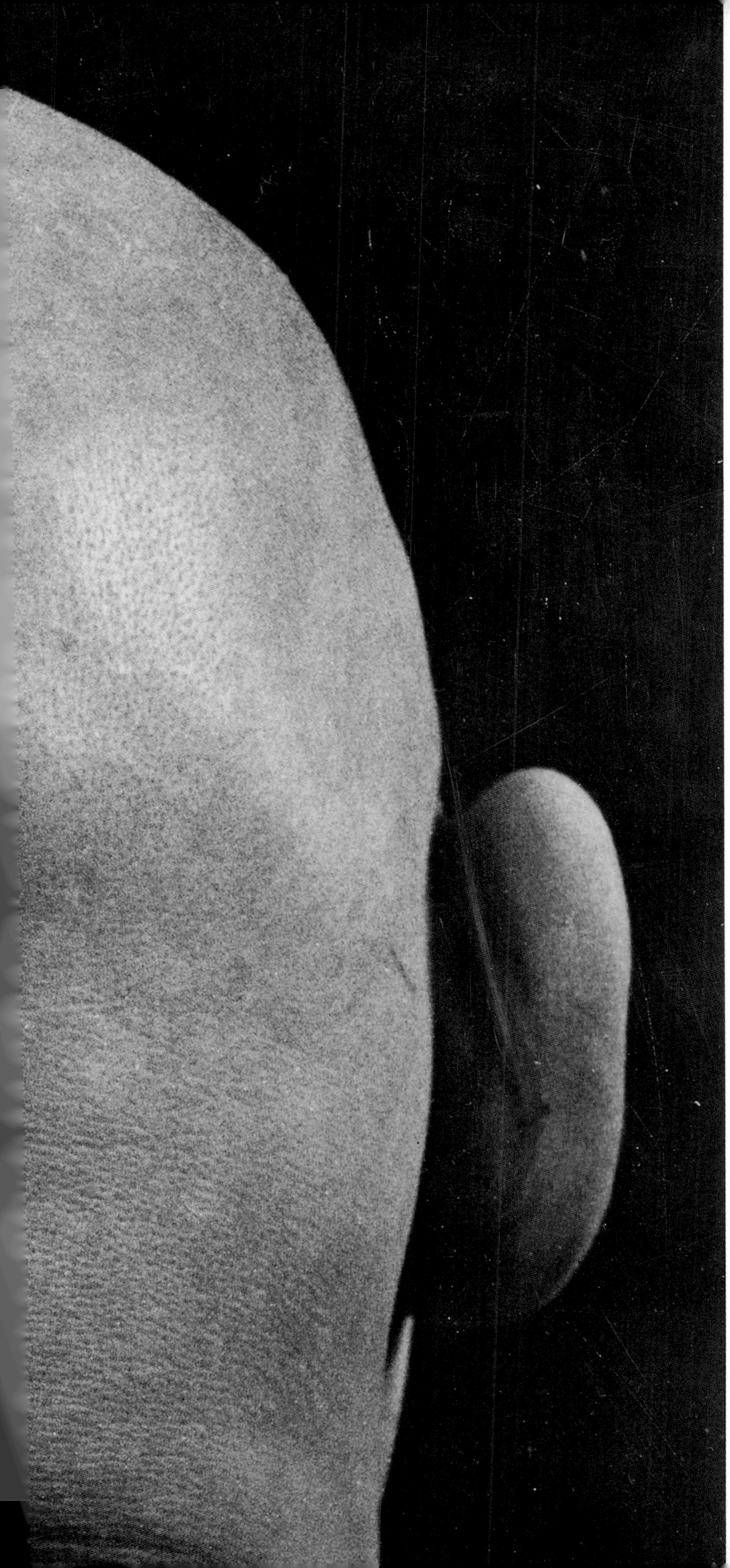

4

CULTURAL HEROES

HEROES OF THE PAST LIVING IN THE FUTURE

Natalia Murray

No generation had a fate like that in history, and maybe there was no such generation yet.
Anna Akhmatova, 1942[1]

OCTOBER 1917 REPRESENTED A CLEAR DIVIDING line between the old and the new. Three years after the Bolshevik Revolution Lenin announced: 'It is with absolute frankness that we speak of this struggle of the proletariat; each man must choose between joining our side or the other side. Any attempt to avoid taking sides in this issue must end in fiasco.'[2] Shortly after this statement was made, many writers and scientists, philosophers and artists who refused to join the side of the proletariat were forced to leave the country.

The renaissance that had occurred in the visual arts at the turn of the century was cut short when most members of the World of Art (*Mir Iskusstva*) group – those artists, poets and musicians who were hostile towards the Imperial Academy of Arts and nineteenth-century Realism, and were often referred to as the 'Russian Secession' – left the country. In the new Bolshevik state, Realism had to develop without Ilya Repin, Nikolai Feshin and Filip Maliavin, Impressionism without Konstantin Korovin, Neoclassicism without Vasily Shukhaev, Alexander Yakovlev or Zinaida Serebriakova, and the avant-garde without Vasily Kandinsky and Marc Chagall.

But at least in 1917–18 most leaders of the Russian avant-garde welcomed the October Revolution as the dawn of new hope. The Futurist composer Arthur Lourié (fig. 58) wrote: 'It was unbelievable what was going on at the period. For the first time we, young dreamers, were told that we could make our dreams come true and no politics would interfere with our pure art, for which we joined the Revolution without hesitation.'[3] After the October Revolution Lourié found himself appointed head of the music division of the People's Commissariat of Enlightenment (NARKOMPROS). However, like many other members of the artistic intelligentsia, he soon became disenchanted with the new regime. On 17 August 1922 he went on an official visit to Berlin, and never returned to Russia.

By 1918 all private art collectors, commercial art dealers and galleries had been replaced by the one all-powerful patron: the new Communist state, which denounced all previous patrons of the arts in order 'to liberate artists from exploitation'. Like any other regime, 'the Bolsheviks aspired to attract representatives of artistic circles to co-operate with them, trying to decorate their ruling with talents'.[4]

The art of the newly emerging country would have to be established by art's representatives, and many avant-garde artists and art critics were appointed to important positions. Bolshevik leaders accepted that culture, in all its manifestations, should play a key part in achieving both solidarity and advancement in this new society, but what that culture should comprise was still under debate. When, following the October

Fig. 57
Nikolai Punin, 1918. Photograph. Punin Family Archive, St Petersburg

Fig. 58
Petr Miturich, *Portrait of the Composer Arthur Lourié*, 1915. Oil on canvas, 102 × 101.5 cm. State Russian Museum, St Petersburg

Revolution, the Bolshevik government decided that art was of the utmost importance for the education of the proletariat, they entrusted Anatoly Lunacharsky (cat. 61; fig. 59) to determine the direction of artistic policies in the new Russia. He was appointed Commissar of Public Enlightenment and head of NARKOMPROS.

'The revolution is most wonderful for its lack of logic,' wrote the art critic Nikolai Punin (cat. 63; fig. 57) in his diary in November 1919.[5] Educated in a prestigious school at Tsarskoe Selo and famous for his articles in the rather elitist journal *Apollon*, Punin was not perhaps the most likely person to represent the new culture of Bolshevism. However, when in November 1917 Lunacharsky invited 120 cultural figures to gather and show support for the new regime, only five of them turned up: Punin, Lourié, Vsevolod Meyerhold, Alexander Blok and Vladimir Mayakovsky. They spoke about the creation of a new proletarian culture, and the participation in it of members of the intelligentsia. Their conversation was followed by a succession of meetings between Lunacharsky and Punin. In January 1918 the Department of Visual Arts (IZO), formed within NARKOMPROS, was established in Petrograd and Moscow. At the time, Punin felt that life itself had ordained him to be at the centre of the Revolution, participation in which became inevitable.

But Punin's excitement about the new Russian culture did not last long. By February 1920 he was writing in his diary: 'One quality of the revolution – life gets to be a risk.'[6] In May 1920 an order was issued by the Communist Party Executive Committee to clear IZO NARKOMPROS of avant-garde artists (the Department of Visual Arts was itself liquidated in 1921). Unable to relate to art without obvious content, Lunacharsky wrote:

> *'Left' artists – as long as they remain true to themselves – can give as much to ideologically revolutionary art as a dumb person can make a revolutionary speech. They principally deny the ideological context and imagery of paintings and statues, for example. They have also gone so far in the deformation of natural materials that the proletariat and peasants, who, together with the greatest artists of all time, demand first and foremost clarity in art, just raise their hands in front of these products of the autumn of Western European culture.*[7]

Punin still refused to bend his artistic principles. In 1921 he announced: 'We were persecuted and will be persecuted, not because we are anti-bourgeois, or the other way around, but because we possess the gift of creative art. This is the reason we cannot be tolerated by mediocrity, even by Communist mediocrity.'[8]

Following this brave statement, in August 1921, Punin and the leading Symbolist poet Nikolai Gumilev were arrested in connection with a fabricated plot called the 'Case of the Petrograd Military Organisation', which followed a mutiny of the formerly loyal Kronstadt Garrison. Overnight, around two hundred people were imprisoned, and soon 60 of them, and then another 34, were shot without explanation or investigation. Among them was Gumilev, leader of the Acmeist movement in poetry[9] and an honoured veteran of the First World War,

Fig. 59
Nikolai Feshin, *Portrait of Anatoly Lunacharsky*, 1920. Oil on canvas, 142 × 100 cm. National Museum of Fine Arts of the Republic of Tatarstan, F-745

Fig. 60
Boris Kustodiev, *Portrait of Fedor Chaliapin*, 1922. Oil on canvas, 99 × 80 cm. State Russian Museum, St Petersburg

who returned from Paris to Petrograd in 1917, and ran a workshop for aspiring proletarian poets. Lunacharsky managed to secure Punin's release, but he was arrested again in 1935, and in 1949 sent to the Gulag, where he died in 1953.

In 1921 Alexander Blok (cat. 69), one of the greatest of Russian poets, who was originally inspired by the Revolution, replied to the writer Kornei Chukovsky, who had asked him why he did not write poetry any more: 'All sounds have stopped. Can't you hear that there are no longer any sounds?'[10] Blok would recite his poems with his eyes closed 'so as not to see those apes'.[11] His faith in the Bolshevik Revolution was first shaken by his arrest in 1919. His brief imprisonment on suspicion of conspiracy ruined his belief in the new State and by 1921 he was mentally and physically exhausted. He developed inflammations of the inner lining of his heart and of his brain. Maxim Gorky (cat. 73) and Lunacharsky appealed to Lenin to allow Blok to travel to Finland for treatment, but the Politburo refused. When they finally changed their mind, it was too late: he died on 7 August 1921 aged forty-one. Lunacharsky, jaded, wrote a secret letter to the Central Committee of the Bolshevik Party: 'There will be no doubt and no refutation of the fact that we killed Russia's most talented poet.'[12]

Blok's death signified the beginning of the end of artistic freedom in Russia. This was a time of disillusionment for the cultural intelligentsia, and it was only to be exacerbated by the 1917–22 Civil War, rooted as this was in the distress caused by the way the Bolsheviks had seized power. Many famous artists and major writers and poets started heading for the West, among them Ivan Bunin, Alexander Kuprin and Konstantin Balmont. They chose to emigrate in order to preserve their artistic freedom.

In 1922 the most famous Russian opera singer, the bass Fedor Chaliapin (fig. 60), also left Russia. Like so many others he had initially welcomed the overthrow of the monarchy and the Bolsheviks made him the first recipient of a new honorary title, People's Artist, but he had seen the reality of the new regime. By 1921 he believed that under the Bolsheviks 'liberty had been turned into tyranny, fraternity into Civil War, and equality meant stomping down anyone who dared raise his head above the level of the swamp'.[13] Chaliapin never returned to Russia.

Many intellectuals who wished to stay were forced to emigrate in the autumn of 1922 when Lenin personally drew up a list of 220 'undesirables' – mostly philosophers, scientists, academics and journalists – whom he wished to be deported before the creation of the Soviet Union in December of that year. Famous theologians and philosophers, such as Nikolai Berdiaev and Sergei Bulgakov (cat. 136), were forced to board so-called 'Philosophers' ships' in Petrograd and travel to permanent exile in Berlin, Prague and Paris.

Those lucky enough to be excluded from this list, who decided to stay in their beloved Russia, consciously chose their fate, and many later suffered for it. In 1926 one of the most acclaimed Russian poets and figurehead of the late nineteenth- and early twentieth-century Russian poetic movement the Silver Age, Anna Akhmatova (cats 62, 66; fig. 61), whose poems were hardly published throughout the 1920s and 1930s, said:

> *To make it clear, there can be two scenarios: either everyone had left or everyone stayed. First: Everyone left. No more Hermitage, Rembrandt's canvases are used instead of tablecloths and rugs, since nobody can explain their value. Winter Palace – a mountain of ashes inhabited by homeless. Total disintegration … Foreigners would not have interfered – they would prefer to wait, in case Russia might become a New America, which they could discover and divide. Second scenario: Nobody left. In this case, we could have had a public, which does not exist now since too few of*

Fig. 61
Anna Akhmatova in Punin's Study, 1926. Photograph by Nikolai Punin. Punin Family Archive, St Petersburg

66
Moisey Nappelbaum
The Poet Anna Akhmatova, 1924
Gelatin silver print, 30 × 21 cm
Alex Lachmann Collection, London

67
Moisey Nappelbaum
The Theatre Director Vsevolod Meyerhold, 1929
Gelatin silver print, 23 × 17.5 cm
Alex Lachmann Collection, London

68
Moisey Nappelbaum
The Composer Dmitri Shostakovich, 1930s
Gelatin silver print, 22 × 15.3 cm
Alex Lachmann Collection, London

69
Moisey Nappelbaum
The Poet Alexander Blok, 1921
Gelatin silver print, 19 × 14.1 cm
Alex Lachmann Collection, London

70
Alexander Rodchenko
The Poet and Painter Vladimir Mayakovsky, 1924
Gelatin silver print, 41.2 × 29 cm
Alex Lachmann Collection, London

5

KAZIMIR MALEVICH

Красная Армия
геройски
сражается
НА ФРОНТЕ.
Красный тыл
должен
помочь
КРАСНОМУ ФРОНТУ.
ХЛЕБ
ХЛЕБ
Рабочий—ты должен удвоить выработку.
Крестьянин—ты должен сдать продуктов вдвое больше чем разверстано.
Железнодорожник—усиль ремонт паровозов и вагонов.
А вы,—остальные граждане—шлите подарки бойцам на фронт.
СМОЛРОСТА.
СМОЛРОСТА.

KAZIMIR MALEVICH

John Milner

THE PAINTER KAZIMIR MALEVICH WAS ARRESTED in 1927 following his return from a visit to Poland and Germany. He was released after several days of interrogation, but found himself precariously caught between success and failure. His post-revolutionary development of Suprematism had attracted many followers who respected his achievements and spread his message; even Marc Chagall, Director of the People's Art School in Vitebsk, responded to the dynamics of Suprematism, as his study *The Traveller (Forward!)* (fig. 5), designed for a street decoration, illustrates. Chagall had invited Malevich to teach in Vitebsk with El Lissitzky, along with colleagues and students Nikolai Suetin, Ilya Chashnik, Vera Ermolaeva, Lazar Khidekel, Nina Kogan and others working on Suprematist painting, posters, ceramics, decorations on buildings and trams, stage designs, publications and experimental architectural projects. Suprematism spread to Orenburg and Smolensk (fig. 62). Working collectively, these artists formed the group UNOVIS (Affirmers of the New Art), asserting innovation in art and exhibiting anonymously.

Malevich was subsequently employed at the Leningrad State Institute of Artistic Culture (GINKhUK) near St Isaac's Cathedral. He worked there closely with Nikolai Punin and Mikhail Matiushin across the yard from Vladimir Tatlin, who worked at the Museum of Pictorial Culture in the same building. In 1926 Malevich had a major display at GINKhUK showing architectural prototypes (*arkhitektoniki* or architectons) together with related drawings (fig. 63).

None of these was a design for a specific building, and they were not functional architectural projects. Like his Suprematist paintings, they occupied another realm,

Fig. 62
Władysław Strzemiński, *The Red Army Is Fighting Heroically at the Front. The Red Rear-guard Must Help the Red Front. Worker – you must double production. Peasant – you must hand over twice as much as the quota. Railworkers – strengthen repairs on engines and wagons. And you, remaining citizens, hand over gifts to soldiers at the Front*, 1920. Chromolithograph, 73 × 44 cm. Published by Smolensk ROSTA. The National Library of Russia, St Petersburg, inv. 218012

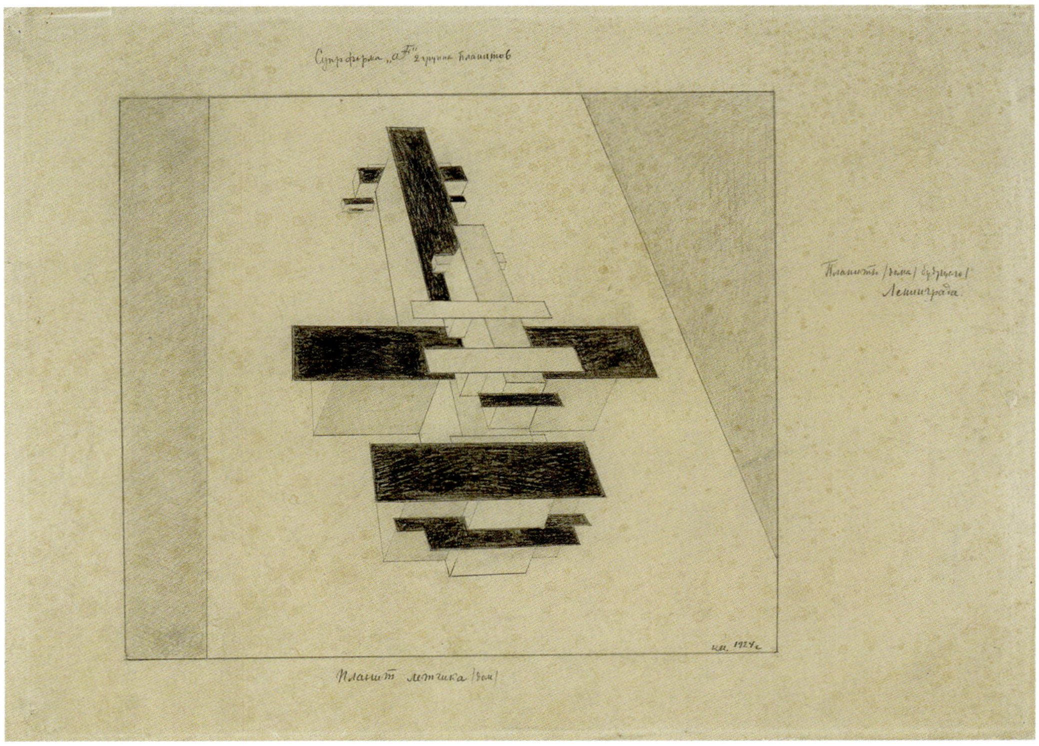

Fig. 63
Kazimir Malevich, *Future 'Planiti' for Leningrad: The Pilot's House*, 1924. Pencil on paper, 30.5 × 45 cm. Collection Stedelijk Museum Amsterdam, inv. A 7698

one in which buildings might fly in cosmic space. In 1926 Malevich called this exhibition 'The Suprematist Order', as if to supersede the classical orders of Vitruvius and the Renaissance (fig. 65). Suetin and Chashnik worked with him. Lissitzky, who had international commitments and a broader perspective, was often in Germany, but he too remained alert to Malevich's continued research (fig. 64).

Yet Malevich was facing a moment of crisis. He had applied to visit Berlin for a retrospective display of his work. When his request was refused he seems to have protested in person, threatening to take his paintings there on a handcart. He eventually took a large proportion of his output with him, ranging from early gouaches through to works illustrating the whole Suprematist experiment. He exhibited first at the Hotel Polonia in Warsaw on 29 March 1927, where he was enthusiastically received by Władysław Strzemiński (fig. 62), Katarzyna Kobro and the Polish Blok group. In Germany he met Walter Gropius and László Moholy-Nagy at the Dessau Bauhaus on 7 April 1927, and so consolidated a Russian connection that included his former colleagues Vasily Kandinsky and Lissitzky. His book *The Non-objective World* (1927) was published in the series of Bauhaus books. His extensive display at the Grosse Berliner Kunstausstellung, running from 7 May, made a great impact: Malevich had very much arrived in Germany.

He may have dreamed of a career in the West, but his sudden recall to Russia forced him to leave many paintings in Germany. Although the recall and his arrest must have been seriously alarming, an opportunity arose in 1929 for a one-man exhibition at the State Tretyakov Gallery in Moscow. With many of his paintings still in Germany, this placed him in a predicament. He repainted some works and displayed other recent paintings.

Malevich's later display within the 1932 anniversary exhibition (figs 66, 68, 69) should be considered in the light of these difficulties. It helped that his colleague Nikolai Punin was one of the curators of the vast undertaking, and that Malevich was allowed to display his own exhibition within the larger show, in a hang that encompassed the origins of Suprematism through to his new figurative paintings. As if to assert that his revolution in art preceded or in some way predicted the political revolution, Malevich gave a primary position to a *Black Square* (cat. 78) and to *Red Square (Painterly Realism of a Peasant Woman in Two Dimensions)* (cat. 79), which he had first exhibited in December 1915 in Petrograd. He made the *Black Square* shown in 1932 to match the latter painting. In hanging these two works, he was suggesting a foundation myth that linked Suprematism to the Revolution, a connection that he urgently needed to make in 1932 (fig. 66). Below them hung a row of three Suprematist works dating from 1916–17, painted at the moment of the Romanov dynasty's collapse.

At that time Malevich was creating paintings with new perspectives of dynamic flight and effortless motions in clean colour without a hint of the mud and blood of war. He hung *Supremus 56* (fig. 67) centrally, like the middle panel of a triptych above an altar. Lower still was a display of plaster architectons (cat. 95) symmetrically

Fig. 64
El Lissitzky, *Proun 30T*, 1920. Oil on canvas, 50 × 62 cm. Sprengel Museum, Hanover

Fig. 65
Nikolai Punin, *Malevich's Personal Exhibition at GINKhUK, Leningrad*, 1926. Photograph. Punin Family Archive, St Petersburg

77
Kazimir Malevich
Desk and Room, 1913
Oil on canvas,
79.5 × 79.5 cm
On loan from
a private collection

78
Kazimir Malevich
Black Square, 1932
Oil on canvas,
53.5 × 53.5 cm
The Stage Hermitage
Museum, St Petersburg

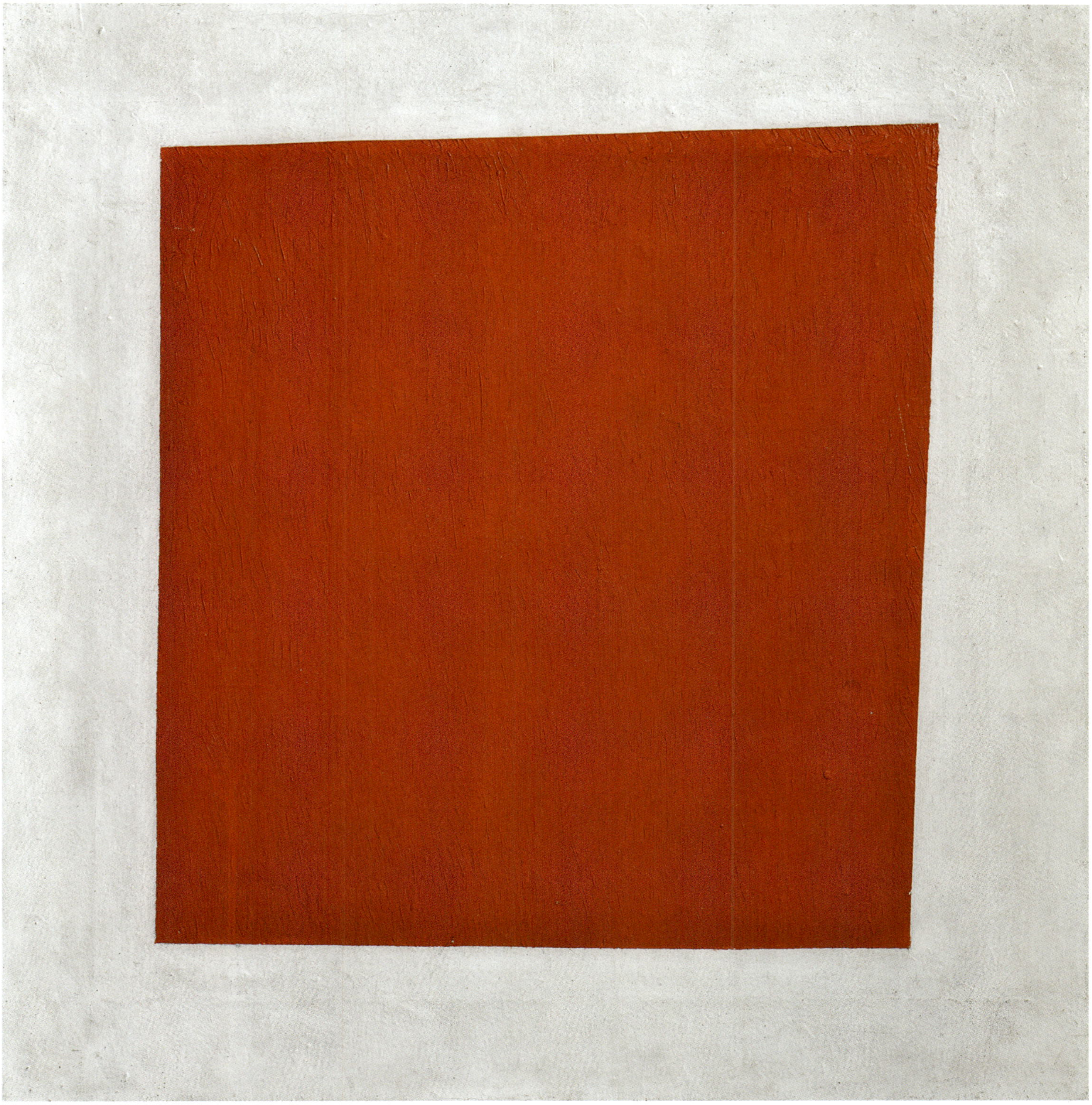

79
Kazimir Malevich
Red Square (Painterly Realism of a Peasant Woman in Two Dimensions), 1915
Oil on canvas, 53 × 53 cm
State Russian Museum, St Petersburg

80
Kazimir Malevich
Dynamic Suprematism Supremus, c. 1915
Oil on canvas,
80.3 × 80 cm
Tate: Purchased with assistance from the Friends of the Tate Gallery 1978

81
Kazimir Malevich
Suprematism, 1915–16
Oil on canvas,
81 × 80.5 cm
State Russian Museum,
St Petersburg

82
Kazimir Malevich
Suprematism (Supremus No. 58), 1916
Oil on canvas,
79.5 × 70.5 cm
State Russian Museum,
St Petersburg

83
Kazimir Malevich
Suprematistic Construction of Colours, 1928–29
Oil on plywood,
72 × 52 cm
State Russian Museum, St Petersburg

84
Kazimir Malevich
Peasants, c. 1930
Oil on canvas, 53 × 70 cm
State Russian Museum,
St Petersburg

85
Kazimir Malevich
Woman with Rake,
1930–32
Oil on canvas, 99 × 74 cm
State Tretyakov Gallery,
Moscow

86
Kazimir Malevich
To Reaping (Marfa and Vanka), 1928–29
Oil on canvas, 82 × 61 cm
State Russian Museum, St Petersburg

87
Kazimir Malevich
Three Female Figures, c. 1930
Oil on canvas, 47 × 63.5 cm
State Russian Museum, St Petersburg

88
Kazimir Malevich
Landscape with Five Houses, 1928–29
Oil on canvas, 83 × 62 cm
State Russian Museum, St Petersburg

89
Kazimir Malevich
The Red House, 1932
Oil on canvas, 63 × 55 cm
State Russian Museum, St Petersburg

90
Kazimir Malevich
Sportsmen, 1930–31
Oil on canvas,
142 × 164 cm
State Russian Museum,
St Petersburg

91
Kazimir Malevich
Female Portrait, 1928–29
Oil on plywood,
58 × 49 cm
State Russian Museum,
St Petersburg

92
Kazimir Malevich
Female Torso, 1928–29
Oil on plywood,
58 × 48 cm
State Russian Museum,
St Petersburg

93
Kazimir Malevich
Torso (Prototype of a New Image), 1928–29
Oil on canvas, 46 × 37 cm
State Russian Museum,
St Petersburg

94
Kazimir Malevich
Red Cavalry, *c.* 1932
Oil on canvas, 91 × 140 cm
State Russian Museum,
St Petersburg

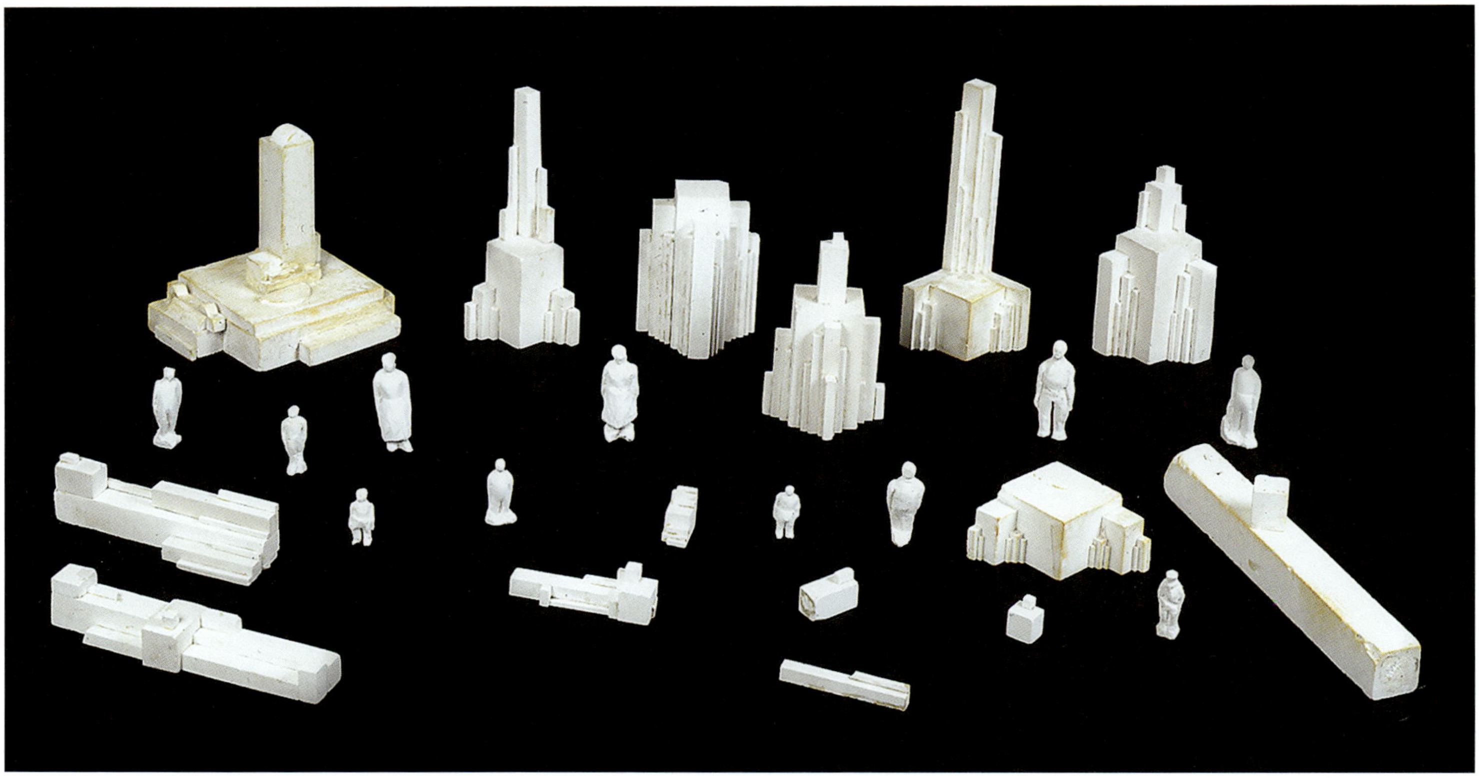

95
Kazimir Malevich
Architectons and Figurines, late 1920s
Plaster, various sizes
Collection of Vladimir Tsarenkov

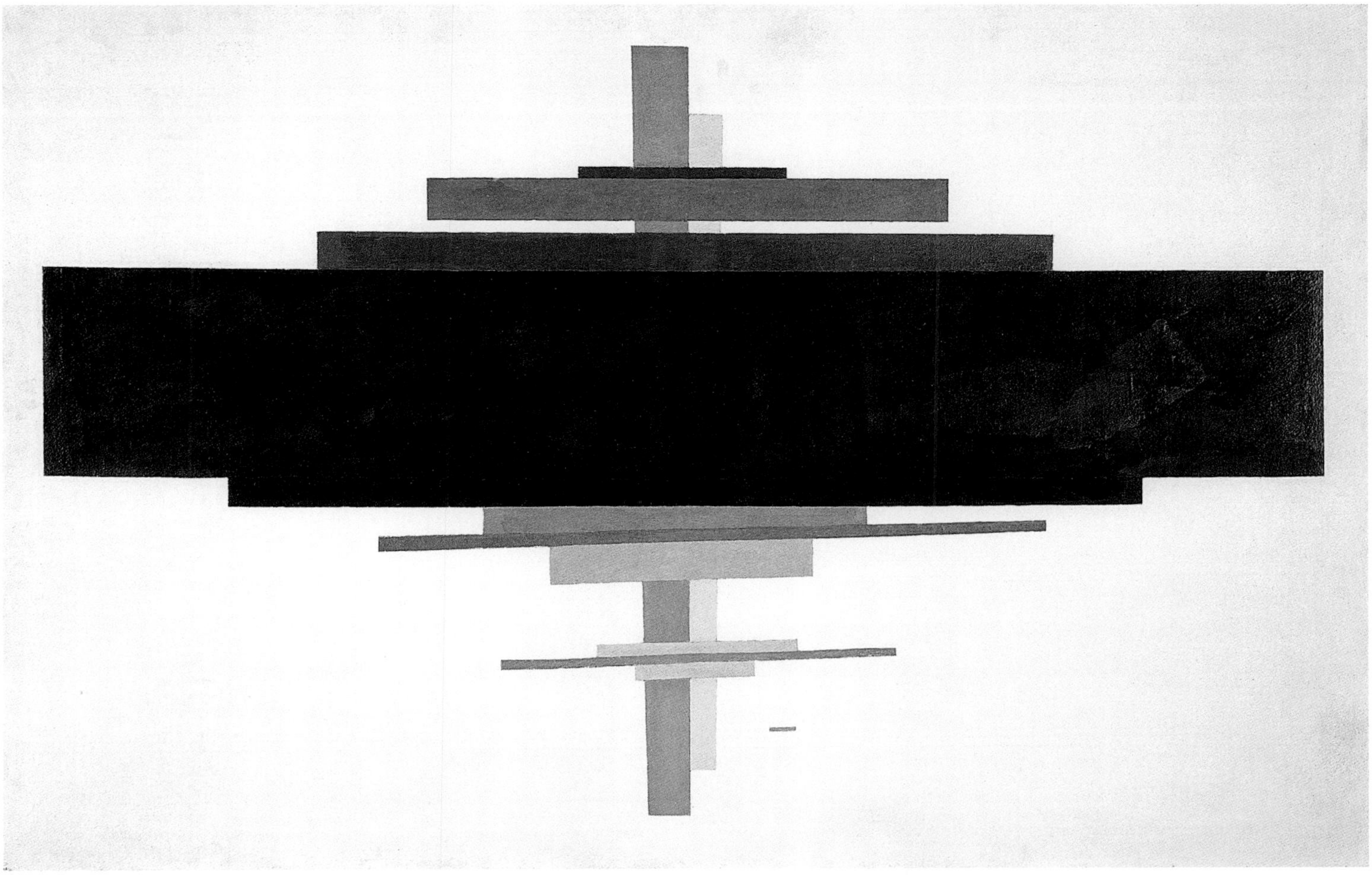

96
Ilya Chashnik
Suprematism, 1924–25
Oil on canvas,
80.2 × 127.5 cm
State Tretyakov Gallery,
Moscow

97
Nikolai Suetin, State Porcelain Factory, Leningrad
Coffee Pot, 1925
Vitrified enamel paint on porcelain, height 18.5 cm
The Petr Aven Collection

98
Kazimir Malevich
Plate with Suprematist Composition, 1923
Vitrified enamel paint on porcelain, diameter 23.4 cm
The Petr Aven Collection

99
Nikolai Suetin, State Porcelain Factory, Petrograd
Plate with a Suprematist Drawing, 1923
Vitrified enamel paint on porcelain, diameter 23.5 cm
The Petr Aven Collection

100
Kazimir Malevich
Plate with Suprematist Decorations: Dynamic Composition, 1923
Vitrified enamel paint on porcelain, diameter 23.4 cm
The Petr Aven Collection

101
Nikolai Suetin, State Porcelain Factory, Petrograd
Suprematist Inkwell (with a Disc) with Removable Cover, 1923
Vitrified enamel paint on porcelain, gilding, etching on gold, 12.5 × 14.8 × 13.7 cm
The Petr Aven Collection

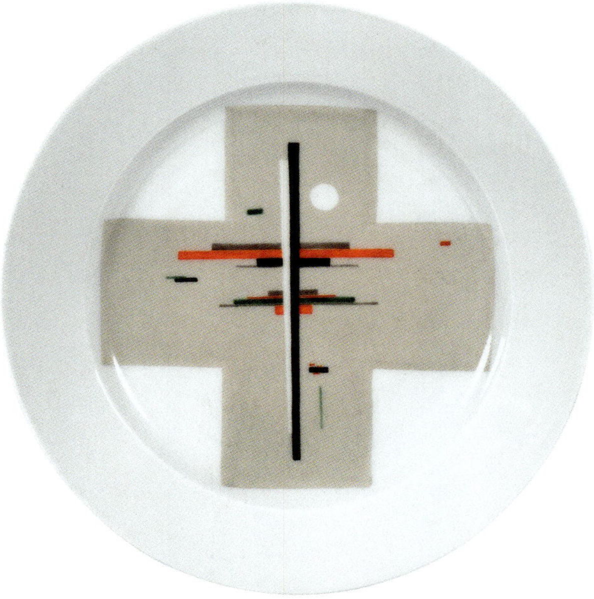

102
Nikolai Suetin, State Porcelain Factory, Leningrad
Plate 'Coloured Silhouettes' ('Three Women'), 1929
Paint on glazed porcelain, diameter 24.7 cm
The Petr Aven Collection

104
Nikolai Suetin, State Porcelain Factory, Leningrad
Plate with a Woman Depicted in a Suprematist Manner, 1934
Vitrified enamel paint on porcelain, diameter 25 cm
The Petr Aven Collection

103
Ilya Chashnik, State Porcelain Factory, Petrograd
Plate 'Grey-green Cross', 1923
Vitrified enamel paint on porcelain, diameter 25.1 cm
The Petr Aven Collection

105
Nikolai Suetin, State Porcelain Factory, Petrograd
Cup and Saucer with Suprematist Painting, 1923
Vitrified enamel paint on porcelain, cup: height 6.2 cm; plate: height 14.4 cm
The Petr Aven Collection

106
Nikolai Suetin, State Porcelain Factory, Leningrad
Vase with Ornamental Suprematist Elements, 1930
Vitrified enamel paint on porcelain, height 15.5 cm
The Petr Aven Collection

И. КЛЮН. 1921 г.

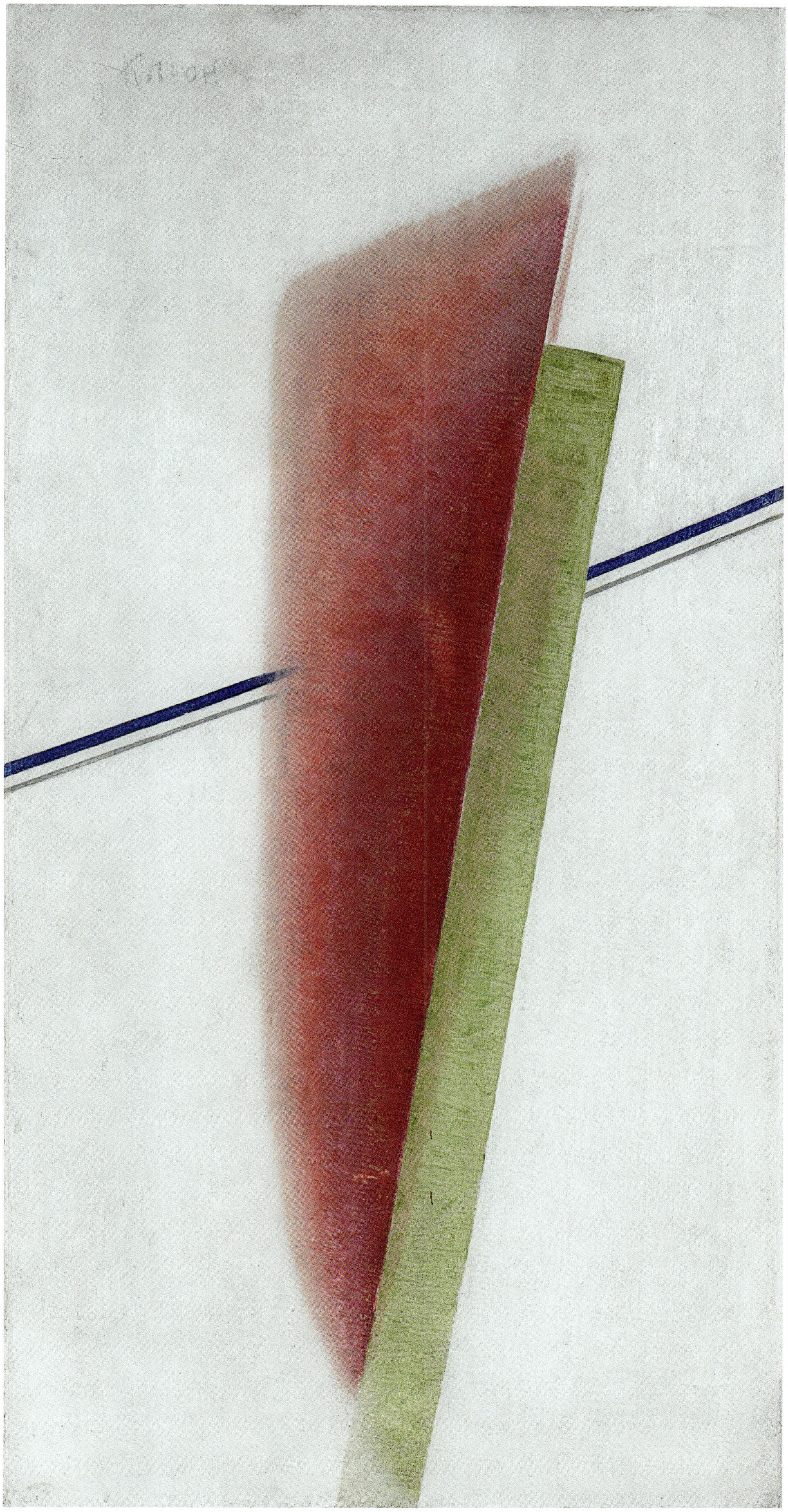

107
Ivan Klyun
Non-objective Painting According to the Principle of Light-Colour, 1921
Oil on cardboard, 86 × 59 cm
State Tretyakov Gallery, Moscow

108
Ivan Klyun
Composition, 1920
Oil on cardboard, 72.3 × 38.5 cm
State Tretyakov Gallery, Moscow

6

FATE OF THE PEASANTS

КОМСОМОЛЬЦ
НА УДАРНЫ
СЕ

FARMING AND FAMINE

John Milner

DESPITE, OR PERHAPS BECAUSE OF, THE VASTNESS of the Russian landscape, peasants are often seen as the very core of Russian identity, each generation retaining the same time-worn features as their forbears after centuries of stubborn survival in extreme conditions. But Russian peasants undoubtedly felt the impact of great national events. Until their emancipation by Tsar Alexander II in 1861, they had been *owned* in vast numbers, working on feudal estates. In the nineteenth century they frequently featured as the subject of paintings as well as in debates about a distinct Russian culture. Often they worked on family smallholdings, sometimes joining forces with other families to allocate strips of land for individuals to farm. Between 1905, in itself a year of revolution, and the outbreak of the First World War in 1914, some peasants began to form larger collaborative farms.

The peasant lifestyle was recognised as a vibrant element in the Russian identity, featuring in books, in music, on the stage and in art. It was celebrated for its vitality in the Russian Arts and Crafts movement, and in the Great International Exhibitions of 1889 and 1900 that were held in Paris. The Russian Futurist painters Natalia Goncharova and Mikhail Larionov, for example, who were among the most influential, dynamic and inventive artists of their day, seized upon peasant costumes, customs and folklore as essential ingredients of their work, adopting decorative motifs from embroidery, architecture and cheap prints. In 1913 Goncharova called on Russian artists to look to the East. She made spectacular designs for Sergei Diaghilev's Ballets Russes, asserting the peasant as a vigorous component of the Russian spectacle.

Although Goncharova's imaginative designs were brilliantly colourful, daily life in a peasant hut, or *izba*, could be desperate and grim.

> *The corner farthest from the door was filled with a huge square oven, usually built of brick and clay, that rose to within a couple of feet of the eaves. The oven warmed the interior, cooked the family's bread and other scant stores of food, and its flat top provided sleeping space for the elderly and infirm. Because few izby had chimneys, smoke from the oven drifted into the interior, and over time, covered everything it touched with a coating of black, greasy soot. Diagonally from the oven, in the corner nearest the door was the 'place of honour' where the family hung the icons towards which everyone bowed and murmured a brief prayer as they entered ... Beetles were everywhere, although bedbugs and even cockroaches tended to diminish in numbers in the most impoverished households.*[1]

Nevertheless, healthy and well-cared-for peasants could be found working the land on country estates, as Goncharova's depictions from the life attest. In his *Midday. Summer* (cat. 188) Kuzma Petrov-Vodkin made a beautiful panorama of the landscape as if seen from

Fig. 70
Gustavs Klucis, *The Komsomol Sows the Ground!*, 1931. Photomontage lithograph, 102.2 × 71 cm. Marx Memorial Library, London, inv. 084

Fig. 71
Arkady Shishkin, *The Sower I. E. Okulov, from the Village of Kharino, Viatsk Region*, 1924. Gelatin silver print, 53.7 × 36.6 cm. Archive Photos, London

a high viewpoint: he seems to include the curve of the horizon, a device that opens up to the gaze many different areas, each containing distinct scenes of the peasants' experience. These are presented as stages of life played out in the cycle of the seasons. Small farms stretch towards the horizon across this fruitful landscape, complemented by scenes of lovers and of a young mother feeding her child in a sunlit field. There are preparations for the coming harvest, and also a funeral procession without a priest, perhaps indicating that this a kind of idyll in the eternal countryside that encompasses the cycle of birth, love and death. The painting's title, *Midday. Summer*, fixes the historical moment between the revolutions of February and October 1917: the Tsar has abdicated, the Provisional Government is in power and the October Revolution is yet to come. Petrov-Vodkin's celebration of peace is unperturbed by premonitions of conflict.

This idyllic landscape stands in stark contrast to life in the peasants' dark *izby*, although it tells us nothing of the individuals depicted. The painter Boris Grigoriev had a sharper eye for facial detail. His *Old Dairy Woman* (cat. 112) has a stolid character, even as she is almost pushed over by her cow. Grigoriev's astutely observed studies of peasants were part of his series *Land of Peasants* (cat. 109), a portrait of Russia through its people.

The peasants' image was transformed by the Bolsheviks after the October Revolution. On his return to Russia on 16 April 1917 Lenin had promised the people 'Peace, Land, and Bread'. Soon the peasant was being promoted as the equivalent to the industrial worker, as the industrial hammer was brought together with the agricultural sickle, forming the Soviet emblem. This promotion of the urban and rural proletariat as equals belies the fact that many peasants had almost no means of survival, especially after the Civil War (1917–22) and the catastrophic famine of 1921–22. Images of industry and agriculture forming a new society were undermined by hunger, poor food distribution and empty fields.

We see none of this in Elizaveta Rozendorf's *Dish with a Depiction of a Reaper* (cat. 124), an exquisitely painted porcelain plate of 1920. The precious crop shines with gold, enough to astonish the reaper herself. Rozendorf's other painted plate (cat. 126) is apparently more modest but is still a brilliant celebration of food, even if it depicts only carrots, beetroot and pumpkin. She shows no sign of the desperate shortages of War Communism. Haymaking and harvest were being promoted in times of hardship (cats 118, 125), whereas, in practice, they were more a goal to reach for than a satisfying success.

Official signs of agrarian change appeared in Moscow in 1923 with the All-Russian Agricultural Exhibition. The wooden pavilions were constructed in a variety of traditional, classical and avant-garde styles. Peasants were bussed to the exhibition in their thousands to see new methods of agriculture and to behold the plentiful produce of all Russia. The official coloured poster by Ivan Lebedev and S. N. Ridman (cat. 123) indicates precisely this abundance. But times were hard for the peasants, with prices fixed at low levels by the government. The All-Russian Agricultural Exhibition was the first sign of the State's new general methods of organising the peasants and their essential work. The adoption of the New Economic Policy (NEP) in March 1921 reintroduced commercial activity and tolerated the profit motive. In the countryside, as in the cities, a conflict of ideology was inevitable in the competition of commerce and communism.

Petrov-Vodkin's *Fantasy* of 1925 (cat. 194) is a mysterious and suggestive painting that makes his position clear in this respect. The red horse leaping upwards and forwards is ridden by a peasant figure. Beneath him lies a village, such as those Marc Chagall depicted, without a cross on its church. The great leap forward of the horse recalls that of the Monument to Peter the Great, erected by Catherine the Great near the Hermitage Palace in St Petersburg, which had recently been renamed Leningrad after Lenin's death in 1924. But the evident differences between Etienne Maurice Falconet's sculpture and Petrov-Vodkin's painting are revealing. The painted horseman has no imperial swagger, no armour, no saddle and no stirrups. He wears the simplest clothes and no shoes: this time a worker-peasant is leaping into a new Russia. This energetic, mythical hero has no trace of arrogance, wealth or modernity. Nor is he interested in private enterprise, although his painter may be.

Fig. 72
Max Alpert, *Iskra Concert*, undated. Period gelatin silver print, 7.6 × 10.5 cm. Private collection

Fig. 73
Semyon Fridlyand (Simon Fridland), *On the Stalin Collective Farm*, undated. Vintage gelatin silver print mounted on an envelope, 6 × 9.7 cm. Private collection

The Church, which had always provided the focus for village communities, lost its vital role, and icon-painting workshops managed to survive only by changing their imagery from Christian to Communist, as in the painted box from the *Kolkhoz* at the village of Palekh (cat. 122).

The traditional anonymity of the vigorous peasant, seen in Alexei Pakhomov's *Reaper (Harvest)* (cat. 111), is emblematic, standing for the type and not an individual. But Malevich was more radical than this. The figure in *To Reaping (Marfa and Vanka)* (cat. 86) is faceless because she is walking away, but in his *Head of a Peasant* (cat. 115) Malevich has modernised his subject, whose face and beard are painted flat and bright in red and white sections. In the background, peasants work in lines in the fields of an extensive collective farm. Strips of different crops stretch away towards the horizon, as colourful and decorative as patchwork. In the metallic grey sky, aeroplanes pass, symbolising the transformation of the old by the new. The *Kolkhoz* has grown immensely and has been industrialised by tractors, as fabric designs by Sergey Burylin (cat. 128) and Vladimir Maslov (cat. 129) attest. In April 1929 government goals were increased calling for 20% of farmland to be collectivised by 1933.

Fig. 74
Semyon Fridlyand (Simon Fridland), *Untitled (Woman Worker)*, undated. Vintage gelatin silver print, 11 × 7 cm. Private collection

Fig. 75
Mikhail Ozersky, *First Tractor*, 1931. Photograph. Moscow Photo Museum (House of Photography)

An important shift of policy and ideology began with the proposal in 1927 that collective farms should be formed in each village to share equipment, increase productivity and thus produce a surplus to feed the urban populations. Sharing equipment and land was anathema to farmers who had become successful during seven years of the New Economic Policy. The NEP ended in 1928 and the collectivisation of agriculture commenced, coinciding with the consolidation of Stalin as leader.

This return to centralised planning aimed to increase production through mechanisation and the amalgamation of farms into much bigger units. In the process the individual ownership of land, equipment, stocks and animals was undermined, although collectivisation was resisted by those who had developed their farms efficiently. The movement grew rapidly in the next few years. When resistance increased, collectivisation became compulsory, combining farms into ever-larger Agricultural Communes (or *Kolkhoz*), which could only be organised at the expense of individual identity, as Kazimir Malevich's faceless peasants (cat. 84) testify. People were uprooted and traditional village life was destroyed.

All sense of individual ownership was rapidly disappearing, and individual identity was vanishing with it. Everyone and yet no-one owns this collective farm. Work on these Agricultural Communes was compulsory, and leaving was dangerous and difficult. Malevich's *Peasants* (cat. 84) stare back at us without opinion or appeal, while the figures in Konstantin Rozhdestvensky's *Family in a Field* (cat. 110) look away in blank contemplation of the endless prospect before them.

The photographer Arkady Shaiket captured the arrival of electricity in *Electrification of Lapatino Village* (cat. 130), and recorded also the arrival of an electric lamp in a peasant's wooden house (cat. 131), where its brilliance surpasses both the dim glow of the icon lamp and the kerosene lamp. Malevich in particular had been making a long series of paintings of peasant life since 1913, adopting in the pre-war years a Cubo-Futurist style to depict the peasants' orderly dedication to woodcutting, carpentry and harvesting. In his painting *To Reaping (Marfa and Vanka)* (cat. 86) Malevich has reworked that earlier composition and style. Marfa and

УДАРНИЦЫ
ЗАВОДОВ И
СОВХОЗОВ,
ВСТУПАЙТЕ
В РЯДЫ ВКП [б]
ПРАВДА
В. КУЛАГИНА -32
ЦЕНА 50 КОП.
ОГИЗ — ИЗОГИЗ
Москва 1932 Ленинград

Vanka move off to join the other reapers in a vaster landscape. These peasant themes were still vital to him in 1928–29, despite the passage of fifteen years that included war, revolution and now collective farming. Even in his Suprematist exhibition in 1915 he included a single *Red Square (Painterly Realism of a Peasant in Two Dimensions)* (cat. 79). The deep red of her kerchief is all we have to recognise the peasant. Malevich had never abandoned Suprematism, still evident in his architectural prototypes in the late 1920s. But now that Malevich was obliged to address the demand for figurative painting, he made paintings of figures once again, strangely constructed and puppet-like new prototypes for the new era of vast fields. Malevich's *Woman with Rake* (cat. 85) is one of these prototypes, and among his followers Nikolai Suetin pursued the same idea in *A Woman with a Saw* (cat. 114).

The bigger the *Kolkhoz*, the more it needed organisation and discipline. Collective farmworkers were usually divided into brigades (cats 117, 132) led by a brigadier. A large *Kolkhoz* in July 1929 might comprise 200 to 400 units divided into sections of 15 to 30 brigades. Within these brigades were shock-workers (*Urdarniki, udarnitsy*), who persistently exceeded work targets, and so were held up as examples to others in order to increase production, as seen in Alexei Pakhomov's *Portrait of Shock-worker Molodtsova* (cat. 116), and in Valentina Kulagina's poster *Women Shock-workers of Factories and Collective Farms Join the Ranks of the CPSU [Communist Party]* (fig. 76). This contrast indicates that Kulagina's printed poster could embrace political rhetoric and communicate to thousands, while contemplative single paintings, being less collective and less public, were also less effective in political terms. The *Shock-worker from Dneprostroi* by Isaak Brodsky (cat. 19) shows an industrial shock-worker. It also shows Brodsky learning from the dynamic composition of posters.

Fig. 76
Valentina Kulagina, *Women Shock-workers of Factories and Collective Farms Join the Ranks of the CPSU [Communist Party]*, 1932. Lithograph in red and black, 89.6 × 60 cm. State Russian Museum, St Petersburg

As the collective farm grew ever larger, the atmosphere became more like that of a factory than a farm, as can be seen in Boris Ignatovich's *Reading the Newspaper at the Collective Farm* (cat. 133). Collectivisation extended across Russia, and was in place when Pavel Filonov painted his *Collective Farm Worker* in 1931 (cat. 113). Since his pre-war Futurist days, Filonov had witnessed the whole process and the transformation it caused. It seems likely that his approach to painting in 1931 reflected his response to government advice. *Collective Farm Worker* has none of the crystalline fracturing that had been a defining feature of Filonov's important paintings in the early revolutionary period, such as *Formula of the Petrograd Proletariat* (cat. 53). In this portrait of an anonymous man with an appearance like granite and a character to match, Filonov achieves a remarkably sculptural effect. Though clearly no longer young, his sitter is intense, his eyes are penetrating and he seems somehow unapproachable. His resemblance to a saint suggests he might be a modern icon for an atheist age. Despite every effort, including harsh discipline, confiscations and arrests, famine was returning in 1932–33.

Grigory Ryazhsky's *Collective Farm Team Leader* (cat. 117) is a less enigmatic and more assertive image. The women in charge of this *Kolkhoz* were powerful and effective. There is nothing decorative about the painter's handling of his subject. Ryazhsky is frank and direct: this is an image of an efficiently run *Kolkhoz* that would please the government and might hang in the head office of an extensive collective farm.

Life on the *Kolkhoz* was promoted widely in posters, periodicals and films as an exemplar of Soviet power and energy, fuelling a new, collective and increasingly mechanised way of life. Posters by Valentina Kulagina (fig. 76), by Gustavs Klucis and others were designed to show the positive side of what was being achieved, how a life of committed and heroic hard labour would soon be transformed into a relaxed and harmonious future. In Klucis's photomontage poster *The Komsomol Sows the Ground!* (fig. 70), the young farmworkers are seeding crops from a long procession of wide agricultural machines with red flags, all preparing for the harvest to come.

This projected happiness was continually postponed, and very many people died in the interim. The individual's experience was of little or no consequence to the new society.

109
Boris Grigoriev
Land of Peasants, 1917
Oil on canvas,
90 × 215 cm
State Russian Museum,
St Petersburg

110
Konstantin
Rozhdestvensky
Family in a Field, 1932
Oil on cardboard,
70 × 52 cm
State Tretyakov Gallery,
Moscow

111
Alexei Pakhomov
Reaper (Harvest), 1928
Oil on canvas, 85 × 106 cm
State Russian Museum,
St Petersburg

112
Boris Grigoriev
Old Dairy Woman, 1917
Oil on canvas, 62 × 71 cm
State Tretyakov Gallery, Moscow

113
Pavel Filonov
Collective Farm Worker, 1931
Oil on canvas, 69.5 × 53 cm
State Russian Museum, St Petersburg

114
Nikolai Suetin
A Woman with a Saw,
c. 1920
Oil on wood,
55 × 33.3 cm
State Russian Museum,
St Petersburg

115
Kazimir Malevich
Head of a Peasant,
1928–29
Oil on plywood,
71.7 × 53.8 cm
State Russian Museum,
St Petersburg

116
Alexei Pakhomov
Portrait of Shock-worker Molodtsova, 1931
Oil on canvas,
56.5 × 39.2 cm
State Russian Museum,
St Petersburg

117
Grigory Ryazhsky
The Collective Farm Team Leader, 1932
Oil on canvas,
209 × 164 cm
State Tretyakov Gallery,
Moscow

118
Alexei Pakhomov
Haymaking, 1925
Oil on canvas, 64 × 105 cm
State Russian Museum,
St Petersburg

119
Natalia Danko, State Porcelain Factory, Leningrad
On Guard: Women's Watch, 1938
Vitrified enamel paint on porcelain, height 25.5 cm
The Petr Aven Collection

120
Natalia Danko, State Porcelain Factory, Leningrad
Dancer, 1929
Vitrified enamel paint on porcelain, height 23.8 cm
The Petr Aven Collection

121
Naum Kongiser, State Porcelain Factory, Leningrad
A Radio for the Village, 1927
Vitrified enamel paint on porcelain, height 25.6 cm
The Petr Aven Collection

122
Unknown
Kolkhoz Box, c. 1923
The banner reads 'Kolkhoz for the New Lifestyle'
Lacquer, tempera and gold paint on papier mâché, 15.3 × 20.2 × 4.7 cm
The Petr Aven Collection

123
Ivan Lebedev and S. N. Ridman
All-Union Agricultural Exhibition (Moscow), 1923
Poster, 107 × 71 cm
Alex Lachmann Collection, London

КТО НЕ С НАМИ, ТОТ ПРОТИВ НАС.

124
Elizaveta Rozendorf,
State Porcelain Factory,
Petrograd
Dish with a Depiction of a Reaper, 1920
Vitrified enamel paint on porcelain,
diameter 32.9 cm
The Petr Aven Collection

125
Sergei Chekhonin,
Proletariat Porcelain and Faience Factory,
Bronnitsa, Novgorod Region
Great Star with a Sheaf of Corn 'Who Is Not With Us Is Against Us', 1922
Vitrified enamel paint on porcelain,
diameter 23.4 cm
The Petr Aven Collection

126
Elizaveta Rozendorf,
State Porcelain Factory,
Petrograd
Dish 'Girl with a Pumpkin', 1920
Vitrified enamel paint on porcelain,
diameter 32 cm
The Petr Aven Collection

127
Ivan Ivanovich Riznich,
State Porcelain Factory,
Leningrad
Large Vase with Peasant Dance, 1929
Vitrified enamel paint on porcelain, height 42 cm
The Petr Aven Collection

128
Sergey Burylin
Tractor, late 1920s
Roller print on calico,
52 × 32 cm
State Russian Museum,
St Petersburg

129
Vladimir Maslov
Tractor, 1925
Ornamental chintz,
cotton fabric, 36 × 49 cm
The Burilin Ivanovo
Museum of Local History,
Ivanovo

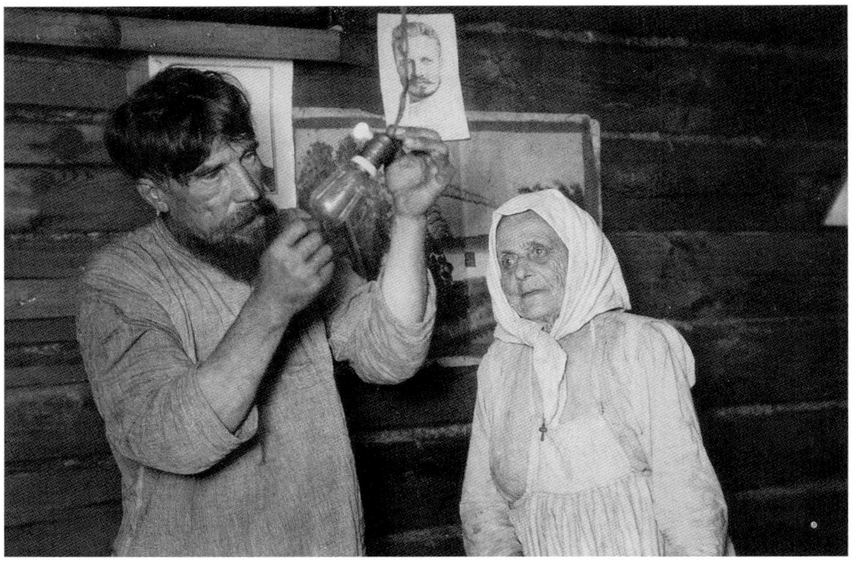

130
Arkady Shaiket
Electrification of Lapatino Village, 1925
Gelatin silver print, 20 × 30.5 cm
Alex Lachmann Collection, London

131
Arkady Shaiket
Lenin's Lamp: Light Bulb in a Peasant House, 1925
Gelatin silver print, 11.7 × 17.3 cm
Alex Lachmann Collection, London

132
Georgi Zelma
Brigade Meeting on the Collective Farm, 1929
Gelatin silver print, 37 × 48 cm
Alex Lachmann Collection, London

133
Boris Ignatovich
Reading the Newspaper at the Collective Farm (Kolkhoz), 1930
Gelatin silver print, 28.2 × 19.6 cm
Alex Lachmann Collection, London

7

ETERNAL RUSSIA

ECHOES OF ORTHODOXY

Nicoletta Misler

IN 1916, IN THE MIDST OF THE GREAT WAR and on the eve of the October Revolution, Mikhail Nesterov completed his ambitious painting *In Russia (Soul of the People)* (fig. 78), a panorama that was meant to embody – visually and philosophically – the meaning of the 'Russian idea'. Nesterov had been working on this subject for almost a decade, endeavouring to synthesise the spirit of Christian Russia into a grandiose historical and religious fresco bearing testimony to the burgeoning self-consciousness of the Russian people. Here we see a young peasant lad, a group of women surrounding a holy man, a metropolitan, a patriarch, a grand prince or tsar, famous writers such as Fyodor Dostoyevsky and Leo Tolstoy – all figures who, in Nesterov's opinion, symbolised the 'adolescence' of Christian Russia. The particular choice of imagery and the Neo-Nationalist aura of the painting associated Nesterov immediately with other artists, writers and intellectuals who had sought refuge from the approaching apocalypse in the protective precinct of the Lavra (Monastery) of the Holy Trinity at the Sergiev Posad (in Soviet times – Zagorsk). Father Pavel Florensky, the writer Vasily Rozanov, the theologian Sergei Bulgakov,[1] the icon scholar Yurii Olsuf'ev,[2] the biologist Pavel Kapterev[3] and the artist and critic Igor Grabar had all gravitated towards the Lavra, a magnet for those who could not welcome, let alone accept, the imminent upheaval, even though many were convinced that the storm would not last.

Konstantin Yuon should also be mentioned here. He lived at the Lavra from 1917 to 1921, painting scenes such as *Cupolas and Swallows: The Cathedral of the Assumption at the Trinity Lavra of St Sergius* (fig. 77) showing the be-crossed and golden cupolas of the Sergiev Posad not as ruins from the past, but as vigorous symbols reverberating in the spring sunshine. Yuon repeated this strangely inopportune appreciation in *The Day of Annunciation* (cat. 137), another sunny day at the Lavra with the faithful gathered and rejoicing before the churches. Even if by then the Bolsheviks had closed and sealed the Cathedral of the Trinity (on 31 May 1920), Yuon went ahead and published an elegant portfolio of lithographs illustrating the life of the Lavra and its surroundings and, thereby, paying immediate homage to Old Russia.[4] On the other hand, it was Yuon who had represented the October Revolution in the ambiguous iconography of his *New Planet* (cat. 52), an apocalyptic interpretation close to the viewpoint of many intellectuals of the time, not least, Rozanov, who published a set of pamphlets entitled *The Apocalypse of Our Time* – at his own expense – between November 1917 and October 1918.[5] These important facts should prompt us to correct the misapprehensions and prejudices that often accompany the conventional understanding of Russian culture and the October Revolution, to the effect that celebrations of Orthodoxy suddenly vanished in the wake of the atheist onslaught.

Indeed, Florensky, Rozanov, Yuon and other thinkers and artists constitute an 'alternative tradition' in the 1920s, one which coexisted with, and, in some measure, countered, some of the more raucous claims of the avant-garde on the one hand, and of the proto-Socialist Realists on the other. In the twilight of Symbolism, they were the last representatives of the Russian Silver Age: adducing scientific criteria, they pleaded for the retention of Orthodox beliefs, and at a time of State nationalisation and confiscation of private and ecclesiastical property, they argued for the preservation of churches, of personnel serving the Christian faith and even of the former nobility as an intrinsic and organic component of Russian history.

Immediately after finishing *In Russia (Soul of the People)*, Nesterov entertained the idea of painting a double portrait of two philosophers who could represent the Orthodox idea, i.e. Sergei Bulgakov and Pavel Florensky,[6] a double rendering that also testified to the cataclysm overtaking Russia in the Great War, the Civil War and the Revolution. Dedicated to Old Russia, *In Russia (Soul of the People)* was organically linked to the political context of the Great War, which had wrecked so many human lives. But Nesterov had also intended his picture to express the spiritual values of Holy Russia, telling the story, however, in a rather obvious kind of Realism of which Florensky made a delicate, but apt, critique.[7] The double portrait *Philosophers* (cat. 136), on the contrary, in its serene and intimate mood, was charged with numerous meanings and presentiments of doom. Started one fateful evening in May 1917, in

Fig. 77
Konstantin Yuon, *Cupolas and Swallows: The Cathedral of the Assumption at the Trinity Lavra of St Sergius* (detail), 1921–22. Oil on canvas, 71 × 89 cm. State Tretyakov Gallery, Moscow

the kitchen garden of Florensky's house at the Sergiev Posad and close to the Lavra, the portrait became the fulcrum of events beneath the aura of the Lavra and a strong witness to that eschatological moment.

Nesterov borrowed his structure for the double portrait from the Renaissance: the image of the two profiles in very close proximity becomes, in fact, a single portrait, because it joins the two figures emblematically and inextricably. As Bulgakov remarked:

> *According to the artist's notion, this was not only the portrait of the two friends created by a third friend, but also the spiritual vision of an era. To the artist, both faces expressed the same moment of comprehension, but in different ways, one seeing terror, the other seeing a world of joy, of surmounting triumph. At first the artist had doubts about the first image and even tried changing the portrait by replacing terror with idyll and tragedy with placidity. However, it quickly became apparent just how false and intolerable that was so the artist felt compelled to restore his initial perception. On the other hand, the image of Father Florensky with its artistic and spiritual self-evidence, seemed eminently appropriate, so there was no need for change. Here was the artistic clairvoyance of two images of the Russian Apocalypse and on both sides of our earthly life – the first in conflict and confusion (in my heart of hearts this really regarded the destiny of my friend) and the second on the path to victorious fulfilment which we can observe right now.*[8]

The tranquil landscape beyond the lake and the pink sky of twilight evoke the various feminine apparitions that had long haunted Russian poets and philosophers, from Mikhail Lermontov to Vladimir Solov'ev and Viacheslav Ivanov. As Florensky observed in his essay 'Celestial Signs': 'Sophia appears as pink or red. She appears pink or red as God's image for his creature, as the manifestation of God on earth, as that "rosy shadow" to which Vladimir Solov'ev prayed.'[9] In the midst of the Revolution Bulgakov and Florensky discussed Sophia, a subject that the Symbolists had confronted through

their various forms of the Beautiful Lady and which had been spiritualised in Orthodox discussions of Sophia as Divine Wisdom – something that Bulgakov himself investigated in his concurrent tract *A Light not Crepuscular: Observations and Speculations*, published by the Sergiev Posad, also in 1917.[10]

The two philosophers' distance from external or topical events – war and revolution – in the portrait is, no doubt, far from actuality. Old Russia had literally been swept away by the Revolution (a metaphor captured in the imagery of brooms in the Russian Telegraph Agency [ROSTA] posters of Vladimir Lebedev [fig. 35] and Vladimir Mayakovsky), but she still had her paladins, well-armed and sober. In any case, opponents of the vandalism of the Revolution – which even the Bolshevik leaders, from Lenin to Anatoly Lunacharsky, People's Commissar of Enlightenment, were trying to stem – needed to be well equipped with practical tools as well as ideals. For example, from the very first, Grabar, a highly respected artist (cat. 143) and art historian, played a vigorous role in the various State institutions charged with registering, making inventories of and restoring monuments and works of art – and, therefore, with deciding what exactly constituted these.[11] Enforced nationalisation often led to a former owner of a collection being appointed its director, as happened with Aleksei Bakhrushin, Ivan Morosov and Sergei Shchukin.[12]

When it came to the physical place and environment in which objects needed to be preserved, Soviet museologists, in their more audacious moments, argued that museums should be regarded not as mirrors of the past, but as living entities. For example, in his 1923 booklet 'The Museum as a Work of Art' Boris Shaposhnikov declared that the single aim of a museum was 'to demonstrate the lifestyle of a bygone era' and that even the 'museum of everyday life … strives to show objects of the past in the settings for which they were intended'.[13] With this justification in mind, Shaposhnikov had organised a 'Museum of Everyday Life in the 1840s' in the so-called Khomiakov house in Moscow under the auspices of the State Historical Museum so as to re-evaluate the objects and values of the nobility, the bourgeoisie and the intelligentsia, which the Revolution was intent on destroying.[14] An ardent protector of

Fig. 78
Mikhail Nesterov, *In Russia (Soul of the People)*, 1916. Oil on canvas, 206 × 484 cm. State Tretyakov Gallery, Moscow

pre-revolutionary values, Shaposhnikov wanted to recompose objects rescued from the vandals of the Civil War into an organic totality, almost a history of material culture and a sociological rebuilding, so as to safeguard not only the objects themselves, but also the historical memories that accompanied them and their complex stratification of values.

The tightness of these bonds can be seen from the professional career of Vladimir Zgura, who, in 1922, of all unlikely dates, managed to establish a Society for the Study of the Russian Country Estate. Zgura had a broad knowledge of history and archaeology, and also began publishing a magazine on the history of the country estate – in the very heyday of the Soviet regime[15] – whose goal was to compile a register of the numerous country houses that had been abandoned as well as to record the less explicit legacy of the country life that had been lived by the nobility (and perhaps even to restore some aspects of it). Here was a 'soft' opposition to those who wanted to create a *novyi byt* (literally, a new way of living) in keeping with revolutionary theory or who were pushing for the 'life-construction' and 'reconstruction' of everyday life. Although some of the most prestigious intellectuals of the *ancien régime* occupied important posts in the Soviet government, albeit briefly, they now countered with the authentic organic nature of old Russian culture, which was democratic, they argued, because it had taken root in the soul of the people.

On 30 July 1917 Florensky wrote to Alexandra Mamontova, daughter of the celebrated entrepreneur and art patron, Savva Mamontov, and curator of the Museum of Abramtsevo, then, as now, dedicated to the promotion of the popular arts:

> *What's going on around us is, of course, agonising. However, I do believe and hope that once this Nihilism has exhausted itself and has demonstrated its impoverishment and everyone is fed up with it, our hearts and minds will then turn to the Russian idea, to Russia, to Holy Russia, after the collapse of all this abomination. Worse: if Abramtsevo were to be physically destroyed and, in spite of the enormity of such a crime, the idea of Abramtsevo were to continue to live, well, not everything would be lost for the Russian people.*[16]

Even the landscape of the Sergiev Posad and Abramtsevo, with the hills and lake surrounding the Lavra, were to be safeguarded at the wont of Florensky, Nesterov and their friends, together with the icons, because all were an essential part of the spiritual configuration of the territory of the Lavra itself.[17] It was precisely this landscape that Nesterov included in his double portrait of Bulgakov and Florensky, demonstrating the intrinsic proximity of the two

Fig. 79
Pavel Korin, *Sketch for Requiem: Vanishing Russia*, 1935–59. Tempera on paper, 65 × 107.5 cm. State Tretyakov Gallery, Moscow

Fig. 80
Studies for *Requiem: Vanishing Russia*, whose dimensions would have been 450 × 941 cm, photographed in Pavel Korin's Moscow studio in 1993

Fig. 81
Pavel Korin, *Young Hieromonk (Priest-monk) Fyodor*, 1932. Oil on canvas, 196 × 73.5 cm. State Tretyakov Gallery, Moscow

Fig. 82
Pavel Korin, *Alexander Nevsky*: central panel from the *Alexander Nevsky* triptych, 1942. Oil on canvas, 275 × 142 cm. State Tretyakov Gallery, Moscow

Fig. 83
Pavel Korin, *An Ancient Tale*: from the *Alexander Nevsky* triptych, 1943. Oil on canvas, 266 × 250 cm. State Tretyakov Gallery, Moscow

philosophers to this specific territory. And this was not only because Nesterov had spent the summer of 1917 there, but, rather, because he wanted to underline the symbolic and affective value that this landscape retained for those who had been at the Lavra at this tumultuous moment: here was an oasis of nature and culture that could still offer relief from the catastrophic events outside.

Nesterov's endeavour to synthesise the entire history of Russia into a grandiose painting was in turn taken up by his pupil Pavel Korin, an artist much appreciated by the Soviet regime despite his initial training as an icon restorer, and generally regarded as an 'official' artist, if not as an exponent of Socialist Realism.

On 7 April 1925 Korin observed the enormous crowd bidding farewell to the body of the deceased Patriarch Tikhon of Moscow in the Cathedral of the Donskoy Monastery, where almost a million people overflowed into the square and adjacent streets. Yet the year before, on 27 January, another crowd of the faithful, this time in the cause of the October Revolution and also numbering a million, had attended the funeral of Lenin in Red Square. The two events were apparently antithetical. Present at the Patriarch's burial service were metropolitans, archbishops, father superiors, monks and nuns, all the representatives of the power of the Orthodox Church. Korin himself attended the service and, in the following years made portraits of its attendees dressed in their liturgical vestments; many were arrested or liquidated or obliged to compromise in order to maintain their positions. Korin's intention was to connect the individual portraits into a single, grandiose canvas called *Requiem: Vanishing Russia*,[18] the second part of the title having been suggested by the writer Maxim Gorky, which Korin welcomed as a strategic justification of the picture's content. True, Korin never finished the painting (he ceased working on it in 1959), but he did create 29 portraits and studies related to the potential masterpiece (figs 79, 80), which, in many ways, would have been the logical conclusion to the work initiated by his mentor Nesterov.

Several years later, in 1943, Korin reworked a figure from *Requiem: Vanishing Russia*, the portrait (fig. 81) of the youngest novice or hieromonk (Father Fyodor Pavlovich Bogoyavlensky, 1905–1943), into his huge *Alexander Nevsky* triptych (figs 82, 83) – as a valiant warrior for Russia as well as for Nevsky. Was it just by chance that Korin chose one of the leaders of the ecclesiastic resistance from the 1920s and 1930s and holy martyr of the Russian Orthodox Church? Certainly not. But why, then, did the Soviet regime not protest or arrest Korin for counter-revolutionary propaganda? Perhaps because the triptych as a whole is strong symbolic testimony to the transformation of Russia's historical iconography from the October Revolution onwards: the phantom of the *bogatyr'*, a legendary knight armed with cross and sword, has vanquished the Russia of Communism, while the phantom of Communism and the October Revolution has been banished from the steppes now occupied by holy men and chivalrous warriors of old.

134
Aristarkh Lentulov
Gates with Tower: New Jerusalem, 1917
Oil on canvas, 102 × 98 cm
State Tretyakov Gallery, Moscow

135
Aristarkh Lentulov
Tverskoy Boulevard, 1917
Oil on canvas, 229 × 215 cm
State Tretyakov Gallery,
Moscow

136
Mikhail Nesterov
Philosophers, 1917
Oil on canvas, 126 × 126 cm
State Tretyakov Gallery, Moscow

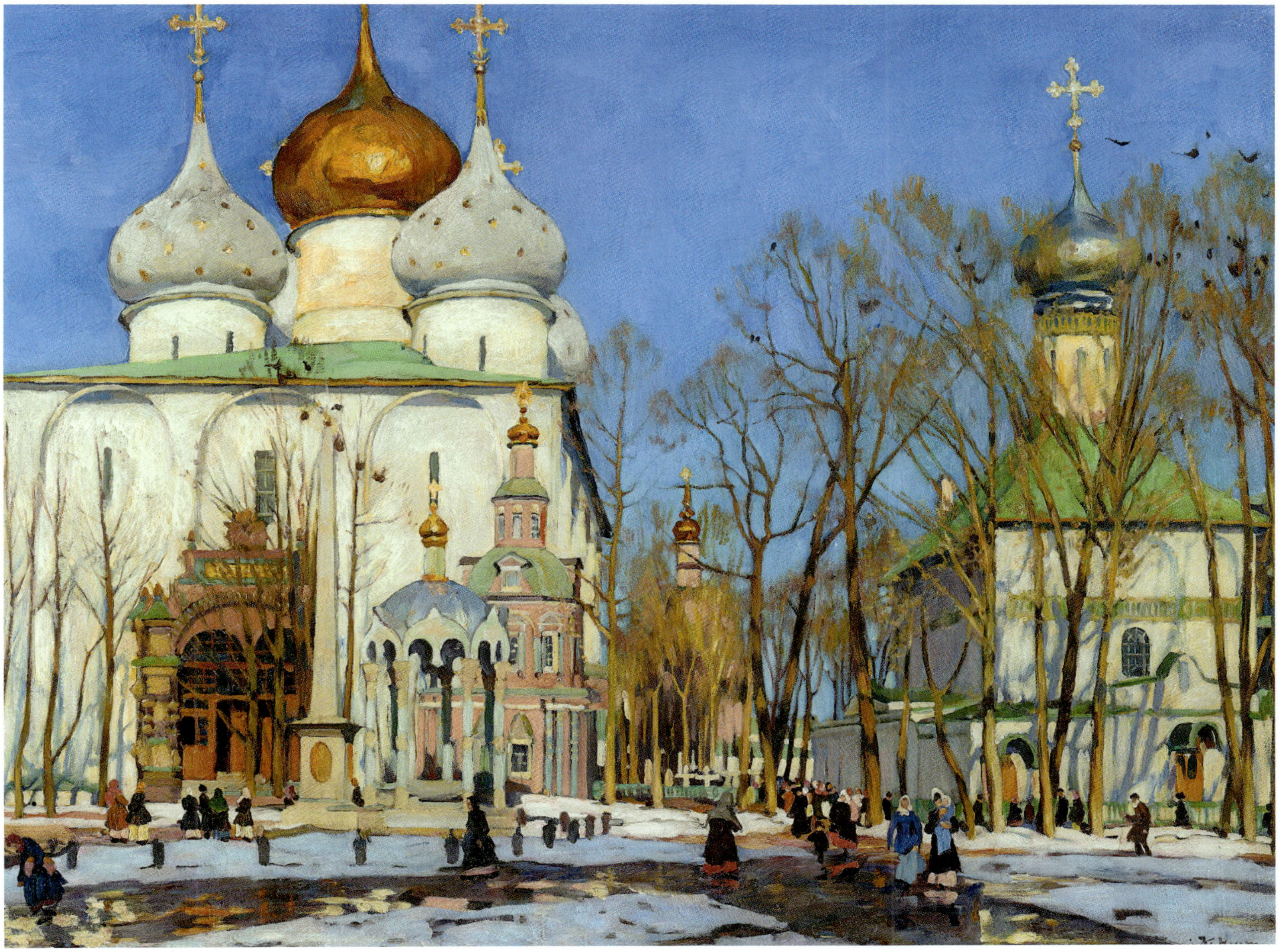

137
Konstantin Yuon
The Day of Annunciation,
1922
Oil on canvas,
73.3 × 100.6 cm
State Tretyakov Gallery,
Moscow

138
Boris Kustodiev
Carnival, 1919
Oil on canvas, 71 × 98 cm
The Russian Academy of
Fine Arts Museum,
St Petersburg

139
Filip Maliavin
Troika, 1933
Oil on canvas, 201 × 224 cm
Private collection

140
Marc Chagall
Promenade, 1917–18
Oil on canvas,
175.2 × 168.4 cm
State Russian Museum,
St Petersburg

141
Marc Chagall
Window over a Garden, 1917
Oil on paper mounted on
cardboard, 46.5 × 61 cm
The Russian Academy
of Fine Arts Museum,
St Petersburg

142
Vasily Baksheev
Blue Spring, 1930
Oil on wood, 44 × 56.5 cm
State Tretyakov Gallery, Moscow

143
Igor Grabar
By the Lake, 1926
Oil on canvas, 77 × 80 cm
State Russian Museum,
St Petersburg

144
Anna Golubkina
Birch Tree, 1927
Bronze, 96 × 27 × 26 cm
State Tretyakov Gallery, Moscow

145
Mikhail Larionov
Cover illustration for *Jar-Ptitza* (*Firebird*), 1922–26
Monthly Russian art and literary journal, Berlin, Dr Selle & Co
14 issues, bound in two volumes, each 32.5 × 25 × 4 cm
Alex Lachmann Collection, London

JAR
PTi TZ A
Ш
T
ЖАРZ
ПТИЦА
№ 1

ЦТКА
ПЕРВАЯ КОННАЯ

8

NEW CITY, NEW SOCIETY

КТО
НЕ РАБОТАЕТ
ТОТ
НЕ ЕСТ
1921

THE LIFE OF ARTISTS IN 1920s RUSSIA

Evgenia Petrova

Detail of cat. 165

SIMPLY TO DIVIDE RUSSIAN ARTISTS WORKING in the period from the mid-1910s to the early 1930s into right and left – those who accepted the Revolution and followed its precepts and those who rejected it – does not reflect reality. Letters, reminiscences and archival documents, many of which are yet to be published or translated, evince the complex and often contradictory states of mind of the artists who experienced this historical watershed. Of course, this holds for ordinary people, too.

On 6 March 1917 the famous portraitist Boris Kustodiev noted delightedly: 'Here [in Petrograd] everything is on the boil, the streets are still full of people ... you have to wait centuries for streets like this.' He adds: 'Everything has shifted, moved, and many things have been turned upside down.'[1] Just under two years later, on 6 February 1919, the same Kustodiev wrote: 'We're living poorly here, cold and hungry, all people talk about is food and bread.'[2] A few months later still, he complains bitterly: 'We are terribly tired! This is our second year without leaving the city [for the dacha]', and adds, as if there had been no proletarian revolution in 1917 to do away with class oppression, 'without servants; now my wife is in the kitchen all day, all our time is taken up in searching for groceries and the prices are horrible!!! *How we are to survive all this*, God only knows.'[3]

Like others, Kustodiev allowed his attitude towards events to be reflected in his work, but it did not always correspond precisely with historical changes. Indeed, in 1918–21 he painted such images from the pre-revolutionary past as *Merchant's Wife at Tea* (fig. 84). And yet at almost the same time he painted *Demonstration on Uritsky Square on the Day of the Opening of the Second Comintern Congress in July 1920* (cat. 1) and *The Bolshevik* (cat. 50). Whereas the former contains at least outward signs of joy and triumph, *The Bolshevik* is an entirely brutal metaphor for the powerful and crude force that had risen over the country, and one that accords fully with the artist's remarks quoted above.

Although he too did not accept the new order, Boris Grigoriev reacted in a different way. A figurative painter famous in Russia from the beginning of the twentieth century, he observed events with interest, wanting to feel the people's mood for himself. On one of his trips around the country, Grigoriev chose a train carriage in which 'the people travelled'. He listened to peasants' stories of violence and requisitions.[4] One man in his carriage said that only the 'unconscious' could speak like that, and that he would be forced to 'denounce' people who stood against the Soviet regime; Grigoriev recounted that the man was practically ejected from the train.[5]

This episode formed part of Grigoriev's attempts to find answers to his questions about the effects of the Revolution of 1917 on the life of the country and its people. He felt that the repercussions of the Revolution were not completely acceptable and sometimes downright criminal.[6] During that trip, he 'tried to see the people in their entirety, find their sources ... And I saw', he wrote, 'the country they called "land of the *bast* shoes [made with bark fibre]"',[7] by which he meant that it was inhabited by simple folk, primarily peasants.

These impressions were the basis for Grigoriev's cycle of paintings and drawings entitled *Rasseya* (i.e. Russia) (cats 109, 112). They contain no irony, no satire and no hatred. They are not portraits of specific individuals, but generalisations, metaphors expressing the artist's profound dismay about the fate of the people he was depicting.

Fig. 84
Boris Kustodiev, *Merchant's Wife at Tea*, 1918. Oil on canvas, 120 × 120 cm. State Russian Museum, St Petersburg

Fig. 85
Nadezhda Udaltsova, *Restaurant*, 1915. Oil on canvas, 134 × 116 cm. State Russian Museum, St Petersburg

Fig. 86
Alexander Labas, *The Train is Coming*, 1929. Oil on canvas, 98.3 × 75.8 cm. State Russian Museum, St Petersburg

Although both Kustodiev and Grigoriev may seem to have belonged to a generation that was overly attached to the old order, both socially and artistically, even those artists who were usually considered radical avant-gardists had a surprisingly ambivalent attitude towards the new. Unlike many of her contemporaries, Nadezhda Udaltsova, daughter of a general and author of the painting *Restaurant* (fig. 85) and other non-objective works, could not accept the new ways. In 1917 she observed wryly (in reference to the then-popular slogan 'Workers of the World, Unite!'): 'General anxiety. *The workers of the world are somehow not uniting.*'[8] 'My heart aches. *The Leninists will doom the revolution*,'[9] she wrote, concluding: 'Social revolution is a complete *mess, deceit and self-deception … violence and rebellion are so vile*.'[10]

Udaltsova's fate was eventually to confirm that she was right. Her father, the general, was arrested and shot in 1918.[11] Her second husband, the artist Alexander Drevin, was arrested in 1938 and also shot.[12] Having replaced her extreme avant-garde methods with a more measured figuration in the early 1920s, Udaltsova found that she still could not meet the demands of the socialist era. From the 1920s to the 1940s her works were almost never shown nor sold. But poverty could not stifle her pride: in 1948, yet another newspaper having branded her a 'Formalist', Udaltsova considered the label an honour.[13]

Artists younger than Kustodiev, Grigoriev and Udaltsova, and descended from a different social background, welcomed the Revolution. Alexander Labas, author of romantic canvases depicting dirigibles and trains travelling at great speed (fig. 86), saw the meaning of modern art in 'expressing feelings, sensations, and being an artist of one's revolutionary time'.[14] Despite hunger, cold and inconvenience, Labas and his fellow thinkers 'laboured ceaselessly decorating travelling theatres and scenery, painting the walls of trains, posters at the stations, entire thematic paintings on train carriages and building walls. Work is feverish,'[15] he wrote, describing the activities of the creative intelligentsia in the propaganda of the new social order (cat. 295). The decoration of cities, using revolutionary and proletarian subjects in posters, on clothing and in porcelain – this was work for many artists in the late 1910s and 1920s against a backdrop of horrifying poverty, starvation, cold and disease. 'Where are we to seek poetry and romance?' Labas asked, answering his own question: 'Poetry and romance are in us. We hoped that it would be better, and we saw in everything around us the seeds of the marvellous future.'[16]

This reaction to the Revolution was not uncommon. Even Marc Chagall, whose work is not characterised by strong social themes, wrote: 'The Revolution shook me with a full force that overpowered the individual, his essence, pouring across the borders of imagination and bursting into the most intimate world of images that turn themselves into part of the Revolution.'[17] In 1917 Chagall created one of his most striking masterpieces, *Promenade* (cat. 140). The painting was primarily inspired by his love for his wife Bella, of course, but the work's spirit of freedom, flight, infinite joy in life and its prospects – all of which differ from the gloom of the majority of his paintings of his Russian years – is in complete accord with Chagall's optimism concerning the Revolution, which was widespread among Jewish people. Many Jews hoped that a new social order with new rules would permit their legalisation in Russia's large cities.

But the Revolution was swiftly followed by Civil War, which brought additional disasters and suffering, and more cold, more disease and hunger. 'I'm walking along Nevsky Prospekt,' recalled Sofya Dymshits-Tolstaya. 'It is filled with banks of snow … A sledge ahead of me … is piled with the corpses of those who have died from typhus. I came home, looked in the mirror … and decided to go to Vitebsk to buy food…'[18]

Belorussia (now called Belarus) was a haven to which many went to save themselves from starvation. Bread and *salo* (fat back bacon) were still available there. Chagall was in Vitebsk, his native city, and invited

Kazimir Malevich to teach there. Malevich arrived with Vera Ermolaeva, Ilya Chashnik, Lazar Khidekel and others. Malevich described the journey: 'We rode three days and nights … the train carriages were full, so we had to crawl with kind permission over bent backs, we gathered firewood for the steam-engine … You really have to have energy to endure this horror.'[19]

And these artists did! Moreover, once in Vitebsk, they quickly joined in the project of decorating the city for the anniversary of the Revolution. When Dymshits-Tolstaya arrived she wrote, 'The city was still flaming with Malevich's circles, squares, dots and lines of various colours and Chagall's flying people.'[20] The residents of Vitebsk, she said, 'became Suprematists at that time'.[21] But Chagall's fantasies with flying green cows were not appreciated by Party officials, who asked him what they had to do with Marx and Lenin.[22]

Chagall did not argue with the Suprematists or with the authorities in his beloved Vitebsk. He left for Moscow, but nothing good awaited him and Bella there. They lived in a tiny room, with water dripping down the walls: 'We had no money … Not that we needed any – there was nothing to buy.'[23] But despite these difficulties, 'I did not complain, everything suited me.'[24] Chagall went on working, painting murals on the walls of the Jewish Theatre and teaching homeless children in Malakhovka near Moscow, travelling there each day, queuing up first for tickets and then to get into the railway carriage.[25] When at last the train moved off, the carriages were filled with mournful songs. Chagall recalled: 'I felt that along with those stocky peasant women and bearded peasants, who kept crossing themselves, *I was flying into the sky, soaring among the birches, banks of snow, and clouds of smoke*.'[26] Chagall's poetic metaphor could have been embodied in a painting, enriching his iconography of subjects. But he left Russia in 1922, forever retaining his affection for his native country.

Malevich, the antithesis of Chagall, unleashed works in Vitebsk that went beyond decorating the city. He and his colleagues created the association known as the Affirmers of the New Art (UNOVIS), gave lectures and wrote articles and books about Suprematism. Malevich's approach was surprisingly in tune with the demands of his time. Suprematism was by definition anti-bourgeois, and responded to the contemporary enthusiasm for other worlds, the planets and the cosmos.

The new social order, which had wrought such changes in people's ways of life – in architecture, interior design, furniture, ceramics and ornament – was in perfect alignment with the ideas of non-objectivity. In Vitebsk Malevich and his colleagues developed new designs in the 1920s in porcelain (fig. 87) and textiles. When he returned to Leningrad, Malevich continued his theoretical work on Suprematism, including the development of a curriculum for the State Institute of Artistic Culture, one of several new institutions in which avant-garde artists were to play a leading role, albeit briefly. Some of their stories about everyday situations are amusing. For example, as staff directors of the Department of Visual Arts at the People's Commissariat of Enlightenment (NARKOMPROS), Vladimir Tatlin and Dymshits-Tolstaya were expected to look after the accounts as part of their responsibilities. They were paid in 'large sheets of coupons' (paper money was then known as *kerenki*). Dymshits-Tolstaya remembered: 'Tatlin wrapped them around himself under his clothes and then we would hang onto the outside of the tram that went to his studio … The tram was free and people hung from it on all sides, like bunches of grapes.' To protect him from thieves, Dymshits-Tolstaya hugged Tatlin, 'vigilantly guarding him'.[27] Tatlin kept the money under the floorboards in his studio, but these were hungry times, even for rats, and concern grew that they might eat them. So Tatlin made a metal box, and that became the treasury of the Department of Visual Arts at the People's Commissariat of Enlightenment.

Such details of the lives of the new artistic and social elite reveal the unpretentiousness and the sincere desire of some to participate in the process of transformation despite everything. Dymshits-Tolstaya describes a paradoxical situation at the Winter Palace (the State Hermitage Museum) during a museum conference. Tradition called for a concluding banquet: 'Refreshments were served – two thin slices of black bread and pieces of saccharine [artificial sweetener] on small plates of the finest porcelain. Servants in formal livery handed around tea in marvellous crystal glasses. It was not real tea, but made with fruit … The delegates to this museum conference, dressed in fur coats, felt boots and ear-flapped hats, sat and discussed museum issues on the broadest scale.'[28]

Fig. 87
Kazimir Malevich, *Teapot, Design for the State Porcelain Factory*, 1923. Ceramic, height 16 cm. State Russian Museum, St Petersburg

Back at the People's Commissariat of Enlightenment, members, including Lenin's wife Nadezhda Krupskaya, 'lined up at the serving window' for lunch. 'Having received our soup, in which a few grains floated, we waited hungrily', wrote Dymshits-Tolstaya, 'for the famous *vobla* [dried and salted roach]. We sat on a bench with our soup and *vobla*, and lunch began with preparing the fish, which we softened by beating one side and then the other against the table.'[29] Similar tales told by many other authors. In the still-lifes of Kuzma Petrov-Vodkin (cat. 192), David Shterenberg (*Herring*, 1919) and others, the scant fare of those years became the object of wonder.

Tatlin began to use found objects from the street to construct still-life reliefs from materials available at the time (fig. 88). Marble, so assiduously worked by artists of the past, was no longer prized in the harsh post-revolutionary era. Dymshits-Tolstaya, who spent much time with Tatlin, wondered 'how an artist raised in the old ideology *can learn a new life* and new goals ... Never stepping away from glass, I painted five glass pieces with agitational slogans [cats 44, 45, 46]'.[30] But it was not enough, she felt: 'One should stand closer to the new man, one should go into production.' So she immersed herself in preparations for the magazine *Rabotnitsa i krest'ianka* (*Female Worker and Peasant Woman*).[31] Later, in the early 1930s, she went even further. 'Returned to realism', as she put it, she began making portraits of new heroines, including *Woman Agitator* (cat. 170), her sitter a poet and member of a literary circle.

The creators of the radical avant-garde and adherents of figuration alike accepted that the changes wrought by the times had brought a need for new heroes. 'You can't paint our *udarnik* [shock-worker] in the pose of a merchant or factory owner,' noted Alexander Deineka. 'He has a different stance ... and the artist must see that stance and be able to show it.'[32] 'Life has promoted the new – most importantly the new, socialist man, new youths, Komsomol members ... worker students ... And these new times', said Alexander Samokhvalov, 'must be dragged onto the canvas.'[33] Such characters became Samokhvalov's *Tram Conductor* (cat. 173) and *Girl in a Football Jersey* (cat. 203). The power of electricity, hitherto controlled by the prophet Elijah and the god Zeus, now resided in the hands of an ordinary female worker. 'The woman conductor', wrote Samokhvalov, 'giving the go signal in some way resembles Oranta [the Great Panagia, an Orthodox depiction of the Virgin Mary with extended arms] ... The spirit of the conductor is the spirit of that era.'[34]

Everyone sought new themes, a new artistic language capable of expressing the changes that were taking place in society. Of course, there were many different interpretations of the 'grand style' then being discussed. Paradoxically, the principal figurative painters, such as Petrov-Vodkin, Alexei Pakhomov, Samokhvalov and Deineka, found inspiration in the icons and frescoes of ancient churches, as did the Suprematist Malevich. This continued into the 1920s, when religion and the Church were effectively declared hostile to the new ideology.

'I tried to imagine', wrote Pakhomov, 'how great the impression must have been on a pious peasant when he entered, hat in hand, a majestic tall church, where in the golden flickering light of numerous candles, he was surrounded by festive walls, covered in paintings '[35] And if churches could have such a powerful effect on the souls of people 'under the tsars', he concluded, 'as many houses and palaces of culture, imbued with the spirit and beauty of the new art, can be built by the victorious people'.[36]

One might assume that Malevich, whose principles in art were in opposition to Pakhomov's, would nevertheless be moving in the same direction in his thinking about church traditions and their role in contemporary art. But both his philosophical and non-objective artistic conclusions were completely different, and much more radical. Firstly, because he saw a 'great resemblance' between the Church and the current State as institutions: 'Both the former and the latter have martyrs and heroes, whose names are entered as if in the church calendar...'[37]

Malevich and others saw a profound meaning in the Houses and Palaces of Culture. Like former churches, these buildings were to be dedicated to glorifying the heroes and prophets of the new

Fig. 88
Vladimir Tatlin, *Corner Counter-relief*, 1914. Iron, copper, wood and cables, 79.5 × 44 × 7.3 cm. State Russian Museum, St Petersburg

Fig. 89
Kazimir Malevich, *Self-portrait*, 1933. Oil on canvas, 73 × 66 cm. State Russian Museum, St Petersburg

society, its martyrs and saints. But in contrast to pious adherence to the visual methods of the Old Church, Malevich rejected the use of fresco in their interiors: 'Fresco is a wrong-headed phenomenon in a proletarian state. Fresco is a monastic hush, whereas now we need new forms, themes, and ideas…'[38]

From the late 1920s he began a cycle of paintings devoted to the peasantry. His use of icons as their source is obvious, as is the metaphorical embodiment of their fate as heads without faces (cat. 84), sometimes painted an alarming red or black colour (cat. 115). They appear before the viewer exactly as martyrs and saints, ready to be transported to the church-like spaces of the new faith: the Houses and Palaces of Culture.

The sense of the tragic fate of the faceless figures expressed in Malevich's peasant cycle coincided not only with the period of repressions of the peasants but also with testing circumstances in the artist's personal life. Although he had lived through periods of poverty in the past, the conditions he experienced in the mid-1920s were unbearable. In 1925 he was deprived of support for being an 'idealist and mystic'.[39]

His inability to manage this deprivation stopped him from sending Suprematist works to an exhibition abroad.[40] His lack of paints and materials prevented him from making works in porcelain to appear in an exhibition, which would have been 'the first in the world'.[41]

In 1930 Malevich told his friends: 'It's cold and chilly – still chillier in my room – and firewood is nowhere to be found.'[42] In Leningrad the populace unloaded firewood from barges and received it as part of a food parcel. 'Emptiness is everywhere and vast horror weighs on the soul.'[43] '… I am like a lighthouse that the unceasing, raw, accursed, ominous wave of life, foaming at the mouth, wants to swallow … to douse the fire of my work in art that has been burning for 34 years.'[44]

Yet despite all this, and his poor health and the cold, hunger and humiliations, Malevich launched into an active correspondence with architects about his ideas on a synthetic architecture that would combine plasticity and painting. In the same years, he painted *Sportsmen* (cat. 90) and *Red Cavalry* (cat. 94) – subjects close to the works of Pakhomov, Petrov-Vodkin and Deineka. But in fact these works, like his others in the late 1920s and early 1930s, correspond to his own ideas about new painting, the new image 'thrust into the foreground by the Proletarian Revolution'.[45]

What then did he understand thematic paintings to be? He urged his students to avoid realism.[46] In his opinion, reality 'can never be achieved and tangible'.[47] The artist, according to Malevich, can and must present an *image*, a sense of reality, which he achieves with colour and rhythm and combinations of the two.

In his late years he painted such works as *Portrait of Nikolai Punin* (cat. 63) among other portraits (fig. 89). Despite their clear echoes of Renaissance masterpieces, these late works embodied something new: they are monumental and integrated images of his contemporaries within the intelligentsia, figures who, like the peasants, are fit to be shown in the Palaces and Houses of Culture as heroes and martyrs of their era.

However, his paintings from the late 1920s of peasants, workers and members of the intelligentsia did not suit the authorities. On 12 December 1932 he wrote to his old friend Ivan Klyun about the 'base' treatment he was receiving: 'general acknowledgement, honour, respect, but not a whit more: they *don't let me go anywhere and they give me nothing … like a total blockade*.'[48] 'At the exhibition they isolated our brothers like wild Formalists, like enemies…'[49]

And then laughingly he recounts the article in which his *Black Square* (cat. 78) is called the dead end of bourgeois art. 'If they only understood what they were writing, they'd have to erect a monument to me in my own lifetime…'[50] 'Yes, I'm a real hero, a revolutionary, having brought Bourgeois Art to a dead end, when actually the Socialist Bolsheviks did,'[51] he said, summarising the drama of his relationship with the Soviet regime.

The fate of another genius of the Russian avant-garde, Pavel Filonov, was perhaps even more tragic. For a long time, Filonov's name and work were unknown outside the Soviet Union. His works began to appear in exhibitions in the mid-1980s, attracting the attention of art historians outside Russia. Nevertheless, to this day he remains one of the most mysterious of twentieth-century artists. The reason probably lies in his preference for privacy and his reluctance to talk about himself and his art. Even in his diaries (1930–39), recently published in Russian,[52] Filonov rarely bares his soul.

By the early 1910s he had formed his artistic method, which he labelled analytical. Its fundamental tenet was that the artist should not attempt to re-create the visible world. Using oils, watercolours, pencil or pen on canvas or paper, Filonov 'grew' the subject he was depicting, rather as the laws of nature dictate the process of growth in plants and other living things. He painted and drew works with different subjects in this style. It made no difference to him whether they were executed in non-objective or figurative forms. The important thing for him was to express his ideas within his analytical method.

One of his main themes was 'Universal Flowering'. The theme's very name contains the philosophy of universal Communism, which was popular in the 1920s and close to Filonov's heart. The principle that united Filonov's works in the 'Universal Flowering' cycle is still not clear, but it included such works as *Formula of the Petrograd Proletariat* (cat. 53), a picture clearly dedicated to revolutionary events, and *Peasant Family* (fig. 90), as well as paintings about the cosmos. People and animals form an important strand of his work, which deserves greater study. The artist makes no distinction: for him people and animals alike are creations of nature. Depicting them with his particular method, he analyses the processes that occur in their organisms and concludes that they are similar.

Fig. 90
Pavel Filonov, *Peasant Family*, 1914. Oil on canvas, 160 × 117 cm. State Russian Museum, St Petersburg

Naturally, such an approach to art was not officially acceptable in the 1920s and 1930s. Filonov's paintings were rarely purchased in the Soviet period, and when they were, they brought him a negligible price. Foreigners offered him good money for his work, but he always refused to sell or to allow exhibitions to be organised. As Filonov's wife Ekaterina Serebryakova recalled, the American artist Charles Baskerville considered him the 'greatest artist in the world'.[53] In trying to persuade Filonov to sell him something, Baskerville told him that in New York, '[the Russian portraitist Ksaveri] Sorin gets $5,000 to $7,000, while Pavel Nikolaevich [Filonov] would be paid up to $25,000'.[54] 'The irony of life,' noted Serebryakova in 1929: 'I'm sitting here sewing him underpants and shirt, so as to save a few roubles from his pension of 50 roubles.'[55]

Her ascetic husband, frugal, even harshly so towards himself, became almost a legend. In 1921 he allowed himself one bottle of milk and one kilogram of bread made from sifted flour for 25 kopecks per day: 'nothing more'.[56] 'He buys nothing but bread,' complained Serebryakova in August 1927. 'He has bread with tea or tea with bread or bread with salt…'[57] In 1929 she wrote, 'He says that any food other than tea and bread is too heavy for him.'[58]

This economising way of life was most probably only partly a result of his financial difficulties. 'He's prepared to spend his whole life having 50 roubles a month, and he doesn't need anything more; he is prepared never to leave his room and work and work. He is prepared to sleep but a few hours a day on his boards and in an unheated room, with nothing but a thin blanket.'[59] Asceticism was part of Filonov's philosophy of life. It gave him freedom and independence from circumstances unrelated to art. He regretted profoundly the few times that he acted against his principles.

On the eve of the 1920s, the situation around him grew very tense. By the end of the decade, in 1929, the censors kept an exhibition of his work at the Russian Museum on hold for almost a year. His works were rejected by other shows. He was forced to live on the money his wife received, a situation he found intolerable. Seeking to help him, his close friends

Fig. 91
Pavel Filonov, *Portrait of Joseph Stalin*, 1936. Oil on canvas, 99 × 67 cm. State Russian Museum, St Petersburg

Fig. 92
Pavel Filonov, GOELRO *(State Commission for the Electrification of Russia)*, 1930. Watercolour and graphite pencil on paper, 44.5 × 35.5 cm. State Russian Museum, St Petersburg

arranged several commissions for him to execute two or three realist works on themes of production. Filonov resisted, but eventually relented under enormous pressure from his friends and wife.

One of these paintings was to depict a leading worker in a sewing factory. Filonov visited in search of models and saw an elderly woman whose very ordinariness attracted his attention. He began to paint her, accenting her commonplace face and the reflections in her glasses.[60] When he showed the work, it drew harsh criticism. An optimistic image of a heroine shock-worker had been anticipated, but Filonov had depicted an unattractive elderly woman. His painting was not accepted, although it was turned into a postcard.

His friends tried again to have him involved in official commissions. He was engaged to paint *Tractor Workshop at the Putilov Factory* (cat. 20). When Filonov described his plan to a friend, he was told painting in that way would be counter-revolutionary.[61] But Filonov held his ground: 'I'll make it the way it is ... and it will not be what you need.'[62] In the end he stopped work on the painting and refused to complete it.[63]

These commissioned works, with a portrait of Stalin (fig. 91) and sketches for a poster for the State Commission for the Electrification of Russia (GOELRO) (fig. 92),[64] stand apart in Filonov's work, and in the history of Russian art. Depicted naturalistically, the industrial scenes and the image of the leader may have reflected the reality the artist observed, but they did not correspond to the doctrine of Socialist Realism. These enforced compromises neither solved Filonov's financial problems nor assisted his friends' attempts to bring his work into the mainstream.

Filonov grew anxious.[65] It was clear that he could not work to other people's dictates. 'I want to do my own works,' he told his wife. 'I cannot take commissions. I am a researcher. A commission leads to other commissions, and I must do my own works. I cannot follow the path of official art. I do not need fame. My ideology will find its own path...'[66] Filonov's statements often repeat this last sentence, defining his sense of self and his attitude towards art.

After his few realist works, painted under duress, Filonov made no more compromises. For the rest of his life he painted compositions about the cosmos, people and animals in his own style. He starved to death in the Siege of Leningrad in the winter of 1941, leaving a vast number of works, most of which his sister donated to the Russian Museum. Her gift effectively made his dream come true; by giving the State his works, she preserved intact his idea of his museum of analytical art.

In 1932 Filonov's works and those of many other artists, both figurative and non-objective, were brought together for the last time in the rooms of the State Russian Museum for the exhibition to commemorate the fifteenth anniversary of the Soviet regime. After this major show, which demonstrated the variety and wealth of Russian-Soviet visual art, the doors to other exhibitions were closed for many decades on artists who did not completely share the ideology and stylistics of Socialist Realism. 'Works by the artists Drevin and Udaltsova,' a newspaper wrote in 1933, 'close to expressionism and echoing Filonov's work, speak to the self-isolation of these artists from the tasks of the working class, from participation in cultural construction ... Their art does not go in the direction of the realistic art of socialism, but in the direction of individual remoteness, another rehash of formal moments in painting that they had previously achieved...'[67]

Quite a few such texts of this kind were published, both about non-objective artists, such as Malevich, Filonov and others, and those who followed the figurative line, among them Petrov-Vodkin, Pimenov and Samokhvalov. Neither themes of labour and sport nor similarity to realism could save them. Nothing defying official doctrine was permissible in exhibitions until almost the 1970s. Hidden by families or in museum storerooms and some private collections, the works of many artists who worked enthusiastically between the 1920s and the 1940s have only recently been made public.

146
Eduard Alma Tenisman
Worker Seated at the Table, 1927
Oil on canvas, 179 × 85 cm
The State Museum of the History of St Petersburg

147
David Shterenberg
Aniska, 1926
Oil on canvas,
197 × 125 cm
State Tretyakov
Gallery, Moscow

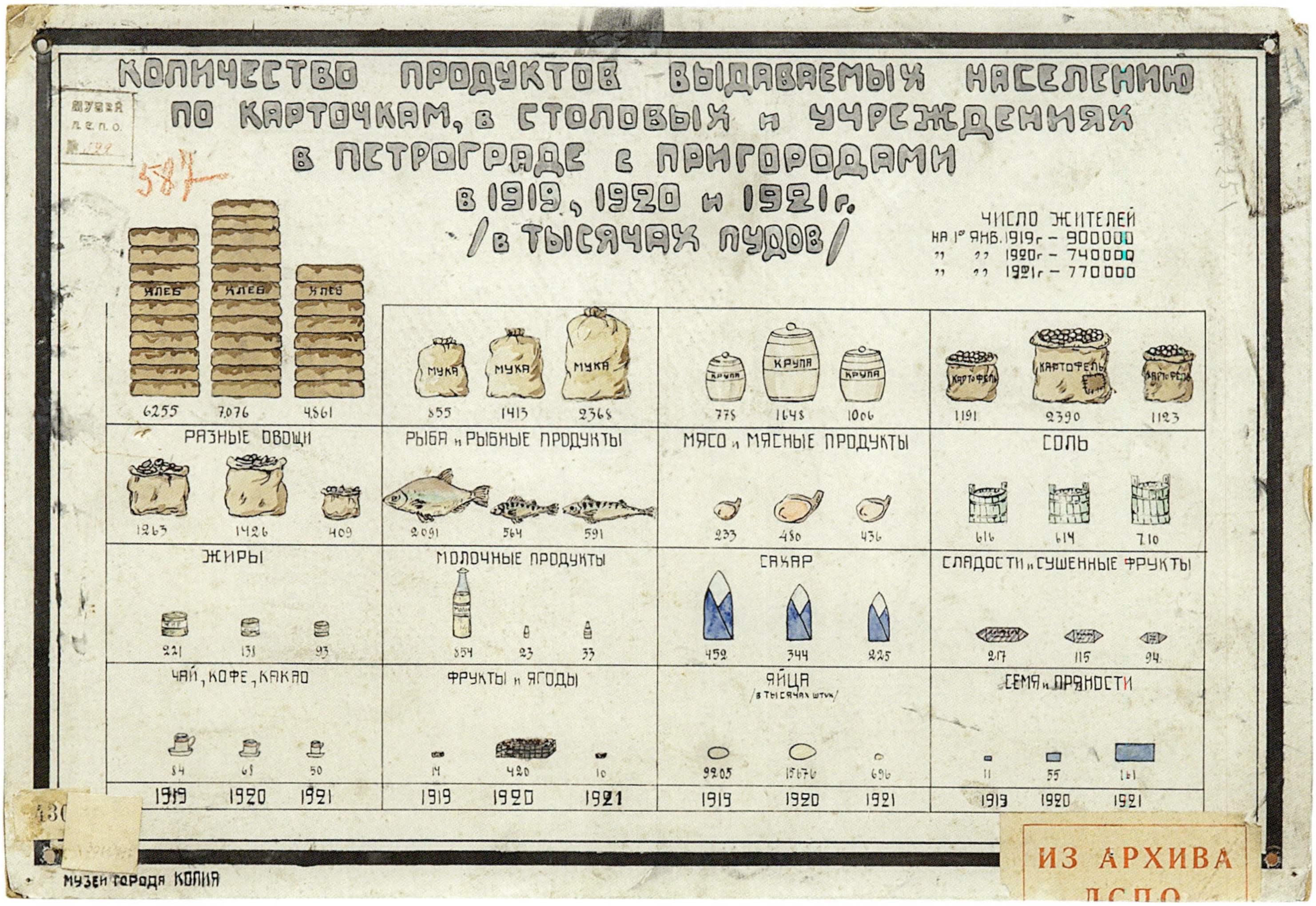

148
Unknown
Diagram 'The Quantity of Products Given to the Citizens in Exchange for Coupons in Canteens and other Establishments in Petrograd and the Suburbs in 1919, 1920 and 1921', 1920s
Ink, pen and watercolour on paper mounted on cardboard, 33 × 48 cm
The State Museum of the History of St Petersburg

149
Unknown
Diagram 'The Quantity of Food for Children in Petrograd (January–October 1918)', 1920s
Coloured ink, pen and watercolour on paper mounted on cardboard, 64 × 99.5 cm
The State Museum of the History of St Petersburg

150
Unknown
Diagram 'In One Year a Mature Man Consumes Approximately …', 1920s
Ink and pen on paper mounted on cardboard, 75 × 47.8 cm
The State Museum of the History of St Petersburg

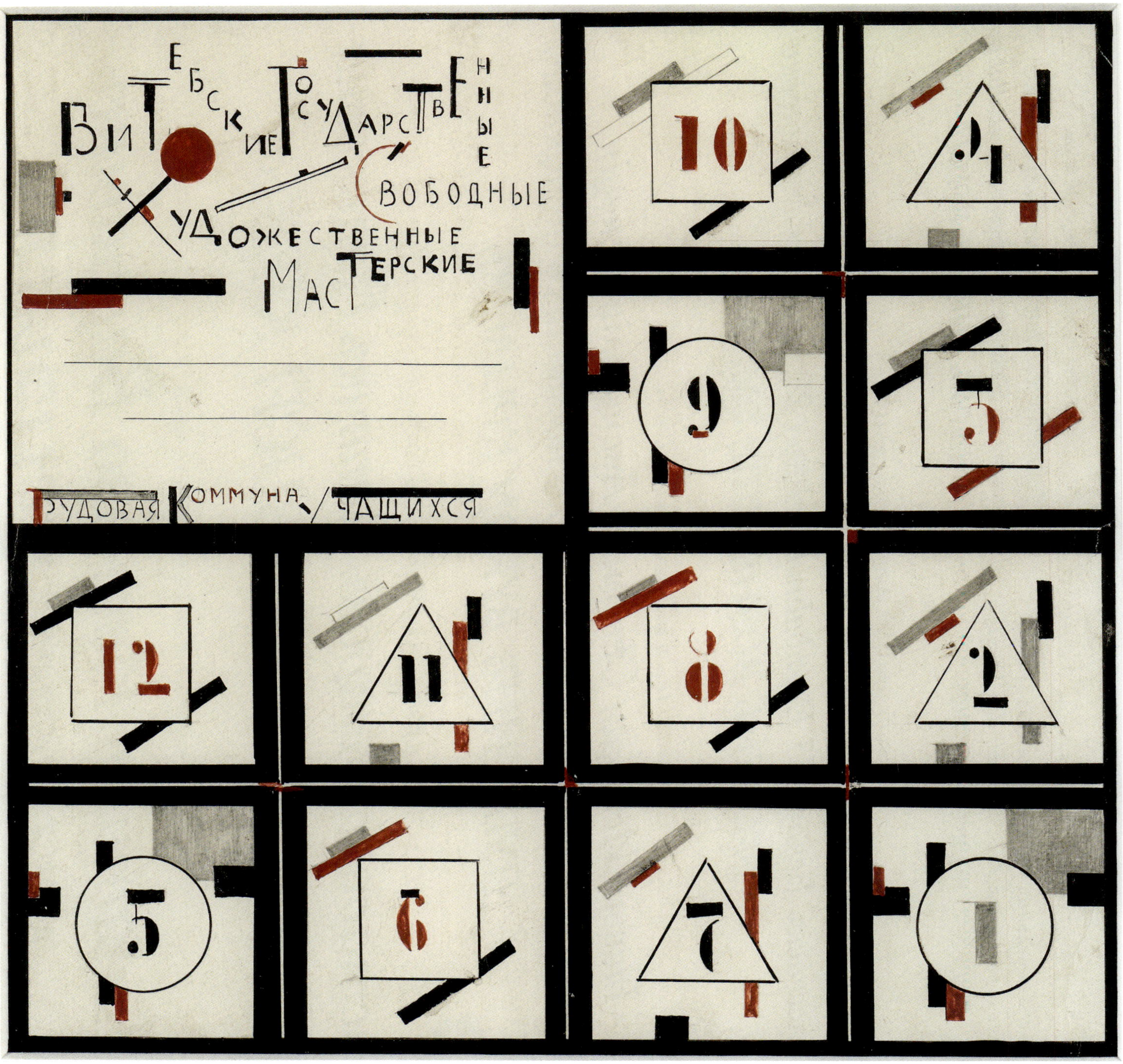

151
Boris Tseitlin
Food Coupon, 1920
Pencil and ink on paper,
17.6 × 18.8 cm
State Tretyakov Gallery,
Moscow

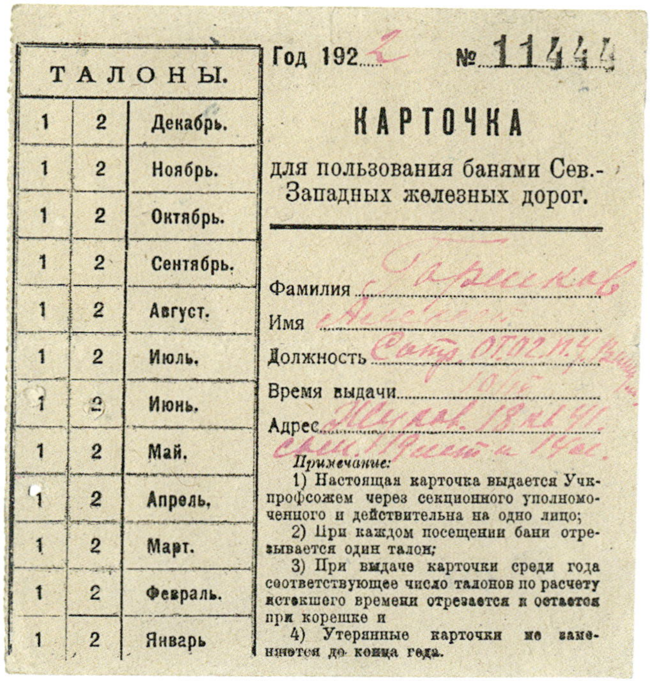

152
Unknown
Voucher for Use of the Bathhouse of North-western Railways in the Name of Gorshkov A. [H.], 1922
Typographical printing and handwriting on paper, 11.7 × 11.1 cm
The State Museum of the History of St Petersburg

153
Unknown
Food Coupon of the 2nd Category for July in the name of Felkergam [Felkerzam] A., 1920s
Offset printing and handwriting on paper, 9.8 × 13.7 cm
The State Museum of the History of St Petersburg

154
Unknown
Additional Bread Coupon for the Member of the Family of the Red Army Soldier, Issue No. 3, 1920 in the Name of Smirnova I[rina], 1920
Offset printing and handwriting on paper, 11.3 × 19.5 cm
The State Museum of the History of St Petersburg

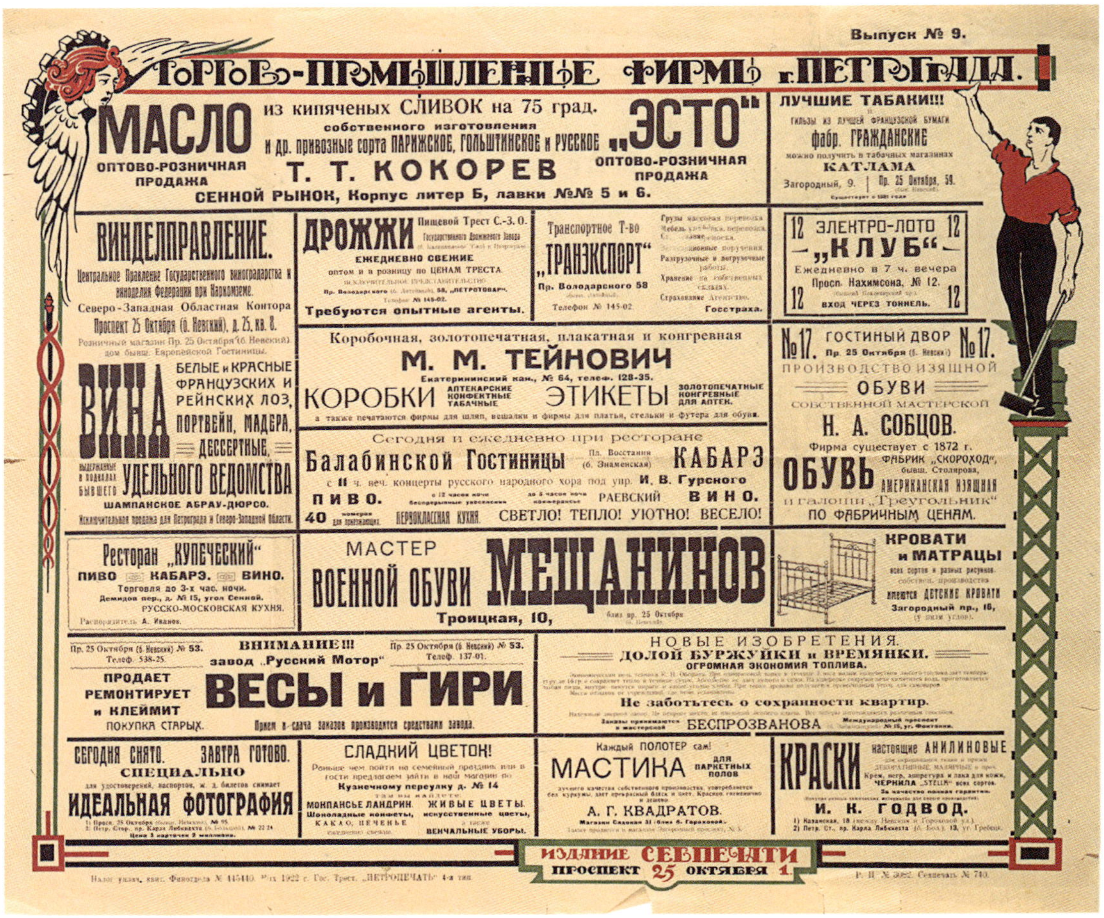

155
Unknown
Poster for the Commercial and Industrial Companies of Petrograd, 1922
Chromolithograph on paper, 46 × 56.2 cm
The State Museum of the History of St Petersburg

156
Unknown
Calendar for 1922 after a Drawing by Boris Kustodiev, 1921
Chromolithograph on paper, 32 × 37.5 cm
The State Museum of the History of St Petersburg

157
Unknown
Restaurant Menu,
after June 1924
Oil on plywood,
94 × 58 cm
The State Museum of the
History of St Petersburg

158
Vladimir Lebedev
Food Tax Poster.
Give a Part of the Harvest to the City, and Keep the Rest, 1921
Linocut, 64 × 55.5 cm
The State Museum of the
History of St Petersburg

159
Alexander Labas
Red Army Soldier in the Russian Far East, 1928
Oil on canvas, 98 × 78 cm
State Russian Museum, St Petersburg

160
Solomon Telingater
Red Army: First Cavalry [collage 2], c. 1928
Photomontage, paper, card, gouache, 52 × 42 cm
Alex Lachmann Collection, London

161
Unknown
Advertisement 'Of Course, Cream-soda!', 1926
Chromolithograph (1st state) on paper, 46 × 29.5 cm
The State Museum of the History of St Petersburg

162
Alexander Deineka
Ping-Pong, 1928
Gouache and watercolour on paper, 39 × 34 cm
Alex Lachmann Collection, London

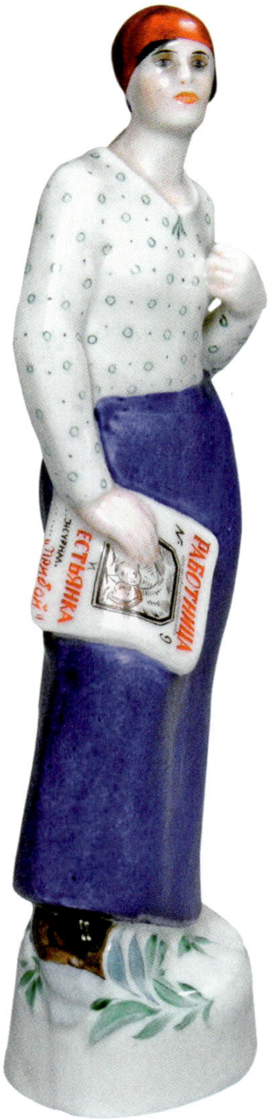

163
Natalia Danko,
State Porcelain
Factory, Petrograd
Woman Worker Making a Speech, 1923
Vitrified enamel paint on porcelain, height 17.5 cm
The Petr Aven Collection

164
Alisa Brusketti-Mitrokhina,
State Porcelain Factory,
Petrograd
Bourgeois Woman Selling Her Wares, 1918
Vitrified enamel paint on porcelain, height 28 cm
The Petr Aven Collection

165
Alexandra Shchekotikhina-Pototskaya, State
Porcelain Factory,
Petrograd
Plate with Inscription 'He Who Will Not Work Shall Not Eat 1921', 1921
Vitrified enamel paint on porcelain, underglaze cover in cobalt, gilding,
diameter 32.3 cm
The Petr Aven Collection

166
Vasili Timorev, State Porcelain Factory, Petrograd
Plate Decorated with an Image of Identity Papers and Work Papers in the Name of Vasili Andreevich Prokhorov, all Surrounded with a Red Banner Inscribed 'He Who Works Shall Eat', 1920
Vitrified enamel paint on porcelain, gilding, diameter 22 cm
The Petr Aven Collection

167
Alexandra Shchekotikhina-Pototskaya, State Porcelain Factory, Petrograd
Dish 'Sailor's Walk. 1 May 1921 in Petrograd', 1921
Vitrified enamel paint on porcelain, silvering, gilding, etching, diameter 35.9 cm
The Petr Aven Collection

168
Alexandra Shchekotikhina-Pototskaya
'Commisar' Bowl, 1921
Vitrified enamel paint on porcelain, diameter 30.1 cm
The Petr Aven Collection

169
Unknown
XIV Years of the Red Army,
1932
Lacquer, tempera and
gold paint on papier
mâché (Palekh),
diameter 37.5 cm
Alex Lachmann
Collection, London

170
Sofya Dymshits-Tolstaya
Woman Agitator, 1931
Oil on canvas, 124 × 71 cm
State Russian Museum,
St Petersburg

171
Izrail Lizak
Walk, 1928
Oil on canvas,
202.5 × 121 cm
State Russian Museum,
St Petersburg

172
Vladimir Lebedev
Portrait of the Dancer and Choreographer Nadezhna Nadezhdina, 1927
Oil on canvas, 65 × 50 cm
State Russian Museum,
St Petersburg

173
Alexander Samokhvalov
Tram Conductor, 1928
Tempera on canvas,
130 × 112 cm
State Russian Museum,
St Petersburg

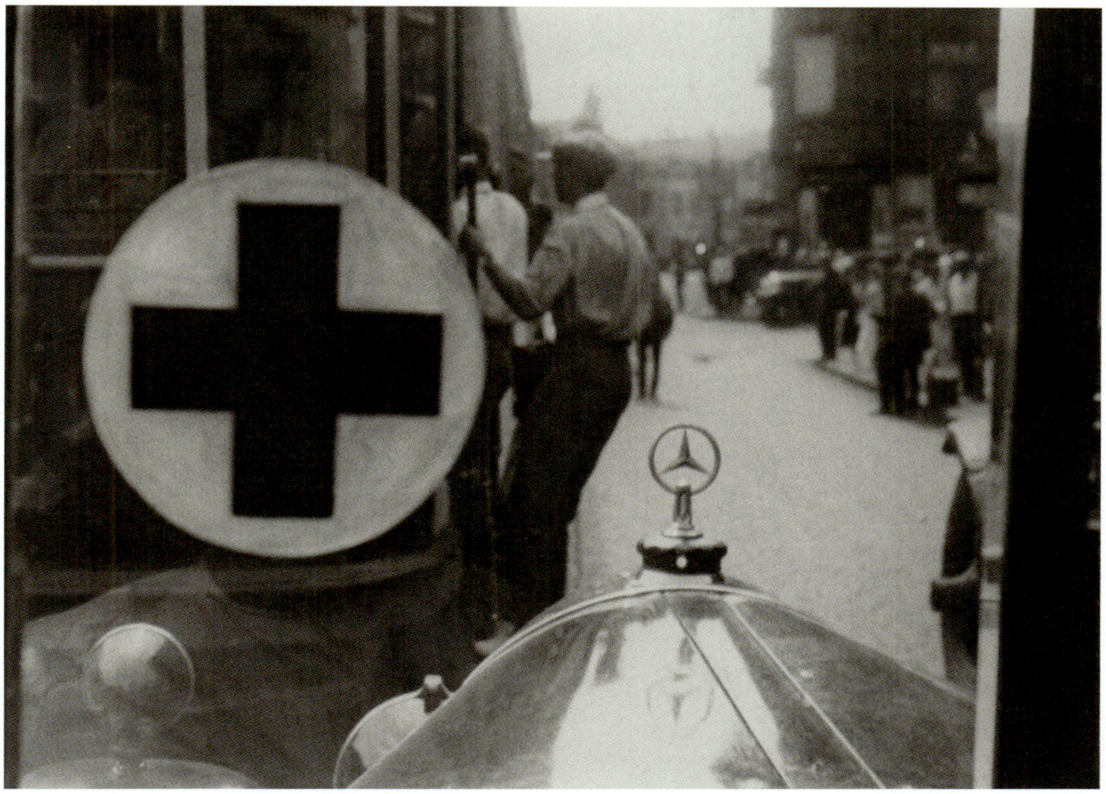

174
Arkady Shaiket
In the Café, 1920
Gelatin silver print,
42.5 × 29.3 cm
Alex Lachmann
Collection, London

175
Alexander Rodchenko
Mercedes Ambulance Car, 1929
Gelatin silver print,
16.5 × 23 cm
Alex Lachmann
Collection, London

176
Alexander Rodchenko
Cigarette Vendor, Pushkin Square, Moscow, 1926
Gelatin silver print,
29 × 44 cm
Alex Lachmann
Collection, London

177
Boris Ignatovich
The Hermitage, 1929
Gelatin silver print,
38 × 50 cm
Alex Lachmann
Collection, London

178
Eleazar Langman
Old and New: Church and Universal Store, 1930–31
Gelatin silver print,
42 × 26.8 cm
Alex Lachmann
Collection, London

УНИВ

БУЛОЧНАЯ
КОНДИТЕРСКАЯ
КОММУН
374

BUILDING FOR SOCIALISM

Christina Lodder

THE OCTOBER REVOLUTION OF 1917 PRESENTED architects with the challenge of designing buildings that would not only reflect the new ideology, but also assist in realising the new Communist society. Inevitably, avant-garde figures identified their own rejection of tradition and their enthusiasm for innovation with the new order. In April 1918 the Suprematist artist Kazimir Malevich declared: 'The Avant-Garde of revolutionary destruction is marching over the whole wide world ... and on the square of the fields of the revolution there should be erected corresponding buildings.'[1] A few years later, the theorist Alexei Gan was more explicit. He argued that the styles and buildings of the past were no longer relevant, as capitalism and individualism had to give way to socialism and the collective client. Mansions, luxury flats and churches were rooted in the economic, social and cultural life of the past, and were now not only inappropriate, but were also the harmful 'allies of counter-revolution'.[2] It was essential to develop new building types, such as communal housing and workers' clubs, which would help to foster a Communist way of life.[3] As El Lissitzky explained, the task of architecture was 'to comprehend the new conditions of life, so that by the creation of responsive building design it can actively participate in the full realisation of the new world'.[4]

Unfortunately, the widespread economic disruption and devastation produced by seven years of almost continuous conflict (the First World War followed by the Civil War in Russia) meant that few designs got beyond the drawing board until the building season of 1924, by which time the New Economic Policy (NEP), implemented in 1921, had begun to revive the economy and the construction industry.

Fig. 93
El Lissitzky, *Wolkenbügel*, 1924–25. Photomontage with ink and coloured pencil, showing the Wolkenbügel superimposed on a photograph of Nikitsky Square, Moscow, 40 × 55.5 cm. Russian State Archive for Literature and Art, Moscow

MODERNIST EXPERIMENTS

The 1920s saw architectural modernism flourish in Russia to such an extent that for a while it became the professional establishment.[5] Modernists developed new building types, elaborated new theories of design and explored new construction technologies. In 1924 Nikolai Ladovsky and Vladimir Krinsky founded the Association of New Architects (ASNOVA) to develop and promote their theory of aesthetic Rationalism, which stressed the importance of the psychological perception of space and form in the design process.[6] Although they actually built very little themselves, the group's members were very influential through their teaching on the Basic Course and in the Architecture Faculty at the Moscow Higher State Artistic and Technical Workshops (VKhUTEMAS). El Lissitzky worked with them on their design for the Moscow Sports Stadium of around 1925 (cat. 210), contributing a project for a clubhouse. Their ideas were also integral to his Wolkenbügel project of 1925 (fig. 93). This was a striking, three-legged skyscraper, which consisted of large, boldly cantilevered horizontal structures for the offices of 'central institutions', eight of which were to be built over intersections on the Moscow ring road.[7] Although extravagant in its use of space and materials, the Wolkenbügel possessed enormous visual vitality, as its configuration of horizontals and verticals changed dramatically depending on the angle of viewing. The building's sculptural qualities reflected ASNOVA's emphasis on form over function, although Lissitzky stressed that it was completely functional and envisioned placing a bus station and facilities for an underground railway system in the building's supports.

In contrast, the Constructivists of the Society of Contemporary Architects (OSA), set up by Alexander Vesnin and Moisei Ginzburg in 1925, emphasised utility, technology and internal organisation. They regarded buildings as 'social condensers' or instruments of social change, which had to answer the needs of the State, the collective client and the new way of life. At the same time, OSA adopted innovations in construction methods, and contributed to the task of establishing standardised norms and types. The Constructivists developed a functional method that established a spatial diagram and a series of volumes by analysing the practical requirements of a building and its flows. The result was 'a logical building ... freed from handed-down modes of style'.[8] Initially the Constructivists revealed unadorned structural frameworks on the exterior, as in Alexander and Viktor Vesnin's Leningrad Pravda building (fig. 94) and their entry to the Palace of Labour competition (with Leonid Vesnin, 1923). Soon, however, they embraced the geometric clarity and purity of the international style. The Narkomfin building (cat. 182), for instance, designed by Ginzburg and Ignaty Milinis (1928–30), incorporated many of Le Corbusier's ideas in its use of smooth exterior surfaces, pilotis, ribbon windows and a roof garden, but presented these features within a building that was organised according to strictly functional principles. The Narkomfin building epitomised a new concept for collective housing, intending to facilitate the transition to a socialist way of life by combining 50 apartments suitable for single people, couples and families (in one block) with a wide range of communal facilities, including a dining room and a library (in visually distinct, but attached premises).[9]

Fig. 94
Alexander and Viktor Vesnin, *Competition Project for the Offices of Leningrad Pravda in Moscow*, 1924. Perspective drawing, project photograph. The Shchusev State Museum of Architecture, Moscow, VIII 27567

THE LENIN MAUSOLEUM

Lenin's death on 21 January 1924 affected the whole of Soviet life. Politically it led to the glorification of the dead leader and the cult of Lenin, which eventually helped Joseph Stalin to consolidate his power. The accompanying proliferation of commemorative images helped to enshrine figurative art as the official art of the Soviet Union, paving the way for Socialist Realism. In architecture, Lenin's death led to the erection of his mausoleum on Red Square (cat. 12), just outside the Kremlin's walls; the building became a place of pilgrimage and worship, replacing the previous shrines of Russian Orthodoxy.

The first temporary structure (fig. 95), made of wood, consisted of a series of simple cubes, two on each side to house guards, and a slightly larger cube in the centre, inscribed with Lenin's name and surmounted by three tiers of steps. The structure's simplicity and the symbolic use of colour reflected the influence of the revolutionary period, with its festivals and decorations embodying a synthesis of painting, sculpture and architecture.[10] The architect Alexei Shchusev, assisted by the artist Ignaty Nivinsky, used black and red, the colour code of the revolution, for the staircase and for the mourning hall in which Lenin lay.[11] The walls were covered in red fabric, the pilasters were black, while red and black fabric radiated out from the central form of the hammer and sickle on the ceiling. The second mausoleum (fig. 96), commissioned in February 1924[12] and also constructed from wood, was a more monumental structure, resembling a flat-topped pyramid, surmounted by a lantern consisting of five columns on each side, which appropriately (in view of the Bolsheviks' hatred of Christianity) recalled

Fig. 95
Alexei Shchusev, *Lenin Mausoleum, Moscow, first temporary structure*, 10 February 1924. Photograph. ITAR-TASS collection

Fig. 96
Alexei Shchusev, *Perspective drawing of the Lenin Mausoleum, Moscow, second temporary structure*, 1924. Project photograph. The Shchusev State Museum of Architecture, Moscow, XI 36679

such ancient sepulchres as the tomb of Cyrus the Great at Pasargadae in Iran and the Step Pyramid at Saqqara in Egypt. Lenin's permanent mausoleum (cats 184, 185), also designed by Shchusev and completed in 1929–30, preserved the essential features of the second wooden structure, with its bold simplicity, modest ziggurat composition and revolutionary colour code. The latter was now translated into stone: polished black marble and labradorite, with red porphyry and granite. Although the austere geometry of the mausoleum had affinities with modernism, its monumentality and antique allusions pointed forward to the more rhetorical style that was eventually to be promoted as Socialist Realism.

The mausoleum acted not only as a monument to Lenin, but also as 'a monument to the entire revolutionary period'.[13] In this respect, it possessed continuities with Lenin's plan for monumental propaganda of 1918, which aspired to inculcate socialist values by replacing Tsarist monuments with statues and inscriptions to important revolutionary and cultural figures. Lenin's mausoleum also served to reinforce the legitimacy of subsequent leaders when they stood on it during official parades on Red Square.

By 1930, despite their efforts to create an architecture that would be revolutionary in both style and substance, the modernists were in retreat. The Society of Contemporary Architects (OSA) and the Association of New Architects (ASNOVA) were under attack from the All-Union Association of Proletarian Architects (VOPRA), which viciously denounced modernist architecture as formalist, bourgeois and counter-revolutionary, and condemned the Constructivists as utilitarian engineers. At the same time, the modernists were losing ground to architects and officials who stressed the importance of the historical heritage and the notion of accessibility to the masses. They argued, for instance, that a truly contemporary architecture could only be created by combining classical principles with socialist ideals.[14] In this respect, the venerable Tsarist academician Ivan Zholtovsky was exemplary. Inspired by Palladio and the Italian Renaissance, he frequently employed Corinthian columns, lavishly decorated architraves and a plethora of sculpted forms in his designs for Soviet buildings, such as that for the USSR State Bank (fig. 97). The important roles that he had occupied in government organisations since 1918 indicate that the regime had consistently favoured his approach.

THE PALACE OF THE SOVIETS

One of the most significant events in determining the future of architecture under Stalin was undoubtedly the competition for the Palace of the Soviets. Conceived as a great administrative and congress centre to be built on the banks of the Moscow River, just along from the Kremlin, the building was intended to commemorate 'the founding of the Union of Soviet Socialist Republics',[15]

Fig. 97
Ivan Zholtovsky, *Gosbank, Neglinnaya Street, Moscow* (completed 1929), c. 1930. Postcard. Private collection

ДА ЗДРАВСТВУЕТ
III-и ИНТЕРНАЦИОНАЛ !

and to replace, both physically and symbolically, the enormous edifice of the Cathedral of Christ the Saviour, which was later demolished. Announced in February 1931, the project was steeped in the long-held desire to create a significant building to symbolise the Revolution and the new society. This aspiration had inspired several earlier projects, including the competition for the Palace of Labour (fig. 99) and Vladimir Tatlin's vision of a *Monument to the Third International* of 1920 (fig. 98), a vast structure of iron and glass that was intended to be a third higher than the Eiffel Tower and a centre for fomenting world revolution. With similar motives, in 1922, the Bolshevik leader Sergei Kirov had called for 'a work of great architecture', 'a palace for workers and peasants ... a symbol of our future power, of the triumph of Communism here and in the West'.[16]

Fifteen entries were submitted during the first round of the competition in July 1931 from invited individuals and groups, including such modernists as Ladovsky, the Vesnin brothers and Ginzburg, as well as architects espousing more historicist approaches, such as Shchusev, Zholtovsky and Boris Iofan. On the basis of these, the programme for the second, open stage of the competition was published in July 1931.[17] This elicited 272 projects, including designs from eminent foreign modernists, such as Le Corbusier, Walter Gropius, Erich Mendelsohn and Hans Poelzig.[18] The submitted designs offered a variety of functional solutions and embraced a wide array of styles, ranging from the ornate to the austerely functional, from neo-gothic, neoclassical and historical eclecticism to art deco and the international style. Prizes were awarded to Zholtovsky's and Iofan's historicist designs and Hector Hamilton's stripped-down neoclassical project. Nevertheless, no single entry was considered completely satisfactory, with the result that the competition underwent two further closed phases: March to July 1932 (with fifteen invited entrants) and August 1932 to February 1933 (with only five invited architects). Eventually, in May 1933, the Construction Committee of the Council of People's Commissars announced that Iofan's design would form the basis for the final building, which would be developed by him in collaboration with Vladimir Shchuko and Vladimir Gelfreikh. Stalin suggested that the building should be surmounted by a statue of Lenin some 50 to 70 metres in height,[19] and it was this feature that dominated subsequent versions (see cats 186, 187).

The results of the competition sealed the fate of modernist architecture and ensured that for the next few decades, Soviet buildings would be traditionally conceived and highly decorated in an eclectic mixture of historical motifs. Stalin and the Party had spoken – Socialist Realism in architecture had arrived.

POSTSCRIPT

The Palace of the Soviets was never built, although the Cathedral of Christ the Saviour was demolished in December 1931, and the palace's foundations were completed by 1939, when war intervened. After 1945 the site was cleared and eventually used for a swimming pool. Nevertheless, the design for the Palace of the Soviets inspired the construction of seven monumental, wedding-cake buildings in Moscow (1947–53), all of which are still standing. They include the Ministry of Foreign Affairs, Moscow State University on the Lenin (now Sparrow) Hills, and the Hotel Ukraina (now the Radisson Royal Hotel). Since 1991, and the fall of Communism, architects have been busy rebuilding Moscow as a contemporary capitalist city, and a reconstructed Cathedral of Christ the Saviour was consecrated in 2000. Several modernist buildings have been restored, although sadly the Narkomfin building still languishes in a state of drastic disrepair. Its derelict condition eloquently reflects the Revolution's discarded dreams of communal housing and its abandoned visions of a new world.

Fig. 98
Vladimir Tatlin standing in front of his *Model for a Monument to the Third International*, on display in the Mosaics Studio of the former Academy of Art, Petrograd, November 1920. Moscow Photo Museum (House of Photography)

Fig. 99
Alexander, Viktor and Leonid Vesnin, *Competition entry for the Palace of Labour in Moscow*, 1922–23. Project photograph. The Schusev State Museum of Architecture, Moscow, VIII 27567

179
Vladimir Tatlin
Letatlin, 1932
Reconstruction by Henry Milner, 2013
Green ash, cork, leather, steel, calico, cotton, webbing ply and twine
wings: height 185 cm, length 530 cm, width 177 cm; body: height 100 cm, length 400 cm, width 80 cm
Courtesy GRAD: Gallery for Russian Arts and Design, London

180
Georgy Petrusov
New Building, 1931
Gelatin silver print,
41.7 × 28.6 cm
Alex Lachmann
Collection, London

181
Georgy Petrusov
New Building from Above (Kharkov), 1930
Gelatin silver print,
42 × 26.8 cm
Alex Lachmann
Collection, London

182
Alexander Rodchenko
Narkomfin [People's Commissariat of Finance] Building, 1932
Gelatin silver print, 24 × 30 cm
Alex Lachmann Collection, London

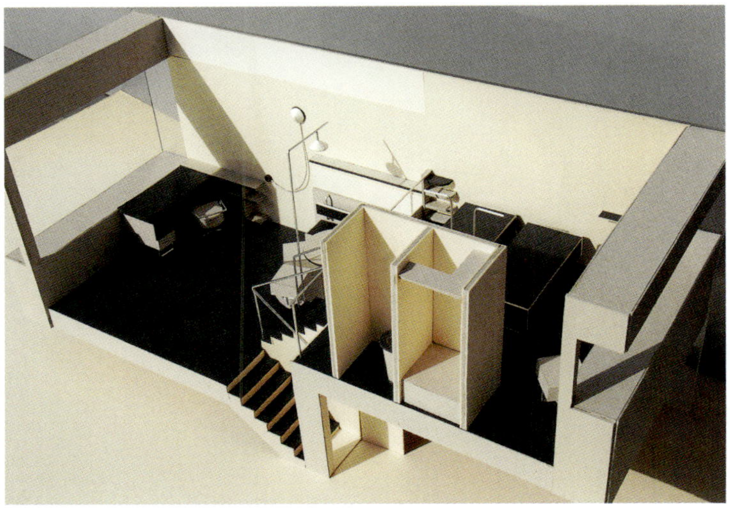

183
El Lissitzky
Design for an Apartment for the Narkomfin [People's Commissariat of Finance] Building, 1932
Maquette for Lissitzky's apartment design.
Reconstruction by Henry Milner Ltd (Henry Milner and Marta Isabel Ferreira), 2012
Card, 23.3 × 51.7 × 19.8 cm
Collection of the Van Abbe Museum, Eindhoven

184
Alexei Shchusev
Lenin Mausoleum, 1929
Gouache, ink and pencil on paper, 38.8 × 56.5 cm
Alex Lachmann Collection, London

185
Alexei Shchusev
Model of Lenin's Mausoleum, 1924
Wood, 14.5 × 37 × 20 cm
Alex Lachmann Collection, London

186
Boris Iofan
Palace of the Soviets,
Perspective, 1935
Ink on paper, 49 × 71 cm
Alex Lachmann
Collection, London

187
Boris Iofan
Palace of the Soviets, 1932
Wood, 42 × 25.3 × 48.7 cm
Alex Lachmann
Collection, London

9

KUZMA PETROV-VODKIN

THE ACTIVE GAZE[1]

John E. Bowlt

THANKS TO NUMEROUS PUBLICATIONS AND exhibitions over the past decades, the trajectory of modern Russian art has become very familiar, if not canonical, to the Western public – from the Realists of the late nineteenth century, such as Ilya Repin and Vasily Vereshchagin, to the stylists of the *fin de siècle*, such as Léon Bakst and Mikhail Vrubel, from the avant-garde, such as Kazimir Malevich and Vladimir Tatlin, to the Socialist Realists, such as Alexander Deineka and Isaak Brodsky. Along the way, however, many gifted visionaries have been omitted from this dialectical history and continue to be disregarded or underrated in Western scholarship – among them Leonid Chupiatov, Vasily Denisov, Alexander Labas and, above all, Kuzma Sergeevich Petrov-Vodkin.[2]

Such artists were not always iconoclastic and, if deeply affected by the tumultuous events of the October Revolution, the Civil War and the first Five-Year Plans, were still guided by a persistence of memory, by a Classical verdict of ages and even by academic convention. Their presence demonstrates that, in parallel to the radical nature of Suprematism and Constructivism, figurative easel painting was alive and well, and still evolving in many directions, culminating eventually in Heroic Realism and then Socialist Realism. Likewise, even if he did 'endeavour to liberate painterly trends from the fortuitousness of polyglot confusion',[3] Petrov-Vodkin, in particular, maintained his distinctive style almost intact, while still adapting his traditional thematic repertoire to the new socio-political exigencies of the Soviet Union, as for example in *First Demonstration*, also called *The Worker's Family on the First Anniversary of October* (fig. 100).[4] Some might view this adjustment as an ideological and strategic compromise, although, in essence, what mattered to Petrov-Vodkin was the craft of representation rather than the representation itself. Put differently, if, before 1917 Petrov-Vodkin painted vestal maidens and Apollonian youths, in the 1920s he often recast them as robust Soviet workers, his 'planetary' or 'spherical' style remaining constant and cohesive. He may have shifted his 'search for the ideal' to a 'search for types' – compare, for example, *Mother* of 1913 (fig. 101) with *Girl in a Red Scarf (Worker)* of 1925 (State Russian Museum, St Petersburg)[5] – even if as late as 1925 he was still painting a Madonna and Child. True, from the first and of humble origin, Petrov-Vodkin supported the new republic, he welcomed democracy, he contributed readily to Lenin's Plan of Monumental Propaganda by designing *panneaux* (hoardings) for Theatre Square in Petrograd, he designed murals for the touted 'All-Union Agricultural Exhibition' in Moscow in 1923 and he painted Lenin lying in state (cat. 13); but at the same time his art remained a reflection of the spirit, of a metaphysical harmony and of the natural cycle of life. His was an art untrammelled by overt political propaganda or didactic message, an innocence that can be identified with most painters of the 4 Arts group, of which Petrov-Vodkin was a founding member – and, not surprisingly, therefore, in the 1930s he was criticised, if not censured, for being Formalist, nostalgic and even alien to the working masses. As Yuri Rusakov observed in his monograph, Petrov-Vodkin's works 'incited furious polemics, passionate collisions and often very contradictory opinions and evaluations'.[6]

As for the muted reception he has received in the West, Petrov-Vodkin was not radical or raucous in the way the Cubo-Futurists were and, for many, his celestial

Detail of fig. 104

Fig. 100
Kuzma Petrov-Vodkin, *First Demonstration* (also called *The Worker's Family on the First Anniversary of October*), 1927. Oil on canvas, 129 × 156 cm. The State Central Museum of Contemporary History of Russia, Moscow

mothers and babies owe too much to tradition, for example to Fra Angelico, Giotto and Raphael on the one hand, and to Puvis de Chavannes and the Nabis on the other, while his rendering of non-Euclidean space often baffles and disturbs. Even so, Petrov-Vokin elaborated an original and distinctive style of painting based on spherical perspective, according to which he tried to depict the 'sensation of each individual phenomenon or object on Earth as being particles in the vast space surrounding us'.[7] Rather like Pavel Filonov's 'knowing eye' of the same time,[8] Petrov-Vodkin's was a formulaic perspective that took account of multiple viewpoints and, therefore, of spatial progression through time, portraits and self-portraits (cats 197, 198) and still-lifes (cats 191, 192) becoming his most experimental genres. Always figurative and concrete, Petrov-Vodkin's paintings conjure up not only a synthetic representation of everyday reality (a mirror, a tumbler, a coffee pot, a samovar), as in *Morning Still-life* (cat. 190) and *At Samovar* (cat. 196), but also a pristine silence (cat. 195) – what Petrov-Vodkin described as an 'optical magic'.[9] In the still-lifes, at least, the effect is as if this or that object (a bowl of flowers, a sprig of cherry [cat. 189]) has been placed at a certain juncture by a higher will and its inclusion has been preordained and exclusive – rather like the saintly sequence in an iconostasis. We can recognise the same kind of hieratic placement in the static groupings of Puvis de Chavannes, the impression being that only this particular grouping, this particular configuration, is possible, being part of an incontestable and, surely, divine order, something implicit in Petrov-Vodkin's statement on the importance of the still-life: 'The impression which an object produces upon us is the sum of perceptions and we receive them thanks to the various positions which that object assumes with relation to us and as a result of our moving round the object and of the movement of the object itself.'[10]

Petrov-Vodkin matured during the Symbolist age of the Nabis, Vrubel and Viktor Borisov-Musatov, and his painting, early and late, often elicits an intimate mood and a mystical dimension. There may even be a theosophical or anthroposophical connection, given the fact that he portrayed the novelists Andrei Bely and Olga Forsh, adepts of Helena Blavatsky and Rudolf Steiner. In any case, Petrov-Vodkin was important not only as a painter, but also as a theorist of pictorial space – of a 'spherical perspective' in which 'form conditions colour' and in which 'symptoms of growth are visible in object-phenomena';[11] interested in non-Euclidean geometry, he based the composition of his paintings on a planetary perception. Both form and colour were of equal import to him, and his early works, such as *The Bathing of the Red Horse* (fig. 102), owed much to his analyses of the techniques and compositions of Novgorod icons, which inspired him to investigate what he identified as their coloured trinity of blue, yellow and red and an elliptical space with its 'cosmic, religious feeling'.[12] In his 'Letters about Painting and Art in General' (1928) he observed: 'Objects surrounding us possess form and colour, i.e. while absorbing these or those rays of the solar spectrum, they also reflect the remaining ones (the result being a kind of paradox: let's suppose that an object is blue, but actually, in itself it does not contain blue, but radiates or throws off a scale of blue).'[13]

The positioning of the subject (person or object) was central to Petrov-Vodkin's pictorial world view and he developed his spatial theory, sometimes coinciding with Mikhail Matiushin's Zorved system (whereby the artist was to depict the object from 360 degrees),[14] in order to register the unit in space, calculating with mathematical precision the singular and exclusive location of the figure, the window, the matchbox or the mirror. As Vladimir Kostin observed, Petrov-Vodkin 'responded to the aspiration to imprint on the surface

Fig. 101
Kuzma Petrov-Vodkin, *Mother*, 1913. Oil on canvas, 102.5 × 134.6 cm. State Russian Museum, St Petersburg

Fig. 102
Kuzma Petrov-Vodkin, *The Bathing of the Red Horse*, 1912. Oil on canvas, 160 × 186 cm. State Tretyakov Gallery, Moscow

Fig. 103
Kuzma Petrov-Vodkin, *Our Lady of Tenderness for Angered Hearts*, 1914–15. Oil on canvas, mounted on wood, 100.2 × 110 cm. State Russian Museum, St Petersburg

of the canvas not only what you can see right before you, but also what is to the side, at the back and all around'.[15]

Ultimately, the majesty of the tactile world and the physiology of things inspired Petrov-Vodkin, irrespective of philosophy, ideology and sociological agenda – a constancy of structure that accompanied all phases of his art, whether Symbolist, Acmeist or Realist. As he asserted in his tract on Euclidean space in 1932: '[One must] encounter the object, but only after renouncing one's preliminary information about that object, as if seeing the object for the first time … Deaf mutes sometimes glimpse the very acute characteristics of visible phenomena about which we, their guides, may have no idea. They take account of both the binocularity and the particular quality of the foreshortenings and the densities of the materials.'[16] Petrov-Vodkin remained loyal to his own formal system despite a full immersion in modern European painting when he lived in France in 1924–25 and the imposition of Socialist Realism in the early 1930s.

Thanks to their structural common denominator, some of Petrov-Vodkin's Soviet paintings might be regarded as belated extensions of his pre-revolutionary repertoire, and ongoing exercises in the application of his triad of blue, yellow and red. *Our Lady of Tenderness for Angered Hearts* (fig. 103) anticipates *1918 in Petrograd (Petrograd Madonna)* (cat. 193) and *Madonna and Child* (1923; private collection, St Petersburg). Even the iconic *Bathing of the Red Horse* is recast as *Fantasy* (cat. 194), not to mention, perversely, perhaps, as Malevich's *Red Cavalry* (cat. 94). The constancy of this arc is so present that even the early genre scene entitled *A Family at Table* (1902; Scientific Research Museum of the Academy of Arts, St Petersburg) can be read as the prototype for the *1919. Alarm* (fig. 104). However, rather than criticise these pictures as mere variations on a theme or narrative repetitions, we might regard them as laboratorial exercises in form, colour, texture, gravity and rhythm, a procedure especially manifest in Petrov-Vodkin's swift and masterful experiments in pencil, ink and watercolour.[17]

An especially striking parallel is to be found between Petrov-Vodkin's *On the Firing Line* (fig. 105) and *Death of a Commissar* (cat. 199). The former, painted in the autumn of 1915, identifies the Russian contribution to the Great War as one of human sacrifice, showing a rural Russia fighting at dawn and entrapped in an endless conflict within an elliptical space which will ever return. Yet, if the ensign, weapon-less, has received a mortal wound, his gaze is one of inspiration and

Fig. 104
Kuzma Petrov-Vodkin, *1919. Alarm* (also called *1919. Air-raid Warning*), 1934. Oil on canvas, 169 × 138 cm. State Russian Museum, St Petersburg

revelation – and the fire becomes the fire of spiritual illumination. Curiously enough, the ghost of the ensign reappears in the dark-blue background of Petrov-Vodkin's Bolshevik painting, *After Battle* (cat. 200), and then *Death of a Commissar*, in which the ensign is now a Red Army officer, even if his troops are still the humble soldiers on the elliptical hill and still threatened by the puffs of cannon fire.

So was Petrov-Vodkin's Soviet production uninventive and repetitive, simply variations on a theme? Not entirely, because just as Vasily Polenov discovered and transmitted the light of the Holy Land in his biblical sketches, or as Pavel Kuznetsov moved from the muted palette of his Blue Rose phase to the ultramarine sky and ochre earth of Kirghizia (today Kyrgyzstan), so Petrov-Vodkin succumbed to the spell of the East when, as member of a State expedition to Central Asia under the auspices of the Academy for the History of Material Culture, he visited Samarkand in 1921. Still reliant upon his non-Euclidean theory, the ensuing Central Asian masterpieces such as *Shakh-i-Zinda (Samarkand)* (fig. 106) with their stark depictions of Uzbek village life – beasts of burden, dazzling mosques, scorched earth and bronzed indigenes – constitute a refreshing exception to his hallowed, if rather saccharine, vocabulary of mothers and babies, Soviet or otherwise.

Petrov-Vodkin's rigorous formulations, his elaboration of a stylistic canon and his lucid theoretical explications were an essential part of his more public career as a pedagogue and administrator during the 1920s and 1930s. Teaching at the Petrograd Free State

Fig. 105
Kuzma Petrov-Vodkin, *On the Firing Line*, 1915. Oil on canvas, 196 × 275 cm. State Russian Museum, St Petersburg

Fig. 106
Kuzma Petrov-Vodkin, *Shakh-i-Zinda (Samarkand)*, 1921. Oil on canvas, 75.5 × 68 cm. State Russian Museum, St Petersburg

Art Studios (SVOMAS), the Higher State Artistic and Technical Workshops (VKhUTEMAS) in Moscow and then the Academy of Arts, he left a profound impression on an entire generation of Soviet students, including Chupiatov, Evgenia Evenbakh, Alexei Pakhomov and Alexander Samokhvalov. In turn, they carried forward their mentor's concepts of perspective, palette and subject-matter to establish what is now known as the School of Petrov-Vodkin,[18] even if, fresh and malleable, they often paid concurrent homage to other Leningrad masters – and rivals – such as Filonov and Matiushin.

Petrov-Vodkin was fascinated by space or, rather, by our perception and rendering of space, and his quest informed some of the major icons of early Soviet culture, such as *1918 in Petrograd (Petrograd Madonna)* (cat. 193), *Portrait of the Poet Anna Akhmatova* (cat. 62), *Death of a Commissar* (cat. 199) and *1919. Alarm* (fig. 104). Yet, however accomplished and engaging, these pictures often seem to be but exercises towards a greater and more panoramic surface – towards the sacred and majestic surfaces of Giotto and Michelangelo. In the summer of 1938, a year after his grand retrospective exhibition in Leningrad and Moscow and yet at the height of Stalin's inquisition, Petrov-Vodkin was invited to paint gigantic murals for a different kind of cathedral – the Palace of the Soviets. Ironically, this prestigious commission might have granted him the spatial freedom for which he yearned throughout his life and, finally, might have fulfilled his dream to paint the 'big picture'. But destiny decided otherwise.

188
Kuzma Petrov-Vodkin
Midday. Summer, 1917
Oil on canvas,
89 × 128.5 cm
State Russian Museum,
St Petersburg

189
Kuzma Petrov-Vodkin
Cherry Blossom in a Glass, 1932
Oil on canvas, 73 × 60 cm
State Russian Museum, St Petersburg

190
Kuzma Petrov-Vodkin
Morning Still-life, 1918
Oil on canvas, 68 × 90 cm
State Russian Museum,
St Petersburg

191
Kuzma Petrov-Vodkin
Still-life with a Violin, 1918
Oil on canvas,
66 × 81.5 cm
State Russian Museum,
St Petersburg

192
Kuzma Petrov-Vodkin
Still-life with a Herring,
1918
Oil on canvas,
56 × 88 cm
State Russian Museum,
St Petersburg

193
Kuzma Petrov-Vodkin
1918 in Petrograd (Petrograd Madonna), 1920
Oil on canvas, 73 × 92 cm
State Tretyakov Gallery, Moscow

194
Kuzma Petrov-Vodkin
Fantasy, 1925
Oil on canvas,
50 × 64.5 cm
State Russian Museum,
St Petersburg

195
Kuzma Petrov-Vodkin
Still-life with Glass, Fruit and Photograph, 1924
Oil on canvas, 50 × 61 cm
The Petr Aven Collection

196
Kuzma Petrov-Vodkin
At Samovar, 1926
Oil on canvas,
81.2 × 65 cm
State Tretyakov Gallery,
Moscow

197
Kuzma Petrov-Vodkin
Portrait of a Boy (Vasya),
1921
Oil on canvas,
36.5 × 51.5 cm
The Petr Aven Collection

198
Kuzma Petrov-Vodkin
Self-portrait, 1918
Oil on canvas, 72 × 54 cm
State Russian Museum,
St Petersburg

199
Kuzma Petrov-Vodkin
Death of a Commissar, 1927
Oil on canvas, 72.5 × 91.2 cm
State Tretyakov Gallery, Moscow

200
Kuzma Petrov-Vodkin
After Battle, 1923
Oil on canvas, 155 × 123 cm
The Central Armed Forces Museum of the Russian Federation, Moscow

10

STALIN'S UTOPIA

КЛУЦИС 1923 г.

SOVIET SPORTS AND GAMES AS PROPAGANDA

Mike O'Mahony

IN OCTOBER 1920 THE THIRD ALL-RUSSIA CONGRESS of the Young Communist League, notably attended by the Soviet leader Vladimir Ilyich Lenin, passed a resolution: 'The physical culture of the younger generation is an essential element in the overall system of communist upbringing of young people, aimed at creating harmoniously developed human beings, creative citizens of Communist society.'[1] Lenin's staunch belief in the transformative potential of sport and physical culture (or *fizkultura*, as it was officially designated in the Soviet Union) ensured that it would play a vital role in Soviet society following the Bolshevik Revolution. Like many Western nations at this time, the Soviet authorities perceived sport not simply as a leisure activity but as a means to develop fit and healthy minds and bodies, thus better equipping the populace to serve the State both in labour productivity and in military service. To promote this ideology, artists were specifically called upon to play their part in both celebrating and articulating ideas about *fizkultura*. For example, as early as 1922 Gustavs Klucis and El Lissitzky, two artists strongly associated with Constructivism, produced works overtly celebrating sport as an integral element of the new Soviet life (figs 107, 108). Employing the new medium of photomontage, they combined geometrical forms, influenced by Kazimir Malevich's Suprematism, with figurative photographs of sportsmen in action, thus emphasising how participation in *fizkultura* would contribute to the transformation of the Soviet citizen into a new Soviet person (or *novyi chelovek*). But it was not just the representation of the sporting figure that was of concern to artists associated with the early Soviet avant-garde. In 1924 Varvara Stepanova shifted her attention to designing specific sports costumes for both men and women. Her *sportodezhda*, or sports clothes (fig. 109), emphasised freedom of movement and, through their use of uniform, geometrical patterning, enhanced their wearers' collective identity. As the poet and cultural commentator Mikhail Kuzmin argued in the fashion journal *Atele*, wearing such costumes would itself contribute to the overall transformation of personality.[2] Clothes, it seemed, would indeed make the new Soviet man and woman.

Fig. 107
Gustavs Klucis, *Sport*, published in the magazine *Proletarskoye studentchestvo* [Proletarian Students], no. 2, 1923. Letterpress, 25.8 × 16.6 cm. Latvian National Museum of Art, Riga, inv. VMM Z-8750/48

If the more radical wing of the Soviet avant-garde took the lead in embracing sport and *fizkultura* after the Revolution, other artists soon followed suit. Thus while the Constructivists increasingly rejected painting and sculpture as valid genres for the new regime, artists associated with the Society of Easel Painters (OST) sought a way to bring together traditional media with the new aims and objectives of the Bolshevik State. Chief among these were Alexander Deineka and Yury Pimenov (cats 201, 205), both of whom produced paintings inspired by the simplicity of form and bright colours of modern Western artists such as Henri Matisse.[3] Following their graduation from the Higher State Artistic and Technical Workshops (VKhUTEMAS) in Moscow, Deineka and Pimenov initially found employment as illustrators for popular journals such as *Searchlight* (*Prozhektor*) and *Atheist at the*

Fig. 108
El Lissitzky, *Footballer*, 1922. Photomontage with ink, graphite pencil, gouache, varnish and drawing tools on cardboard, 33 × 24.2 cm. State Tretyakov Gallery, Moscow. Designed to illustrate the story 'Vitrion' in the book by Ilya Ehrenburg, *Six Tales with Easy Endings*, Berlin, 1922

Factory Bench (*Bezbozhnik u Stanka*). For these they produced countless images of modern life, including representations of sport. The latter subject, however, was not restricted to their illustrations. Indeed, their prominent emphasis on the *fizkultura* theme in paintings displayed at the first Society of Easel Painters' exhibition in Moscow in 1925 was enough to draw the approval of Anatoly Lunacharsky, the Commissar of Enlightenment for the Soviet State. Deineka later went on to forge a whole career based predominantly on his representations of *fizkultura*, gaining success both as an avant-garde painter during the 1920s and as a Socialist Realist after 1934.

In August 1928 the city of Moscow played host to one of the major sporting events of the early Soviet period, the First Workers' Spartakiad. To open the event, in a foretaste of the mass sports parades of the 1930s, 30,000 athletes paraded through Red Square, before marching on to the newly built, Art Deco-influenced Dinamo sports stadium. There athletes from over a dozen nations participated alongside sportsmen and women from the Soviet Union.[4] These, however, were not the elite athletes who had competed just a few weeks earlier at the 1928 Amsterdam Olympic Games. Rather, all the competitors came from socialist-worker organisations and the vast majority were explicit supporters of the politics and ideology of the Soviet Union. Even the games' name, 'Spartakiad', derived from that of Spartacus, the Roman slave rebel, signalled a revolutionary contrast to Western games' emphasis on the gods of ancient Olympia. Given its importance to the State, artists were officially recruited to promote, celebrate and document the First Workers' Spartakiad. Most famous among these was Klucis, who was commissioned to produce a series of nine photomontages, which were widely disseminated as postcards, representing the various sporting activities at the Spartakiad (fig. 110). Klucis was by no means the only artist inspired by this major sporting festival. In 1929, at the annual Moscow exhibition of the Society of Russian Sculptors (ORS), Iosif Chaikov, a sculptor who had trained in Paris before the Revolution and gained a reputation as an avant-garde practitioner during the early 1920s, exhibited an innovative work entitled *Football Players*. The work, just 83 cm in height and executed in plaster, painted to give a bronze-like patina, represents two players competing for a ball. Chaikov's work exemplifies physical balance, control and movement while also demonstrating its sculptor's technical ability, as the entire work is supported solely by the connection between the lower player's right boot and the pedestal. Despite its overt emphasis

Fig. 109
Varvara Stepanova, *Costume Designs for Sportodezhda* (sports clothing), 1924. Lithograph. Russian State Library, Moscow. Published in *LEF*, no. 2, 1923, pp. 65–68

Fig. 110
Gustavs Klucis, *Postcard for the 1928 Moscow Spartakiad*, 1928. Offset lithography, 14.1 × 10.5 cm. Purchase 449.1992.7. Jan Tschichold Collection, gift of Philip Johnson. The Museum of Modern Art (MoMA), New York, 714.1999

Fig. 111
Antonio del Pollaiuolo, *Hercules and Antaeus*, c. 1475. Bronze, height 46 cm. Museo Nazionale del Bargello, Florence

Fig. 112
Iosif Chaikov, *Football Players*, 1938. Bronze. State Tretyakov Gallery, Moscow

on a modern subject, the work is also reminiscent of Renaissance bronzes, such as those produced by Antonio del Pollaiuolo and Giambologna representing the battle between *Hercules and Antaeus* (fig. 111).[5] When, a decade later, Chaikov's small-scale sculptural representation of footballers in action was notably enlarged (fig. 112), cast in bronze and sent for display at the 1939–40 New York World's Fair, the centrality of sport and *fizkultura* as a theme for Soviet artists was fully affirmed.[6] Throughout the 1920s and early 1930s, representations of sport permeated Soviet society, playing a major role not only in art exhibitions but also in the popular form of ceramic figurines by Natalia Danko and in the design of such ephemera as kerchiefs (cat. 33) and even wallpaper.

Before the Revolution, the social development of sport in Russia had largely been restricted to the wealthy leisured classes and dominated by men. Under the new regime, however, efforts were made to bring all classes, and especially women, into the sporting fold. Thus the representation of sportswomen became a vital component in the campaign to promote *fizkultura*. The most famous artist to contribute to this was undoubtedly Alexander Samokhvalov, whose two works, *Sportswoman with a Shot-put* (cat. 202) and *Girl in a Football Jersey* (cat. 203), both appeared in the exhibition 'Fifteen Years of Artists of the Russian Soviet Republic'.[7] These works were produced at a fascinating moment for Soviet art, that is following the April resolution of 1932, which demanded the reformation of literary and artistic organisations, and the official declaration, at the 1934 Soviet Writers' Congress, that Socialist Realism would henceforth be the only approved style for artistic practice. On the one hand, Samokhvalov's two works can be read as clearly conforming to the expectations of the Soviet authorities, presenting strong, determined young women, clearly willing participants within the officially approved *fizkultura* programme. Their gaze is notably directed beyond the frame, into a light-filled, heroic Communist future. At the same time, however, the works adopt a strikingly modern approach in their deployment of loose, sketchily applied paint and bright colours. Here they contrast markedly with the more traditionally realist styles adopted by artists who found approval as Socialist Realists. Samokhvalov's works might thus be read as transitional, standing between the experimentalism of the avant-garde of the 1920s and early 1930s, and the Socialist Realism of the later Stalin years. However, the works also make an allusion to a specifically, and significantly older, Russian cultural model. Shortly after they were first exhibited, the Soviet art critic Natan Strugatsky drew an explicit parallel between Samokhvalov's new images of Soviet sportswomen and traditional Russian icons.[8] The artist's simply defined single figures presented against a predominantly empty background, executed using oil paint mixed with the more traditional medium of tempera, perhaps inevitably evoked this tradition.[9] Here, however, the focus on sport as a signifier of modernity transformed the religious dimension of the former works into a more secular version of worship. The Soviet sportswoman now effectively became a new image of devotion for the Soviet populace, an exemplar not only to celebrate but also to emulate. Sport's potential to transform the population into the 'harmoniously developed human beings, creative citizens of communist society' as outlined at the Third All-Russia Congress thus operated as a consistent and powerful metaphor throughout the early years of the Bolshevik regime. It also came to acquire increased importance during the later Cold War years when the Soviet Union competed with the United States at the post-war Olympic Games. The role of artists in promoting this vision of sport thus remained paramount throughout the Soviet era.

201
Alexander Deineka
Race, 1932
Oil on canvas,
180 × 135 cm
The Association
of Historical and
Regional Art, Tula

202
Alexander Samokhvalov
Sportswoman with a Shot-put, 1933
Oil on canvas,
124.5 × 65.8 cm
State Tretyakov Gallery,
Moscow

203
Alexander Samokhvalov
Girl in a Football Jersey,
1932
Tempera on canvas,
102 × 64 cm
State Russian Museum,
St Petersburg

204
Alexander Deineka
Football, 1924
Oil on canvas,
104 × 113 cm
Collection of
Vladimir Tsarenkov

205
Yury Pimenov
Football, 1926
Oil on canvas,
134.5 × 89.5 cm
The Astrakhan State
Art Gallery

206
Alexander Deineka
Who is Winning?, 1932
Gouache and collage on paper, 63 × 99 cm
Alex Lachmann Collection, London

207
Nizhny Novgorod
Commemoration of the Flight of a Russian Dirigible from Moscow to New York Piloted by Three Soviet Airmen, c. 1932
Lacquer, tempera and gold paint on papier mâché (Palekh),
44 × 17 cm
Alex Lachmann Collection, London

208
Arkady Shaiket
Physical Training (Morning Gymnastics), 1927
Gelatin silver print, 31.5 × 41 cm
Alex Lachmann Collection, London

209
Boris Ignatovich
Demonstration, 1927
Gelatin silver print, 17.8 × 24 cm
Alex Lachmann Collection, London

210
Boris Ignatovich
Dinamo Stadium,
Moscow, 1932
Gelatin silver print,
22.8 × 16.4 cm
Alex Lachmann
Collection, London

211
Boris Ignatovich
May Day, Red Square,
Moscow, 1927
Gelatin silver print,
24 × 18 cm
Alex Lachmann
Collection, London

212
Alexander Rodchenko
Pioneer with Trumpet,
1930
Gelatin silver print,
44.7 × 37.5 cm
Alex Lachmann
Collection, London

213
Boris Ignatovich
Dinamo Factory
Brass Band, 1926
Gelatin silver print,
18 × 24 cm
Alex Lachmann
Collection, London

214
Varvara Stepanova
Result of the Five-Year Plan, 1932
Photomontage, 41 × 56 cm
Alex Lachmann Collection, London

215
Moisey Nappelbaum
Joseph Stalin, c. 1934
Gelatin silver print, 56.5 × 37 cm
Alex Lachmann Collection, London

216
Nikolai Punin. Portrait Photographs from His Personal Investigation File as a Prisoner, 1949
Photograph. Punin Family Archive, St Petersburg

13144 Пунин Николай Николаевич 1888

ENDNOTES

INTRODUCTION

John Milner (pp. 15–21)

1 Early in 1922 Lunacharsky's journal *The Press and the Revolution* announced that INKhUK was setting up an investigation into art and production, leading to a published set of essays, *Representation to Construction*, which would make clear 'the ideological position and bases of creative work of those groups seeking a way into production'. Proposed contributors included Vladimir Tatlin, Alexandra Exter, Alexander Rodchenko and Alexander Vesnin, together with the theorists Osip Brik, Boris Arvatov and Boris Kushner. See 'Khudozhniki i Proizvodstvo', in *Pechat' i Revolutsiya*, 1, 1922, p. 334.
2 Alexei Gan, *Konstruktivizm*, Tver, 1922, pp. 3, 5.
3 Ibid., pp. 12, 13, 14.
4 Ibid., pp. 18, 45.
5 Ibid., p. 57.
6 Ibid., p. 70.
7 Arvatov's book *Art and the Classes* was published in Moscow and Petrograd in 1923. He contributed essays to *The Press and the Revolution*, spoke at INKhUK and wrote for the LEF journal. See Boris Arvatov, 'Na putyakh k proletarskomu iskusstvomu' ('On the Routes to Proletarian Art'), in *Pechat' i Revolutsiya*, 1, January–March 1922, pp. 65–75.
8 Arvatov reviewed articles published in a revolutionary art newspaper in Petrograd in 1919. Here he praised Nikolai Punin's 'Art and the Proletariat' and Osip Brik's 'Artist and the Commune', both of which debated the nature of art produced by the proletariat. See Arvatov's review of *Izobrazitel'noe Iskusstvo*, 1, 1919, Petrograd, in *Pechat' i Revolutsiya*, 2, August–September 1921, p. 216.
9 Arvatov 1922, p. 71.
10 Boris Arvatov, review of 'Kazimir Malevich, *Bog ne skinut: iskusstvo, tserkov', fabrika*', in *Pechat' i Revolutsiya*, 7, September–October 1922, p. 344.
11 Arvatov 1922, p. 68.
12 Ibid., p. 74.
13 René Fülop-Miller, *The Mind and Face of Bolshevism: An Examination of Cultural Life in Soviet Russia*, London, 1927, cited in Ronald Hunt and Katja Waldén (eds), *Poetry Must Be Made by All! Transform the World!*, exh. cat., Moderna Museet, Stockholm, 1969, pp. 50–51.
14 Nikolai Tarabukin's book *From the Easel to the Machine* was published in Moscow in 1923 (Izd. Rabotnik Prosveshchenia). He traced the development of Constructivism into the production phase. A French translation with a critical essay was published as Nikolai Taraboukine, *Le Dernier tableau*, A. B. Nakov (ed.), Paris, 1972, pp. 39, 40.
15 'Kogo Pedostregaet Lef?' ('Whom Is Lef Warning?'), LEF, 1, 1923, pp. 10–11.
16 N. F. Chuzhak, 'Pod znakom zhiznestroenie' ('Under the Sign of Life-construction'), LEF, 1, 1923, pp. 12–39.
17 In Germany, Russia and across Europe, Kandinsky was known for his book *Concerning the Spiritual in Art* and for his leading role in the Blaue Reiter that had brought together Russian artists, such as Alexei Jawlensky and Marianne Werefkin, and Germanic artists, such as August Macke, Franz Marc and Paul Klee. In the early Soviet period in Russia, Germany was not altogether forgotten as the enemy, and the Bolsheviks preferred materialism to a quest for the spiritual.

Fig. 113
Fridrikh Ermler directing *Fragment of an Empire*, 1929. Photograph.
Ronald Grant Archive

'THE NEW WORLD OF THE MASS MAN'

Natalia Murray (pp. 23–25)

1 René Fulöp-Miller, *The Mind and Face of Bolshevism: An Examination of Cultural Life in Soviet Russia*, London, 1927, p. 4.
2 Nikolai Punin, diary note, 1 September 1917, in Nikolai Punin, *Mir Svetel Luboviu. Dnevniki, pis'ma*, Leonid Zykov (ed.), Moscow, 2000, p. 112.
3 Igor Golomstock, *Totalitarian Art in the Soviet Union, the Third Reich, Fascist Italy and the People's Republic of China*, Robert Chandler (trans.), London, 1990, p. xii.
4 T. Goriacheva, '"Tsarstvo dukha" i "Tsarstvo Kesaria": Sud'ba futuristicheskoi utopii v 1920–1930h godah', *Iskusstvoznanie*, 1, 1999, p. 286.
5 Solomon Volkov, *The Magical Chorus: A History of Russian Culture from Tolstoy to Solzhenitsyn*, Antonina Bouis (trans.), New York, 2009, p. 56.
6 Christina Lodder and Martin Hammer, *Constructing Modernity: The Art and Career of Naum Gabo*, New Haven and London, 2000, p. 57.
7 Joseph Brodsky, 'Catastrophies in the Air', in *Less Than One: Selected Essays*, Harmondsworth, 1986, p. 268.
8 Quoted in Evgeny Kovtun, *Russian Avant-garde*, Nick Cowling and Marie-Noelle Dumaz (trans.), Hoo, Rochester, 2007, p. 104.
9 The Wanderers (Peredvizhniki) evolved into the Society for Travelling Art Exhibitions in 1870 with the aim of giving people from the provinces a chance to follow and appreciate the achievements of Russian art, and to teach people to appreciate art.
10 *Pis'ma Kazimira Malevicha, El Lisitskomu i Nikolaiu Puninu*, Moscow, 2000, p. 34.
11 See Punin 2000, p. 266.
12 The Makovets group was named after the hill where the spiritual centre of the Russian Orthodox Church, the Trinity Lavra of St Sergius, was founded in 1345.
13 Letter from the group of artists to I. O. Stalin (Joseph Stalin), in the archive of the Russian Centre for Preservation and Study of the Documents of Newest History, f. 17, op. 60, d. 805, l. 56–66.
14 Ibid., l. 65.

SOVIET ART IN REVIEW: 'FIFTEEN YEARS OF ARTISTS OF THE RUSSIAN SOVIET REPUBLIC' IN LENINGRAD, 1932

Masha Chlenova (pp. 27–31)

1 The displacement of the avant-garde's legacy from the Soviet public sphere was completed at the Moscow version of the retrospective, held at the State Historical Museum from June 1933 to February 1934.
2 An art historian and critic, from 1926 Nikolai Punin was the founder and chief curator of the Department of Newest Trends at the State Russian Museum. Dobychina owned an Art Bureau in St Petersburg in 1911–19, where she held numerous exhibitions, including the landmark 'The Last Futurist Exhibition of Paintings 0–10' in 1915.
3 Ivan Matsa, *Sovetskoe Iskusstvo za 15 Let: materialy i dokumentatsiia* (*15 Years of Soviet Art: Materials and Documents*), Moscow, 1933, p. 5. Matsa completed his initial exhibition plan in February 1932 and his editorial work on the volume of primary documents in July 1932.
4 Ibid., p. 234.
5 'Materials for the Organisation of the Exhibition "Artists of the RSFSR"', Russian State Archive of Literature and Art, f. 645, op. 1, d. 470, l. 66.
6 Mikhail Arkadiev, 'Introduction', in *Khudozhniki RSFSR za 15 let. Katalog iubileinoi vystavki. Zhivopis', grafika i skul'ptura* (*15 Years of Artists of the RSFSR. Catalogue of the Anniversary Exhibition. Painting, Graphics and Sculpture*), Leningrad, 1932, pp. 5, 7.
7 Igor Grabar, 'Prazdnik masterov kisti, karandasha i reztsa' ('Celebration of the Masters of the Brush, Pencil and Chisel'), in ibid., p. 9.
8 Ibid., p. 10. The emphasis is mine.
9 Nikolai Punin, 'Zhivopis'

Oktiabr'skogo piatnadtsatiletiia – vystavka v Russkom Muzee' ('Painting of Fifteen Years after October – An Exhibition at the Russian Museum'), *Rabochii i teatr*, 32–33, December 1932, p. 22. On Punin's leading role, see Andrei Chegodaev, 'Vystavka 1932 goda', in *Moia zhizn' i ludi kotorykh ia znal: vospominaniia*, Moscow, 2006, p. 219.

10 Malevich joked about the ostentatious opulence of the dinner for 300 people, with an abundance of exotic dishes and numerous waiters: 'it seemed that we suddenly moved and fell from the threshold of socialism to the year 1910.' Letter from Malevich to Kliun, 12 December 1932, in *Malevich o sebe, sovremenniki o Maleviche: pis'ma, dokumenty, vospominaniia, kritika*, Irina Vakar and Tatiana Mikheenko (eds), Moscow, 2004, vol. 1, p. 233.

11 This pun is based on the double meaning of the Russian verb 'vystavit', which literally translates as 'to put out' in the sense of 'throw out' and/or 'put on display'. Evgeny Katsman, diary entry, 9 April 1933, in Tatiana Khvostenko, *Vechera na khutore bliz Dinamo*, Moscow, 2003, p. 125.

12 Igor Grabar, manuscript of the essay 'Artists of the RSFSR over 15 Years. An Anniversary Exhibition in Leningrad', Manuscript Division of the State Tretyakov Gallery, Moscow, f. 106, op. 1, d. 1243.

13 Nikolai Punin, 'Obchshiy kharakter vystavki' ('The General Character of the Exhibition'), in ibid., pp. 19–20.

14 Ibid., pp. 14–15.

15 Igor Grabar, manuscript of the essay 'Artists of the RSFSR over 15 Years. An Anniversary Exhibition in Leningrad', Manuscript Division of the State Tretyakov Gallery, Moscow, f. 106, op. 1, d. 1243.

16 For details see documents in *Malevich o sebe*, vol. 1, pp. 566–72.

17 Iosif Gurvich, 'Fifteen Years of Soviet Power and the Russian Museum', *Memoirs*, 1968. Manuscript Division of the State Russian Museum, St Petersburg, f. 221, d. 2, l. 37. Gurvich directed the museum in 1932–34. His letter to Kirov shows that the State Russian Museum planned to exhibit more leftist artists, anticipated criticism and was prepared to stand its ground.

18 This argument is developed in Masha Chlenova, 'Kazimir Malevich', in 'Abstraction, 1910–1925: Eight Statements', *October*, 143, Winter 2013, pp. 19–27.

19 Letter from Kazimir Malevich to Ivan Kliun, 12 December 1932, in *Malevich o sebe*, vol. 1, p. 233. This was to be the last extensive public display of Malevich's works in the Soviet Union until 1989.

20 Minutes of debates at the Moscow Union of Soviet Artists (MOSKh), 8 December 1932. Russian State Archive of Literature and Art, f. 2943, d. 1128, l. 10.

21 Osip Beskin's essay 'Formalizm v zhivopisi' and the critical historical survey by Mil'da Bush and Aleksandr Zamoshkin, 'The Path of Soviet Art, 1917–1932', appeared in the leading art journal *Iskusstvo* in the spring of 1933, and within two months had been published as books with a wide circulation.

22 Igor Grabar, manuscript of the article 'Anniversary Exhibition of Soviet Art in Leningrad. Observations and Thoughts of an Artist', Manuscript Division of the State Tretyakov Gallery, Moscow f. 106, op. 1, d. 1252.

'THE MOST IMPORTANT ART'? SOVIET FILM-MAKING IN THE 1920S

Ian Christie (pp. 33–37)

1 Quoted in Jay Leyda, *Kino: A History of Russian and Soviet Film*, London, 1950, p. 268. Alexandrov's account of this meeting with Stalin, Molotov and Voroshilov was published ten years later in the journal *Iskusstvo Kino* under the title 'Great Friend of Soviet Cinema', and is not corroborated by any other account, which suggests it may have been 'adjusted' in the light of Stalin's later obsessive control of Soviet cinema.

2 Sergei Eisenstein, 'Through Theatre to Cinema', in his *Film Form: Essays in Film Theory*, New York, 1949, pp. 3–17.

3 See review of *Expiation* by H. D. [Hilda Doolittle], *Close Up*, 2, 5, May 1928; reprinted in James Donald, Anne Friedberg and Laura Marcus (eds), *Close Up, 1927–1933: Cinema and Modernism*, Princeton, 1998, pp. 125–30.

4 Literally 'spinning top'. Vertov was born Denis Kaufman, in Białystok, with two brothers who retained their family name: Mikhail, who served as Vertov's cameraman, and Boris, who emigrated and worked for Jean Vigo in France and later on such celebrated American films as *On the Waterfront* (1954), *Baby Doll* (1956) and *The Pawnbroker* (1964).

5 Dziga Vertov, 'The Cine-eyes. A Revolution', LEF, 3, June/July 1923. Translated in Richard Taylor and Ian Christie (eds), *The Film Factory: Russian and Soviet Cinema in Documents, 1896–1939*, London, 1988, p. 94.

6 For details and an analysis of the film's opening, see Yuri Tsivian, '*Man with a Movie Camera*, Reel One: A Selective Glossary', *Film Studies*, 2, Spring 2000, pp. 52–53.

7 'There is, I believe, only [Viktor] Turin and *Turk Sib* ... *Turk Sib* is an affair of economics, which is the only sort of affair worth one's time or patience.' John Grierson, 'Films and Talkies: Cinema of State', *The Clarion*, NS, 2, 8, August 1930, p. 235. *Turksib* [as it is normally referred to] was one of the few Soviet films to be passed by the British Board of Film Censors, and was widely shown around Britain in 1930–31, 'especially in cinemas that had yet to convert to sound', according to Henry K. Miller, in notes accompanying a British Film Institute DVD release of the film in 2012. Miller also quoted the film-maker Basil Wright, writing in 1967: 'this was the only Soviet documentary ... which really influenced me permanently'.

8 *A Severe Young Man* was withheld from distribution, and both Room and the scriptwriter Yuri Olesha suffered lasting disapproval as a result. The film remained unseen by foreigners until the 1980s.

9 'The Results of Cinema Construction in the USSR and the Tasks of Soviet Cinema', Report, 1929, in Taylor and Christie 1988, p. 211.

10 The historian Oksana Bulgakowa has suggested that Stalin 'specialised' in cinema, while Trotsky and Bukharin were more attuned to literature and the traditional arts. Oksana Bulgakowa, *Sergei Eisenstein: A Biography*, Berlin and San Francisco, 1998, 2001.

11 See, for example, the denunciation of this new trend in Soviet cinema by formerly enthusiastic American critics: Dwight McDonald, *On Movies*, Englewood Cliffs, NJ, 1969, reprinting his essays from *Partisan Review* in the 1930s; and Robert Warshow, 'Reviewing the Russian Movies', *Commentary*, October 1955, reprinted in *The Immediate Experience*, Garden City, NY, 1962.

12 On Stalin's distinction between 'socialist realism' and 'revolutionary romanticism', see Sarah Davies and James Harris, *Stalin's World: Dictating the Soviet World Order*, Princeton, 2014, p. 251.

CREATING THE SOVIET MYTH

Natalia Murray (pp. 55–57)

1 Kliment Redko, *Dnevniki, vospominaniia, stat'i* (*Diaries, Memoirs, Articles*), Moscow, 1974, p. 66.

2 James von Geldern, *Bolshevik Festivals, 1917–1920*, Berkeley, CA, 1993, p. 3.

3 Quoted in V. P. Lapshin, *Khudozhestvennaya zhizn' Moskvy I Petrograda v 1917 godu*, Moscow, 1983, p. 122.

4 Quoted in Alexei Yurchak, 'Bodies of Lenin: The Hidden Science of Communist Sovereignty', *Representations*, 129, University of California, Winter 2015, p. 122.

MECHANISATION TAKES COMMAND

John Milner (pp. 75–79)

1 The engineer Vladimir Shukhov was an inventor of self-supporting tensile structures that needed no armature, though to facilitate access one was later inserted into his Shablovka Radio Tower in Moscow. This tower functioned for many years as a radio mast, broadcasting Radio Moscow. In 2015 it was saved from demolition and is now the focal point of a cultural and entertainment centre.

CONSTRUCTORS OF THE FUTURE IN SEARCH OF THE NEW

Zelfira Tregulova and Faina Balakhovskaya (pp. 101–05)

1 Nadezhda Udaltsova, 'We Want', first published in the journal *Anarkhiya* (*Anarchy*), Moscow, March and April 1918, 38, cited in A. D. Sarabianov, with chronology and texts by N. A. Gurianova, *Neizvestnyi russkii avangard v muzeyakh i chastnykh sobraniyakh* (*The Unknown Russian Avant-garde in Museums and Private Collections*), Moscow, 1992, p. 265. The full text can be found in Nadezhda Udaltsova, *Zhizn' russkoi kubistka* (*To Live as a Female Russian Cubist*), Moscow, 1994, p. 44.

2 'The Intelligentsia and the Revolution' was first published in *Znamia truda* (*The Flag of Labour*), 122, 19 January 1918. Alexander Blok, *Sobranie sochinenii*, 8 vols, Moscow, 1962, vol. 6, p. 12.

3 Georgy Fedotov, 'Pravda pobezhdennykh', in *Sovremennye zapiski*, Paris, 1933, p. 360. 'The Twelve' was Alexander Blok's most celebrated revolutionary poem. It was completed on 29 January 1918.

The twelve of the title are a group of Red Army soldiers searching through a blizzard: they glimpse a figure with a blood-red rag and crowned with white roses or flowers of snow. The poem was first published in *Znamia truda* on 3 March 1918.

4 'O politike partii v oblasti khudozhestvennoi literatury', 18 June 1925, in Alexander Yakovlev (ed.), *Vlast' i khudozhestvennaya intelligentsiya. 1917–1953*, Moscow, 1999, p. 56.
5 'Itogi vystavki gosudarstvennykh zakazov k desyatiletiyu Oktyabrya', *Izvestia*, 40, 16 February 1928, in Anatoly Lunacharsky, *Ob izobrazitel'nom iskusstve*, vol. 2, Moscow, 1967, p. 210.
6 Letter from a group of artists to Stalin in Yakovlev 1999, p. 63.
7 For example, the 'old writers', who were a separate group among those listed as 'writers politically close to us at the present moment' in a memorandum to Stalin regarding the situation among writers by Yakov Yakovlev, deputy leader of the department of agitation and propaganda. Ibid., p. 39.
8 Fedotov 1933, p. 360.
9 El Lissitzky, 'Suprematizm mirostroitel'stva', *Almanakh UNOVIS*, 1, 1920.
10 *Chevengur* by Andrei Platonov (1899–1951) was written in 1927–28 but not published in the USSR until 1988, in Moscow. The book comprises a series of satirical scenes of Soviet life in the years of the New Economic Policy (NEP).
11 Letter from Boris Kustodiev to Vasily Luzhsky, 6 March 1917, in *B. M. Kustodiev*, Leningrad, 1967, p. 156.
12 Regardless of the continuing discussion of the role of letters, and especially texts; this new context appeared in collages by Picasso.
13 Abram Efros, *Profili. Ocherki o russkikh khudozhnikov*, Moscow, 1930, p. 213.
14 'Kaplya degtya', 1915, in Vladimir Mayakovsky, *Polnoe sobranie sochinenii*, 13 vols, Moscow, 1955, vol. 1, p. 343.
15 Nikolai Punin, 'Obzor novykh techenii v iskusstve Peterburga', *Russkoe iskusstvo*, 1923, p. 24.
16 Ibid., pp. 24–25.
17 From Vladimir Mayakovsky's poem 'Left March!', 1918.
18 'Opyt khudozhnika novoi mery', 1926, in Mikhail Matiushin, *Tvorcheskii put' khudozhnika*, Kolomna, 2011, p. 240.
19 Vasily Kandinsky, 'Khudozhestvennaya vesna v Rossii', 1919, first published in German as 'Kunstfrühling in Russland', *Die Freiheit*, Berlin, 9 April 1919. See Vasily Kandinsky, *Izbrannye trudy po teorii iskusstva*, 2 vols, Moscow, 2008, vol. 2, p. 17.
20 From the play 'Black and White', 1910s, published in 'Vasily Kandinsky, Stikhotvoreniya i stat'i 1910–1920-kh godov "Shramy zazhivayut. Kraski ozhivayut"', *Znamya*, 2, 1999.
21 As noted in Stepanova's diary on 2 September 1910, in Varvara Stepanova, *Chelovek ne mozhet zhit' bez chuda*, Moscow, 1994, p. 127.
22 This is one of the slogans that hung on the wall of Rodchenko's studio at the Higher State Artistic and Technical Workshops (VKhUTEMAS). See Alexander Rodchenko, *Lozungi. Opyty dlya budushchego*, Moscow, 1996, p. 126.
23 Lyubov Popova, typewritten catalogue of the 1921 exhibition '5 × 5 = 25' published in Moscow. Rodchenko Stepanova Archive, Moscow.
24 Letter from a group of artists to Stalin, no later than 3 February 1926, in Yakovlev 1999, p. 63.
25 Pavel Filonov, *Deklaratsiya 'Mirovogo rastsveta', Zhizn' iskusstva*, 20, 1923, p. 15.
26 Pavel Filonov, Anna Kirillova, David Kakabadze, Elsa Lasson-Spirova, Evgeny Pskovitinov, *Intimnaya masterskaya zhivopistsev i risovalshchikov 'Sdelannye kartiny'*, St Petersburg, 1914.
27 Sergei Tretyakov, *Perspektivy futurizma*, Moscow, 1923.

HEROES OF THE PAST LIVING IN THE FUTURE

Natalia Murray (pp. 127–31)

1 Anna Akhmatova, quoted in T. Pozdnyakova and N. Popova, *Under the Roof of the Fountain House*, St Petersburg, 2005, p. 9.
2 Speech delivered at an all-Russia conference of political education workers of Guberniia and Uezd education departments, 3 November 1920.
3 Quoted in V. P. Lapshin, *Khudozhestvennaya zhizn' Moskvy I Petrograda v 1917 godu*, Moscow, 1983, p. 122.
4 A. V. Krusanov, *Russkii avant-garde: 1907–1932: Istoricheskii Obzor*, 2 vols, St Petersburg, 1996, vol. 1, p. 70.
5 Entry for 14 November 1919, in Sidney Monas and Jennifer Greene Krupala (eds), *The Diaries of Nikolay Punin: 1904–1953*, Jennifer Greene Kupala (trans.), Austin, TX, 1999, p. 61.
6 Ibid., p. 62.
7 From the article by A. V. Lunacharsky, 'The Soviet State and Art' ('Sovetskoe Gosudarstvo I Iskusstvo'), in *A. V. Lunacharsky ob iskusstve*, I. Saz and A. Ermakov (eds), Moscow, 1982, vol. 2, p. 104.
8 Nikolai Punin, 'Art and Revolution', in Viktor Woroszylski, *The Life of Mayakovsky*, Boleslaw Taborski (trans.), London, 1972, p. 258.
9 Acmeism, or the Guild of Poets, was a transient poetic school, that emerged in 1910 in Russia under the leadership of Nikolai Gumilev and Sergei Gorodetsky. Their ideals were compactness of form and clarity of expression. The term was coined after the Greek word *akme*, i.e. 'the best age of man'.
10 Ibid., pp. 290–91.
11 Ibid.
12 Quoted in Solomon Volkov, *The Magical Chorus: A History of Russian Culture from Tolstoy to Solzhenitsyn*, Antonina Bouis (trans.), New York, 2009, p. 72.
13 Ibid., p. 41.
14 Anna Akhmatova, quoted in Pozdnyakova and Popova 2005, p. 25.
15 Quoted in Nadezhda Mandelstam, *Hope Against Hope: A Memoir*, Max Hayward (trans.), London, 1975, p. 190.
16 Diary entry, 18 February 1926, in Leonid Zykov (ed.), *Mir Svetel Lubov'iu. Dnevniki, pis'ma*, Moscow, 2000, p. 263.
17 Proletkult is an abbreviation of Proletarskaia Kul'tura (Proletarian Culture), an experimental organisation established in Russia in 1917 in conjunction with the October Revolution, to provide the foundations for the development of proletarian art.
18 Sergei Eisenstein, *Selected Works*, vol. 4, *Beyond the Stars: The Memoirs of Sergei Eisenstein*, Richard Taylor (ed.), William Powell (trans.), London, 1995, p. 263.

KAZIMIR MALEVICH

John Milner (pp. 149–54)

1 Selim O. Khan-Magomedov, *Aleksandr Nikolsky*, Moscow, 2009, p. 48 et passim.
2 Andrei B. Nakov, *Kasimir Malevich, Catalogue raisonné*, Paris, 2002, p. 349, cites a document written by Malevich and preserved in the Russian State Archive of Literature and Art (RGALI) in Moscow, in which Malevich describes his 'architectural artistic Column, a monument to the Land of the Soviets, with stone and marble for the figures. K. Malevich, 25.4 1932g'. RGALI, Moscow, f. 643, op. 1, ed. hr. 4.

FARMING AND FAMINE

John Milner (pp. 183–87)

1 W. Bruce Lincoln, *In War's Dark Shadow. The Russians before the Great War*, DeKalb, IL, 2003, p. 46.

ECHOES OF ORTHODOXY

Nicoletta Misler (pp. 209–13)

1 Sergei Nikolaevich Bulgakov (1871–1944), priest, philosopher and economist. Born into a priest's family, Bulgakov studied at the Moscow Theological Seminary, announcing his religious and philosophical beliefs in the collection of essays *Ot marksizma k idealizmu*, St Petersburg, 1903. Ordained in 1918, he was exiled from Russia in 1922. See Catherine Evtuhov, *The Cross and the Sickle: Sergei Bulgakov and the Fate of Russian Religious Philosophy, 1890–1920*, Ithaca, NY, 1997.
2 Count Yurii Aleksandrovich Olsuf'ev (1878–1939) was a connoisseur of early Russian icons and wrote the first scholarly catalogue raisonné of those at the Lavra before the opening of the Historical and Art Museum of the Sergiev Posad in April 1920. See his *Opis' ikon Troitse-Sergievoi Lavry do XVIII veka i naibolee tipichnykh XVIII i XIX vekov*, Sergiev Posad, 1920; and Gerol'd Vzdornov, 'Zabytoe imia', *Pamiatniki Otechestva*, 1987, 2, 16, pp. 85–92.
3 Pavel Nikolaevich Kapterev (1889–1953), the son of the theological historian Nikolai Kapterev (1847–1917), graduated from Moscow University in biology in 1911 and in philosophy in 1916. In 1924 he was appointed Director of the Hypnosis Society in Moscow and the following year Director of the Commission for the Study of Artistic Creativity at the Russian Academy of Artistic Sciences. In the late 1920s he gave increasing attention to the natural sciences. See his 'Lichnoe delo', in the Russian State Archive of Literature and Art, Moscow, f. 941, op. 10, ed. khr. 268; see also his 'Iz istorii Troitskoi Lavry', in Pavel Florensky, Pavel Kapterev, Yurii Olsuf'ev et al., *Troitse-Sergieva Lavra*, Sergiev Posad, 1919, pp. 30–45.
4 Konstantin Yuon, *Sergiev Posad*, Moscow, 1922 (dated 1923 on cover).
5 Vasilii Rozanov, *Apokalipsis nashego vremeni*, November 1917 – October 1918.
6 For a recent reconsideration of this work, see Nicoletta Misler, 'Mikhail Nesterov', in *Tret'iakovskaia galereia*, 2007, 2, 15, 2007, pp. 48–57; and S. Trubacheva, 'P. A. Florensky i M.

V. Nesterov', in S. Trubacheva et al. (eds), *P. A. Florensky. Izbrannoe. Stat'i i issledovaniia*, Moscow, 2005, pp. 345–59.
7 See Igumen Andronik (Aleksandr Trubachev), Mariia Trubacheva and Oleg Genisaretsky (eds), Pavel Florensky. *'Analiz prostranstvennosti i vremeni v khudozhestvenno-izobrazitel'nykh proizvedeniiakh'*, Moscow, 1993, pp. 252–53.
8 Sergei Bulgakov, 'Sviashchennik Pavel Florensky', *Slovo*, 12, 1989, p. 29.
9 Pavel Florensky, 'Nebesnye znameniia', *Makovets*, 1922, 2, pp. 14–16.
10 Sergei Bulgakov, *Svet nevechernii. Sozertsaniia i umozreniia*, Sergiev Posad, 1917.
11 Under the aegis of the Committee for the Preservation of Artistic Treasures, Grabar published the pamphlet *Dlia chego nado okhraniat' i sobirat' sokrovishcha iskusstva i stariny*, Moscow, 1919.
12 V. Kuchin (ed.), *Iz istorii stroitel'stva sovetskoi kul'tury 1917–18*, Moscow, 1964.
13 Boris Shaposhnikov, 'The Museum as a Work of Art' ('Muzei kak proizvedenie iskusstva'), *Experiment*, 1997, 3, p. 233.
14 Boris Shaposhnikov, *Bytovoi Muzei sorokovykh godov*, Moscow, 1924. During the brief life of the Museum (1924–28), Shaposhnikov published annual guides to its holdings under the auspices of Moscow's State Historical Museum.
15 A. Grech, 'V. V. Zgura', *Iskusstvo*, 1927, II–III, pp. 210–11. On the history of this association see G. Zlochevsky, *Obshchestvo izucheniia russkoi usad'by (1922–1930)*, Moscow, 2002.
16 Pavel Florensky, 'Pis'mo A. S. Mamontovoi', in Igumen Andronik (Aleksandr Trubachev), Pavel Florensky and Mariia Trubacheva (eds), *Pavel Florensky. Sochineniia*, Moscow, 1994–99, vol. 2 (1996), pp. 409–10.
17 See Pavel Florensky, Pavel Kapterev, Yurii Olsuf'ev et al., *Troitse-Sergieva Lavra*, Sergiev Posad, 1919. Of particular note were Florensky's and Kapterev's projects to safeguard the territories delineated by the Commission for the Preservation of Monuments of Antiquity and Art at the Monastery of the Holy Trinity at the Sergiev Posad. See Mariia Trubacheva, 'Komissiia po okhrane pamiatnikov stariny i iskusstva Troitse-Sergievi Lavry 1918–1925', *Muzei*, 1984, 5, pp. 152–64.
18 Natalya Aleksandrova et al., *Pavel Korin. 'Rekviem'. K istorii 'Rusi ukhodiashchei'*, exh. cat., State Tretyakov Gallery, Moscow, 2013–14. Also see Natalya Aleksandrova and Vera Golovina, 'K istorii "Rusi ukhodiashchei"', in *Tret'iakovskaia galereia*, Moscow, 2014, 2, p. 43; and Ekaterina Kiseleva, *Dom Pavla Korina*, Moscow, 2015.

THE LIFE OF ARTISTS IN 1920S RUSSIA

Evgenia Petrova (pp. 229–35)

1 Boris Mikhailovich Kustodiev, *Pis'ma. Stat'i. Zametki. Interv'iu. Vstrechi i besedy. Vospominaniia (Letters. Articles. Notes. Interviews. Meetings and Conversations. Reminiscences)*, Leningrad, 1967, p. 156.
2 Ibid., p. 161.
3 Ibid., p. 163. The italics in quotations throughout this essay are my own, and have been used for emphasis.
4 Boris Grigoriev, *Liniia / Literaturno-khudozhestvennoe nasledie (Line / Literary-artistic Heritage)*, Moscow, 2006, p. 83.
5 Ibid., p. 106.
6 Ibid, p. 49.
7 Ibid., p. 106.
8 Nadezhda Udaltsova, *Zhizn' russkoi kubistki. Dnevniki, stat'i, vospominaniia (The Life of a Russian Cubist: Diaries, Articles, Reminiscences)*, Moscow, 1914, p. 37.
9 Ibid.
10 Ibid., p. 38.
11 Ibid., p. 49.
12 Ibid., p. 121.
13 Ibid., p. 76.
14 Alexander Labas, *Vospominaniia (Reminiscences)*, St Petersburg, 2004, p. 25.
15 Ibid., p. 27.
16 Ibid., p. 29.
17 Marc Chagall, *Angel nad kryshami (Angel Above the Rooftops)*, Moscow, 1989, p. 151.
18 *Vospominaniia Sof'i Dymshits-Tolstoi (Reminiscences of Sofya Dymshits-Tolstaya)*, Manuscript Division of the State Russian Museum, St Petersburg, f. 100, op. 1, ed. khr. 249, l. 58.
19 *Malevich o sebe. Sovremenniki o Maleviche. Pis'ma. Dokumenty. Vospominaniia. Kritika, (Malevich About Himself. Contemporaries About Malevich. Letters. Documents. Reminiscences. Criticism)*, vol. 1, Moscow, 2004, p. 111. Irina A. Vakar and Tatiana N. Mikhienko (eds), *Kazimir Malevich: Letters, Documents, Memoirs, Criticism*, 2 vols, London, 2015, vol. 1, p. 111.
20 *Vospominaniia Sof'i Dymshits-Tolstoi (Reminiscences of Sofya Dymshits-Tolstaya)*, Manuscript Division of the State Russian Museum, St Petersburg, f. 100, op. 1, ed. khr. 249, l. 59.
21 Ibid.
22 Marc Chagall, *Moia zhizn' (My Life)*, Moscow, 1994, p. 136.
23 Chagall 1989, p. 158.
24 Ibid.
25 Ibid., p. 166.
26 Ibid., p. 167.
27 *Vospominaniia Sof'i Dymshits-Tolstoi (Reminiscences of Sofya Dymshits-Tolstaya)*, Manuscript Division of the State Russian Museum, St Petersburg, f. 100, op. 1, ed. khr. 249, l. 38.
28 Ibid., p. 44.
29 Ibid., p. 46.
30 Ibid., p. 63.
31 Ibid.
32 Alexander Deineka, *Zhizn'. Iskusstvo. Vremia (Life. Art. Time) / Literaturno-khudoznestvennoe nasledie*, Moscow, 1989, p. 90.
33 Alexander Samokhvalov, *Moi tvorcheskie put' (My Creative Path)*, Leningrad, 1977, p. 48.
34 Ibid., p. 116.
35 Alexei Pakhomov, *Pro svou rabotu (About My Work)*, Leningrad, p. 48.
36 Ibid., pp. 93–94.
37 Kazimir Malevich, *Sobranie sochinenii (Collected Works)*, 5 vols, Moscow, 1995, vol. 1, p. 248.
38 Vakar and Mikhienko 2015, vol. 1, p. 243.
39 Ibid., p. 181.
40 Ibid.
41 Ibid., p. 182.
42 Ibid., p. 228.
43 Ibid., p. 229.
44 Ibid., p. 229.
45 Ibid., p. 245.
46 Ibid., p. 266.
47 Malevich 1995, vol. 5, p. 363.
48 Ibid., p. 250.
49 Ibid., p. 254.
50 Ibid.
51 Ibid.
52 Pavel Filonov, *Dnevniki (Diaries)*, St Petersburg, 2000.
53 *Dnevniki Ekateriny Serebryakovoi (Diaries of Ekaterina Serebryakova)*, Manuscript Division of the State Russian Museum, St Petersburg, f. 156, 1929, ed. khr. 39, l. 51.
54 Ibid., l. 52.
55 Ibid., l. 55.
56 Ibid., ed. khr. 41, l. 71.
57 Ibid., ed. khr. 35, 1930, l. 48.
58 Ibid., ed. khr. 39, 1929, l. 40.
59 Ibid., l. 59.
60 Ibid., ed. khr. 41, 1931, l. 56.
61 Ibid., l. 73.
62 Ibid., ed. khr. 41, 1931, l. 41.
63 Ibid., l. 47.
64 In 1931 friends arranged two more official commissions: *Portrait of Stalin*, intended for a poster, and one on the theme of electrification, with Lenin as the main personage (both in the State Russian Museum, St Petersburg). The works were difficult for Filonov and were not accepted for exhibition because of their strikingly individual manner.
65 Ibid., ll. 63, 65–5 verso.
66 Ibid., ed. khr. 43, l. 12.
67 M. Bush and A. Zamoshkin, 'Put' sovetskoi zhivopisi' ('The Path of Soviet Painting'), *Iskusstvo*, 1933, 1, p. 34.

BUILDING FOR SOCIALISM

Christina Lodder (pp. 257–61)

1 Kazimir Malevich, 'Arkhitektura kak poshchechina betono-zhelezu', *Anarkhiya*, 37, April 1918, p. 4; Kazimir Malevich, *Essays on Art, 1915–1933*, Troels Andersen (ed.), Xenia Glowacki-Prus and Arnold McMillin (trans.), Copenhagen, 1968, vol. 1, pp. 60–64.
2 Aleksei Gan, *Konstruktivizm*, Tver, 1922, p. 63; Aleksei Gan, *Constructivism*, Christina Lodder (trans.), Barcelona, 2013, p. 63.
3 *Iskusstvo kommuny*, 2, 1918; K. Afanas'ev (ed.), *Iz istorii sovetskoi arkhitektury 1917–1925 gg. Dokumenty i materialy*, Moscow, 1963, p. 231.
4 El Lissitzky, *Russia: An Architecture for World Revolution*, Eric Dluhosch (trans.), London, 1970, p. 27.
5 Catherine Cooke and Igor Kazus, *Soviet Architectural Competitions 1920s–1930s*, London, 1992, p. 8.
6 'Osnovy postroeniya teorii arkhitektury – pod znakom ratsionalisticheskoi estetiki', *Izvestiya Asnova*, 1, 1926, p. 3; Catherine Cooke, *Russian Avant-garde Theories of Art, Architecture and the City*, London, 1995, pp. 178–79.
7 L. Lisitskii [El Lissitzky] 'Seriya neboskrebov dlya Moskvy: WB1', *Izvestiya Asnova*, 1, 1926, p. 2; Cooke 1995, p. 198.
8 Moisei Ginzburg, 'Konstruktivizm kak metod laboratornoi i pedagogicheskoi raboty', *Sovremennaya arkhitektura*, 1, 1927, pp. 160–66; Cooke 1995, p. 90.
9 Moisei Ginzburg, 'Dom sotrudnikov Narkomfina', *Sovremennaya arkhitektura*, 5, 1929, pp. 161–62; Cooke 1995, p. 120.
10 V. E. Khazanova, *Sovetskaya arkhitektura pervykh let oktyabrya 1917–1925 gg*, Moscow, 1970, p. 164.
11 Ibid.
12 *Izvestiya*, 5 March 1924; Afanas'ev 1963, pp. 225–26.
13 Khazanova 1970, p. 165.
14 A. Nekrasov, 'Puti architektury. K problemu stiliya sovetskoi arkhitektury, *Pechat' i revolyutsiya*, 4, 1928, p. 69.
15 *Dvorets Sovetov: Byulleten' upravleniya stroitel'stvom dvortsa sovetov pri Prezidiume TsIK SSR*, Moscow, 1, 1931, p. 1; 'Competition Brief', Christina Lodder (trans.), in Helen Adkins (ed.), *Naum Gabo and the Competition for the Palace of Soviets, Moscow 1931–1933*, Berlin, 1993, p. 202.
16 Sergei Kirov, 'Rech' na s'ezde Sovetov SSSR' ('Speech to the Congress of Soviets of the USSR'), 20 December 1922; Afanas'ev 1963, p. 148.

17 *Dvorets Sovetov*, 1, 1931, pp. 1–8; 'Competition Brief', in Adkins 1993, pp. 202–09.
18 Cooke and Kazus 1992, p. 59.
19 Karl Schlögel, 'The Shadow of an Imaginary Tower', in Adkins 1993, p. 179.

THE ACTIVE GAZE

John E. Bowlt (pp. 273–77)

1 'Active gaze' is the translation of 'zhivoe smotrenie', a phrase that Petrov-Vodkin often used to explain his visual theory. See Vera Donets, *Kuzma Petrov-Vodkin*, Moscow, 2011, p. 39.
2 Petrov-Vodkin is the subject of numerous publications. Of particular importance are the following monographs: Vladimir Kostin, *Kuzma Sergeevich Petrov-Vodkin*, Moscow, 1966; Yuri Rusakov, *Risunki K. S. Petrova-Vodkina*, Moscow, 1978; Yuri Rusakov, *K. S. Petrov-Vodkin*, Leningrad, 1986; Jelena Selizarova (ed.), *K. S. Petrov-Vodkin. Pisma. Stati. Vystupleniia. Dokumenty*, Moscow, 1991; Vladimir Leniashin, *Kuzma Sergeevich Petrov-Vodkin*, St Petersburg, 2001; Tamara Grodskova (ed.), *K. S. Petrov-Vodkin i XXI vek*, exh. cat., Radishchev State Art Museum, Saratov, 2008; Maria Petrova-Vodkina, *Moi velikii russkii muzh*, exh. cat., Radishchev State Art Museum, Saratov, 2008; Elena Gribonosova-Grebneva, *Tvorchestvo K. S. Petrova-Vodkina i zapadnoevropeiskie 'realizmy' 1920–1930-kh*, Moscow, 2010; Vasily Uspensky, *Kuzma Sergeevich Petrov-Vodkin. Materinstvo*, St Petersburg, 2010; Donets 2011; Sergei Daniel, *Kuzma Petrov-Vodkin*, St Petersburg, 2011; Tatiana Khristoliubova, *K. S. Petrov-Vodkin. Mirovozzrenie i tvorchestvo*, St Petersburg, 2014; Natalia Adaskina, *K. S. Petrov-Vodkin. Zhizn' i tvorchestvo*, Moscow, 2014. Petrov-Vodkin's memoirs and commentaries on art are of particular interest. See Yuri Rusakov (ed.), *K. Petrov-Vodkin. 'Khlynovsk. Prostranstvo Evklida, Samarkandiia'*, Leningrad, 1970 (2nd edition, 1982).
3 Inessa Levkova-Lamm, '"Narodnye massivy" Petrova-Vodkina', in *Novoe russkoe slovo*, New York, 19 August 1983, p. 4.
4 For a discussion of Petrov-Vodkin and the European 'Realisms' of the 1920s and 1930s, see Gribonosova-Grebneva 2010.
5 Adaskina 2014, p. 169.
6 Rusakov 1986, p. 3.
7 Kostin 1966, p. 88.
8 For a discussion of what Filonov called the 'seeing eye' and the 'knowing eye', see Nicoletta Misler and John Bowlt, 'Vidiashchii glaz, znaiushchii glaz', in Gleb Ershov et al., *Pavel Filonov. K 125-letiiu so dnia rozhdeniia khudozhnika*, St Petersburg, 2008, pp. 145–54.
9 Kirill Sokolov, 'Extracts from "Euclidean Space". The Book by K. S. Petrov-Vodkin (1878–1939)', *Leonardo*, Paris, 1978, vol. 11, p. 143.
10 Kostin 1966, p. 86. Kostin quotes from unpublished material that had been compiled by Petrov-Vodkin's wife, Maria.
11 Rusakov 1982, pp. 487, 554.
12 See Tatiana Stepanova, 'Kosmicheskoe religioznoe chuvstvo', in Grodskova 2008, pp. 46–48. Kirill Sokolov suggests that Petrov-Vodkin may have arrived at his formula after learning of Kandinsky's identical colour triad; see Sokolov 1978, vol. 11, p. 140.
13 Kuzma Petrov-Vodkin, 'Pisma o zhivopisi i ob iskusstve voobshche', in Selizarova 1991, p. 300.
14 On Matiushin and his theory of Extended Viewing, see Alla Povelikhina, *Mikhail Matiushin. Tvorcheskii put' khudozhnika*, exh. cat., Museum of Organic Culture, Kolomna, 2011, and Isabel Wünsche, *The Organic School of the Russian Avant-garde*, Farnham, 2015.
15 Kostin 1966, p. 76.
16 Kuzma Petrov-Vodkin, 'Prostransto Evklida' (first published in 1932), in Rusakov 1982, pp. 458, 459.
17 See Rusakov 1978.
18 On the Petrov-Vodkin 'school', see Evgenia Petrova et al., *Petrov-Vodkin's Circle*, exh. cat., State Russian Museum, St Petersburg, 2015; and Ildar Galeev (ed.), *Shkola Kuzmy Petrova-Vodkina*, exh. cat., Galeev Gallery, Moscow, 2015.

SOVIET SPORTS AND GAMES AS PROPAGANDA

Mike O'Mahony (pp. 295–97)

1 James Riordan, *Sport, Politics and Communism*, Manchester, 1991, p. 25.
2 Mike O'Mahony, *Sport in the USSR: Physical Culture – Visual Culture*, London, 2006, p. 27.
3 Matisse visited Russia before the Revolution and many of his works, originally acquired by the collector Sergei Shchukin, remained on display in Leningrad (St Petersburg) throughout the inter-war years.
4 Reported in *Izvestiya*, 12 August 1928, p. 1.
5 O'Mahony 2006, p. 36.
6 After its display in New York, *Football Players* returned to Moscow and was displayed outside the Tretyakov Gallery. It remained there until the 1980s and, following recent restoration, is now a key work in the Tretyakov's collection.
7 Both works were purchased for the State and exhibited abroad over the next few years, *Sportswoman with a Shot-put* at the Venice Biennale in 1934 and *Girl in a Football Jersey* in the Soviet Pavilion at the Exposition Internationale des Arts et Techniques dans la Vie Moderne in Paris, 1937. See O'Mahony 2006, p. 40.
8 Natan Strugatsky, *Aleksandr Samokhvalov*, Leningrad, 1933, p. 21.
9 Samokhvalov had studied icon painting as a student at the Academy of Arts in Petrograd (St Petersburg). See Alexander Samokhvalov, *My Creative Journey*, Leningrad, 1977, p. 43.

SELECTED BIBLIOGRAPHY

Helen Adkins (ed.), *Naum Gabo and the Competition for the Palace of Soviets, Moscow 1931–1933*, exh. cat., Berlinische Galerie, Berlin, 1993

Konstantin Akinsha (ed.), *Russian Modernism: Cross-currents of German and Russian Art, 1907–1917*, Munich, London and New York, 2015

Anne Applebaum, *Gulag: A History of the Soviet Camps*, London, 2004

Simon Baier (ed.), *Tatlin: New Art for a New World*, exh. cat., Museum Tinguely, Basel, 2012

Achim Borchardt-Hume (ed.), *Malevich*, with contributions by Alexander Bouras, Iria Candela, Masha Chlenova, Nicholas Cullinan, Maria Gough, Maria Kokkori, Christina Lodder, John Milner, Fiontán Moran and Evgenia Petrova, exh. cat., Tate Modern, London, 2014

El'vira Borisovna Samietskaia (ed.), *Sovetsky Farfor: mezhdu oktiabr'skoi revolutitsiei i otechestvennii voinoi*, 3 tom., Moscow, 2014

John E. Bowlt, Nicoletta Misler and Evgenia Petrova, *The Russian Avant-garde: Siberia and the East*, exh. cat., Palazzo Strozzi, Florence, 2013

Joseph Brodsky, 'Catastrophes in the Air', in *Less Than One: Selected Essays*, Harmondsworth, 1986

Oksana Bulgakowa, *Sergei Eisenstein: A Biography*, Berlin and San Francisco, 1998/2001

Masha Chlenova, 'Kazimir Malevich', in 'Abstraction, 1910–1925: Eight Statements', *October*, 143, Winter 2013, pp. 19–27

Katerina Clark, *Petersburg, Crucible of Cultural Revolution*, Cambridge, MA, 1996

Catherine Cooke, *Russian Avant-garde Theories of Art, Architecture and the City*, London, 1995

Catherine Cooke and Igor Kazus, *Soviet Architectural Competitions 1920s–1930s*, London, 1992

Rainer Crone and David Moos, *Kazimir Malevich: The Climax of Disclosure*, Chicago, 1991

Robert William Davies, *The Soviet Collective Farm, 1929–30*, Cambridge, MA, 1980

Sarah Davies and James Harris, *Stalin's World: Dictating the Soviet World Order*, Princeton, 2014

James Donald, Anne Friedberg and Laura Marcus (eds), *Close Up, 1927–1933: Cinema and Modernism*, Princeton, 1998

Ilia Dorontchenkov (ed.), *Russian and Soviet Views of Modern Western Art, 1890s to Mid-1930s*, Berkeley, CA, 2009

Matthew Drutt, *Kazimir Malevich: Suprematism*, exh. cat., Solomon R. Guggenheim Museum, New York, 2003

Sergei Eisenstein, *Film Form: Essays in Film Theory*, New York, 1949

Sergei Eisenstein, *Selected Works*, vol. 4, *Beyond the Stars: The Memoirs of Sergei Eisenstein*, Richard Taylor (ed.), William Powell (trans.), London, 1995

Catherine Evtuhov, *The Cross and the Sickle: Sergei Bulgakov and the Fate of Russian Religious Philosophy, 1890–1920*, Ithaca, NY, 1997

Sheila Fitzpatrick, *Stalin's Peasants*, Oxford, 1996

René Fülop-Miller, *The Mind and Face of Bolshevism: An Examination of Cultural Life in Soviet Russia*, London, 1927

Naum Gabo, *Gabo: Constructions, Sculpture, Paintings, Drawings, and Engravings*, London, 1957

Ildar Galeev (ed.), *Shkola Kuzmy Petrova-Vodkina*, exh. cat., Galeev Gallery, Moscow, 2015

Aleksei Gan, *Constructivism* (1922), Christina Lodder (trans.), Barcelona, 2013

James von Geldern, *Bolshevik Festivals, 1917–1920*, Berkeley, CA, 1993

Igor Golomstock, *Totalitarian Art in the Soviet Union, the Third Reich, Fascist Italy and the People's Republic of China*, Robert Chandler (trans.), London, 1990

Maria Gough, *The Artist as Producer: Russian Constructivism in Revolution*, Berkeley, CA, 2005

Tamara Grodskova (ed.), *K. S. Petrov-Vodkin i XXI vek*, exh. cat., Radishchev State Art Museum, Saratov, 2008

Boris Groys, *The Total Art of Stalinism: Avant-garde, Aesthetic Dictatorship, and Beyond*, Charles Rougle (trans.), London, 2011

Nina Gurianova, *The Aesthetics of Anarchy: Art and Ideology in the Early Russian Avant-garde*, Berkeley, CA, 2012

Geoffrey Hosking, *A History of the Soviet Union*, revised edn, London, 1985

Ronald Hunt and Katja Waldén (eds), *Poetry Must Be Made by All! Transform the World!*, exh. cat., Moderna Museet, Stockholm, 1969

Pamela Kachurin, *Making Modernism Soviet: The Russian Avant-garde in the Early Soviet Era, 1918–1928*, Evanston, IL, 2013

Ernst Kallai, *Egyseg*, Vienna, 1922

Christina Kiaer, *Imagine No Possessions: The Socialist Objects of Russian Constructivism*, Cambridge, MA, and London, 2005

Christina Kiaer and Eric Naiman, *Everyday Life in Early Soviet Russia: Taking the Revolution Inside*, Bloomington, IN, 2006

Maria Kokkori, *A Historical Contextualization of Selected Paintings by Kazimir Malevich, Ivan Kliun and Liubov Popova c. 1905–1925*, PhD thesis, Courtauld Institute of Art, London, 2007

Evgeny Kovtun, *Russian Avant-garde*, Nick Cowling and Marie-Noelle Dumaz (trans.), Hoo, Rochester, 2007

Tamara Kudryavtseva, *Circling the Square: Avant-garde Porcelain from Revolutionary Russia*, London, 2004

Alexander N. Lavrentiev (ed.) with an introduction by John E. Bowlt, *Aleksandr Rodchenko: Experiments for the Future. Diaries, Essays, Letters, and Other Writings*, Jamey Gambrell (trans.), New York, 2005

Jay Leyda, *Kino: A History of Russian and Soviet Film*, London, 1950

W. Bruce Lincoln, *In War's Dark Shadow. The Russians before the Great War*, DeKalb, IL, 2003

El Lissitzky, *Russia: An Architecture for World Revolution*, Eric Dluhosch (trans.), London, 1970,

Nina Lobanov-Rostovsky, *Revolutionary Ceramics: Soviet Porcelain 1917–1927*, London, 1990

Christina Lodder, *Russian Constructivism*, New Haven and London, 1983

Christina Lodder, *Constructive Strands in Russian Art 1914–1937*, London, 2005

Christina Lodder and Martin Hammer, *Constructing Modernity: The Art and Career of Naum Gabo*, New Haven and London, 2000

Christina Lodder, Maria Kokkori and Maria Mileeva (eds), *Utopian Reality: Reconstructing Culture in Revolutionary Russia and Beyond*, Leiden and Boston, 2013

Dwight McDonald, *On Movies*, Englewood Cliffs, NJ, 1969

Kazimir Malevich, *Essays on Art, 1915–1933*, Troels Andersen (ed.), Xenia Glowacki-Prus and Arnold McMillin (trans.), Copenhagen, 1968

Nadezhda Mandelstam, *Hope Against Hope: A Memoir*, Max Hayward (trans.), London, 1975

Jean-Hubert Martin (ed.), *Malévitch: œuvres de Casimir Severinovitch Malévitch, 1878–1935, avec en appendice les œuvres de Nicolaï Mikhaïlovitch Souiétine, 1897–1954*, reconstructions by Poul Pedersen, Paris, 1980

John Milner, *Kazimir Malevich and the Art of Geometry*, New Haven and London, 1996

John Milner and Elena Sudakova (eds), *Re-constructivism*, London, 2013

Sidney Monas and Jennifer Greene Krupala (eds), *The Diaries of Nikolay Punin: 1904–1953*, Jennifer Greene Kupala (trans.), Austin, TX, 1999

Natalia Murray, *The Unsung Hero of the Russian Avant-garde: The Life and Times of Nikolay Punin*, Leiden and Boston, 2012

Museum Jean Tinguely, *0.10, Ivan Puni: Works from the Herman Berninger Collection, Zurich and Photographs of the Russian Revolution from the Collection Ruth and Peter Herzog*, Basel, 2003

Andrei Nakov, *Kasimir Malevich, Catalogue raisonné*, Paris, 2002

Andrei Nakov, *Kasimir Malevich*, Paris, 2007

Mike O'Mahony, *Sport in the USSR: Physical Culture – Visual Culture*, London, 2006

Evgenia Petrova et al., *Petrov-Vodkin's Circle*, exh. cat., State Russian Museum, St Petersburg, 2015
T. Pozdnyakova and N. Popova, *Under the Roof of the Fountain House*, St Petersburg, 2005

Ada Raev and Isabel Wünsche, *Kursschwankungen: russische Kunst im Wertesystem der europäischen Moderne*, Berlin, 2007
Kliment Redko, *Diaries, Memoirs, Articles*, Moscow, 1974
James Riordan, *Sport, Politics and Communism*, Manchester, 1991
Margit Rowell and Deborah Wye, *The Russian Avant-garde Book, 1910–1934*, exh. cat., The Museum of Modern Art, New York, 2002

Alexander Samokhvalov, *My Creative Journey*, Leningrad, 1977
Simon Sebag Montefiore, *Stalin: The Court of the Red Tsar*, London, 2014
Robert Service, *Lenin: A Biography*, London, 2010
Jane Sharp, *Russian Modernism between East and West: Natal'ia Goncharova and the Moscow Avant-garde*, Cambridge, 2005
Aleksandra S. Shatskikh, *Vitebsk: The Life of Art*, New Haven and London, 2007
Aleksandra S. Shatskikh and Marian Schwartz, *Black Square: Malevich and the Origin of Suprematism*, New Haven and London, 2012
Kirill Sokolov, 'Extracts from "Euclidean Space". The Book by K. S. Petrov-Vodkin (1878–1939)', *Leonardo*, Paris, 1978, vol. 11, pp. 140–4
Andrew Spira, *The Avant-garde Icon*, Aldershot, 2008
Richard Stites, *Revolutionary Dreams: Utopian Vision and Experimental Life in the Russian Revolution*, Oxford, 1989
Natan Strugatsky, *Aleksandr Samokhvalov*, Leningrad, 1933

Nikolai Taraboukine, *Le Dernier tableau*, A. B. Nakov (ed.), Paris, 1972
Richard Taylor and Ian Christie (eds), *The Film Factory: Russian and Soviet Cinema in Documents, 1896–1939*, London, 1988
Margarita Tupitsyn, *Gustav Klutsis and Valentina Kulagina: Photography and Montage after Constructivism*, New York and Gottingen, 2004
Margarita Tupitsyn (ed.), *Rodchenko and Popova: Defining Constructivism*, exh. cat., Tate Modern, London, 2009

Irina A. Vakar and Tatiana N. Mikhienko (eds), *Kazimir Malevich: Letters, Documents, Memoirs, Criticism*, 2 vols, London, 2015
Solomon Volkov, *The Magical Chorus: A History of Russian Culture from Tolstoy to Solzhenitsyn*, Antonina Bouis (trans.), New York, 2009

Alex Ward (ed.), *Power to the People: Early Soviet Propaganda Posters in The Israel Museum, Jerusalem*, Aldershot, 2008
Robert Warshow, *The Immediate Experience*, Garden City, NY, 1962
Nicolas Werth, Karel Bartošek, Jean-Louis Panné, Jean-Louis Margolin, Andrzej Paczkowski and Stéphane Courtois, *The Black Book of Communism: Crimes, Terror, Repression*, Cambridge, MA, 1999
Robert C. Williams, *Artists in Revolution: Portraits of the Russian Avant-garde, 1905–1925*, Bloomington, IN, 1977
Viktor Woroszylski, *The Life of Mayakovsky*, Boleslaw Taborski (trans.), London, 1972
Isabel Wünsche, *The Organic School of the Russian Avant-garde*, Farnham, 2015

Alexei Yurchak, 'Bodies of Lenin: The Hidden Science of Communist Sovereignty', *Representations*, 129, University of California, Winter 2015, pp. 116–57

LENDERS TO THE EXHIBITION

ASTRAKHAN
The Astrakhan State Art Gallery

IVANOVO
The Burilin Ivanovo Museum of Local History

LONDON
GRAD: Gallery for Russian Arts and Design
Tate

MOSCOW
The Central Armed Forces Museum of the Russian Federation
JSC Trekhgornaya Manufactura
The State Historical Museum
State Tretyakov Gallery

ST PETERSBURG
The Russian Academy of Fine Arts Museum
The St Petersburg State Museum of Theatre and Music
The State Hermitage Museum
The State Museum of the History of St Petersburg
The State Russian Museum

TULA
The Association of Historical and Regional Art

The Petr Aven Collection
Alex Lachmann Collection, London
Collection of Vladimir Tsarenkov

and others who wish to remain anonymous

PHOTOGRAPHIC ACKNOWLEDGEMENTS

All works of art are reproduced by kind permission of the owners. Every attempt has been made to trace copyright holders. We apologise for any inadvertent infringement and invite appropriate rights holders to contact us. Specific acknowledgements are as follows:

PHOTOGRAPHIC CREDITS

Amsterdam, © Stedelijk Museum: fig. 63

© Petr Aven Collection: cats 2, 3, 4, 5, 6, 16, 28, 29, 30, 64, 97, 98, 99, 100, 101, 102, 103, 104, 105, 106, 119, 120, 121, 122, 124, 125, 126, 127, 163, 164, 165, 166, 167, 168, 195, 197

Berlin, © Deutsche Kinemathek: figs 19, 21, 23

© 2009 Christie's Images Limited: cat. 139

Florence, © 2017. Photo Scala: figs 111 (courtesy of the Ministero Beni e Att. Culturali); 64 (BPK, Berlin. Photo: Michael Herling / Aline Gwose); 71, 76, 98 (Photo: Fine Art Images / Heritage Images); 25, 46, 110 (Digital image, The Museum of Modern Art, New York)

Photo © GRAD: cat. 179

© Alex Lachmann Collection: cats 11, 12, 34, 35, 37, 38, 40, 41, 42, 43, 59, 66, 67, 68, 69, 70, 73, 74, 76, 130, 131, 133, 174, 177, 180, 181, 184, 186, 187, 208, 209, 210, 212, 213, 215; 25, 39, 61, 71, 72, 75, 123, 145, 160, 162, 169, 176, 178, 185, 206, 207, 211 (Photo © Alex Fox at Roy Fox Fine Art); 36, 132, 175, 182, 214 (Photo © Patrick Schwarz)

London, © akg-images: figs 5; 3 (Photo: Elizaveta Becker); 35 (Pictures From History); 55 (Picture Alliance / Friedrich-Schiller-Universität, Jena)

London, © Alamy Stock Photo: figs 1, 7, 40, 48 (Fine Art Images / Heritage Image Partnership Ltd / Stock Photo); 30, 34, 54 (Heritage Image Partnership Ltd); 31 (World History Archive); 39 (INTERFOTO)

London, Bridgeman Images: fig. 56

London, Kobal Collection: figs 20; 27 (SOVKINO)

London, Marx Memorial Library: fig. 70

London, Mary Evans Picture Library / SOVKINO / Ronald Grant Archive: fig. 113

London, Richard Saltoun Gallery: figs 6, 45, 51

London, © Slava Katamidze Collection / Hulton Archive / Getty Images: fig. 42

London, © Sputnik Images: fig. 2

London, © Tate, London 2017: cat. 80

London, © topfoto.co.uk / SCRSS: fig. 26

Photo © Henry Milner: cat. 183

Moscow, © State Tretyakov Gallery: figs 43, 77, 78, 79, 80, 81, 82, 83, 102, 108, 112; cats 7, 8, 10, 13, 15, 18, 24, 26, 27, 47, 48, 50, 52, 55, 56, 85, 96, 107, 108, 110, 112, 117, 134, 135, 136, 137, 142, 144, 147, 151, 193, 196, 199, 202

Moscow, The Russian State Archive of Literature and Arts: fig. 93

Moscow, The Schusev State Museum of Architecture: figs 47, 94, 96, 99

Moscow, State Central Museum of Contemporary History of Russia: figs 8, 28, 44, 100

Paris, courtesy DIGARD AUCTION: figs 72, 73 (neg. at Dalbey Photographic Collection at the University of Denver. University Art Collections, Denver, Colo.), 74

Paris, Lobster Films: figs 29, 32, 33, 38

Private collection: fig. 97

© Private collection. Photography: Robert McKeever: cat. 77

Riga, Latvian National Museum of Art. Photo Normunds Brasliņš: fig. 107

RussianArchives.com: figs 9, 14, 15 (The Russian State Film and Photo Archives)

St Petersburg, The National Library of Russia: fig. 62

St Petersburg, Punin Family Archive: figs 11, 12, 49, 57, 61, 65; cat. 216

St Petersburg, Photograph © The State Hermitage Museum / Vladimir Terebenin: cat. 78

St Petersburg, © 2017, State Russian Museum: figs 13, 16, 17, 18, 58, 60, 66, 67, 69, 76, 84, 85, 86, 87, 88, 89, 90, 91, 92, 101, 103, 104, 105, 106; cats 1, 20, 21, 23, 44, 45, 46, 49, 51, 53A, 53B, 54, 58, 60, 62, 63, 79, 81, 82, 83, 84, 86, 87, 88, 89, 90, 91, 92, 93, 94, 109, 111, 113, 114, 115, 116, 118, 128, 140, 143, 159, 170, 171, 172, 173, 188, 189, 190, 191, 192, 194, 198, 203

© Provided with assistance from the State Museum and Exhibition Center ROSIZO: cats 9 (The State Historical Museum, Moscow); 14, 31, 32, 129 (The Burilin Ivanovo Museum of Local History); 17, 19, 138, 141 (The Russian Academy of Fine Arts Museum, St Petersburg); 22, 205 (The Astrakhan State Art Gallery); 33 (JSC Trekhgornaya Manufactura, Moscow); 57, 200 (The Central Armed Forces Museum of the Russian Federation, Moscow); 65 (The St Petersburg State Museum of Theatre and Music); 146, 148, 149, 150, 152, 153, 154, 155, 156, 157, 158, 161 (The State Museum of the History of St Petersburg); 201 (The Association of Historical and Regional Art, Tula)

© Collection of V. Tsarenkov: fig. 68; cats 95, 204

Wiesbaden, © Fine Art Images, Germany: figs 4, 22, 24, 36, 37, 41, 50, 52, 53, 59, 75, 95, 102, 109

INDEX WITH BIOGRAPHIES OF ARTISTS

Biographies by Lauren Warner, index by Hilary Bird

All references are to page numbers; those in **bold** type indicate catalogue plates, and those in *italic* type indicate essay illustrations.

2 Stenberg 2 *see* Stenberg, Vladimir and Georgi
4 Arts Society (4 Iskusstva) 25, 29, 47, 48, 50, 273
'5 × 5 = 25', Moscow (1921) 46
XIV Years of the Red Army **248**
1905 Revolution 102
1932 anniversary exhibition *see* 'Fifteen Years of Artists of the Russian Soviet Republic'

Academy of Art, Petrograd 44, 75, 277
Academy for the History of Material Culture 276
Acmeist movement 128, 275
ADAMOVICH, MIKHAIL MIKHAILOVICH (1884–1947). Painter/ceramicist. Studied at Stroganov School of Arts and Industry (1894–1907), decorative art on scholarship in Italy (1907–09). Designed agitprop decorations for Pokrovsky Square, Petrograd (1918). Served in Red Army (1919–21). Worked at State Porcelain Factory (1918–19; 1921–23), Volkhov Ceramic Factory (1924–27), Dulevo Porcelain Factory (1937).
Cup with Leon Trotsky's Portrait **61**
Plate with Depiction of the Second Interim Wooden Mausoleum of Vladimir Lenin **60**
Additional Bread Coupon for the Member of the Family of the Red Army Soldier **241**
Adlivankin, Samuil 46
The Adventures of Oktyabrina (film) 34, *34*
Advertisement 'Of Course, Cream-soda!' **245**
Aelita (film) 19, 34, *34*
Affirmers of the New Art (UNOVIS) 18, 44, 149, 153, 231
agriculture, collectivisation of 48, 49, 153, 185–87
Akhmatova, Anna 127, 129–31, *130*, **134**, **138**, 277
AKhRR *see* Association of Artists of Revolutionary Russia
Alexander II, Tsar 183
Alexander Nevsky 213, *213*
Alexander Nevsky (film) 37
Alexandra, Tsarina 41
Alexandrov, Grigori 33, 37
October 48
All-Arts Union 41
All-Russia Collegium of Museum Affairs 42
All-Russia Congress of Trade Unions 44
All-Russian Agricultural Exhibition, Moscow (1923) 184, **199**
All-Russian Congress of Workers, Peasants and Cossack Deputies (1918) 43
All-Russian Congress of Soviets 41, 42, 45
All-Russian Museum Conference, Petrograd (1919) 44
All-Russian Proletkult Conference (1918) 43
'All-Union Agricultural Exhibition', Moscow (1923) 273
All-Union Association of Proletarian Architects (VOPRA) 259
All-Union Congress of Soviets, Second (1924) 47
Alone (film) 37
Alpert, Max
Iskra Concert 184
ALTMAN, NATAN ISAEVICH (1889–1970). Painter/graphic artist/sculptor/designer. Studied at Odessa School of Art (1901–07), Free Russian Academy, Paris (1910–12). Major designer of agitprop decorations: Palace Square, Petrograd for first anniversary of Revolution (1918), then responsible for all Petrograd decorations (1919). Taught at Department of Visual Arts, People's Commissariat of Enlightenment, Petrograd (1918–21).
general references 17, 41, 47
Russia. Labour **85**
Andreev, Nikolai 47
Angelico, Fra 274
ANNENKOV, YURY PAVLOVICH (1889–1974). Painter/draughtsman/stage designer. Studied at Savely Zeidenberg's studio (1908–09), Yan Tsyonglinsky's studio (1909–11), Maurice Denis's studio, others, in Paris (1911–13). Returned to St Petersburg, worked as stage designer, including collaborations with Meyerhold; illustrated books and magazines (1910–20s). Founder member, Society of Easel Painters (1925).
general reference 48
Portrait of the Theatre Director Vsevolod Meyerhold **136**
anniversary exhibition (1932) *see* 'Fifteen Years of Artists of the Russian Soviet Republic'
architecture 154, 257–61, **264–69**
Arkadiev, Mikhail 28
Arkhangelsk 43
Arkhipov, Abram 25, 46
Arsenal (film) 34
Art of the Commune (newspaper) 44
Art Deco 296
'Art in the Epoch of Imperialism', Leningrad (1931) 154
'Art of the Great Industrial Bourgeoisie on the Eve of the Proletarian Revolution', Moscow (1932) 50
Art Historical Committee 41
Artel of Ancient Painting 47
Article 58 48
Arts and Crafts movement 183
Arvatov, Boris 16–17
ASNOVA *see* Association of New Architects
Association of Artists of Revolutionary Russia (AKhRR) 25, 29–30, 46, 47, 48, 153
Association of New Architects (ASNOVA) 257, 259
'Association of New Trends in Art', Petrograd (1922) 46
Association of the Workers of Revolutionary Posters (ORPP) 50
Atele (journal) 295
Atheist at the Factory Bench (journal) 295–96
Avraamov, Arseney
Symphony of Sirens 17, *17*

Bakhrushin, Aleksei 211
BAKSHEEV, VASILY NIKOLAEVICH (1862–1958). Painter. Studied at Moscow School of Painting, Sculpture and Architecture (1878–88), taught there (1890s–1918). Academician (1913); Soviet Academician (1947). Member, Association of Artists of Revolutionary Russia (1922–27); founder member, Association of Realist Artists (1927). Order of Lenin (1953, 1958); People's Artist of the USSR (1956).
Blue Spring **222**
Bakst, Léon 273
Baku 17
Ballets Russes 183
Balmont, Konstantin 129
banners 56
BARNET, BORIS VASILIEVICH (1902–1965). Director/actor/screenwriter. Studied at Moscow School of Painting, Sculpture and Architecture (1918), Central Military School for Physical Education (1923), in Lev Kuleshov's film workshops (1923). Director at various studios (from 1925). Artist of Merit of the RSFSR (1935). Stalin Prize (1948). Artist of Merit of the Ukrainian SSR (1951).
general references 34, 35
The House on Trubnaya Street 49
Barr, Alfred H. 20, 34
Baskerville, Charles 234
The Battleship Potemkin (film) 32, 35, 47
Bauer, Evgeni 34
Bauhaus 18, 46, 150
Bed and Sofa (film) 35
Belorussia (Belarus) 230–31
Bely, Andrei 274
Benois, Alexandre 41
Berdiaev, Nikolai 129
Berkeley, Busby 37
Berlin 15, 18, 33, 46, 129, 150
Bezhin Meadow (film) 37
Bible 102
Bilibin, Ivan 41
Blavatsky, Helena 274
Blok, Alexander 46, 128, 129, **140**
'The Intelligentsia and the Revolution' 101
'The Twelve' 101, 102
Blok group 150
Bogdanov, Alexander 42, 48
Bogoyavlensky, Fyodor Pavlovich 213
Bolshevik Military Revolutionary Committee 42
Bolsheviks *see* Communists
Bolshoi Theatre, Moscow 48, *101*
Borisov-Musatov, Viktor 274
'Bourgeois Art in Crisis', Moscow (1931) 154
Brest-Litovsk Treaty (1918) 42
Brik, Osip 17
BRODSKY, ISAAK IZRAILOVICH (1884–1939). Painter/graphic artist/collector. Studied at Odessa School of Art (1896–1902) and St Petersburg Academy of Arts (1902–08). Agitprop designer for Petrograd (1918). Joined Association of Artists of Revolutionary Russia (1924). Director of Academy of Arts in Leningrad (1934–39). Known for paintings of revolutionary events and leaders.
general references 15, 16, 46, 47, 273
Lenin in Smolny 15, **65**
Portrait of Alexander Kerensky 22
Portrait of Joseph Stalin 15, *28*, **70**
Shock-worker from Dneprostroi 77–78, **80**, 187
Vladimir Lenin and a Demonstration 25, *56*, **64**
Brodsky, Joseph 25
Bruni, Lev 25, 41, 47
BRUSKETTI-MITROKHINA, ALISA YAKOVLEVNA (1872–1942). Sculptor/ceramicist. Studied at Moscow School of Painting, Sculpture and Architecture (1901–05). Worked at Savva Mamontov's ceramics studio, Moscow (until 1905). Taught at commercial school in Tver (1905–09), Society for the Encouragement of the Arts (1909–15). Invited to Imperial Porcelain Factory by Evgeny Lanceray (1915).
Bourgeois Woman Selling Her Wares **246**
Bubnov, Andrei 27, 48
Bukharin, Nikolai 48, 49, 57
BULANOV, DMITRI ANATOLIEVICH (1898–1942). Graphic artist. Studied at Free State Art Studios (c. 1918–20). Head, department of art and agitprop, Russian Telegraph Agency, Nikolaev region (1920–22). Head of Art Department, *Life of Art* magazine (1923). Designed and illustrated children's books (1924–26). Worked at Leningrad Proletkult, Department of Visual Arts (1926–32).
Advertisements in the Tram Are Read by Millions of People Every Day 48
Bulgakov, Sergei 129, 209–11, 212–13
A Light not Crepuscular: Observations and Speculations 211
Bulla, Viktor
The Shooting of Demonstrators on Nevsky Prospect, Petrograd 40
Bunin, Ivan 129
BURYLIN SERGEY PETROVICH (1876–1942). Textile artist. Born into a family of engravers and worked in Ivanovo-Voznesensk. Received no specialist arts education and began working aged 17 at Great Ivanovo-Voznesensk Textile Mill. With factories throughout Ivanovo printing fabrics from his designs, he was a pioneer and innovator of Soviet textile art *Tractor*.
general references 185, **202**
By the Law (film) 34
Bytie (Being) group 25, 46, 48

Calendar for 1922 after a Drawing by Boris Kustodiev **242**
'Case of the Petrograd Military Organisation' 128
Cathedral of Christ the Saviour, Moscow 50, 154, 261
Catherine the Great, Empress 184
Central Asia 276
ceramics 21, **58–62**, **86–87**, 102, 153–54, **176–77**, 184, **198**, **200–01**, *228*, 231, *231*, **246–47**
Cézanne, Paul 17, 29
Chagall, Bella 18, 230, 231
CHAGALL, MARC ZAKHAROVICH (1887–1985). Painter/graphic artist/designer/sculptor/ceramicist/writer. Studied at Yehuda Pen's studio, Vitebsk (1903/04–06), and in St Petersburg at Society for the Encouragement of the Arts (1907), Zvantseva School (1908–09). Left Russia permanently (1922). Became French citizen (1937). Powerful colourist and pioneer of modern art with corresponding international reputation.
general references 18, 44, 48, 75, 127, 184, 230–31
Promenade **220**, 230
The Traveller (Forward!) 18, 149
Window over a Garden **221**
Chaikov, Iosif
Football Players 296–97, *297*
Chaliapin, Fedor 41, 129, *129*
Chapaev (film) 37
Chaplin, Charlie 34
CHASHNIK, ILYA GRIGORIEVICH (1902–1929). Painter/graphic artist/designer. Studied at Yehuda Pen's studio, Vitebsk (1913–18), State Free Art Studios (1918), Vitebsk Art School under Chagall, then Malevich (1919–22). Joined Affirmers of the New Art (1920). Strong adherent of Suprematism. Worked at State Porcelain Factory on Suprematist compositions at Nikolai Punin's request (1923–24).
general references 44, 149, 150, 154, 231
Plate 'Grey-green Cross' **177**
Suprematism **175**
Cheka 42, 43, 46
CHEKHONIN, SERGEI VASILEVICH (1878–1936). Graphic artist/ceramicist/painter/stage designer. Studied at Society for the Encouragement of the Arts (1896–97); Princess Maria Tenisheva's art studio (1897–1900). Worked at Savva Mamontov's Moscow ceramics studio (1902–07). Renowned illustrator in pre-revolutionary Russia. Artistic director, State Porcelain Factory (1918–23; 1925–27). Director, Volkhov Ceramic Factory (1923–24). Immigrated to Paris (1928).
general reference 21
Great Star with a Sheaf of Corn 'Who Is Not With Us Is Against Us' **200**
Chief Committee for Political Education 44
Christianity 209, 258
Chukovsky, Kornei 129
Chupiatov, Leonid 273, 277
Cine-eye (film) 35, *36*
Circle of Artists group 25, 29, 48
Civil War (1917–22) 16, 24, 25, 33, 37, 42–47, 77, 101, 129, 184, 209, 230, 257
Class War 48
Close Up (journal) 34
Cold War 297
collages 102
Comintern Congress, 2nd (1920) **58–59**
Commemoration of the Flight of a Russian Dirigible from Moscow to New York Piloted by Three Soviet Airmen **303**
'Commission for the Immortalisation of Lenin's Memory' 57
'Commission for the Organisation of Lenin's Funeral' 57
'Commission for the Preservation of Lenin's Body' 57
Commission for the Protection of Art Valuables 41
Committee for Art Industries 154
Communism
and avant-garde artists 24
Bolsheviks come to power 23
control of art 23–25, 28
and film-making 35
importance of art to 15–21, 55–56, 127–28
use of propaganda 23
Congress of Soviets of the USSR, First (1922) 47
Constituent Assembly 42
Constructivists 16–17, 104, 105, 295
and the 1932 exhibition 31
and architecture 257–58, 259
exhibitions 18
and film-making 35
'Realistic Manifesto' 44
and Socialist Realism 20
Cossacks 55
Crimea 45, 47
Cubists 102
Cubo-Futurists 34, 185, 273
Cultural Revolution 19–21, 48
Cyrus the Great, King of Persia 259

Dada 18
DANKO, NATALIA YAKOVLEVNA (1892–1942). Ceramicist/sculptor. Studied at Stronganov School of Arts and Industry (1900–02); Vilnius State Art School and Yalmar Yanson's studio (1906–08). Worked at studios of Maria Dillon and Leonid Shervud (1908–09), as Pavel Kuznetsov's assistant at Imperial Porcelain Factory (from 1914). Director, sculpture workshops at State Porcelain Factory (1919–41).
general references 21, 297
Dancer **198**
On Guard: Women's Watch **198**
Woman Embroidering a Banner **62**
Woman Worker Making a Speech **246**

Decorative Institute, Leningrad 44, 48
DEINEKA [DEYNEKA], ALEXANDER ALEXANDROVICH
(1899–1969). Painter/graphic artist/designer. Studied at Kharkov Art School (1915–17), Higher State Artistic and Technical Workshops, Moscow (1921–25). Founder member, Society of Easel Painters (1925). Member, later Vice-president, St Petersburg Academy of Arts (1947, 1962–66). Awarded Hero of Socialist Labour (1969). Often focused on interplay between people and space.
general references 16, 20, 25, 29, 49, 50, 232, 233, 273, 295–96
Construction of New Workshops **83**
The Defence of Petrograd 15–16, 103, 105, **120–21**
Football **300**
Let's Mechanise Donbass **84**
Ping-Pong **245**
Race **298**
Study for The Defence of Petrograd 104
Textile Workers 77, **82**
Who is Winning? **302**
DEMKOV, NIKOLAI SEMENOVICH
(1897–1959). Textile artist. Received no specialist arts education. Participated in exhibitions (from 1928). Worked as an artist at the cotton mills in Strunino (1912–34) and Karabanovo (1934–58). Member, Association of Artists of Revolutionary Russia (1929–32). Designed textiles for dresses and headscarves.
Kerchief with Portrait of Lenin in the Centre and Trotsky's Corner Portrait Cut Out **67**
Deni, Viktor 50
Denisov, Vasily 273
DENISOVSKY, NIKOLAI FEDOROVICH
(1901–1981). Painter/graphic artist. Studied at Stroganov School of Arts and Industry (1911–17), Free State Art Studios (1918–19). Created posters for Russian Telegraph Agency (1919–20). Illustrator for Moscow and Leningrad satirical magazines (1920s). Founder member, Society of Easel Painters (1925). Taught at Higher State Artistic and Technical Institute (1928–30).
Cast Iron Output **84**
Department of Visual Arts *see* IZO
Derain, André 43
The Devil's Wheel (film) 34
Diaghilev, Sergei 183
Diagram 'In One Year a Mature Man Consumes Approximately...' **239**
Diagram 'The Quantity of Food for Children in Petrograd' **239**
Diagram 'The Quantity of Products Given to the Citizens in Exchange for Coupons...' **238**
Dickinson, Thorold 34
Dinamo Stadium, Moscow 257, 296, **305**
Dish 'Moulding Workshop' **87**
Dobychina, Nadezhda 27
Dr Mabuse the Gambler (film) 35
Donbas region 37
Donskoy Monastery 213
Dostoyevsky, Fyodor 209
DOVZHENKO, ALEXANDER PETROVICH
(1894–1956). Director/screenwriter. Studied at Glukhov Teachers' Institute (1911–14), Kiev Commercial University (1917–20), Kiev Academy of Arts (1918), in Erich Heckel's studio in Munich (1921–23). Worked as secretary of trade commission, Ukrainian consulate, Berlin (1922). Directorial debut in Ukrainian cinema (1926). Order of Lenin (1935).
general references 33–34
Earth 46
Drevin, Alexander 47, 230, 235
Dulevo Porcelain Factory, Moscow **60**
Duma 41
DYMSHITS-TOLSTAYA, SOFYA ISAAKOVNA
(1889–1963). Painter/graphic artist. Studied in St Petersburg at Sergei Yegornov's studio (1906–07), Zvantseva Art School (1908–10); in Paris, Charles Guérin's studio (1910–11). Head of Publications, Department of Visual Arts, People's Commissariat of Enlightenment, Moscow (late 1920s). Enjoyed experimenting with glass: 'being flat, it is simultaneously three-dimensional...'
general references 103, 230, 231–32
Propaganda Glass 'Labour is the Foundation of the RSFSR' **108**, 232
Propaganda Glass 'Peace to the Sheds, War on the Palaces' 103, **107**, 232
Propaganda Glass 'Workers of the World, Unite!' **106**, 232
Woman Agitator 232, **249**
Dzerzhinsky, Felix 42, 43, 46

Earth (film) 46
Egypt 259
EISENSTEIN, SERGEI MIKHAILOVICH
(1898–1948). Director/screenwriter/designer/theorist. Studied at Petrograd Institute of Civil Engineering (1915–18); under Meyerhold at State Higher Directors' Workshops, Moscow (1921–22). Joined Proletkult (1920). Directed first film, with Vertov's assistance (1923). Taught at State Institute of Cinema/All-Soviet State Institute of Cinema (from 1932). Order of Lenin (1939).
general references 16, 17, 33, 34, 35, 37, 49, 131, **142**
The Battleship Potemkin 32, 33, 35, 47
The General Line 33, 37, 151
October 33, 37, 43, 48
The Strike 34, 35, 35
Ekaterinburg 42, 43
The End of St Petersburg (film) 33
Ender, B. 25
Ender, K. 25
Ender, M. 25
Enthusiasm (film) 37
ERMLER, FRIDRIKH MARKOVICH [BRESLAV, VLADIMIR MARKOVICH]
(1898–1967). Director/screenwriter. First used his pseudonym as a spy behind Russian-German frontline (during 1918–21). Studied at Leningrad Institute for Screen Arts (1923–24). Founder member, experimental cinema workshop (1924). Stalin Prize (1941, 1946). Grand Prix, Cannes Festival People's Artist of the USSR (1948).
general references 35, *312*
Ermolaeva, Vera 25, 149, 231
Evenbakh, Evgenia 277
'Experimental Comprehensive Exhibition of the Art of the Capitalist Era', Moscow (1931) 50
Experimental Laboratory, State Russian Museum, Leningrad 50
'Exposition Internationale des Arts Décoratifs et Industriels Modernes', Paris (1925) 18, *19*, 35
Exter, Alexandra 15, 34, 46, 48
The Extraordinary Adventures of Mr West in the Land of the Bolsheviks (film) 33, *33*, 34

Factory of the Eccentric Actors (FEKS) 34, 37
Falconet, Etienne Maurice 184
The Fall of the Romanov Dynasty (film) 35
famine (1921–22) 46, 184
The Famine in Russia (film) 33
February Revolution (1917) 23, 41, 55, 56, 102
Federation of Groups of Soviet Artists 49
Fedotov, Georgy 101
FEKS group *see* Factory of the Eccentric Actors
Feshin, Nikolai 127
Portrait of Anatoly Lunacharsky *128*
'Fifteen Years of Artists of the Russian Soviet Republic', Leningrad (1932) 15, 19, 21, 25, *26*, *27–31*, *28–29*, 50, 150, 151, 153, 154, 235, 297
Film Truth (newsreel series) 34, 35
Film Weekly (newsreel series) 34
films 33–37, 77, 131
FILONOV, PAVEL NIKOLAEVICH
(1883–1941). Painter/graphic artist/poet. Studied at Society for the Encouragement of the Arts (1897–1901), Lev Dmitriev-Kavkazsky's studio (1903–08), St Petersburg Academy of Arts (1908–10). Founder member, Union of Youth (1910). Inventor, Analytical Realism (from 1912). Established Collective of Masters of Analytical Art (1925). Key figure of Russian modernism.
general references 30–31, *30*, *47*, *48*, *104*, *105*, *233–35*, *274*, *277*
Collective Farm Worker 187, **193**
Formula of the Petrograd Proletariat *30*, **116**, 187, 234
GOELRO (State Commission for the Electrification of Russia) 235, *235*
Heads (Human in the World) **117**
Peasant Family 234, *234*
Portrait of Joseph Stalin 235, *235*
Tractor Workshop at the Putilov Factory *30*, **80**, 235
Finland station, Petrograd 41, 48
'First German Exhibition', Moscow (1924) 47
'First Russian Art Exhibition', Berlin (1922) 18
'First State Free Exhibition of Works of Art', Petrograd (1919) 44
First Workers Group of Constructivists 16
First Workers' Spartakiad, Moscow 296, *296*
First World War 15, 23, 33, 41, 42, 44, 55, 209, 257, 275–76
First Writers' Congress (1934) 101
Five-Year Plans 27, 37, 48, 50, 273
fizkultura (physical culture) 295–97
Florensky, Father Pavel 209–11, 212–13
Food Coupon of the 2nd Category for July in the name of Felkergam A. **241**
food coupons **238**, **240–41**
Food Industry Workers 56
Formalism 153, 230, 273
Forsh, Olga 274
Fragment of an Empire (film) 51, *312*
Free State Art Studios (SVOMAS) 43, 44, 277
Freedom of Arts 41
FRIDLYAND, SEMYON OSIPOVICH [SIMON FRIDLAND]
(1905–1964). Photographer. Self-taught, then studied at State Institute of Cinematography (1930). Worked as a photographic laboratory assistant at *Ogoniok* and began taking photographs (1925). Professional photojournalist for Unionfoto agency (later Soyuzfoto) (1930–32), *USSR in Construction* (1932) and *Pravda* (from 1933). Appointed head of *Ogoniok* photographic department (1932).
Construction at the Cherepovets Factory: Welding 79, *79*
On the Stalin Collective Farm 184
Fulöp-Miller, René 23
Futurists 24, 34, 44, 183

Gabo, Naum 76
'Realistic Manifesto' 44
Galerie Van Diemen, Berlin 18
Gan, Alexei 16, 49, 257
Gardin, Vladimir 34
Gelfreikh, Vladimir 261
The General Line (film) 33, 37, 151
Gerasimov, Alexander
Lenin on the Tribune 25, *28*
Giambologna 297
Gilded Rot (film) 35
GINKhUK *see* State Institute of Artistic Culture
GINZBURG, MOISEI YAKOVLEVICH
(1892–1946). Architect/theorist/urban planner. Studied abroad, primarily at Accademia di Belle Arti, Milan (graduated 1914), Riga Technical University (Moscow) (1914–17). Founder member, Association of New Architects (1925). Taught at Moscow Higher State Artistic and Technical Workshops (1920s). Board member, Union of Soviet Architects (1932). Academician, Soviet Academy of Architecture (1939).
general references 49, 154, 257, 258, 261
Giotto 274, 277
The Girl with the Hat-box (film) 35
GLAVISKUSSTVO 48
Glavpolitprosvet 44
Glumov's Diary (film) 34
'Godless Five-Year Plan' 50
GOELRO *see* State Commission for the Electrification of Russia
Golomstock, Igor 23
Golopolosov, Boris
Lenin is the Leader of the Proletariat 57
GOLOVIN, ALEXANDER YAKOVLEVICH
(1863–1930). Stage designer/painter. Studied at Moscow School of Painting, Sculpture and Architecture (1881–90); in Paris, Jacques-Emile Blanche's studio (1889), Witte studio (1897). Began producing theatre designs (1898). Adviser to Imperial Theatres (1902–17), also became principal designer (1908). Stage designs for Vsevolod Meyerhold and Sergei Diaghilev (from 1908). Academician (1912).
Portrait of the Theatre Director Vsevolod Meyerhold **137**
GOLUBEV, ANDREY GRIGORIEVICH
(1884–1943). Textile artist. Studied at Ivanovo-Voznesensk Drawing School (1901). Worked at Vitova and Sons Factory, Gandurin and Brothers Factory (prior to 1917), Central Art Studios at Great Ivanovo-Voznesensk Textile Mill (from 1922), Sosnevsk Amalgamated Mills (from 1931), Tashkent Cotton Mill (from 1934).
Red Spinner **88**
GOLUBKINA, ANNA SEMENOVNA
(1864–1927). Sculptor. Studied at A. Gunst's studio (1889–90), Moscow School of Painting, Sculpture and Architecture (1891–94), St Petersburg Academy of Arts (1894); in Paris, Académie Colarossi (1895–96), also studied independently and advised by Auguste Rodin (1897–99). Founder member, Society of Russian Sculptors (1925). One of Russia's premier sculptors in Paris.
Birch Tree **224**
Goncharov, Andrei 29
Goncharova, Natalia 48, 183
Mystical Images of War 15
Gorky, Maxim 41, 46, 101, 129, **143**, 213
Gosbank, Moscow 259, *259*
Gosplan 45
GPU 46
GRABAR, IGOR EMMANUILOVICH
(1871–1960). Painter/collector/museum director/art historian. Studied law at University of St Petersburg (1889–93). Later studied at St Petersburg Academy of Arts (1894–96), Ažbe School, Munich (1896–98). Edited multi-volume *History of Russian Art* (1909–16). Academician (1913). Director, State Tretyakov Gallery (1913–25). Organised State Art Restoration Workshops (1918–30).
general references 28, 29, 30, 31, 47, 48, 209, 211
By the Lake **223**
Great International Exhibition, Paris (1889) 183
Great International Exhibition, Paris (1900) 183
Great War *see* First World War
Gregorian calendar 42
Grierson, John 35
GRIGORIEV, BORIS DMITRIEVICH
(1886–1939). Painter/graphic artist. Studied at Stroganov School of Arts and Industry (1903–07), St Petersburg Academy of Arts (1907–12), Académie de la Grande Chaumière, Paris (1912–14). Taught at Free State Art Studios (1918). Immigrated to Paris (1920). Taught at Academia Chilena de Bellas Artes, Santiago (1928–30). Dean, New York School of Applied Arts (1935).
general references 229–30
Commissar (People's Commissar Anatoly Lunacharsky) **133**
Land of Peasants 184, **188–89**
Old Dairy Woman 184, **192**
Rasseya 229
Gropius, Walter 150, 261
Grosse Berliner Kunstausstellung 150
Grosz, George 18
Gulag 25, 129
GULAG (Directorate of Camps) 49
Gumilev, Nikolai 46, 128–29
Gurvich, Iosif 30–31

Hamilton, Hector 261
Harvest Day 48
Hermitage, Leningrad 41, 44, 48, 129, 184, 231
Heroic Realism 273
Higher State Artistic and Technical Institute (VKhUTEIN) 48, 49
Higher State Artistic and Technical Workshops (VKhUTEMAS) 44, 46, 48, 257, 277, 295
Hodler, Ferdinand
Students of Jena in the Fight for Freedom against Napoleon 103, *103*
Hollywood films 37
Holy Land 276
Hotel Polonia, Warsaw 150
Hotel Ukraina, Moscow 261
House of the Press, Leningrad 48
House of Trade Unions, Moscow 57
The House on Trubnaya Street (film) 35, 49
Houses of Culture 232–33

icons 75, 185, 232, 233, 274
IGNATOVICH, BORIS VSEVOLODOVICH
(1899–1976). Photographer/journalist. Chief editor, *Mineworker*, Moscow (1921), satirical magazines in Leningrad (1922–25). Entered photography (1923). Worked as photojournalist (from 1926), film camera operator (1930–31). Founder member, October group (1930). Organised 'Igantovich Brigade' for Soyuzfoto agency (late 1930s). Worked as photographer for *Fighting Battalion* newspaper (1941–45).
Crankshafts **95**
Demonstration **304**
Dinamo Stadium, Moscow **305**
Generator **95**
The Hermitage **254**
May Day, Red Square, Moscow **305**
Reading the Newspaper at the Collective Farm (Kolkhoz) 187, **205**
Stretching Cables **93**
Tightening the Bolt: Lever Controls for Tramways 78, **92**
Young Worker 79, *79*
Ilyinsky, Igor 34
Imperial Academy of Arts, Leningrad 41, 42, 127
Imperial Porcelain Factory, Leningrad 21, 42, 154
Impressionism 127
Institute of Artistic Culture (INKhUK) 16, 17, 18, 24, 44, 47, 104
International Workers' Solidarity Day 41
IOFAN, BORIS MIKHAILOVICH
(1891–1976). Architect. Odessa School of Art (1911). Regio Istituto Superiore di Belle Arti, Rome (1916). Practised in Rome (1917–24). Joined Communist Party (1921). Returned to USSR (1924). Most famous design, Palace of Soviets (1933, never completed). Travelled to USA to study innovations in the construction of high-rise buildings (1934).
general references 154, 261
Palace of the Soviets **269**

Iran 259
Ivan (film) 34
Ivan the Terrible (film) 37
Ivanov, Viacheslav 210
IZO (Department of Visual Arts) 24, 42, 44, 46, 128
Izvestia 44

Jack of Diamonds 25, 45, 46, 48
Jar-Ptitza **225**
Jazz Comedy (film) 37
The Jazz Singer (film) 37
Jews 18, 230
Joint State Political Directorate (OGPU) 49
Jolly Fellows (film) 37
Julian calendar 42
'July Days' (1917) 41

Kamenev, Lev 47, 48
KANDINSKY, VASILY VASILIEVICH
(1866–1944). Painter/printmaker/stage designer/theorist. Studied law at Moscow University (1886–92). Ethnographic expedition to Vologda Province (1889). Active in People's Commissariat of Enlightenment; taught at Free State Art Studios (both from 1918) and the Bauhaus (1921–33). Key figure in the twentieth-century transition from representational to abstract art.
general references 17, 18, 21, 24, 44, 46, 75, 127, 150
Black and White (play) 104
Blue Crest **111**
Horseman. St George 24, *24*
Steps (autobiography) 44
Troubled **110**
Kaplan, Fanya 43
Kapterev, Pavel 209
Katka's Reinette Apples (film) 35
Katsman, Evgeny 29
Kaufman, Mikhail *78*
Kerchief Commemorating the Second Congress of the Trekhgornaya Textile Workers **89**
Kerensky, Alexander 22, 23, 41
Khidekel, Lazar 149, 231
Khomiakov house, Moscow 211–12
Kiev 44
Kiev Picture Gallery 49
Kino-fot (journal) 35
Kinoki 35
Kirghizia 276
Kirov, Sergei 31, 261
KLUCIS, GUSTAVS [KLUTSIS, GUSTAVS GUSTAVOVICH]
(1895–1944). Painter/sculptor/graphic artist/designer. Studied at Riga Art School (1913–15), Society for the Encouragement of the Arts (1915–17), Free State Art Studios/Higher State Artistic and Technical Workshops (1918–21), where, with Senkin, founded new, experimental agitprop studio (1922–23) and later taught (1924–30). Founder member, October group (1928).
general references 19, 49, 76, 154, 296
The Komsomol Sows the Ground! 182, 187
Long Live Our Happy Socialist Motherland 77
Postcard for the 1928 Moscow Spartakiad 296
Sport 294, 295
KLYUN, IVAN VASILIEVICH
(1873–1943). Painter/sculptor. Independent study in Kiev (1880s). Studied at Ilya Mashkov's studio, Bolshakov School of Painting and Sculpture, Moscow (early 1900s), Fedor Rerberg's studio (1903–07). Director, Central Exhibitions Bureau, Department of Visual Arts, People's Commissariat of Enlightenment (c. 1918). Based his 'constructive realism' on Purism (1920s).
general references 31, 233
Composition **179**
Non-objective Painting According to the Principle of Light-Colour **178**
Kobro, Katarzyna 150
Kogan, Nina 25, 44, 149
Kogout, Nikolai
With the Rifle We Defeated the Enemy, With Our Labour, Comrades We Shall Win Our Bread 76–77, *77*
Kolkhoz (Agricultural Communes) 185, 187, **205**
Kolkhoz Box **198**
Komsomol 78, *182*, 232
The Komsomol – Sponsor of Electrification (film) 35
KONGISER, NAUM ALEXANDROVICH
(1904–1984). Sculptor. Studied at Higher State Artistic and Technical Institute, Leningrad (1920–26). Taught at secondary schools in Leningrad (1920–28). Assisted with street decorations in Moscow for revolutionary celebrations (1930s) Created marble reliefs on historical revolutionary themes for the House of Penal Servitude and Exile building project (1934).
A Radio for the Village **198**
Korin, Pavel 213
Alexander Nevsky 213, *213*
An Ancient Tale 213
Requiem: Vanishing Russia 213
Sketch for Requiem: Vanishing Russia 212, 213
Young Hieromonk (Priest-monk) Fyodor 213, *213*
Kornilov, General Lavr 23, 41
Korovin, Konstantin 127
Kostin, Vladimir 274–75
KOZINTSEV, GRIGORY MIKHAILOVICH
(1905–1973). Director/screenwriter/theorist. Studied at Kiev School of Art (1919–20), Free State Art Studios/Petrograd State Free Artistic Workshops (1920–22). Founder member, Factory of the Eccentric Actor (1921–32). Joined Sevzapkino/Lenfilm Studio (1924). Collaborated with Trauberg on film projects (1924–45). Taught at All-Soviet State Institute of Cinema (1941–64). People's Artist of the USSR (1964).
general reference 37
The Adventures of Oktyabrina 34, *34*
New Babylon 35, *37*
KOZLINSKY, VLADIMIR IVANOVICH
(1891–1967). Graphic artist. Studied at Maksimov School, Zvantseva School, various private studios, including Dmitri Kardovsky's (early 1910s). Audited courses at Imperial Academy of Arts (from 1912). Agitprop designer in Petrograd (1918). Established Petrograd Russian Telegraph Agency (1920–22). Taught at Moscow School of Higher Art and Industry (1952–66).
general reference 76
Despite the Best Efforts of Our Enemies Over Three Years the World Revolution Proceeds with Gigantic Steps! 14
Krasnaya Gazeta (The Red Newspaper) 43
KRINSKY, VLADIMIR FEDOROVICH
(1890–1971). Architect/graphic artist. Studied at Society for the Encouragement of the Arts (1907–10), Imperial Academy of Arts (1910–17). Taught at Higher State Artistic and Technical Workshops (from 1920). Explored issues of colour, form and composition through a series of experiments (1920–23). Founder member, Association of New Architects (1923).
general reference 257
Collective Figure 76, 77
Kronstadt mutiny (1921) 45, 46, 128
Krupskaya, Nadezhda 232
Kulagina, Valentina
Women Shock-workers of Factories and Collective Farms Join the Ranks of CPSU (Communist Party) 186, 187
kulaks 49
Kuleshov, Lev 34
The Extraordinary Adventures of Mr West in the Land of the Bolsheviks 33, *33*, 34
Kuprin, Alexander 47, 129
Kuptsov, Vladimir
The First of May, 1929 55
KUSTODIEV, BORIS MIKHAILOVICH
(1878–1927). Painter/graphic artist/stage designer. Studied at Pavel Vlasov's studio, Astrakhan (1893–96), Academy of Arts, St Petersburg (1896–1903), René Menard's studio, Paris (1904). Founder member, New Society of Artists (1904–06/08?). Academician (1909). Agitprop designer in Petrograd (1918). Created designs for State Porcelain Factory (from 1923).
general references 25, 46, 229–30, **242**
The Bolshevik 76, 102, 103, **112–13**, 229
Carnival **218**
Demonstration on Uritsky Square on the Day of the Opening of the Second Comintern Congress in July 1920 56, **58–59**, 229
Merchant's Wife at Tea 229, *229*
Moscow I. Entry 102, *102*
Portrait of Fedor Chaliapin 129
Kuzmin, Mikhail 295
Kuznetsov, Pavel 47, 276

LABAS, ALEXANDER ARKADEVICH
(1900–1983). Painter. Studied at V. Mushketov's studio (1908), Stroganov School of Arts and Industry (1912–17), Free State Art Studios (1917–19), Higher State Artistic and Technical Workshops (1921–24); also taught there (1922–24). Served with Red Army in the Far East (1919–20). Founder member, Society of Easel Painters (1925).
general references 29, 31, 230, 273
Red Army in the Russian Far East **244**
The Train is Coming 230, *230*
Ladovsky, Nikolai 257, 261
Lang, Fritz 35
LANGMAN, ELEAZAR MIKHAILOVICH
(1895–1940). Photographer. Studied at Odessa Art School, Moscow Conservatory. Took up photography (late 1920s). Joined October group (1931). Worked for Izogiz Publishing House and the journal *USSR in Construction* (from 1935). His photographs were published in *Evening Moscow*, *Pioneer* and elsewhere. Presidium Member, Photography Section, Union of Film Camera Operators (late 1930s).
Old and New: Church and Universal Store **255**
Larionov, Mikhail 48, 183
Cover illustration for *Jar-Ptitza* **224**
'Latest Trends in Art', Leningrad (1927) 48
Lavra of the Holy Trinity at the Sergiev Posad *208*, 209–10, 212–13
'Law on Defectors' 49
Le Corbusier 258, 261
League of Nations 49
Lebedev, Ivan
All-Union Agricultural Exhibition (Moscow) 184, **199**
LEBEDEV, VLADIMIR VASILIEVICH
(1891–1967). Painter/illustrator/graphic artist. Studied at St Petersburg Academy of Arts (1910–14), School of Drawing, Painting and Sculpture, St Petersburg (1912–16). Professor, Free State Art Studios, Petrograd (1918–21); assistant head of poster department at Petrograd Russian Telegraph Agency (1920–22). Art editor of Detgiz Publishing House, Leningrad (1924–33).
general reference 211
Food Tax Poster **243**
Portrait of the Dancer and Choreographer Nadezhna Nadezhdina **250**
The Red Vision of Communism is Sweeping over Europe 47
LEBEDEVA, MARIA VASILIEVNA
(1895–1942). Painter/ceramicist/graphic artist. Studied at the Society for the Encouragement of the Arts (graduated 1917). Toured northern Russia with Shchekotikhina-Pototskaya during their studies. Worked in graphic art and monumental painting (until 1917); at State Porcelain Factory (1919–23; 1934–40). Taught at Vitebsk Art School (1924–27) and Minsk Art Institute (1933–36).
Decorative Vase 'The Liberated People' **61**
LEF (journal) 17–18, 35
Left Front of the Arts ('LEF' group) 16, 105
Lenin, Vladimir 15, 41, 42, 48, 211, 231, 295
and 1932 exhibition 29
assassination attempts 42, 43
attitude to art 24
cult of Leninism 47, 56–57, 258
death 18, 25, 47, 57, 184, 213, 258
and film-making 33
'Letter to Congress' 47
list of 'undesirables' 129
Mausoleum 49, 57, 57, **60**, 258–59, 258–59, **268**
nationalises art galleries 44
'On the Proletkult' 45
Palace of the Soviets competition 261
and peasants 184
Plan for Monumental Propaganda 55, 273
portraits of 15, 20, 21, 25, 28, 56, **64–67**
Red Terror 43
and Stalin 47
on the struggle of the proletariat 127
Lenin Institute, Moscow 56–57
Leningrad, Siege of (1941–44) 235
Leningrad Regional Union of Soviet Artists (LOSSKH) 50
Leninism 47, 56–57
LENTULOV, ARISTARKH VASILIEVICH
(1882–1943). Painter/stage designer. Studied at Penza Church Institute and Seminary (1889–98), Selivertsov Drawing Institute, Penza (1898–1900). Private study under Dmitri Kardovsky in St Petersburg (1906–07). Founder member Jack of Diamonds (1910). Studied at Académie La Palette, Paris (1911–12). Taught at various major institutions (1918–43).
general references 48, 50
Gates with Tower: New Jerusalem **214**
Portrait of the Theatre Director Alexander Tairov **132**
Tverskoy Boulevard **215**
Leo Tolstoy and the Russia of Nicholas II (film) 35
Leporskaya, A. 25
Lermontov, Mikail 210
lettering 102–103
'Life and Customs of the USSR Peoples', Moscow (1926) 48
LISSITZKY, EL [LAZAR] MARKOVICH
(1890–1941). Painter/graphic designer/architect/theorist. Studied at Technische Hochschule, Darmstadt (1909), Riga Technical University (Moscow) (1915). Creator, Soviet flag (1917). Worked at Vitebsk Art School (1919). Active member, Affirmers of the New Art (from 1919). Made head of architecture, Higher State Artistic and Technical Workshops (1921). A key figure linking East and West.
general references 16, 18, 76, 79, 101, **144**
architecture 154, 257, **267**
faceless figures 153
photography and photomontage 20, 77
and Suprematism 150
teaches at People's Art School, Vitebsk 44, 149
Beat the Whites with the Red Wedge 44
Constructor (Self-portrait with Dividers) **123**
Design for an Apartment for the Narkomfin [People's Commissariat of Finance] Building **267**
Footballer 295, *295*
Proun 153
Proun 1E: The Town 153
Proun 30T 150
The Story of Two Squares 19
Wolkenbügel 256, 257
LIZAK, IZRAIL LVOVICH
(1905–1974). Painter/restorer. Studied at Free Art Educational Studios (later Free State Art Studios, then Academy of Arts) in Petrograd (1918–25). Member, Commune of Artists (1925–28). Founder member, Circle of Artists (1926–30). Taught at College of Art and Design, Leningrad (1946–48). Worked in restoration studios (1950s–60s).
Walk **250**
London 56
London, Jack 34
LOSSKh see Leningrad Regional Union of Soviet Artists
Lourié, Arthur 127, *127*, 128
Lunacharsky, Anatoly *18*, 27, 41, 46, 211, 296
drive for literacy 15, 79
as head of NARKOMPROS 23–24, *23*, 128–29
on importance of art 101
lectures 42
lists paintings for State purchase 43
portraits of *128*, **133**
removal from power 48, 49
Lvov, Prince Georgy 23, 41

'Machine Shop' group 29
MAI group see Masters of Analytical Art Group
Makovets see Union of Poets and Painters
MALEVICH, KAZIMIR SEVERINOVICH
(1878–1935). Painter/printmaker/graphic artist/writer. Studied at Kiev School of Art (1894–96), Stroganov School of Arts and Industry and Moscow School of Painting, Sculpture and Architecture (1904–05), at Fedor Rerberg's studio (1905–10). Joined Jack of Diamonds (1910). Inventor, Suprematism (1915). Taught at Vitebsk Art School (1919–22). Founder member, Affirmers of the New Art (1920). Visionary innovator.
general references 16, 17, 18, 25, 48, 57, *147–54*, *153*, *273*, *295*
and the 1932 exhibition 15, 21, 30–31
architectons 149–50, 151
on architecture 257
arrested 49, 149
ceramics 21, 153–54, 231, *231*
on the Church 232–33
and the Decorative Institute 44
exhibitions 48, 49, 149–51, 150–51, 153, 154
figurative paintings 151, 187
in First World War 15
and food coupons 75
and GINKHUK 149, 154
and IZO 24
lists paintings for State purchase 43
opposition to AKhRR 25
paintings of peasants 233
and UNOVIS 44
in Vitebsk 231
Architectons and Figurines **174**
Black Square 150, **156**, 233
Desk and Room **155**
Dynamic Suprematism Supremus **158**
Female Portrait **169**
Female Torso **170**
Future 'Planiti' for Leningrad: The Pilot's House 149, 151
Head of a Peasant 185, **195**
Landscape with Five Houses 151, **166**
Monument to the Land of the Soviets 154
The Non-objective World 150
Peasants **162**, 185
Plate with Suprematist Composition **176**
Plate with Suprematist Decorations: Dynamic Composition **176**
Portrait of the Art Critic and Curator Nikolai

Punin **135**, 233
Red Cavalry 153, **172–73**, 233, 275
The Red House 151, 153, **167**
Red Square (Painterly Realism of a Peasant Woman in Two Dimensions) 150, **157**, 187
Self-portrait 233
Socialist City 50
Sportsmen 153, **168**, 233
Suprematism **159**
Suprematism (Supremus No. 58) **160**
Suprematism: White Square on White 20
Suprematistic Construction of Colours **161**
Supremus 56 150, 151, 152
Teapot, Design for the State Porcelain Factory 231
Three Female Figures **165**
To Reaping (Marfa and Vanka) **164**, 185–87
Torso (Prototype of a New Image) **171**
Woman with Rake **163**, 187
MALIAVIN, FILIP ANDREEVICH
(1869–1940). Painter/draughtsman. Studied at St Panteleimon Monastery, Greece (icon painting) (1885–91), St Petersburg Academy of Arts under Ilya Repin (1892–99). Member, Union of Russian Artists (1903). Academician (1906). Taught at Free State Art Studios (c. 1918). Exhibited with Association of Artists of Revolutionary Russia, immigrated to France (1922).
general references 47, 127
Troika **219**
Mamontov, Savva 212
Mamontova, Alexandra 212
MAN RAY
(1890–1976). American photographer/painter/draughtsman. Studied at Ferrer Center, New York (1912). Founder member, Society of Independent Artists (1916). Moved to Paris (1921). An innovative artist: created rayographs (1922), cine-rayographs (1923), solarised prints (1930–31). Moved to Los Angeles (1940). Returned to Paris (1951). Key figure in Dada and Surrealist movements.
The Film Director Sergei Eisenstein **142**
The Man with a Movie Camera (film) 35, 45, 77
Manchester 56
Mandelstam, Osip 131
Mars (planet) 15, 19, 34
Marx, Karl 15, 231
Marx Brothers 37
Mashkov, Ilya 24, 47, 48
MASLOV, VLADIMIR I.
(?-1928). Textile artist. Studied at Stroganov School of Arts and Industry (1909). Worked at Karetnikov and Son Factory, Teikovo. Best known for his *Tractor* fabric design, which appeared in the 1928 exhibition 'Soviet Domestic Textiles' in Moscow.
Tractor 185, **203**
Masters of Analytical Art Group (MAI) 47, 48, 50
Matisse, Henri 295
MATIUSHIN, MIKHAIL VASILIEVICH
(1861–1934). Painter/patron/musician/writer/publisher. Married to Elena Guro. Studied at Moscow Conservatory of Music (1878–81); then concertmaster (1881–1913), Society for the Encouragement of the Arts (1894–98), Yan Tsionglinsky's studio (1903–05), Zvantseva School (1906–08). Founder member, Union of Youth (1910). Active Futurist (from 1912). Published Russian translation of Albert Gleizes and Jean Metzinger, *On Cubism* (1913).
general references 25, 44, *149*, 154, *274*, *277*
Movement in Space 103–04, **122**
Matsa, Ivan 27–28, 29
MAYAKOVSKY, VLADIMIR VLADIMIROVICH
(1893–1930). Poet/playwright/graphic artist. Studied at Stroganov School of Arts and Industry (1908–09), Moscow School of Painting, Sculpture and Architecture (1911–14). Designed posters for Russian Telegraph Agency (1919–22). Founder member, Communist Futurism (1919). Head and editor, *LEF* group and magazine (1921–25). Primarily known as a poet and playwright.
general references 15, 17, 35, 49, 103, 128, **141**, **143**, 211
The Bedbug 19
Blacksmith 50
Mystery Bouffe 44
'*Workers: Expensiveness and NEP Don't Scare Us' (Bread Advertisement for Mosselprom Store)* 47
MELNIKOV, KONSTANTIN STEPANOVICH
(1890–1974). Architect. Studied at Moscow School of Painting, Sculpture and Architecture (1905–11, 1912–17). Worked at Higher State Artistic and Technical Workshops (1921–23). Joined State Academy of Artistic Sciences (1925). Constructed six, career-making, workers' clubs in the Moscow area (1927–29). Appointed Studio No. 7 head at Mossoviet (1933).
general references 18, 57
Mendelsohn, Erich 261
Mensheviks 41, 42, 50
MEYERHOLD, VSEVOLOD EMILIEVICH
(1874–1940). Stage director/theorist/actor. Studied at Moscow Philharmonic Society's Music and Drama School (1896). Founder member, Society of New Drama (1902). Head, Theatre Department, People's Commissariat of Enlightenment, Petrograd (1920). Established State Higher Directors' Workshops, Moscow (1921). Inventor, biomechanics acting system (1921). People's Artist of the RSFSR (1923).
general references 17, 19, 34, 41, 128, 131, **136–37**, **139**
Michelangelo 277
Milinis, Ignaty 154, 258
Milner, Henry
Letatlin (reconstruction) **262–63**
Design for an Apartment for the Narkomfin [People's Commissariat of Finance] Building (reconstruction) **267**
Ministry of Foreign Affairs, Moscow 261
Miturich, Petr 47
Portrait of the Composer Arthur Lourié 127
modernist architecture 257–58, 261
Moholy-Nagy, László 150
MOKH, MIKHAIL NIKOLAEVICH
(1911–1978). Ceramicist/graphic artist. Studied at Slutsk Art School, Pavlovsk (1922–29). Worked at State Porcelain Factory (1929–33; 1935–41). Member, Union of Arts Workers (from 1929), USSR Arts Fund (from 1950). Military service (1933–35). Restorer at Hermitage (1941–48). Principal artist and deputy director, State Porcelain Factory (1954–60).
Tea Set **86**
Molotov, Vyacheslav 50
Moor, Dmitry 50
Help! 45
Morosov, Ivan 16, 211
Morosov collection 44
Moscow Laughs (film) 37
Moscow Radio Mast 74, 75, 76
Moscow Regional Union of Soviet Artists 50
Moscow Salon 45
Moscow School of Painting, Sculpture and Architecture 43
Moscow State University 261
The Mother (film) 33, 35
MUKHINA, VERA IGNATIEVNA
(1889–1953). Sculptor/decorative artist. Studied under Konstantin Yuon and Ilya Mashkov (1911–12), at Académie de la Grande Chaumière, Paris, under Antoine Bourdelle (1912–14). Alexandra Exter's design assistant at Moscow Kamerny Theatre (1915–16). Founder member, Monolith (1919–20). Member, Society of Russian Sculptors (from 1926). USSR's premier Socialist Realist sculptor.
Flame of the Revolution 55, **63**
Municipal Museum, Leningrad 47
Museum of Abramtsevo 212
Museum of Artistic Culture, Moscow 44
Museum of Artistic Culture, Petrograd 43, 46, 47
'Museum of Everyday Life in the 1840s', Moscow 211–12
Museum of Modern Art, New York 20
Museum of the October Revolution, Petrograd 44
Museum of Pictorial Culture, Leningrad 149
Museum of Visual Arts, Moscow 47
museums 211–12
music 17

Nabis 274
Nadezhdina, Nadezhna **250**
Nansen, Fridtjof 33
NAPPELBAUM, MOISEY SOLOMONOVICH
(1869–1958). Photographer. Apprentice at Boretti studio, Minsk (1884). Worked in studios in Smolensk, Moscow, Odessa, Vilnius, Warsaw, USA. Returned to Minsk, opened own studio (1895). Published in *Sun of Russia* (from 1910). Focused on portraits. Produced Lenin's first official portrait (1918). Established first State Photographic Studio (1919).
The Composer Dmitri Shostakovich **140**
The Composer Sergei Prokofiev **143**
Joseph Stalin **309**
The Poet Alexander Blok **140**
The Poet Anna Akhmatova **138**
The Theatre Director Vsevolod Meyerhold **139**
Vladimir Ilyich Lenin **66**
The Writer Maxim Gorky **143**
Narkomfin building, Moscow 154, 258, 261, **266–67**
NARKOMPROS *see* People's Commissariat of Enlightenment
Neoclassicism 127
Neo-Nationalism 209
Neradovsky, Petr 27
NESTEROV MIKHAIL VASILIEVICH
(1862–1942). Painter. Studied at Moscow School of Painting, Sculpture and Architecture (1877–81; 1884–86), Academy of Arts, St Petersburg (1881–84). Created icons for St Vladimir's Cathedral, Kiev (1891–95). Member, Wanderers (from 1896). Artist of Merit of the RSFSR, Order of the Red Banner of Labour (both 1942).
general reference 212
In Russia (Soul of the People) 209, *210–11*
Philosophers 209–11, 212–13, **216**
New Association of Painters 25
New Babylon (film) 35, 37
New Economic Policy (NEP) 33, 45, 48, 184, 185, 257
New Society of Painters (NOZh) 46
New York 33, 234
New York World's Fair (1939–40) 297
Nicholas II, Tsar 23, 41, 43, 55, 75, 184
Nikolsky, Alexander 154
Nivinsky, Ignaty 258
Nizhny Novgorod 17, **303**
Nomenklatura process 44
Novgorod 274
NOZh *see* New Society of Painters

OBMOKhU *see* Young Artists Society
Obshchestvo Molodykh (Society of the Young) 25
October (film) 33, 37, 43, 48
October Revolution (1917) 23, 42, 44, 55, 101, 102, 127
Odessa 47
Oktiabr (October) group 49
The Old and the New (film) 37, 151
Olsuf'ev, Yurii 209
Olympic Games 296, 297
OMKh *see* Society of Moscow Artists
'On the Reformation of Literary-Artistic Organisations' 50
Ordzhonikidze, Sergo 48
Orenburg 149
Orgburo 44
Orlova, Luba 37
ORPP *see* Association of the Workers of Revolutionary Posters
ORS *see* Society of Russian Sculptors
Orthodox Church 46, 76, 185, 209, 213, 232–33, 258
OSA *see* Society of Contemporary Architects
OST *see* Society of Easel Painters
Ostroukhov collection 44
Ostrovsky, Alexander 34
Ozersky, Mikhail
First Tractor 184

Painters of Moscow group 25, 47, 48
'Paintings by Realist Artists to Help the Starving' (1922) 46
PAKHOMOV, ALEXEI FEDOROVICH
(1900–1973). Painter/graphic artist. Studied at Stieglitz School (1915–17), Higher State Artistic and Technical Institute (1922–25). Founder member, Circle of Artists (1926–32). Board member, Leningrad Union of Artists (from 1932). Taught at Leningrad Institute of Painting, Sculpture and Architecture (1948–73). Academician (1964). People's Artist of the USSR (1971).
general references 232, 233, 277
Haymaking **197**
Portrait of Shock-worker Molodtsova 187, **196**
Reaper (Harvest) 185, **191**
PAKULIN, VYACHESLAV VLADIMIROVICH
(1900–1951). Painter/stage designer/graphic artist. Studied at Stieglitz School (1917/19(?), 1920–22), Higher State Artistic and Technical Workshops (1922–25), also stage production with Meyerhold (1918). Founder member, Circle of Artists (1926–32). Board member, Leningrad Regional Union of Soviet Artists (from 1932). Created powerful cityscapes while in Leningrad during Second World War.
Turbine Shop at the Factory 'Elektrosila' **81**
Palace of the Soviets competition 21, 154, 258, 259–61, *261*, **269**, 277
Palaces of Culture 232–33
Palekh 47, 185, **268**, **303**
Palladio, Andrea 259
Paris 18, 19, 33, 129
The Parisian Cobbler (film) 35
Pasargadae 259
Pasternak, Boris 17
Path of Painting Society 48
peasants 181–87
PEGOSKhUM *see* Petrograd State Free Artistic workshops
People's Art School, Vitebsk 18, 44, 149
People's Commissariat of Enlightenment (NARKOMPROS) 23–24, *23*, 28, 42, 43, 44, 45, 46, 127–28, 231–32
Perm 44
'Permanent Exhibition of Avant-garde Art', Moscow (1928–30) 48, 49
Peter the Great, Tsar 76, 184
Petrograd Musical Drama Theatre 44
Petrograd Proletkult (Proletarian Culture Organisation) 42
Petrograd State Free Artistic Workshops (PEGOSKhUM) 42, 43
PETROV-VODKIN, KUZMA SERGEEVICH
(1878–1939). Painter/draughtsman/writer. Studied at F. Burov's studio, Samara (1893–95); Stieglitz School (1895–97); Moscow School of Painting, Sculpture and Architecture (1897–1905); Ažbe School, Munich (1901); Académie Colarossi, Paris (1906). Agitprop designer, Petrograd (1918). Professor, St Petersburg Academy of Arts (1921–33). First president of Leningrad Regional Union of Soviet Artists (1932).
general references 21, 41, 47, 50, 232, 233, 235, 271–77
1918 in Petrograd (Petrograd Madonna) 275, 277, **284**
1919. Alarm 275, *275*, 277
After Battle 276, **291**
At Samovar 274, **287**
The Bathing of the Red Horse 274, *274*, 275
Beside Lenin's Coffin 25, **67**, 273
Cherry Blossom in a Glass 274, **280**
Death of a Commissar 275, 276, 277, **290**
A Family at Table 275
Fantasy 184, 275, **285**
First Demonstration 273, *273*
Girl in a Red Scarf (Worker) 273
'Letters about Painting and Art in General' 274
Madonna and Child 273, 275
Midday. Summer 183–84, **278–79**
Morning Still-life 274, **281**
Mother 273, *274*
On the Firing Line 275–76, *276*
Our Lady of Tenderness for Angered Hearts 275, *275*
Portrait of a Boy (Vasya) **288**
Portrait of the Poet Anna Akhmatova **134**, 277
Self-portrait 274, **289**
Shakh-i-Zinda (Samarkand) 276, *277*
Still-life with Glass, Fruit and Photograph **286**
Still-life with a Herring 274, **283**
Still-life with a Violin 274, **282**
PETRUSOV, GEORGY GRIGORIEVICH
(1903–1971). Photographer. Worked as photo-journalist for *Labour* and *Pravda* newspapers (1924–30). Produced series depicting construction of Magnitogorsk Steel Works while its Head of Information Department (1928–30). During Second World War, served as war photographer and reached Berlin with Soviet forces. Worked for *Soviet Life* and other magazines (1957–71).
Caricature of Alexander Rodchenko **145**
New Building **264**
New Building from Above **265**
Pevsner, Antoine 44
'Philosophers' ships' 47, 129
photography 20, 77–79, 153, **252–55**
photomontage 20, 77, 256, *294–95*, 295, 296
Picasso, Pablo 17, 43
PIMENOV, YURY IVANOVICH
(1903–1977). Painter/graphic artist/stage designer. Studied at Higher State Artistic and Technical Workshops, Moscow (1920–25). Founder member, Society of Easel Painters (1925–28). Member, Moscow Regional Union of Soviet Artists (from 1932). Taught at Institute of Cinematography (1945–72). Academician (1962). Laureate, Lenin Prize (1967). People's Artist of the USSR (1970).
general references 25, 235, 295–96
Football **301**
Plan for Monumental Propaganda 42, 55
Poelzig, Hans 261
Poland 44, 45
Polenov, Vasily 276
Politburo 44, 47, 48, 49, 129
Pollaiuolo, Antonio del
Hercules and Antaeus 297
POPOVA, LYUBOV SERGEEVNA
(1889–1924). Painter/designer. Studied at Konstantin Yuon and Ivan Dudin's art school, Moscow (c. 1906/97), Académie de la Palette, Paris (1912–13). Travelled extensively,

including Samarkand. Worked at Tatlin's studio (1912–15). Taught at Higher State Artistic and Technical Workshops (1920–23). Designed textiles for First State Textile Print Factory (1923–24).
general references 15, 46, 75
Space-force Construction 105, **118–19**
porcelain *see* ceramics
Poster for the Commercial and Industrial Companies of Petrograd **242**
posters 14, 15, 19, 20, *36*, 51, **242–43**
Poussin, Nicolas 48
Pozemskiy, P. 25
Prague 129
Pravda 34, 49, 56–57, 258, *258*
PREKHNER, MIKHAIL GRIGORIEVICH
(1911–1941). Photographer. No specialist training. Worked at *Radio Listener, Moscow Speaks* (1928–30), Soyuzfoto (from 1930), Izogiz Publishing House (1931), *USSR in Construction* (1932). Featured in *Soviet Photo* under 'Profiles of Masters' (1935). Worked as photojournalist in Tallinn; killed during a bombing raid (28 August 1941).
El Lissitzky **144**
PREOBRAZHENSKAYA, DARIA NIKOLAEVNA
(1908–1972). Textile artist. Studied at Higher State Artistic and Technical Institute (1924–29). Textile section member, Union of Youth of the, Association of Artists of Revolutionary Russia. Worked as a textile designer at Central Art Studio, Great Ivanov-Voznesensk Textile Mill (1929–31), then at Trekhgornaya Factory, Moscow.
Five Years in Four **88**
Production Art 31, 105
Prokofiev, Sergei **143**
Proletariat Porcelain and Faience Factory, Bronnitsa **200**
Proletarskoye studentchestvo 294
Proletkult 45
Proletkult Theatre 131
propaganda 20, 23
PROTAZANOV, YAKOV ALEXANDROVICH
(1881–1945). Director/screenwriter. Studied at Moscow Commercial School (1900). Travelled extensively abroad (1904–07). Joined Iosif Ermolev's film company (1915) and emigrated with them (1920). Made several films in Paris and Berlin (1920–23). Returned to Russia to join Mezhrabpomfilm Studio (1923). Artist of Merit of the RSFSR (1935). Prolific film director.
general reference 19
Aelita 34, *34*
PROTOPOPOVA, LIUDMILA VIKTOROVNA
(1906–1981). Ceramicist. Studied at Leningrad Artistic Industrial Technical College (1926–30). Member, Union of Porcelain Industry (from 1920), Union of Arts Workers (from 1929), Leningrad Regional Union of Soviet Artists (from 1940). Worked at Lomonosov Porcelain Factory (1930–41; from 1944). Medal of Honour for porcelain (1944). Deputy, Leningrad Soviet (1947–50).
A Cup for Serving Tea **87**
Provisional Government 23, 41
PUDOVKIN, VSEVOLOD ILLARIONOVICH
(1893–1953). Director/screenwriter/theorist/actor. Studied at Moscow University prior to joining military (1914). Studied at State Film School (1920). Joined Lev Kuleshov's workshop (1922), then Mezhrabpomfilm Studio (1925). Stalin Prize (1941, 1947, 1951). Elected president of All-Union Society for Cultural Relations with Foreign Countries (1944). People's Artist of the USSR (1948).
general references 33, 34, 35
PUNI, IVAN [POUGNY, JEAN]
(1892–1956). Painter/graphic artist/designer. Studied under Ilya Repin (1900–08) at Académie Julian and Académie Colarossi, Paris (1910–11). Joined Union of Youth (1912). Created relief paintings (from 1915). Agitprop designer (1918). Taught at Free State Art Studios (1918). Left Russia (1919), settled in Paris (1924). Became French citizen (1946).
general reference 48
Spectrum: Flight of Forms **114**
Punin, Nikolai 17, 25, 29, 48, 76, 126, 131
and the anniversary exhibition 27, 28, 30
arrested 19, 46, 128–29
and the Decorative Institute 44
and Freedom of Arts 41
and GINKhUK 149
portrait of **135**, 233
on the Revolution 23
Anna Akhmatova in Punin's Study 130
Malevich's Personal Exhibition at GINKhUK, Leningrad 150
Portrait Photographs from His Personal Investigation File as a Prisoner **311**
Punina, Irina 25
Purism 18
Pushkin State Museum of Fine Arts, Moscow 19
Puvis de Chavannes, Pierre 274

¡Que viva México! (film) 37

Rabotnitsa i krest'ianka (*Female Worker and Peasant Woman*) (magazine) 232
Radakov, Alexei
The Illiterate Man is Like a Blind Man 15, *16*
Raphael 274
RAPKh *see* Russian Association of Proletarian Artists
RAPP *see* Russian Association of Proletarian Writers
Rationalism 257
Realism, nineteenth century 127, 273
see also Socialist Realism
Red Army 19, 21, 42, 44, 45, 105, 153
Red Guard 23
Red Square, Moscow 15, 19, 258, 259, 296, **305**
Red Terror (1918) 43
REDKO, KLIMENT NIKOLAEVICH
(1897–1956). Painter/graphic artist. Studied at icon painting school of Kiev-Pechersk Monastery (1910–14), Society for the Encouragement of the Arts (1914–18), Kiev Academy of Arts (1918). Attempted to combine art and science: founder member, Electro-organism. Returned to Moscow (1935), worked for Telegraph Agency of the Soviet Union (1940s).
general reference 55
Insurrection **68**
Rembrandt 48, 129
Renaissance 150, 210, 233, 259, 297
Repin, Ilya 47, 101, 127, 273
Restaurant Menu **243**
'Revolution, Daily Life and Labour', Moscow (1925) 47
'Revolutionary Art of the West', Moscow (1926) 48
Riazhsky, Grigory 46
RIDMAN, SERGEI NIKOLAEVICH
(c. 1890–after 1930). Architect/graphic artist. Studied at Higher State Artistic and Technical Workshops. Along with fellow students Andrey Burov and Sergei Kozhin, awarded third-place in open design competition for All-Union Agricultural Exhibition's layout and buildings (December 1922). Many prize-winners were students or junior architects; they were compelled to assist the older, more conservative architects, who then reaped the rewards.
All-Union Agricultural Exhibition (Moscow) 184, **199**
Riga 47
Riga, Peace of (1921) 45
'Right Opposition' 49
RIZNICH, IVAN IVANOVICH
(1908–1998). Ceramicist/sculptor/graphic artist. Studied at Pavlovsk Art School (graduated 1926). Worked at Lomonosov Porcelain Factory (1926–30; 1933–41; 1945–57; 1960–68; 1976); principal artist (1951). Awarded silver medal, International Exhibition in Brussels (1956). Specialised in overglaze and underglaze techniques in painting ceramics. Order of the Red Banner of Labour (1944).
Large Vase with Peasant Dance **201**
RODCHENKO, ALEXANDER MIKHAILOVICH
(1891–1956). Painter/sculptor/designer/photographer. Married to Stepanova. Studied at Kazan Art School (1910–14), Stroganov School of Arts and Industry (1914). Active in Department of Visual Arts, People's Commissariat of Enlightenment (from 1918). Taught at Higher State Artistic and Technical Workshops/Higher State Artistic and Technical Institute, Moscow (1920–30). Key figure of Constructivism.
general references 15, 16, 18, 20, 75, 76, 79, **145, 154**
on Constructivism 105
exhibitions 46
faceless figures 153
and film-making 34
and Freedom of Arts 41
and IZO 24
and the Museum of Artistic Culture 44
photography and photomontage 19, 20, 77
posters *36*
theatre designs 19
'Beer Beats Poteen!' (Advertisement for Mosselprom Store) 47
Cigarette Vendor, Pushkin Square, Moscow **253**
Dinamo Factory Brass Band **307**
The Last Painting 17
Mercedes Ambulance Car **253**
Narkomfin Building **266**
Pioneer with Trumpet **306**
The Poet and Painter Vladimir Mayakovsky **141**
Spatial Constructions 78
Steering Wheels **94**
Varvara Stepanova at Work in Her Studio 20
Worker's Club Installation 18, *19*
'Workers: Expensiveness and NEP Don't Scare Us' (Bread Advertisement for Mosselprom Store) 47
Rodin, Auguste 17
Romanov dynasty 150
Room, Abram 35, 37
ROSTA *see* Russian Telegraph Agency
Rozanov, Vasily 209
The Apocalypse of Our Time 209
Rozanova, Olga 24
ROZENDORF, ELIZAVETA BERNGARDOVNA
(1898–1984). Ceramicist/painter/graphic artist/stage designer. Studied at Stieglitz School (1916–20). Worked at State Porcelain Factory under Chekhonin (1919–20). Moved to Tallinn (1923). Married poet and artist Karl Hershelman (1926) and was listed as 'Rozendorf-Hershelman' in exhibition catalogues (1929–32). Moved to Poznań, Poland (1940), then Germany (1945).
Dish 'Girl with a Pumpkin' **200**
Dish with a Depiction of a Reaper 184, **200**
ROZHDESTVENSKY, KONSTANTIN IVANOVICH
(1906–1999). Painter/graphic artist/designer. Studied at Mitrofan Poliakov's studio, Tomsk (1919–22). Worked at Museum of Artistic Culture, Petrograd (1923), State Institute of Artistic Culture, Leningrad (1924–26). Master of exhibition design (from 1940s). Secretary, Union of Artists for Applied Arts (1963–88). People's Artist of the RSFSR (1976). Academician (1979).
general reference 25
Family in Field 185, **190**
Rubens, Peter Paul 48
RUBLEV, GEORGY IOSIFOVICH
(1902–1975). Painter/graphic artist. Studied at State Free Art Studios, Lipetsk (1919–22), Higher State Artistic and Technical Workshops/Higher State Artistic and Technical Institute, Moscow (1923–30). Joined Union of Soviet Artists (1933). Taught at Moscow Institute of Decorative and Applied Arts (1946–52), Mukhina Higher School of Art and Design (1952–75).
general reference 48
Portrait of Joseph Stalin **71**
Rumiantsev Museum, Moscow 48
Rusakov, Yuri 273
Russian Academy of Artistic Sciences 46
'Russian Art of the Imperialist Era', Leningrad (1931) 50
Russian Association of Proletarian Artists (RAPKh) 50
Russian Association of Proletarian Writers (RAPP) 48, 50
Russian Social Democratic party 23
Russian Telegraph Agency (ROSTA) 44, 211
RYAZHSKY, GRIGORY GRIGORIEVICH [GEORGY GEORGIEVICH/ EGOR EGOROVICH]
(1895–1952). Painter/graphic artist. Studied at Prechistensky Workers' Drawing Courses (1910–15), M. Leblanc's studio (from 1912). Served in the army (1915–17). Studied at Proletkult (1918) and under Malevich at Free State Art Studios (1918–19). Founder member, New Society of Painters (1922). Academician (1949).
general reference 50
The Collective Farm Team Leader 187, **196**
Rykov, Alexei 48, 50

Samarkand 276
SAMOKHVALOV, ALEXANDER NIKOLAEVICH
(1894–1974). Painter/graphic artist. Studied at Petrograd Academy of Arts (1914–17), Free State Art Studios/Higher State Artistic and Technical Workshops under Petrov-Vodkin (1920–23). Travelled to Samarkand with Petrov-Vodkin (1921). Member, Circle of Artists (1926–29), October group (1930–32). Taught at Mukhina Higher School of Art and Design (1948–51).
general references 25, 56, 235, 277
Girl in a Football Jersey 232, 297, **299**
Sportswoman with a Shot-put 297, **299**
Tram Conductor 232, **251**
Saqqara 259
'Scissors crisis' (1923) 47
Searchlight (*Prozhektor*) (journal) 295–96
Serebriakova, Zinaida 127
Serebryakova, Ekaterina 234
Sergiev Posad *208*, 209–10, 212–13
A Severe Young Man (film) 37
SHAIKET, ARKADY SAMOILOVICH
(1898–1959). Photographer. Self-taught, worked as retoucher in a Moscow commercial studio (1922). Worked as photojournalist for *Ogoniok* magazine (1924–30), photographer for *USSR in Construction* (from 1930), *Front Illustrated* during the Second World War. Skilful in capturing changes in Soviet society and known for his frontline imagery.
Brigade of Shock-workers **96**
Construction of the Moscow Telegraphic Centre **90**
Electrification of Lapatino Village 185, **204**
In the Café **252**
Komsomol at the Wheel 78, **91**
Lenin's Lamp: Light Bulb in a Peasant House 185, **204**
Moscow Radio Mast 74, *75*
Physical Training (Morning Gymnastics) **304**
Red Square **66**
Shakhty 48
Shaposhnikov, Boris 211–12
'The Museum as a Work of Art' 211
SHCHEKOTIKHINA-POTOTSKAYA, ALEXANDRA VASILIEVNA
(1892–1967). Ceramicist/graphic artist/stage designer. Studied at Society for the Encouragement of the Arts (1908–15), Académie Ranson, Paris (1913). Worked for Sergei Diaghilev (1913–14) and at State Porcelain Factory (1918–23). Lived and worked in Paris with husband Ivan Bilibin (1925–36). Returned to Leningrad, worked at Lomonosov Porcelain Factory (1936–56).
'Commisar' Bowl **247**
Dish 'Sailor's Walk. 1 May 1921 in Petrograd' **247**
Plate with Inscription 'He Who Will Not Work Shall Not Eat 1921' **246**
Shchukin, Sergei 16, 211
Shchukin Gallery 44
Shchuko, Vladimir 261
SHCHUSEV, ALEXEI VIKTOROVICH
(1873–1949). Architect/restorer. Studied at St Petersburg Academy of Arts (1891–97), awarded bursary to Europe (1898–99). Director, State Tretyakov Gallery, Moscow (1926–29). Designed Lenin's mausoleum (final version 1929–30). Organised and served as first director of State Research and Scientific Museum of Russian Architecture (renamed in his honour after his death) (1946–49).
general references 49, 57, 261
Lenin Mausoleum **268**
Lenin Mausoleum, Moscow, first temporary structure 258, *258*
Model of Lenin's Mausoleum **268**
Perspective drawing of the Lenin Mausoleum, Moscow, second temporary structure 259
Shekhonin, Sergei 41
Shishkin, Arkady
The Sower I. E. Okulov, from the Village of Kharino, Viatsk Region 183
shock-workers 187
Shostakovich, Dmitri **140**
SHTERENBERG, ABRAM PETROVICH
(1894–1979). Photographer. Brother of David Shterenberg. Commenced photographer apprenticeship (1909), military service during First World War. Worked in B. Tapuskyansky's studio, Tashkent, then joined Red Army's art and photography department (1919). Photojournalist in Moscow (from 1926). Joined October group. Worked for Novosti Press Agency (until 1979).
The Poet and Painter Vladimir Mayakovsky at his Last Exhibition **143**
SHTERENBERG, DAVID PETROVICH
(1881–1948). Painter. Studied in Odessa (1905) and Vienna (1906), then Paris at Ecole des Beaux-Arts and Académie Vitti (1907–12). Major figure in post-revolutionary reorganisation of visual arts, including as Commissar for Art (1917–18). Agitprop designer, Petrograd (1918). Founder member, Society of Easel Painters (1925) and its president (until 1930).
general references 17, 18, 25, 29, 42
Aniska **237**
Herring 232
Shub, Esfir 35
Shukhaev, Vasily 127
Shukhov, Vladimir 75, 76
Silver Age 129–31, 209
slogans 21, 102
Smolensk 149
'Socialism in One Country' 47
Socialist Realism 21, 235, 273
architecture 261

cult of Lenin and 258, 259
as official Communist art 19–20, 25, 50, 101, 154, 297
and photography 153
Society of Artists Named After Ilya Repin 47
Society of Contemporary Architects (OSA) 257–58, 259
Society of Easel Painters (OST) 25, 29, *29*, 31, 47, 295, 296
Society of Moscow Artists (OMKh) 25, 29–30, 48, 50
Society of Russian Sculptors (ORS) 47, 296
Society for the Study of the Russian Country Estate 212
Sologub, Fedor 23
Solovetsky Islands 47
Solov'ev, Vladimir 210
Sophia 210–11
Sorin, Ksaveri 234
Soviet Art group 50
Soviet Writers' Congress (1934) 297
Sovnarkom (All-Bolshevik Council of the People's Commissars) 42, 44, 47
Spartacus 296
sports 295–97
Stalin, Joseph 19, 46, 131, 277
and 1932 exhibition 29, 30
collectivisation of agriculture 48, 49
and film-making 33, 37
Five-Year Plans 21
'Godless Five-Year Plan' 50
and Lenin 47
and opposition to AKhRR 25
Palace of the Soviets competition 154, 261
portraits of 15, 20, 21, *28*, **69–71**, 235, *235*, **308–09**
rise to power 185, 258
Socialist Realism 19–20
and Trotsky 44, 47
Stalin as the Glorious Leader **69**
Stalingrad 47
State Commission for the Electrification of Russia (GOELRO) 45, 235, *235*
State Higher Theatre Workshops 131
State Historical Museum, Moscow 31, 211–12
State Institute for Art History, Leningrad 154
State Institute of Artistic Culture (GINKhUK) 25, 47, 48, 149, *150*, 154, 231
State Institute of the History of Art 48
State Lomonosov Porcelain Factory, Leningrad 154
State Museum of Fine Arts, Moscow 50
State Museum Fund 48
State Museum of New Western Art, Moscow 48
State Porcelain Factory (GFZ) 42, 50, **60–62**, **86–87**, **176–77**, **198**, **200–01**, *231*, **246–47**
State Russian Museum, Leningrad 21, 26, 27–31, *28–30*, 41, 48, 50, 154, 234, 235
State Tretyakov Gallery, Moscow 41, 43, 47, 48, 49, 50, 150, 154
Steiner, Rudolf 274
STENBERG, GEORGI AVGUSTOVICH
STENBERG, VLADIMIR AVGUSTOVICH
(Georgi: 1900–1933; Vladimir: 1899–1982). Sculptors/designers. Studied at Stroganov School of Arts and Industry (1912–17), Moscow Free State Art Studios (Georgi: 1917–20; Vladimir: 1918–19) and railway and bridge construction on military engineering courses in Moscow (1917). First collaborated under the name 2 Stenberg 2 (1917). Founder members, Society of Young Artists (1919). Joined Institute of Artistic Culture (1920). Kamerny Theatre artists (1922–31). Cinema poster designers (from 1923). Official designers of holiday decorations for Red Square (from 1928). Founder members, Moscow Regional Union of Soviet Artists (1932). Principal artists, House of Unions, Moscow (1932).
poster for *Fragment of an Empire* 51
Step Pyramid, Saqqara 259
STEPANOVA, VARVARA FEDOROVNA
(1894–1958). Painter/designer. Married to Rodchenko. Studied at Kazan Art School (c. 1910–11). Worked at Department of Visual Arts, People's Commissariat for Enlightenment (from 1917). Created numerous designs for First State Textile Factory (1920–24). Taught at Higher State Artistic and Technical Workshops (1924–25). Worked as graphic designer (1930s–50s).
general references 19, 20, *20*, 46, *77*, *104*, 153
Costume Designs for Sportodezhda 295, *296*
Result of the Five-Year Plan **308**
De Stijl 18
'The Storming of the Winter Palace', Petrograd (1920) 45
The Strike (film) 34, 35, *35*
Stroganov Art School, Moscow 43, 44
Strugatsky, Natal 297
Strzemiński, Władysław 150
The Red Army Is Fighting Heroically at the Front *148*
SUETIN, NIKOLAI MIKHAILOVICH
(1897–1954). Painter/graphic artist/ceramicist. Studied at Vitebsk Art School under Malevich (1918–22). Joined Affirmers of the New Art (1920). Followed Malevich to Petrograd (1922). Member, State Institute of Artistic Culture (1923–26). Worked at State Porcelain Factory, Petrograd (1923–54; principal artist from 1932), Leningrad Institute of Art History (1927–30). Major Suprematist artist.
general references 50, 149, 150, *153*, *154*
Coffee Pot **176**
Cup and Saucer with Suprematist Painting **177**
Plate 'Coloured Silhouettes' (Three Women) **177**
Plate with a Suprematist Drawing **176**
Plate with Woman Depicted in a Suprematist Manner **177**
Suprematist Inkwell **176**
Vase with Ornamental Suprematist Elements **177**
A Woman with a Saw 187, **194**
Suprematist Ballet 44
Suprematists 17, 18, 149–54, 187
ceramics 21, 153–54
exhibitions 44
and food coupons 75
Malevich's architectons 149–50
and photomontage 295
in Vitebsk 149, 231
Sverdlov, Yakov 55
Svilova, Elizabeta 35
SVOMAS *see* Free State Art Studios
Symbolists 209, 210–11, 274, 275

Tairov, Alexander **132**
Tambov province 44, 46
Tarabukin, Nikolai 17
TATLIN, VLADIMIR EVGRAFOVICH
(1885–1953). Painter/designer/constructivist. Merchant sea cadet (c. 1899). Studied at Moscow School of Painting, Sculpture and Architecture (1902–03), Penza School of Art (1904–10). Various teaching posts (1918–33). Director, Department of Visual Arts, People's Commissariat of Enlightenment, Moscow (1918–19). Founder member, Union of New Tendencies in Art (1921–22). Key figure of Constructivism.
general references 15, 16, 17, 75, 79, 273
and the 1932 exhibition 31
and the Decorative Institute 44
exhibitions 50
and Freedom of Arts 41
and IZO 24
at the Museum of Pictorial Culture 149
at NARKOMPROS 231
Corner Counter-relief 232, *232*
Letatlin 19, 21, 50, **262–63**
Model for the Monument to the Third International 45, 75–76, *75*, 78, 103, 260, *261*
TELINGATER, SOLOMON BENEDIKTOVICH
(1903–1969). Graphic artist/typographer. Lived in Baku (1910), studied at various studios. Attended Higher State Artistic and Technical Workshops, Moscow (1920). Returned to Baku (1921), worked as technical editor and artist for *Young Worker* and *Labour*. Returned to Moscow (1925). Typographer, *Polygraphic Productions* (1925–27). Founder member, October group (1928–32).
general reference 77
Red Army: First Cavalry **244**
TENISMAN, EDUARD ALMA
(1898–1941/42). Painter/graphic artist. Studied at Higher State Artistic and Technical Institute, Petrograd (1918–25). Attended Filonov's classes and became member of Collective of Masters of Analytical Art (1925–30). Contributor to the open letter 'Artists at the Front of Atheism', published in the Collective's name (4 May 1930).
Worker Seated at the Table **236**
TERPSIKHOROV, NIKOLAI BORISOVICH
(1890–1960). Painter. Studied at Konstantin Yuon and Ivan Dudin's art school; Vladimir Meshkov's School of Painting and Drawing, Moscow School of Painting, Sculpture and Architecture (1911–17). Military service (1917–22). Member, Moscow School Society of Artists (1917–25), Association of Artists of Revolutionary Russia (1922–32). Multiple trips to Central Asia (1929, 1935, 1939).
First Motto 56, **62**
textiles **88–89**, **202–03**, 231
Theatre Square, Petrograd 273
Tikhon, Patriarch 46, 213
TIMOREV, VASILII PORFIREVICH
(1870–1942). Painter/graphic artist/ceramicist. Studied at the Association for the Encouragement of the Arts; St Petersburg Academy of Arts (1890–92); Elizaveta Kruglikova's studio in Paris (1905–07). Worked for publisher Joseph Knebel in Petrograd (1918–21) and at the State Porcelain Factory (1918–23; late 1920s).
Plate Decorated with an Image of Identity Papers and Work Papers in the Name of Vasilii Andreevich Prokhorov **247**
Tisse, Eduard 37
Tobolsk 42
Tolstoy, Alexei 34
Tolstoy, Leo 209
TRAUBERG, LEONID ZAKHAROVICH
(1902–1990). Director/screenwriter. Studied at Odessa Comical Opera Theatre's studio school. Established own studio theatre in Odessa (1919). Founder member, Factory of the Eccentric Actor (1921). Collaborated with Kozintsev on film projects (1924–45). Taught at Leningrad Institute for Stage Arts (1926–34). Stalin Prize (1941). People's Artist of the RSFSR (1987).
general reference 37
The Adventures of Oktyabrina 34, *34*
New Babylon 35, *37*
Tretyakov, Sergei 17
Tretyakov Gallery, Moscow
see State Tretyakov Gallery
Trotsky, Leon 37, 42, 44, 47, 48, 57, **61**, **67**, 101
Tsaritsyn 47
TSEITLIN, BORIS VIKTOROVICH
(1902–1921/44?). Graphic artist/painter. Studied at Yehuda Pen's studio and Vitebsk Art School (1919–22). Assisted with Malevich's lithographic book *On New Systems in Art* (1919). Member, Affirmers of the New Art (1920–22) and a creator of the group's first *Almanac* (1920).
Food Coupon **240**
Turin, Victor 35, *37*
Turksib (film) 35, *37*
TYSHLER, ALEXANDER GRIGORIEVICH
(1898–1980). Painter/graphic artist/stage designer/sculptor. Studied at Kiev School of Art (1912–17). Worked at Alexandra Exter's studio (1917–18). Poster designer, Russian Telegraph Agency, Melitopol (1919). Studied at Higher State Artistic and Technical Workshops (1921–23). Founder member, Society of Easel Painters (1925). Principal artist, Moscow State Jewish Theatre (1941–49).
general reference 31
Formal-Colour Construction of Red Colour **109**

Udaltsova, Nadezhda 24, 47, 230, 235
Restaurant 230, *230*
'We Want' 101
Ukraine 44, 50
Union of Artistic Affairs 41
Union of Musicians 19
Union of Poets and Painters (Makovets) 25, 45, 48
Union of Soviet Artists 19, 25, 28–29, 31, 46, 50, 101
Union of Writers 101
United Opposition 48
United States of America 297
UNOVIS *see* Affirmers of the New Art
Uritsky, Moisei 43
Uzbekistan 19

Van Dyck, Anthony 48
Vasiliev, Georgi 37
Vasiliev, Sergei 37
Veniamin, Metropolitan 46
Venus de Milo 56
Vereshchagin, Vasily 273
Veronese, Paolo 48
Versailles, Treaty of (1918) 44
VERTOV, DZIGA [KAUFMAN, DAVID ABELEVICH]
(1896–1954). Director/theorist. Studied at Białystok Conservatory (1906), Bekhterev Psychoneurological Institute, Petrograd (1916). Established experimental sound studio (1916). Editor for newsreel series, *Film Weekly* (1918–19). Joined Moscow Committee for Cinematography (1918). Founder member, Cine Eye group (1919). Created *Film Truth* series charting everyday life (1922). Influential documentary film-maker.
general reference 17, 34–35, 37
Cine-eye (film) 35, *36*
The Man with a Movie Camera 35, 45, 77
Vesenkha (Central Economic Council) 42
Vesnin brothers 46, 258
Competition Entry for the Palace of Labour in Moscow 261, *261*
Competition Project for the Offices of Leningrad Pravda in Moscow 257–58, *258*
VILDE, RUDOLF FEDOROVICH
(1867–1937). Graphic artist/ceramicist. Studied at Stieglitz School (1895–99). Head of painting workshop at Imperial Porcelain Factory (1906; joined 1905). Awarded gold medal, International Exhibition of Decorative Art, Paris (1925). Director, Lomonosov Porcelain Factory (from 1930). Head of artist section, Volkhov Ceramic Factory (from 1936).
Plate with the Inscription 'Workers' Victory 25 Oct' **60**
Vilyams, Petr 44
Vitebsk 18, 44, 149, 230–31
Vitruvius 150
VKhUTEIN *see* Higher State Artistic and Technical Institute
VKhUTEMAS *see* Higher State Artistic and Technical Workshops
Vladivostok 56
Volga region 46
VOPRA *see* All-Union Association of Proletarian Architects
Voucher for Use of the Bathhouse of Northwestern Railways in the Name of Gorshkov A. **241**
Vrubel, Mikhail 273, 274

The Wanderers 25, 30, 43
Warsaw 150
White Army 42, 44, 45, 47, 131
The White Eagle (film) 34
White Sea Canal 49
Winter Palace, Leningrad 23, 41, 42, 43, 129
Wolkenbügel, Moscow 256, 257
'Woman in Art', Moscow (1925) 47
Workers' Opposition group 44, 45
World of Art (Mir Iskusstva) group 29, 43, 44, 45, 47, 127
Wrangel, General 45

Yakovlev, Alexander 127
Young Artists Society (OBMOKhU) 44
Young Communist League 295
The Youth of Maxim (film) 37
Yudenich, General 44
Yudin, L. 25
YUON, KONSTANTIN FEDOROVICH
(1875–1958). Painter/writer. Studied at Moscow School of Painting, Sculpture and Architecture (1894–98), Valentin Serov's studio (1899–1900). With Ivan Dudin, established a Moscow art school (1900); students included Popova and Stepanova. Joined Association of Artists of Revolutionary Russia (1925). First Secretary, Union of Artists of the USSR (1956).
general references 46, 50, 209
The Creation of the World: The Realm of the Living 102
Cupolas and Swallows: The Cathedral of the Assumption at the Trinity Lavra of St Sergius *208*, 209
The Day of Annunciation 209, **217**
New Planet 101–02, 103, **115**, 209
Study for a Theatre Curtain for the State Academic Bolshoi Theatre 101

Zamiatin, Evgeni
We 19
ZELMA, GEORGI ANATOLIEVICH
(1906–1984). Photographer. Moved to Moscow from Tashkent (1921). Worked at film studio Proletkino. Correspondent for Russfoto Agency, Central Asia (1924–27), Soyuzfoto (from 1930), then Izvestia newspaper. Photographed defence of Odessa, Battle of Stalingrad, during the Second World War. Later, worked for Novosti Press Agency.
Brigade Meeting on the Collective Farm **204**
Crane Operator **92**
Red Army Soldiers by Power Cable **97**
ZERNOVA, EKATERINA SERGEEVNA
(1900–1995). Painter/graphic artist/illustrator. Studied at Fedor Rerberg's studio (1915–18), Higher State Artistic and Technical Workshops (1919–24). Also physics and mathematics at Moscow State University (1917–19, 1921). Member, Society of Easel Painters (1928). Made sketches on the Red Army's 1st Baltic Front (1943–44). Meritorious Artist of the RSFSR (c. 1947).
Tomato Paste Factory **81**
Zgura, Vladimir 212
Zhdanov, Andrei 37
Zholtovsky, Ivan 259, 261
Gosbank, Neglinnaya Street, Moscow 259, *259*
Zinoviev, Grigory 47, 48
Zvenigora (film) 33–34